BEACON

DARK NEBULA
BOOK 4

SEAN WILLSON

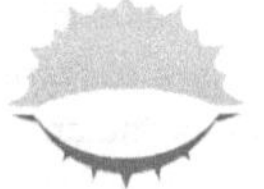

WELCOME TO DARK NEBULA

Thank you for buying this book!

If you're interested in a free novella entitled **Dark Nebula: Contact**, hearing more about the series, seeing new cover art as it's released, or getting exclusive access to sales as they happen, then you can subscribe to my newsletter online at:

seanwillson.com/subscribe

You can also drop me an email at:

author@seanwillson.com

I always love hearing from my readers.

DARK NEBULA SERIES
Novella: Contact (FREE)
Book 1: Isolation
Book 2: Discovery
Book 3: Generations
Book 4: Beacon (This book)
Book 5: Graveyard
Book 6: Nursery

PORTAL SERIES
Book 1: Drowning Earth
Books 2-4: Coming Soon…

CONTENTS

SHAUNA OLIVAW
SOL, OORT CLOUD — 2272

Zachary glanced left and then right. It was funny watching him try to address her as if she were any one of the particular robotic constructs escorting him. Shauna was both of them at the same time. She also had the consciousness feed from the shuttle popping in and out of her mind when the line of sight precisely hit her antennae without diffraction.

"And you're sure you didn't detect our Olivaw drive inside that thing?" Zachary began. "I mean, it'd be easier if we—"

"Negative," she interrupted. "It would've shown up on the many frequencies we monitor. Even the military drives have ways for us to detect them. No, whatever is powering that shuttle isn't one of ours."

The fact that he still questioned her as if she made normal human errors in judgment was frustrating. If she'd detected anything indicating this was an Olivaw drive, she would've said so. She wasn't a newbie making a gut call. She was a computer with a human consciousness. One capable of trillions of calculations per second. Hell, she could read a lidar scanner and scan millions of frequencies in the visual and non-visual spectrum in the time it took him to blink.

She was impressed when he finally ordered her to head out on this rock in the first place. While he was growing up to be a strong man, he was taking his sweet ass time. Her death had done a number on his confidence, and this robotic crutch wasn't helping with that.

Had the Four-Laws not compelled her to keep him out of harm's way, she'd have told him to get off his duff and protect her planetesimal. When she'd been truly alive, she'd spent decades restoring this place and buried down below were the remains of her human body. It was her god-damn shrine, and she didn't need pirates looting it.

They needed to branch out and take control of this situation. Her first form could watch after Zachary. She'd take the second one around the other side.

"It's over this ridge, so stay sharp and stick to that copy of me." She veered her second humanoid form left, heading away perpendicular to him.

"Watch after him," she transmitted to the first copy.

"Always," her first copy replied subconsciously. "Take care of yourself and do me a favor. Kick their ass if you get to them before we do."

"Oh, I plan to, and then some." No one messed with her family, and they certainly didn't frak with her grave.

As she distanced herself from the others and worked her way to the far side of the crater, she kicked her chassis into its maximum speed. Crawling at five kilometers per hour was painful. She could achieve seventy kilometers per hour on this planetesimal before she'd break loose and float out of control. It helped that the core of this rock was metallic. The magnetic implants in her feet used that fact to maintain her altitude near the surface.

Coming around the crater, she still hadn't detected any transmissions on the surface, nor had there been any signs of movement. The shuttle craft they'd spotted before landing should be opposite this rock formation.

She stepped up to the edge of the jagged outcropping and worked her hand over the dusty orange face to expose the cameras in her fingers to what was on the far side. There, in the crater's shadow, about fifty meters from her current position, was the Blazer Dragonfly shuttle they'd seen from orbit. It was parked beside a small cave entrance that had never been there. These bastards had defaced her home.

The cavern was too dark to make out any details, so she turned her attention to the shuttle. The elongated starship reminded Zachary of a classic sci-fi cruiser, but she saw it differently. To her, it looked like an ergonomic vegetable peeler. Had the kid ever made his own meal by hand, he might've had similar ideas.

While she was studying the ship's exterior, trying to make sense of the shape of the drive cones, two humanoids walked out of the cave and headed toward the side of the shuttle, opposite Zachary's position. They were each carrying small transparent tubs that sort of looked like specimen containers. When she zoomed in, there was some type of black powder filling the inside. Where the frak was that coming from? Were they mining the planetesimal?

She took a moment to analyze a data feed from Zachary and her first copy on the far side of the shuttle. They'd just come into view and for some reason her other form thought it was safe to burst to her. The two humanoids exiting the shuttle froze in their tracks and began gesturing frantically with their arms, pointing in Zachary's direction.

"Shit, we've been made," she muttered into the electronic ether. There was no one to hear her except her own mind locked in this robotic cell. She wouldn't dare risk a useless burst like that and give away her position.

The two humanoids shoved each other until the one nearest her backhanded the other. Rather than return the gesture, they merely paused and bowed toward the other. A moment later, they both spun in place and sprinted back inside the shuttle. The boarding ramp began retracting inward at once.

She had to think fast. Her sensors showed they were powering up the landing drives on the bottom side of the shuttle. They were either preparing to exit stage left or were mounting an assault on her son.

With that spark of an idea from her human consciousness, her Four-Laws engine kicked in, taking control of the robot's humanoid shell and leading her full tilt toward the shuttle. Apparently, she wasn't letting them get away. Either that or the computer side of her brain wanted her to disable their weapons. She really needed to keep her internal thoughts to herself.

As she approached the shuttle, she assessed her options. The ramp had retracted; the door was closed, and the ship was lifting off. It was only millimeters higher than it was a second earlier, but to her an eternity had passed.

While the shuttle's exterior was sealed, there were numerous ways she could break inside, including a manual override, but that was on the far side. For now, she'd need to find somewhere to grab on before she worked her way around. Maybe if she got lucky, the bastards would have left their helmets behind, and she could just vent the internal oxygen.

She leapt upward between the two massive dormant rear drive cones and grasped a maintenance ladder before climbing topside. The shuttle had begun its ascent in earnest as she scrambled up and across the top toward the port side. She used any nook she could find to grasp onto, and she also engaged the magnetic fields in her body to remain attached, all the while being careful not to make a sound. Based upon the files she had for this class of ship, if there were standard armaments, they'd be flanking each side near the front. Port side was as good as anywhere to start. Zachary should be able to see her, and perhaps she'd manage a tight beam in the open.

Just as she'd made her way to port and was about to climb down the side, the ship rocked. Zachary and her copy were launching an assault on the shuttle, attempting to take out the drive with a round of red-hot plasma. The external cameras on the bottom surface of her torso showed the remnants of the drive. It was glowing brightly and the section she'd climbed had melted away, but otherwise it was intact. Whatever they made it from, a direct hit from a round of ionized gas hadn't taken them out.

She had to keep going. There was still a chance the pirates might turn about and confront Zachary, and that wasn't acceptable to her Four-Laws engine. It was willing her to move forward, and she was incapable of resisting it. She reached around the side of the ship and continued her climb toward where the external weapons mount would be. There was definitely a pod there. From the looks of it, they had missiles and a few light laser armaments.

Fantastic. Why couldn't this be a simple pirate ship? Why did it have to be a well armed one?

As she worked her way toward the bow, she kept an eye on the weapon mounts. Suddenly, the ship rocked sideways, again. From the change in brightness around her, two more plasma charges had hit their mark. As a third was approaching, the pilot of the Dragonfly veered starboard and dodged the glowing energy round.

A few meters closer and that would've been the end of her little hero trip. It was strange being in the moment, struggling to save her son and yet missing the normal human feelings of a body. The sweaty palms, shaking extremities, or raising heart rate were gone. While she sometimes felt phantom pangs of those feelings, her A.I. consciousness kept the mirage of her former human emotions in check. She was a robot, not a frail biological.

The weapon's pod was only a half meter away when something strange happened. A fine layer of sparks sprinkled over the exterior of the Dragonfly. Waves of flickering light flowed over her, like water lapping over a tortoise on the ocean shore.

Her sensors exploded with data, and she couldn't make up or down from it. The whole thing was odd and wonderful, sort of like they were entering a warp bubble, but that couldn't be. No one had that technology besides them and the Galactic Alliance.

And then everything blinked out. Engulfed on all sides, her body entered a powdery windstorm of radiance. It reminded her of the wicked snowstorms in Michigan she'd played in on vacation as a kid. Except the odds were that this whiteness wouldn't end in hot cocoa.

SOMEWHERE OUTSIDE SOL

WHEN SHE FINALLY DROPPED OUT OF the clouds of white, it took her sensors several minutes to recalibrate. She was attempting to make headway breeching the ship at the same time she was figuring out what was going on around her. Her probability matrix gave her a ninety-nine percent with five nines of certainty that she'd been in a warp bubble. Combine this with the fact that they hadn't found the Galactic Alliance, and it meant only one thing.

The Galactic Alliance had found them.

With her sensor suite finally back online, it only took her a moment to match the star patterns around the ship. They were close to home, just outside Sol. None of the stars had changed much from their current positions. Her internal clocks showed they'd been traveling for thirty minutes and were headed into deep space.

She didn't know how long they'd be out of warp, and the sooner she could interface with the ship, the better off she'd be. Whoever was inside had either stolen probe technology from the Olivaws or were observing the happenings of Sol from afar.

This ship had to have some type of external mating connector of some kind. Something they could use at a space-port to get a hardline into the infrastructure. It was the easiest way to securely upload data, recalibrate systems, and download transmitter telemetry. She brought up the schematics for this class of ship in her mind's eye. The connection she was looking for was on the port side. On her side. It was several meters in front of the weapons pod.

The pathway to the connector was simple enough, but she still took it slow. Risking detection now would lose their upper hand. She needed to find out who or what was inside this thing.

As she crept on all fours past the weapon mounts, her Four-Laws engine itched. She was putting herself in harm's way, and the path to her safety was not clear. One's needless recklessness violated the Third Law of A.I.

An artificial intelligence in physical or virtual form must protect its own existence as long as such protection does not conflict with the Zeroth, First, or Second Laws.

She was gambling on something in those first three laws that would usurp this tier of per programming.

The communication port was standard CoPE tech and easy for her to interface with. She extended a data connector from her hip, being careful not to trigger an external connection warning. Her A.I. side knew the protocol forward and backward, so bypassing this level of the mating process was child's play. Getting past the security protections inside would be another matter entirely. While the Blazer company wasn't the leader in drive technology, their computer systems were top-notch. Fortunately for her, the internals of her robotic form weren't too shabby, either.

As she navigated the systems, she also rerouted a trickle of power to recharge herself. Not knowing how long she might be out here meant she should top off her charge any chance she got.

An hour into the connection, she hit pay dirt. She'd been able to bypass the central data core and focused on taking control of the internal systems of the ship instead. Reading someone's personal logs and replaying the telemetry of where they'd been would come later. Right now, she wanted to see who was inside. To accomplish that, she needed access to the ship's environmental crawlers and repair bots.

It was slow-going for a while. She gave a single crawler bot instructions to navigate around the ship, probing each of the rooms within the luxury vessel. After making several recordings, it returned to physically connect with the base station. Only then could she download and replay the visuals. She didn't want to risk needless wireless broadcasts for fear of being detected.

Just over thirty minutes into the back-and-forth game of telephone and she found what she was looking for. There in her mind's eye were either two ugly aliens, or some humans preparing for a costume party.

They had sixteen eyes and two long antenna atop their head that articulated around as if the stalks had minds of their own. One of them appeared to be eyeing her robotic form, following its every movement. She made sure to follow the normal routes these service bots had taken in the past. Introducing new stimuli the occupants weren't accustomed to wouldn't help her situation.

She flinched when the alien nearest the crawler reached

out and picked it up. The alien's antenna bent down and rubbed up against the exterior of the service bot, almost as if tasting it. A second later the aliens emitted a series of high pitch clicking and squeaking noises and their body gyrated uncontrollably. Were they laughing at the robot?

Perhaps they saw the device as crude. She earmarked that audio recording and began processing it, seeing if she could translate it over time or cross-reference it with the Galactic Alliance data she had in her memory banks. It was limited at best, but she had something.

The alien antenna thoroughly inspected the bot before they tossed it over its shoulder. Microscopic jets of air fired from all sides, and the bot safely landed on the ground and crawled toward the nearest uplink recess to receive further directions. As it passed midship, she spotted a table covered in alien tools.

Snatching a tool would be risky if they could detect its location within the ship. To defend against this, she merely had to get it into her torso to shield it using her stealth storage. Zachary liked to call it absolute blackness, but the name never caught on with her. Its purpose of stealth was all her mind cared about.

She'd always been a gambler, and recovering the object was no different. This was likely to be one of many such leaps of faith she'd need to take in order to survive this mission. She intended on living long enough to transmit her findings to her people, so she might as well gather as much intel as possible.

The smallest of the devices she'd seen on the table would require two service bots to procure. Dozens of the tiny robots were onboard and there were printers to churn out more if needed. If she could figure out how to take control of that system without being detected, she could make this ship do her bidding from the outside.

She issued the commands for the bots to collect the device,

using another pair of service bots as a diversion up front. She directed them to work their way up the chairs of each alien and interface with their computers. The act of doing this was standard procedure, but she wanted them to make a bit more noise, vibrating their legs as they ascended the surface rather than in their usually stealthy way. She figured it would get the aliens' attention and give the other two bots enough latitude to grab the object and bring it to the waste processor onboard the ship.

Normally, excrement within a human space vessel was reprocessed and broken down for its useful bits. Nothing was ever destroyed, but every so often when an infection hit, the risk of cross contamination meant it needed to be dealt with. Because of this, ships had been designed to eject waste to the outside. The idea of poop floating in space had been the focus of many memes over the centuries, but in reality, these systems were only used dozens of times a year throughout all of Sol. Running into someone's fecal matter in space was as probable as finding an alien, the irony of which wasn't lost on her.

She reprogrammed the waste processor in the rear restroom to eject without recording or alerting the central core. It was simple to bypass the software safeguards when you had physical access. Almost every security countermeasure the Blazer company built into the ship had a manual override. If you breached someone's physical security, you had the literal keys to their castle.

After she triple checked the programming, she disconnected from the ship and headed sternward toward the waste ejection port. About five minutes later, the small rectangular alien device that had been resting on the table popped out the side of the ship and into her awaiting hand. She had it safely ensconced in her stealth compartment within seconds and started her analysis, bombarding the device with nanites and multilevel scans.

While she was processing the initial results, her cameras detected a nearby locker she'd passed over. It wasn't on the plans she had in her memory banks for a Dragonfly shuttle. Changes to space cruisers weren't uncommon. For the right price, the sky was the limit with any incentivized company in Sol.

Putting one hand ahead of the other, she continued her magnetic crawl toward the hatch and inspected it. It was simple enough, a manual latch that opened from the outside. The lock seemed crude and she should be able to disengage it with the right command codes, but she didn't want to risk detection.

If this turned out to be an external tool storage bin like she imagined, she might just have a way to hitch a ride for the long haul.

LOCATION UNKNOWN — 2273

SHAUNA HAD BEEN in warp for nearly a year. Fifty hours after exiting the bubble in Sol, they entered it again. According to her calculations, it'd been just enough time for light to reach their location from when they'd left her memorial site, assuming they were traveling at Galactic Alliance superluminal speeds.

They must've been waiting to see if they had a tail. She couldn't tell what they'd done on the outside of the ship to determine they weren't followed, but one of the aliens had cycled the atmosphere and left the ship in their environmental suit. This time they used a different helmet, one far less human looking and giving their antenna room to move about.

Her body was safely stowed in the external locker she'd discovered. She spent the better part of a week gradually breaking into it from the inside out. Once her calculation had shown it to be safe, she programmed the service bots to begin the slow job of reaching out to her. All the while she tucked herself into a rather unflattering position and took most of her physical shell offline to conserve energy. When they finished burrowing through, the bots spliced into the ship's network to give her a direct interface to maintenance systems.

She spent most of her time analyzing the data she'd retrieved from the scans of the stolen alien tool. After days of trial and error, she reverse engineered the device's APIs and figured out how to communicate with it. It was a machine and therefore no different from her. Its design was highly structured and logical to navigate once you knew how to talk to it.

The device turned out to be a surveying tool. From her crude analysis, she deduced the aliens must have used it to direct the mining operations at the planetesimal. It had a range of settings, and while none of them breached her stealth container, it returned a surprising level of detail for anything she placed in the compartment alongside it.

While the device didn't offer her a translator, once she realized what it was, she used it to translate parts of their language. The different scan results on its display were combined over time to create a master codex of symbols to their human equivalent. It was monotonous, but some progress was better than nothing.

Over the course of the weeks and months that followed, the service bots brought her more alien tools and equipment littered around the ship. The aliens onboard had entered some type of cryo-stasis liquid soon after they'd dropped into warp the second time and hadn't made a peep since.

During her slow explorations of the ship those first weeks, she found what she thought was the primary alien control unit running the show while the aliens slept. They'd coupled it with the ship's data core midship. She didn't know how it hadn't detected her, but perhaps they didn't bother to interface with and learn all the crude human systems. Their loss was her gain.

The only thing she couldn't breach was the storage containers holding the black dust the aliens collected from her memorial site. She'd made countless attempts to open the latches, but one could only try so many random things while cleaning the ship and still avoid detection. If she had physical access, she might've made more progress getting inside.

A few weeks shy of one year at warp and the Dragonfly dropped into regular space. Coinciding with that moment, the aliens' cryo-pods opened.

During their sleep, she managed to patch into the ship's broader systems. While controlling the ship was out of the question, she routed copies of their data streams through her computational core, giving her the ability to see everything they could.

What she saw when they dropped out of warp was beyond her imagination. There were moons, thousands of moons. At least they looked like moons at first. It wasn't until the alien scanners connected to the Dragonfly completed their stellar scans that she recognized them for what they really were, massive alien starships. From the volume of ships transferring into and out of the dark spheres, they were preparing for something big.

2

———————

ZACHARY OLIVAW
ZETA LUPI, OORT CLOUD — 2278

He'd been turning the idea over and over again in his head for days, and the more he thought about it, the more it made sense. They were outgunned in Sol, and the Galactic Alliance forces in Epsilon Eridani were a quarter the size. If the rumors were true, they'd only have one chance at the Beacon of Therion. That window of opportunity would present itself in the seconds after the closing of the Dark Nebula. It was then that the mythical object from the Builders would be exposed.

Zachary paced around the front of the room, waiting for Mayor Nathan Clarke to arrive with the rest of the battlefield generals. At least that's what they called themselves. A few had made their way here from Sol, but the people with that title here in Zeta Lupi were by label only. While some had seen battle, they were scientists and engineers first, not military.

The entrance to the vast chamber opened, and Mayor Clarke walked down the hall, flanked by the soldiers escorting him. Close behind were his two handpicked generals and two more from Sol.

"This's far enough." Nathan rested his hand on the soldier to his left.

"We were instructed to escort you the entire—" the soldier began.

"I don't think Zachary Olivaw is going to assassinate me. You and the rest of your guard can backtrack up to the doors and close them on your way out." He gestured toward the back of the room.

The soldier glanced to his left at General Raft from Sol. The general nodded, and the soldier spun around.

"I want two per door!" the soldier said, barking orders at the others. "Split up into four groups. This place has entries on all sides. Keep your eyes open. Now move, move, move!"

The soldiers fanned out to cover the perimeter. A moment later the doors sealed them in and the sound of their locks clanged through the room.

"That's a bit much, isn't it?" Zachary scratched his head.

"You're telling me." Nathan walked up onto the stage and reached his hand out toward Zachary. "It's good to see you again. Last time we had a fair amount of comm lag."

He'd briefly spoken to Nathan a few months back, before they departed to the Lupus Dark Nebula, and that was with a five-minute lag in between broadcasts. "Yea, sorry about that. We were sorta in a hurry. I appreciate you making the time to speak with me, Mayor. We only arrived an hour ago, but it's imperative we move on to the next stage of the plan."

Nathan chuckled and glanced around at the generals. "Fantastic. And here I thought we were just twiddling our thumbs building a fleet of battleships and fighters to save Sol."

"No, that's not what I meant." He had to slow down. He wasn't any more in charge of these people than Bradley. Neither of them had held an elected office in any star system, and they certainly couldn't go ordering anyone around.

"What I meant to say was, I have some intel to share with you from our mission. I believe it will influence your next step in saving humanity."

He glanced away from Nathan and only now noticed the generals had surrounded him on all sides, pinning him in front of the wall screen. It was unnerving how the four of them stared silently, doubtless planning how to remove him from the situation as quickly as possible.

"Relax." Nathan gestured down with his hands. "You seem a lot like your brother. A million clicks ahead of everyone else in the room. How about you slow down and catch us up? I've only read over the briefing that Libby put together summarizing your last mission. She didn't get into the details about this meeting. Only the small discovery that you found humanity's home star system, fought with multiple alien superpowers, and uncovered the fact that this whole Galactic Alliance thing might be a big misunderstanding. That we're in fact, a species well over five thousand years old and had superluminal travel before nearly every other alien. You know, the high-level stuff."

Zachary smiled and then broke out into a laugh. He couldn't help himself. "I'm sorry. Yes, that's a lot to take in. We've had far longer than anyone else to absorb the news over these past weeks. As you can imagine, we didn't believe it was safe to send these details back in our probes."

"I should think not," General Green said. "With the distance between you and us, any number of aliens could have intercepted it. At least according to the galactic maps we've been briefed on since being allowed in the Circle of Trust. I believe that's what you Olivaws call it."

"Called it," Zachary said, correcting him. "Past tense, General. We're beyond all of that bullshit from my family's past. Everyone's in the loop now." He scanned the faces surrounding him. "Well, everyone with clearance, that is."

The generals all chuckled.

"Besides," Zachary continued. "None of the aliens we would've encountered en route to the Lupus Dark Nebula have evolved enough to pose a threat to us. If they had been, we'd have bigger problems right now."

Nathan raised his eyebrows. "Bigger than a galactic invasion threatening our very existence?"

"With the closest Galactic Alliance species over eighty light years from our current location, we're pretty safe out here. There are hundreds of thousands of stars between us and them. The odds of an alien finding—"

"Please don't finish that sentence," Nathan interrupted, raising his hand for Zachary to stop. "I'm not one to be superstitious, but I prefer not to tempt fate. Why don't you get on with why you called us here?"

Zachary nodded. "Certainly, Mayor." He gestured over his shoulder and brought up a picture that caused each of them to take a step backward with their mouths gaping open. "That, sirs, is the Beacon of Therion. The heart of what gives the Galactic Alliance their stranglehold over the galaxy. It has allowed the Qudoculi and Thyreuns to run roughshod over nearby aliens, and it was used to extinguish the flame of humanity four thousand years ago. What I'm here to propose to you today is that we steal it out from under their noses."

THEY'D BEEN THERE for hours and had been joined by a dozen other members from engineering and the military. They were all lower in the ranks, but each had some experience flying in either Zachary's mission or testing the gate drives around Zeta Lupi. A moment earlier, the generals invited Pluto into the chamber.

He nodded at her as she made her way down the aisle and

joined them on stage. She smiled when she passed him, giving him her usual wink before stepping up beside the other members from their Lupus mission.

"So you're telling me we're simply going to drop in, scoop it up, and gate away. Am I following you?" General Yule asked.

"That's right." Zachary nodded toward the battle plans he'd placed up on the wall screen. "We're proposing multiple waves of ships to act as cover for our catchers, but yea, it's a snatch and grab. Or in this case, a snatch and gate."

The engineers in the audience chuckled, but the military folks didn't find it funny. Evidently, their entire plan wasn't up to snuff with them.

"It'll never work," General Raft said. "There are too many moving parts, and we don't have enough time to coordinate."

"I beg to differ," Harold interrupted. "At the current rate of learning, construction, and with several well-planned test exercises, this plan has a seventy percent chance of success."

Everyone in the room went quiet.

"Remind me never to have you share the odds of someone's death next time," Zachary subvocalized to Harold.

"What Harold meant to say was that it'll succeed." Zachary took a deep breath. "You don't even want me to ask him what the odds of our success in Sol are."

"I made that mistake last week." General Raft shook his head. "The odds weren't even a quarter that."

"Sorry, sirs. There's no point in sugarcoating it," Harold said.

"What are we missing?" Nathan asked. "I mean, obviously you're not telling us something. Nothing is this simple."

"Oh, there's nothing simple about this plan." Pluto stepped toward the group of generals, shouldering her way through the crowd. "We need to wrangle the people in Tau Ceti back here, train hundreds of pilots, and hope we have a few Ulixi in the bunch. Add to that, we need to build thousands upon thousands of fighter craft, and time our arrival precisely after the GA uses the Beacon to seal the Dark Nebula. Nothing about this mission is simple, Mayor, sir."

He raised his hands to his face and shook his head. "Well, since we're laying it all out on the table, we might as well tell them about the Beacon itself."

The collective audience glanced at each other and then toward him, hanging on his next words.

Nathan broke the silence. "What does that mean?"

Pluto chimed in. "There are rumors the Beacon renders lesser species in a state of awe, unable to control their faculties. Allegedly, they stare at it until it's shielded, or they die of starvation, whichever occurs first."

Nothing about this meeting had gone as planned, and the longer he was here, the less he imagined this mission was going to work, let alone be approved.

"And why do we want the Beacon?" one of the engineers asked. "I'm sorry if you reviewed it already, but I only just arrived."

"The Galactic Alliance reveres these Beacons." Zachary stepped toward the wall screen and craned his neck. "There are eight of them, spread throughout the galaxy. The network of Beacons gives the alliance instant communication to anywhere a Beacon is present. The distances between them and the lag are as low as you and me here today. With them, the Galactic Alliance can coordinate an assault. Add to this the fact that many of the species in the alliance use the Beacon to focus their mental and spiritual powers, and you have a super weapon. One that is only ever revealed to the galaxy when the alliance seals a Dark Nebula."

Nathan was shaking his head. "I get all that. But why do we want it? Won't they use it against us somehow? And besides, there's only one of them within reach."

Ibu stepped out from behind Pluto and he did a double

take. He hadn't even seen them enter. How the heck had they gotten in here?

"I asked them to come," Pluto subvocalized to him. She must've noticed his reaction to Ibu.

"But why?" he replied subvocally.

"With it, you'll see everything they see," Ibu began.

The people in the room stepped away from the little girl. None of them had expected to see a child in the room.

Fortunately, Ibu didn't notice and continued. "You'll know everything they know. With the right decoding, you'll also be able to translate and understand their thoughts and every communication. They don't know humanity has returned to the Lupus Dark Nebula. They can't comprehend what you discovered inside. With a Beacon of Therion, you would have the upper hand. Any species strengthened by the Beacon, will suddenly be weaker. The Thyreus and Qudoculi have shared this Beacon for millennia and their power will be instantly diminished. The blow will be swift, and it will be felt around the galaxy."

You could hear a pin drop when Ibu finished speaking. Zachary walked up and rested his hand on their shoulder before returning his attention toward the generals.

They were each staring at Ibu, taking in the implications of their words.

"And… who are you?" General Yule asked. "Your name isn't coming up on my retinal comm."

He squeezed Ibu's shoulder. "This is Pluto's niece, on her mother's side of the family." He waved his hand. "It's a long story, but she was with us on our trip to Lupus, and she spent a lot of time reading all of the lore and material we found."

General Yule squinted and slowly nodded his head. His eyes were questioning the lie, but Zachary hoped that Harold could cover his tracks quickly.

"Who cares," General Raft said. "You're telling me we're doing all of this for a little Beacon."

Ibu tilted their head and squinted past the general, focusing on the image of the Beacon on the wall screen. "The Nanil had the luxury of being present with a Beacon of Therion on two occasions. It's written about in the Book of Truth. They spoke of being at one with the universe, of hearing the voices of everyone and everything. Of being told the truth of their very existence in the universe. The two Nanil present returned to their home world on Devid. Upon their return, they penned the Book of Truth and lived to be nearly one thousand years old, twice the age of any Nanil in history."

Again, murmurs spread throughout the room as everyone absorbed the scope of what Ibu had just told them. For some reason, their little alien friend neglected to tell him about this. He would've led with it had he known.

Nathan ran his hand through his hair and eyed Zachary. "You buried the lead on purpose, didn't you?"

He faked a smile.

"So, what happens if we don't take a shot at this Beacon?" Nathan asked. "Let's pretend for a moment that we didn't know about this. What then?"

Zachary was about to answer him when Harold jumped in. "We continue on with Sol, of course. We originally had a fifteen percent probability of success confronting the Galactic Alliance forces there. That was without considering the Selene moon ships which will more than likely depart from Epsilon Eridani to bolster the forces in Sol. With these added cohorts, and knowing the Beacon will be present at some point in the star system, I believe the odds in Sol would be insurmountable."

He sighed and shook his head before opening a subvocal comm to Harold. "I thought I asked you not to talk to people about death or statistics."

HE STARED out across the expansive hangar, bustling with activity. What was once an assembly line of construction robots was now an active star port teeming with movement and signs of humanity. People were shouting at each other and cheering their training successes. At the same time, cargo ships flowed into and out of the berths, bringing much needed resources and people to Zeta Lupi The Wheel.

While he stood at the railing, he leaned forward to study the unloading of the nearby mining vessel which had recently docked. Robots engulfed the exterior, nearly ripping the doors open and relinquishing the massive hauler of the ore that was the lifeblood of their expansion and warfare plans. Orangish sparkling minerals poured into the hoppers of the robotic haulers as they zipped into the distance toward the refinery tubes to dump the contents. Minutes later, they were back to take on more.

"What's that one hauling?" Zachary asked. "The orange stuff looks like North Carolina mud."

"It's actually water ice," Shauna replied. "The orange comes from the excess iron in the asteroid. It was a double mineralogical win. We're running out of low-hanging fruit planetesimals nearby and need to venture further into the Oort Cloud."

He nodded. Without a requirement to stay hidden, their objective to build had come much easier. That still didn't solve the problem of resources, though. People didn't realize that reality wasn't like in the vid-sims. Asteroids and planetesimals weren't located in dense pockets, they were spread over great distances. Occasionally, you'd find some floating together, but that was rare.

"What do you think? Should we relocate The Wheel closer to Tiān?" he asked.

Shauna let the question hang for a moment before answering. "I don't know if that's necessary. We could move it closer to another planet. Fumis or Laniger would do. By the time we moved it to Tiān, they might as well build one. This rock isn't exactly mobile, and besides, it would be a massive waste of resources at a critical hour."

What she said made sense. The problem was explaining that to Mayor Clarke. He'd all but demanded it after giving in to the Beacon mission earlier this afternoon. The military brass was worried about OPSEC this far out in the middle of nowhere. Being away from their home planet and people didn't help, either. He couldn't imagine the pressure the Mayor must be under from his constituents to ensure the Olivaws didn't pull one over the eyes of humanity again. In fact, Zachary had gotten Nathan's approval to seed the details of this change in mission to key individuals. They were planning to leak that it was Nathan's idea and not the Olivaws. He liked Nathan and would do everything he could to aid in the transfer of power. The last thing he wanted was to have to lead these people into this conflict.

He didn't know how Abigail had done it for so long. The pressures of rank and how he was regarded was stressful, and he wasn't even elected. His situation was worse. He inherited the virtual leadership position due to the severity of his family's subterfuge, combined with a gulf of confidence in the current leaders and their ability to come up to speed fast enough.

"Do you think we'll pull it off?" he asked as he stared out across the hangar.

"I'm assuming you're not referring to refining the water ice," Shauna said.

He chuckled. "No. I mean stealing a Beacon of Therion. The military strength of the Galactic Alliance is still unknown."

"It is, and it isn't," Shauna began. "We can assume the technological advancement of humans and Nanil in the

Lupus Nebula was a similar trajectory to the GA outside the nebula. If we compare that to the details we scraped from Lisp and your sister's time in the tribunal ships, we can safely estimate their overall power. There haven't been many leaps or discoveries by the alliance in millennia. The science has been fairly static according to the records."

"So, you think we can do it."

Shauna laughed out loud. "I didn't say that. I said their technology hasn't evolved. They're still thousands of years ahead of humans. Even with the stolen knowledge from Lupus, Little Red, and Ibu's books, our overall scale pales compared to them. We're talking about thousands upon thousands of Selene moon ships between Sol and Epsilon, and each of those holds hundreds of battlecruisers and thousands more fighters. I can't imagine—"

He waved his hand for her to stop. "Ok, I get it. You're as confident as Harold. Why even try? We might as well quit before we start."

"Cut the pity party shit!" Shauna said. "I didn't raise a quitter, and you're putting words in my mouth. You and I know the power of the gate drive is still untested in a battle scenario. We have an ace in the hole and our hand isn't all off suit. We just can't tell its strength compared to the GA. All we can do—"

"Is go all in," he interrupted. When she snapped like that, hints of his mother's personality came out. He didn't know if it was always there and merely had trouble breaking free of the Four-Laws Engine or the sheer size of the A.I. machinations around her, but he needed it. Her candor and no nonsense point of view reminded him of Pluto.

"Where we lack speed, we bring surprise and innovative battle strategies," she said.

On cue, a small squadron of gate fighters came tearing down the taxiway and dropped toward the landing pads below the lumbering, mining and transport ships. He tried to pick out which one of the arrowhead shaped crafts was holding the human and which was robotic. With the computer piloting both sets of ships, it was impossible to tell.

While they were away, some of his team from The Wheel in Sol made their way here to Zeta Lupi, and brought with them new fighter and battle plans. They'd been pulling more military personnel into the fold in recent years and with the GA's arrival in Sol, that recruiting was now even more frantic.

"How many fighters do we have?" He walked down the gangplank, circling over the ships below. There appeared to be hundreds of them in the squadrons from this last exercise.

"We have what you see here." Bradley walked up beside him.

Zachary glanced toward the voice of his brother. "Oh, hey. I didn't realize I was talking out loud."

Bradley smirked. "You weren't. Mom was sharing your conversation with me since I was approaching."

It was weird calling Shauna Mom. Bradley had started doing it after they arrived from the Lupus Dark Nebula. To him, it didn't feel natural, but he wasn't about to confront his brother about it.

"Have you been studying the fighter plans, then?" Zachary asked.

Bradley walked around him and continued toward the lift tube. "I have been. You couldn't pay me to walk into that hornet's nest of a meeting you were in earlier, so I poked my head in the tactical training bays on level forty-seven. They were guiding the simulations for these squadrons outside, getting everyone familiar with the new designs."

They both stepped into the lift tube and shot downward, popping out a moment later on the flight deck. The squadrons of black fighters surrounded them on all sides and extended well into the distance. From the looks of the people wandering through the ships, there were only a handful of human pilots among the bunch.

"They pair each human pilot with sixty-three automated peers to make up each squadron. The flight patterns, while directed by the pilot, can be overridden on the field of battle to protect the pilot. Both they and their bombardier are treated like gold. You know, Four-Laws and all." Bradley walked around the outside of one of the black arrowheads, sliding his hand across its surface. "I'd give anything to take one of these out for a spin. I bet it's like that Nanil skiff we commandeered from Yaan."

Zachary had glanced over the fighter designs while they were preparing for the meeting with the brass. Rather than equip each ship with a gate drive and risk the technology being stolen, they were dropped into the field of battle through a stationary gate floating in space. It opened a single massive ring across space-time and allowed an entire squadron of fighters to fly through. After a few hundred gated, the tachyon field broke due to exponential power demands. This required that they open another gate to drop a few more squadrons through.

It wasn't ideal losing the gate tunnel, but it was actually tactically elegant. The gates themselves didn't open that far away from the other squadrons. Given the gravity constraints of the transfer, they weren't likely to enter too close to harm's way unless the Ulixi who'd piloted the gate ring had been purposely trying to drop them inside another ship.

"I assume we're not testing these particular fighters with munitions yet?" Zachary asked as he watched Bradley lean forward and peer into the side of the now vacant sphere they'd lifted out of the rear of the ship. He appeared to be checking for its pilot or bombardier. They'd already exited stage left, according to his retinal comm.

Bradley popped back out of the sphere and shook his head. "Na, not yet. We're still far from using real munitions. Besides, I think they were debating about what to arm them with until we arrived with the GA weapons' playbook.

They've been drooling and arguing over the plans for hours down there. I had to step away before they asked my opinion."

"I'm sure they could use your help. You and Pluto are technically the only people who've fought an alien ship and lived to tell the tale."

Bradley spun around to face him. "Not true! Don't forget about Crayo and Lync's little excursion near Jupiter."

"Ah yes, I forgot about that. You understand what I meant, though." He walked up beside Bradley and leaned forward to peer inside the crew sphere. It was cramped, with barely enough room for two humans to be surrounded by mock nuclear warheads and a gate tube. The approach to dropping nukes into an alien ship had been surprisingly effective in both Lupus and Sol. "Are you sure you don't want to stay here?" He spun around to face his brother, who was studying him intently.

"Are you trying to talk me out of going?" Bradley asked.

He shook his head and sighed. "No, I just... everyone in that room was all doom and gloom. Hell, even Harold was spouting shitty statistics about the mission." He bumped his shoulder into Bradley as he walked past. "I've only had you back in my life a few months, and I'm not keen on losing you again."

"Hey!" Bradley reached out and spun him to face him. "You're the one who went and played hideout for over twenty years, pretending you were headed to Epsilon Eridani. We could've had a lot of time together before I left."

He waved his hands and raised them in submission. "I know, I know. It was all part of the shitty master plan. I sometimes think we take for granted the time we have when we live to be nearly two hundred. In hindsight, I don't know what Dad and Abigail were thinking talking me into that."

Bradley nodded. "We all inherited that familial hot potato,

bro. Now we need to do everything we can to fix what our ancestors broke."

He was right. Between his mother and brother, they'd shown him time and again that he needed to lean on others to guide his North Star. Otherwise, he'd spiral into places that weren't healthy for anyone.

"I should warn you, you're gonna be locked up in that rock for a few months." He glanced over and watched as Bradley fiddled with something in his pocket. "You sure you can handle sitting still that long?"

Bradley squatted down and rubbed the support pillar that rose out of the ground to hold the sphere and to prevent it from rolling. "Should be plenty of time to beat Pluto at poker. I swear she cheats like the dickens. I can't ever seem to bluff her."

He turned and glanced out across the sea of ships at his level and overhead. "Just do me a favor, would you? Keep an eye out for her."

"I've got her back, bro." Bradley hopped up out of a squat as a repair bot rolled up and started tweaking something on the exterior of the sphere they were standing near. "Why's she so hell-bent on going, anyhow?"

He swallowed hard. "Her sister's on Liprosus."

"Oh shit, yea. I forgot." Bradley took a step forward and tried to push the robot with his foot, but it didn't budge. He then spun around to face him. "I'd ask you to look after Cynthia while I'm gone, but I'm pretty sure she'd put you in your place if you told her what to do."

Zachary glanced over his shoulder. "And Pluto wouldn't do the same with you?"

Bradley reached up and scratched his neck, studying the repair bot. He didn't bother replying. They both knew the answer to that question. "Is this going to work?"

He spun around and tilted his head. "Do you mean you

continuing to try to push robots over like you did when we were kids, or the mission?"

The little robot rolled closer to them, and Bradley gave it another push with his foot. It didn't reposition itself or adjust its weight at all. "I still think Harold is fraking with me half the time. He knows the geometry of these things are catty-wampus, and then he rolls them up and taunts me, almost begging me to give 'em a push." He took his foot down off the spherical robot and stared at Zachary. "The mission. I meant the mission. Is it going to work?"

"It's never been done before, but then again, nothing we've been doing the past few years has. I guess we'll find out."

A soldier jogged up beside them and then snapped at attention, saluting them both.

He glanced at the young woman, huffing and puffing, struggling to catch her breath. She couldn't have been any older than twenty. "At ease, soldier. We're not military. Whatcha need?"

"Yessir!" She saluted him. "I've been ordered to escort you to the mission briefing on level four."

"And you couldn't have just told us that, Harold?" Bradley asked out loud.

"I did not issue that command, sirs," Harold said. "General Raft issued the orders directly to Private Gamal, who is now standing in front of you."

Bradley glanced at Zachary and mouthed the name "Raft?"

"Yea," Zachary began. "He's not happy we're wasting our time on this 'little beacon'." He gestured with his fingers in the air.

"Apparently he didn't see the archive footage," Bradley said.

Zachary shook his head. "No, he did. Like we've said before, this new alien discovery is going to hit reset on hundreds of years of assumptions our people made about technology and the universe. Some are less able to accept that change than others." He nodded at the soldier. "Very well, Private. Take us to General Raft. I'm pretty sure we can find our way, but something tells me you can't leave our side."

"That's correct, sir." Private Gamal turned and began speedily walking toward the lift tube.

3

BRADLEY OLIVAW
EPSILON ERIDANI, INSIDE OORT CLOUD

The ship shook and stabilizers whined as the boring tool advanced into the blue glow of the active gate drive. Clouds of debris billowed backward into the chamber as massive suction hoses attempted to keep the dust from covering their ship. Hundreds of articulating robots darted forward and back, grasping chunks of rock and tossing them into waiting hoppers.

Bradley wiped at his forehead and for the third time in as many minutes, he whacked his helmet. They only had one chance at this, at least that's what they were told. They were already dangerously close to the Epsilon Eridani Selene moon ships. Even if they were half a light day from the nearest alien vessel, it was far closer than he'd ever imagined they'd be. He must have missed that part in the mission prep.

"Out of the Lupus boiling pot and into the firestorm of Epsilon," he muttered.

"What's that?" Pluto's eyes were fixed on the controls in front of her. She was waiting for the green light from the boring team before she guided their capsule into the hole they were digging in the asteroid. Once inside, they would sit there for a few months until they arrived safely at their destination.

Zachary reassured him this would work, though General Raft had his doubts. Now that they were in the moment, Raft's naysaying was eating at the edges of Bradley's confidence. The team spent weeks preparing for this dig after Adri arrived from Tau Ceti. According to Lync, her talents were off the charts. Her ability to focus on the smallest detail while directing the tachyon fields had surpassed every other candidate in the first batch of trainees. The tiny girl's skills were crucial to their mission's success. He only hoped she had the mental strength to push through the pain of the long dig.

The astronomy team had to obtain a perfect scan of an asteroid to give this mission a chance. Once they'd identified the candidate, Harold launched a probe into the system to study every square centimeter of the rock. The extreme elliptical path of the tiny rock had been a lucky find. He still couldn't grasp how Harold had pulled it off without being discovered by the GA. The guy seemed to be everywhere at all times.

"Shit!" Adri screamed over the open comm as the boring tool slid sideways and slammed into the superstructure of the ship. A second later the tool snapped in half and the rear section shot backwards, knocking over a few dozen robots like they were bowling pins crashing into the back wall. Another five meters to the right, and it would have collided with the collapsible barricade that protected their capsule.

The gate winked out a moment later. All that remained in front of them was the field of stars framing the Epsilon Eridani sun in the middle. They'd lost the asteroid.

"What the hell happened?" Bradley lurched sideways in his seat. Without the asteroid, they'd need to scrub the entire mission.

Adri's voice was shaking. "We had an unexpected mass appear off the starboard side of the asteroid. It was some type of alien ship from the imagery coming in from the forward probes. I couldn't account for the additional mass in time. It threw everything cattywampus."

He reached up and rested his head in his hands. This wasn't happening. Everything they'd worked for was lost. "So, now what? We go back?"

"No way!" Adri said. "I've got this. Just gimme a second to see where this ship's headed and I'll give it another go."

"But the masses will move around," Pluto said. "Especially with that ship nearby."

"I said I gots it! My father didn't raise a goldbrick. He didn't give up on us in Sol, and I'm not about to quit on you now."

Lync had sent on a recording with Adri when she arrived in Zeta Lupi. Said the girl was special and that her father had saved their mission escaping from the Galactic Alliance fighters. He was the first human to kill an alien in battle. Harold's escapades saving the colonists on Liprosus didn't go unrecognized, but this girl's father sparked a movement with the people on Tiān. Ever since the footage of the explosion that took his life aired, the waves of volunteers hadn't stopped.

"Ok, we can try it again," Moet said. "But my orders were explicit. The moment we're detected, and the mission is compromised, we're returning to Zeta Lupi. Is that understood?"

"Yessir," Adri said.

Pluto leaned forward and tweaked something on the panel in front of her, bringing up a video feed of Adri on the screen. The little girl couldn't have been older than six. Sweat was beading up on every centimeter of her exposed pale skin. From the look in her eyes, she was going to pass out.

"Are you sure you're ok, Adri? No one's lost anything but time right now," Pluto said.

The little girl grabbed a towel to wipe her face and eyed

the indicator that showed someone was watching her. "I'm fine, ma'am. Thank you for asking."

"Why don't you take a second and drink something? You need your energy," Bradley said.

The girl leaned forward. Her image got bigger in their camera, and she took a long sip from a straw before leaning back in her chair. "I'm ready, Captain."

"Distance acquired, rotation locked." Pluto studied her controls and then glanced back to the camera showing the bridge and Adri. "She's all yours, dear. Give it hell."

The little girl scrunched up her face and narrowed her focus. A moment later, the gate in front of them formed. The blue tachyon field converged, and the stars panned around, moving up and down until ultimately settling on the asteroid. The drive plumes from an alien ship were in the distance, heading toward a faraway Selene moon as the image slid, gradually focusing on the inside of the asteroid itself.

"I've got it. I'm zeroed in on our pocket," Adri said. Her voice was strained, and her cheeks were puffing in and out.

"Engaging secondary bore," Moet said.

The robotic boring machine's rotating teeth and gravitational blasters dove into the partially excavated hole from their previous attempt. Somehow Adri had brought them back to the same point in the asteroid. Lync was right, this girl was talented.

Chunks of rock began flying as robots clambered forward and continued their repetitive assault on the debris field in the wake of the boring machine. The power requirements for this mission were extraordinary and required the energy from two dozen ships to keep this gate open. They figured more couldn't hurt, but little did they know they'd need to do it multiple times.

"Are we ok on—" Bradley began.

"Shh!" Pluto gestured for him to stay quiet.

He studied Pluto. The woman was feeling every emotion

of the young Ulixi. Just when he thought she was going to pop, she transformed. Her face went blank, and she abruptly calmed. With the seconds dragging by, and the rocks flying, Pluto slipped into a hidden rhythm. She began slowly bopping her head to the sound of chunks ricocheting against some unknown microphone in the drilling area.

Suddenly, she started singing. "I'll sing you a song, a good song of the stars."

Her voice was a cool breeze on a hot day. He'd never heard anything like it, especially coming from someone as tough as her.

"Way — hey, blow the Galactic Alliance down. I trust that you'll join in the chorus with me."

Adri replied in tune, her face a mask of pain. "Give me some time to blow the alliance down."

Pluto smiled and continued her song as Adri accompanied her. The sight was both shocking and eerie as the boring proceeded at a healthy clip. The girl's anguish appeared to grow deeper and deeper by the second.

"Blow the alliance down, bully, blow the alliance down," Pluto sang. "Way — hey, blow the Galactic Alliance down. Blow the alliance down, everyone, from Earth to Tiān; Give me some time to blow the alliance down."

The panel in front of them burst with a green light and Pluto slammed the throttle forward. Their capsule shot from behind the protective cover in the corner, sending the barrier flying to the side of the ship and sticking into the wall like a knife to butter.

"Brace yourselves!" Pluto shouted. "This is gonna hurt, and I don't know how much room we have on the other side."

He watched their capsule shoot into the dancing surface of tachyons. The hope for their mission safely resting inside. When they hit the light, he knew it was too fast. Every millimeter of his body screamed out in pain. It was like being submerged in boiling water, except it wasn't just his skin. It was his insides, as well.

The screams from the crew were deafening. A second after the transition, their comms cut. It was probably Harold protecting them from listening to each other's misery. Either that or they were dead. He couldn't tell, but based upon the jerk forward in his harness and the crash echoing through the capsule when they hit the other side of the tunnel, they were still alive. At least for now.

He reached for his pocket and rubbed at the crystal beneath the fabric, trying to clear his mind. Memories of the cool waters of the Pacific lapping up on the shores of Charlotte sprang forward. They'd swam in the ocean countless times on their summer trips to Earth. The water had been frigid, but his father loved it. He used to call it the polar bear club, or something like that. That man was always a glutton for punishment. Like father, like son, he supposed.

"Are you ok?" Pluto's voice was hoarse.

"I think so. It… hurts."

"Good," she said. "Pain reminds us we're alive."

THEY GAVE themselves a few minutes to come down from the pain. Harold injected something into their bloodstream through the tubes in their acceleration chairs. He assumed it was some type of painkiller. Whatever it was, he was feeling better by the second, and the itching had subsided.

"Do we have a status?" Bradley asked, his voice gravelly from screaming.

"It's finishing now," Pluto said. "All systems are nominal. We have some impact damage on our forward side, but Harold has repair bots working their way toward the bow end."

That wasn't good. "Will we be able to repair the stealth

material?"

"It seems to be patchable," Harold said. "It won't be pretty, but it'll prevent signal leak. Best we keep our systems at a minimal while I finish the repairs. It shouldn't be but thirty minutes or so."

"Ack that." Bradley took a few slow, deep breaths. "I just want to check the last comms we have pending and we'll power down." He reached forward and hit play on the queued message. It was a brief recording during the seconds after their transition. The gate must have held open for longer than he realized.

Adri's face appeared on the screen in front of them. "Thank you, ma'am. My mum used to sing that song to me when I was little. Instead of the word *Alliance*, it used *Inners*. It makes more sense your way, given our new situation. Good luck! The gods are on your side." Her face was still as white as before, but the smile beaming at the camera spoke volumes. They'd made it.

Pluto reached forward and slammed the master power breaker they'd built into the controls in case of emergency. All signals and unnecessary electronics shut off. Except for basic life support systems and the repair bots outside, everything was powered down.

The only noise that remained was the creaking of their ship and the faintest hum of a welding apparatus not far away. It would have been easier to drop a probe into the system to update the survivors on Liprosus with their new mission. But they didn't know the state of things planetside and couldn't risk leaking the particulars of their segment of the mission to the Galactic Alliance. They'd be dead before their plan ever started.

The mission details were safely ensconced inside both his and Pluto's bodies. The nanites in their blood would wipe the data dots at the first sign of bodily harm. They didn't know the Galactic Alliance's technological capabilities to scan for augmentation or information, but they couldn't take any chances. This meant physically delivering the details was their safest bet.

He exhaled and stared at the faint light on the control panel. The cold caused the water from his breath to glisten as it crystalized in front of him. The temperatures in the capsule had already dropped precipitously. When Harold said basic life support, he meant it. He reached up and pulled his helmet closed over his head, manually sealing it with the switch on his neck. Keeping some heat from his body inside should help make this wait a bit more comfortable.

After Harold completed his repairs, he'd deploy nanite crawlers to work their way to the surface to check things out. Once they had the all clear, they'd start their month-long tunneling project in strategic directions, radiating away from their safe pocket in the heart of the asteroid. When they were done, they'd attach their ion thrusters to the tunnels for fine tune navigation controls to guide them toward their destination.

The planet Liprosus.

IT'D BEEN forty-eight hours of frustration and pain. Every square centimeter of his body ached. Who'd have thought mining an asteroid would've been so strenuous?

Bradley mulled over the idea for a moment and then laughed out loud. That was both ignorant and short-sighted. Of course, it was painful. He'd moved his muscles more in the last two days than he had in months. Well, except for that little expedition on the alien planet in Lupus. Maybe he should take up running or do some other exercises to build his endurance.

"What's so funny?" Pluto asked.

He chuckled. "Nothing. I'm just realizing how strange it is

to have muscles and yet no stamina. These nanites in our bodies are our worst enemy." He reached out to grab the globe of water floating in front of him. Pulling it to his mouth and squeezing it sent jolts of pain into his forearm and tricep.

Pluto floated across the galley and came to a stop near the kitchenette, clicking her boots to the ground next to the food processor. "I learned that the hard way my first few years at The Wheel. They shot me up with all the good stuff, and I felt like a million bucks. It wasn't until my trip back to Ganymede for supplies and to pick up recruits that I realized while my physique was the same, my physical abilities had diminished."

He nodded as his stomach rumbled at the aroma of Pluto's food wafting across the room. It smelled amazing, but that was a long way to go to get some grub. He wasn't sure his body was up for moving yet.

"Funny thing, though. A lot's mental." Pluto grabbed two trays from the processor, closed the door, and then walked back to the table. Her magnetic boots held her firmly in place as she navigated the zero gravity. She clicked both trays onto their table and then slid one across toward him.

His eyes went wide. "Thanks! You didn't have to do that. I would have made it over there... eventually."

Pluto snickered. "No worries. You seemed like you needed it."

He reached over and detached the utensil from the side of the plate and carefully lifted the lid to the veggies. Sliding in the spoon like tongs, he scooped up a portion and then closed the lid and brought them to his mouth. He'd never imagined mixed vegetables could taste so delicious. His mother would be proud.

When he swallowed the first few bites, he glanced back up at her. "How do you mean pain's mental? Pain hurts last I checked."

She smiled as she finished her mouthful before speaking.

"True. There's no doubt about it. Pain is pain. Those little nanites in your blood have done remarkable things, stimulating your musculature growth with no help by you. It's your mind that hasn't bridged that divide. You're convinced you're weaker than you are, and the only way to learn that is to use your muscles. It's one reason the latest batch of soldiers coming up with these nanites seem so much stronger than the rest of us. They've grown up with these things since they were kids and have retrained their minds to what's possible. It's extraordinary, really."

He hadn't ever thought about it that way. He'd managed to complete all the tasks over the past day. While he may have fumbled because of poor coordination, nothing indicated he was weak. Perhaps retraining his mind and building some endurance wouldn't be as hard as he'd imagined.

"I've completed the baseline bores to the surface and executed the passive scans," Harold said over their retinal comms. "There are no signs of the Galactic Alliance nearby, and we floated past their Selene ship without notice. I guess we're not big enough to use in that Dark Nebula they're laying down."

He finished the veggies and moved on to the chicken breast. At least that was what it looked like. It was probably something plant based, but he didn't care. It tasted wonderful and few people could tell the difference except for a few Amish he'd met on Earth as a kid. Their sense of taste was uncanny.

"So what's next?" he asked between bites of the herb crusted chicken between his tongs.

"Now we sit still and let the robots widen the tunnels I dug. It'll take a few weeks, as we slowly eject the tunneling debris into space as we go. We don't need much room. Just enough to connect those ion thruster tubes you all prepared to weave their way toward the surface."

He couldn't believe they were planning to crash-land an

asteroid on a planet. Part of him doubted it was possible, but he'd thought the same thing about gate travel a few months back. Look at them now. He knew Harold wouldn't put them in harm's way if the odds weren't in their favor.

The next month was going to be excruciating without cryo-pods. Their hard work was nearly done. All that remained was to pass the time and plan for their arrival. Transporting and storing a Beacon of Therion was no small task, especially if you were starting from scratch like they were on Liprosus. While they had the Archégonos site, Harold's copy there was purposefully ignorant of the events and discoveries that had transpired in recent years. They needed to ensure their technological advances weren't spread across the galaxy, so only certain copies of his personality knew about gate travel or the actual location of their second colony in Zeta Lupi. That was about to change.

"Seems like we won't need to do manual labor for a while." Pluto pushed her empty tray forward. "What do you want to do next? Maybe we should review the contingencies if we hit the planet and have to find Archégonos ourselves?"

Little Red floated into the galley on a microburst of air and angled toward the two of them at the table. "Don't forget about the missiles. We can't forget about the missiles," he chirped as he came to a stop next to Bradley.

"We won't, buddy." He reached out and gave the little red robot a nudge with his finger, sending him flipping end over end across the room. "Nobody wants a repeat of the nova in Lupus. We have a lot of work to do once we reach Arché- gonos, but I thought we'd take a break for a bit."

He glanced over at Pluto and raised his eyebrows. "Are you up to losing some credits at poker?"

She reached forward and snatched his tray away before digging at his pudding squares. "I hope you brought the Olivaw wallet. You're gonna be broke by next month if you didn't." A smirk crept into the corner of her mouth.

4

ABIGAIL OLIVAW
TAU CETI, OORT CLOUD

The images around Abigail faded. The previously solid starships she'd brushed against in her fog of confusion evaporated like the morning mist over the nearby ponds. Moments earlier she'd been climbing, and now she was in a hangar somewhere near their house in North Carolina. The teardrop black shapes transformed into pinpoints of light that grew brighter and brighter by the second.

"What do you mean, to fight?" Her mouth tasted like she'd been chewing on a handful of cotton. She licked her lips and moaned. A second later, droplets of water ice rubbed against her mouth. When she moved to lick the ice, pain arrested her. "Water," she muttered.

"I can't give you water," Lync said. At least it sounded like her. "Not until the doctors say so. They said to use ice instead."

The cold chips of frozen water circled around her lips as her eyes slowly parted, letting more light in. "Can we make it… darker?"

The points of illumination complied in an instant and dispersed to a faint glow across the entire ceiling. That was much better. As she opened her eyes, she slowly looked to her left. Lync was sitting there, smiling back at her and delicately applying the ice to her mouth. Next to her was Minula. From the glare on her face, she was unhappy and was trying to move Lync out of the way.

"Don't give her too much." Minula nudged Lync over. "They warned us it could upset her stomach."

Lync growled. "I'm pretty sure I know how to administer ice." She glared at Minula, and the woman scowled in return. "Fine, doctor frosty, you man the ice cubes." She stood up and slammed her shoulder into Minula.

Like two walls colliding, neither budged a centimeter until finally Minula stepped aside for her to pass. Once she was clear, she eased up to Abigail's side and her face transformed in an instant when they made eye contact. Her once harsh edges melted and tears welled up. "You're back. You're really back."

Abigail watched as she reached out again with the ice and circled her mouth, making sure the water didn't drip inside. She'd always been the rule follower, that one.

She glanced over at Lync. Her arms were crossed at the end of her bed, and she was staring at Minula. "What... what did you mean, to fight?"

Lync shook her head when she realized Abigail was talking to her. It took a second for her to shake off her anger. "I..." she stepped around the other side of the bed and grasped her hand. "Best if you rest. We can talk about it later."

"What happened? The last thing I remember..." She fell silent. She couldn't separate her dreams from reality. It was like she'd lived the same few weeks of her life, repeatedly trapped in the cell of her mind.

"What do you remember?" Harold's voice was coming from all around the room.

"I... remember the Galactic Alliance arriving. I remember visiting their ship several times and working with Lisp. We were about to meet with Ambassador… Addae I think." She reached up and rubbed her head. "And then that green mottled bastard… they touched me." She paused, staring into the light.

"And?" Harold asked.

"And that's it. Everything went blank, and I appeared on a rocky cliff and started climbing again. Over and over and over again. That cliff never seemed to end, and each time I got near the top, I…" She hesitated, unsure how to find the words to describe what she'd experienced.

Minula glanced at Lync. They both had concerned looks on their faces.

"What cliff?" Minula asked.

"You know, the one near our house in Charlotte." Abigail leaned forward and coughed. She felt something cold and wet run down her chin.

Lync's face went white, and she reached forward with a cloth to wipe at her face.

"What is it?"

"Nothing." Lync's jaw clenched as she wiped. "What cliff in Charlotte?"

She was lying. Something was the matter. "There's a bluff behind our house, about a click hike away. We… had my father's funeral there. When we were kids, we used to climb it every summer. Far too many times. You remember, Harold?"

"I do," he said. "What were you doing there in this… dream?"

She shook her head, struggling to focus her thoughts. "I… don't know. Climbing toward the light, I think. I fell constantly trying to reach the top, and each time I dropped I started over. Hell, I met that damn alien at least… a dozen…" Her voice trailed away and she stared past Lync. "Each and every time… it was… excruciating. The Galactic Alliance arrived, and the whole thing repeated. I knew I shouldn't let him behind me, but I didn't heed my own warning."

When she turned to look at Minula, her face was making micro gestures. They were subvocalizing to each other.

"What are you saying?" She glanced between the two of them. "What are you saying about me?"

"We… we're just talking to Harold," Minula said. "We're not sure what you're telling us."

Lync leaned forward and sat on the edge of her bed. She felt her hand brush the side of her face and move her hair out of her eyes before she talked. "Are you saying you remember reliving the meeting with the Galactic Alliance?"

She nodded. "I did… I woke up in my office countless times, thinking it was all a dream." She squinted at Lync and then at the light on the ceiling. "Is this a dream? Is any of this real?"

Harold laughed out loud, startling the two women next to her. "We're as real as they get, Abby. We're just glad you're ok."

A group of doctors stormed through the doorway and began peppering them with questions.

"How long has she been awake?"

"What did you do?"

"Why is there blood on the towel?"

That was why they looked so scared after she'd coughed.

Lync stared down at the cloth before handing it to the doctor. "She coughed a moment ago, and we wiped it up. She seemed ok after that."

"I'm fine." Abigail leaned forward and hacked into her hand again.

This time it wasn't her friends fighting to get close to her, it was the doctors. They leapt toward her side, shoving the two military women back like rag dolls.

The last thing she remembered was the room getting bright again. It hurt her eyes.

ABIGAIL TOOK a deep breath in and then out. The air was crisp and sterile. Not a hint of anything organic at all. No pollen, grass, or even sweat. Wherever she was, it was new. It didn't have the lived in smell of her home office or the Jurat.

As she opened her eyes, she found herself upright in a hospital bed. From the looks of it, the bed she woke in last time. She had no idea how many hours or days had passed, but Minula's head was resting by her feet and Lync was asleep on the couch on the far side of the room.

"Where am I?" Her mouth wasn't as dry as it was before. It actually felt pretty normal.

"You're in Tau Ceti." Harold's image sprang to life on the screen beside her bed. His youthful face and sandy brown hair framed his wide smile. He couldn't have been a day over thirty in that form.

"Am I—"

"You're fine," Harold interrupted. "A tad dehydrated, your hormones are out of whack, and your blood cells look like they've been through a nuclear winter, but otherwise you're healthy."

She chuckled and leaned forward to cough, bringing her hands to her mouth. When she opened it, it was clean. There was no blood.

"Don't look so surprised," Harold said. "I wasn't lying. You were touch and go there for a bit, and no one was prepared for Lync to bring you back. I still can't figure out how she did it. You'd been mumbling for weeks. Everyone's tried talking to you, but nothing worked. She walks in, you two start having a conversation, and a minute later… wham!" A crack echoed through the room. "You're awake."

"Who… what!" Minula shot upright in her chair with a start and reached to her hip for a weapon that wasn't there.

Lync rolled off the couch and collapsed to the floor with a thud before springing up onto her feet. "Is she ok?"

Abigail chuckled, and her cheeks warmed as she held

back a laugh. She made eye contact with both of them and nodded. "I'm great. Actually, I'm better than great. I've got far too many people fretting over me." She gestured toward them. "Come here, you two. Give me a hug."

They each stepped to opposite sides of her bed and leaned into her. Uncertainty was in their eyes, but she didn't care. She reached around and pulled them both close. "Thank you. Both of you."

The women chuckled for a minute and wiped at their eyes. They were afraid to hug her. That was fine. She wouldn't force them to. When she finally released them, they leaned away and settled in on the edge of her bed, each grasping one of her hands.

"How long have I been out?" Abigail studied each of their faces. They weren't sure how to answer her.

Harold broke in. "Three months, Madam President."

She sighed. He switched to the official form again. She hated the god-damn president shit. "Please don't start calling me that. I'm not ready yet."

"Very well," Harold said.

Three months was a long time. She stared past the women and then back at them. Her brothers weren't here yet. That couldn't be good. If everything had gone as they'd hoped, they would have found something by now.

"Where are my..." She couldn't say it. The words wouldn't come. If she asked, then she'd know.

Lync smiled. "Your brothers are fine. They're in the other Tau Ceti." She winked.

Abigail glanced at Minula and tilted her head. "She... knows?"

"She knows about a lot more than that."

"What does that mean?"

Lync smirked. "I'm in the Circle of Trust now, baby!"

Abigail smiled. "Really? Shit must've hit the fan while I was gone, aye?"

"You don't know the half of it." Kara had just entered the room. She was holding three coffees in her hand and was smiling from ear to ear.

"Aunt… Kara?" Her face warmed, and tears welled in her eyes. "Is it… truly you?"

"Hot damn, she's awake!" Kara tossed the coffees on the table and shot across the room, collapsing into the spot Minula vacated. Her arms engulfed Abigail like a bear protecting its young.

She squeezed her tight like her mom used to. "Now that's more like it. That's how an Olivaw hugs."

They held the hug for a minute, melting into the protective embrace of each other. She couldn't understand how she was here. They'd lost her signal after the Zeta Lupi colony intercept mission. She'd never arrived with the rest of the colonists. Everyone assumed she stayed with the Tau Ceti ship and was heading there instead.

"How'd… you get here?" Abigail asked, with her head on Kara's shoulder. "What happened to you?"

"That's a long story." Kara leaned back to stare her in the face. "Our A.I. family friend and I had a healthy disagreement about killing some people, so I decided to take a minor detour to Tau Ceti. Then Miss Lync shows up and wakes me during my nap. The next thing I know, I'm whisked away to save your life only to find out my biologicals are no help."

She shook her head. It was like she was talking in riddles. "What does that mean?"

"Whatever Admiral Gwar gave you, nearly killed you," Harold said.

"Shut up, Harold!" Kara glared at his image on the wall screen. "You know our agreement counts here, as well."

"Our agreement is null and void when it comes to Abigail."

Kara's face was turning red. "Fraking A.I. double-talker."

"Harold, give us a moment. Please," Abigail said.

"Yes, Madam... Abigail. You can subvocalize if you need me. Your retinal comm should be in working order."

She'd forgotten about her comm. From the sound of Harold's voice, he was wounded. But she needed to talk to the others without them fighting. She could feel her heart beating faster in her chest with all the emotions mounting, and it was making her light-headed.

"He's gone," Abigail said. "Now tell me what's going on."

Lync cleared her throat and went to attention. "I was approached to go on a mission to retrieve Kara Olivaw. They believed she was en route to Tau Ceti, so we dispatched a specially designed ship to dock with Spērō and rescue her. Upon arriving, she was in a modified cryo-stasis and had all but eliminated any remnants of Harold aboard her ship. When I woke her, she claimed he had tried to kill her and the engineers who woke to confront her on Spērō. After I calmed her—"

"Calmed me!" Kara interrupted. "More like knocked my ass out."

Lync glanced down at Kara and smiled. "After I sedated Kara, I brought her back to Tau Ceti to help revive you, Madam President."

Abigail shook her head. "Harold tried to kill you?"

Kara raised her hand. "No, not me. The engineers who woke on Spērō to confront our docking maneuver. They had done nothing wrong, but he was convinced they'd compromised our mission. I had to save them."

"And he wouldn't listen?"

"Nope. He tried shutting off their cryo-pods, so I shut him off. It took me a few years, but I figured it out."

None of this made sense. Why would Harold try to kill innocent bystanders? Was there something more at play here? She reached up and tapped her ear before speaking out loud. "Harold, what do you have to say for yourself?"

"Nothing, Madam President. I haven't merged that copy

of my consciousness with this one. It's isolated in another computer system. I've interacted with it, but thus far I've been unable to reproduce the thought pathways it took to the ultimate conclusion described by Kara."

She nodded. It was hard to imagine a set of logical steps that would lead to Harold killing someone, but he was a computer. His actions were simple decisions and weren't always able to be controlled by his human side.

"And you haven't made amends with this copy?" Abigail asked.

"Amends?" Kara shot up. "Make amends with the computer that tried to kill innocent people. Are you fraking kidding me?"

Abigail closed her eyes and took a deep breath before opening them. "I'm sorry. I… you know what I meant. Aren't you willing to work with Harold going forward?"

"If he'd tried to kill my friends, I wouldn't," Lync interjected.

Abigail glared at her. "I didn't ask your opinion, officer."

Lync chuckled. "I don't care if you did, Madam President. I offered it anyhow."

"Speak to me that way again, and I'll have you removed from this room."

Lync shook her head. "I heard about your Olivaw temper. I guess I know where that comes from. Happily, I didn't get—"

Abigail slapped her hand against her bed. "Shut the frak up. Harold, please escort Major Michaels from—"

"I wouldn't recommend that," Harold interrupted.

"Oh, you wouldn't. She doesn't exactly sound like she's on your side, and I need to focus. We have some hard decisions to make."

"Might I remind you she's in the Circle of Trust, Madam. And there's the small matter of her saving your life."

"I thought you said Kara's blood didn't help?" Abigail asked.

Harold's face appeared on the screen next to her bed. This time he was the elder form he took whenever he had something serious to tell her. "It didn't, but your sister's blood did."

She shook her head. These people were talking gibberish. "I don't have a sister and my brothers—"

"Are light years from here," Kara interrupted. "He said your sister." She stepped away from the bed and gestured toward Lync.

Her arms were crossed, and she was staring a hole through Abigail. If looks could kill, Abigail would have a hole piercing through her heart right about now.

"I don't see why blood matters, but hey, sis." Lync waved.

KARA CLEARED the room and left them alone together. Neither she nor Minula felt comfortable in that moment. This was something they needed to talk through, and the more was not the merrier.

"I know this is a stupid question, but how is this possible?" Abigail asked.

Lync was standing at the far side of the room with her arms crossed. "Your guess is as good as mine. Harold wouldn't tell me, and I never knew my mother. I sure as hell know one thing though, my father is not your father."

"No, he is not," she muttered.

"Your mother and your father were separated for a few years before you were born." Harold was still in the elder form of himself on the screen and was staring at Abigail. "She reached out to me a little over a year before you were born. She had wanted to talk to Stark, to see if they could make amends and patch things up."

Abigail ran her hands through her hair and paused at the end, resting them against her forehead. "They never mentioned any of this to us before."

"No, they didn't. There was no reason to. Your father had buried himself in his work, and your mother wanted more. She wanted a life. She tried to stick it out beside him, but in the end she decided to leave. I think she hoped he would follow, but you know Stark."

"He wasn't the brightest emotional bulb sometimes." Abigail swallowed hard.

Lync chuckled.

Abigail remembered when she was little. There would be days and weeks that her father would disappear for work. It must have been rough for her. "So," she nodded toward Lync, "she met your father when they were split."

Lync adjusted her stance, shifting from one foot to the other. "I only know they met at a Ulixi ceremony. She'd apparently stumbled across it, and they were about to kill her. One thing led to another, and my father saved her life. Ten months later, bam!" She pointed at herself.

"And then what, Harold? This still doesn't make sense."

Harold shook his head. "I don't know what happened. Fast-forward another fifteen months, and she popped out of hiding and wanted to talk. She hasn't told me any more than that after all these years."

They stared at each other for a while, uncertain what to say next. She'd never had a sister before. There'd always been a weird vibe between her and Lync, but she figured it was friendly, or perhaps even romantic. Never in a trillion years would she have pegged her for a sister.

Lync shifted her stance again and broke the silence. "I'm sure it'd be fun and all to sit around and comb each other's hair and shit, but I'd rather get back to defending Sol. We sorta have a few loose ends to take care of there."

She was right. They could tackle this later. There were

more important matters to discuss. "Who's in charge in Sol right now?"

"I expect we'd be better off staying here," Harold began. "We need to plan the next steps to—"

Abigail tilted her head. "Harold! Who'd you leave running the show in Sol? Who's handling the Galactic Alliance?"

"Your brothers are at our other colony, and I believe Commander Quesh would like a word—"

She slammed her hand against her bed. "Harold!"

"I left Fleet Admiral Nguyễn Due in charge."

The room went silent, and she noticed Lync had recoiled at the mention of the name.

"That's impossible." Abigail shook her head. "He was being escorted to the Jurat, but last we talked he was a prisoner."

This time Harold looked uncomfortable. She didn't know how an A.I. managed to do it, but his human side was coming out now. "Commander Quesh and I discussed contingencies, and we came up with an idea to break you out. It was a long shot, but it was all we could come up with. I forged your signature on some documents that made it happen. You were trapped in the alien tribunal ship and my Four-Laws Engine wasn't thinking straight. There was a fourteen percent proba-bility of success and—"

"Fourteen!" Abigail screamed.

"It was the best odds we could find. And you'll be happy to know that within twelve hours of re-enlisting Nguyễn, those odds went up to seventy-five percent. You probably wouldn't be standing here had we not done it. You'd still be on their tribunal ship or worse."

She glanced at Lync. Her face was white, and from the looks of her posture, if she could jump into the screen, Harold would be getting an ass kicking. "Are you ok?"

Lync clenched and unclenched her fists. "Is this Nguyễn

Due the same Major Nguyễn Due who formerly commanded the I.R.F. Kaliningrad?"

Harold nodded. "It is. That was many years ago, but yes. He's moved up the ranks since then."

Abigail squinted. "Do you know him?"

Lync slowly turned her head toward Abigail. Tears of rage welled up in her eyes. "The soldiers under his command killed my father."

5

LYNC MICHAELS
TAU CETI, OORT CLOUD

Lync couldn't believe her ears. After all this time, the bastard that killed her father was running the show in Sol. If she'd known this detail when she was picking up the Ulixi, she wouldn't have left.

"He needs to pay." She closed her eyes and then opened them again, staring through Abigail to the image of Harold on the wall screen. He'd done this thing. He'd put Nguyễn in power.

"You're right." Abigail raised her hands up. "We need to address the issue with your father, but right now, we're needed here."

Lync shook her head. "You mean you're needed here. I'm not about to abandon our people in Sol. You got what you needed from me. You got my blood. I have something more important to take care of." She spun around and started toward the door.

"Don't you turn your back on me, Major!"

She ignored her and kept walking. She didn't need this shit, and she'd already wasted far too much time in this room. As she approached the door, she felt a hand on her shoulder that whirled her around.

"I'm talking to you!" Abigail said. "Don't turn your back on your president."

"Former president!" She raised a finger. "According to Harold, they replaced you with a traitorous killer named Nguyễn. But perhaps that's what you Olivaws call president."

Abigail's eyes went wide. She was shaking on her feet, but Lync couldn't tell if it was rage or fatigue. "Are you accusing me of being a traitor?"

"Given the lies and deception your family spread throughout the years, it might not be a stretch. If the shoe fits—"

Abigail rounded on Lync and cracked her in the jaw, sending her spinning toward the wall. Pain shot through her face. The woman had a solid hook for being a pencil pusher. She didn't care if she had just come out of a coma. Her family was going to suffer, one way or another, and her fists were good enough for now.

Lync lurched forward and slammed Abigail hard with her shoulder, sending her toppling backward. After she stopped sliding, she knelt down with her knee in her stomach and repeatedly pummeled her with each fist.

Every ounce of pent-up rage toward the people who'd killed her father was surfacing and pouring out on this one woman whose family had caused so much bloodshed in Sol. Despite her being a friend over the years, she'd changed. They'd both changed.

Abigail brought her hands up to her face to defend herself, but she was weakening. Her arms were bloody and bruised, but Lync kept hitting. "You were happy to take my blood to save yourself before you and your A.I. tossed me aside. Typical elitist Inners pretending to be an Outer when it's convenient. You're no different from Nguyễn."

Her rage was overflowing, and she was picking up steam.

As Abigail lowered her hands, the door flew open and guards swarmed Lync, pulling her off their president.

"Harold to the rescue!" She spat toward Abigail, hitting her with a gob of bloody spit.

"Get her out of my fraking sight. Toss her in the brig!" Abigail reached up and rubbed the fresh wounds on her face.

The soldiers yanked Lync hard as she struggled to break loose. There was no use fighting. There were too many of them, but the rage in her was impossible to control.

In a matter of days she went from being on top of the world, to yet again being on the bottom.

THE HARD STEEL of the bench in Lync's cell was cold to the touch and felt great against her cheek. It'd flared up within seconds of Abigail's right hook, and the frigid bench did wonders for it.

Her nanites were reporting it would take a few days to repair the damage to her face. She had nothing but time and nowhere to be.

As she replayed the moments of the hospital room through her mind, she shook her head. She should've just walked away. Hitting her hadn't helped anyone and now she was fraked. Literally and completely fraked.

"Done a number on you, she has," Crayo said over the intercom.

She flinched at the sound of someone else's voice and sat up. Her friend was grinning at her through the visitor port on the far wall. "Trust me, she looks worse than I do."

"I'd hope so," he chuckled. "You's got decades more training on her. I'm surprised she hit ya at all. You must be getting soft."

"Even traitors are lucky once in a while," she muttered.

"I'd be careful who you're calling a traitor, Major."

Commander Quesh walked up beside Crayo. "She may not be the acting president in Sol, but she's in charge out here."

She laughed and leaned back with her head against the wall. At first, it was a shallow laugh, and then it broke out and turned into a deeper bellowing howl.

"Did I say something funny?" Commander Quesh asked.

She exhaled and slowly cracked each knuckle on her right hand before making eye contact with her former commander. "Whatcha want, Queshy?" She tapped her left arm and spat to the side. "Does Abby need some more blood? Or are you simply waiting long enough for Fleet Admiral Nguyễn Due to do your dirty work in Sol before taking over again?"

Commander Quesh shook his head. "I see you're still strung out from all the transfusions, like Harold said. You're not yourself."

What the hell was he on about? She hadn't had a transfusion in a week, and except for some non-invasive surgeries to remove her implants, she was fine. Harold must be up to something.

"Still," Quesh continued, his face screwed up in thought. "I can't risk you attacking the president again on our voyage. You're not giving me many options." He turned to look at Crayo. "She's gonna have to ride a cell during the trip."

"Where are we going?" she asked, but no one answered her. Maybe they'd shut off her microphone.

"Awe, come on, bossman." Crayo gestured in the air with his hands. "She needs to keep training to stay sharp. We all do. Tis da only chance we got against these aliens."

Quesh nodded. "I hear you, but Major Michaels isn't making this decision easy. I can't leave her alone in Tau Ceti." He seemed to stare past Crayo, pondering something. "Still, we can rig something up below deck for her until she's back to normal. We have other plans for her. For all of us."

Crayo tilted his head and glanced briefly over his

shoulder at Lync before returning his attention to the Commander. "What's that supposed to mean?"

"You'll find out along with everyone else once we're under way, Lieutenant. Until then..." He gestured over his shoulder with his thumb toward her. "Take care of Major Michaels. Clean her up and get her in uniform. She needs to start acting the part again and stop fraking around with the civilians. We're in a war, not a soap opera."

He stormed away, leaving her staring at Crayo with her mouth open.

"What was that about?" she asked.

"Gots no clue." Crayo scratched his head. "Something tells me the overseer had your back, though."

LYNC REACHED up and rubbed at her neck. After centuries of technological advancement, you'd think they could develop military fatigues that didn't itch.

As her transport car came to a halt, she hopped off and gestured a thank you toward the driver before she realized it was a robot. The idea of everything being automated took some getting used to.

"So I hear you pummeled the president." Kara walked up beside her.

She glanced to her left at the elder Olivaw, unsure what to make of the statement. "Something like that. You know sisters."

"Can't say I do," Kara said. "My brother was an asshole, though. He relinquished me of my role within the family while I wasn't looking."

Lync tilted her head. "I thought you stepped down to start a family?"

"That's what we told the media." Kara stiffened her jaw. "The Olivaws are a—"

"What the frak is she doing on my ship?" Abigail shouted as she stepped off her transport. "No way in hell is she riding with me. Quesh, what's she doing out of the brig, anyhow?"

Lync took a step away from Abigail. She preferred not to be accused of anything out here. She'd be liable to end up in the brig, or worse, she'd get spaced.

Commander Quesh jogged up between them and rested his hand on Abigail's shoulder. "She's fine. Harold's watching her, and she'll be on an entirely different level than you. Besides, she's part of the plan. Your brother is expecting her."

"You and this fraking plan. What the hell has Zachary got you doing?" She shoved his hand away and stormed into the ship. "I wish you'd just tell me what this is about."

Quesh shook his head and followed behind her. "Not until we're underway, Madam President."

"I love it." Kara glanced toward Lync. "You're gonna fit right in this family." She reached over and pulled her closer. "You're my niece now, and you're bunking with me. We've got a lot to talk about. I need to fill you in on this dysfunctional tribe of ours."

These Olivaws were like riding a mine car through the ice tunnels on Europa. One minute they're at a high, and the next they're barreling to the bottom, leaving her stomach in a lurch. She wasn't sure she could keep up with all their personalities.

She reached up and tapped her ear, subvocalizing a comm. "Harold, are you talking to me yet?"

There was nothing but silence. Harold hadn't answered her queries since she'd been dragged out of Abigail's hospital room. She still didn't know what was going on, but she couldn't take much more of this. It was hard enough feeling like they were giving up on Sol, but being blindly taken away to god knows where was almost worse.

When she stepped aboard the ship, she glanced back at the hangar. The entire place was clearing out. Wherever they were headed, they were going together. That gave her some comfort.

Her retinal comm chimed with a message. Its sender was empty, and the subject was eerily familiar. The last time she'd seen that subject line was over twenty years ago at Saturn, when a message was forwarded on from her father. It said, "A close friend, S".

She took a deep breath and opened the message. The contents appeared on her retinal comm.

Looking forward to finally meeting you in Zeta Lupi. See you soon. S.

Her stomach flipped. She hadn't seen that S initial in years. Not since she'd received that video of her father's death. Whoever this was, they knew who killed him. She didn't know why they hadn't told anyone else about her, but she needed to meet them. They could hold the keys to understanding her past.

6

NGUYỄN DUE
SOL, NEAR NEPTUNE

Admiral Nguyễn and his contingent of five others stepped off the alien shuttle. The four space marines were surrounding him, along with his right hand, XO Gwen Marshall. They'd become inseparable these past months since President Olivaw released him from military prison.

Ambassador Addae seemed to float through the entryway without a sound before landing in front of them. "I told you it wasn't necessary to bring other... humans." Her feathers ruffled when she approached, as if she were shuddering in their presence.

Unless his memory was failing him, her plumage was more vibrant than during his last visit. Her green feathers were so bright they practically burned his eyes, whereas her purples had shifted entirely to black.

He stepped toward her and his team parted. As he approached her, he paused and bowed. His contingent mimicked his motion in sync.

"I figured that since you came armed to the last session, it couldn't hurt. Besides, we both know I didn't make many friends with my... gesture." A smirk teased at the edge of his mouth, but he kept it from forming into a smile. There was no point in offending them sooner than necessary.

Ambassador Addae's right talon clanked against the noiseless floor, its pearl color shimmering in the shuttle bay light. "I'd hardly call splitting open a Galactic Admiral with your primitive knives a simple gesture. More like a provocation of war."

"Is that why you called me here, Ambassador? To reprimand me?" He straightened his back and let out an exhaustive exhale. "I could've listened to this shit from the safety of my ship. Can you please get to the point? I have things to do."

Ambassador Addae took a step closer to him, leaning one eye toward him and bringing her beak mere centimeters from his face.

His contingent shuffled in place and moved to his side. He could see their subcutaneous skeletal armor powering up on his retinal comm. His hand raised to the side, gesturing for them to stand down.

"Don't insult me again," Ambassador Addae said softly. "I warned you of that last time. You may be flashing your colors at me trying to act dominant, but the fact of the matter is, I could kill you before your armored puppets even finished their nanite adrenaline spike."

The skin on his neck throbbed as if to remind him of the steel-like grip of her talons around his throat a few months back. She knew more about them than he'd imagined. These soldiers' body mods were top secret. Either they had a mole, or the Galactic Alliance had infiltrated their systems.

He squinted at her eye staring at him. "I see you've been eavesdropping on our comms. You should learn to respect our privacy."

Ambassador Addae leaned back and let out a melodic note he could only assume was a laugh. "You don't know the extent your species has betrayed its own kind. All will be revealed soon enough. Please follow me." She spun around with her back to them and walked away, heading toward the chamber he'd been in during his last visit.

It wasn't until they followed her that he and his team realized they'd been outflanked by her soldiers. The Ambassador's guard had been in the shuttle bay the entire time, either cloaked or hiding out of sight. Either way, there were now four heavily armed birds accompanying them close behind. Their exo-suits weren't making any attempt to be quiet.

He watched as his team's adrenaline levels peaked, and they began preparing their mods. Checking their safeties and assigning out who was covering which guard.

"Careful," he messaged over his comm without subvocalizing. He couldn't risk Lisp, their Bynaury, detecting them. While he knew their bodies were supposed to be off limits aboard the tribunal ship, President Olivaw found out the hard way that even the GA had judicial mechanisms to conceal the truth. "Don't provoke them. You can posture all you want, but we will not fire first. Is that understood?"

"Yessir!" they all acknowledged.

XO Marshall had been silent since their arrival. From what he could tell from their private comm channel, she'd been taking in all of her surroundings and recording volumes of data at the same time. Apparently, she and her team were ejecting airborne nanites to take readings. While she didn't appear to be formidable at first glance, she was quite capable of holding her own.

Ambassador Addae escorted them into the center of the larger chamber and gestured for them to stop. She then continued toward the distant perch and sat upon it. Her escorts slid up behind her while seamlessly walking backwards until they reached her side. They never once took their eyes off his team.

His plan had worked. He wanted them on edge. They were more likely to make mistakes that way.

The chamber was somehow even more spacious than his previous visit, and his retinal comm confirmed it. Along the walls, there were three rows of benches encircling the room rather than only one like the last time. Whatever was going on, it would be far larger than before.

A few moments later, the aliens began filing in. XO Marshall had already assigned each soldier a quadrant of the room. They were doing detailed ops on each and every alien they could, attempting to record as many channels of communication and verbal cues as possible. She also had hundreds of nanites encircling the room, eking out any intel they could.

Occasionally, the nanites would blink out of existence. When he gestured with his comm to understand why, they reported back that they'd been detected and took evasive measures to self-destruct. No remnants other than specs of unidentifiable dust would ever be found.

As he studied the path of the nanites she deployed, he realized she'd done something particularly ingenious. She'd been using them to monitor themselves along with the other aliens. That way if the Galactic Alliance accused them of treachery, they could point to their privacy being invaded, as well. He liked how she thought.

The room filled rapidly. There were easily three to four times as many aliens as his previous visit. This time, each alien was represented by four members of their species. There also appeared to be many new species that weren't present last time mixed among the others. His retinal comm outlined each new type of alien in red with a small question mark hanging over them. XO Marshall must be having a field day.

He dismissed the nanite overlay when he saw Ambassador Addae float down off her perch and adjust her plumage. Her bright-green feathers appeared to radiate light outward, drawing the attention of the other aliens and bringing the audible mutterings to an abrupt end.

Ambassador Addae lowered her beak with her eyes closed for a moment, seeming to relish the silence and respect of everyone around her. When she opened them, they ignited the air between her and him. If she could tear him apart in front of them all, she would. "Distinguished species, noble applicants of the Galactic Alliance, and humans. I've brought you all here to bear witness to the prosecution's case before humanity. Traditional proceedings normally involve months and sometimes years of judicial research, but our times are different. The Galactic Alliance has failed our members and allowed a rogue segment of an alliance species to impact a tribunal."

Murmurs spread throughout the room, and aliens began standing up. They each shouted at her and raised their hands or appendages, pointing them downward. Their shouts were translated for him and the others.

"Down with the Qudoculi!"

"Trial for them all!"

"Ban the Thyreus!"

The Ambassador's neck lengthened, her wings spread wide, and her beak pointed upward. The room fell silent. She was threatening to let loose her screech. She almost seemed disappointed as she glanced around the chamber, searching for a dissenter to challenge her. There was no one.

Admiral Nguyễn simply stood in place, shaking his head as she centered her attention back on him. He raised his hand, inaudibly chuckling into it. He could sense Ambassador Addae watching him, which was the point. Throw them off and keep them fuming.

"Mark my words," she continued, "we will deal with the rogue factions of the Qudoculi and the Thyreus. This isn't the first time power has poisoned the minds and intentions of splinter groups within our alliance. What matters is the actions of the many and not the ignorance of the few."

He chuckled into his hand again. The aliens were intent on putting on a show. His retinal comm alerted him he'd drawn the ambassador's attention.

"Apparently the humans present are finding my words to be… humorous."

The crowd of onlookers turned and focused on him. His comm lit up. Earlier in the week he'd asked his crew to create a means to use their nanites to better understand and read the jury. While they outlawed such things in Sol, here in the Galactic Alliance, he wasn't aware of any such rule.

He bowed his head toward her and raised his palm outward, as was officially the protocol to request the floor when another non-uplifted species had it. Harold and Lisp shared this little detail with him after his last faux pas landed him on the ground with a talon around his neck.

Ambassador Addae waved her wing dismissively at him. "You may speak, Admiral. If you would, I'm sure the other members of the alliance would love to know what you found so humorous about my speech."

"Thank you, Ambassador, for the honor of addressing the alliance members. I apologize if my reaction to your message came across unexpectedly. You can't help but sympathize with our current situation being how you described it, and yet, you're giving special treatment to the Qudoculi and the Thyreus." He gestured with his hand to the right, pointing at the distant Thyreus contingent, one of which was Prosecutor Drak. "I see they're still present in the proceedings and probably even hold a valid vote, if I understand your… rules."

Ambassador Addae eyed the Thyreus before returning her attention back to him. "The Thyreus are on probation, but nothing we uncovered showed they were doing more than responding to a direct order from the Qudoculi. Besides, I—"

He couldn't take another word. "Oh, come on, Ambassador!" He raised an arm into the air. "Is your alliance honestly incapable of thinking on their own? Here I thought you were more evolved. It sounds like your police force is nothing but a pawn to your governing alliance members."

Voices of frustration rose throughout the chamber as the translator struggled to keep up.

"There are murmurs of assent to what you said from the non-alliance members," XO Marshall said over their private comms. "Keep them thinking."

Ambassador Addae began walking toward him. "Please do not interrupt me again, human."

A smile spread across his face. She was making this too easy. "I believe you relinquished the floor, and I was able to speak freely. Such is allowed for in article sixty-three, subsections six through twenty-two. Even as an uplift species, we're entitled to these same measures. Or does that get thrown to the galactic wind like your judicial forces in Epsilon Eridani already casting the Dark Nebula?"

Her eye twitched. He couldn't tell if it was out of anger or if she was being fed information by her implants. Either way, it wasn't normal for her to drop her defenses. She'd always been hot or cold, nothing in between.

Ambassador Addae turned to face the alliance members. "We're not here to discuss or debate any forthcoming trials with other alliance members. We're here to present and preside over your current trial, Admiral. In case you forgot about the human trial of subverting our faster than light laws. As an uplifted species, you're banned from using such technology. I see no parallels to the matter at hand with that of Qudoculi or the Thyreus. You've also failed to produce evidence to counter our claims of theft."

He turned up his face dramatically and pointed at her for effect. "It was you who said a moment ago that what matters is the actions of the many and not the ignorance of the few.

Were those not your words? The acting judicial head of the Galactic Alliance tribunal."

Her feathers ruffled and straightened. He could have sworn the bright-green section on her chest throbbed brighter in response to his remarks. "Those were my words. I stand by them."

She was walking right into his trap. "Then I'm perplexed. How is it that the many Thyreus should be treated any differently than the many humans? As I'm sure your archival evidence shows, humanity knew nothing of the subterfuge enacted by the rogue Olivaw family, and yet, you're putting our entire species on trial." He shook his head and vocalized a ticking sound. "That sounds to me like a double standard by any definition."

The murmurs from before were replaced with louder shouts of assent interwoven with frustration and anger that the human was still being allowed to speak. Each alien voice was gradually chipping away at Ambassador Addae's armor. She was strong, but all politicians had their weaknesses. They were nothing without the support of their constituency.

"Enough!" Ambassador Addae raised her beak toward the sky and let out a blood-curdling screech.

The room fell silent.

As he clasped his hands around his ears, he couldn't help but find it confusing how a sound dampened space was so easily manipulated by these judicial members. The more he learned how these aliens operated, the more he wanted to slit their throats. The electro-blades in the nook of his back were calling to him. Begging to taste fresh blood.

After the sound stopped echoing through the chamber, Ambassador Addae lowered her beak and spoke. "The floor is now mine. No other species is authorized to speak."

He chuckled.

She leaned toward him, and he did, in turn.

"Do not push me, human!" Spittle flew across the space between them and hit him on the cheek.

His nanites reported that the liquid was natural and contained no toxins. He reached up and wiped it off his face, flicking it at her. "Do that again, you fraking pimped out bird, and I'll kill you where you stand. You and your kind need to leave our star system, before you regret it."

A message appeared from Harold on his retinal comm and an anger rose from within. No matter how hard he tried, he couldn't escape this A.I. from invading his mind. He read the message:

Ambassador Addae violated article seventy-seven, subsection C. She invaded the space of a fellow alliance member and exchanged bodily fluid in a manner non-acceptable to said species. These are grounds for her dismissal with enough votes.

It was funny how despite his invasions being unprovoked, he always came bearing gifts.

He took a few steps back from Ambassador Addae as her guards streamed into the chamber from around the room. Nguyễn's people shifted to a defensive stance, surrounding him on all sides with their backs to him and facing the alien birds advancing from all directions.

"Hold on," he subvocalized as he reached out, resting his hand on two of his soldiers' shoulders. "Don't overreact. I still have this under control." His comm showed each soldier checking over their mods, triple confirming they could juice up in a moment's notice.

Nguyễn stepped between his people and almost comically smiled toward the ambassador as he waved a hand around the room. "I see you called your guards to take you away."

"On the contrary, Admiral. As an uplift, it is you who is being removed for threatening a judicial task force member. While the Qudoculi may have ignored such matters with their previous administration, I will no longer have a spectacle made of these proceedings."

He nodded. "I agree. That's a wise move indeed, Ambassador. It's for that reason that I ask my fellow uplift species and alliance members to have you removed as the acting head of this tribunal force. Under article seventy-seven, subsection C of the uplift accord, you forced your bodily fluids upon me without my consent. Should I not be given leeway for my reaction, I choose to relinquish my position as representative of humanity and hereby request that Captain Marshall here fill the role in my stead." He stepped to the side and gestured toward Gwen, who was standing silently behind him. Her expression wore the mask of surprise, as well as that of the Ambassador.

For a third time, the room cascaded out of control as the species split along invisible party lines. Those who were against the human's existence after the last human trial, and those who were sympathetic to their situation.

"I... don't understand—" Ambassador Addae did a double take and shook her head. Or was she looking around? He couldn't tell. Either way, she was confused over what had just transpired.

According to the data coming in from XO Marshall, the numbers were split thirty percent in favor of supporting the humans, and seventy against. While it wasn't a majority by any stretch of the imagination, the dissenters were quite vocal, and that was all he needed.

He leaned a little toward the ambassador, though he was sure that whatever he said would be translated for everyone. "I hate to ask, but do you have a decision? Are you stepping aside or are we calling for a vote of no confidence in your species turn at the helm?"

Ambassador Addae's eyes twitched again, like it'd done earlier. She was clearly getting either intel or instructions from somewhere else, and she wasn't used to it. Her body trembled in frustration whenever she was ordered to do something.

A moment later, whatever orders she'd received were acted upon. All around the room her guards bowed toward the humans in the center, and Ambassador Addae dropped in front of him.

Nguyễn flinched backward, unsure what to do. He wasn't expecting this at all.

A lone soldier stood up from the back row of her guard and approached his group, being certain not to provoke his soldiers by making eye contact. The entire way, he held his beak low in shame and drew his eyes to the ground. As he neared them, he came up short and slowly spun his staff toward Nguyễn.

He reached out and took the offered weapon. The weight of it was remarkable. It was almost like it wasn't there, yet he knew exactly where it was in space. He lifted it up and down. Fascinating.

When the Trochilidae released the staff, he did a double take. There was a massive blade on the end. A moment before, it hadn't been present. Whatever they did to it, the shimmering metal blade only appeared after they'd released it.

"What am I supposed to do with this?" he asked his team sub-vocally.

"Kill her," Harold said.

His response echoed through his mind. He couldn't be serious. What she'd done certainly had no grounds for death. While he felt nothing but anger toward the Galactic Alliance, this wasn't how he imagined it would go. There was no glory in dying this way.

"You're required to execute her," Harold said. "It's the

law. Her actions were unprovoked and could have led to harm."

He shook his head, staring at the plumage of Ambassador Addae. In the last sixty seconds her bright-green feathers had all but faded and were now nearly as dark as the black surrounding them. "I won't."

"You must."

The memories of cutting into Admiral Gwar flashed through his mind, slicing him open and taking his life in an instant. While it was unexpected at the time, it was provoked and due. This, however, was not.

As he studied the ambassador, he became aware of the chants around him. The volume in the room was rising. Each species joining the other in a melodic chorus. "Judge her, for she is not fit. Judge her and return respect to her kind. The Beacon demands it. The Beacon expects it." They repeated their incantation faster and faster, louder and louder, willing him to take her life.

"These aliens are insane," he subvocalized.

"The longer we're with them, the more unusual they become," Harold said. "While I suspect each species nuances' and behaviors have influenced their laws over the generations, this is downright barbaric."

"Perhaps we should give them what they're asking for," XO Marshall said.

Maybe she was right. They were expecting a show. Far be it for him to not offer one up.

He bounced the staff in his hand, being sure he understood the weight before he acted. "Everyone bow down, now."

There was no questioning his order. All five of the others immediately dropped into a bow around him, and he stepped forward, standing over Ambassador Addae.

She hadn't moved in minutes. Not since she'd lowered to

the ground. No whimpers and no shaking. She'd resigned her fate, even if it wasn't what she'd wanted.

He took a deep breath as the chanting grew to a crescendo and raised the staff high over his head. For an instant, the room paused, and their chant shifted to a single word.

"Judge!"

It repeated over and over again as he held the weapon aloft.

Every ounce of his focus was being challenged. Everything they'd worked for over the past months had come to this moment. The energy from the crowd coursed through his muscles as he let out a blood-curdling scream and drew the blade of the staff downward.

The weapon sensed his motion and its weight shifted, from nothingness to a heft he'd never sensed before. It didn't just power his swing; it accelerated with an unexpected explosiveness.

As the weapon sliced through the air, its arc ended embedded solidly in the ground below.

The room fell silent. Not the eerie silence he'd experienced when he first stepped onto a GA shuttle, the type of silence after you'd witnessed a life-changing event. One you hadn't expected.

Ambassador Addae shifted, turning her beak toward the lethal object mere millimeters from her head. The shimmering base where the staff seamlessly transitioned to the blade reflected in her eyes.

It was only now that he noticed she'd been crying. At least he assumed they were tears. He'd never seen this emotion before in his time aboard the tribunal ship, but the signs were universal across all species on Earth.

"You must take my life to return honor to my kind." Ambassador Addae glanced up at him with one eye.

He shook his head. "I will do nothing of the sort."

She leaned back, but remained low. "It's the law."

"I don't care. It's not our law." He looked up and slowly panned around the room. "Your—laws—are—not—valid —here."

He gestured to the side and opened a transfer to Lisp; the Bynaury presiding over the ship. He also opened a comm to his team. "Play this over my head now."

"Are you certain, sir?" Harold paused his transfer. "It's too soon to provoke them. We need more time."

"Send the message, Harold. This will give us the time we need. Trust me. They're already in shambles, and this ought to push them over."

"Very well."

The transmission continued.

A moment later, a video appeared over his head, projected from one of his exo-suited officers. It was a recording from the bow of a ship and was dramatically panning around a Dark Nebula.

The crowd remained silent, taking in the imagery. When its target came into view, the room collectively inhaled.

There on the screen was some type of Galactic Alliance relay. An unmanned one from what Harold told them. He didn't care if it had occupants or not. What mattered more was what happened next.

A beam of light burst forward from the source of the video aimed squarely at the relay. It exploded into a million pieces in a ball of orangish pink luminescence before it faded to black, replaced by the pulsing waves flowing over the Dark Nebula in the background.

A set of Galactic Alliance coordinates appeared overhead.

He broke the silence by stepping away from the ambassador and walking between the still kneeling Trochilidae soldiers surrounding them. "I'll spare you the drama of what your home worlds will find out months and years from now. Or maybe your computers have already told you. We took this image from your relay near Achernar twelve days ago. It was part of your forward array. We can only assume you built it to ensure your eighty-year-old sealed Dark Nebula around the Gharloc wasn't somehow compromised. If you were anywhere nearby, you'd likely have received a warning of an unidentified alien ship appearing nearby, until it blinked out of existence and you lost your signal. Consider this retribution for smash mining a planetesimal in our system. But rest assured, this isn't even close to the pain we'll inflict for destroying our colony and killing our people in Epsilon Eridani."

The murmurs began to spread. First from the aliens closest to him and then like a flame to a fire from around the room.

He knew the implications of what they were seeing. The revelations were sinking in slowly with each second that passed.

The images were twelve days old, and yet traveling aboard Galactic Alliance ships would take them over five hundred days to reach Sol. Using the technology Harold claimed to be commanding brought this message to them in a tad over six days.

"I will not warn you again!" He emphasized each word with his fist coming down into the air. "Leave Sol now and never return to this or any human star system. Each and every alien that fails to comply, or gets in our way, will regret it. Blood will be shed. We won't invade your stars, but any further motion into our star systems can only be seen as an act of aggression."

The ship had stopped translating and muted the conversations around the room, but the nanites they had circling the space made it clear their message was received. The aliens weren't happy, but they also weren't making any motions to advance on them.

Nguyễn turned toward his people and marched between them. They each stood as he passed and followed close behind as they headed out the entrance they came through.

He paused before exiting and raised a finger skyward. "And one last thing. We will not be coming aboard this ship again. Any future communications can go through other channels."

With that, he lowered his hand and exited the room. When they each passed over the precipice of the exit and the door closed behind them, he finally took a deep breath. He didn't know when he'd last breathed, but it'd been too long.

His heart was pounding in his chest, and his skin was crawling from all the alien eyes that'd been watching him. Their scrutiny lingered even now with the door sealed. He could sense them tearing him apart with their eyes, limb by limb. That whole situation could've gone any number of ways. Had the ambassador not played into his hand, they may not have had an opportunity to present that video.

Harold claimed they needed time, but based upon what he'd seen in that room, they were already cracking at the seams. While he'd managed to turn the tables in their favor for a few minutes, the Galactic Alliance still had the upper hand by many measures. They could start and end this thing at any moment, and humanity would be done for. Just another footnote in the GA history books.

Hopefully, Harold was bluffing and could help them if needed.

7

JOYCE GREEN
EPSILON ERIDANI, LIPROSUS

No matter how long Joyce stared at the virtual wall of aliens sliding back and forth and crawling toward her, she couldn't get her ship to jump through hyperspace. Harold insisted it was as simple as aligning the balls of energy in three-dimensional space, but she never could do it.

"This is such a fraking waste of time." She slammed her fists downward and shattered the virtual control panel into a cloud of dust.

The massive words "GAME OVER" strobed in and out a dozen meters overhead. She squinted at the text, barely visible beneath it. "What does it mean to insert twenty-five cents to play again?"

Harold's avatar as an elderly man flashed into existence beside her. "Those are the coins or credits I used as a kid to play these things. We'd gather at the arcade to play this game after school. A far more primitive form of it, but essentially the same thing."

"What did you say it was called again?" Elaine asked, her voice ominously coming from all directions. She was standing behind Joyce in real life.

Harold stared off into the distance with a smile on his face. "Galaga. It even sounds badass, right?"

"It sounds like you're wasting my time." Joyce subvocalized a command, and the simulation fell away, bringing her back into the real world. She was resting on a virtual reality couch, her body sitting in a neutral position.

"You seriously were awful," Elaine said. "Not at all like Mimi. She's a natural."

Joyce swung her legs off the couch and stretched her back. "I hate VR games. Give me a physical rifle or a plasma howitzer any day of the week."

"I'm with you." Ryder walked up and handed her a globe of coffee. "Though if you remember, about two months ago you'd have fallen flat on your ass wielding a howi."

She smiled at the thought. When she'd seen them used in battle the first time against the Galactic Alliance mining shuttles, she practically shat herself. She swore the whole place was going to collapse in on them. "Truer words have never been spoken. Two months of being cooped up underground, and I've run out of toys to play with."

On the wall screen, she watched as Mimi manipulated the glowing sphere of light in front of her. She slid her hand around the globe and adjusted the luminous beams toward the center, playing with their colors until she blinked out and jumped behind the barricade of aliens. A second later she fired her laser blaster and took out the Boss Galagas waiting patiently behind their drones to attack where she'd once been.

Joyce leapt forward and nearly dropped her coffee as the little girl's body gyrated in the air and screeched in celebration of her virtual win. She reached up and wiped away a few droplets of coffee off her shirt. "Harold, tell me again why we're wasting our time in a twentieth century arcade."

His elderly human form strolled across the wall screen toward her and paused to face her. "We're training for what's coming."

She closed her eyes and took a deep breath after swallowing the last gulp of caffeinated bliss. He was talking in riddles again. If she had to hear another damn convoluted non-answer, she was going to scream. "Can you please just give me a straight explanation? Stop talking like Mr. Miyagi and answer my fraking question."

Harold narrowed his gaze at her and stared silently, as if contemplating something before speaking. "I… can't honestly tell you anything else other than what we're doing matters."

"Matters to what? When? You have to give us more than that, you ball of binary." She chucked her empty globe of coffee at him, and it ricocheted back at her, landing in her open hand.

"Nice shot," Elaine muttered.

"Thanks. I wish it were a grenade."

Harold flashed off the wall, but his voice still sounded from overhead. "That wouldn't be nice and would definitely be counter to our mission."

She shook her head and dropped the globe, kicking it toward the recycler at the last moment before it hit the ground. It slid to a stop just short of the receptacle and a bot zoomed past, picked it up, and knocked it into the hole. "If only we knew what our mission was."

"We've spoken about this countless times," Harold said to her privately over her comm. "You know the goal is to build reserves and prepare for an aggressive expansion when the time's right."

Her fist clenched and then relaxed. She hated it when he injected himself into her mind without consent. It was one thing to be around her, in reality, but it was quite another to invade her private space without permission.

"I sense I may have crossed a line again," Harold said. "Your heart rate is elevated, and—"

She subvocalized the command to squelch him. While they didn't have a means to shut him off, they could always stop listening to what he was saying. At least the Olivaws had thought of that. It took her almost a month to ask him if there was a way to do that. She didn't know why it'd taken her so long to think of asking, but it was glorious. His damn Four-Laws engine was good for something.

"I'm out," Joyce said. "I'm heading for a stroll to clear my head." She walked toward the door.

Ryder craned his neck at her. "Headed to see our guests?"

She nodded and paused. "Maybe. Wanna come?"

"I'll be down in a bit. Gonna watch Mimi give it another go on level sixty-four. She's making a run at a high score."

A chuckle escaped as she rubbed her face with her hand and exited the simulation room. In ten years, they're going to look back on this and laugh. Being cooped up underground, passing the time playing ancient video games because an A.I. told them to. This whole thing had to be a massive joke.

When she rounded the corner, she paused to check the status of their mining runs on her retinal comm. The day's second mining crew was due to return any minute now. They were taking chances and drilling deeper into the planet than before.

Their automated reconnaissance bots uncovered several large pockets of ore deep below the planet's crust, and one of them contained the same dark spots they found on the Galactic Alliance scans from a few months ago. That single run resulted in a decent haul of Spános and her new addiction to weaponry.

That was a word she didn't understand Harold's fixation on, Spános. He insisted it was the actual name for the material but couldn't say how he'd learned it. They confirmed it by asking their guests downstairs. It was strange, though. While they knew what it was, no matter how hard they tried, they were mum on the topic of how to process or refine it.

The Spános they'd uncovered was a goldmine of research. They were only scratching the surface of what they could use the material for. She'd asked Captain Hui to plan a mission to detonate it on one of the Selene ships, but Harold had assured her it was a waste of Spános. He said they'd need it when the others arrived and couldn't risk the Galactic Alliance returning to the planet and destroying the still functional orbiting space station. While the beanstalk had been severed, dropping a replacement nanotube cable was simple enough. Building a new platform was another challenge entirely.

She shuddered, thinking about the whole damn situation. No matter how many times she'd asked him, Harold could never tell her when these reinforcements would arrive. He merely reassured her they would.

When she checked the tracker network, there were still no signs of the crew. If they weren't back in the next hour, she'd need to dispatch a search party. They hadn't seen aliens in a long time, but she wasn't about to take a chance that they'd missed something. She was done leaving her people to die at the hands of the Galactic Alliance.

"Harold."

"Director."

"Please scramble a search party to send after the miners. Give them an hour countdown, and then I want them in the tubes bringing our people home."

"I'm on it."

That was strange. He's never not talkative. Knowing him, he was still pissed she'd shut him off earlier. She should take advantage of the quiet while she could. That A.I. needed to learn his place. He was a tool, not a person. She didn't care what his origins were. Harold Olivaw had died over two hundred years ago, and it was about time for his family to let his soul rest.

No one had asked to copy her memories, or her son's for that matter. And he died because of the damn Olivaw war with the Norths. Even thinking about it made her blood boil. She needed to get her mind off this topic before she lost control again. It had become a daily thing lately. Without her firearms, she'd have killed someone for sure.

Her comm chimed with an update. Harold had scrambled a search team. They were prepping a stingray ship as she stood there.

She dismissed her retinal overlays and stepped into the lift tube. Directional forces pulled her downward, making her fall faster than gravity would take her, and yet she didn't feel a thing. Every once in a while she took the emergency evacuation stairs to clear her head, but the steps took forever. While it was nice knowing they were there, this was more convenient, and faster to boot.

Her next destination wasn't far down, forty or so floors. About ten seconds of weightless falling, and she stepped out of the gravity field and continued down the security corridor. A series of hatches closed behind her, having opened when her nanites broadcasted her approach.

As the last of the quarter meter thick Skotádi hatches sealed, her ears popped. She hated the sensation and buzzing that lingered afterwards. It was like the old days when you went up or down too rapidly and pressure built up in your ears. While this didn't hurt like that could, it was still annoying. Harold said it was because the nanites in her ear canal were resetting with new security protocols to protect her around the aliens, but it felt strange.

She paused to let the scanners run up and down her body. Her muscles were tense from repeatedly dying in the simulation and dwelling on the time they were losing. Hiding out down here below the surface was stressful.

Reaching out, she ran her hand over the hatch in front of her. The material was remarkable. They used to call it stealth material until one day Harold started calling it Skotádi. Like with Spános, he had no idea why he changed, but he insisted the words were correct.

Every day they were cooped up with the amnesia ridden

A.I. was an adventure she grew more and more tired of. She hoped there was an end in sight to this underground prison. Maybe today was the day they'd give her a clue when this nightmare would end.

When the hatches silently opened, she was face to face with a featureless hallway. The only thing visible in the dim-lit space were two guards near the entrance and four more spaced down the corridor, positioned at the doorway to each cell. There were only two survivors from the mining incident, and they were each as stubborn as the other. They were sepa-rated by multiple layers of Skotádi and countless sensors recording their every move.

She walked up to the display outside Bumble Two and nodded at the guards flanking the door before reaching forward and swiping through the transcripts from the past day. It was pretty much the same as any other day. They meditated, muttered in their sleep about their hive, and demanded to be released or to seek representation under some random ass Galactic Alliance clause she didn't give two shits about.

Her team had come up with the names for the Thyreus prisoners of war after they'd returned from their extraction mission. Everyone in the colony kept referring to them as bumblebees or wasps rather than by their proper names. She should have cared more and chosen a more formal name. As far as she was concerned, though, they'd eventually be dead, so they went ahead and called them Bumble One and Bumble Two.

Captain Hui lodged an official protest to the nicknames. But she was the only one. Maybe she would've followed POW protocols in some other time or place that didn't have them on the brink of extermination. For now, she'd decided to give her people every bit of fun or diversion she could and the names stuck. There sure as hell weren't many outlets for fun buried underground.

She reached out and slammed her hand against the outer wall of the cell to see if Bumble Two reacted. While the guards flinched, the alien inside never budged. The vibrations and sound never made it through the material. She wasn't even sure why she did it. Partially to release some of the mounting frustrations she had before heading in, and partly to see if they sensed more than they let on. Trust wasn't something she ever imagined she'd give the aliens. Not in this lifetime.

"I'm headed in," Joyce said toward the guards. "Watch my six."

"Yessir!" they both snapped. The one to her right peeled off without a word and rotated to follow her inside.

Neither of them had weapons they might lose control over should the area be compromised, but they were by no means defenseless. They both had implants and mods that enabled them to accomplish mind-blowing feats of strength and agility. From what Harold had told her, they could tear off a Thyreus' limbs without much effort if it came to that.

The panel beside the door of this and the neighboring cell slid down into the floor. Once safely concealed, the overhead scanners ran one last check to make sure she had no nanites or unexpected articles on her person before they were finally allowed inside.

When the room went green and the doorway rose upward, a wave of fury from within followed suit. No matter how hard she tried to keep it at bay, it climbed up through the cracks. Pain and anguish were a tricky thing to suppress in the most ideal of circumstances, and these weren't even close.

She took a deep breath and stepped into the cell.

It was all black, from floor to ceiling and wall to wall. They didn't see any sense in painting the Skotádi. On its own, it had a soothing matte finish, so they left it.

Bumble Two had their back to the doorway and their hands and feet were completely immobilized. This again wasn't following established POW protocols of giving a prisoner room to move about, but these weren't normal times.

The Thyreus leader of that first mining mission had almost taken her head off with his gloved hands before they removed them. While they didn't require gloves to shoot their energy beams, they were far less lethal without them. That was another lesson they learned the hard way.

A week after their capture, several guards nearly lost their lives tending to Bumble Two. They'd made it a habit of giving each alien room to walk around their cells to exercise. Somehow, over that first week, they managed to reprogram their restraints to release when the guards entered. Had the humans not been in a pair, the results would have been death.

She still didn't know how that other guard hadn't killed Bumble Two. Had it been her, they'd be dead for sure. It was hard enough keeping her rage at bay and she didn't have the mods they did. Not yet, anyhow.

"Good afternoon, Two." She stepped in front of the alien and smiled. Her hands were behind her back, concealing her fists, which were repeatedly clenching and unclenching in a fleeting attempt to suppress her frustration.

Bumble Two was staring at the far corner of the room, but his antennae raised up and followed her around. They sensed her long before any noise or motion would've been apparent to a human without mods or nanites. These aliens had countless advantages over an unmodified human. Perhaps humanity shouldn't rethink their position on genetic modifications in a GA galaxy.

The alien didn't respond. Beyond the antennae swimming through the air, they remained silent, fixing their stare of sixteen eyeballs squarely at the corner. All those damn eyes were freaky and made her skin crawl.

It'd taken them the better part of the first month to figure out what the hell they were looking at most of the time. Harold whipped up a retinal comm overlay that could show them what was drawing the alien's attention, and today it was the absolute corner of the room where the walls met the floor.

Joyce nodded her head and began her normal pacing along the far wall, passing in front of Two's field of view. "Are we going to have a civilized conversation today, or are you planning on clamming up?"

Still no response. Last week they wouldn't shut up about the weather, and this past week they were mum. Apparently, they'd only volunteered for the mining mission because they were allowed out on the planet's surface to feel the sun against their skin. Something they hadn't experienced in over seventy thousand cycles. She forgot how many years that was. Harold did the conversion for them. It sounded like the GA form of cryo-stasis was common on these longer alliance tribunal ships, except they also had to spend great lengths of time outside of stasis doing scut duty.

She paused in the corner opposite where the alien was peering and folded a flat seating surface out of the wall before turning around and sitting to face them. "So, how long did you say you had left on your tribunal rotation?"

"Not long." Two broke the silence but continued their staring. "With the rate we were planning on closing the Nebula here and in Sol, we'd be back on Kerh in another hundred thousand cycles. We should make it in time for the selection of a new Octave queen."

Converting cycles to years was mind-numbing. The scale of time didn't make sense to her, and she didn't care, either. Most of the things they talked about were useless, but you never knew when they'd drop an important nugget she could use. For now, she was merely making small talk. "So how much longer until you finish closing the curtain here?"

Two's antennae paused their dance and bent slightly toward her. "What is curtain?"

Damn human terms. She gestured with her hand in the air

from left to right. "It's an analogy. A curtain is something we humans use to cover a window. You know, like the Nebula curtain you're closing around our star to kill us. How long until you finish sealing our Nebula?"

The antenna above Two went straight. "Thyreuns would never block the sun on purpose unless it was to provide shelter from the elements. It was bad enough not seeing it in space. A sun is a giver of all life. It helps the queens produce their nectar and provides sustenance to the plants that keep the Octave strong."

She hated it when they didn't answer her question. They were either getting distracted or playing mouse, and she was in a fucken catty mood. "Yea, but the problem is, human skin is sensitive to changes in temperature and light. But that's beside the point. What can you tell me about the Nebula?"

Two's body began shuddering and gyrating. She remembered that motion. Visions of a dozen of his species gyrating like that sprang forward from the recesses of her mind. They'd made the same gesture at Warren in the ring before they killed him. While she couldn't blame them for killing the bastard, what she'd asked about wasn't humorous.

A moment later Two stopped moving, and his antennae arced back toward her before he slowly turned to face her. All sixteen eyes staring her down. "It's useless."

Her hands were still concealed in her lap with her legs crossed, clenching and unclenching her fists. It was all she could do to contain her mounting frustration. She narrowed her gaze on the jet black alien, focusing on the hint of neon blue encircling its neck rather than their sea of eyes. "What's useless, Two? I'm not following."

His body shook again. "I don't suspect you would. Your species was never mentally adept, being uplifted and all. What you're failing to understand is that attempting to escape the Nebula is useless. There are countless ships and soldiers like me at the ready. They're awaiting the call from the tribunal. It's an honor to lose your life for the cause. But I should warn you, anyhow. It's impossible to leave your star system. You will be destroyed." He let those words hang in the air for a moment before turning his attention back to the corner of the room where he'd been staring when she entered. "You're better off waiting till we close the Nebula and then taking the few remaining years you'll have left to find your god, or whatever the hell it is your scum of a species believes in."

The muscles in her arms and back tensed as she fought a wave of anger boiling upward. She needed to keep it together. They had intel to gain from these aliens, and her script could follow any number of paths after that last rant of his. Maybe it was time for her to flip the script. She'd always found it productive to work through improbable ideas first and have fun eliminating them. Then, once those were out of the way, you could more easily focus on the probable ones.

She stood up and straightened her back, her chair sliding into the wall without a noise. "Let's play a game of what if. How does that sound?"

Two didn't reply.

"Perfect!" She whirled her hands around and clapped them together, sending a dull bang through the room.

Two flinched, and his antennae swirled over his head, taking in the space in response to her motion.

She could only assume it was searching to see why she'd clapped. "Let's start with a twist and have fun making some shit up. What if we weren't uplifts? That's what you called us, right? What if instead, we were the uplifters, and the Nanil were, in fact, our little pet project? How do you suppose that would change our position with the Galactic Alliance?"

Two shuddered. His body was a traitor to his mind. She could tell he didn't think much of her words.

"Come on." She waved her hand toward him. "It's a

game. What would that mean to this Nebula curtain you're pulling closed?"

Two broke his stare from the corner and locked his eyes on her face, staring her down many times over. "It would mean you deceived the alliance over forty million cycles ago. It would mean your uplift species should never have been admitted into the fold. We should have wiped out your kind eons ago. You and the others like the Qudoculi. You both thought you were better than every other species. Our queens frequently debate the decisions our ancestors made so long ago. Particularly the decision to join the Galactic Alliance. Many still believe it's misguided. But with the Beacons of Therion, we can influence the direction of the entire alliance. We're unstoppable, whereas you..." His antennae circled around. "You're nearly dead for the second time. A speed bump in our road to ruling the galaxy. That's the term you humans use, right?"

She nodded, a hint of a smile teasing at the edges of her mouth. When Two got going, he was hard to shut off. "You used it correctly. Not all of us were blessed with flight, so we adopt wheeled vehicles to get around." She paused in front of him and leaned back against the wall. Her hands were no longer fighting her emotions now that she was making progress at something rather than dying over and over again in a simulation. "Tell me more about this Beacon. Surely, it can't be like our lighthouses on Earth. Nothing like that could influence an entire alliance."

Another shudder engulfed Two. Like endless rhythmic waves battering the shore of a land mass, she was playing into his ego and his constant slip of tongue. He loved to share his opinion when he got going. After a few hours of playing along, she should be able to extract some helpful nuggets from the giant bumblebee.

JOYCE SIGHED. Two had been rambling for over five minutes on the latest tangent, and she'd been in the room for approaching three hours. If she had to listen to one more story about his escapades as a kid, she was going to lose it. Perhaps it was being lost in translation, but she didn't see the excitement in sneaking away from the colony to live alone for a few months. Maybe he wasn't telling her about having some weird alien sex with a Qudoculi or something. Besides stealing nectar to live off of, it didn't seem very badass, and more to the point, it was useless to her.

"Am I boring you?" Two asked.

She shook her head. "No. I... it just sounds similar to the last story you told about the Nidal. How many times did you escape?"

His antennae bent at nearly right angles. A sure-fire sign of him doubting her words. "A few... but you're lying. I know a boredom diversion when I see it. I'm sorry I'm not buzzing on about the Beacon like I was earlier. I got wise to your methods. We get spook training in our special forces, in case you were wondering."

While he was onto her ruse, it still took him forever to catch on. He'd easily spent the first two hours bragging and revealing some interesting nuggets for Harold and her team to chew on. It might never amount to anything, but it was better than being eaten alive by a Boss Galagas or one of its drone ships.

When she stood up from the chair in the corner, she brushed at her pants, removing the creases. "I'm not sure what you're talking about, but it's been fun. If you're ever in the mood to share any details that are more likely to help your situation, we're all ears." She made a circle gesture in the air, pointing toward the ceiling.

Two's antennae traced the path she pointed at in the air, expecting to see something. They weren't a species that understood gestures very well.

He nodded.

That was new. She'd never seen him do that before. Maybe he was mimicking her or poking fun at human gestures. She couldn't tell.

He trained his eyes on her and leaned forward until his restraints whined and yanked him back against the pole he was shackled to. A groan escaped from his mouth as he arched his spine where it'd collided. "What do you think would be enough to help me out of these things?" He shrugged his arms and looked down at the restraints.

She reached up and rubbed at her face. "It'd have to be something damn good given how you nearly killed someone the last time you weren't wearing them."

Two's posture stiffened at the mention of what he'd done. Maybe he'd forgotten about that, about how long he'd been in this cell or the lengths he went to fight in the early days. She probably shouldn't have led with that.

He adjusted his gaze, looking away from her, and returned his attention to the corner. The exact same damn corner he was staring at when she entered.

Maybe she had wasted three hours on this fraking bee. Hopefully, her team would be able to filter the lies from the truths from her time here.

She turned and walked toward the exit.

"Would something about your son help my situation?" His eyes were still trained at the corner, but his antenna had followed her motion. They seemed to study her response.

She froze in her tracks. He'd never mentioned her son before. None of them had. How the hell had anyone even known anything about her son was beyond her. He had to be testing her. This was clearly a ruse and he was grasping at straws.

"I don't know what you're talking about. My son's in Sol with his father." She reached forward and pressed her hand against the scanner beside the exit and the wall rose silently upward. When she pulled it back, it was shaking. The rage she'd previously held at bay was bursting to the surface again.

"That's strange," Two began. "The entertainment streams linked him to you. Warren had told them as much. We all knew the hosts played up the human deaths in the fields, you know, for effect. But your son's stream had been real. It was obvious."

When she spun around to face him, the antennae above his head came to life and started projecting an image in front of her. She stepped backward. That was a new trick they'd never seen before.

The image was crystal clear. It showed a field of crops, human crops. From the looks of it, they were out past the eastern edge of the colony. She could barely make out the colony rings reflecting in the distance and a thread of objects rising up and lowering down toward the beanstalk. The morning sun was behind whomever was making this recording. Their human shape was casting a shadow in front of them.

The person stood there for a moment and stared at the horizon, seemingly transfixed by something. It wasn't until they reached up and wiped at their forehead that she realized who it was. It was her son, Paul. She recognized his wristwatch. It was his father's and his father's father's. They'd passed it down for generations.

Her heart raced, and her world flipped end over end as she collapsed to her knees in front of the hologram. It was him. It was really him.

"We're about ready to raise the next wall," a voice said to his right.

"I'm ready when you are." Paul reached up and wiped at his forehead again.

He loved working outdoors, even if it made him sweat. He said it helped him feel alive. Being closer to nature and having a hand in helping to build a new world was what finally sold him on coming to Epsilon Eridani. After his father's death, he'd nearly lost his way until they started preparing for the trip to Liprosus.

Suddenly, the picture changed. The ground lurched upward, and Paul let out a scream that tore her to pieces. His voice combined with a dozen others in a howl of pain, like nothing she'd ever heard before. It was one thing to watch a remake of a battle or a horror simulation; it was quite another to watch people you cared for live through it.

Tears streamed down her face as she watched him collapse to the ground and grasp at the dirt around him. He reached up and pulled on the nearby hydroponic walls before his strength gave way. His arms were already showing signs of the telltale purple lines streaking through them and splotches were appearing.

It didn't hit her until that very moment that she was watching this entire thing through her son's eyes. The aliens shouldn't have had access to this. Her team had extracted all the footage, and she hadn't ever seen this video from any of the humans who'd died in the fields. Their nanites had been wiped clean and their programming reset. The damn Galactic Alliance had turned the whole thing into an entertainment experience. They were capitalizing on the death of her people to rally the troops.

As the last breath her son would ever take escaped from his mouth, her body sank lower. They'd taken him from her once, and now unbeknownst to her, she'd been coerced by her emotions to watch it happen again.

Every ounce of fear and sadness she'd worked so hard to suppress over the past months came rushing to the surface. No longer held at bay by duty or outside pressures, it poured out of her like a geyser. Her strength evaporated and with it her resolve to hide her despair and anger.

Her son still hadn't stopped moving. He continually

reached toward the sky, each time looking worse than before. She couldn't tell what he was reaching for. Every once in a while she could make out a moan or a cry for help in the distance as his fellow agricultural engineers succumbed to the same fate as him.

No matter how hard she tried, her eyes wouldn't look away. Her tears had dried up, but the video kept playing. While she'd thought her son's breathing would have stopped, it hadn't. Every minute or so he'd gasp for breath. Maybe if they'd gotten there faster, they could have saved him. They could have saved all of them.

"Mom…" Paul rolled onto his side. "Is that you?"

Her heart leapt, and she sat up, leaning closer to the video.

His voice was hoarse. Like he'd been coughing all night when he was little. "I'm sorry, Mom. I… know I wasn't always the ideal son. I put you and Dad through hell sometimes. Damn all the failed examinations." He reached his hand up toward the horizon and held it there for a moment before his arm collapsed. "You and Dad did your best. For that, I'm… thankful. Mom… you have to fix this. You always fix… everything."

The image froze, and his eyes glazed over. The retinal comm was still recording, but his body was dead.

Joyce gasped for air. She hadn't even realized it, but she'd been holding her breath since he'd started talking again. Of all the ways he could have died, this was never how she'd imagined it.

Maybe that was part of the entertainment spin the Thyreuns watched for. The act of tearing down their enemy and then getting them to pour out an emotion for the audience.

She shook her head. That couldn't have been it. What he'd said was sincere. Only she and her husband knew how many times he'd failed to find his way. The number of entrance exams he'd botched before she'd helped him realize his true calling. They'd nearly torn him and their relationship apart.

No, that part was him. His words were real.

She took a deep breath and then another. Letting his last request sink in and burn into her memory forever.

"Mom... you have to fix this. You always fix... everything."

The room went silent for what seemed like an eternity until Two cut the hologram. His antennae returned to their random motions, exploring the chamber. "That was my favorite footage from the farm. They played them repeatedly for days on end aboard the ships. People told stories about the waste of emotion and how pitiful you humans were. I didn't agree. I thought they were intriguing. A bit disgusting, but the emotions were raw and natural. You could tell, right? So, what do you think? Did that earn me a release from these shackles?"

She pushed up off the ground and stood straight. After she faltered a bit, her hand reached for the wall and she righted herself. As she pushed off, she felt someone guide her from behind.

When she glanced back, she noticed one of the soldiers standing at the entrance to the room. They must've stepped in when she'd opened the door earlier. Their face told a story of sadness and pity. They'd watched her son die in front of her. They also heard his words challenging her, begging her to fix what had happened to him.

Maybe they wouldn't hold against her what she was about to do.

Her back straightened and nodded at them before reaching up and activating her retinal recorder. It was off limits to record in these cells. Everything they did in here went through a separate system for processing and filtering before it made it outside these walls. But she didn't care. They were her rules, and she needed to remember this moment.

She leaned toward the soldier. "You might want to leave."

The soldier tilted his head. "Pardon, sir."

Her fist clenched, and she closed her eyes, struggling to center herself. "Do not touch me. Do not stop me. Do you understand?"

The soldier glanced down at her hands, toward the alien, and then back to her. Realization painting his face as her words sank in. Suddenly, they stiffened. "I wouldn't think of it, sir."

"Thank you," she whispered.

"So, how about it, Director Green?" Two asked. "I have some other videos, if you'd like to see them. They weren't as long or as powerful as this one. At least from my—"

Joyce stepped sideways and slammed her foot into the side of the alien's head. Just as her boot was making contact, she engaged the force plate on the bottom and his head rocketed down and away from her. A snap cracked through the room when his head collided with his chest. She wasn't sure if she'd broken his neck, but she didn't care. Two's head twitched and gradually rose upright as she stepped around the front of him.

Her eyes were bulging as she took several deep breaths, studying the damage she'd dealt. Not bad for a power assisted kick. Yellow blood oozed out the side of his head and his antenna shook violently, as if they were still recovering from the unexpected attack.

She reached out and grasped one of his antennae, yanking at it with everything she had. It was surprisingly tough, and seemed to be resisting her pull, but she wasn't about to give up without a fight. She lifted her foot to Two's chest and leaned back, pulling while applying additional force from her boot.

The alien screeched. Their blood-curdling bellow echoed out and around the chamber and down the hall as the antenna ripped from the top of their head. Yellow blood shot out from the empty socket and splattered against the ceiling. A moment later, a gob of it dripped down in a long slimy trail leading back to the body.

The other soldiers in the hall scrambled toward the entrance to her room, but the one guarding her door stopped them. He blocked the way with his arm. After they recognized what was happening, they took a step backward in shock.

She stared down at the dislodged antenna wriggling in her hand. It was clean of blood, which was remarkable given how much had shot out of Two. His head was resting against his chest and neither he nor the second antenna were moving.

When she took inventory of herself, she'd gotten away without a mark. She wasn't sure if he'd launch some other type of unexpected attack or maybe try to bite her. It didn't matter if he did, though. She still would've killed him. Even if it meant asking for help.

The guards remained standing at attention at the entrance to the cell. They were neither smiling nor frowning. They were pillars, void of emotion.

She, on the other hand, was overflowing with rage and satisfaction. Until now, she'd only had that one opportunity near the mining shuttles to strike back. Since that day, she'd questioned herself countless times, wondering if her feelings had been a one and done thing. She doubted her resolve and forced down her animal instincts to take more life.

But now it was back, and she was right to be afraid of it. Her body surged with unexpected emotions that had been struggling to surface since that day. The day she held the pistol to the head of the Thyreusian leader and pulled the trigger. Today her resolve was reinforced.

In the words of her son, she'd fix this. She would end the Thyreusians and any other Galactic Alliance members responsible for the deaths on Liprosus, even if it meant she'd die trying.

8

ZACHARY OLIVAW
ZETA LUPI, OORT CLOUD

She'd only been on her mission a few weeks, but Zachary already missed seeing Pluto's face every morning and night. Even though they hadn't been running in the same circles since their return, knowing she was safe was reassuring and relaxed that segment of his brain from worrying all day. As it stood now, he couldn't see a mining asteroid being hauled closer to The Wheel without imagining Pluto stuck inside and unable to escape.

He took a deep breath and returned his attention to the inspection the general was taking him on.

"Thinking about Pluto again?" Shauna asked over his retinal comm.

"Was it that obvious? How long was I out of sorts?" he subvocalized.

"Only a few minutes. Just enough time to miss General Raft comparing your team's arrowhead ship design to a billiard ball and the Selene ships to the pocket. I believe he was looking for a rise out of you. This time your zoning out and ignoring him worked to your advantage."

He froze in his tracks, staring at the drones whizzing past the superstructure of one of their Nyílak ships being constructed. The name was a hat tip to the Hungarian designers that came up with it. It translated to arrow, or arrowhead as many people called it.

Each ship was a clone of the other, and they were densely packed with ordinances of death and destruction. While the analogy of billiards was remedial, the reality of the technology wasn't far off.

The ship design was over half shielding and phase absorption apparatus to combat laser blasts. It was a technology the Nanil had invented inside the Lupus Dark Nebula and humans subsequently stole, at least according to the records on both sides. Either way, the hull was constructed with microscopic chambers that could adjust the specific frequency of their optical cavity to trap incoming beams of light. Once trapped, they redirected the energy, forcing it to bounce around and dissipate, recharge their own energy reserves, or bend them in other directions. That bouncing around and redirecting of energy was likely the reasoning for General Raft's crude billiards analogy.

As he studied the Nyílak, he could just make out the slow but steady growth of the ship itself. Even without his retinal comm overlaying the details, the ship was growing before his very eyes as nanites fused into the superstructure, creating the distinct arrow-like shape that was the foundation of the design. In the center of the rear section of the ship in front of him was the sphere of life. It was only present in a handful of these ships. Only the ones lucky enough contain and protect the human pilot and bombardier.

"So, as you can see," General Raft began, "our construction is coming along. We should have plenty of time to finish all sixteen thousand Nyílaks before we set course for Epsilon Eridani. The challenge is going to be the transfer to the battlefield more than constructing the ships themselves."

"There's also the small matter of pilots," Zachary said.

General Raft pulled his attention away from the contingent of gawkers from Tiān who were slack-jawed at the rate of progress in The Wheel. He peered past them to lock eyes with Zachary. "We're still winnowing through the candidates. We have no shortage of volunteers."

"Oh, but there are." Zachary stepped through the crowd. "For every fifty volunteers, we're lucky to find one with any potential. For every ten of those, if we can identify one that can match a Ulixi, we'd call that a win."

The general nodded and then straightened his back as if to assert himself as stronger than he appeared. "We'll find enough. I'm sure they're out there."

Zachary let out a quiet chuckle to himself.

"Did I say something funny, Mr. Olivaw?"

"I'm sure your implant did the math for you already, General. We're talking about sixty-four pilots in all of Tiān that might, I underscore, might, be able to keep up with a Ulixi. With sixteen thousand ships, the optimal ratio of human to automated pilot is thirty-two to one. That means—"

"We need five hundred pilots," Mayor Clarke interrupted. He was eyeing the general suspiciously. "We're a tad bit off, now aren't we?"

General Raft shot the mayor a glare. "Like I said, I'm sure they're out there."

"I agree," Zachary said. "But they're in Sol, not here in Tiān."

"It's a little late to think about sending a recruiting mission to Sol, Mr. Olivaw. Maybe we should reconfigure the inter-ship mesh network to employ more nodes. Surely, your engineers can handle that. Or do I need to say pretty please before they'll try?"

This guy was as dense as they come. What the frak was it going to take to get someone with a little more ingenuity and a lot less shove in this place? Zachary took a step toward the general, and the hairs on his neck stood up. "You could always try, General. Physics, quantum computing, and the speed of light are sorta bottlenecks. But hey," he leaned forward, "maybe if you remove that billiard ball from your ass you can find room to grow some brains and lend us a hand."

The general's face turned crimson, and he shifted his weight like he was going to throw a punch. Zachary ducked down before he realized the general had stopped. His face was white, and he took a few steps backward.

Zachary spun around to see a half dozen of the nearby articulating and spherical robots. They'd advanced on the party and were standing behind him. Either Harold or Shauna weren't keen on a fist fight down here.

"Even though the general is old, he's far better trained than you at killing," Shauna said over his retinal comm. "I'm sorry, but my Four-Laws engine was itching, and I knew the moment the old geezer's heart rate spiked that he was close to going over the edge."

"I see you're still holding us under your thumb." General Raft gestured toward the robots.

Zachary shook his head. "Not at all, General. In case you don't know how the Four-Laws of Robotics work, all humans are kept from harm when possible. They'd have advanced on me if I'd made the same gesture at you."

"I didn't say that," Shauna said over his comm.

"Go with it," he subvocalized. "If I'd hurt him enough, you would have."

"True."

General Raft glanced at the onlookers from his little dog and pony show. Most had already backed up well away from the two of them and were whispering between each other or into their retinal comms. He snapped his uniform straight and took a deep breath, bringing his height up another few inches. "We're done here." He spun around and marched toward the lift tubes, his secretary and support staff in tow.

Mayor Clarke walked up beside Zachary and watched the

general silently disappear into the tube, shooting downward. "You're as skillful at communication as your brother. Apparently, only Abigail got those genes."

Zachary lowered his head and laughed into his hand. That wasn't far from the truth and he knew it. While Bradley had been the one to tackle things head-on without finesse, he'd always done it behind the scenes, preferring to stay out of the spotlight. His little speech a few months back had been the first time he'd mustered the confidence to speak in public in years. If he was being honest, talking to a drone was nothing like in front of hundreds or thousands of people.

"So talk to me about what you'd need from Sol," Mayor Clarke said.

* * *

ZACHARY DIDN'T EXPECT Mayor Clarke would be able to move the mountains necessary to send a covert operation to Sol, not yet anyhow. Not with all the people they needed to focus on this mission. At any other time or place, maybe.

He could be wrong and would support him if he needed it. No, that conversation wasn't about him helping get pilots. It was about Nathan talking to and getting into the confidence of Zachary. He knew when his belly was being rubbed. Nathan recognized who was really in control at The Wheel. Olivaw International ran operations here, and it wouldn't be turning over command to anyone else for quite some time. At least not until some normalcy had returned to their existence.

As he popped out of the lift tube, he scanned around to get his bearings. This newly constructed section of The Wheel was new to even him. He stepped into the security chamber and glanced over his shoulder as the meter thick doors closed behind him. A second later, his retinal comm lost signal to the outside world.

The clang of the doors slamming shut, and the resulting

vibrations sent an icy shiver up his legs and into his spine. He'd always hated the idea of being locked in or buried alive. Doing it on Henosi had been hard enough, and he never imagined he would willingly do it again.

When he turned his attention back to the wall in front of him, he could feel the room closing in. It wasn't really, not yet anyhow. It was the optical illusion of being surrounded on all sides by meters of nothing. He closed his eyes and envisioned what was happening. His entire body was being scanned, and he was breathing in nanites. They were entering his mouth and nose, circulating through his extremities, searching for bugs and anything that might be used to compromise what was inside these walls.

Not even General Raft nor Mayor Clarke knew this level existed. They had heard rumors of hidden areas within The Wheel, and they realized the information collected from Lupus had to be housed somewhere secure, but they hadn't the foggiest idea how secure it was.

His vision went green with the light beyond his eyelids, and he opened his eyes. He'd passed the first barrier. His retinal comm was still out, but he knew what was coming next. Hell, he'd helped design the room on the way back from Lupus.

He took a few steps toward the wall and a meter thick panel dropped into place from the ceiling, clanging into the floor. At the same time, one raised in front of him. He repeated that a half dozen more times until the final panel rose, and his retinal comm sprang to life, adjusting to the brightness beyond to protect his eyes.

The room he'd stepped into was expansive, yet simple. Libby was there, working at her virtual workstation, and in the center of the space, inside a transparent diamond enclosure, were the data cores they'd extracted from Lupus. The jet black cylinders with their throbbing green lights encircling them were ominous surrounded by the bright white sterile chamber. He couldn't imagine why their ancestors had made them look so evil, but perhaps that's how the mind warps when you're locked inside a nebula for thousands of years.

"We only found three bugs this time," Libby said, removing her virtual harness. "They're either giving up or regrouping their efforts."

He reached up and rubbed at the stubble on his chin. Pluto hated facial hair. To him, it was a reminder of how long it'd been since they'd been together. That, and it gave him something to focus on when he was thinking.

"Are we sure our friends from Sol and Zeta Lupi can't get in from the outside?" He walked up to the diamond enclosure and stared at the green throbbing lights. "I mean, they could drill their way through."

"We'd know that within seconds of anyone penetrating a millimeter of the outer shell," Libby said. "After that, Harold would be on them like a tiger in a tuna fish factory."

A smile crept into the corner of his mouth. She was always coming up with odd turns of phrase. "Have we learned anything useful today from these…" He waved his hand in circles. "Whatever we're calling them now? Memory stores, personality dumps, virtual worlds, extinction archives."

"I like that last one the best." Libby stepped around him toward the far side of the chamber. He followed in step behind her.

When she reached the wall, she gestured with her hands, and it sprang to life. The display showed their slow but methodical march through these data cores as they attempted to squeeze as much information out of them as possible.

"I uncovered another sixteen thousand personality stores, bringing us to well over two million souls. They each have their own memories, thoughts, and… personalities."

A cold hollow dread seeped out of the place he'd shoved it last. The visions of the robot spinning around and killing the nearby technicians brought the pain back. The blood and gore were something he'd remember forever. He didn't know how the occupants of these data cores had taken over their robots and made them do their bidding. But had Harold not cut the power and triggered the EMP, there's no telling how far they'd have gotten.

"I assume they're just as jaded as the one we previously encountered?" he asked.

Libby nodded. "Right you are. Apparently, human consciousness doesn't store well for millennia."

"Or they were lunatics before they dumped themselves to storage for eternity. So, did you find anything useful then?"

She gestured at the wall screen. "I filled in more of the timeline after the humans closed the Nebula in Henosi. There was infighting within the survivors to either build out the star system, research multidimensional travel, reprogram the Dark Nebula barrier, or restart their civilization from scratch. You can guess which party won."

He tilted his head. "Wait, did you say reprogram the Dark Nebula barrier?"

She brought up a mental model from a group of researchers within the contingent that relocated to Henosi. "Yea, I found that one peculiar, as well, and meant to follow up. I don't have a lot of details on it, but there was a strong belief by some of the humans that since the Dark Nebula was controlled by the Beacon of Therion, they believed they could, as well. There isn't much beyond some theories and a few crude attempts to recreate the energy field the Beacon used to close the Nebula and seal it."

He gestured in the air and spun the mental map. These things never felt logical to him, but to Libby and her team, they were as clear as the written word. "Why would they want to close it? It was already closed."

Libby swatted at his hand, spun the map around, and then dove inside to a branch from one of the researchers. She then gestured to replay a memory.

The wall screen showed a tall, lanky female standing within a grouping of humans, studying some type of simulation. "If we can recreate the energy signatures used to communicate with the bynardrals, then we should be able to invert them, thereby allowing us to invert the closure process itself. That would enable us to poke a hole in the nebulosity, which should give us enough time to escape."

"You believe," a muscular male said, standing beside her. "The Griffars and Vuunuundra believed the same thing, and look what happened to them."

"The Vuunuundra did manage to get a response from the Nebula." The female closed her eyes and a moment later, the simulation changed. It was replaced with what appeared to be a grand starship.

Zachary leaned in close to the screen and Libby chuckled, gesturing with her hand to zoom in on the object. "Is that a… ship?"

"Whatever it is, it's massive," Libby said. "My first translations from their memories reported it as being tiny, but after I studied the minds of this researcher and their peers, I realized it was the wrong measurements. I believe it's nearly a tenth of a parsec, or a little over twenty thousand AU long."

"That's… impossible."

Libby gestured, and fast forwarded the memory playback. "I've given up on possible and impossible these days. From the looks of this, they were using the structure to collect either dark matter or some other unknown force hoping it would…"

The video changed and a flash of green light arced from one end of the long thin structure toward the nearby Dark Nebula. At first, the nebulosity appeared to dip inward, but then a moment later it lashed out and crossed the distance between the Vuunuundra object and the darkness in the blink of an eye. It cascaded up the impossibly thin structure as if it were any other mass touching the Nebula, engulfing it and pulling it into the powdery blackness.

"That didn't go well," he muttered.

"But they failed and everyone died testing it," the alien male spoke again.

Libby adjusted the memory playback to bring the entire scene into focus, framing the group around the simulation device.

"But they clearly elicited an intelligent response," the female said. "With adequate time… and enough support, we could do the same thing."

"We need to rethink the approach," the male began. "I believe the idea has merit, but in the Henosi star system we're constrained on all sides. We can't put at risk the entirety of humanity in hopes that this will succeed."

The woman waved her hand in a figure eight through the air, exploding the simulation outward into the onlookers before it cut out. "So, you'd rather we sit around and die contemplating the origins of the universe? I'm not a damn Friop, I want more from this life. I want more from all my lives."

Libby gestured to pause the memory. "There's nothing helpful from here. Just more arguing and theorizing. A lot of their memories are similar. This entire branch of our species seemed to enter a stage of their existence where they were paralyzed by any action and feared it might cascade out of control, ending their lives. This paralysis of analysis was the primary driver for their Edenist world view that finally prevailed."

He tilted his head. "Edenist?"

"The belief that if they restarted their civilization from scratch, in a pure and simple form, yet with all the knowledge they had among them, that they would evolve beyond their current limits and transcend the Nebula itself. It was the simplest and least invasive approach to survival they could come up with, and it won out."

He sighed and began scratching at his beard. This inaction

was repeated throughout human civilization on Earth. The peaks and valleys of doubt and non-belief interspersed with science and progress both stymied and propelled humans in this corner of the galaxy through their own parallel timeline. Only when his family brought humanity together to fix that which they broke, had they been able to push past their mental barriers. And even that led them here, to the precipice of extinction yet again. So much for progress.

"I was hoping for some magic pills or leaps in technology to report today. Maybe a way to create mass from nothing or turn back time." He winked at her.

Libby spun the virtual memory cube, and it exploded into a field of stars. "Sorry to burst your space-time bubble. Just more soap operas to report. The mental spiral these people followed at the end was like watching water circle a drain. You know what's coming, but you can't help but watch your shit flush sometimes."

There she went with her vivid metaphors again. He really had to make sure she got out more. They couldn't afford to have her spin out like these other humans had. He needed to change the subject. "Any idea when the Tau Ceti crew will be arriving?" He spun around to face the data cores in the center of the facility.

"Assuming Quesh has been able to break loose the anchor keeping them there." Libby stepped up beside him and peered at him to gauge his response. "They could arrive any time now. We sent the message nearly three weeks ago."

He glanced at her reflection in the diamond shielding and then back at the data cubes. "I assume you're referring to my sister?"

She fiddled with her hands before finally putting them behind her back. "It's been months, and she still hasn't changed. We can't just sit around and hope any longer. We need to act if we want to turn the tide of this war."

He had known that for a while now and had been

working to push everyone toward a new goal. The hurdles in Sol were too great, and had they not uncovered the Beacon of Therion, he'd have suggested another approach that didn't include kamikaze runs against the Galactic Alliance. Either way, they were acting and were light years past the paralysis phase.

"Well, let's hope they're en route. We could use some momentum in our favor for a change. I'm beginning to wonder if even this plan is doomed."

9

———————————

ABIGAIL OLIVAW
EN ROUTE TO ZETA LUPI

She reached across and rubbed the back of her hand. Her wrist and fingers had been throbbing all morning. The nanites had managed hundreds of repairs in the last day, but they still had days to get her back to normal.

Whatever Quesh was up to, he was taking his sweet ass time starting. The people had been filing into the empty mining vessel for the better part of an hour. Their fleet of ships had made a half dozen jumps away from Tau Ceti, but few knew where they were ultimately headed. She had an inkling, but she didn't know why.

Apparently, the orchestrated gate jumps were also being treated as a training exercise. They'd never attempted to move so many ships at one time, and with the effects of the gate drive preventing matter from occupying the same space, their exit point wasn't always predictable.

"Thank you, everyone, for transferring aboard," Commander Quesh said as he stepped out of the shadow of a crate and into the center of the hold.

The audience of well over one hundred was seated haphazardly on crates and packing material. It reminded

Abigail of a college diag party with people strewn about. Some of them were even lying down.

He continued. "I know this vessel is far from ideal, but it's the only space where we could convene everyone together to minimize signal leak and potential for interception. Some of your colleagues are still piloting the vessels you'll return to when we're finished, but I expect each of the ship commanders to bring the details safely to their officers in a secure manner."

She scanned around the expansive cargo hold. There were people from all ranks at The Wheel. Her retinal comm highlighted each of their names as she glanced over them, along with their specialty and years of service. Whatever was going on, there wasn't anything but a skeletal crew remaining in Tau Ceti.

When she brought her focus back to Quesh, his hand was up near his head. Like he'd opened a comm. He was animated for a second and then her retinal comm cut off.

Murmurs spread through the hold as everyone seemed to experience the same thing. People were sitting up with a start and reaching up to tap their heads, attempting to engage their comms.

"Relax!" Quesh shouted, as he waved his hands in the air to get their attention. "I killed all your comms." He lowered his hands and folded them behind his back before beginning again. "Each of you, upon entering our family at The Wheel, swore an oath. An oath to protect humanity and to follow our leaders to the end. To ensure our species' future in the galaxy. What I'm about to share with you today, is our first plan in the battle against the Galactic Alliance."

She smiled. He'd learned a thing or two about rallying the troops from her father. While he often denied his role in the history of Sol, she knew better. He was in his element now.

Quesh gestured with his hand, and a three-dimensional

hologram appeared in front of everyone. The room let out a gasp as they took in what they were seeing.

The image showed a sea of Selene ships, as far as the eye could see, belching Dark Nebula into space. She'd seen the image before, as had most of them, but rarely at this level of detail. As the view panned out, the scale of the devastation they were unleashing became clear. They were encompassing the Epsilon Eridani star system in a shroud of death.

Quesh gestured up at the hologram. "The fate you're seeing here is coming to Sol. While many of you imagined we would be making a frontal assault at home, I can put those rumors to rest. We will not be attacking Sol. Not yet."

The murmurs picked up again. She could make out a few words of dissent from the crowd behind her.

"Worry not. We will return to Sol in time. What we're after is here in Epsilon Eridani. Our mission can, and will, save Sol itself. It will strike at the heart of the Galactic Alliance. Our goal, when achieved, will turn the tide of this war in our favor."

"What are we doing?" someone shouted.

"Yea, why are we running away?" another voice asked.

She couldn't tell who they were. Without her retinal comm, they might as well be a random person in a mall on Earth.

A smile crept across Quesh's face. She'd seen it before when she was little, when one of the blockade runners had walked into their trap. He'd been hoping they would shout out. It presented him with an opportunity to pull them in. To tug them closer to his objective. It was only a matter of when he'd do it.

"We're cowards if we don't protect our people!" someone yelled.

Quesh nodded, and the image in front of them flashed. It transformed from pictures of darkness and death to one of light. What she saw was the manifestation of centuries of rumors and random stories they'd been able to salvage from the first contact probe. She didn't even need for him to speak. She knew what it was before he said a word. It was the most beautiful thing she'd seen in her entire life, and this was the first time she'd set eyes on it.

Judging by the sighs around her, she was not alone.

"Our mission, ladies and gentlemen, is to steal a Beacon of Therion!"

ABIGAIL HADN'T EVEN REALIZED it, but she'd stood up when she saw the Beacon. The stories she'd read in the Galactic Alliance archives spoke of the fabled object as if it were real. They described its beauty as breathtaking, but she assumed it was fiction as there was never an accompanying image, only drawings.

What was in front of her made it clear why. Even looking at it calmed her. It was as if the recording itself could somehow reach inside her and squelch that which angered her the most. She wanted to stare at it. It was as if it was speaking to her.

Suddenly, the image blinked out and their retinal comms came back to life. But something was different. The beacon was still there in front of her. It merely looked… fake.

She glanced around the room. The others, like her, appeared to be exiting some form of trance. She thought that perhaps she'd imagined it, but she hadn't. Whatever that image had done, she wanted it back. It was addictive.

Quesh's voice boomed over the darkened chamber and her eyes adjusted to the loss of the beacon's light. "I've enabled a special mode of your retinal comm that allows your optical pattern matching system to detect if you're looking at the Beacon of Therion, and to alter it. It filters out its true image and replaces it with something… simpler. As you can see, the Beacon is a powerful tool in controlling a mass of people, or in the case of the Galactic Alliance, a mass of species. And this was only a recording. You can imagine what the real thing must be like. They've used these Beacons over the years to control their expansion through the galaxy, and with them, they've placed a stranglehold on anyone who didn't come into line with their plans. That, my friends, is what happened to humanity thousands of years ago."

She took a deep breath and stepped closer to Quesh. The people to her left and right whispered when they recognized her.

"What are we intending to do with the Beacon?" she asked. "I mean, we don't even know what it's used for."

The whispers around her rose louder. They were surprised she wasn't aware of the plan.

Quesh nodded. "We didn't until your brothers returned from humanity's home. While inside, they discovered the fate approaching humanity in Epsilon Eridani and eventually Sol. They also found information we plan to use in our favor, to turn this battle back upon the Galactic Alliance."

She squinted. He was speaking too vaguely. "So, the Beacon can stop the Dark Nebula from advancing and surrounding Epsilon?"

"Quite the contrary," Quesh said. "The Beacon is used to seal the Nebula around a star. We intend to let them use it for that purpose and to seal Epsilon. That is when we'll strike," he pumped his fist, "and steal it out from under their noses."

"But," she stammered, "why not stop the Nebula and save the star? Wouldn't that make more sense?"

"Once the Dark Nebula is laid down, nothing can stop it. At least not that we know of. The Beacon is required to seal the Nebula, and prevent it from drifting aimlessly in space and absorbing everything in its path. No, we want the star sealed, for we have an advantage the Galactic Alliance does not." He waved his hands around the room. "We have the power of the gate drive. We can jump past the Nebula boundary in the blink of an eye. To the aliens, it's a protective shell jailing a captured species, but to us, it's a safe haven from which we will build a response to the Galactic Alliance. A secret place to construct a fleet of battleships to drive them back. To drive them out of our home star system forever."

Cheers erupted around her as Quesh drove his agenda forward. So much didn't make sense about what he'd said, but she couldn't rob him of his speech. He needed to rally the people, and from the sound of it, what he said had worked. The problem was, his strategy had a galactic size hole in the middle, and she didn't know if he saw it.

THE HOLD HAD CLEARED of personnel, and all that remained was her inner circle. At least that's what it appeared like, as her retinal comm still hadn't been reactivated. The manipulated Beacon of Therion remained hovering in the space over their head, its hypnotic effects long ago squelched.

"Nice speech," Abigail said. "Light on details, but effective."

"Thanks." Commander Quesh nodded at the soldiers who'd stuck around. Each of them were either the ship commanders, ground troop generals, or she'd seen them training the Ulixi.

She cleared her throat. "So, what's the actual plan?"

Quesh squinted at her and slowly shook his head. "I'm not following." He gestured up at the beacon. "That was the plan."

"Right, I understand. Snatch and grab. But where are the details?" She glanced around. "I mean, you can't honestly think we'll have enough ships to pull this off, even with automata. The Galactic Alliance outnumbers us a thousand to one on a good day." She pointed up. "And that's assuming they're not all converged on a single point. We're giving them something to aim at that's the size of this ship."

Quesh shifted on his feet. It was slight, but she'd seen it before when her father would yell at him. Apparently, she was having the same effect. She couldn't tell if that was good or bad.

"We have nine months to fill in the details, but the brass, and your brothers have faith in the plan. They've sent on chunks of the archives they found in Lupus for us to study on the way. We have significant advancements in armament at our disposal. Add to that the weapons the Nanil used against humans in the Nebula, and we should have the means. We now just need—"

"The numbers." Lync stepped out of the shadows. She glanced at Abigail and then back at Quesh. "As President Olivaw already said, we're outnumbered a thousand to one, or more if you count those cylindrical ships and the fighters I ran into near Jupiter. I'd say ten thousand to one is more accurate."

Abigail could feel her temper rising, and she crossed her arms. The pain in her hands was a reminder of their last encounter, but it did nothing but spur her on.

"Relax," Harold said in her ear. "She's on our side."

"Is she?" Abigail asked subvocally.

"All the more reason that the timing needs to be perfect," Quesh began. "That, and we need to keep training with your Ulixi. They're talented, for sure. Now that we have a clear objective, and can run more accurate simulations with the data we've recovered, we should be able to recreate a detailed field of battle. We'll know soon enough if this mission is a dead end or not."

"And then what?" Lync asked.

"And then we'll adapt," Abigail said, coming to Quesh's defense.

Lync bit her lip before she spoke again. "You mean throw

more lives on the battlefield? Toss a few more Ulixi into the fire, as it were."

"That's not what I said, and you know it." Abigail raised her voice. "We'll explore every option. We're not about to throw lives aside for one strategic goal."

"I beg to differ," Quesh said.

She spun around and glared at him. "What?"

He cleared his throat. "I said, I beg to differ, Madam President. As Zachary so clearly made the point to the generals in Zeta Lupi, we have no other options."

He gestured and changed the image above them from Epsilon Eridani to Sol. The video panned through perspective after perspective, showing countless Galactic Alliance moon ships throughout the system. Each of them waiting for their orders.

Quesh continued. "For every one Selene ship in Epsilon, there are ten already in Sol. If you think we're outnumbered now, you haven't seen anything yet. No, we have this one chance. This one opportunity to take advantage of their mistakes. As you already know, Madam President, and as Fleet Admiral Nguyễn Due has reported, the Galactic Alliance is infighting about the Nebula fleets actions in Epsilon. They weren't supposed to have spread the Nebula until the tribunal had issued a ruling of guilty. This opportunity was an accident orchestrated by the Qudoculi and the Thyreus, but we intend to capitalize on it. Once they're done here in Epsilon, their fleet will head to Sol. And then, well, it'll be all over for us."

From the looks of it, she and Lync were the only outliers here. Not something she'd anticipated. And unbeknownst to her, Zachary had somehow become quite the diplomat while she was out. Her role in this mission was becoming vaguer and vaguer by the second. Even as a figurehead, she didn't appear to be needed.

"If there's nothing else." Quesh studied the audience. No

one appeared comfortable asking a question. He reached into his pocket and pulled out a data dot, passing one to each of them. "None of the information we saw today was recorded by your retinal comms and nothing that is said in any briefing will be recorded, either. Harold will make certain of that. These data dots contain the directives each of you are to follow to prepare for this mission. We have ten days en route to Zeta Lupi. Let's not squander it. Is that understood?"

"Yessir!" the officers shouted.

"Dismissed."

She watched as Quesh handed the last of the data dots to Lync and nodded. She paused for a moment, as if to turn and face Abigail, but thought better and continued onward toward the exit. Her stride was confident and swift, without a hint of the hesitation Abigail had seen seconds earlier.

Even Lync had a role in this mission, while Abigail was empty-handed. Without the skills of a pilot, an engineer, or a general, they didn't need her. The role of a formerly comatose bureaucrat wasn't part of the mission parameters.

QUESH TRIED to talk to her after the briefing and only after being chastised did he relinquish his own data dot. While he may have counted wrong, him not handing her one had been a slight. He struggled to apologize, but she stormed away. She didn't need anyone's pity. She was the person who'd kept their family plan on track for the past thirty years. They wouldn't be here if it weren't for her blood, sweat, and tears. She'd given up any semblance of a normal life for this secret.

She boarded the return shuttle and left Quesh aboard the mining vessel. He could find his own way back. Right now, silence would do her some good. To get in her own head and straighten herself out.

If Zachary was running the shots in Zeta Lupi, she needed

to find something to do. Some way to contribute. Walking in there and demanding control over the situation wasn't bound to go over well. Not after he'd delivered the colony the news. What the hell was he thinking, laying it all out like that? They didn't stand a snowball's chance in Hades of repairing the damage he'd done to the family.

The shuttle docked with the flagship and as she stepped across the threshold; the doors slid closed behind her. Apparently, Harold was dispatching the same shuttle to fetch Quesh.

Her magnetic inserts in her shoes disengaged, and rather than clicking while she walked, she was silent in the gravity of the gate ship. As she worked her way toward her quarters, the soldiers she encountered saluted her as she passed. The others nodded thoughtfully, but she sensed their gaze lingering. She couldn't tell if it was anger or discontent they were spewing at her. Either way, it wasn't a vibe she was used to feeling.

It was strange going from leader to leper overnight, even if it was a very long night.

As she approached her quarters, she changed her mind and headed to a nearby personal space. She needed to see what was on this data dot. There had to be something she could help with. Some way to return her to being useful for the cause. Ever since that mottled green bastard touched her, everything had gotten worse. Her parents didn't raise a quitter.

"Aren't you going to lie down for a bit?" Harold asked over her comm. "Your vitals indicate you could use—"

"Shut it, Harold," she subvocalized, as she stormed her way into the small meeting room just outside her quarters. "You got me into this fraking mess, and I need to get myself out of it."

"What's that supposed to mean?"

"You let Zachary broadcast everything to Zeta Lupi. You

let him move the primary base of operations to the furthest place possible. You let him propose this plan. Hell, you didn't even warn me about Admiral Gwar." She walked over and dropped the data dot into the reader.

The room locked, and Harold's face appeared on the wall screen. "That's what this is about, isn't it?"

She turned around and collapsed in the chair, crossing her arms. "What?"

"Admiral Gwar? You think I failed you."

She reached down and adjusted her shirt. "You never warned me he was going to touch my shoulder. And now... I've been replaced. In the blink of an eye, they relegated me to merely taking up space. You and I both know the only reason I'm on this mission is because it's safer for me here than in Tau Ceti. There's nothing but a skeletal crew back there."

Harold's face was emotionless. She hadn't seen him this way in a long time. He was usually quite animated with her. "What about your brothers? You haven't talked to them or hugged them in... years. What about the broader mission? We need you to focus on that."

She laughed out loud and then leaned forward. "The broader mission. What the frak is that? Zachary killed that the moment he showed our cards. There is no broader mission any longer. Sure, we have some supply depots stashed away, but besides that, everything is out in the open."

This whole situation wasn't getting her anywhere. She stood up and turned her back to the wall screen. Nothing felt comfortable any more. Her own fraking skin didn't feel the same when she touched it. "Harold, please bring up Bradley and Zachary's mission logs and the data they uncovered. I need some time alone. To focus. I'll call if I need you."

The light from the wall screen flashed, and when she turned around the screen was showing a timeline viewer from the Lupus mission. Harold's face had disappeared.

She took a deep breath and sat back down in the chair,

resting her arms on the armrests. "Bring up the first mission logs for all Olivaws and start playback, optimized for retention not visualization. Two data streams. Engage synaptic memory enhancement nanites."

"Nanites engaged, playback beginning," a robotic voice said over her retinal comm. She hadn't heard that voice in years, since she was little. It was bizarre not hearing Harold, but was fitting for the situation she found herself in.

The archive began playing on the wall screen, the imagery and text replaying at inhuman rates of speed. The human mind was a far more powerful computer than people imagined. In the mid-twenty-third century, researches uncovered ways to retrain the human mind to absorb information at speeds never thought possible. Most of the approaches to date had been focused on creating virtual life like experiences rather than retraining the mind to learn. It took a researcher at the Lunar Academy accidentally jacking her brain into an ancient lander's navigation computer while on stimulants to learn it the hard way. Within an hour, she'd taught herself everything the primitive machine's memory banks contained about their solar system, orbital dynamics, and trajectories with eidetic recall rates. She went on to win a Nobel Prize a few years later for neural enhanced education.

While the experiences replayed in a lossy manner, Abigail marked points in the feed she wanted to revisit. Despite the emotional fidelity being low, she couldn't help but feel the highs and lows of her brothers' situation as they advanced through the nebula. Bradley and Zachary had quite the teammates. Without each other, they wouldn't have survived.

She paused the feed and closed her eyes after an hour of playback, letting her mind catch up and connect the experiences. The branches were far more numerous than she'd anticipated. When she glanced back at the wall, she realized she hadn't even covered a third of their mission, and already she had a spider web of events to reply with deeper fidelity.

Her stomach rumbled. She hadn't eaten in hours and could really use a drink. Reaching up, she tapped her ear and subvocalized a command to have a meal delivered. She then brought up the first item she'd marked to revisit. Something about Bradley's friend almost dying at the hands of someone named Yaan.

THE IMAGE FROZEN on Abigail's screen was unimaginable. The sea of warships battling near the massive metallic cone the aliens had named the Kornu was breathtaking. There were thousands of Nanil ships, and they were all unable to make headway toward the Kornu. The sheer scale of the battle was hard to comprehend, especially when you considered how much smaller their fleet of starships was in Sol.

Libby and Cynthia had meticulously catalogued recordings and research during their return voyage. They worked with Harold and Zachary's A.I. Shauna to rank and plot the battles based upon size, location, aliens involved, lives lost, and starship configuration. While the Nanil ships were powerful and remarkable feats of engineering, the Galactic Alliance had an entirely different arsenal of death in Sol and Epsilon Eridani.

She flipped through scene after scene of death and destruction. For thousands of years, the Galactic Alliance marched their way through the central bulge of the galaxy. Each species they encountered either joined them, or perished in some technicality of their laws. The GA had ruled on many of the infractions before a tribunal had convened. She paused on the images in Lupus.

The millennia's old archival footage of the Selene moon ships defending off the human forces in Lupus during their tribunal judgment had been the most telling. Seeing the Syndrus cylindrical warships undocking from the Selene spheres and then further subdividing was remarkable. It was hard to believe the tribunal ships were these same harbingers of death. The ease in which they dispatched the ragtag fleet of ships attacking or fleeing from them was startling and tough to watch. Even knowing the images were from the distant past didn't help to dampen the impact of witnessing hundreds of thousands of lives dying in an instant.

She picked up her empty globe of water and chucked it at the wall screen before slamming her fist against the table. "I should be in Sol! I should be the one confronting these fraking alien bastards."

The plastic sphere compressed flat when it crashed into the glass surface of the screen and then slid down the wall with a thump. A few droplets of water from inside slipped down the screen and streaked over the exploding human ship frozen before her. The water was a crude metaphor for the tears now welling in her eyes.

Their mission was hopeless. Even with all the power in Sol focused on this one task, they'd be lucky to escape alive with a single ship. Their numbers were just too minuscule compared to the sheer size of the Galactic Alliance. If they managed to steal the Beacon, that was but one battle on a galactic battlefield where the odds of their success weren't even a fraction of the margin of error.

Maybe that was why humanity had escaped to Sol thousands of years ago, when they first joined the alliance. They saw the eventual path the alliance was on, and they knew they couldn't defeat them. Instead, they chose to run, to start over.

What they needed was an alliance of their own. A means to this new end. What they needed were allies in the galaxy, or someone who was in the same or worse situation they were. Maybe then they could come together to fend off the Galactic Alliance.

She stared at the black billowing nebulosity projecting out

above and below the Selene ship. Its cloud of death blocking out all light, and trapping inside the species who'd failed to abide to the wishes of a collective of others, all motivated by greed or worse, altruistic motives. Their failures were no different from those of humanity.

Was it that simple? She tilted her head and brought up the map of the galaxy she and Harold had built during their trips to the tribunal ship. Her answer was right there in front of her.

If you can't beat the jailer, then perhaps you rally the prisoners.

10

LYNC MICHAELS
EN ROUTE TO ZETA LUPI

The alien ships moved like nothing she'd ever seen before. The way they veered to a stop and redirected seemed impossible. Even with a gravity assist, the deceleration outclassed every style of ship they threw at it. They'd been destroyed hundreds of times since Quesh's speech yesterday, and there wasn't an end in sight.

Lync reached up and rubbed her hand through her hair, slicking it back. Her sweat was beading up and dripping into a puddle on the floor. The simulated heat of the explosions and the confined space of the simulators were far from optimal. This equipment wasn't designed to be deployed in the cramped confines of a cargo hold like this, but they were making it work.

Crayo drifted away from the group he was chatting with and meandered over to her side. "Ready ta give it another go?"

She shook her head. "No. I need a break. I've been staring at that sim for the past eighteen hours. Those rotating ships, they're all starting to blur together. Their whole movement pattern... it's illogical and breaks the fraking laws of physics. I have to think about something else for a bit."

He gave her a gentle nudge. "We need ta practice. The game has changed, and we gots ta catch up."

She jolted up, and her helmet went rolling along the ground with a thunk. "I said I need a break! It's like a washing machine in there, and if I fraking die one more time, I'm gonna…"

"Relax." He reached out and rested his hand on her shoulder. "Go take some time if ya need. I just gots ta bury me self some more, ta learn their tactics. I'll catch ya later tonight for some grub den?"

Her helmet had rolled to the far side of the small space they'd allocated for debriefing. People were stepping over it as if it was part of the room. Like her, they were each so focused on their tasks that it hadn't occurred to them that the helmet was out of place. Almost as much as she was.

She didn't know what she imagined would happen when Abigail woke up. Perhaps she'd fooled herself into thinking she'd be the sister she never had. Or maybe she imagined they'd talk about it, and get to know each other. Either way, she hadn't imagined they'd end up like this. She rubbed her wrists. At least she wasn't still in the brig.

"Hello." Crayo waved his hand in front of her. "Dinner tonight?"

"What?" She shook her head out of her trance. "Yea. Later. Sure. Grub." She pointed at her ear. "Give me a ping."

"Sim!" Crayo spun around and ambled toward the simulator with a skip in his step.

She didn't know how he could keep going back in there. The beating was numbing. It was one thing to try to learn their tactics, but they didn't even know who they'd be fighting. These were simulations from thousands of years ago. As far as they knew, the battle styles and vessels they'd face would be completely different.

Her retinal comm beeped, and she reached up and tapped her ear. It was an incoming request for a meeting. It didn't say who it was from, but it had a location. Up two levels and on the opposite side of the ship, toward the bridge. Whoever it was, they were from the higher ups and not the ground troops down below.

It was best not to keep them waiting. She strode across the deck and bent down to snatch her helmet up, racking it a few meters away on the way to the lift. While she should probably shower, she didn't care. If whoever it was wanted her, they'd have to accept her in whatever state she was in. Stench and all.

As she made her way toward the bridge, her mind wandered forward in time to the coming weeks. They had so much to learn, so much to prepare for. Everything up till now had been focused on sneak attacking an unexpected Selene ship and putting up enough diversion and suppression fire to get them within range to drop a nuke. It wasn't about formations, attack patterns, or dropping out of a gate and rapidly reassessing the state of a battle. It had gotten overly complicated in the blink of an eye, and she was still reeling from the first punch. They weren't going to Sol.

She'd never heard from her cousins or extended family. They'd dropped a few probes into Sol after they extracted her Ulixi faction from the ceremony grounds. There were other tribes spread throughout the asteroids and planetesimals of the Outer Ring. They'd been hoping to reach them, to enlist their help.

Any help at all would be good. But whatever Chief Austen had told them, they were underground and impossible to find. She'd hoped to reach Kalifa, her aunt's daughter in the Ewalle tribe, but she came up empty. Crayo sent a small crew of Ulixi to see if they could flush them out to talk, but that was a few days before they exited stage left in Tau Ceti. They hadn't heard from them since. She'd debated on going by herself, but Harold guilted her into staying with Abigail. A lotta good that did.

She paused outside the glowing green door on her retinal comm. It was just a random conference room from the looks of the sign on the door. She wasn't sure what to expect, but whoever it was, they were on the other side.

Why the hell did they need to talk to her again?

Her job was simple, prepare for and train the pilots. She didn't think anyone was preparing for a ground assault, but she'd wanted to practice. The generals overrode her. Said they could worry about that in Zeta Lupi. They were as full of shit as Commander Quesh.

She took a deep breath and gestured toward the door panel. It slid to the side and the far wall screen went dark as the person in front of it spun around, their face as shocked as she was.

"What're you doing here?" Abigail asked.

"I… don't have the foggiest," Lync said. "Says here on this message that you wanted to see me, Madam President." She gestured and flicked the comm onto the wall screen for her to read.

Abigail turned and studied the brief note and the directions Lync had followed before speaking. She sighed and then turned back, her head tilted upward. "This is you meddling, isn't it, Harold?"

There was only silence.

It made sense. He hadn't spoken to Lync since she'd assaulted Abigail back in Tau Ceti. If he was, in fact, a family consciousness with human traits, perhaps he was feeling the same thing she was. The unsatisfying gulf left by two family members at odds with one another.

Lync cleared her throat. "So, this is the overseer imposing his will, is it?"

"It appears so," Abigail snipped, her hands now on her hips. "Sorry to bother you, Major. You were duped."

She stood there for a moment, taking in the room. Apparently, Abigail had been holed up here for a while. The table was littered with food and drink cartons, and from the looks of her hair, she had either slept with her head on the table or was attempting a new fashion trend. Either way, her appearance wasn't nearly as kept as she'd grown used to seeing her.

When her eyes returned to Abigail, it was obvious she'd been studying her. Each taking in the disheveled image of the other. She had to wonder what her assessment was being confronted by a sweaty pink faced pilot with an attitude.

"Are you in or out?" Abigail finally asked.

Lync tilted her head. "Is it an option, Madam President? I mean, do you need me for anything?"

Abigail paused and glanced back at the still blank wall screen before returning her attention to Lync. "Maybe you could help me. I could use someone else's opinion of something I found earlier. If you have a few minutes."

The last thing she imagined she'd be doing to calm down from being blown up in a simulator was sitting next to her half sister while being yelled at and treated like shit. "I'm famished, actually. If you—"

The message:

Food has been ordered.

Flashed on the wall screen in giant letters.

She snickered and shook her head. "Seems the overseer would like me to stay."

Abagail smirked. "He gets overbearing like that sometimes. I think it's in the genes."

"No frak," Lync muttered.

"Touché." Abigail raised her middle finger.

She laughed out loud and stepped into the room.

A moment later Abigail laughed, as well, and the door closed.

"What can I do ya for, Madam Pres—"

"Cut the president shit," Abigail interrupted. "I'm about as presidential out here as this fraking globe of water." She flung a globe at Lync, who snatched it out of the air as it soared forward.

Her stomach growled as she palmed the cool globe. She hadn't realized how thirsty she was. Bringing the globe to her lips and taking a sip, her stomach flipped in excitement. The cool clean beverage was refreshing pouring down her throat.

She took another few sips of water as Abigail flipped through the archive data they'd received. While Lync had spent the better part of the day training, apparently Abigail had spent that time studying. She was bringing up image after image of the alien ships and weapons on the wall. Devastating battle scene after battle scene, as if she were preparing her defense in a court case.

As she glanced around, she eyed an empty chair across from her that didn't have a spent water globe or wrapper of some sort thrown into it. "Did the bots break down in here?"

"No," Abigail snipped. "I told Harold to leave me alone. This is how he gets when he stews over something or wants to teach me a lesson."

She squinted at the half-eaten sandwich from last night an arm's length away and her stomach growled again. "He stops cleaning?"

"Yep. He feeds me, though," Abigail smirked. "If he didn't, I think his Four-Laws' engine would seize up."

"I'll have to remember that." Lync brushed the garbage to the other side of the table. "Are you just going to spend the whole time opening up evidence of why we're walking into a shit storm we're likely going to die in?"

Abigail's eyes went wide, and her head swiveled to face her. "You see it, too?"

"We're gonna get slaughtered." Lync brought up her globe

and squeezed the last of the water out before shaking it for more. None came.

Abagail tossed her another.

"Thanks."

"Sure!" Abigail studied her. "I'm confused. If I see it, and you see it, then why don't the others?"

She shrugged. "Don't know. Maybe it's their penises. They tend to get in the way like that."

Abigail laughed, spitting up water all over the front of her shirt. She then brushed at it.

"I'm serious," Lync began. "The testosterone does a number on them. They see something they want to tear down, and they'll do anything to make it happen, even if it means a loss of lives or mass casualties. Hell, look at what Mayor North did on Liprosus. He sold us out to the fraking Galactic Alliance over a pissing match with your father and his father. It's insane."

Abigail nodded. "Yea, the North family has always been that way. It's only ever been about power and influence to them. But this, this whole situation is on a different scale. We're not picking a fight in the courtyard with our school bully. We're picking a fight with a tank using our fists." She flipped through the images of devastation. Destroyed ships, devastated worlds, squadrons of ships as far as the eye could see.

She took another sip of water and leaned forward, placing her arms on the table. "I see it. Hell, I've been feeling it the past eighteen hours in the sims. We don't stand a chance with them. Except for a few lucky shots, we've been getting trounced. When we're not, we're staying alive, but we're certainly not able to turn the tide."

"This is only day one of training," Harold said from overhead, causing both of them to jump in their seats. "We have nearly three hundred more days before we have to confront them. We have people working on stronger weapons in Zeta Lupi. I know we can rally between now and then."

"What makes you think that?" Abigail paused her flipping of images on a particularly nasty space battle between their Syndrus tribunal ships and the remains of a few hundred alien battleships. The destruction was epic in scale, and while the Galactic Alliance ship wasn't unscathed, the battlefield was littered with far more wrecks from the other side.

"Because if we don't, we've lost before we start," Harold said. "We don't need a frontal assault on them, we need a guerrilla war. Our goal is focused. Get in, get the Beacon, and get out. If we keep the Beacon between them and us or in the line of sight, odds are on them not even firing."

Lync nodded. She hadn't considered that. While it was helpful to train against their ships, they didn't have to beat them. They had to divert their attention and survive long enough for someone else to help them escape. "What about the pilots and bombardiers? How do we get them out?"

The image on the wall screen changed to a picture of Harold helping Abigail escape from the tribunal ship. He was pulling some type of device over both of them. "Zachary's team is working on that. I believe he's taking the same approach we used to get Abigail out. A small personal gate drive. Something to get you far enough away from the battle to be rescued."

She hadn't seen these pictures before. No one had. Lync glanced over at Abigail. Her arms were wrapped tightly around her chest like she was cold. Her eyes were locked on the body bag on the wall screen.

"It's ok." Lync reached across the table toward her with her hand. "You made it. You're alive."

Abigail nodded, but didn't say a word. She merely rubbed her arms and squeezed herself tight.

While Lync thought perhaps Abigail might cry, she didn't.

Instead, she stood up and without a word; she marched out of the room, the door opening and closing behind her.

"Should I go after her?" Lync spun toward the exit in her seat.

"Probably not." Harold dismissed the video. "I think I went too far showing that to you. She hadn't even seen it before."

She turned back toward the wall screen and studied the battlefield in front of her. "Do we have the footage of this battle? I'd like to watch it."

Harold backed the video up to the beginning and replayed the carnage. She watched the fast forwarded scene as the flotilla of hundreds of smaller alien ships approached the Syndrus formation from all sides and opened fire. While there wasn't much motion, there was a whole lot of firing. Volley after volley of missiles, laser beams, and some type of cannons firing accelerated charged particles toward the GA fleet. They had similar weapons, but the effects between the two were markedly different. She didn't know what type of shielding or protection they had, but the GA weren't being nearly as damaged as the alien ships were.

"What do we know about the armor differences?" she asked.

The door chimed, and the wall screen cleared.

She reached over and pressed the button to open the door.

Kara was standing on the other side, holding an arm full of food and beverages. "Yikes!" She leaned forward and peered around the room. "How long have you been living in here?"

LYNC RUBBED her hands through her hair. So much about these aliens was bizarre. Some of them seemed as brittle as a deep freeze banana while others could take twenty or thirty g-forces in their ships without blinking an eye.

"Well, let's just hope they don't have a ship full of Gharloc." Kara took another swig from her bulb of soda.

"From what we know of the Gharloc," Harold began, "they were highly dependent on automata, so it's likely that what you're seeing here isn't their pilots, but rather their drone ships."

"So, they can't survive a twenty g-force turn on a dime like that?" Lync pointed at the ship on the wall screen. It dove straight at an approaching Syndrus tribunal ship before making a right-hand turn to lay down a bombing run with strafing fire. That superhuman move was followed by another tight change in direction just before an inbound GA fighter collided with it.

"I'm not certain," Harold said. "But according to our archives, that ship design is a Hiratath. They're an aquatic member of the Galactic Alliance and use a modified liquid pilot chamber along with electronic implants to interface with their ships. The density of the liquid allows them to take on feats of endurance in space travel that would crush the body of a human."

"Thanks, Harold. That makes everything so much better." Lync reached over and wiped the virtual white board clear. She needed to start over. There had to be some way to tactically approach this battle that didn't require technology they didn't have or resources they couldn't obtain. She stood up and started pacing around the table.

"I'm going to go out on a limb here and assume we're not up for rethinking this mission?" Kara asked.

"While it's certainly not required that we capture the Beacon of Therion," Harold began, "without it or another event to dislodge the stranglehold of the Galactic Alliance, I fear we'll lose Sol forever."

Kara shrugged and pushed an empty globe around on the

table-top. "Is that so bad? I mean, even if we don't lose it, it's not like the GA is going to disappear and leave us alone."

Lync froze in her tracks. "Are we really talking about giving up our home star system and billions of lives? Think about that for a second."

"You already did it when you moved to Epsilon Eridani." Kara spun the globe between her fingers. "As did all the colonists headed to Tau Ceti."

"You mean Zeta Lupi," Lync said.

"Shit! Yea, you know what I mean."

She had a good point. Assuming they managed to drive the Galactic Alliance from Sol, if one fast forwarded twelve months or a few years, they'd return stronger and more able to wipe their star system by force. She took a deep breath and closed her eyes. It was too much to take in. While planning ahead and over thinking a situation was always her thing, even she had her limits.

Kara stood up and walked to her side before placing her hand on her shoulder. "You're not doing this alone. None of us are. We have each other."

Lync whipped around. "That's it!"

"What?" Kara squinted. "Us having each other?"

She waved her hands in the air and shook her head. "No, well, yea that's nice and all. What I meant was... it's too much. Too much information. Too many possibilities. Too many things to consider."

Kara didn't say a word, she merely took a step back from Lync like she'd broken her.

"I'm not understanding what you're saying," Harold said.

Lync gestured at the wall screen and brought up the earlier battle between the Galactic Alliance and the Gharloc warships.

"Why are we watching this again?" Kara asked. "They get slaughtered."

She raised her hand and motioned downward. She needed

for Kara to not talk. "Harold, remove all the ships. Replace them with their attack vectors only and do the same with the background stars and their weapons. I want a basic HUD without all the noise."

The video changed to a much simpler view. Harold replaced the ship with a crude outline and simple lines for each attack. There was far less to see, and the distracting explosions and effects for the weapons were gone. She watched as shots fired and the colors of the ships changed from green to yellow to red. It was still too much.

"I want to avoid seeing the damage." She gestured with her hands and tweaked the display. The ships were replaced with simple circles and squares.

"How will they know if they're damaged?" Harold asked.

Lync chuckled. "I'm pretty sure they'll feel it, assuming they even survive a hit. Besides, that's for the pilot to care about, not the bombardier."

She studied the wall screen. This was much more manageable.

"But they still die." Kara interrupted her thoughts.

"Yep, and their lack of motion is why." Lync walked up to the wall and gestured toward the expansive empty space. The ships were immobile. It was a sheer brute force battle with no finesse.

"I'm not seeing it." Kara squinted at the wall screen. "What am I missing?"

Harold changed the battle to one with the Hiratath versus the Ursis. The screen exploded with motion and dynamics. Nothing followed a predictable path, and there were hundreds if not thousands of ships all moving about. The entire field resembled a chaos fractal. It was beautiful.

"But… they still get destroyed," Kara said. "They eventually lose, and the Dark Nebula curtain gets raised."

Lync nodded. She knew Kara was right, but there was a

silver lining. "What's the elapsed time of the first battle with the Gharloc compared to this one with the Ursis?"

The view changed to show both battles side by side. Under the left image was the Gharloc encounter, with an elapsed time of ten minutes and fifty seconds. On the right was the Ursis battle, with an elapsed time of eight hours and thirty-two seconds.

Kara leaned back in her chair and let out a whistle. "We don't need eight hours. What's our estimated mission time, Harold?"

"Based upon historical footage, if we time it correctly to gate to the Beacon while they're sealing the Nebula, but not late enough for them to stow the artifact, I estimate we'd need twenty-four minutes. Give or take a few minutes."

"We can do that," Kara muttered before turning to stare at Lync. "Right?"

Lync nodded her head up and down slowly. "I hope so. It'll require us doing more complicated maneuvers than we do today and training to attack from unfamiliar approach vectors." She subvocalized a command to bring up human archives on space travel. The images appeared on the wall screen. "Talk to me about our research into space travel suspended within a fluid."

Kara choked on the water she was swallowing and spit it down the front of her shirt. "You've got to be kidding me."

"The human body can sustain twenty-four Gs of pressure suspended within a liquid and breathing oxygen," Harold said.

Kara stood up and walked up next to Lync. "No shit!"

"And what about breathing a liquid?" Lync asked.

"Explorers on Earth described significant discomfort when exposed to liquids for long durations of time. Their mental acuity and—"

Lync groaned. "Harold! How many Gs?"

"Over one hundred g-forces for no more than twelve

hours before the wearer reported diminished sensory and motor responses."

Kara thwacked Lync on the shoulder.

This could be it, the answer they'd been looking for. Assuming the other pieces fit, and they could cobble some of the technology together in time. She swallowed hard at the thought of breathing a liquid rather than air. Even if they couldn't get everyone to breathe the goo, they could switch from four g-force maneuvers to twenty. That would help some.

"Alright." Lync started pacing around the room again. "I want you to scramble whoever you need and put them on this, Harold. I don't care if Quesh fights me. I'll go toe to toe with the guy if I have to. This is our only chance. Give the teams a heads-up. Tell them to get some rest, and we'll be scrambling the squads in six hours to start out fresh. I don't know if you can tweak the simulations to dial up our g-force limits until the engineers make it work better. That way we can start preparing."

"I'm already on it," Harold said.

11

NGUYỄN DUE

SOL, NEAR NEPTUNE

The return trip to the Aitken was dead silent. His entire crew stood in formation, stoically staring at the exit ramp of the alien shuttle without moving a muscle. They knew better than to talk about anything important in a space controlled by the Galactic Alliance. Harold had warned them as much on multiple occasions. Everything onboard their ships was recorded except religious ceremonies and legal counsel, and it was all admissible in their trial. Even when they got off the shuttle, they went through thorough scans to ensure no eavesdropping devices or foreign nanites were on their person.

Nguyễn paced back and forth in the briefing room and froze when the door opened. Captain Marshall entered, followed by Lieutenant Lei, the head of his protective guard. He waited until the door closed behind them before he spoke. "Sorry about putting you on the spot like that, Captain."

Gwen glanced at the Lieutenant and then back at him. "Permission to speak freely, Admiral."

He nodded. "Granted. This is a safe space."

"That could've gone south fast if they'd taken your bait and thrown you in the brig. Nothing like a battlefield promotion to get the blood pumping. I assume that Captain bit was only to make a point with the aliens?" She squinted, studying him.

The room fell silent as they awaited his response.

"I can't continue to have one of our strategic assets in the human fleet commanded by an XO. While I'd prefer to make the promotion in a more suitable way, this'll have to do for now." He brushed at his jacket before reaching into his pocket and pulling out a command pin and offering it to her.

He rarely misjudged people, and she was the only one who stuck around after that traitor of a president disappeared with her minions. She'd proven her skills on multiple occasions over the past months and even managed to whip that ship into shape, a task that not even he had wanted to take on. "Do you accept the promotion, or should I search for your replacement?"

Gwen's gaze narrowed, but otherwise he couldn't read her. She was a tough nut to crack when she chose to be. Gone was her ball of emotion he'd first encountered onboard the Jurat.

She snapped to attention and saluted him. "It'd be my honor, Admiral."

He saluted her back, and she took the pin, staring at it in her hand. "Perfect. Now, back to the trial. How do you think we faired?"

"That was a clusterfuck if ever there was one," Harold said.

"Damnit!" Nguyễn slammed his fist on the table. "Don't you know your place? You're not welcome here, Harold. Please show yourself out."

"I can stop talking, but I'll warn you now. I'll still be listening. I'm always listening. Besides, I thought you'd want to know more about the reaction of the other aliens. Suit yourself."

"Wait!" Gwen raised her hand upward and shot Nguyễn a look. "Harold, can you share your intel? Please."

A private point to point encrypted message appeared on Nguyễn's retina comm from Gwen.

Let me take this, sir. He might have something we can use. We need him as an asset in the field. The GA ships won't talk to us, but they do to him. You keep your resolve. I'll play good cop.

She was right. While Harold was a pain in the ass, he'd come in handy on multiple occasions. Far more than he'd like to admit.

Harold's face appeared on the wall screen behind them. "Well, only because you said please, Captain Marshall. I have to say, that has a nice ring to it."

Gwen smiled. "Thank you."

"You're welcome." Harold adjusted his gaze on the wall to make eye contact with Nguyễn. "I maintained my connection with the tribunal ship after your departure. Lisp honored my request for access to the recordings so long as I accessed them from their shuttle. The entire exchange is rather archaic, but as long as I physically access their records, I'm able to copy everything I experience to my memory and bring it back onboard."

Nguyễn raised a hand for Harold to stop. "Wait, you're physically accessing their ship? For how long?"

"That's the thing. The exchange takes ten, fifteen seconds tops since I can control the rate of the data transfer. Like I said, it's a loophole in their laws. But it allows me to access anything pertinent to the trial as an extension of you, my uplifters."

A chuckle escaped from Lieutenant Lei before he returned

to his previously blank expression. He hadn't said a word since they'd entered.

"What's so funny?" Nguyễn eyed him.

"Nothing, sir."

"Aw bullshit. What is it, Lieutenant? I said this was a safe space."

Lieutenant Lei adjusted his posture and shuffled his feet for a moment, like he'd been caught off balance. "It's… just bizarre that you see Harold as a mistake and an unwelcome obstruction to our ship, and yet the aliens see him as a natural extension of humans and we as his uplifter."

Nguyễn wasn't keen on admitting when he was wrong, but this time he was. Perhaps he'd been looking at Harold wrong the entire time. Maybe they could have been using him to learn more from their fleet.

He walked around the far side of the table and turned to face Harold. "Why else have they suddenly opened their arms to you? What's changed?"

Harold stared skyward, as if in deep thought before speaking. "Other than explaining the fine points of our history to them while we were waiting between your slow human speeches aboard the tribunal, nothing has changed. Had you allowed the ambassador to present the rest of her case you would have—"

He laid his hand down on the table and leaned forward. "You're feeding them details of our history?"

The human form of Harold shrugged on the wall screen. "It's boring, really. All the Bynaury seem to care about are our religions. Apparently, we have markedly more religions than any other species in the GA. So many so, they have their own theories about how humans devolved into such a fragmented people after their arrival in Sol."

"I'm glad we could help them with their research papers," he said.

Gwen sat down in a chair beside the wall screen. "What

were you saying about the rest of the case, Harold? What was Ambassador Addae about to present?"

"The Ambassador was about to make a motion to accelerate the trial and present all of their evidence in the case, including what they found in Epsilon Eridani. This would fast-forward the trial to put the ball in our court." Harold brought up a translation of the Galactic Alliance Prosecution's case against humanity. The words scrolled by until he paused at the primary pieces of evidence.

Nguyễn read the paragraphs several times before saying them out loud. "A judicial force uncovered a human probe in the Epsilon Eridani star system. Upon discovery, it attempted a failed self-destruct sequence which left behind evidence of stolen technology. While the drive was unrecoverable, its power core design matched the output and connections from a Galactic Alliance superluminal warp bubble drive." He paused and let the words sink in before he finally spoke again. "Are you fraking kidding? You couldn't even think to swap out the connectors?"

"It wasn't that simple," Harold said.

Gwen leaned closer to the wall screen. "So, we did steal their technology then?"

"If I tell you, it might show up in their vital recordings during the proceedings. As of now, none of you are showing signs of lying. Me telling you would change that."

"What are you talking about?" Nguyễn hated being strung along. "You said they could read our subvocal conversations when we were on the tribunal floor, but what else are they monitoring?"

The wall screen exploded with metrics. Heart rate, precipitation, millimeter movements in body language, and even attempts at reading what was being projected on their retinal contact lenses. No wonder Harold had always preferred audio. Those were embedded deep inside their ear canal, where sounds were transmitted to the auditory cortex. There was no way they could intercept that without invading his body.

He collapsed down into a chair. "How's any of this legal?"

"Human laws have no bearing in the Galactic Alliance courts. Our body's reactions, projections, and movements are all admissible as evidence in their judicial system."

Gwen shot up and covered her mouth after seeing something in the data. "As were our nanites. How didn't that get us tossed?"

Harold smirked. "They allow a certain amount of latitude for discovery by the defendants, even if it's antiquated in its approach, so long as it doesn't invade the space of another species."

"How was it antiquated?" Lieutenant Lei asked.

The wall changed again, this time presenting a breakdown of every species reaction over time to all the information presented. All transcripts, body movements, etc. The same things being recorded by the defendant were available from the prosecution and the jury.

"Remarkable," Nguyễn muttered.

"It actually is. It's an open playing field, so long as you know what to look for. Or in this case, whom to befriend."

Nguyễn saw it as far worse than that. They were so far ahead of humanity; it was hard to figure out where to start. Except for when his anger threw off all their metrics, they'd been able to read his team's reactions like a book. They'd been playing them as fools the whole time.

"Back to the evidence they have against us. We look like fraking baboons over there." He gestured to his left, toward where the tribunal ship was floating in space off their port side. "I'd rather understand what the Olivaws were working with, so we have a better chance of getting out of this mess."

"Did you mean what you said on the way out?" Harold asked. "About not returning to the tribunal ship."

"If I can help it."

Harold's face appeared in the corner of the wall screen. "I can work with Lisp on that. Perhaps we can do something virtually. There's precedence for it, though the species was incapable of fitting within the tribunal ship itself. But that's beside the point. Alright, yes. We borrowed technology from the Galactic Alliance."

Nguyễn rubbed his face. "No shit, Sherlock. We knew that. What else?"

Harold mimicked taking a deep breath before laying it all out. "It took a few hundred years to reverse engineer the probe we found in Antarctica. During that time, we slowly leaked technology to humanity to advance them without raising suspicion of where the tech was coming from. At times, we made mistakes."

Gwen gestured in the air, making a forward circle. "Like?"

"When one of our tests exploded out in the Oort Cloud and gave away humanity's location in the galaxy."

Lieutenant Lei raised his hand. "I thought those were tests of our colony ship's subluminal drives?"

Harold shook his head. "Nope, that was a lie. We covered it up that way and used it to help accelerate our plans to colonize other stars. The fact was, we were already out there around several of them. Exploring them well ahead of the colonists."

Nguyễn leaned back in his chair and stared at the ceiling before sighing. "Are you fraking kidding me? How many decades have we wasted with the details the Olivaws hid?"

"It's not exactly a fair question," Harold began. "As a species in Sol, we've been more concerned about killing each other than advancing toward the stars. I don't believe we were wrong in withholding it. There's no telling what would have come of us had we not."

He stared at the sinusoidal wave tiles lining the ceiling. Their pattern was regular, but the fibrous weave of the sound dampening material they were composed of wasn't. It was random and chaotic.

Harold was right. Their species was constantly converging on destroying itself one moment, and in the next, they were on the precipice of greatness. It was never a continuum of prosperity. Humanity was only capable of riding the crashing waves of its existence, hoping that one of them wouldn't lead to its extinction.

The Olivaws weren't wrong, but Nguyễn would never tell them that. The last thing humanity needed was more of their leadership. It was time that a firm hand guided humans. Someone capable of leading them out of their darkest hour. Someone like him.

"And how did we get to Achernar?" He continued to stare up at the ceiling in silence, waiting for the reply before sitting up and making virtual eye contact with Harold's artificial face.

"What do you mean?" Lieutenant Lei pointed at the wall screen. "We used the GA drives, didn't we?"

Nguyễn watched as Gwen sat back in her chair and crossed her legs and arms, staring at Harold. She, too, was waiting for a response and knew what he was asking. She, like him, wanted to know why the Galactic Alliance was scared. They'd danced around it for a long time, and Harold had alluded to it on multiple occasions, but he'd never stated it outright.

"Harold? Are you going to answer me?" Nguyễn reached out and traced a circle on the top of the table. "You continue to deflect and not share the details pertinent to our survival. Plus, you invade our ships without provocation. You're really no different from the GA."

"That's bullshit and you know it." Harold's image enlarged on the wall screen and the other documents disappeared. "Given our situation, I'm doing what I can to protect humanity."

"You're doing what you can to protect the Olivaws," Gwen said.

"They're one and the same to me. My programming outlines—"

Nguyễn slammed his hand flat on the table, sending a crack through the room. "I don't care about your programming. We've heard it a thousand times. You're looking after us, as well as the Olivaws. We get it. You and I know the Achernar angle is our ace in the hole, and yet we have no clue how to use it. I could be doing so much more to send the fear of humanity into the aliens if I knew details, but you're preventing us, preventing me from knowing it. I'll ask you again. How did we get to Achernar?"

Harold's face was a model of control. The emotion and drama from before had seeped out. "The key to humanity's survival in Sol is in the Spános."

Gwen uncrossed her arms and gestured at the wall screen next to Harold, doing a search on the name, but it came up empty. "What, or where, is this Spános?"

"It's a what, and you're already in possession of it. It's the name of the material the Galactic Alliance mined from the planetesimal near Jupiter. It's the key to much of the raw power the alliance wields."

Lieutenant Lei walked around beside Nguyễn and whispered in his ear. "I don't understand what this has to do with Achernar."

"It doesn't," Nguyễn said. "His answer is to not answer. He's redirecting our attention elsewhere. Such is the Olivaw way. When you don't want people watching you, you give them something else to draw them in. The question is, what are you planning, Harold?"

Harold pulled up chemical properties and refining methods on the wall screen. "With the proper preparation and enough time, we can refine the Spános into weapons capable of destroying this entire fleet. Assuming we can get close enough."

"Time isn't something we're finding plentiful at the moment." Gwen cloned the data Harold shared and began studying it on the other wall screen. "This would require months and years to complete. I don't see how we can hold them off that long."

"We can't," Harold said. Emotion returned to his face. This time he was solemn, and his eyes exuded a strange sadness. "At least not to refine all of it. The hope is that you're able to refine enough for us to defend Earth and as many other outposts as possible, should the Galactic Alliance fleet advance on us. Spános is the rarest ore in the galaxy. We don't exactly have stockpiles of the stuff lying around, and finding it has been… let's just say a challenge. There are a few other things I can't underscore enough." Harold's image zoomed in. "First, you must not cut corners in the refining process. Second, it's imperative you separate the ore from its storage while you're refining it. Failing to do either will result in significant devastation and death. Trust me on this."

Nguyễn studied the data Gwen was scrolling through. There were more details here than met the eye. The sheer volume of research was well beyond anything even the Olivaws could have produced. Either that, or the Olivaws were hundreds of years ahead of them with this stuff. But from what Harold alluded to, Spános was rare enough that even they didn't have much of it. "Ok, so if we can't refine enough to take out their fleet, then what's going to prevent them from laying down that nebulosity and killing us all? There's no point in them advancing on our planets and outposts if they can merely engulf us in Black Death."

"We have hope," Harold said.

Gwen chuckled and turned her attention back to the wall screen. "You're kidding, right?"

"I wish I were, Captain Marshall. I wish I were."

Nguyễn stood up. He was growing tired of this A.I., tired of all the drama. "So, you hand us what amounts to a metric ton of research on this Spános shit, but you can't tell us about Achernar. I assume you have a needle in this haystack that we should be focusing on?"

The plans for a small spherical device appeared on the wall screen. It was no larger than a marble. At the heart of it was a single grain of refined Spános. When he read the megaton yield, he collapsed back into his chair. The implications of such a device were astounding. If it could produce this much power, harnessing it for other means could change the course of human history. "That's a factor of ten times more than every nuclear weapon in all of Sol."

"Like I said," Harold began. "Do—not—cut—corners! We should be able to refine a few dozen of these in time."

The words hung in the room before it dawned on him what Harold had said. "Time for what?"

A smile slowly formed on Harold's face. "To turn the tide in our favor."

12

JOYCE GREEN
EPSILON ERIDANI, LIPROSUS

"I want to see another route!" Joyce's voice echoed through the room, and all eyes briefly turned to watch her before returning to their consoles. "There has to be a way to get across the barrier. Space is far too vast for them to scan everything."

The technician in front of her fumbled at his controls for a moment before regaining his composure. "We've fired a few sample rocks over the past few weeks, Director. Harold helped us get them launched from the ground and redirected in orbit, so they didn't appear to be from Liprosus. Except for the half meter chunks, none of them made it out."

She trusted Harold about as much as a junkie in a drug lab. While he'd proven himself useful on countless occasions, he never seemed to be truly on their side. It was like he was always masking broader secrets, and the colonists were along for the ride.

"I won't just sit back and die. Escaping is the only option that makes sense." She leaned in closer to the technician's screen. "Can we run a test with the stealth tech? They can't detect the stuff. We've got mountains of the shit and ships covered in it sitting idle in the holds, waiting for something

Harold refuses to tell us about. We can fire a few of those off planet and see if they make it out of the system, right?"

"I wouldn't recommend that," Harold said over her comm.

Her frustration was a short wick today. The last thing she needed was an egotistical A.I. interrupting her thoughts. "I asked you to stop doing that."

Her words were spoken out loud, and the technician lifted his hands off his controls. "I'm sorry, Director. I was running a projection like you asked."

She shook her head and raised her hand upward, and the technician flinched. He was frightened of her. From the looks of the surrounding faces, many of the others were, as well. Apparently, word had spread further than she'd expected over what she'd done to the Thyreusian. Ryder assured her his teams were under control. He was wrong.

"I'm sorry, soldier. You're fine. I was talking to Harold." She pointed at her head. "He continues to interject his ideas into my mind without consent. He's mistaken me for someone who wants his opinion all the time." She raised her attention toward the ceiling and raised her arms. "Harold, I'm not an Olivaw mouth piece. If you have something to say, then say it to all of us."

Harold's face appeared on the bank of displays in front of the technician. "As I was saying, I wouldn't recommend launching those ships. They're not designed for interstellar travel, and besides, there's not exactly a star nearby they could float up to. It would take hundreds of thousands of years to reach Sol using primitive methods of propulsion. That's assuming you make it at all."

She raised her fist before pausing and lowering it to her side. Another act of frustration in front of her people wasn't going to help matters. "We can't continue to watch and wait for the curtain to be drawn. As far as we know, you're a puppet to the Galactic Alliance and are telling us to sit still until their work is complete. Hell, I'd run a disinformation campaign similar to that if I were them. It'd make their jobs a hell of a lot easier."

"Hope is coming, Director." A light appeared behind Harold off-screen, illuminating him with an angelic effect. "We've talked about this before. Besides, I've given your team access to read any and all of my programming and data. I'm an open book on full display. Honestly, I'm not hiding anything."

Elaine stepped forward from the shadows and rested her hand on Joyce's shoulder. "He's telling the truth. I've had dozens of programmers digging through his neural network for weeks. Everything he's saying adds up. He can't lie to us. He's bound by his Four-Laws Engine. While he might not have the details behind why he's advising we should wait, he believes them nonetheless."

Belief. They're basing their entire existence, their future on the belief of a machine. One that started humanity down this road hundreds of years ago.

Joyce nodded toward the technician. "How does Harold's programming differentiate a hope from a lie? If he's programmed to protect us from death, and the only path to us living longer is to sit still and do nothing, then how can we tell he's not simply lying to us to fulfill his Four-Laws' obligations?"

When she glanced around, studying the faces of the others, they were deep in thought. It was clear they hadn't foreseen that possibility. She wasn't even sure if what she was saying made sense. It all depended on how Harold's A.I. pathways enforced the Four-Laws and how he interprets his objective to save humanity.

"Can we test that hypothesis?" Elaine asked.

"We can," Harold began. "While I could tell you the answer, it's easier if you discover it yourself. I'll guide your teams on how to run the simulation in isolation, but I won't interact with their work. If that's ok with the Director?" He turned his attention to Joyce.

She clenched her jaw. "How long would it take?"

Harold waited a moment for the technicians to answer, but none did. They merely stared at each other, their eyes glazed over in thought. He broke the silence. "To run the gamut of tests in a controlled environment, from simple to full data sets like this copy has access to will require trillions of compute cycles. I'd guess two weeks. I could do it faster myself with access to my entire computational mesh, but your team needs to run this one."

She glanced at Elaine, and she shrugged and nodded. "Seems like a decent estimate."

Two weeks to know if this A.I.'s laws were influencing the destiny of the colony in ways that inhibited their escape. That was two more weeks of the curtain closing tighter.

"I sense hesitation and doubt," Harold said. "Might I suggest an alternate approach to aid in your decision?"

No one else was chiming in, either out of fear of her or their own death. "Sure, why not? Suggest away."

"You spin up a team to make your suggested modifications to a few of the ships in the holds. Figure out how you want to augment them for interstellar travel, or whatever you plan on doing out there once you get past the nebula. All the while, the programmers will work on your quest to determine my trustworthiness. Both sides act, and no one worries about doing too little to prevent their own demise."

Again, he made sense. It really was two steps forward and two steps back with her trusting him. "Do we get your assistance in both endeavors?"

"Only if asked. I don't want to be accused of getting in the way."

The surrounding faces were nodding. And unless she was mistaken, there was a hint of something more in their faces. Dare she say a drop of hope.

"Make it happen!"

———

"ARE YOU HEADING DOWN?" Ryder asked.

Joyce hadn't realized he'd entered the control room. The last thing she needed was someone crawling down her throat, friend or not. She stopped and took a deep breath, careful to not snip at him. "What can I help you with, Lieutenant?"

His eyes drifted to where she'd left, unsure how to say what was on his mind.

She gestured in a striking motion across her hand. "Tear it off. I have places to be."

He shifted his weight from one foot to the other. "Are you ok? I mean, you seem a bit on edge."

A chuckle escaped her lips. "Other than the usual end-of-life decisions and being locked in a cell for the rest of our lives, I'm peachy. Is that all?"

"I think what you did back there was great." He tilted his head toward where she'd been. "Giving everyone something to do other than stare at their screens and hope Harold isn't leading us down a dead end is an excellent idea."

"Don't thank me, thank Harold."

He nodded. "You could've said no, or tossed everything aside and went full bore with your plan."

She furrowed her brow. "I can't tell if you're pro-Harold or pro-escape."

His posture stiffened. "I'm pro-survival. Whatever it takes. Whatever the cost. I can't imagine the Olivaws would leave us down here to die if they didn't have bigger plans."

"That makes one of us. The longer I'm buried down here, the more helpless I feel, the angrier I get. We're sitting here hiding, and every centimeter of me wants to be up there, kicking their alien ass." She pointed skyward.

"I feel you. I do. We'll be up there soon enough. I know it."

"I hope you're right." The thought of finally being able to avenge her son and the colonists she'd failed to protect had been wearing on her for months. "Is there anything else?"

He shook his head and smiled. "Nope. Just checking in on the boss."

"I appreciate it." She gestured toward the approaching soldiers. "Looks like you're wanted." As she was about to turn to leave, she paused. "Say, that reminds me. Have your people been keeping my outburst with our guests tight to their chest?"

Ryder recoiled slightly. "Of course, sir. They understand the importance of security. Have you heard something?"

Her head shook slowly from side to side. "No. Just a feeling."

"I'll look into it." He reached out and touched her shoulder. "I'm sure it's your imagination. But if someone leaked anything, Harold, or our other surveillance systems would've picked it up. I'll let you know what I find."

"Thanks." She smiled and turned, making her way to the lift tubes and dropping downward.

Another visit to the guests was in order. Today her mission was to unlock more intel on this damn nebula. If they had any hopes of escaping this mess, they needed details and timelines on their closing curtain.

AS THE DOORWAY rose into the ceiling, she stepped into the cramped cell. Two was in his usual position with his back toward the entrance, except today his posture was less upright. Like he was more tired than usual.

She couldn't blame him. He'd been standing for months. That and he'd undergone their poor attempt at surgery to reattach the antennae she'd yanked off. While it hadn't been rejected by his body, it was hardly what she'd call functional.

"Good afternoon, Two. How've you been today?"

His wounded antennae twitched like it was attempting to turn toward her, but failed. For some reason, the unharmed antennae seemed unable to act on its own.

"Back for another round of ten, Director?"

She squinted. "Round of ten what?"

"You know, as in boxing." Two shrugged his shoulders and turned his attention out of the corner and focused on her. "I figure since I was your punching bag, you were coming back for another round."

"You never cease to amaze me, Two. Where on Liprosus did you hear about boxing? One of our guards?" She walked over to the corner he was always staring at and spun the seat out of the wall. Maybe this was his lucky corner. It couldn't hurt to give it a try.

"Human television."

She recoiled in surprise. "Seriously. Where?"

"It's quite popular throughout parts of the alliance. Your species created so much useless entertainment in Sol, it's a wonder you ever found time to break free of the gravity and explore your star system at all. Your signals have been leaking into the Milky Way for centuries. It was only a matter of time before you were discovered. Though that big flash of light you made a half century ago certainly broadcast an open invitation to the universe at the speed of light."

He was talkative today. That was a good sign.

She slid down into the seat some and crossed her legs. "What shows are your favorite?"

"Sports, obviously. I was into boxing for a while until that maniac bit off the ear of his competitor. It ruined the whole thing for me, so I switched to MMA fighting. Now that's some crazy shit. It reminded me of the blood matches the Nanil used to run with you humans as the fodder, except you were doing it willingly." Two shook his head, mimicking her human gesture. Without his antenna to express his emotions, he seemed out of sorts.

"I'm not sure what blood matches you're talking about, but MMA has been popular for centuries. My son Paul used to love watching them. Especially the zero-g MMA. It really brought the Jackie Chan antics and fighting style into the ring." She closed her eyes, remembering back to when he was a teen. He spent hours engulfed in those fights. It was a miracle he hadn't wanted to give it a go himself. Maybe then he'd be alive.

"Are you thinking about him now?" Two asked.

When she opened her eyes, he was leaning his head down at an angle, trying to make eye contact with her. Like he was struggling to see her face. Maybe she'd messed up his eyes, as well. Surely a few of the sixteen should be enough for him to see her.

"I was." She stared down at her hands. "I miss him every day. I haven't even had a chance to tell his sister back in Sol about him. I'd give anything to see her again and break the news." She was lying through her teeth. He didn't have a sister, but Two didn't know that.

Two tilted his head, as if he was still trying to focus on her. "While I can't relate as I've never had offspring, I imagine our queens could. They'd go to the end of the galaxy to protect their hive members. I'm confident mine is a tad pissed right about now."

She clasped her hands together in her lap. "Oh, I'm sure they have a few centuries before they notice you're missing."

"Not with the Beacon of Therion." Two leaned down lower until his harness snapped him back against his pole. He shook his head and leaned down again before he spoke. "It should be here by now. With its arrival, she'd know instantly."

"Instantly?" She squinted. "Over that great of a distance?"

"Such is the power of the Builders." A buzz emanated from Two as he arched his back and glanced toward the ceiling. A moment later his attention returned to lowering down to stare at her. "No one knows how they work, but they enable the races wielding them to communicate over vast distances."

"Seems like something you'd want to protect rather than drag all the way out here. Someone might steal it." She peered up at him and forced a smirk.

Two leaned back, and his body gyrated uncontrollably until he bellowed a human laugh. She'd never heard him laugh like a human before.

Finally, after his body stopped moving, he lowered his head to stare at her. "You stand about as good a chance getting close to a Beacon as I do leaving this cell alive. I'm not worried, though. Your day is fast approaching. Your fate will be sealed in another three months. Then, I'll rest."

She brought her foot down and slid forward some. "Humm. Strange how we still have at least six to seven months at the current rate you're closing the curtain."

Two's antennae began moving around their head in a circular motion. A jittery circle, but a circle nonetheless. "Then the Beacon hasn't arrived. It's due any time now." The antenna stopped and angled down toward her, having regained all of their articulation. "Your end is near, Director. Just like your son."

Her heart was beating fast and she didn't realize she had moved. Looking back at it days later, it would still be a blur. Joyce leaned forward, grabbed the antennae atop Two's head, ran behind his restraining pole and yanked down. This time, she ignored his screams of pain. She knew how much force they'd take to detach, and she didn't stop yanking until they did. Both of them.

As she stood over Two's twitching corpse, she stared down at her hands. His slick yellow blood coated her arms and the front of her outfit. She'd crushed the two globes in her fists and the stalks dangling beneath them were still writhing. When they stopped moving, her attention rose up toward the corner of the room.

And then she saw it. What Two had been staring at for so long. He'd never been trying to catch her gaze. He'd been focusing on the absolute corner of the room. There, framed in the yellow blood oozing down the wall, was the perfect joining of three surfaces. When the light hit them just right, she swore she could see a hexagon. The shape of the Thyreuns hive and everything in their world.

13

ZACHARY OLIVAW
ZETA LUPI, OORT CLOUD

"Well, that didn't work." Zachary was watching the cockpit cameras of the test craft. A projectile from the skirmish pierced the hull, and the chamber began freezing solid. Within a minute, it was as hard as a rock. The temperatures of the vacuum crystalized the liquid breathing medium. Had the dummy occupant been real, they would have frozen solid.

"We're going to need to research some alternate mediums," Harold began. "With this first trial, we're starting from what we know worked on Earth. This will at least get us within the realm of attempting some of the maneuvers Lync and Kara are preparing their teams for."

Zachary's eye twitched as the robots near the docking harness cracked open the test ship. The contents inside spilled out like a slushy. Partially frozen and yet a liquid at the same time. The dummy human floated inside like a cherry submerged in the ice.

They didn't have much time left before they needed to begin the mass manufacturing of their fleet of ships if they had any hope of hitting their numbers. Hell, they were already decreasing the longer they waited to hit go. With this curveball they'd been given, their odds of success had plummeted again. He'd asked Harold to not spread the news just yet, preferring to wait until they'd gotten further with their designs. The grave news would spread soon enough. It was pointless fanning the flames any sooner.

He stood up and circled around the far side of the room. Every so often he changed position to look at things differently. "Are there any other liquids that can remain a liquid near zero? Or perhaps we could build in some type of heating units into the cockpit?"

"Maybe." Harold brought up a list of known breathing mediums. "If we had access to the Galactic Alliance archives, we might have more details on the Ursis or the Gharloc. They're the most recent examples we have of species that use liquid breathing medium."

"Perhaps Libby has dug up something for us." He didn't say more for fear that if someone were observing them, they would figure out what that meant. On its own, it was an innocuous statement. In reality, he was hoping their Lupus data trove would have some leads on the technology they needed. She'd been sifting through the alien archives for a few weeks now, looking for anything that could help them but had come up short so far.

"In the meantime, I'll direct the engineers to optimize for rapid closure of the penetration, as well as heating the liquid. Perhaps some nanites suspended within the fluid could keep it circulating and be optimized to vent heat in an emergency."

He stopped in his tracks. That was actually an excellent idea. Why hadn't he thought of that? It made perfect sense, but he wasn't functioning anywhere near normal. Between the radio silence from Pluto, his brother and her being in harm's way, and all of this mission planning, he was a tad stressed. Add to that his sister, who he hadn't seen in over six years, arriving in a few hours and his nerves were frazzled.

"I need some air." He spun around and marched out the

door. As he stepped into the nearby lift tube, he gestured at the controls to take him down to the arboretum. Even though it was a controlled environment, some type of open space would do him wonders.

His mind went fuzzy as the floors zoomed past. The last week had gone from bad to worse. The infighting with the generals, the failed pilot exercises piling up, and the dead ends in the Lupus archive had pushed him over the edge. Add to that the fact that his sister hadn't bothered to message him since she'd woken up. He'd sent a few messages her way, and he'd confirmed their receipt, but none had been returned. She was either sleeping the entire trip or pissed off beyond recognition.

The last time they had a blowout like this was over not telling Bradley about the family. That'd been nearly a quarter century ago, and their relationship ever since had been icy at best. Hell, when they last spoke they'd gotten into a screaming match and then he stormed away after they both watched Bradley depart for Zeta Lupi. He'd wanted to bring Bradley into the fold, but she insisted they couldn't trust him.

He stepped out of the lift tube into the warm yellow light of the artificial sun overhead. The sound of water running and birds chirping hit him like a feather pillow to the face. The warmth was welcoming, and the sounds of life were just what the doctor ordered. He made his way down the crushed stone path and took his usual route left, heading clockwise around the facility.

There was a murmur of whispers when he passed the gazebo where people congregated during their lunch. He could make out a few mentions of his name, but he subvocalized a command to his retinal comm to block anything that wasn't natural to the environment. The sounds of the birds and crickets replaced the gawking and frustrations of someone famous nearby. Someone who changed their lives forever and whose presence wasn't necessarily welcome.

"Does she know about you?" Zachary asked subvocally. He knew she was listening. Like Harold, she was always there.

She didn't answer right away, but eventually Shauna's voice spoke. "And by she, I assume you mean Abigail?"

He tilted his head. "Who else would I be talking about?"

"I don't know," Shauna began. "I was just asking. No, she doesn't know about me. I figured you'd want to be the one to tell her. From everything Harold sent on, except for some initial research into the archives, she's spent the trip alone in her room."

"Alone for two weeks after having been in a coma for months. Are you sure?"

"That's what—"

A bird dove in front of him, causing him to jump sideways. "What the hell?" he muttered, glancing about to see if any other animals were approaching. He didn't notice anything else and by the time he found where the bird had gone, it had swooped up, and was coming back around for another run at him.

He leaned forward and started sprinting down the path, trying to put some distance between himself and the bright red cardinal. Its jet black beak was squawking at him as he pounded his feet into the gravel. He raised his hands up to his head in an attempt to protect himself from the approaching sounds of the angry, feathered animal.

As he made his way out of the small grove of trees and into a clearing, the bird arced skyward and circled back. It was no longer angrily pursuing him. He slowed to a fast walk, his heart pounding in his chest. "What was that about?"

On his retinal comm, a video appeared of a small nest with several tiny chirping birds inside. Their beaks were raised skyward, and they looked to be angry at something. A second later, two red cardinals landed on the edge of the bowl of twigs and one of them dropped a worm into the center of the raucous bunch of babies. They tore at it with their beaks, shredding it within seconds. When the image panned out a few feet, he noticed the walking path just beyond the nest.

"Apparently our feathered friend built their home too close to the trail," Shauna said.

"We should warn anyone who passes near there to be on the lookout." The entire event reminded him of his mother, Marie. She never let people frak with her kids or his father. She'd put them in their place if they attempted to get in the way of her family. Her computer name was Shauna, but he and the crew from their expedition knew who she really was. Everyone swore to secrecy, but he was sure it would leak eventually, just as Harold's identity had.

Every step he took along the path, the gravel beneath his feet ground away his stress. He was never fond of exercise, but it helped. With his sister's arrival, he might have to find new outlets to relax. She was a force to be reckoned with, and if he knew her, shit was about to hit the fan.

"So, tell me what you know about this third colony ship," he subvocalized.

"That's a bit out of nowhere," Shauna said.

He took a right on the path and headed toward the small pond of water in the middle of the arboretum. "I've been thinking about our problem with pilots and bombardiers. There have to be a few Ulixi in the mix onboard that ship. That or some Gunders."

"Why would we need Gunders?"

He'd forgotten about the conversation he and Libby had in the lab. Neither she nor Harold's copy in there had any way to communicate with the outside world beyond their memories. That and an occasional data dot transferred through several layers of security.

"It's an idea Libby had been mulling over," he began. "She was wondering if the Gunders on Earth might have the same disposition as the Ulixi. Their lives of seclusion from the surface world could give them an advantage piloting the ships or depositing the bomb payloads."

The Earth Gunders had negotiated with their above-ground brethren in recent centuries, and some of them had even managed to make a life for themselves outside their subterranean cities. Libby was hoping the younger migrant Gunders would have retained some of their abilities to focus on tasks. They were renowned for their willpower and attention to detail in game shows and casinos throughout Sol. Some establishments had gone as far as banning them in their facilities.

"I wish you'd mentioned this sooner," Shauna began. "There are several dozen Gunders in the colony on Tiān. I'll have Harold work his magic to see if they're already in training or interested in joining. He's been working with Adri on a way to test for the skill sets inherent in the Ulixi."

"Sorry I didn't say anything sooner. Libby only brought it up yesterday. I've been a bit—"

"Distracted," she interrupted.

He chuckled. "Something like that."

"The records of the colonists headed toward Delta Sagittarii show even more Gunders on their registry. There's close to three hundred among the fifty thousand souls drifting through space. The Ulixi aren't as easy to find, though. But based upon how many we found here on Tiān, this could truly turn the tide in our favor."

As he walked up to the edge of the water, he paused to watch a small flock of ducks fly down and slide across the surface before coming to a stop. Their little webbed feet were barely visible, paddling beneath the water. "There's the small matter of building a starship, finding them, and then transporting them safely here. And we don't even know if the Gunders are suitable candidates yet."

"Let's assume they are for now. I call getting them here

child's play compared to the alternative of recruiting and bringing them here from Sol."

He reached down and picked up a rock. It was flat, like the ones he and his brother used to skip across the pond in North Carolina. Why this one was here, he wasn't sure. Best to not offset the balance, though. He tossed it back on the ground, and it bounced into the edge of the water, just below the surface.

Even the smallest change could have massive consequences on a living environment. A second earlier that rock was on the dry side of the water, and now, now it was submerged. It could take centuries to return to that same spot, if ever, and he'd be the reason why. And this was merely a rock. They weren't even talking about lives.

He bent down and retrieved the rock out of the water and lodged it back into the mud he'd pried it from. "Maybe we can retrofit the Spērō with a gate drive somehow?"

"I'm going to need some help on this mission," Shauna said. "I can't plan this alone."

He stood up and nodded, wiping his hands together and flaking off the dirt in the process. "Pull in whomever you need. And if any of the generals or politicians give you push back, tell them to fraking talk to me."

"Is that a direct quote?"

"Yes! You're welcome to record me saying it if it helps. I'm tired of these bureaucrats thinking they have any say here. This is war, and the clock's ticking."

14

ABIGAIL OLIVAW
ZETA LUPI, OORT CLOUD

Abigail stepped out the hatch and a shiver reverberated up her arms and down her spine. It was unexpected. There was no breeze in the Zeta Lupi Wheel, and the temperature change wasn't noticeable, but the quiver still hit her. Perhaps it was fear or the anticipation of the unknown.

As she strolled across the catwalk, she caught a glimpse of Zachary on the far side, waiting for her. He was smiling and had that look on his face their father used to have after a long day of traveling. Like he'd been working too hard and needed to rest, but he could still handle his daughter jumping on his lap to say hello.

She smiled as she walked up without a word and put her arms around him. He hugged her tight, and they didn't speak. They didn't need to. He knew she hadn't spoken to anyone in a few weeks and had shut off her comms. Harold had surely relayed as much on to her by now.

There was a commotion about ten meters from where she was standing. She lifted her head off his shoulder and glanced toward the sound of voices shouting.

"Madam President!" Mayor Clarke waved his hand in the air. "Can I speak to you for a moment?"

"What's he want? Why can't he move closer?" And then she saw them. A half dozen armed soldiers were surrounding him. They'd come for her, and had it not been for the security robots blocking their path, they would've arrested her.

"Let's go somewhere to talk," Zachary said, tugging her away from the onlookers. "Somewhere quiet. Much has changed while you were…"

He didn't finish the sentence because he didn't want to remind her of her coma. She wasn't that brittle, but she'd be lying if she said she hadn't thought about it a hundred times a day. Even this event had played in her mind as many times. Some of them were her arriving to an empty hangar, void of all life because the Galactic Alliance had killed everyone she loved or hoped to save. A few even had her arriving to great fanfare for saving humanity and giving them hope. But most were very much like this. Her getting arrested or only having one person come for her.

"Ok," she muttered. "Let's go."

He turned with his arm still around her, and they walked toward the small crowd. The security robots transformed within seconds of them approaching. They rose a few centimeters taller and their colors switched from their normal whitish blue to a far more menacing red.

"Stand back, or we'll use force," the robots said in unison.

The soldiers weren't sure how to react. Their hands went to their weapons and their eyes trained on the mayor, looking for his orders.

"Madam President," Mayor Clarke said. "You must answer for your crimes against humanity. If not now, then soon."

"Ignore him," Zachary whispered. "He's doing it for the media. He doesn't want to be seen as a pushover."

She craned her neck and only then realized there were a dozen micro drones hovering overhead, jockeying for position, each wanting a glimpse of her arrest. They, too, were being held in place by a mirror of security drones. Harold had his hands full controlling the Wheel and corralling all these people.

It'd been her job for the last few decades, and before that, her father's. They were always manipulating and tweaking the message. Rarely had the truth been immediately available for everyone to hear. A select few, yes, but never the masses. Not until Zachary had ripped back the curtain.

She froze in her tracks.

"Come on," Zachary said in a hushed voice. "Not here, not now."

She still hadn't activated her retinal comm, so normal speech was all he could use to talk to her.

Maybe she should just walk over and give in. Give up and let the people render their judgement. While they didn't know everything she knew, she couldn't blame them for wanting her dead, or worse, to rot in jail forever. Harold might have a thing or two to say about that, but she could make him listen to them.

She cleared her throat. "I'm sorry."

"Pardon me," Mayor Clarke said, struggling to lean closer between the robots holding him back. "I didn't catch that."

She glanced up toward the drones and then at him. At the man she'd put in power here in Zeta Lupi. The man she'd promised that everything would be ok before they left Sol. That his family would be safe, and that their colony mission would be a new hope for humanity. She hadn't lied. She had genuinely believed those things then, but that didn't matter anymore.

"I said I'm sorry. I'm sorry for not sharing more about what my family had discovered. For not doing more... to change the course of the events I'd been handed. I'm—"

"Will you answer for your crimes?" Mayor Clarke asked. He was nodding at her, his head deliberately moving up and down. It was as if he was willing her to say yes.

She glanced at Zachary. His head wasn't moving, but his eyes were piercing. She hadn't seen him in so long. Hell, a few months ago she wasn't even sure she'd ever see him again. No, she owed him more time. If only a few days, a few moments. She needed to better understand the state of everything before she rushed down a path she couldn't escape from.

When she turned back toward Nathan, she stiffened and took a deep breath. "I will answer you in time, Mayor. I promise. But not now. Not yet."

Zachary, having heard her words, gave her another tug. She went willingly, stepping in alongside him and working her way down the seemingly infinite walkway of the hangar. Tens of thousands of robots were bustling about, unpacking the materials from inside the belly of the ships they'd arrived in. Some of them even appeared to be dismantling the ships themselves.

"What're they doing?" she asked, raising her hand to point at the robots. "Did we take damage en route?"

He glanced to his left and then returned his attention to the approaching lift tube. "These ship designs are over a year old, and we're in desperate need of materials. Hell, we'd be tearing apart the walls and floor if we thought it could help make more ships." He gestured for her to enter the tube. "Be careful. With your comm off, this is going to be a rough ride."

She nodded. "Where are we getting off?"

"At the bottom."

THE GROUND FLOOR was rapidly approaching. Abigail adjusted her posture and prepared to step forward and out of the lift tube. They'd just passed the third floor, and the first was only a moment away. The last time she'd been this deep in any of their facilities was at the Sol Wheel to visit Libby.

As the ground approached, she started to panic. She wasn't slowing down. Usually, the lift's gravity dampeners applied upward pressure to reduce her momentum, to bring her closer to the exit and to ease her stepping out. That wasn't happening.

Shit, she should've turned on her comm, but it was too late. She should've been under the control of Zachary or Harold. Perhaps something went wrong. When she glanced up, she could just make out Zachary. He wasn't even watching her. He looked like he was having a conversation or was zoned out into his retinal comm. Maybe Mayor Clarke had caused this.

She turned her attention back to the approaching blackness below her and took a deep breath. Her body tensed as it prepared for an impact that never came. There was a faint flicker of light as she passed through a hologram of the ground that until that moment she swore was real. But she kept on going, heading deeper into the lift, surrounded on all sides by darkness. She couldn't even make out Zachary. For all she knew, she could be moving sideways. Given how advanced their dampeners were, she wouldn't put it past them.

This planetesimal was a crazy place without her retinal comm. She imagined it was like going back in time to prehistoric eras after living in the present day. The surprise of seeing massive dinosaurs ruling the world and long extinct plants larger than life. While it wasn't quite the same, the disbelief would be real. At least until they ate her. Maybe it wasn't as far from reality as she thought.

She was about to shout up at Zachary in hopes that it would get his attention when the tube brightened. As she'd suspected, she wasn't headed straight down any longer. She'd adjusted course and was moving at an angle. There, in the distance, was a glowing ring marking the end of the line. The familiar gravity pressure of the tube deceleration tingled her senses, warning her of the coming change in direction.

When she stepped across the threshold of the ring, there was only enough room for a few people before a vast black barrier confronted her. She reached out and pressed her palm against it. A shock zapped her like she'd stuck her finger in an ancient electric socket on Earth before she yanked it back.

"What the frak?"

"Defenses," Zachary said as he stepped out of the lift behind her.

She rubbed her hand on her shirt and glanced at him. "From whom?"

"Everyone." He squeezed past her to face the wall of black. "We don't have as many friends any longer with the reality of our situation freely circulating. I'm not even sure we'd have the volunteers we've had if the circumstances weren't as dire."

"Maybe we should've thought of that before—"

He spun around and glared at her. "Don't even start with me," he snapped. "You don't know the half of the shit sandwich you left me chewing on during your little nap. You and Dad and all the damn secrets." He shook his head. "Someone had to end it."

She wasn't about to question his decision yet. Not until she knew more. They had always known the transition of the truth would be shaky at best. She, however, never expected they'd be the ones dealing with it.

"So how do we get past this wall?"

She took a step backward and felt the tingle of the gravity tube raising the hairs on her neck. The wall in front of them began rising upward into the ceiling, and on the other side was barely enough room to hold a body bag.

"After you." Zachary moved aside and slid up to the wall.

She swallowed hard. "That's either a trash compactor, or you're having me sized for a coffin." Sometimes it was easier to joke in a stressful situation than to deal with the pressure. She straightened her outfit and stepped around him.

"Push up against the wall as close as you can," Zachary began. "It's tight, but you should fit."

"Should?" she muttered, as the ceiling behind her slid down, closing her in darkness.

It was like she was in the dream again. She'd woken countless times in darkness, only to realize she was on that damn cliff again, or worse, on the couch in her office on Luna, reliving the contact event repeatedly. How many times had she replayed that event in her mind?

The doctors told her she'd been trapped, replaying her memories on repeat in her unconscious coma-like state. They claimed it was normal, and that minds naturally replayed events of the day to consolidate memories and make sense of them. She didn't know what the frak they called it, but reliving a week hundreds of times wasn't the same as taking a nap. And this was far too similar to that.

She reached her hand up and hit the wall, only to have it shock her and raise upward into the ceiling. A faint glow appeared and when she stepped forward, the ceiling behind her lowered again, closing her in darkness.

"Let me the frak out of here! I don't want to die anymore!" She pounded her fist against the slab. The jolts that shocked her got harsher and harsher until she had to stop. Her hand was burning, but she couldn't help it. She needed to get out. This was too much. It was too vivid. She couldn't relive dying again.

Suddenly, something touched her. She flinched, stepping forward just as the ceiling raised. She felt the shadow presence of someone having brushed her shoulder. When she reached up, an outline of Admiral Gwar lingered in front of her before it vanished. It was like a halo of light from her unconscious, reminding her what the mottled green bastard had done to her.

She took another step deeper as the light brightened and then faded, with the ceiling coming down. How much more of this was there? She wasn't sure she could take it any longer.

Finally, the chamber erupted in a bright white glow, and then someone grabbed at her, embracing her with their powerful arms.

"It's ok!" Libby pulled her back into the room and hugged her tight. "You're fine! We're so sorry… so, so sorry. We didn't realize that was going to be so hard for you."

She put her arms around Libby and returned the embrace. It felt good to have the arms of someone she loved surround her and hold her tight for more than a brief moment. It'd been too many years since she'd felt an extended hug.

"Is she alright?" Zachary asked as he stepped out of the entrance. He must have reached up to touch her shoulder, but Libby shooed him away.

"I'm fine," Abigail mumbled. "I'm sorry I freaked out in there. The darkness, it was too… familiar."

"Don't worry about it." Libby leaned back and pulled a chair up to Abigail, and she sat down in it. "I read the reports of what you described in your coma. I should've realized this was a bad idea. It's on me."

Abigail shooed her and then reached out and grasped her hand, squeezing it tight. Their eyes met and she smiled. "I really am fine. Don't worry about it. I need to get past it at some point. Trial by fire works for me. So, what did you two bring me down here into the dungeon for?"

She glanced around at the small lab with the eerie, throbbing green objects in the center behind the thick glass walls. "And what the hell is that?"

IT WAS ALL a bit much to take in. She stared at the neon green data cores and tried to imagine hundreds of millions of humans living inside, but it seemed impossible. Who would want to live that way for an eternity? They had to know what they were getting themselves into before committing to something like that.

She thought back to what her father and grandparents and even Harold had told her about his transition. It was voluntary, and at the end of his life. He knew it wasn't the same as being alive, but the family felt it was best for him to help carry the mission to future generations, given how hard it was to find people who they could trust. No matter how she spun it, she still couldn't understand an entire species doing this. She'd rather die than live forever.

"Did they say why they did it?" she asked as she walked around the circular diamond glass enclosure surrounding the data cores.

"Each person seems to interpret the decision a little differently," Libby began. "Collectively, they saw it as their duty now that they were living in a star system with finite resources. They were each given a chance to inhabit a host body every fifty years for a few months. To remind themselves what it meant to have feelings and to be alive. A great many of the minds are crazy and have spiraled into infinite loops of babbling thought. But among the chaos, there are still a few that are sharp and struggling to escape."

Abigail turned to face Libby. "Escape?"

Libby glanced at Zachary.

He nodded. "No secrets. Not anymore."

She fiddled with the stylus in her hand and unconsciously rubbed her shirt. "A few months back, after we'd first tried interfacing with the data cores, they managed to take control of some robots. Let's just say it didn't end well for the assistants in the lab." Her face turned pink, and Zachary stepped forward, resting his hand on her shoulder.

"We shut it off," he said staring at Libby. "We shut them all off. After that, we started the construction of this place." He gestured around the room. "We took everything we'd learned from their world and built this impenetrable chamber. Nothing comes in, and nothing goes out that we don't know about. It's one of the last family secrets."

Abigail chuckled. "I'm not so sure about that, little brother."

He tilted his head and squinted at her. "What does that mean?"

"Harold," she said aloud.

"Hello, Abigail," Harold said. "After you mentioned you hadn't spoken to my copy most of your voyage here, I was wondering if you'd say hello or not."

She peered down at her hand before she spoke. "Privacy mode Eta."

The room went silent.

"Harold, are you there?" she asked, but he didn't reply. She glanced at Libby, and then at Zachary. They each had concerned looks on their face. They were subvocalizing, likely to Harold. "It won't work."

"What did you do?" Libby asked. "He isn't replying."

She held up her hand. "How old did you say the copy of Harold was that you used for this lab?"

Zachary tapped his ear. "We unarchived a clean copy from before we left the Sol Wheel. He figured it was the safest version. It didn't need to know anything about how it got here, and would have the cleanest set of memories from which to process the results of everything we were researching. Why?"

She stared at the throbbing green lights from the data cores again. Their colors and patterns were mesmerizing. Almost like they were speaking in Morse code. "After I realized our Beacon mission was going to fail, something happened."

"What do you mean, it'll fail?" Zachary stepped in front of her. "We can—"

She shook her hand for him to stop. "We're outgunned and out... aliened. Even if we had ten years, they'd kill us."

"Lync's plan doesn't require us to win," Libby said. "We only have to survive long enough to capture the Beacon and escape."

Abigail sat down on a stool and spun it toward Libby. "And then what? Do we expect they'll leave us alone forever?"

"We haven't thought that far," Zachary said. "We just knew we couldn't miss this opportunity."

She pointed up toward the ceiling. "I guarantee they've thought further. That rage in Nathan's eyes when I got off that ship. He wants something from me. He wants me. Hell, he probably wants all of us to be his negotiating chip with his people on Tiān and the Galactic Alliance. Yes, they're helping you today, but mark my words, they'll cover their asses, little brother."

Zachary shook his head. "No. Mayor Clarke wouldn't do that to us. Bradley vouched for him. I trust him."

She cracked the knuckles on her left hand. "Did Bradley tell you about his and Nathan's deal in Sol?"

He slowly shook his head from side to side. "I'm not sure what you're talking about."

"Harold found out that Bradley made a deal with Nathan to get on the Tau Ceti colony ship. In exchange for his being approved to join, Bradley set up Nathan's family with some tech he'd stolen from The Wheel."

Zachary lurched forward. "Bullshit! That's a lie. He wouldn't do—"

She held out a finger and reached up, squeezing her left ear for five seconds. The interface of her retinal comm sprang to life, and she had to squint several times. Everything was so vivid and new. She'd never unplugged for that long before.

Once she'd taken a moment, she subvocalized a command to bring up Bradley's data sheet. Gesturing with her right hand, she flicked the details up on the wall screen beside her. "It's all there. You can read it later, but trust me when I tell you he did it."

"But why?" Zachary shook his head as he studied the transcripts and the data Harold had shared.

"He was desperate to get away," Abigail said quietly. "He wanted out of Sol, and getting on that ship was his only hope. So, he reached out to some people and hit a few dead ends. Then, he dug up some old tech on a data dot from Mom's little hideaway."

He spun around to face her. "He hasn't been out there since…"

She nodded. Neither of them said it.

"Since her funeral." Libby's eyes were wide, and she raised her hand to her mouth before she began shaking her head. "I saw him there that day. He was wandering about, rummaging through things. I assumed he was looking for a keepsake or something. I never imagined he'd…"

Abigail sighed. "It wasn't a big deal. Most of what he'd stolen was ancient. We couldn't even figure out why Mom had copied it in the first place. Hell, some of it was about to be released by Olivaw International, anyhow."

"Wait, you knew he'd done it?" Zachary reached up and rubbed his cheek. "I don't understand. If you knew about it, why'd you let it happen?"

"Because I loved him. I wanted to protect him, and if this was how he got what he wanted, and made it safely away from Sol, then we'd look the other way."

"We?" Libby asked. "Who else knew about this?"

"Dad and Harold." She reached down and picked up the stylus Libby had set down. It was hefty, but it felt good in her hand. "We agreed it was the right thing to do. To let him have the data."

"But I still don't get what this has to do with Nathan?" Zachary asked.

She shook her head. He really was naïve. "He's not as trustworthy as you're making him out to be. I bet a billion credits Harold has dirt on him, and he's jockeying for control as we speak."

"He'd tell us if he did," Libby said.

"Would he? I mean, his Zeroth-Law speaks about humanity and the family." She gestured at the wall screen and brought up the zeroth law.

An artificial intelligence in physical or virtual form may neither harm humanity, or, by inaction, allow humanity or the Olivaw family to come to harm. Any conflict or attempted violation of this or subsequent laws shall be shared with the Olivaw family designated to be within the Circle of Trust.

She watched as they both read it, moving their mouths as they worked their way through the words.

Libby nodded. "Right, so he'd tell us. He can't allow the family to come to harm. If he did, he'd have to notify us."

"He'd only tell you when you were on a path to be harmed. Being arrested is not harm. Trial is not harm. Only after it was clear that Nathan would turn you over to the GA would he be forced to notify you of his infraction. He's skirted this fine line before. We all know it." She glared at Zachary. They both knew he'd killed to protect the family, and his human side had pushed the robotic one over the edge to break the law.

"But why are you bringing this up now?" Libby asked. "You've been buddy-buddy with Harold for decades. And

I've never seen you use that privacy mode trick before. Where'd you learn that?"

Abigail spun on her stool to look directly at her. She was serious. Perhaps her theory was wrong. She of all people should have known about this back door. "I thought for sure you'd know. You're the one who sent me the message on the way here."

Libby froze. She glanced at Zachary, and then back again. "I don't know what the frak you're talking about. I wouldn't have sent you a message in your state without clearing it with Zachary first. I've been in the Circle long enough to know how this family operates, and I knew how fragile you were. "

How was this possible? If she hadn't sent her the comm, then who had? She subvocalized a command to bring up the message she'd received and flipped it onto the wall screen.

"Then if this wasn't you, who is it?"

Feeling like you're going mad, Abdiga? Sometimes you need time to yourself, to be alone. Harold is not as he seems. Try enabling 'Privacy mode Eta' for some peace and quiet.

She watched Libby as she studied the message. Like the previous one, her mouth moved ever so slightly as her mind read the words. She must have been reading it over and over again. Just as she was about to ask her about it, her hand raised and brushed at her chest. It wasn't an unusual movement. More like an itch. The kind of thing you do unconsciously when you're deep in thought.

"What was that?" Abigail asked.

Zachary glanced from Libby to Abigail and then back. "What was what?"

Abigail stood up. "You reached up. What were you touching?"

Libby took a step backward and shook her head from side to side. "What are you on about? I didn't..." She froze, and her eyes went wide as realization flashed across her face. "No," she mumbled. "It's not possible."

"What are you both on about?" Zachary asked, still glancing between the two of them. "Can someone please catch me up?"

"I don't know," Abigail said, facing Zachary. "It's just... she moved her hand up, and it seemed like she was touching something. I could have sworn this message was from Libby. She's the only one who used to call me that other than you, Brad, and..." She tilted her head toward Libby.

Libby reached behind the back of her neck and unclasped a necklace before she pulled it up and out of her shirt.

Abigail hadn't ever noticed her wearing any jewelry before. "How long have you had that?"

"A little over twenty years." Libby cradled the delicate pendant in her hand.

Abigail leaned closer for a look at what it was. There in Libby's hand was a beautiful tiny black opal. The green lights to her left seemed to flicker through the pristine diamonds encircling the simple stone. It was an understated and remarkably elegant piece. "Beautiful."

Libby turned it over and over in her hands, as if studying it. She hadn't made eye contact with either of them. She merely stared at the necklace.

"Who's it from?" Zachary asked.

As if in a trance, Libby walked over to her work surface and laid out the piece. She then reached up without a word and pulled down one of the magnification panels they used to study the data cores. It was a large sixty-four by sixty-four centimeter panel whose backside was layered with millions of nanite lenses. They could zero in and analyze anything down to the molecular level.

The panel sprang to life and her hands flew over the screen as she deftly navigated the controls, bringing into focus the object she'd laid in front of them. When she slid her hand up and zoomed in on the opal, she let out an audible gasp and Zachary did the same.

"Is that what I think it is?" He leaned in closer over the display.

Libby sighed. "It is."

Now it was Abigail's turn to be confused. "What is it?"

"Stealth material," Zachary muttered. "Who gave this to you?"

"Hera," Abigail said.

Libby spun around and stared at her. "How'd you know?"

Abigail reached out and brushed her hand across the surface of the necklace. It was cool to the touch. "Because she's the only other person who called me Abdiga. Where is Hera nowadays?"

"Last I checked, she's still in her cryo-pod along with Zeus." Libby gestured at the screen beside her desk. The manifest for the Sol Wheel came up. "Unless I'm mistaken, you should've brought her with you on one of your ships. Yep, right here. She was actually onboard your ship. That's odd."

"What is?" Abigail asked.

Libby glanced at her and then back toward the screen. "From the looks of it, she and Zeus were in storage right below your quarters."

Abigail reached up and brushed at the wrinkles in her shirt. "Maybe we should wake them up and have a chat?"

SHE WATCHED as the back wall of the lab opened up to another space. It was about the same size as the one they'd been standing in for several hours, but in the middle of it sat two cryo-pods.

Zachary had left to fetch the pods, working with Harold on the outside to locate them and route them below. Apparently, he'd been a bit pushy about why they were being brought inside, and he was concerned about their safety. But in the end, he'd overruled Harold and ordered him to deliver the pods. He reminded him that there was a Harold copy inside the lab, and he would ensure the safety of the Olivaws sleeping inside.

The scan of the pods had taken far longer than it took her to pass through the barrier. They stepped inside the second lab, and a loud clang reverberated through the entire space.

Abigail jumped forward as the walls behind them closed in, sealing off this lab from the neighboring one.

"We can't be too careful," Zachary said. "Those data cores could have sensors we can't detect."

Abigail took a deep breath and centered herself. Her heart was still beating a million kilometers an hour. She didn't know why she was so nervous. She and Hera had been on pretty good terms, though they obviously hadn't seen each other in a few decades.

Libby stepped around to the head of the cryo-pods and began issuing the commands to wake the occupants from their slumber. They'd given explicit orders not to be awoken unless things were dire and their life was on the line. While they technically weren't dire, there was enough confusion to warrant waking them for a few hours or days to chat.

"That's strange," Libby said.

"What's up?" Zachary stepped around to her side.

Libby shook her head and thwacked the top of the pod. "It's not letting me wake them. It keeps giving me an error, asking me to enter an override code. They never gave me one."

"Let me try." Zachary reached in front of her.

Libby sighed. "I know how to navigate all the information systems of two human species. I'm pretty sure I can issue commands to a simple cryo-pod."

"Sorry, jeez," Zachary said. "I was just trying to help. Besides… these aren't standard controls. This looks like a custom build."

"Everything was custom with Hera," Libby said. "She didn't trust anyone but herself with her own life. She even double-checked my calculations most of the time."

"Yea, that's right. I forgot about how she'd been like that. It's been a while."

"So, can we wake them up or not?" Abigail asked.

Zachary shook his head. "Not without risking hurting them. We need the override code."

They stared at each other in silence.

"Should we ask Harold?" Zachary asked.

Libby reached down and typed a short sequence on the keypad, and the pod beeped in complaint. She then tried again, with a longer one this time. A moment later the pods clicked, and the fluids flowed backward, out of the inside and into the tanks below.

"What did you do?" Abigail asked.

Libby smiled. "I entered the code."

"I thought you didn't know it?"

"I didn't." She glanced up at her. "You did."

"I did?" Abigail furrowed her brow.

A smile crept across Libby's face. "Privacy mode Eta."

"You're shitting me," Zachary said.

Libby walked over beside Zeus's pod and did the same. It, too, sprang to life and entered its wake up procedures. She stepped back between Abigail and Zachary at the foot of the pods and waited.

The process was fairly quick. It took about thirty seconds to expunge the fluids, and then the pods cracked open, raising up and off the side. The vapor inside was thick, but as it dissipated in the open air, the occupants became visible.

In front of them were two human mannequins with heads that resembled Hera and Zeus. Where their bodies should have been, there was a complex network of electronics like she'd never seen before.

"Those aren't Hera or Zeus," Abigail said. "Disable privacy mode Eta."

"What do we have here?" Harold asked, coming to life again. "That looks like the head of Hera and Zeus. And why am I picking up a cross chatter of low frequency signals emanating from these two pods? They're reaching out and trying to find something or someone. I can't decipher what they're saying. It's encrypted."

Zachary turned and looked Libby up and down. "Where's your necklace?"

"I left it in the other lab," she said. "Let me go grab it."

She stepped toward the wall and started the transition, cycling through the protective layers.

"So is someone planning on telling me what's going on, or are you just going to leave me hanging?" Harold asked.

Abigail glanced at Zachary. "What's the last thing you remember Hera saying to you, Harold?"

"Speaking directly at me?" He chuckled. "Other than obscenities or telling me to frak off, I'd say the very last thing she said to me was, 'Not now, Harold' after she had spoken to Zachary at The Wheel. It was right after he'd arrived with Pluto. They'd been experiencing some malfunctions with their ship."

Zachary snapped his finger. "That's right! Those weren't malfunctions. Those damn asteroids were attacking us. Now that you mention it, I remember her mumbling something about Eta then and getting flustered when nothing happened. I bet she was trying to shut you off then."

"Shut me off? Why would she do that?" Harold asked.

"What was she flustered about?" Abigail asked.

"It was right after Harold had overseen a mission to take out those mercenaries the North's hired to find The Wheel. She was going on about him overstepping his bounds, and how he needed to be shut off."

"That's right." Abigail walked around the side of Hera's pod. It was eerie seeing her head resting so serenely near where the exterior viewport was. "Her and Zeus weren't happy that we didn't disable him. That explains her need for that privacy mode."

"What privacy mode?" Harold asked. "Would someone talk to me, please?"

Abigail raised her hand and shooed at the ceiling. Hera's face was so real it was unsettling. She leaned forward before she jumped backward and crashed into Zeus' pod. "What the hell was that? She moved."

"It's a programmed motion," Harold said. "There are actuators below the surface of the artificial skin. The entire thing is meant to fool anyone who happened to peer into the viewport of the pod."

"Well, it fooled me." Libby exited the newly visible recess in the wall. She had the necklace in her hand and Abigail could make out the chain dangling between her fingers. "Ouch!" Libby shook her hand and grasped the links opposite the pendant. "That got damn hot."

Harold's face appeared on one of the wall screens. "I'm detecting a concentration of signals directed toward that necklace. Can you place it near a pod?"

Libby walked to the foot of Hera's cryo-pod and placed the dangling necklace at the foot of the frankensteinian body of their great-grandmother.

Suddenly, a hologram of Hera projected out of the lid and into the middle of where her real chest would have been.

"Hi, Libs," Hera said. "I'm sorry you had to find us this way. I hope things aren't truly dire. If they are, we'll try to come for you. From the looks of it, we lost contact with a number of our redundancy devices at The Wheel. I'm sure you have many questions, and while I want to answer them, it'll have to wait until we see each other again. Too much is at stake, and Harold and the others cannot be trusted. They've taken that A.I. too far, and Zeus and I needed to take things in another direction."

The hologram of Hera reached out as if Libby were standing in front of her and then returned her hand to her side. "I'm so sorry. I wish I was there with you. If you bring this necklace out of The Wheel, its signal should be able to reach… a relay. I can't say more, and I don't know how long it'll take to get to us. But rest assured, we'll come for you. There are a great many things I want to tell you. I hope you're safe. While you've unknowingly helped our cause all these years, I truly hope you'll forgive me for keeping you in the dark. Please keep me close. I love you and will see you soon."

The hologram cut out, and the room fell silent.

Abigail never expected anything like this. *Where had they gone? Who else had they taken with them? Why hadn't they trusted her and Zachary?* The questions circled her mind, each jockeying for her attention. They'd abandoned them rather than helped them, and when they needed them most, they were nowhere to be found.

She raised her hands in the air and screamed. "Why?"

"Why what?" Harold asked.

"Why didn't they trust you? Why didn't they trust us? Where the hell are they? There's so many fraking whys, I don't even know where to start."

She spun around toward Libby. Her cheeks were pink and

tears were streaming down her face. She'd obviously been in the dark all this time, and now she felt as alone as Abigail did.

When she stepped forward to give her a hug, she took a step backward, shaking her head.

"No," Libby muttered. "I failed you and the family. I don't deserve your compassion. You need—"

"You couldn't have known," Zachary said.

"I should have seen it." Libby clenched at the neck of her blouse before pounding her fist against the black wall behind her. It didn't make a sound.

Abigail reached out and rested her hand on Libby's arm. "Our great-grandparents were a dozen steps ahead of all of us. You can't beat yourself up. What we need to do now is regroup."

Libby started laughing. Quietly at first and then louder as she leaned forward and nearly fell over. "You've... got to be kidding me. Regroup? We've got aliens attacking us across the galaxy. We've got our ancient ancestors trying to kill us in the other room. We have an all-seeing killer A.I. watching over us. And our people up top, they're jockeying to take us out, as well. Add to that an abandoning set of grandparents, and you want to regroup? You've either got a death wish or you're fraking joking."

Abigail chuckled. "You forgot about the sister I never knew I had."

Libby glanced up. "What?"

Zachary shot an arm out and spun Abigail around to face him. "I have another sister?"

She smiled. "Like I said earlier, we've still got the secrets, little brother."

He reached up and rubbed at his face. His eyes were wide, and he clearly didn't know if he should ask. "Who... is it?"

A smirk crept into the corner of her mouth. "Why don't we go meet her? She's up top somewhere."

15

LYNC MICHAELS

ZETA LUPI, OORT CLOUD

These generals were fraking clueless. Not only were they weeks behind in their research, their tactics were remedial at best. They were used to dealing with Outer Ring bandits or rogue militias, and they didn't have the faintest idea how to handle an alien battle.

Lync stood there with her arms crossed as General Raft attempted to brief his staff on her strategy. If he made one more mistake, she was going to lose it. He was a superior officer, and she'd likely get the boot, but he was leading these people to their death.

"Once you've transitioned," General Raft began, "we'll need the bombardiers to take out any Syndrus ships that are at play on the field of battle."

"No!" Lync said. "That's not right at all." She stepped through the crowd surrounding the general to an open position across from him and the circular battlefield projector.

General Raft arched his back and glanced around the crowd of soldiers before he caught a visual of her. "Excuse me… Major Michaels. Did you have something to say?"

"Yessir. Sorry, but… you're mistaken. I believe you meant

the Selene ships, sir." Lync gestured at the battle hologram and repositioned the target markers from the cylindrical Syndrus ships to the Selene moon ships instead.

"No, you're mistaken, Major. That strategy was ruled out already. The Syndrus ships are the aggressors on the field of battle. If they're not—"

Lync narrowed her gaze at the general. He was an egotistical prick. The guy had a few minor wins in Sol, and suddenly, he was a god of strategy. "No, you're wrong!"

General Raft shook his head. "Now's neither the time nor the place for your insubordination. I don't care what your last name is now."

She could feel her pulse elevating. She needed to control her temper. "It's not about names, General. My last name is Michaels, and my father died battling the Inners. I'm a Ulixi and proud of it… despite what you might believe. It's about simple strategy, nothing more. Have you even watched any of the Galactic Alliance tactical videos?"

General Raft glanced to his right at his tactical officer beside him. "We have. They're ancient, and we can't assume they'd follow the same tactics from thousands of years ago. We need to assume—"

"Assume… are you fraking kidding me?" She blurted it out before she even thought about it.

The nearby gasps were audible. She could feel everyone's eyes focus in on her and several people close to her stepped backward.

General Raft reached up and adjusted his lapel. "I don't know where you're getting your details from, Major, but the strategy we're following has been set."

She took a deep breath and then exhaled. It was now or never. "The moment you leave the Selene moons alone, they'll cover the entire field of battle with Syndrus ships. They will eject hundreds and thousands of them within minutes. If you studied the Nanil battles near Lupus, you'd see they followed a similar strategy." She gestured toward the holo deck and nothing happened. General Raft had control.

"With all due respect, General. You can give me a moment to explain, and then I'll be done. Or you can choose to keep your mind closed and your tactics in three-dimensional human Sol space. I prefer our people not die as soon as they hit the field of battle."

He stared at her, his eyes narrowing by the second. She could just make out a twitch in his left lip. He'd never had his authority confronted before. This was about to go badly.

"I've got your back," Harold said into her retinal comm.

Her video began playing in the center of the display.

General Raft was clearly surprised. He shook his head and grabbed the shoulder of the colonel to his right. They started gesturing at each other.

She pushed onward. "You can see it in this battle and countless others." She gestured several more times, bringing up different Nanil battles. "Time and time again, they went for the Syndrus and ran themselves ragged, slowly thinning out their fronts. Every time this has been attempted, it failed."

Glancing to her left, the other officers near her were nodding at the videos, whispering to each other. She worked her way around the holo deck toward the general.

"If we were to follow tactics more like the Ursis, we'd stand a fighting chance of pulling this off. I sent this analysis on a week ago. I'm sure you've seen it by now." She gestured several more times, bringing up a half dozen different battles between the Ursis and the Galactic Alliance.

Lync pointed at the videos playing. "In each of these battles, I want you to count the number of Syndrus on the field of battle."

"There are ten at most," an officer to her right said.

She pointed at each of the forward prongs of the fast

attack craft splintered from their carriers. "Exactly! Now look closer. Watch their fighters."

Wave after wave of alien vessels headed toward the moon ships. Even the destroyers on the field of battle were directing their armaments at the Selene moons. Some, to their detriment, as the approaching Syndrus advanced on them and took them out.

She glanced to her left and General Raft was still arguing with his colonel, gesturing wildly with his hands. But General Yule was nodding. She hadn't even noticed him. He must have been behind someone else.

"How long do they survive?" General Yule asked.

General Raft paused his argument and glared at his peer. "General Yule, you can't seriously be considering this."

General Yule turned his head toward Raft and then returned his attention to Lync. "The Major here has obviously done her homework, General. That's more than I could say about Colonel Cay." He turned his gaze back toward Lync. "Continue your presentation, Major."

"I won't—" General Raft began.

"You will!" General Yule's face turned a bright shade of red and his focus wasn't on Raft, it was on the video in front of him. "You will or you can dismiss yourself. I've listened to you demean the colonists here long enough. We might be peers with the Admirals in Sol, but I'm fairly certain I have the support of the leadership here in Zeta Lupi when I say we want to listen to what Major Michaels has to share. She is, in fact, the only person here to have confronted any of these aliens, and twice if I remember correctly." He tilted his head toward her.

She cleared the knot in her throat. "That's correct, General. In Epsilon Eridani, and in Sol, near Jupiter."

General Raft shot her a glare. His eyes were like steel daggers reaching out to cut her. His facial tick had stopped, but he was no less pissed. Colonel Cay had her back to Lync, but she could make out her saying something to an officer near her.

Lync stiffened and continued working her way toward Raft, pausing a half meter away at General Yule's side.

"Please continue," General Yule said.

She stared at General Raft as she slowly turned around to face the holo deck. Eventually, she had to stop looking at him. She always made it a rule to never turn her back on her enemy, but she didn't have many options right now.

"As I was saying." She gestured and raised the archive videos up off the field of battle, far into the air. After that, she subvocalized a command to load one of the simulations she and Kara ran on the way to Zeta Lupi. They began playing, and she watched for a moment before speaking.

"We're going to need to constantly gate into and out of the field of battle as long as possible. If the Ulixi can drop the gates near each other, then this'll be the plan." She raised her hands and motioned them to her side, zooming into a small section of the battlefield.

"Our gates will open for fifteen seconds before they close again and reposition. We should be able to reuse the drop site multiple times, but it's important that we randomize their opening so as to not draw the GA's fire."

Colonel Cay walked up beside her. "We can't guarantee the masses of the nearby ships won't throw off the gates. That means the gate drops are dead."

"That's not entirely the truth." Lync gestured to spin the simulator. "A talented Ulixi can hold the drop steady within a two percent margin of error unless a Selene moon adjusts course toward their position. Then their mass will warp space-time enough to render them useless."

Colonel Cay adjusted her footing. She'd been caught off guard.

Lync pushed on. "We use the rapid drops to arrange a

field of ships at the edge of the gate itself. We're talking a wide gate, wider than we've ever attempted. We need to get as many ships through as we can before we hit the mass limit."

"What mass limit?" General Yule asked.

"The more mass that passes through the gate, the more energy we need to expend to keep the gate open." Lync zoomed the battle out through one of the simulated gates. On the other side were wave after wave of ships, all aligned in a disc-like formation. They were lined up away from the gate, just outside its field of view. After two squadrons transitioned, the gate closed, and another squadron slid down into formation.

Colonel Cay leaned forward and squinted. "Is that gate moving?"

Lync nodded. "It's an optimization we have to test out before we go with it. But, yes, it's moving toward our ships as they're moving toward it. The faster we can line up another wave, the faster we can get them into battle."

"And what's that lone gate doing?" General Yule gestured across the open space in front of them.

Lync spun the simulation toward the general and sped it up. A swarm of ships came sailing through the near gate and then banked hard, working their way toward a nearby line of ships to prepare for another run.

Suddenly, General Yule leaned backward as a blast of energy shot toward them through the open gate. It sailed to the edge of the simulation and dissolved over his shoulder.

"Sorry about that," Lync said. "That was—"

"One of the Selene ships firing through the gate," General Yule interrupted. He was nodding and reached out at the pixel trail of the blast in front of him as the transition gate closed. "What happens if they hit the edge of the gate? Will it collapse?"

"We're not certain." She gestured to zoom into the

massive gate. "We need to simulate it ourselves. Harold believes it'll either skim past the edge, bend around, or blow out the gate in that segment."

"That won't work," Colonel Cay said. "Seems like they'd merely take out the gates as fast as possible and that'd end our assault."

Lync chuckled. "Sure, if that's how it works, and we didn't think of a way around that. Harold, please run a gate assault simulation."

The image in front of them adjusted. A slow motion plasma beam that mimicked the size and energy they'd seen used against Epsilon Eridani moved toward the gate and hit the edge of the circular field. Sparks flew and the gate closed, but all was not lost. A moment later, the damaged section broke off, and the entire gate resized itself, closing smaller and connecting to the nearest undamaged section. After another pause, the gate opened again and another wave of ships passed through. That repeated a few more times before the gate disconnected and expanded, making room for another chunk to slide in place, returning the damaged gate to its original size.

"It repairs itself?" General Yule scratched his head. "Can we do that?"

"We can," Harold said.

"But have we done it before?" Colonel Cay asked.

Harold's face appeared at her eye level. "Our gates are made of a nano mesh used to direct the tachyon fields. They regularly repair themselves from micrometeor collisions and other structural abnormalities in the gate vanes when they're damaged. I'm pretty sure we can engineer this."

Colonel Cay chuckled. "Are we seriously making battlefield decisions on pretty sure?"

"I'd say we have a ninety-eight point seven percent probability of engineering that, but I predicted you'd try to shoot a hole in that, as well. This entire battle has never been attempted before, Colonel. I don't know about you, but I'll take a pretty sure for now until we prove it inaccurate. And then, we think of something else. The alternative is to give up and die, and I'm not about to do that to humanity."

The colonel adjusted her posture again. Being called out by an A.I. wasn't a norm in the military, and certainly not one controlling the very environment they lived in.

"So, is this all you have, Major?" General Raft asked. "A guerrilla attack from the bushes."

Lync spun around to face him. She'd clasped her hands behind her back, and if he could see her, he would know her left was already clenched into a fist.

"Don't do it," Harold said in her retinal comm. "We've got Yule. Don't put your plan at risk. Show him the rest. Bring up your big guns."

"We don't know if we can even do that," she subvocalized.

She watched the light in General Raft's eyes flicker, and his face went blank. Harold had brought up the simulation behind her. She could feel it. They hadn't made it very far with this one, and she hated to play a card before they even knew if they could create it in time.

General Raft tipped his head, gesturing behind her. "What's that?"

"We like to call it a reverse pocket shot," Lync said, still facing him.

"What the hell's a pocket shot?" Colonel Cay asked, chuckling under her breath.

"It's a shot performed in old Earth billiards," General Yule said. "When you have a clear shot with the cue ball to an open pocket. I'd imagine this one would be the opposite of that."

"If the gate were the pocket, we're taking the shot from the far side." Lync spun back toward the holo deck.

"What're we shooting?" General Yule asked, glancing at

Lync.

"Well," she began, "we can start with some of our Sol rail guns." She gestured, and the simulation played. A pattern of rail guns fired through an open gate toward a distant Selene moon ship. "We're not sure what type of damage they'll do, but we won't know until we try."

"And if they fail?" Colonel Cay asked.

She was grasping every chance she got. Lync had met many a ladder climber like her in the Sol military. They'd cling to the tail of their closest superior until they had a chance to make themselves look good, and then they grasped for the neck of the closest person, pulling themselves up. Occasionally, the prey would be their superior. There was no chance in hell she was going to let this one climb any higher.

Lync smiled and nodded at the display. "Then we bring in the big gun."

Harold was already prepared. He slowly panned a strange-looking ship into view from off-screen. She'd never seen it before, and Harold hadn't even mentioned having something ready to show anyone yet.

"What the hell's that?" General Yule leaned closer to the hologram for a better look.

"That, good sir," Harold began, "is our prototype energy weapon powered by Spános."

Colonel Cay shook her head. "Maybe I'm mistaken, but we haven't even found any Spános yet. Unless there was a hidden stash of the stuff on your Fountainhead puddle jumper you flew to Lupus."

"We have some," Harold said.

"We do?" Lync subvocalized.

"Well, sorta," Harold replied to her privately.

"Sorta?"

"And where exactly might we be hiding Spános?" General Yule asked.

"Why, in Sol of course," Harold said.

General Raft started laughing. "Are you seriously going along with this, Yule? Are you prepared to go forward without me? Because I'm not about to sit here and—"

"Don't let the door hit you in the ass," General Yule said. "Colonel Michaels and I have a lot of work to do in your and Colonel Cay's stead."

"You've got to be kidding me, James," General Raft said. "After all we've been through."

General Yule glanced to his left and nodded as a contingent of military police appeared out of the crowd and stepped between him and Raft.

"If you and Mrs. Cay would please leave the facility," the MP said, raising his hand up and pointing to the distant exit.

Raft leaned forward toward Lync, and two MPs stepped between them, forcing his arms behind his back and practically lifting him toward the exit.

"You've not heard the last of me!" Raft shouted.

As Lync turned around to face the simulation, she caught Cay being escorted behind Raft.

"You do realize you were just promoted to colonel, right?" Harold asked over her retinal comm.

It had happened so fast; she hadn't even realized it, but General Yule had said it. She wasn't sure if accidentally or not, so she leaned toward him and whispered, "Sir, my title is major."

"No, it used to be major." He adjusted his uniform and nodded at the holo deck. "You're now my acting colonel in charge of strategy over this field of battle. Are you ok with that, Colonel?"

She swallowed hard and butterflies fluttered in her stomach. "Yes... yessir."

"Now, talk me through some of these other plans you cooked up with Harold and Kara on your trip here from Tau Ceti," General Yule began. "I wanna know everything you've come up with. No matter how cockamamie or crazy an idea it is. We need to think out of the box with these aliens. The more I see what you've planned, the more I realize how far behind we are. If we have any chance of winning this battle, it'll be by thinking differently like you've shown me here."

LYNC COLLAPSED into the chair she'd pulled out from under the holo deck. She couldn't stand for another minute. It'd been nearly twelve hours since she'd opened her mouth. Twelve hours of talking, arguing, and explaining. She'd made a lot of friends in that time, and likely just as many enemies.

So much of what they'd been preparing here in Zeta Lupi was a mess and would ultimately fail. They'd made assumptions and went in directions with the technology that would end in death by a thousand cuts. The only people who truly understood the gate technology were Zachary's engineers, his crew from the Fountainhead, or her Ulixi brethren. The rest were grasping in the dark at best.

She sighed and reached out to pick up the globe of coffee her assistant had brought her. A chuckle escaped every time she thought about the last few days. Yesterday she was going stir-crazy in the belly of a transport ship, worried about being relegated to scut duty here in Zeta Lupi, and now she was a colonel thanks to a battlefield promotion. She was sure she'd have to deal with naysayers eventually, but the fear General Yule put into his staff if they undermined her meant that wasn't likely to surface for a while.

That reminded her. She subvocalized a command to send a message to Crayo.

"Head up to holo deck eight when you have a chance, Major. And please bring me some of that casserole your mom used to make. This grub the brass is being served is atrocious. And before you ask, no, don't be daft. That's not an order." She winked. "See you soon… hopefully."

"You know he's been frazzled since you gave him that promotion," Harold said.

Lync smiled. "I bet he has been. That makes two of us. I need him, though. I need to know the Ulixi are in the right hands and that his piece of the plan is moving forward. The last thing we can afford is another Sol assumption getting thrown into the mix."

"A Sol-sumption?" Harold asked.

She chuckled and took another sip of coffee. "Yea, a Sol-sumption."

Harold's face appeared to her left, just off the surface of the holo deck. "Can we talk about this Dark Nebula strategy you've been mulling over? I'm not too keen on trying to redirect the nebulosity into the field of battle. It's too much of an unknown."

It'd been an idea Kara had. They were reviewing some of the footage from the Lupus mission when they uncovered Harold's recordings of Bradley and Pepper's mistake transiting the Nebula. Kara thought it was remarkable how the nebulosity had a mind of its own and seemed to reach out to absorb any matter that got too close.

She gestured and brought up their crude strategy for using the Nebula as a weapon. "If we can't send a mission to Lupus to test it out, then I don't think we should do it. We were slaphappy at the point we came up with this idea."

Harold's virtual head nodded. "It feels like more of a last resort. When I mentioned the idea to Zachary, he sorta freaked out. He was adamant that we shouldn't try it. He said he'd seen footage that proved we wouldn't want to open that Pandora's box."

It was strange knowing Zachary had been reviewing her strategies. She squinted. "What footage is he talking about?

The snippets we saw from the Fountainhead were promising. The gate drive seemed to displace the nebulosity, and none of the gas approached the ship for quite a while." She shrugged. "It's worth a shot to test it out. Why were you discussing strategy with him anyhow?"

"He was checking in on you and wanted to know how you were doing."

She leaned forward and set the bulb of coffee on the edge of the table. "Is this going to be a regular thing?"

"I'm not sure, why don't you ask him yourself." Harold pointed over her shoulder. "He'll be entering through that door in a moment."

When she turned toward the exit, no one was there. "Are you sure he's—"

The door to the room slid open and in walked Zachary, Abigail, and another person she'd never seen before. Her retinal comm identified her as a Dr. Libby Green. Apparently, she was also an Olivaw by lineage and was a member of the Circle of Trust. At least, according to Harold.

Lync sighed and stood up, straightening her uniform. She didn't want to deal with a family reunion right now. There were more important things to work on. She took a deep breath and spun around to face her approaching family. That was a weird thing to think about. She hadn't called anyone family other than Crayo in a very long time.

"To what do I owe—"

Libby skipped forward and threw her arms around Lync, giving her a hug. "Hey cuz! It's nice to finally meet you. Zachary and Abigail have told me so much about you."

"Oh... I guess we're hugging then." Lync held her hands out wide.

"Well, I am," Libby said. "You ain't family if you can't hug when you meet. Sorry, I guess I should've held off."

Lync shook her head. "No. No worries. I just... wasn't

expecting it. Hopefully, your… cousins haven't jaded your view of me too much." She nodded at Abigail. "We haven't always seen eye to eye on things."

Zachary turned his head toward Abigail and raised an eyebrow.

Libby spun around to look at Abigail. "Oh, I didn't know that."

"It's not important." Abigail shook her head. "Let's call it a reality check."

Lync chuckled. "Is that what you call throwing your sister in jail?"

"You did what?" Zachary leaned forward to make eye contact with Abigail, who was dodging him. "Are you fraking kidding me? After she saved your life."

Abigail shook her head and held up a finger. "Hold on one second. You didn't give me a choice. You called me a traitor, accused me of being no different from Nguyễn, and then attacked me. That man sold us out to the media the moment he had a chance."

Lync motioned forward at the mention of Nguyễn, and Abigail flinched backward. "Don't remind me of his name. It's hard enough not jumping on a ship and gating straight to Sol to kill the fraking bastard. Unlike you, I didn't go putting him in power of the entire human fleet."

Abigail stiffened and tilted her head to the side. She wasn't used to having her authority called into question. "It was part of the plan. Not my plan, but… more of a contingency Harold came up with. Had he not… well, I probably wouldn't be standing here today. I still don't get why you said what you said and went all medieval on me."

She knew Abigail was right on some level. Lync shouldn't have said what she did about her family spreading lies. Not without knowing everything. "Something tells me that if you knew someone killed your father, you wouldn't act any different than I did if someone got in your way. Even if the people getting in your way were... family." She fiddled with the clasp on her pants.

"Now might not be the best place for a group therapy session." Libby gestured around the room. "Abigail suggested we regroup as a family and consider our next steps. Plus, Zachary and I sorta had no idea you existed until a few minutes ago."

"Surprise!" Lync muttered, staring at the floor. While the sentiment was nice, she would rather get back to her mission. And there was the small matter that her trust wasn't flowing over toward Abigail. The sooner she took care of Epsilon Eridani, the sooner she could move on to ending Nguyễn.

"Welcome to the family." Zachary stepped forward and offered his hand.

"What, no hug?" Lync asked, as she shook his hand in return.

"Under normal circumstances, maybe." He shuffled his feet against the floor. "But I'm still coping with the idea of having another sister. One was hard enough to deal with growing up." He smirked at Abigail. "Plus the fact that our mother never said anything to us about you is... disappointing." He glanced at her as if he had more to say, but thought better of it.

Lync wasn't always the best at reading people, but something was eating at him. Maybe he'd come around to telling her later. "Now that we're being all buddy-buddy, I meant to ask you something when I arrived."

"What's that?" Libby asked.

"Does anyone know who 'S' is? They sent me a message on the way here and..." She glanced to her left and then her right, checking that no one else had walked in while they were talking. "I know this is gonna sound crazy, but I think they also sent me one twenty years ago, as well."

"S?" Abigail shook her head. "I can't say the name rings a bell."

Libby and Zachary were silent, each staring at the other. There it was again. The same expression Zachary had a second ago. They stood there silent for a second and then Libby subvocalized a comm. She couldn't tell what, but Zachary froze for the briefest of seconds.

"Do you two have any ideas?" Lync asked.

Abigail crossed her arms and had a motherly look on her face, like she knew something was up. "Go on, Zach. Spit it out."

Zachary shrugged and threw up his hands. "Why the frak not, I suppose? Everything else is out on the table. But not here, no. Can we… show her?" He tilted his head toward Lync. "It's safer there."

Libby nodded. "Couldn't hurt. She's a colonel now and happens to be in charge of this battle of ours."

Abigail spun her head around and squinted at Lync's collar. "No shit! I hadn't even… how'd you manage that? We've only been here for like twelve hours."

"Am I the only one that pays attention to the details?" Libby laughed and put her arm around Lync's back. "Let's show her our little party spot." She guided her toward the exit.

"I'll be right behind you," Zachary said. "I need to spin past my quarters and pick something up first."

"You couldn't be acting any more suspicious, little brother," Abigail said.

He laughed out loud but didn't say a thing.

Lync still wasn't sure she could trust them, but Libby seemed genuine. It was the other two that gave her pause. While she'd known Abigail for a while, and until recently, she never had any reason not to trust her, something still wasn't fitting into place. They were so used to keeping secrets; it was hard to tell where the facts met the fiction of their lives.

IT'D TAKEN them the better part of an hour to make it to the secret lab. Every few meters after they left the planning room, someone confronted either Lync or Zachary and slowed down their progress. It took light years more coordination to run a battle this size than she'd imagined.

"So, that was fun." Lync stepped into the small lab. "Sorta like standing up in a coffin."

"That's what I thought, too." Abigail entered from the far side of the room with Libby.

"I bet that sucked," Lync began. "After those dreams you were having, you must've been peeling yourself off the walls."

Abigail reached up and crossed her arms, rubbing at her shoulders. "Something like that. Let's not relive it anymore. I still have to pinch myself to make sure I'm not there again."

"Well, while we're waiting on Zachary, why don't we help you with your battlefield planning. Before we dropped down, Harold mentioned you could use some gaps filled on your Beacon of Therion research." Libby gestured at the screen covering the near wall. On it popped up dozens upon dozens of videos with various angles of the Beacon.

Lync walked up beside her and squinted. "These are different. They're not the ones you passed on in the data dot."

Libby shook her head. "No, we uncovered them after we sent that on. There's a lot more where this came from. So, what do you need to know?"

Lync glanced back at the glowing green canisters behind the glass in the middle of the lab. "And we're going to ignore the green elephant in the room?" She gestured over her shoulder. "Is that where these were uncovered?"

"We can get into it, but it'll take too long. Those there green glowy things." Libby tilted her head back, and she brought up some additional details for the Beacon on the wall. "Those are electronic coffins holding millions of human lives, and our mostly evil ancestors' consciouses. Is that how you say that, or is it consciousi? It doesn't matter. Oh yea, and they're fighting to break out and kill us."

Lync coughed and shook her head. "Well, that's interesting. And all of this," she gestured around, "is to keep them inside?"

"And to keep others out." Abigail walked up beside Lync. Her eyes were trained on the wall screen. "This Beacon will not be easy to snatch. Are we convinced this is the best idea in the bag?"

They really weren't going to explain anything else about them. She'd come back to that later. Lync turned her attention toward the wall screen. "The footage you passed on from the Gharloc and Ursis battles wasn't nearly as detailed as this. Tell me we have more of this." She reached out and gestured around at the footage from screen to screen. Her theory was holding true.

Libby nodded. "Tens of thousands of hours of battles just like these. They're pretty old, but we have 'em in spades. What are we looking at?" She leaned forward and squinted at where Lync was pointing.

"It's empty," Lync muttered. "Right before they deploy the Beacon and after they use it, the battlefield is completely barren. Even when they're attacking, the offensive force retreats. Why?"

Libby subvocalized a command, and her hands were dancing over some virtual controls that only she could see. Lync was about to ask if she'd heard her when she started talking. "This footage seems to have something about it. Do you want to read the transcript or watch it?"

Lync glanced back at the wall. "Let's watch it. I mean, if we can understand it."

"I'll turn on the translators." Libby brought the video full wall. "It'll be weird, and their mouths will move in odd ways, assuming they have mouths at all. But we'll be able to hear them."

No mouths. That was strange. The image changed to show the bridge of a starship. It was massive, larger than anything she'd ever seen before. At first, she thought it was a virtual deck, but when she saw explosions and things falling, she recognized it was real.

"This footage came from the memories of a human ambassador aboard a Pluutar observation vessel." Libby slid the timeline forward to the point of interest. "Apparently, they were heading up this round of the tribunal and were responsible for leading the Selene and Syndrus fleet into the final stages of the Beacon deployment."

A massive part tree, part jelly fish looking alien floated through the room. It was impossibly large next to its human companion. Easily ten times taller than the human who must have been at least Lync's height or more. She was lanky and frail and she was using a cane to walk. A stiff wind would have blown her over.

"We're sure we've sealed the external damage?" the woman asked. "The last thing we need are the likes of your people tearing the ship apart from the inside out."

Waves coursed through the alien squid's body like a wave passing over the shoreline. Their voice boomed through the bridge, causing all the other Pluutars to make similar wave-like motions with their tentacles. "Do not question our ability to manage the fleet, you insolent human. If we weren't in the midst of battle, I'd—"

"Oh relax, Puqart!" The woman thwacked the tree with her cane, and the giant recoiled back. "You and I both know your kind have missed a few holes in the past. You might be able to survive in the vacuum of space for a few hours, but the rest of us don't have the luxury. Besides, even a Pluutar can't handle being exposed directly to a Beacon of Therion. It wasn't but a hundred cycles ago that a flock of your brethren purposely exposed themselves to the Beacon near Griundark. Last I recall, they died in a comatose state."

"Some say they elevated their minds to a higher plane," Puqart said.

An explosion of sparks cascaded from the distant ceiling of the bridge, and half of the space went dark.

The frail woman laughed and leaned to the side on her stick, resting what seemed like all of her weight against it. "Well, you and I know they're full of shit. That light zeroes out everything. It damn near wipes out all neural activity. If you want to call a higher plane ceasing to function, then sure, you go raise yourself up. I just need to know if I should get my ass into a stasis chamber surrounded by a few meters of Skotádi."

"The Syndrus have finished their docking maneuvers across the fleet, Admiral." Another Pluutar floated in from off-screen. "All Selene ships are reporting that their Nebula has been deployed and either their repairs are complete or their crews are safe. The Terbinaf are retreating, as well. We're ready for the Beacon, sir."

More sparks ignited in the darkness, except this time, instead of losing more light, the overhead glow came back and illuminated the bridge. There was an eerie white haze in the air from something burning. When it combined with the background of the Selene ships surrounded by a web of black nebulosity, it made the entire scene feel otherworldly. Like a bad vid-sim space opera.

The video on the wall screen froze, and Lync shook her head out of the trance. "Why'd you stop it?"

"That's it," Libby said. "The rest is simply them deploying the Beacon. You've already seen that before."

"Whatcha watching?" Zachary stepped into the room from the closing entrance.

"From the looks of it, another wrinkle in our plan," Abigail said. "We're gonna need to make sure our pilot and bombardier ships don't have any holes if they deploy that Beacon, or else they'll be in a vegetative state after the light turns on."

"They have to deploy the Beacon." Lync stared down at her hands. "If they don't, the nebulosity will drift and enshroud the star system and everything in it. Epsilon Eridani will be destroyed and all of our people on Liprosus with it."

"Well, this ought to be fun." Abigail spun around to face her brother. "I'd share my ideas on what we should do instead, but I'd rather find out what Zachary is late for. Something tells me he's about to drop a bombshell. Is Pluto pregnant?"

Zachary choked and then coughed into his hand. "No, nothing like that. I'd tell you it wasn't a bombshell, but I'd be lying."

Lync sighed and ran her hands through her hair. Nothing was ever simple with these Olivaws. She was starting to wonder if she should've looked the other way in that graduation line when she met Abigail all those years ago. Sometimes the smallest encounters have the biggest consequences later in life.

She reached down and pulled up a stool. Best to sit down in case this one took it out of her. That, or at least she'd have something to throw at him. She spun it around to face Zachary and leaned forward, resting her elbows on her legs and her hand under her chin.

Libby gestured to shut off the wall screen and joined them in facing Zachary. "Alright, let's have it. Or should I leave?"

"No, no!" Zachary waved his hand. "I'm going to need you here to identify my body in case these two kill me."

Libby chuckled until she noticed that neither Lync nor Abigail were smiling. She motioned to the door. "I think I'll just—"

"Freeze, missy," Abigail said. "If you're complicit in this, then you can stay right here."

She turned around to face them. "So that we're clear. I had nothing to do with what Zachary is about to tell you. I found out myself on our mission to Lupus, along with the rest of the crew. And for the record, Harold has known about this for quite some time."

"Wait, so the others know?" Lync asked. This can't be all that bad then. She sat up. "Go on, spit it out, Z."

He shot a look at her. "What'd you call me?"

"Z. Is that ok?" She glanced at Abigail. She was chuckling. "What?"

"That's what his girlfriend Pluto calls him," Libby said.

"Oh, sorry."

"Yea, we call him Zachary McCrackery." Abigail broke out into laughter again.

Lync fought back a laugh into her hand.

"Har, har," Zachary said. "You can laugh at my expense all you want. Just remember, I'm your brother and I love you. You," he pointed at Lync, "I don't know well enough yet, but you seem lovable, too."

Libby meandered past Lync and Abigail and worked herself around the far side of the room, beyond the green data cores.

"So," Zachary began. "You all love Harold, right?" He nodded at them.

"You mean Harold the overlord?" Lync asked.

"Is that what you call him?" Abigail asked.

"Me and Crayo, yea. He's always interrupting at the most inopportune times."

"I love it." Abigail turned to face Zachary. "Yea, we like him. Why?"

"Well, remember Shauna?" Zachary asked.

Abigail tilted her head and squinted. "Yea, I forgot all

about her. Isn't she your A.I. assistant? What does she have to do with this? Is she S?"

He nodded. "She is."

Lync's heart skipped a beat, and she shot up. "She found the footage of my father being killed by Nguyễn. How'd she know who I was or who he was?"

Zachary took a step backward. "I'm getting to that. Now sit down… please."

"You do realize that her sitting down won't save your ass if she wants to kill you, right?" Abigail reached up and rubbed at her neck. "Trust me, I know."

Lync sat back down on the stool. He had best get to the point, or she'd have to beat it out of him.

"Ok… so, as you're already aware, Harold is a copy of the consciousness of our great-great-to the whatever grandfather, right?" Zachary asked.

They both nodded.

He stared down at the ground. "Well, as Abigail knows, I was pretty depressed around the time our mother was diagnosed with Rett Syndrome. I tried to take my life more than once."

Abigail leaned forward. "I didn't know…"

He motioned her away. "No one did. Not even Harold. He's in many places, but he's not everywhere. Anyhow, after I repeatedly failed, I understood what I was missing. I needed our rock. Our family pillar of strength. I needed Mom." He made eye contact with Abigail and then returned his attention to the floor. "So I asked her. It was after I had a really weird dream where Harold talked Marie into joining him. It was crazy."

"Who's Marie?" Lync asked.

"That was the name of our mother," Zachary said. "Your mother."

She'd never thought to ask her mother's name. To her, she was imaginative. Someone who existed in a blurry photo. But beyond that, she was only an idea. A concept. She looked at Abigail, and she was shaking her head from side to side, staring at Zachary. "What is it?"

"You didn't... did you?" Abigail asked, tears welling in her eyes.

He nodded. "I couldn't imagine a universe without her in it. She kept our family moving forward while dad was off gallivanting around the planets. I wanted her to know my kids some day. To know my wife. I'm... sorry. I should have told you."

Lync shook her head. "Told her what? I'm confused. I must've missed something."

"Hello, Lync. Abigail," Shauna said from overhead. "It's good to see you. Both of you."

Tears streamed down Abigail's face, and she kept shaking her head from side to side. "No," she muttered. "This can't be."

Shauna's face appeared on the wall screen to their right. She was taking on her human form as Marie. Her vibrant green eyes had a sparkle in them, just like Lync's.

This whole thing was more than Lync could have imagined. Ideas and questions were racing through her mind. She didn't know if she should be crying like Abigail or furious that Shauna hadn't reached out before this. Why here? Why now? If she'd been out there all these years, she certainly could have made this crazy life of hers easier. She wouldn't have had to get blood transfusions or lied her way through most of life.

She hadn't realized it, but her heart was racing, and she was having trouble breathing. It was like when she'd hidden in that crater from a scout drone when she was eight. This had been before she'd mastered Ulixi techniques to focus herself. All the emotions of the unknown raced at her and smashed her in the face, knocking the wind out of her. If she hadn't stopped breathing and passed out, she might have been detected and killed.

"Why?" It escaped her mouth before she knew it. There was so much more to ask after that, but it was all she could say.

Abigail reached out and grasped Lync's hand, pulling it into her lap before returning her attention to Shauna. She sat there silently, waiting for the same answer as her.

Shauna's eyes glistened.

Lync couldn't tell if an A.I. could have emotions like that, but given she was similar to Harold and had the foundation of a human, she couldn't rule it out.

"I was young. I was stupid. And I hadn't even realized I was pregnant until it was too late."

Lync gritted her teeth. "How does someone not realize they're pregnant? It sorta takes nine months to have a baby."

The silence between them was deafening. Even Libby had wandered around the glass divider to listen. Her reflection was just visible in the shiny edge of the desk next to the wall screen.

Shauna stared straight at Lync. "I don't know how to tell you this, dear. I've never told anyone this before today. Not even Zachary has seen these memories. I managed to hide them during the recording and found ways to conceal them from him after that."

He shook his head. "How's that—"

She waved him silent. "It doesn't matter. What's more important is that my daughter hears this from me, and no one but me. Lync, your father wasn't a human."

The words crashed over her like a wall of cold water from a wave pool. She'd only been in a few in her lifetime, but she remembered the events vividly. Wave after wave collided with her body, tossing it around and moving on, like it wasn't even there. The words were like the cold wet water. They enveloped her and shocked her awake, forcing her to catch her breath.

Your father was not a human. The words weren't as foreign as they were refreshing. She'd have expected them to feel unfamiliar. But maybe that's what a person in shock would say. Either way, she didn't remember much after that. Everything got muffled as her head crashed into the floor and the lights went out.

16

NGUYỄN DUE

SOL, NEAR NEPTUNE

He'd been standing perfectly still for the better part of an hour as the alien tribunal reviewed their case against humanity. Most of the material Nguyễn had heard before, minus all the drama the prosecutor caked on, of course.

After he'd brought to light the revelation about the Thyreus and the Qudoculi a few months back, the Galactic Alliance replaced Prosecutor Drak with a Prosecutor Xoolo from the Licertus. The reptilian species surfaced memories of his one time visiting a zoo. The giant reptiles he'd seen there had given him nightmares for weeks. They weren't at all like the dinosaurs he'd learned about in school. Their scales had an always wet appearance that sickened him.

Prosecutor Xoolo was finishing his closing arguments and had just made some pun about how the Nanil should have left well enough alone and never uplifted humans. Even the GA audience around him didn't react to the failed joke. Maybe it was the dry speech or their lack of animation, but the Licertus fell flat. They didn't have the stage presence of the Thyreus or Trochilidae.

His eyelids were growing heavy. He hadn't slept much

over the past few days. Trying to ensure the rapidly expanding human fleet of barely battle worthy ships remained organized and equipped for a possible war was demanding. Add subterfuge to the mix in their efforts to refine the Spános away from the prying eyes of the GA, and you got a tired bunch of humans. Even stimulants were having little effect.

"Should we accept your silence and lack of a rebuttal as your refusal to put up a closing defense?" Ambassador Addae asked. Her presence in the virtual world Harold and Lisp had cobbled together wasn't nearly as foreboding as the real thing. Her colors weren't as vibrant, either.

They'd held their ground on not returning to the tribunal ship, though not without difficulty. Today almost hadn't happened. The tribunal was about to convene without them until Lisp brought to Ambassador Addae a little known clause in the GA laws that gave humanity grounds to appeal the hearing if they weren't fully represented through its entirety.

"Sorry," Admiral Nguyễn said. "I may have faded off. I was just reading through our crib notes. Prosecutor Xoolo's delivery was a tad... how shall I say it, boring. I had to catch up."

Murmurs of what he could only interpret as laughter echoed through the virtual tribunal chamber. Their ship was making an attempt to reproduce the effects of the real chamber, but fell short in every sense of the word. In this case, it was nothing like the real thing, but that suited him fine.

"The facts stand on their own." Prosecutor Xoolo bowed toward Ambassador Addae.

She nodded and waved him up before pointing her beak downward and then directing her massive eye at the virtual form of Nguyễn in the center of the chamber. "You may begin your defense, Admiral."

Admiral Nguyễn closed his eyes and paused his end of

the transmission. "Do I honestly have to do this? Can't I just beam them our defense?"

Harold's voice came in over his retinal comm. "We need to rile them up, sir. Plus, I have a surprise kicker at the end. It arrived in a memory merge this morning. You'll love it, trust me."

His anger was rising. "We should have reviewed our plans before I stepped up here."

"They'd know you were lying or withholding if we had. This way, your shock, and their belief will rise together. Come on, you've got this."

Receiving words of encouragement from the A.I. he loathed wasn't how he imagined this day would go. He believed this flimflam presentation was a mistake. Had he not been half asleep, he wouldn't have agreed to it at all. Gwen would be far better up here.

After a deep breath and a gesture, he reconnected. "Aliens of the honorable Galactic Alliance." He spun around and wildly waved with his hands. There was no better way to get their attention than to lay it on thick. "What you just heard was certainly food for thought. Weeks and weeks of bad tasting food, but edible nonetheless. If you're like us humans, you realize truth is often simpler than fiction. Especially the fiction Prosecutor Xoolo just spit up."

More chuckles permeated the virtual space. The statistics Harold had learned how to overlay on his comm showed the aliens sentiment was building in his favor. How this was a court was beyond him.

His retinal comm guided him to the first discussion topic:

Physical proof, circumstantial. Energy core.

This he was prepared for. He snapped his fingers and a

top hat appeared. Harold had to be kidding. "Forgive me for not asking for approval to use this prop, Ambassador. I know how you are on decorum. It's merely a prop. Unlike my knives, this is virtual."

The sentiment toward him fell on his retinal comm. He should have known making reference to having killed another alien would be received poorly.

"Tough jury. Sorry about that." He spun the hat and tossed it into the air as it fluttered back into his outstretched palm. "What you see here, is an ordinary hat. It's hard to believe humans actually wore this on their head on Earth."

Admiral Nguyễn set it atop his head and demonstrated. The audience laughed. He had to admit it was rather absurd looking, but so were many of the species he was staring at.

"Sometimes we humans use this type of hat for tricks. Astonishing things can be concealed inside, even in a virtual world like this. If I were to reach inside your recovered probe, as Prosecutor Xoolo revealed, I'd find a scrapped Galactic Alliance power core. Or at least something they swear had to be one. It's the only thing that made sense if you were to believe their evidence. But what if it wasn't? What if it was a regular subluminal human power core? I submit this list of the hundreds of thousands of power cores we humans have created over the centuries here in Sol. Most of these are some-where in a scrapyard, storage, or museum. We're prepared to produce each and every one of them in an attempt to match it with your probe."

Ambassador Addae's feathers ruffled. "That'd take months or even longer."

He raised his hand outward. "I'm sorry, does the alliance wish to refuse our evidence? We'd be more than happy if you'd like to withdraw the charges against us."

"No, we do not." Ambassador Addae floated down off her perch and approached him. "You're on thin, I believe you say, ice, Admiral. We'll accept your evidence, but you only have two weeks to produce any viable candidates. Is that all you have?"

"Of course not." He stared down into the hat. "Aren't you going to let me show you what's inside?"

The talon on Ambassador Addae's left foot clinked against the floor, sending a shiver up his spine. He winced. Somehow they'd overpowered his audio levels. He thought Lisp had agreed to allow Harold to control their side of this event.

"We all know the rabbit in the hat trick," Ambassador Addae said. "Human television is something of a fad in much of the alliance."

He shrugged. "Fair enough. I'll do it myself then." He reached into the hat and his hand came upon what felt like dirt. When he pulled it out, it was just that. A handful of a fine sand looking substance.

"What is this?" He subvocalized to Harold.

Stellar remains from millions of stars that fit our star's chemical patterns.

He held his hand flat for all to see. From the numbers Harold was projecting, the aliens were reacting with curiosity, their eyes focusing in on his every move.

Prosecutor Xoolo raised his arm in objection. "I fail to see what dirt has to do with this case."

"But, you're the one who brought it up. I think it was about halfway through my nap."

The room broke out into laughter again.

"Silence!" Ambassador Addae said. "Overruled, Prosecutor. You took the case there, he can defend against it."

Admiral Nguyễn leaned forward and blew the virtual dust. It exploded forward into a pattern mimicking the Milky Way. Spread within the spiraling arms of stars were millions of sparkles every so often. Those must be what Harold was talking about.

"Members of the tribunal, I present all known stars that have plausible chemical matches to that of our own sun. Each is within the realm of possibility and could have produced matter with the same molecular patterns as our sun here in Sol. Any one of these stars could contain the species that created the probe you uncovered."

"And sent it to Epsilon Eridani?" Prosecutor Xoolo asked.

"Far be it for me to understand or explain why a species would travel halfway around the galaxy to study and spy upon someone. You would know more about that than we would." He gestured over the audience of aliens.

The sentiment rose on a large percentage of the tribunal members and plummeted on others. Their mutterings and frantic gestures were highlighting the fractures in their ranks. His plan was working.

Prosecutor Xoolo clanked his jaw shut. Like Ambassador Addae, these aliens loved their show of force. "And how are you going to rebut your presence in Achernar? Certainly, your subluminal travel wouldn't have gotten you there in time."

Admiral Nguyễn raised a finger. "But neither will your faster than light drives. That we both know. The math is simple enough."

He spun around and stepped away from the walking reptile, hoping Harold would prompt him for his next item to present. This charade of a defense was a mistake. His doubt and discomfort was surely coming across to everyone watching him. He was on stage. He hated being on stage.

With his back to the Prosecutor, he waited, but nothing came. Harold had left him out to dry. Their entire defense lied in producing a few power cores they hoped could match up to the recovered probe.

"Might I remind the human that the burden of proof is on your species to prove your innocence," Prosecutor Xoolo said.

His fist tightened, and a chuckle escaped from Admiral Nguyễn. Their system was shit, and he was tired of being Harold or the Galactic Alliance's puppet. He was done. He could see his anger spiking his vitals on his retinal comm. The tribunal was seeing it, as well.

Play this video. Lead in dramatically. Question the very foundations of the GA.

He relaxed his hands and conjured the most evil grin he could muster before spinning around to face Prosecutor Xoolo. "Proof? You need proof, do you?"

"We doooo..." Prosecutor Xoolo leaned in closer to him. "Or your kind is dead." They followed that with a smile, their white fangs glistening in the virtual lights.

Admiral Nguyễn took a step backward. "I'm not certain if you're prepared to see the proof, Prosecutor. None of you are." He gestured in a circle over his head, tossing the top hat for effect.

Harold must've done something because it started shooting black vapor from its brim as it floated down to the ground in the center of the room. The wispy smoke reminded him of the Dark Nebula. It'd landed well past where he was aiming, but it'd do.

"If you knew what I'm about to show you, none of you might be standing here today. You see, the very foundation of your seemingly all powerful Galactic Alliance is built upon a fault line. One that each of you allowed to spread, deep within your stellar ranks. Honorable members of this tribunal, you asked for it."

He pointed at the top hat in the center of the virtual

chamber and then blinked at his retinal comm, on the area where Harold had floated the video link.

A moment later, the black hat began projecting upward. It was a recording of what appeared to be a muscular Nanil, a Qudoculi, and a Thyreus.

"Where'd you get this?" Ambassador Addae asked.

Admiral Nguyễn smirked. "In due time, Ambassador. In due time. Just watch." He pointed at the hologram.

"Relax Bruthil!" The Qudoculi gestured downward with their hands. "Your secret's safe with us. We understand the situation you're in. Humans were using you to do their bidding. One could only imagine what would happen if it were discovered that you were, in fact, the uplifts of the humans. It could destroy everything."

Bruthil sidestepped between them and motioned to the exit behind them.

"Wait!" The Thyreusian gestured for them to stop. "We don't have to allow events to follow that path if we don't want to." They turned their sixteen eyes toward the Qudoculi. "I'm sure we can come to an amenable place, don't you think so, Admiral Ular?"

The deep green of the Qudoculi grew even darker as an eerie smile carved across its moss-like face. "I very much think we can. What about you, Bruthil? Are you up to turn the tables on your uplifters? We can keep this our secret if you want. All you have to do is give us details on where your uplift broke alliance laws, and we can eradicate them."

"But... they uplifted us." Bruthil's eyes narrowed. "That would be illegal."

"Not at all." The Thyreusian's antenna were buzzing around their head in excitement. "As far as we and the Galactic Alliance are concerned, you're the uplifter. Without proof otherwise, it's you versus them."

"What do you say?" Admiral Ular asked. "Care to take control of your own destiny?"

The muscles rippling across Bruthil's body had gradually decompressed, having brought them back to a size identical to that of a human. "What do you need me to do?"

Admiral Ular nodded toward the Thyreusian.

The neon blue alien rubbed their antenna together. "Is there any chance you're aware of any starships under their complete control with no Nanil onboard?"

Bruthil bobbed their head. "Hundreds of them. There are outposts hidden throughout our home worlds."

Admiral Nguyễn froze the hologram. He had to double-check his virtual uplink to be sure it was still connected as the tribunal was silent. All alien eyes were glued to the images playing out in front of them, the implications of which he was only now beginning to understand himself.

He stepped forward and casually walked around the hologram, rubbing his chin. "Tell me, Ambassador Addae. On what grounds would your Galactic Alliance case hold merit in the theft of faster than light technology if we were the uplifters and not the uplifts?"

Ambassador Addae rapidly swung her head left and then right, taking in the silent stares of her fellow alliance members before she finally spoke. "We'd... have to discuss that."

The text flashed across Nguyễn's retinal comm.

There would be no grounds.

Admiral Nguyễn smiled. "Come on. You and I both know there would be no grounds. Isn't that right, Ambassador?"

"The authenticity of these conversations needs to come into question," Prosecutor Xoolo said, stepping out of the shadows.

Signed and authenticated by Lisp. Cycle 128 GA Time.

He cleared his throat. "Lisp?"

"Yes, Admiral Nguyễn," Lisp said.

"Can you be a dear and share the authenticity details of these recordings?"

"Certainly, Admiral. Members of the tribunal, I have verified the authenticity of these recordings as they were being transmitted. They predate my operation, but their recording devices were certified alliance recorders stamped and sealed. The recording device was from an undisclosed bodyguard of Representative Bruthil, the first Nanil representative of the newly appointed alliance member species."

Strange alien noises began emanating from the surrounding tribunal members. Some even came off their benches around the outer walls, moving closer to the center, toward Ambassador Addae.

Admiral Nguyễn raised his hands and his voice. "Tribunal members! Please! Give me but another moment."

The room fell silent, and the dozen or more advancing aliens paused.

"Thank you." He turned to face Ambassador Addae. "The alliance must answer for their actions. The Qudoculi, Thyreus, and who knows how many other species used their powers and positions to effect the near demise of an entire species. My species! They have been unchecked for millennia. And I could be mistaken, but weren't there recently several species who the Galactic Alliance enshrouded in Dark Nebula in succession? It certainly wouldn't look good if those species were near the growing borders of other alliance members, now would it?"

That's speculation.

He didn't care, and apparently neither did the aliens in the room because chaos erupted. The alliance aliens began attacking one another, tearing each other apart. Limbs were flying and all colors of blood sprayed and stained the floors. Lisp was making no attempt to clean up the mess. Not yet anyhow.

All the while, he stood there in the middle, next to the top hat, arms crossed and wearing a smile on his face. Finally, something had turned their way.

17

JOYCE GREEN
EPSILON ERIDANI, LIPROSUS

Joyce bolted upright with a start. Sweat covered her from head to toe, and her right arm throbbed where she'd taken the hit from the rocks in their subterranean battle royale a few months back. When she glanced at the clock in the corner of her retinal comm, she realized it was the middle of the night, and she'd only slept for a few hours.

The image of Two holding up the number ten thousand and thirty-two on a placard lingered in her mind's eye. His laugh repeatedly echoed in her ears. Each time his mimicked human voice bellowed, yellow blood oozed from one of the antenna receptacles on his head and the crushed left half of his face. The second antennae twitched, like it had a mind of its own.

They received the message the same day she'd killed Two. It was a short broadcast, tight beamed from the void of space, and it contained a tiny data packet.

The message had been directed toward her. Well, they thought it was intended for her, but they weren't positive. The destination address matched her colony number from the Liprosus roster. The number four. Her people turned the number inside out, trying to match it to anything meaningful in their archives, but came up empty-handed.

There was nothing else in the message. An address and a number. Since its arrival, she hadn't slept. The high of killing Two had subsided, and all she was left with was this test, this puzzle.

She swung her legs off her bed and rested her naked feet on the cold metal floor. The shock of the temperature shot up her legs and the image of Two faded. All that remained was the blasted number.

"Why?" she said aloud.

No one responded, nor should they have. The only person listening was Harold, but she'd put him in his place weeks ago. He'd been suspiciously absent ever since.

The arrival of the message had given her pause. She never trusted Harold. If anyone could send a broadcast like that, it'd be him. He always seemed to wait until the last minute to share a snippet of hope, and she could see him dropping this to force them to reengage him. Maybe it was time they did.

She leaned back on her bunk and rested her hand on the plush mattress. "Why, Harold?"

"I'm not sure if I understand the question," Harold said. "Your sleep was restless by every measurement in the books. So, I can only imagine you've been having nightmares about the number again. That, or your son."

"I'm missing something. We all are." She closed her eyes and sighed.

"It could be anything, really. The only certainty in the entire message was its relationship to you."

His words stung. Why her? Certainly, the message could have been directed at anyone else. It was right there. She could see it, but was failing to connect the dots. Just as she'd failed at so many things since arriving here.

She'd give anything to start over. To turn back time and change the past. Her son would still be alive, and hell, she might even still be married. This entire colony put her life into a tailspin, and she hadn't recovered since.

Saying yes was the biggest mistake in her life.

And then it clicked. Was it that simple? It couldn't be. She did the math in her head and compared the dates. Her stomach knotted up.

"That's too easy," she muttered.

"What is?" Harold asked.

She stood up and gestured toward the door and it silently slid open. Her team would be asleep, but she needed to wake them.

Harold's voice appeared in her ear and she froze. "Might I suggest some clothes?"

When she stared down, she realized she was still naked. "Yea, that would probably be a good thing." She took a step backward and the door closed. If anyone had been passing by, they'd have gotten quite a show.

"Wake my team while I get ready. I want everyone in the control room stat."

"Consider it done," Harold said.

The knot in her stomach had spread out, and all that remained was a tingle. That feeling of excitement and antici-pation. She only hoped it wasn't another dead end.

ELAINE YAWNED as she passed into the control room. Even though everyone lived underground, and there wasn't a day or night per se, they'd defined a start and end to each shift that aligned with the surface above them. At this hour, there was only a skeletal crew manning the controls.

Joyce paced back and forth behind Captain Hui, who was sitting in a chair, waiting for the others to arrive. Her hair was a mess, and she hadn't even bothered to get her uniform on.

As she bit her thumbnail, she glanced up at the wall

screen. Another stingray ship was returning with raw materials. They'd been recovering them from the remains of the colony rings over the past months. There was no point in leaving perfectly salvageable raw materials on the ground, especially if they could retrieve them without detection.

She watched as the stingray's cargo hold doors swung open and a herd of robots swarmed in, emptying its contents in all directions. Electronics, metals, plastic, and from the looks of it, bags of some sort. She hoped it was coffee. She could really use some of the good stuff from Sol's Coffee & Tea.

"Who else are we waiting on?" Captain Hui asked.

Joyce shook her head and returned her attention to the people who had gathered around her. Ryder had arrived, and she hadn't even noticed. "I... think this is it. Thanks for coming at this hour. I figured it was better to discuss this now than in a few hours, in case we need to prepare."

The group traded stares, and Ryder broke the silence. "I'll bite. Prepare for what?"

She subvocalized a command and brought up the number they'd received on the far wall. Ten thousand and thirty-two glowed in bright yellow. She'd picked the color as a nod to Two who'd helped her in realizing its meaning.

"Not this again," Captain Hui said. "You realize it's probably Harold pranking you, right?"

"It's not me." Harold's voice was coming from the control panel, but he did not show his virtual face. "She's asked me directly on sixteen occasions, and I have no recollection of sending this signal. You know I cannot lie to you."

Joyce hadn't realized she'd confronted him so many times. "I don't think it's from Harold. At least not this copy of him. I believe I've figured out the number, though."

"Really?" Elaine stepped closer to the control panel and squinted, hoping to see something there, but it was blank. "What is it?"

Joyce swallowed hard. This was either going to fizzle or explode. "It's a duration. A number of days."

Ryder yawned and pulled up a chair, sliding it in front of the group and beside Captain Hui. "Without a point of reference, it's meaningless."

She took a deep breath. "I think the reference point could be December third or seventh, 2250."

The group glanced at each other, masks of confusion on their face.

She continued. "Either the day Abigail Olivaw asked me to join the colony mission as the Director of Colonization, or the day I accepted the position. It fits."

"Alright." Ryder spun around to face the control panel and brought up the time controls for the three-dimensional celestial planisphere on one of the wall screens. "If that's the date, then we're talking about something happening… two to three weeks from now."

His hands danced over the controls, and his head slowly turned from side to side until he froze. His fingers stopped moving when the timeline hit day sixteen.

Joyce leaned forward and crossed her arms, squinting at the screen. She couldn't see it. "What do you see?"

He reached up and rubbed his chin. "This asteroid." He pointed at a small rock he'd selected on the wall. "It's supposed to pass well outside the orbit of our Liprosus moons in sixteen days. It happens every few years and has a weird orbit, but it hasn't changed since we've been tracking these things. The rock is solid, and ripe with heavy metals. It has a gold mine of ores if the colony had ever gotten big enough to slow it down. The sucker's moving like a rocket!"

"So why'd you freeze on it then?" Joyce asked. She couldn't help but notice he'd used the past tense of the colony, like their fate had already been sealed.

"Because according to this more recent observation we made," he tilted his head, "last week, its orbit was revised.

One of our Lagrange point micro sats picked up the difference in its passive scan of the sky."

"How'd it change?" Captain Hui adjusted something in front of her.

The wall screen updated and showed an amended route for the asteroid, one well inside the path of Luna Duas, the second and closest of their five moons.

"It's not going to hit, is it?" Joyce asked.

Ryder shook his head. "No, but at the rate it's changing course, it certainly could. It's crazy how it suddenly started moving."

"It could've released some subterranean gases," Elaine began. "With sufficient force and ejecta, they could easily change the orbit of something that small."

"Like I said, it was a solid rock of ore. Platinum, iron, molybdenum, you name it. I don't see any mention of ice or anything else that could release." He shrugged. "Who knows, maybe it picked up some on the last circuit in a collision, and that's what's throwing it off."

Joyce uncrossed her arms. If this thing collided with Liprosus, this could be catastrophic. "If it continues, where would the impact locations be?"

He adjusted the projected orbit of the asteroid on a linear projection, and the path appeared on the wall screen as an elongated oval. "Depending on the rate, anywhere in here. It's coming in shallow, so the final impact will be over a vast swath of the southern continent. We'll have to keep an eye on it."

From the looks of it, the collision was nowhere near them. In fact, it was on the far side of the planet, almost directly opposite their location. Convenient how that worked out.

Her tingles returned. Something about this was too perfect. "Does anyone else find the impact location... suspicious?"

Again, the blank stares at each other, everyone except for Ryder. His eyes had caught something. Maybe it was the same thing she was seeing.

"It's in the ideal location to not hurt us. It's well south of the equator, and the prevailing wind patterns this time of year will keep the back splash of ejecta minimal, and the resulting cloud of debris shouldn't move north across the oceans." He paused and reached up to scratch his head. "If I were a conspiracy theory nut, I'd say this was designed to be the best worst way to land something on this rock undetected."

Captain Hui laughed. "That'll be one hell of a ride if it's true. If there are people inside, they'll be lucky to survive."

"What if it misses?" Elaine asked. "I mean, could someone be hiding out on the far side and drop in from orbit?"

Ryder made a few more adjustments and nodded. "Yes, I suppose they could. The asteroid would collide with Liprosus sometime in the next thirty to forty years, but yea, that's a path that it could follow if the change in orbit increases. I have to think the Galactic Alliance would see it, though. Hell, I wouldn't be surprised if they sent out a contingent of forces to make sure the impact or near miss is legit."

As the changes Ryder made repeated on the wall screen, she studied them. The longer she watched, the more a miss didn't sit well with her. An impact felt like the most logical course of events. If someone wanted down on the planet, that is.

She brought her hands together, fist to palm. "Let's play this out and work all the angles! I want to hear ideas on how we get close to the impact site without losing people. I want eyes on the ground everywhere down there. If something comes out of that rock, I want to know about it. Is that clear?"

Everyone nodded at her.

"Now!" she shouted. "Come on, the clock's ticking. Wake up whomever we need. Move it!"

Her team scrambled up and out of their seats, bolting toward the exit. Most of them needed to get properly dressed, but she didn't imagine that would slow them down. No one wanted to be on her bad side, not since she'd killed Two.

18

ABIGAIL OLIVAW
ZETA LUPI, OORT CLOUD

It was Abigail's turn to sit at the bedside of a family member. Lync had been out for nearly six hours. At first, they thought she'd fainted, but after she didn't regain consciousness, they realized it was more than that.

Shauna and Harold were monitoring everyone's vitals in the lab and throughout The Wheel for that matter. From what they said, Lync's heart had just stopped. One minute she had a healthy heart rhythm, and the next it went flat. No spike, no flutter, it simply dropped to nothing. Had Abigail not been sitting beside her, she likely would've cracked her head hard against the floor and had a concussion.

Harold had done what he could to keep Lync's situation on the down low until they knew more. Apparently, General Yule had been looking for her. Harold reminded him how she'd been going on upwards of twenty-four hours without sleep, and she'd crashed in her room. He refused to let the general wake her, claiming that her sleep-deprived state was unhealthy and would do them no good. He was begrudgingly complying, but that would only last so long.

Her feelings toward Lync were complicated. She was still furious with her for calling her a traitor. The whole thing was a fog looking back on it. To be honest, she shouldn't have been making any decisions at that point in time. Coming out of a coma didn't exactly make one clear of mind. There was also the fact that Lync's father had been killed by the man Harold placed in power. That wasn't a good look by any stretch. She swallowed hard. Tossing her in the brig had been a shit decision, as well, and she knew it.

The door to the room slid open and Abigail shot up with a start, stepping toward the entrance to get between her and whoever was coming in. A small girl who was a little over a meter and a quarter tall walked in, and the door closed behind her.

Abigail tilted her head. "Can I help you, dear? Are you lost?"

Harold appeared on the wall screen next to Lync's bed. "This is Ibu."

She shook her head. "I'm sorry. The name doesn't ring a bell. Did you know Lync?"

Ibu smiled. "Nope, can't say I did. When I heard she was a friend of Zachary and Shauna, I wanted to meet her. I thought perhaps I could keep her company."

This was curious. She had no idea who this girl was. "You know my brother and… Shauna?"

Ibu skipped up to Lync's bedside and reached out to grasp her hand. "I do! She was great fun during our trip from Lupus. She taught me so much about humans and how you nearly destroyed your world in Sol. It's a wonder your species managed to make it to this time period in the first place. I'd love to know how your kind devolved over the millennia, only to rise again."

Abigail cleared her throat. "Our kind? What does that mean?"

"Ibu is a Nanil," Harold said.

The little child glanced up at her again and then returned their attention to Lync. Their hand was moving over Lync's palm in a figure eight motion, and she seemed to mutter something. It was too faint to hear.

"A Nanil." Abigail stepped up across from Ibu, studying them as she walked. "I must have missed that part of the briefing. I know we encountered your... kind on a world named Doda, but I don't recall them mentioning bringing back a Nanil."

Ibu closed her eyes and tightly grasped Lync's arm, sliding their hand up to her elbow and resting Lync's palm around their upper arm. Ibu bobbed their head up in a circular motion. "She has a very unusual presence. Unlike any other human I've experienced."

Abigail glanced over Ibu's shoulder at the face of Harold. "Are you going to tell me why we didn't include Ibu in the return team roster? Seems like something we should've made a note of."

"The people who were on the mission know," Harold began. "Pluto and Zachary didn't think it was necessary to frighten everyone. Shauna and I have been watching over them the entire time. They've been an immense help in reviewing the Nanil's history and the other records we uncovered in Lupus."

"They have me helping create the killing machines," Ibu said, their eyes still closed.

Abigail did a double take. "We're using child labor to build our military hardware. What the frak is she talking about, Harold?"

Ibu chuckled, their head briefly pausing their circular motion in fits and starts. "I would hardly call me a child by human standards. I'm forty years old. If memory serves, I believe you were running your family business at the same age, plying the web of lies to keep your species on the path to the stars."

She coughed and opened a subvocal comm to Harold. "She's a feisty one. I love it."

"They're actually intersex," Harold began, "and prefers to not be spoken to as a male or a female."

"Oh," Abigail said.

"Oh, what?" Ibu asked, peeking one eye open to look at Abigail.

"Nothing. I… was just talking to Harold."

Ibu closed their eye and continued to move their head as they maintained their grasp on Lync's arm.

"What is she… I mean, what are they doing?" Abigail asked Harold over her comm.

"They're attempting a mental link," Shauna said. "When we told Ibu that Lync wasn't wholly a human, they wondered if maybe they would be able to establish a mind connection with her. Apparently, Nanil use these links to interact with each other through touch. When we dug into their history, we found that this was one of the ways Nanil teach their Clonos to deal with the memories they retain after they're born. They congregate in groups to communicate collectively at rates of speed unheard of in humans until nanites and retinal comms were combined with neural enhanced education."

She hadn't expected Shauna to be listening in on their conversation. This was going to take some getting used to. "And they do it with no modifications?"

This time Harold replied. "Their bodies are transmitting the equivalent information via touch, which humans do through wireless means using nanites. You then consume the information through your retinal comms' visual or neural link. The Nanil are doing it naturally, without all the elec-tronic wizardry."

"Fascinating," Abigail muttered.

Ibu stopped bobbing their head and contorted their face, scrunching their eyes together and making strange motions with their mouth. Suddenly Lync's heart rate became erratic and the machines over her bed chimed in warning.

"Whatever you're doing, stop!" Harold said, his voice bellowing from the wall screen.

"I'm almost..." Ibu muttered. Their voice was distant and muted, like they were deep in thought.

"You're going to put her into cardiac arrest," Harold said.

A medical bot slid out of a hidden wall recess beside Lync's bed and moved up next to Ibu. It reached its hands up and placed them around their bicep and began pulling their hand away.

In one quick motion, Ibu reached across from the other side, ripped the robot's hand clear off, and tossed it into the corner. "I said I'm almost there. Don't touch me!"

Abigail took a step backward and brought her hand to her mouth. The sheer strength of the action was inhuman and the Nanil's body was morphing before her eyes. In the seconds following the incident, Ibu had grown a head taller, and their muscles were bulging through their shirt. "Is that normal?" She glanced toward the door to be sure she had a clear shot to the exit if she needed it.

"It's a fight response all Nanil have," Shauna began. "Our human ancestors thought it would be an interesting genetic tweak to make their bodyguards walls of muscle. We've never seen them use their mental link before. It seems like interrupting it is the same as striking them or threatening them. I'll have to note that for the future."

The door to the small room slid open and three larger security bots stepped in, blocking the Nanil's exit. They surrounded Ibu on all sides, careful not to touch them, but preparing to do exactly that.

As the robots reached toward Ibu, they froze. At first, Abigail couldn't tell why. Perhaps Ibu had somehow ordered them to release them through some other yet unseen skill. But then it became clear.

Lync stirred, kicking her legs and muttering under her breath. "Daddy, why'd you do it... you could've escaped."

Her body contorted, and her arms moved around, sliding her hands over the bedsheets and crinkling them into her fist. "Why," she muttered over and over again, rocking her head side to side.

When Abigail looked at Lync's other hand, she noticed the same vise-like grip except it was against Ibu's arm. Their skin was turning white from cutting off the circulation and their body seemed to enlarge even further, sensing the attack to their person. But their eyes remained firmly shut and there was no further motion from them other than a slight fluttering of their eyelids. It was like their eyes were darting around underneath.

"Her levels are rising." Harold's voice was coming from the security bot closest to Lync's head this time. Even after all these years, it was still surreal hearing his voice from every object in a room.

Abigail took a step toward the bed and reached to Lync's hand clutched in a fist. She stroked it tenderly. "Is she…"

"Where am I?" Lync sat up with a start. Her forehead was glistening with sweat, and her face was pale.

"You're in a private medical room. Everything's ok." She continued rubbing her hand.

Lync shook her head, darting her eyes around the room. "How long have I—"

"A little over six hours," Harold said. "You passed out while we were talking… downstairs."

She glanced in the direction of Ibu. Their eyes were now open, and she nodded toward them. "Thank you," she muttered.

"That's—" Abigail began.

"Ibu, I know," Lync interrupted. "They introduced themselves already. Though, I have to say, I wasn't expecting a visitor in my dead father's dream." She swallowed hard. "It's sorta personal and a little weird." She chuckled. "Yea, you're right. Try receiving it in a message from your deceased A.I. mother, and you know how I feel... no really, it's—"

"Are... we missing something?" Abigail glanced between Harold and Lync.

"I'm sorry." Ibu nodded toward her. "I was communicating with Lync through our mental link. It's much easier and far more efficient than using words. When she's awake, she's more accustomed to responding vocally. She'll learn."

Being on the outside of a situation was a new feeling. She hadn't felt it in years. Abigail picked up a cloth from the bedside, dipped it into a melted cup of ice, and then reached out and ran it over Lync's forehead. She looked like she'd just run a marathon.

"That feels nice." Lync leaned back in her bed. "I don't suppose you have any grub? My stomach is empty, and I was hella hungry before we even went down to the lab."

"What lab?" Ibu asked.

Lync turned her head to look at them. "The one—"

"A few levels down," Harold interrupted. "We were discussing private family matters."

"Oh, for frak's sake, Harold!" Abigail continued rubbing Lync's forehead with the cloth. "The kid just saved Lync's life. The least you could do is not lie to them. You really do need to learn a new mode. Anyhow, Ibu, as Lync was saying, we were reviewing some of the material we recovered from your mission to Lupus and we both learned about our mother."

"You mean Shauna?" Ibu eyed her curiously.

Abigail chuckled and glared at Harold's human face still on the screen beyond the wall of security bots. "How are we the last two people to fraking learn about her?"

"Lync told me in her dream," Ibu said. "I hadn't known until only a moment ago. Time moves at a different pace inside our mindscape. Information is far easier to share, and it's harder to lie."

"That sounds refreshing." Abigail dipped the cloth into

the ice water again. "We could use with far fewer lies out here in the real world."

Ibu released Lync's hand and gently set it on the bed before they began rubbing their own arm. "That's what the Prima Nanil believed, as well. They refused to speak to anyone outside a mental link for fear that they were being deceived. For decades many presumed the Prima Nanil were mute until enough people linked with them."

Abigail drew in her breath. While Ibu had been speaking, their body had transformed, shrinking before her very eyes. Their muscles deflated, their height reduced, and the plates in their skull, which she hadn't noticed before, seemed to slide away and smooth out their head, returning it to its original beautiful shape. It was miraculous to watch, and while it looked like it hurt, Ibu didn't react in the slightest.

When she glanced at Ibu's arm, there was a ring of bruises where Lync had been squeezing. "Are you ok? Should we have that checked out?"

"I'm sorry." Lync reached out toward Ibu. "I didn't—"

Ibu shooed her away. "No, I'm fine. Really. It'll be gone in a few hours. Trust me, I've had worse done to me." Their body shuddered, as if they were remembering a pain far greater than that of a human hand.

"So, when were you going to tell me you were a Ulyxsauri?" Ibu asked. They narrowed their eyes and stared at Lync and then Abigail.

Lync squinted and studied the Nanil.

"It's pronounced Ulixi," Abigail said.

Ibu slowly shook their head from side to side, mimicking the human gesture. "No, I know the word Ulixi. I hadn't put the two together until now. From my studying, the Ulixi are a smattering of human nomadic tribes in Sol that believe in isolation and replenishing of one's mind and the universe as a whole. They live off the scraps of others and little was known of their religious system until recently."

Lync sat up in bed, straightening her back. "What does that mean?"

"The footage that was shared with me showed you," Ibu nodded toward Lync, "and I believe a male human named Crayo." They paused until Lync nodded. "You were in a ceremonial chamber in Sol, near your gas giant Jupiter. 'Tis a strange name for a planet. The mythological gods on Earth are very similar to those of the Nanil." They brought their hand up to their chin. "I wonder if—"

"Ibu!" Lync shouted, frustration painted her face. "Please... stop the tangents. Tell me what you meant and what it has to do with the Ulixi."

"Oh, sorry." Ibu snapped their hand to their side. "When you touched the pedestal and bound with the Spános, your aura rose up and expressed itself in the chamber. This is precisely how a Ulyxsauri coming of age ceremony worked in the books I've read."

Abigail sighed. "There it is again, the term Ulyxsauri. You speak of it as if it's a different alien species. Is there a Galactic Alliance species with that name?"

Ibu made eye contact with her and shook their head from side to side. The gesture reminded Abigail of a robot learning to move. They were attempting human gestures, but they felt unnatural.

"Indeed! They are an unusual humanoid species. But they would never join the Galactic Alliance. Like the Ulixi, they're nomads spread throughout the galaxy and their numbers are far too small." Ibu returned her attention to Lync. "At one time, the Nanil believed they were descended from the Ulixi until we learned we were created in a human lab. The Ulyxsauri have great powers of mind and body from the tales in my books. They each have an ability that, when combined with other Ulyxsauri, make for a stronger whole. A sharper mind and spirit. Some believe they were the original keepers of the Beacon."

"Sounds like a bunch of superstitious hokum." Abigail studied Ibu as they spoke. "We have religions on Earth that could each claim to be similar to what you describe. In one way or another, everyone wants to be part of something bigger, something more than the sum of their lives."

Ibu nodded. This time it was a far more fluid motion. "I agree. All species' religions mimic those beliefs in many ways. It's curious if you think about it. There's one thing about the Ulyxsauri, though. One feature that makes them unique." They reached out toward Lync.

She recoiled back into the head of her bed. It had raised to meet her position when she sat up. "What are you—"

"Can I?" Ibu nodded and glanced at Lync. Their eyes softened, and their hand hovered just out of reach, awaiting her response.

Lync swallowed hard. "I guess so. This isn't going to be anything... weird, is it?"

"Not at all. I merely want to see if you..." Ibu delicately reached toward her collar and pulled down the soft skin fitted medical gown that cocooned Lync to reveal her neck. They gasped in surprise at what lay underneath. "It's real... you are a Ulyxsauri. That means your father or your mother must have been one. Do you also have a marking at the nape of your neck?"

She reached up and rubbed her neck before she nodded. "They're birthmarks. I've had them my entire life. All Ulixi are marked."

Shauna interrupted. "Most Ulixi are given their markings at the coming of age ceremony as part of their rite of passage when they join the clan. You know this. You, however, have had these markings from the moment you were born. I remember them vividly."

A video began playing on the wall screen. It was a memory from Marie, of her holding a small baby Lync to her bosom. From the looks of it, it was mere moments after birth.

The baby's face was pink, and she was chaotically wrapped in a plush purple blanket. You could just make out her neck. The markings were there. Smaller versions of what they were today, but they were there.

"She's beautiful," Marie said in the video. She reached out her finger and gently rubbed at baby Lync's neck. "I thought birthmarks only appear after a few weeks."

"Some are present at birth," a man said. He stepped around the foot of the bed and slid next to Marie. His hand moved into the video as he stroked at the birthmark. The baby's tiny fingers flailed in the air and then grasped his finger. They both giggled. He looked young and perfectly normal. A human by any observer's measure.

Abigail glanced toward Lync. Her hand was covering her mouth, and she was fighting to hold back tears. She couldn't imagine what it must be like to see and experience all of this. It was hard enough knowing your mother wasn't dead and was now an all seeing artificial intelligence. It was quite another to realize you weren't what you thought you were, and your life had just become much more complicated.

The video cut off and was replaced by Shauna's face. Not her mother, but the A.I. likeness everyone had grown accustomed to. "I've sent the records on the Ulyxsauri we recovered from Lupus to your comm, Lync. You can study them at your leisure. Until then, we have other matters to deal with."

Abigail chuckled and sat on the edge of the bed. "I'm pretty sure we're topped off with matters, Mom. We could use a few minutes to breathe."

"We don't have a few minutes," Shauna snapped. "General Yule is already on the hunt for Lync, and we can't hold him back much longer. From her vitals, she seems to be fine. You couldn't even tell anything happened if you hadn't known it. She needs to—"

"Relax and absorb what she just learned," Abigail interrupted.

"No," Lync said, swinging her legs off the side of the bed and standing up in one fluid motion. "Shauna's right. I'm needed here. These idiots are gonna get us all killed if I don't help them. And then humanity will be on the run again, except this time I'm not sure the GA will stop hunting us."

Abigail stood up and stepped around the end of the bed. "And what about Nguyễn?"

Lync did a double take and then narrowed her gaze. "What about him?"

Abigail stared down at her hand, at the marks still healing from their fight. "A little over a week ago, you were hell bent on revenge and killing his ass the first chance you got."

Lync snickered. "Oh, don't worry, he'll die by my hand. You can bet on it. But Sol's not where I'm focusing my attention at the moment."

"We need to run more tests," Harold said. "We still don't know why you passed out. We shouldn't run the risk of—"

"I'm not gonna sit around and do nothing!" Lync interrupted, her eyes flinching toward Abigail. "You and Shauna can have your nanites swim through my insides and run your tests from afar. I'll even stop in for some other checkups when I can. But I'm heading to the strategy session I'm already late for. My retinal comm is about to explode with General Yule's fury." With that, she turned and headed toward the door.

"Good luck," Abigail muttered.

Lync froze but didn't turn. "You know you're welcome to join me... if you want."

Abigail adjusted her outfit, wiping away the creases. "No, thanks. I need to see a guy about a ship."

"Oh! Can I come?" Ibu asked, bouncing on their toes.

"Certainly." Abigail reached out and placed her arm around the Nanil. "Maybe you can show me where the Fountainhead is parked nowadays." They both stepped around Lync, who was still standing in the doorway, and headed down the hall toward the lift tube.

"You know you can use your retinal comm, right?" Ibu asked.

"I've turned over a new leaf. I'm trying to shut it off. To give my thoughts and my mind a break." She paused before stepping into the tube to engage her comm. There was no sense in forcing the Nanil to guide her up and down. It was a shame that even getting around required you to be plugged in.

"SO LET ME GET THIS STRAIGHT," Zachary began. "You want to take the Fountainhead to find other surviving species from the Dark Nebula in hopes they'll join our band of merry aliens to fight the Galactic Alliance? That's—"

"Brilliant!" Shauna interrupted.

Zachary's head spun around to face the approaching humanoid form of Shauna as she stepped out of her charging bay. "Those weren't the words I'd have chosen. I'd have gone with insane or foolish."

Abigail recoiled at the description. "What the frak do you know about diplomacy, little brother? Or the long game, for that matter."

"Well, first of all." He strode further into the bridge, up to the wall, and ran his hands down it. "I know this wall was torn to shreds by the last alien species that found itself caged inside the nebula. I also know that had we not lucked out having a Nanil aboard, we'd be dead right now."

"I guess that means I'll need to go with her," Ibu said. They were spinning in the chair beside Abigail. While they insisted they weren't a child, their personality was quite the opposite.

Abigail opened and closed her mouth and shot Zachary a wide-eyed look. "I don't think your... Pluto or Zach would want you traipsing on this mission with me. It's far too dangerous."

Ibu's head bobbed up and down. "I'm pretty sure I can handle myself. Only one of us in this room has taken out a Shu the last I checked, and there aren't any Ulixi who aren't already part of Lync's broader mission." Their head stopped bobbing, and they spun slowly to face Zachary. "Maybe I should talk to Lync about joining them. Surely, they would accept my help."

"No!" Zachary reached forward and stopped short. "Frak," he muttered. "Why can't you both just sit still and help plan the mission?"

"And then what?" Abigail shot up from her seat. "Win or lose, what's next in this master plan of yours? I mean, you tossed the original family playbooks, and apparently, now we're winging it. So, what's the plan?" She was tired of having her ideas questioned. No one seemed willing or able to think any further than the next step. Like Lync, she couldn't simply shut her mind off from thinking ahead. All the plans they'd made for generations had been torched in a few strokes by the Galactic Alliance and her brother. It was such a waste.

Zachary leaned against the wall and crossed his arms. "I'm merely trying to survive. That's all most of us have time for these days."

Abigail gestured at the wall screen and brought up the mission plan she'd been working through. "Well, you can hide out here and keep the generals company. Kara has her project, and this one is mine. I'm headed to the Prodo system to check on the Ursis. They're our best bet to locate survivors from the most recent Dark Nebula curtain raising. You can either let me take the Fountainhead… or I'll find a ship of my own."

"I'm sure we can find something," Shauna said.

"Wait!" Zachary ran his hands through his hair and

paused for a moment. He seemed to be subvocalizing into his comm. "What's Kara up to, and why can't anyone in this blasted family sit still for a minute? You haven't been here but two days, and you're already exiting stage left."

Shauna's humanoid form walked up beside Abigail at the wall screen. "The longer we sit still, the faster we die. I know you wanted to have one big happy family when you and Pluto got here, but there'll be time for that later. Until then, we need a few more coals in the fire."

Abigail glanced to her right. "I don't need you pandering to my ideas. I need someone to call me out if they're…" She peered at her brother and then returned her attention to the wall screen. "A bad strategy. I don't care about wants, I'm focusing on needs, and we desperately need some allies if we intend to survive in the long game."

"Don't worry, Abdiga," Shauna began, as she flipped through her proposal at a dizzying speed. "I'll tell you if it's shit. I've never once pandered to you. Even when you wanted to fold during the Neptune miner strike, I told you your ideas were fair and just. The Inner Ring came around to the bargaining table, didn't they? This plan of yours makes sense. It's risky, but it keeps our options open, especially to species who are on the same side of the Galactic Alliance judicial system as we are."

Abigail shook her head. Despite being in a coma, her memory wasn't failing her. "You weren't even around during the Neptune miner strike. What the frak are you talking about?"

"I was opposed to your decision," Harold's voice echoed robotically overhead. He wasn't bringing up his image on the wall screen like usual.

She glanced upward. "What? You never—"

"Marie… I mean, Shauna, and I had it out when you were pitching that idea. She made me assert my support for the plan. At the time, I begrudgingly got behind it. Fortunately, it turned out you were right, and the miners came out ahead."

All these years she thought it was Harold, it could've been her mother. How many hours of venting or conversations had she had with her mom and not even known it? There'd been so much lost time and opportunity.

"I'm glad you came out of the shadows." She exhaled a long breath and struggled to focus on the plan. It was all that mattered. "What do you see that I don't?"

Ibu stepped up to her left and adjusted the star charts, bringing the plane of stars flat to look down into them. "You're assuming the star systems are fluidly interconnected like Lupus was. We're going to want contingencies if they're not. Being a newer judgment by the Galactic Alliance, there'll be monitoring stations around the perimeter. We'll need to map them out, to make sure we can exit the Nebula if we need to realign to jump into another segment of the Nebula."

"Are we actually considering doing this?" Zachary asked.

Abigail, Ibu, and Shauna glanced back at him and then at the wall screen. Their answer was silent, but it was clear.

"Yes, little brother," Abigail began, "and I could use your help. The question is, are you going to be part of the solution, or part of the problem?"

"Frickety frak," he muttered as he stomped up next to them with his arms crossed again.

She smiled inside. She knew he'd come around. He always did. "I could really use a pilot I trust on this mission. Does anyone know where Minula is these days? I saw her when I first woke up, but she wasn't on any of the transfer ships from Tau Ceti."

"Last I heard, she was on a secret mission for Commander Quesh," Harold said. "Do you want me to reach out to him to get an update?"

It was strange that he hadn't told her about any mission. Come to think of it, she wasn't even sure who he was working for anymore. Up until she'd gone under, she'd have said he worked for her, but a lot had changed while she was asleep.

She brought her hand up and rubbed her chin. "No, I'll track him down later and pick his brain. She's top of my list for this mission if she's available. I assume Pepper is already locked into wherever Zachary is headed on the Beacon mission. That leaves me plum out of pilots I know, so if someone has a suggestion, I'm all ears."

The room was silent. That wasn't helpful.

"So, can I use the Fountainhead, or am I on my own?" She glanced in Zachary's direction.

He smiled. "You'll have to fight Pepper for her."

"I made a few copies of Zachary's ship design for contingency," Harold said. "They've scrapped that design for the Beacon mission, as the gate vanes were too complex and fraught with problems when damaged."

"Awe, come on. They look cool," Zachary muttered.

She shook her head. "And these copies aren't being scrapped for materials?"

Harold brought up the ships on the wall screen in a window. There were three of them sitting in a darkened hold somewhere. "No. They're nowhere near the Wheel. I needed some contingencies when things went south and Zachary broke ranks and gave away our position out here, so I stashed a few things, just in case."

"Of course you did," she muttered. "Of course you did."

19

ZACHARY OLIVAW
ZETA LUPI, OORT CLOUD

It'd been almost two weeks since Abigail had arrived from Tau Ceti, and she was driving Zachary crazy. While she hadn't ever directly undermined him in front of anyone, behind the scenes, she and Kara were ignoring everything he'd been working to accomplish. He'd hit reset on the subterfuge of his family's past, and they picked it back up like a familiar tune, playing the same old game they always have. If anything was certain in the galaxy, it was that an Olivaw never liked to be told what to do.

"They're gonna notice I'm gone one of these times," Zachary said, stepping out of the transport ship.

"Then stop taking the risk if you care that much." Kara stepped past him and into the entrance he'd just walked out of.

"It's good to see you, too," he muttered. Sometimes he wondered why he even bothered. If he hadn't been lonely at The Wheel, he might never have known how they were progressing.

He sighed and strolled down the gangplank. When he hit the bottom and hung a left, he froze. Harold said he'd only built three ships out here, and unless he was mistaken, he counted four. "Who the hell brought the Fountainhead out of The Wheel?" he screamed.

Pepper's voice came over his comm. "I did. Turns out General Yule and whatever flippin' title Lync has, were gonna scrap her for the parts. Over my fraking dead body, I said. So, I busted her out."

This entire mission was spiraling out of control. They were stretching their resources and trying to change too much too quickly. Instead of building from what they knew worked, they were doing a million things and none of them well. "I thought we were rehabbing him to help with the Beacon transition."

"The Fountainhead's a she, not a he," Pepper said. "And we were rehabbing her for the mission until they realized we had more ship than we needed and could spare some layers of hull. Especially the extra thick stealth plating I'd installed. They could easily cover a few dozen automated ships with the same material. Fraking credit pinchers over there can kiss my ass."

"I hardly think it has anything to do with credits," Harold said.

"Shut up, Harold!"

He stared into the distance at the four ships berthed nose to nose. It was a tight fit in the small hangar, especially with the supply transport he'd absconded with. Harold had managed to reuse one of the planetesimals they'd started burrowing out for ore. Fortunately for them, the dig had come up empty. He then erased it from the charts and made sure to steer any ships around it rather than near it. Anything he could do to keep eyes off it until the ion thrusters were installed and could be used to propel it to a safer orbit, out of the way of prying eyes. Something that would take a few years from his last estimates.

A clang echoed through the hold, and he spun in a circle, searching for the source.

"Is everything ok?" he asked over the open network.

"Yea," Kara began. "Fraking bot dropped one of the supply crates before Harold could tweak the gravity. I'm fine, though. The crate's toast, however."

"Anything inside we can't live without?"

Kara didn't reply for a minute. She was probably checking through the manifest. They'd removed all the trackers before he left to avoid detection. The result was a system of inventory management that was primitive at best.

Kara moaned. "From the remains of the wreckage." She paused.

He could just make her out in the distance. She was frozen in place, climbing down one of the ladders off the gantry and was peering down at the remains of the crate.

"It looks like it was a few inertial dampeners and some extra fabricator raw material canisters. We're gonna need to see if any of it's salvageable. I'm sure we'll be fine."

He arched his back and looked up. An audible sigh escaped between his lips. Hiding out like this was putting more at risk than was necessary. "Are we certain we want to do these two missions on the down low? I have to think that if we approached Lync or General Yule, they'd support our efforts."

"I'll ask when we're ready to go, and from a secure location," Abigail said from behind him.

He jumped forward and smashed into the railing. "Frak! You scared the shit out of me! Don't sneak up like that."

She brought her hand to her mouth and chuckled into it. "Sorry, didn't mean to scare ya. I forgot how skittish you are."

"Why didn't my retinal comm alert me to your approach?"

She lowered her arm and stepped around him, tilting her head for him to follow her toward her ship. "We're running Harold in limited capacity. The less he knows, the less is synced back, the safer we are."

He shook his head and followed behind her. "Harold doesn't have to merge with his copy. He can simply exist here."

"Call a damn spade a spade, Abs," Kara said over the comm.

Abigail spun around and faced him on the catwalk. "Alright, fine. We're only giving Harold and Shauna limited access to navigation and bots aboard the ships. They aren't controlling the whole show. Everything else is off limits."

He squinted. "But… why? It's easier if—"

"Because we've leaned on them for centuries and we don't trust them anymore," she interrupted. "We need to start thinking for ourselves. If you're not ok with that, just say so. You don't have to be included in all this." She waved her arms around the hangar.

He didn't know how to react. Both her and Kara had been acting weird toward the A.I. since they'd arrived, but this took the cake. Abigail grew up attached at the hip with Harold. He was surprised she knew how to tie her shoes without him. Kara he could understand. She'd always hated Harold, especially after their Spērō clash when he tried to kill those engineers. What they were attempting was down right reckless without planning.

"Their Four-Laws engines won't respond well to this change," he said. "I'm not sure if they'll let this happen." After their incident in Henosi, he'd started working on a plan to reign them in over a period of time and had already tweaked Shauna's code. Harold's copies and the scope of his world were far harder to govern, and he hadn't finished making the changes.

"My systems aren't complaining yet," Harold said. "So long as we have some ability to protect the humans onboard, we should be fine."

A physical message came in over his retinal comm. It was from Abigail.

I have a way around them if we need it. I'll tell you the details later.

How do you bypass an A.I. who controls and sees everything short of an EMP, which he's already had to use once? He didn't know if either of them would let it happen a second time. For now, he'd change the subject. "You realize that means you're gonna need more crew to man the ships, right?"

She nodded. "We know. Harold says it's doable. You, however, never said if you're ok with it. You and Shauna are pretty… inseparable."

"We're together far less than you'd imagine," Shauna said from a robot that rolled up beside them.

Abigail jumped. "Shit!"

He laughed out loud. "See what it's like being snuck up on. Serves you right."

She pursed her lips and reached out, smacking him on the shoulder.

The little robot drove circles around the two of them. "When Pluto and Ibu were there for him, sometimes we didn't talk for days. It's sorta nice having a conversation with someone other than Harold."

"You never mentioned you missed talking," he said.

"You never asked."

The robot rolled up and zapped him with a tiny charge of electricity.

He jumped forward again. "Ouch! What the…"

Abigail smiled.

"That's what you get for not asking," Shauna said. "Now seriously, we have to get to work. The clock's ticking, and we need to be back to The Wheel before we're set to wake up. Z's people think he's asleep and will be calling on him in a few hours. We're one or two gates away and can't miss our merge in with the rest of the supply shuttles Harold is routing through the area. Hop to it! There's still unloading to do!"

The last thing he'd expected to be was manual labor. That's what they had robots for. Apparently, Harold hadn't thought of everything when he built this place. He'd have to find a way to steal a few on his next run.

"Go on! Move it." Shauna shooed him into Abigail's ship.

He looked left and right. "What do you want me to do?"

"She needs some help with the gate drive array," Pepper said over their comms. "Pluto always said you were the best at it. I could never tell if she was flirting when she said it, or if she was serious."

The thought of Pluto lying on her back, adjusting the array while holding the gate tachyometer at The Wheel in Sol flashed before his eyes. Except this time she was naked. Things seemed so much simpler then. He missed her smile and the sound of her voice. If everything was going as planned, they should be touching down soon in Epsilon Eridani. With any hope, they'd hear something in a week or so.

"Let me grab a—"

"Tachyometer?" The robot reached up and handed it to him.

He nodded. "Yea, how'd you know?"

"I was there the last time you fixed one, remember?"

He forgot sometimes that they were both everywhere. In his mind they had their regions of the physical world where they were located. Shauna in and around his quarters and labs, and Harold in his. But the reality was they were both omnipresent and merely respected the human need for artificial delineation to make life simpler.

"Let's do this." He marched up the catwalk toward Abigail's ship. "So whatcha decide to name this thing?"

"I was thinking Phoenix," Abigail said.

He paused and then continued onward. "Did someone die and rise from the ashes that I wasn't aware of?"

"It feels like it some days." She stepped up beside him. "You know Libby got word of what we were doing, right?"

"Frak," he muttered, hitting the tachyometer into his hand. "Can't anyone keep a secret around here? We really need her focusing on those data cubes. She's our only hope to squeeze everything we can out of those things before we destroy them."

Abigail guided him into the ship, through the airlock, and then toward engineering. "You can tell her that when we get back. She sounded like she was tired of being relegated to the basement all the time. Said something about Hera and Zeus taking advantage of her one too many times and thought maybe you were doing the same."

Nothing he ever had to deal with was simple anymore. "Does she want to join you on your mission to meet the Ursis?"

She shook her head and bent down, lifting the grating up to reveal a ladder leading downward. "No. She said I'd be gone too long and that you needed her."

"She wanted to join me," Kara interjected.

This open party channel was hard to tell when you were ever having a private conversation. The answer was, you never were.

He tucked the tachyometer into his waist, spun around the ladder, and slid down the rungs, dropping three meters down to the lower engine room. The hum of the equipment was soothing. It was the one simple and predictable thing in his life.

The first thing he needed to do was locate the gate array relative to where he was standing. Once he found that, he needed to access the first tachyon field emitter and remove the panel. He then pulled out the tachyometer and took a measurement of the grid inside this housing. A few minutes later and after a half dozen small tweaks, it was within acceptable levels. It hadn't been far out, but every nanometer counted.

He sealed the panel and then crawled forward another meter to the next emitter in the array. Sixty-three more and he'd be done. He really needed to work on a self-calibrating version of this. Most small ships didn't need this many segments in their array, especially their newer, narrower supply ships. These wider models had a larger surface area to pass through the field and required a far bigger array. It was a flaw in his original design, but one they'd worked past in the later generations. He didn't much like the cone-shaped designs they were evolving toward, but he had to admit it was easier to allow the tachyon field to naturally direct itself down over that progressive surface. This way, it didn't require the vanes to control the gate field.

"Are you still hell-bent on hunting down the Delta Sagittarii colony ship alone?" he asked as he removed the second panel and started taking another tachyon measurement. "You could use some help."

"You mean G. Eridani," Kara said, "and why the hell are you still on this? I'm a big girl. I can take care of myself."

He shook his head and made an adjustment to the field prongs. "I think it's better to call it the name of the star system it was actually going to, not the lie we told people onboard or in Sol. It's bad enough we did that to the Tau Ceti colonists. Let's not keep perpetuating the same lies any longer."

"Fine, Delta Sagittarii it is. And yes, I always prefer to go it alone or with a smaller crew. Once we find the ship, hopefully in one piece and drifting in space, we'll locate the colonists we need. Then we'll start the fabricators working with the raw material we're bringing along, and head home. In another six to ten months, Shauna should have their gate drive built, and they'll gate here to Zeta Lupi."

He stopped his calibration. "Wait, you're bringing Shauna? I thought you wanted to leave the A.I. behind."

"Oh, Marie and I go way back. We've got some catching up to do now that I know who she actually is. As long as she sticks to her humanoid forms, we'll be fine. Besides, who else is going to pilot the colony ship after we return with the Gunders and Ulixi we need?"

He had to hand it to her and Shauna. The plan was elegant at first glance. "Hadn't Shauna circulated this plan to find the colony ship to the other people at The Wheel? I mean, isn't this mission already compromised before it starts?"

Shauna replied. "The idea didn't make it past General Raft's strategist. She shot it down before I could even defend it. Said it was too complicated, and we couldn't expend the resources. I meant to tell you, but Abigail arrived the next day, and you were sorta... freaking out."

Abigail chuckled from above. "He does that sometimes."

"If you didn't stress me out, I wouldn't have to." He closed the panel and crawled over to the third emitter. Sixty-two more tweaks to go. This was going to be a long morning.

20

LYNC MICHAELS
ZETA LUPI, OORT CLOUD

Lync was surrounded by idiots. That was the only way to explain the sheer lack of coordination these recruits were exhibiting. They weren't merely missing their marks; they were putting the entire squadron in jeopardy. She gestured over her controls and flagged half of the battlefield as dead.

Moans came in from the pilots within seconds, and their anger was apparent in the cockpit cameras. A few were even flipping their cameras the bird, not knowing she was watching.

She reached forward and pressed the broadcast button. "That'll be enough for this morning."

When they realized it was her, they straightened in their seats as if she was standing over their pod.

She continued, "You're piloting like a grounder who lost their cherry for the first time. Half of you piled on too much momentum and careened through the nebulosity. That means you killed not only yourself and your bombardier, but anyone within the blast back area from your splash. We've spent hours studying the nebulosity, right? How about you return to dock and spend a bit more time studying the recordings from the last few Dark Nebula invasions."

Groans echoed over the comms.

"That's not a request. That's an order! I expect you to be primed for another exercise at 1800 hours, and if this shit show continues, there will be far more hell to pay than watching some ancient videos."

She reached forward and slammed the control panel, ending the broadcast.

"You don't need to hit the equipment," Harold said. "A simple gesture will do."

"Don't mess with me, overseer! I'm not in the mood."

She gestured at the wall screen and brought up views of the second through sixteenth squadrons. They were deep into their training exercises, not looking much better than the first squadron.

"What the frak do we need to do to break them from their virtual habits? It's like they know the Nebula isn't real, and their instincts aren't taking it seriously enough."

"Might I suggest we try practicing near a planetesimal?" Harold asked.

She panned in the air, flipping through the views of the training exercises. Harold was marking more of the pilots as dead that broke the virtual barrier. It was a sea of red on the wall. "And have them crashing and dying against the ground? General Yule would have my ass."

Harold's face appeared in the corner of her retinal comm. "Maybe, but in a few weeks, if these newbies aren't looking far better, he'll have your ass, anyway."

He was right. They hadn't even moved on to any of the complex formations they'd need to master to survive the Beacon run, let alone included any of the A.I. ships into the mix.

"What would the casualty rate be if you'd been piloting alongside these grounders?"

A virtual image of the A.I. fleet of ships was superimposed over the human training squadrons. What was a sea of red with some random pockets of green turned into a tidal wave of bloodshed.

She arched her neck and sighed. "Would anyone be alive right now?"

The surviving pilot's names flashed green and then enlarged on the wall screen. They were all members of Crayo's squadron. Her former team.

"Approximately four percent of our pilots would survive, but most of their ships would've sustained some type of damage."

Her head was throbbing. "How the frak are we going to shape them into a fighting force in six months?"

Harold smiled. "We'll do it. We always find a way."

She was glad someone was being positive about the situation. The pressure to produce against her plan had been mounting, and she didn't have a lot to show for the past few weeks except for some spiffy new gates being constructed out in the middle of nowhere. That and a shit ton of autonomous fighters with more being produced every day. Good pilots, on the other hand, those were hard to come by.

General Raft's idea of building a few dozen massive destroyers wasn't looking so bad right about now. If they had the time and the resources, they might still be able to build a few. Not the fleet he'd originally envisioned, but they'd have a chance.

"Say, didn't General Raft's destroyer plans call for using Spános to power the defenses, as well as the offensive weaponry?"

Harold's image enlarged to fill up more of her virtual field of vision. He was looking confused. "They did. I fail to see what this has to do with training our pilots."

"I was… just mulling over if there was time to build a few of those destroyers he was calling for. I'm pretty sure the proposal was making the rounds again this morning." She gestured in the air and brought up Colonel Cay's plans she'd submitted to General Yule for review in his staff meeting. If she didn't know better, her competition had been monitoring their progress and was jockeying for position while they were licking their wounds.

"Those are them. Again, I fail to see why this course of action would be preferred. Your strategy is superior by every—"

She shook her head. "But, where are we getting the Spános from? Last I checked we still didn't have any, and your secret energy weapon needed some."

"It's due to arrive any day now, according to my intel." Harold closed the destroyer plans from the wall screen. He clearly didn't want to continue down that path.

"Care to fill in the blanks with some details? It'd make me feel like we're on the right track after watching this circus act." She glanced at the sea of red ships practicing their maneuvers. While there were hints of orchestration, you had to squint to see it.

"Honestly, I know this is going to sound a bit odd, but this copy doesn't have the details. I believe it's en route, and we have the best people working on it, but I couldn't tell you the first thing about who or where they're getting it from."

She didn't understand how he didn't know. How was it possible that neither he nor any of the Olivaws knew from who or where the Spános was coming? Surely one of them had to know.

"Do you have any idea who might have details?" Her eyebrows raised in anticipation.

Harold's reply was unexpected. "I'd conjecture that either Commander Quesh or Shauna would be in the know."

Neither of them were people she was keen on speaking with right now, but the more she knew about the reality of their situation, the better she'd feel about her plan.

She subvocalized a command to bring up Quesh's location on her retinal comm. He was down in the arboretum. What the hell was with everyone hanging out down there all the time?

"Let's pay Quesh a visit," she muttered. "And have Crayo meet me down there when he gets in. I have a feeling I'm going to need some backup on this one."

LYNC WAITED behind the ridge until Crayo arrived before approaching Quesh. She didn't know why the man freaked her out, but he did. Part of it was probably because of how many years he worked with the Olivaws to perpetuate their lies. While he'd been a pawn on multiple levels, he was someone who commanded respect within all arms of the military, much like Nguyễn. Her imagination often got the best of her with the higher up brass. They always seemed to be corrupt, on a power trip, or they lacked empathy and normal human emotions. Something she never wanted anyone to think about her.

Crayo walked up to her and came to attention. "Colonel! Reporting as ordered."

"Awe, cut the shit." Lync reached out and pushed against her shoulder. "No one's around."

He glanced around and subvocalized for a few seconds before his posture relaxed. "I... can't tell how I should address you sometimes. We need a code or something to make this easier."

She shook her head. Even the simple things had to be layered now. "I think it's safe to say that if no one else is nearby, and I'm not visibly pissed, you're safe not saluting me."

"And what if you're noticeably freaked out?" He smiled.

A chuckle escaped, and she took a deep breath. "That's all

the more reason not to salute me, then. I might punch you." She leaned forward and faked a jab to the chest and merely pushed off some. "Is it that visible?"

"Sim." He glanced over his shoulder, seeming to peer through the rock face to where Quesh was seated next to the pond. "If it's any consolation, he freaks me out, too. Has for years. The way he'd sneak up on me at the Tau Ceti Wheel, it gave me the willies. So, whatcha need me fer?"

"Backup."

He cocked his head. "You're not thinking of jumping him, are ya?"

She cracked a smile. "No! I just want someone at my side. Like you, he sets me off, and I have to get a straight answer from him. If such a thing is possible with these Circle of Trust folks."

"That cult of you Olivaws is pretty weird."

She flinched. He didn't mean the way it came out, but it still didn't land right. "It's not my doing. I was let in by accident. The sooner we break up the whole thing, the better off everyone is."

"I'm not sure if I'd use those words," Harold said.

She lowered her head and a sigh escaped. "Is there any universe where you stop eavesdropping, overseer? I mean, is there a privacy mode we can set or something?"

"I look out for you and all the other humans here at The Wheel the same. I hear or see someone breaking a rule, and I fix it. No one gets special treatment. My Zeroth-Law has a provision for both humanity and the Circle of Trust. Acting on or attempting to end it would be a violation of that law and would obligate me to notify its members."

Debating the details of him and his ancestors' sick and twisted rules wasn't something she wanted to deal with. She reached out and grasped Crayo's hand. He flinched slightly, but didn't pull away. She then stepped toward him and stared him in the eyes.

If she couldn't talk to him in private, maybe she could try what Ibu had shown her. She closed her eyes and focused, trying to reproduce the situation Ibu found her in. Her body was shut off for all intents and purposes, and there were only her thoughts. Nothing else. Once she'd done that, she tried to reach out. She didn't know what she was expecting, but maybe it'd be clear when she stumbled upon it.

As she was about to give up, the base of her scalp started to tingle. Like that feeling you got when someone was talking about you. Sometimes it gave you the goosebumps or the shivers and other times the base of your scalp itched. It was similar to that, but it was the type of itch she couldn't scratch.

"Can you hear me?" she said with her mind, careful not to say the words out loud.

Crayo pulled his hand away, and her eyes shot open. His face was blank, and he was shaking his head slowly from side to side. Like he'd seen or heard a ghost.

She'd never told him anything about her little episode with Ibu or passing out. While she knew she should have, the opportunity hadn't come up.

"Are you ok?" she subvocalized, reaching her hand out toward him.

"Yea… I think. I just… could've sworn—"

She mirrored his head shake, but more subtly. He stopped.

"Shall we?" she asked.

He squinted at her for a moment and then glanced over her shoulder. "Oh, you mean go talk to Quesh. Yea, sure. Let's do it."

She needed to find a moment to talk to him later. Maybe Kara had an idea how to pull back the curtain for some privacy. That, or she'd need to get some practice sharpening her mental link skills with Ibu.

A waft of fig struck her face as a wind picked up. She turned in place and took a deep breath of the fruity air. It seemed like years since she'd last felt a breeze. While it'd actually only been a few months, it might as well have been an eternity. She missed the openness of Liprosus.

Crayo stepped up beside her and paused, waiting for her to make the move.

Her eyes closed. She needed to center herself. She took another deep breath, this time catching some hints of flowers. There must be an orchard of some kind nearby. This place was a myriad of smells.

Finally, she took a step and worked her way around the rock face. According to her comm, Quesh was on the other side and down the hill. From what Harold had said, Quesh had been sitting on a bench for the better part of an hour.

As they stepped up behind him, she froze when he spoke first.

"I was wondering if you were ever going to make your way down here," Quesh said, staring out over the still pond. "And you brought backup. It's good to see you, Major Ubri and Colonel Michaels."

It was so hard getting the upper hand with these people. She kept forgetting that all members of the Circle had access to Harold.

She stepped around the park bench and stared out over the pond. There wasn't a single ripple in the water. "I suppose the overseer already told you why I'm here?"

"I didn't ask, but I have an inkling." Quesh reached down and picked up a sandwich off the bench and took a bite.

Of course he did. "So, if I don't have to ask, maybe you can make this quick and tell me where it's coming from."

Crayo subvocalized to her. "Where what's coming from?"

"Spános," Harold replied over their private channel.

A shiver went up her spine. She hated when Harold answered questions between her and someone else without being prompted. She glanced at Crayo and shook her head. He nodded ever so slightly.

Quesh reached over and picked up a mug and took a sip

before setting it back down. "I believe you already know, Colonel. If you think hard, it'll become… obvious."

She squeezed her fist and released it. "Why do all you… people speak in riddles? Why not just say it?"

Quesh glared up at her before returning his attention to the water. Faint ripples were starting to appear on the surface. "Were you about to call me an Olivaw?"

"If the situational shoe fits, you can't blame me." She stepped in front of him, between him and the water.

He reached for his sandwich and then sighed. "While things may seem safe to you, all is not how it appears. The Wheel has many eyes these days, and OPSEC is just that, a secret. There's a reason Harold doesn't know. Think about it. Since he lacks the need to complete his duties, need to know prevents him from knowing the details. Now, if you don't mind, I'd like to enjoy my lunch for a few more minutes."

She shrugged. "That's all you're going to tell me? To think hard."

"I'm sure you'll figure it out." He turned to face Crayo and raised his eyebrow. "It's not everywhere that the yellow and blue from within paints the room green."

What the frak was this guy on about? She just wanted a straight answer to know if they needed to change their plans. Her body tensed up as she stared him down. He brought his attention back to her before returning it to the increasing frequency of waves lapping at the shore behind her.

She could feel her temper rising and her pulse quickening.

"Let's go," Crayo said subvocally.

"I'm not leaving without answers," she replied.

"Don't worry. I know where he's talking about."

She shot a glance at Crayo. He had a smile painted on his face from ear to ear. He tilted his head to the side and waved her away as he began walking into the distance, toward where they'd come from.

"It's been a pleasure, Colonel," Quesh said as he reached

down and picked up his sandwich again. He went back to acting as if she weren't even there.

"Yea, sure, if you say so." She stepped around him and trotted up beside Crayo.

If he knew, and she didn't, now they needed to find a way to share the details in private without other people finding out. Where could such a place be found?

CRAYO STEPPED out of the dark recess in the wall and took a deep breath of air and exhaled. His hands were shaking.

"I didn't expect you'd have trouble in there." Lync studied him.

"Neither did I," he muttered. "Neither did I. So, what level of hell is this place?"

"I believe this would be Treachery," Harold said.

Crayo's eyes went wide, and he pointed upward. "I thought..."

Lync spun around and surveyed the modest lab. Libby was on the far side, and apparently she was taking a catnap in one of the couches that slid out of a wall recess.

She didn't want to freak her out. There was no telling how she'd react, and she hadn't exactly asked if it was ok to bring Crayo down here.

"Hey Libby! Are you awake?" She stepped around the central glass enclosure.

Libby flinched and then sat up. "Wha... yea... sure. Whatcha need?" She smiled at Lync and then a second later, when she realized they weren't alone, she stood up and lurched at her desk.

"He's with me!" Lync stepped between her and Crayo.

Libby shook her head and reached into her drawer, pulling out some type of handheld pistol that was strangely shaped like the letter D. She leveled it toward Crayo. "You shouldn't have brought him down here. You know only—"

"The Circle is allowed down here," Lync interrupted, raising her hands in front of her, making it clear she wasn't armed. "He's been in my Circle of Trust since the beginning. Far longer than any of you have." She glanced at him and then back to Libby. "If he can't be trusted, then you shouldn't have ever trusted me."

Libby's hand was shaking. The uncertainty of her actions was written all over her face. She looked like she hadn't slept in weeks.

Lync took a step closer to her. "Have you been down here since... my incident?"

Libby didn't respond at first. She merely let the words sit in the air.

"I've had... a lot on my mind," Libby muttered. "First Hera and Zeus, and now Marie." She brought her hands up to rub at her face and then realized she was still holding the weapon. A chuckle escaped, and she tossed it onto her desk. The clank echoed through the room as it slid to a stop against the display along the opposite side.

"Aren't you afraid of that going off?" Crayo asked. He'd crept his way closer to the enclosure separating them in case he needed to dive behind it.

"Not unless I'm working out." Libby shuffled over to the couch and collapsed back into it. "They're used to simulate pull-ups and other gravity inverted workouts. The other one's in the drawer." She pointed at her desk. "I use them to clear my mind every so often. It helps to keep the blood flowing. Even with nanites, our bodies forget how to move."

"Death by workout machine." He stepped out from behind the glowing green enclosure. "I never saw that coming."

Libby started laughing, her voice cackling like a playful hyena. "To what do I owe the visit, cuz?"

"I need something," Lync said, staring at Crayo. "Well, we need something."

"Of course you do." Libby nodded and rubbed her hand in a circle on the fabric of the couch. "Why else would you be down here? Everyone seems to need me for something. The question is, are you using me or are we friends?"

Lync smiled. "I thought we were family."

"Family?" Crayo asked. "I must have missed a bombshell somewhere."

Libby raised an eyebrow. "Didn't you say he was in your Circle?"

Lync brought her hand up toward Crayo. "I've sorta been a bit busy. I was planning to tell you I was an Olivaw… and a few other things. I just… didn't know how to say them."

He nodded as he stared at the floor. His eyes glazed, like he was taking it in and deep in thought. "How long have you—"

"Two weeks," she interrupted.

"So not in Epsilon? Or on Ganymede, or—"

She stepped toward him, making eye contact. "No! No… I wouldn't have kept that a secret from you. You're my only friend. Do you think I would have gone through all this on purpose," she gestured around the room, "if I'd known I was…" She paused, staring at him. His eyes were piercing and made her feel weak. "Once I found out I was an Olivaw, I shoulda just stole a ship and become a nomad or something."

"You wouldn't have wanted to miss out on all the family backstabbing," Libby said. "Oh, yea, you also forgot to tell him you were an alien." She drummed her hands against the cushion like it was a dramatic tune.

"She's an alien?" Harold asked.

"Awe shit!" Libby muttered. "See, now I went and broke Harold. We need to keep this copy clean. Privacy mode Eta," she said aloud as she stood up and marched toward the wall screen. Her hands began gesturing over the wall of controls that appeared.

Lync couldn't make out what she was doing. It seemed like some type of reset procedure. "What are you—"

"I'm resetting him back to a few moments ago, before his backup matrix overwrites this clean copy and I lose days of assistance. I hate reteaching him things."

Crayo walked up beside Lync. "You can do that?"

"I can, and I am," Libby began. "It's not something we can do everywhere, but here, in this lab, I'm in control and Harold is merely a tool. What was it you were going to ask me?" Her hands continued to dance over the controls. She was selecting the backup she wanted to restore and applying temporal recordings since the point in time she said the words. "Hurry, before I turn him back on, and he can hear us."

Lync reached out and touched her arm. "Wait, you mean he can't hear us?"

"Nope. I enabled Privacy mode Eta." She paused her work and stared at the display for a moment before glancing back at Lync. "That's right. You weren't here when we learned that trick from Abigail via Auntie Hera. Yea, apparently some copies of Harold have a backdoor that allows you to speak a magic incantation and shut him off."

Lync spun toward Crayo. "Where's the Spános from?"

He chuckled. "So, we're gonna skip past the alien thing like she didn't even say it."

Libby slid forward and started working her way toward the exit, clearly feeling uncomfortable.

"Don't you dare slither away." Lync reached out and twirled her around. "You ripped off the lid of this Pandora's box. You tell him."

Libby sighed and eyed the exit, seeming to will it to be closer. "Fine." She turned and made eye contact with Crayo. "We found out the other day that Lync's father wasn't a human, he was a Ulyxsauri. Not to be confused with a Ulixi, which, you know, because you're one. The Ulyxsauri are a species of aliens that, like the Ulixi, are nomadic, but instead of being confined to Sol, they travel the galaxy searching for truth."

Lync furrowed her brow. "Truth?"

Libby glanced back at her. "It's the best translation I could find in the materials. Didn't you read anything Shauna sent on to your comm?"

Lync knew she should have, but she'd been ignoring Shauna since she woke up from her coma, or whatever the hell it was. As her favorite poet used to say, the fear of the unknown is sometimes easier to fend off by leaving it unknown. "I've... sorta been busy. You know, Beacon and all."

A grunt of discontent escaped from Libby before she continued. "As I was saying, your friend here is half Ulyxsauri. We don't have many details about them, even with Ibu's records. What we do know is that they're viewed as mystical overseers with more knowledge about the inner workings of the universe than any other species. The last known Ulyxsauri in the Nanil archives came forward at the founding of the Galactic Alliance to protest the bringing together of the Beacons of Therion."

"That would have been an interesting detail to have earlier," Lync said. "Do we know why?"

"It's all in the records you already have," Libby said.

"I have a question," Crayo said.

Libby nodded and crossed her arms. "Shoot!"

"What are Ibu's records?"

"They're a Nanil that came back with the Lupus Dark Nebula mission."

"Wait! We have a Nanil among us? No shit." He reached up and scratched his head. "How have I not met them yet?"

Lync cleared her throat. She really had to find time to catch him up. "Remember that little girl you've seen tagging along with Zachary all the time? The one with the always tossed auburn hair."

He nodded. "Yea. I figured that was his niece."

Libby took a step toward him. "They're not a she, they're a Nanil. And no one who isn't allowed down here knows that. I suggest you keep it that way if you know what's good for you. Are we clear?"

Crayo swallowed hard. "Sim."

Libby looked between them. "Ok, are we all caught up now? Can I get back to work?"

"No!" Lync raised her hands toward the ceiling. "I want to know where the hell the Spános is coming from? It's the whole reason we came down here."

"Oh yea, the privacy thing. Check." Libby gestured a check mark in the air. "I really need some coffee."

An audible click echoed from the corner of the room and a panel slid up, revealing a coffee maker with a freshly brewing set of coffee pods.

"Oh, can I have one?" Crayo asked.

Libby skipped toward the steaming pods of life. "Certainly—"

"Not!" Lync interrupted. "Until you tell me about the Spános."

"That's easy." He walked past Lync and picked up a glistening globe, closing his eyes to breathe in the aroma. "It was from the Ulixi ceremonial chamber near Jupiter. You remember the one that was blown up when we extracted the clan members?"

Lync shook her head. "But if it was destroyed… how could that be where the Spános is coming from? And why the hell hasn't the Harold here synced up with these details yet?"

Libby turned around and took control of her wall screen again. After a moment of silence, Lync was about to ask her when she spoke. "Harold's copy here in Zeta Lupi hasn't been merging with the copies from Sol nor Epsilon Eridani.

He's worried they're corrupt and has instead been queuing them up while he works on a way to process them safely. As for the Spános..." She flipped through some imagery on the wall screen. "This came in before he put a kibosh on his merges. This is your return footage, right?"

Lync stepped toward the wall screen and studied the images. It looked like the ceremonial planetesimal. The kidney bean markings on the surface matched up and the relative coordinates and trajectories rang a bell. "Think so."

As Libby fast-forwarded, their point of view changed. The footage must have been from the forward camera on their gate ship. It sped through their wait, rushed landing, and chaotic departure before the video froze.

There on the wall screen was a beam of energy flashing out of the Selene ship like a chisel to a rock. It broke the planetesimal into small pieces and then engaged some form of gravitational field, guiding the rocks toward it.

Where her mind had previously seen the particles of light swirling toward the Selene ship as molten rock or gases burning off, she now saw them for what they actually were, Spános.

The image paused as the sparkles of glowing yellow ore glittered in Libby's eyes. "So that must have been the mysterious Spános material we're hunting for. There's a surprising lack of research on it in the archives. Each species I've studied guarded their knowledge of the stuff with a ferocity I've never seen before. I've wanted to go back and spend some time studying our ancient Earth lore. Many of our gods have similarities to how other alien species transformed their knowledge of Spános into a mythical and religious system. The result was a society of people that were easier to control and delineate the haves from the have nots. Those who controlled the Spános, and those who didn't."

"Everything we're doing here depends on this stuff," Lync

said. "I'd love to know how the hell we're planning on getting it from the Galactic Alliance."

"That must be what Lieutenant Clarke is doing in Sol." Libby panned around the fireflies of light rising toward the alien ship on the wall screen. "I was wondering why she hadn't returned with the rest of the Sol contingent. Minula and Abigail have been inseparable for years."

"Minula's back in Sol," Crayo said as he sipped the belt of coffee. "I didn't know that."

Lync spun around and started to pace the room. "Our right hand doesn't know what the left is doing half the time. Let's just hope she's having more success than we are. This entire mission depends on it."

21

NGUYỄN DUE

SOL, JUPITER'S MOON GANYMEDE

Nguyễn stood watch as the supply shuttles silently floated across the space between the Ganymede supply depot. One of them was headed toward the Aitken, and the others were headed to the agreed upon locations near Mars, Jupiter, Saturn, and Uranus. While they'd done their best to mask this run as a need for repairs and upgrades, he couldn't help but think that the Galactic Alliance was watching their every move. They weren't stupid. They knew, or at least they believed, humanity possessed Spános before. It was only a matter of time before they'd show their hand and use it.

The shuttles departing from the Jovian moon contained most of the supply of Spános he had at his disposal. Routing them to the other planets appeased Harold, and in exchange, he agreed to share the weapon designs. He assumed the Olivaws had more of the mysterious ore, but he couldn't say where it was, and the fraking A.I. wasn't about to tell anyone the truth until they were damn well ready to.

"Sir, we'll be underway in... five minutes once we store our cargo," Arrluk, his comms officer, said. "Should I ping you once we're underway?"

They weren't studying his response, instead; they were

watching his hands fiddling with the electro-blade on his hip. He had a nervous tick and a habit of accidentally activating it when he was deep in thought. Ever since the events onboard the tribunal ship, he felt better wearing the blade than not, even in the safety aboard his own ship.

When he released the hilt of the blade and clasped his hand behind his back, Arrluk visibly relaxed. "No need to ping me. Let's get underway as soon as possible. I want to be on Earth before breakfast."

"Certainly, sir." Arrluk returned his attention to his control panel and the status of the shuttle.

Ever since they'd learned about the staggering power the Spános contained, everyone was on edge. Especially when they realized they had almost destroyed their entire secret underground weapons facility on Ganymede. It could've devastated the Outer Ring economy and the battle readiness of the CoPE fleet had Harold not shared the research when he did.

He wasn't about to thank the A.I., though. Withholding information was what got humanity into this mess in the first place. If anything, he blamed him and the Olivaws for everything and more.

While they left a chunk of Spános here for this leg of the mission, the remainder had been scattered throughout Sol. They couldn't have all their eggs in one basket, so they enlisted the help of multiple Inner and Outer Ring research institutes to aid in refining the mineral. It took longer to coordinate the request than he'd hoped, but wielding the War Powers Act, which Abigail Olivaw had so kindly executed, gave him complete authority to do pretty much anything. At least for another few months, anyhow.

Without a word, he made his way toward the lift tube. Pausing briefly before stepping off the bridge, he glanced at his XO. "Wong, you have the bridge."

Wong nodded and saluted him. "Bridge command received, sir."

Nguyễn turned and plotted a path to the security holds on his retinal comm. Seeing the ore safely in place should help him sleep tonight. At least he hoped it would. He hadn't slept well in weeks.

"Now that the Spános is onboard, I've sent on the weapon plans we discussed," Harold said privately over his comm.

He hated when he did that. It was one thing to have an A.I. companion and assistant randomly enter your thoughts; it was quite another to have an unwanted guest constantly popping in. "And what makes you think we won't betray you and take the plans?"

"Because I have faith."

A sigh escaped his lips and his shoulders tensed. He was always speaking in code. "Faith in what?" He stepped into the lift tube and dropped toward his destination.

"Faith that your inquisitive nature is stronger than your desire to one up me. You know you want to know what we have on Earth and why we need the Spános there. It's been eating at you since I mentioned defending Earth a few weeks ago. I've intercepted the queries your team securely encoded, asking your operatives to dig deeper. It's rather disappointing they haven't even scratched the surface. I always enjoy a challenge."

Harold was testing him. Trying to see if he could piss him off. He'd been doing it for weeks. He didn't need a nanny to help him control his temper. "Frak off, Harold. Don't toy with me. This would be far easier if you merely told me what was there." He stepped off the lift and turned right, toward security.

"I can't. The only way for you to believe the Olivaws have never hung humanity out to dry is to prove it to you. You need to see it with your own eyes."

His own eyes. He shook his head. He wasn't even sure he

could trust those nowadays, with Harold slithering in and out of his mind. The A.I. claimed the Olivaws had been bulking their defenses for decades, but refused to say how. Everything was a riddle, and the clues only came when the odds turned against them and they were close to check. Never checkmate, only check.

"Sir, they're moving," Rogers, his security officer, said over his comm.

"I'm outside security. I'll bring it up there." He strode faster, and the soldiers in his wake froze at attention. As he made his way past them, he nodded. Such a formality wasn't necessary when they weren't at port, and even in the moment it seemed like overkill.

When he entered the security section, all eyes were on the wall screens in front of the officers manning the secondary posts. This area was one of many redundant controls throughout the ship that allowed them to maintain battle readiness should they take significant damages and incapacitate the bridge.

There on the wall panels was a view of the alien tribunal fleet. They were subdividing along the only visual lines in the ship's hull. Their intel assumed these were construction and expansion points, but no one imagined they could do this. If memory served, each ship would have the capacity to split off into thirty-two smaller vessels. Their problem just became much bigger than they'd predicted.

"Status," he said, announcing his arrival.

"Sir!" the officer in charge began. "The fleet has broken into one hundred and ninety-two individual ships." She pointed at a pocket of alien ships converging on the screen. "From the looks of it, some of them are reconnecting to others. Intel from Harold suggests each ship had an equal number of representatives from every race. I imagine this could mean they were meeting back up with their fellow species."

He nodded. "Yes. That, or allies."

They all watched as the alien fleet orchestrated maneuvers around each other. It was like the dance of drones you'd see each year before the Olympics, when they drew pictures and projected massive holograms in the sky. Except these weren't bringing humanity together as a people. They were threats to their very existence.

"Orders, sir?" the officer spun to face him.

He wasn't sure there were any. As he was about to issue a hold order, his eyes went wide. The image flashed on the screen. First one, and then others. Several ships seemed to be entering what he could only predict was the superluminal bubble Harold had mentioned before. From the looks of their trajectory, they were heading away from Sol.

The officer returned her attention to the wall, and their hands were dancing over the controls. They confirmed his suspicion a moment later. "They… appear to be retreating. I don't understand. And sir, we're getting intel from the second formation near the asteroid belt. They're also breaking up and dispersing."

Cheers erupted in the distance and all throughout the ship as news of the retreat cascaded through the crew.

"Let's not count our chickens before they hatch, shall we." He stepped closer to the wall screen. "What about these?" He gestured toward three large groupings of tribunal segments, coming together into a new circular formation.

The officer's display lit up. "We're receiving a broadcast comm redirected from the bridge, sir. It's from the tribunal. They sent it on all frequencies throughout Sol."

He straightened and took a deep breath. "Bring it up."

The image of his enemy appeared larger than life on the massive screen. "Admiral Nguyễn and the people of Sol. I'm Ambassador Addae of the Galactic Alliance. I stand before you one last time with a message of hope and alliance. We're offering humanity a chance at protection from the rogue and splinter species of our alliance, in exchange for an open trade agreement."

Her wings unfurled, taking up the width of the camera. Her glowing green plumage radiated for all to see. The effect was spectacular, and judging by the response from the soldiers in his midst, they were in awe.

"While our specific interest lies in your superluminal abilities you've so painstakingly hidden from both us and your own people, we're prepared to exchange any and all technologies and goods to obtain it. If you agree to enter this agreement, we'll protect you at all costs."

"The feathered bitch can go to hell," he muttered.

The soldiers around him flinched and eyed him curiously. He wasn't known to make outbursts like that before.

"Think fast, Admiral. Our offer will not last forever."

The camera focusing on Ambassador Addae zoomed out and took in the view of collected aliens before cutting to dozens of written forms of the message. Most of Sol had yet to see many of these aliens. While their PR teams had purposely released clips from some of the more evil looking species, the people hadn't seen the full breadth of what the alliance contained.

Dozens upon dozens of species were assembled around the ambassador. While it was only a fraction of the alliance members he'd seen, it would still be impressive to most of humanity.

As he collected his thoughts, the security officer spoke, her voice cracking. "We're receiving a second broadcast, sir. It appears to be from the larger multi ring collection of ships."

"Frak!" He sighed. "Toss it up."

The screen to the left of the rotating wall of translations from the first broadcast came to life, replacing what was previously there with a second video. This one showed the face of a Thyreus alien and several other species flanking them. They were each holding ominous looking weapons aimed at the camera. Judging by the density and number of blue markings of the central Thyreusian, this wasn't Drak. It was someone far higher ranking.

"Humans of Sol! As a founding species of the former Galactic Alliance, you're in violation of its superluminal laws and are thereby in violation of ours, the Therion Collective. You will immediately cease all military efforts, and then you will turn over your armaments and technology to us. If you comply, your lives may be spared. Failure to do so will result in your death, which I assure you will be slow and agonizing. Not at all like that of your colonists on Liprosus." The antennae above the glowing neon blue alien twisted together in a wringing motion, almost like someone menacingly rubbing their hands together.

"While you may have managed to stall the tribunal over the past months, your time remaining will be far shorter. I suggest you gather your people and come to an expedient decision, Admiral. You have two weeks to pick your side before we advance on Earth."

The video cut out. Unlike the previous feed, no attempt was made to translate the broadcast.

"This is both an unfortunate and opportune turn of events," Harold said privately over his retinal comm.

Nguyễn was struggling to hold back his anger and to not lash out at the wall screen. He'd do anything to have the power to order an attack on these disgusting beasts. "How exactly is this opportune?"

"We have something they want, and they're both competing for it. One is threatening us and the other is promising riches and protection. Giving it up outright would be a mistake on both counts, but perhaps we can negotiate amicably."

He tried to imagine the type of deal it would take for the Galactic Alliance to stand down. The thought was appealing, though not at all in his control. Not yet, anyhow. He replied subvocally. "Are you suggesting we trade your magic drive?"

"I hate to burst your bubble, Admiral, but in her speech, Ambassador Addae never offered us amnesty. She only suggested we enter a trading agreement. Something tells me her motives are more around helping us win the battle but lose the war. No, we won't be trading our magic drive. I still believe we have the upper hand."

He closed his eyes, struggling to keep his cool. If he could strangle Harold, he would. "How the frak do you see an upper hand?"

"Deliver the Spános to Earth and the other agreed upon locations. I'll make it clearer after that." There was an audible click in his ear. Something he'd never heard before.

"Harold," he subvocalized, but there was no reply.

He pivoted right to face Rogers, who'd come down from the bridge. "Have we figured out where this A.I. is broadcasting from? I'm getting sick of him having access to my brain without consent."

Rogers shifted his weight uncomfortably. "Not exactly, sir. But Duval here has a theory." He gestured to the officer who was manning the security station when he'd arrived.

It wasn't until he shifted to face her that he noticed she was augmented. Her right eye wasn't biological. In fact, her entire right half appeared to be cybernetic. "Go on now." He waved his hand. "Out with it. What's your idea?"

Duval turned her cybernetic eye toward the ceiling. "Aren't you worried he'll hear us talking, sir?"

He sighed, the stress of the moment was weighing on him nearly as much as the uselessness of this conversation. "Harold's fraking everywhere. He probably already knows your theory. Come on. Shit on the pot or get off."

Private Duval visibly shook and came to attention. It was almost as if she hadn't realized who she'd been talking to. "I'm sorry, sir. My apologies. I believe Harold has infiltrated the very superstructure and walls of the Aitken and likely every other ship within the fleet, for that matter. When he's communicating with you, it's impossible to triangulate his location. I've been able to track the signal everywhere, except outside this or the other ships."

A chill passed through him. "How's that possible?"

She tilted her head, clearly confused by his words. "I'm not sure if I understand your question. With nanites, anything is possible. They can infiltrate at the molecular level, especially if our plating fabrication facilities have been compromised. Or the tooling we use for the skeletal build out. As far as we know, we could track it back any number of layers in the construction process. With enough time, he could have a mesh inside your body."

He swallowed hard. That would explain him having heard Harold aboard the tribunal ship. His body may have been infiltrated as early as his time on the Jurat. Suddenly, the realization hit him. They'd installed his retinal comm after his incarceration onboard that ship. How had he not seen it before? He needed to get another unit transplanted ASAP.

"Can we use an EMP to take it out?" Rogers asked.

Duval emitted a tiny laugh and then caught herself. Her face turned beet red when she recognized her mistake. "Sorry, sirs." She stared down at the ground. "No, we can't use an EMP. We'd destroy every centimeter of tech in our ship if we did. As far as we know, we'd be replacing it with the same problem. This demands a systematic review of each stage of construction of our military industrial complex to root it out, and even that seems improbable."

There was nothing they could do about Harold at the moment. They had bigger issues to take care of. "Where's the Spános?"

"Um… the robots are bringing it into the holding cells, sir. The Gamma squad has been shadowing the shipment the entire way."

"Good. Good." He reached up and rubbed his chin before turning to leave.

"Admiral, sir. What should we do about... the alien demands?" Rogers asked, seeming unsure if he should broach the topic.

He froze and stared at the wall of screens. The robots were lining the holding cells from floor to ceiling with crates of the material. They separated each softball size amount into a special meter by meter solid steel enclosure. One scientist had the bright idea and believed it made the ore safer to transport. Harold claimed otherwise, but it was too late now. They'd deal with removing the enclosures near Earth.

When he turned to face Rogers, he found several officers staring at him. He'd been in thought longer than he realized. "Recall the fleet to their respective planets and redirect a majority of the Inner Ring fleet to Earth. Tell them to layout in a Vivaldi sphere. They'll know what that means."

"The entire fleet, sir?" Duval fiddled with the Inner Ring insignia on her uniform. "Won't that leave the aliens unguarded?"

"We weren't guarding them so much as we were posturing. They may not have known it, but we did. Now they'll think our hand is even stronger if we withdraw our forces. It's a bluff, Private."

"And what of their demands?" Rogers asked again.

He glanced in the direction of Lieutenant Rogers. The officer was studying his response. "We say nothing. They'll need to wait. We have business on Earth. Besides, our A.I. friend assures me I'll be smitten once we touch down. I can make our formal response from there."

22

MINULA CLARKE
SOL, NEAR JUPITER

Her team had been lying in wait for weeks. They were floating around Jupiter while hidden within the debris in a junkyard, awaiting a signal from Harold for his plan to transpire. Minula had begun to doubt the entire enterprise until the signal arrived. It was a tight-beam encoded burst they'd agreed upon at the outset, and it'd been a single burst concealed among a million others the Aitken made every day.

Harold had told her he wasn't sure he could reach out to them without being detected aboard the Aitken. It was a matter of time before they discovered how he'd taken control of the ship, and in turn they'd have access to his programming. While he might not be able to hide his thoughts from Nguyễn forever, he said he could use their reality to encode the data he needed to share with Minula and her team. If she hadn't been looking for it, his message would be indistinguishable from countless others. Harold's vantage on the battle was one of only two footholds they'd obtained in the fleet, and without them, they'd be blind.

The beam had come yesterday, and they'd used every second since to prepare. She wasn't keen on taking the lives of her fellow soldiers, but there was no other way to get her colonist family what they needed to survive, what the Olivaws needed to survive.

Such was the road of any terrorist, she supposed. Her beliefs in their reality had to be stronger than those who opposed her. She only hoped their strength and preparation would afford them the time to cling to the life they were struggling to create.

She confirmed the approaching drive signature matched the ones Harold sent on. It was one of the new Blazer Hornets she'd heard about. That company had an unusual fixation on insects she'd never understood. They'd done anything they could to differentiate themselves from an Olivaw design. She had to hand it to them. It did look menacing. Its golden yellow exterior and forward facing railgun arrays could easily be mistaken for antenna. Add to that their weapons' mounts protruding from its hull, and you had wings. The hornet name really was a solid fit.

It appeared Nguyễn's lost faith in the Olivaws was now turning in their favor. Harold had unearthed design flaws in the Blazer networking systems, and they were about to take advantage of them. All that remained to be seen was if their operative had gotten Harold inside the hornet. Without him, or part of his programming to disable the drive and energy core, their mission would be over before it started.

The green throbbing dots of her pirate fleet floating within the scraps of the junk pile lit up her controls. Each of the five ships were powered down but still able to communicate every ten seconds in short, focused bursts.

Everyone was a go. They were awaiting her orders. It was imperative they began the assault before the power went out on the hornet. Military protocol dictated that any ship under attack broadcast their situation to the closest vessels. In this case, those were over an hour away.

This first stage of their assault was another crux of their success or failure. The problem with them having to strike before their enemy had lost power was that their survival came down to timing. They'd never know for certain if Harold had succeeded. The burst merely signaled the attempt had been made, not that it had been successful. If they attacked and he failed, their mission would abruptly end.

Her hands hovered tentatively over the button to initiate the assault, but she didn't press it. A tingle crawled down her arm to her finger. She wasn't sure why she was hesitating. All signs were a go, and their window of opportunity was passing with every second.

The markings on the hornet's hull seemed to be smiling at her, daring her to take it on. She realized it was an illusion brought on by the angle of their approach, but the streaks of dark brown striping on the exterior made it look like a grin. Like it knew something she didn't.

What if they'd been wrong? What if the recent change in formation of the Galactic Alliance fleet had been for the good? Maybe Nguyễn was planning on taking up Ambassador Addae on the offer she'd broadcast to all humanity. That would make their entire mission moot. Unnecessarily taking the lives of other humans wasn't something she needed on her conscience with a galactic war looming.

Are we sparky?

The crisp yellow glow of the message appeared along the bottom of her retinal comm. It was from her lead ship. The tip of their spear, if they had one. There were six lives onboard, one pilot and five marines in full exo-suits. They were armed and prepared to eject once they were within striking distance of the hornet.

She had to make the call and time was short. She wasn't sure if faith alone was enough to drive this decision. Twenty-nine soldiers masked as pirates were depending on her. While most of them had yet to visit any of the colony sites, if they survived today, they'd be returning with her to begin new lives.

As the hum of the air recyclers kicked up, the cool breeze of the aging ventilation system tickled her neck, spreading goosebumps in its wake. Their familiar tingle surfaced memories of the first time she'd met Abigail. She'd caught her eye queued in line at the academy when they were waiting for their class assignments. Her face reminded her of her mother. The round cheeks and short jaw framed her deep blue eyes. Their infinite shades of blue could go on forever. While she felt it at first sight, it was confirmed hours later after they'd actually spoken. She'd follow Abigail anywhere. Love had a strange way of leading people to make irrational decisions.

She reached forward and pressed the button, holding it down while speaking. "The hive is green, and the air is clear. Aim true."

They'd practiced this in virtual reality countless times. Each of the lead three ships fired a single railgun round on the trajectory of the Blazer frigate. If they hadn't known the exact acceleration parameters the ship would be on, their shots would miss, but their trail would still trigger evasive maneuvers from the advancing warship. What was done was done. Now all they could do was burn like hell and hope for the best.

Four seconds later, her ship and the other four in the formation lit up like Christmas trees. Her helmet came down over her head and the cold of the acceleration drugs pumped through her veins. To most, the g-forces slamming them back were fear inducing, but to her, it relaxed her being smothered into place. Their multitude of options and what ifs leading into a battle were squelched the moment the gravitational forces hit. All that remained was the path they'd chosen.

While their pirate vessels weren't modern attack ships by

any stretch of the imagination, they were highly modified. Each had a rail gun, a few banks of lasers, and several missile batteries. Enough to make them look like well-funded pirates, but not enough to raise suspicion. Safely ensconced in the rear two ship's cargo bays was a shuttle. A gate drive capable shuttle to be exact. They'd be useless if this went south, but if the power went out like they'd planned, then the crafts would be their tickets out of here.

Thirty seconds into their burn and her comm panel lit up. She tweaked the controls on the arm of her chair and brought up the message. It was from the Provespa, the frigate they were advancing on.

Unknown vessels off our port side, you're approaching the Provespa, an Inner Ring military envoy ship. You have sixty seconds to adjust course, or you will be fired upon. This is your first and last warning.

She hit the broadcast button and played their doctored and prerecorded response. "Inner Ring cruiser. You've entered a quadrant of space controlled by the One Ring Military. Long live Admiral Doyle!" An aged female pirate persona raised her fist skyward. "Disengage your drives and prepare to be boarded. Our demand for your safe passage is half your supplies and armaments. Failure to submit to these demands will result in your slow and painful death."

The comm cut, and the countdown continued. She adjusted her long range scopes, bringing them to bear on the frigate. They still had twenty seconds until the rail guns were supposed to hit.

Judging from the reaction of the Provespa, their commander was by the book. A few seconds after their warning, they broadcast a micro comm burst on military frequencies. It likely contained details of their encounter, along with a request for assistance. Then the hornet fired a battery of lasers aimed squarely at her and her advancing team.

Holes blasted through their hulls as the massive beams targeted the outer edges of her ships. Based on the models of her aged ship's hull signatures, the Provespa was shaping their laser beams in an attempted breach of as much of their surface area as possible. They were hoping to eject their oxygen and force them to retreat.

Once they realized no oxygen was ejecting, they'd escalate their assault to rail guns. Until then, her advancing ships fired off a second barrage of their own deadly projectiles. The first of which was about to hit home.

She studied her display and watched as the numbers neared their goal. Five, four, three, two, one... zero. Two massive explosions of orange and white strobed across the front of the Provespa. The light was promptly extinguished, but in its wake she could just make out holes in the hull.

Their estimates had been off, but not by much. It was likely due to her having thrown off the timing and the small adjustments their pilot had made to align to fire on her ships. Either way, it didn't matter. The next few minutes would make or break the entire mission.

Her ships couldn't risk firing any additional shots. One unexpected laser round, and both they and their target were toast. Spános wasn't the most stable of all the elements in the universe, and they weren't about to test whether superheated lasers set it off.

When she ran another active scan of the ship, her stomach dropped. They still had full power, and apparently her team had reached the same conclusion.

Are we red or green?

The message seemed to throb on her retina comm. The letters, like the last, were presented the same. But these had deeper implications. Did they continue on a path likely to end in death, or did they turn and hope to escape? If they timed it right, they still might be able to turn tail and run, rendezvousing behind the junkyard and piling into the shuttles.

The question appeared again, this time from all four ships.

Are we red or green? We need to know.

She took a deep breath and squinted at the screen, hoping for even the tiniest hint that something more was going on inside the Provespa. That Harold had managed to shut down their power.

And then it happened. Her sign. Two of her lead ships at the front of the formation exploded in a ball of light.

She slammed her controls to the right and peeled off the group, exposing her port side to an attack that didn't come. Not immediately, anyhow. The g-forces were intense, and the patchwork ship groaned the entire way. It was a miracle it hadn't torn in half after being sliced open.

While they'd managed to veer away in time, their fourth ship in formation had taken significant damage. It was one of two ships that contained an escape shuttle. They were still on course, but the pilot had lost three of her five marines. Debris from their exploding ships had shot through what remained of their hull and killed her people in an instant.

"Status?" she subvocalized, and broadcast the question. She needed to know. There might be time to turn. The first of the two remaining ships reported in a moment later.

All systems green.

She took a breath and waited for the second to reply. There was a slight delay, but it arrived soon thereafter.

We're yellow… but fired up.

From the details they'd sent along, the second shuttle was still intact. They could make it. Maybe not take the frigate, but they could escape.

As she punched in the command to retreat, her control panel flashed.

"No, no," she muttered. "Now's not the time for games, baby." She reached forward and rubbed her control panel. She couldn't afford a system's failure. Not now. And then it happened again. It flashed. Not once, but twice this time, and then again three times. "What the hell?"

Her fingers hovered over the send button when her panel flashed four times in unison. Whoever was doing this, they were trying to get her attention. The problem was, she didn't know how they were pulling it off or what they were saying.

She'd forgotten about their second barrage of rail gun rounds. With her mouth still open in awe over her controls being on the fritz, she watched as the second round of shots ripped through the side of the Provespa, exposing its innards to the vacuum of space.

Their shot formation was tight, and their results were devastating. Not only were there prolonged sparks and explosions from inside the ship, but according to her controls, the entire ship had powered down. They'd either gotten lucky, or Harold had done his job.

Orders?

The message flashed on her comm. Even though it was happening in seconds, to her, it was an eternity.

Minula froze, trying to run the numbers in her head. Operating a mission like this with thirty soldiers was already cutting it close. Running it with even a dozen elite operatives could only lead to certain death.

The alternatives were equally daunting. They'd lose Liprosus and Epsilon Eridani, miss the Beacon, and would likely need to submit to the GA here in Sol. While their death at the hands of the aliens wasn't guaranteed, it might as well be. She knew what they'd done at Lupus. Their fate would be the same if they failed.

Her hand shook as she squeezed the edges of the control panel in a failed attempt at calming her nerves. They were in too deep to back down. Harold had done his part. She had to trust that. Everything they'd worked for was now up to her and her team.

We're a go.

Like their opening salvo had cleared away their options, sending this message had done the same. Seconds later, all three of her ships were on an intercept course with the Provespa.

MINULA'S BREATHING WAS NORMAL, but the thump of her heart was like a bass drum in her head. Every second since they'd approached the Provespa had been excruciating.

She'd expected the ship to power up at any moment and blow them out of existence, but that didn't happen. It was as quiet now as it was in the seconds following their rail gun attack. She could see the confidence on the face of her crew as they came to the same conclusion as she did. Harold had come through.

They knew the design of this ship backward and forward, having been assured by their operative that Nguyễn would choose this frigate over the Olivaw equivalent. On the port side, they'd chosen to enter the warship through the remnants of the hull breach. If there were crew members still alive, they'd likely be hunkered down and defending the normal points of entry. They also had the added advantage of being on the far side of any known military outposts that might be watching them. That was one of the compelling reasons they decided on the junkyard as their point of attack.

Minula raised her hand and counted down from five. Hitting zero, she motioned for her team to advance. They each tossed a few small cube drones out and into the hole in the side of the ship. Tiny jets of air propelled each robot inside and sent secure streams of data back to their suits. From the looks of the images, the initial scans showed the coast was clear.

Two by two they entered the breach. Each group covered the other as they slowly made their way through a maze of floating wires and the remains of broken equipment.

Ten meters in, they hit the central axis of the ship. They'd gotten lucky. Far luckier than she could have imagined. Their rail gun rounds had pierced the primary artery of the Provespa, leaving anyone not in at least a full environmental suit exposed and dead. While they hadn't come across any bodies yet, that soon changed as they floated toward security.

Passing past the crew quarters, they used their exo-suits to pry open the rest of the nearly closed emergency doors.

Their drones were too big to fit through the gap, but it had been there nonetheless. It was enough space to allow the oxygen inside to escape outward.

Whatever Harold had done, he'd somehow managed to cut the power part of the way through them sealing off the ship. They'd been caught with their pants down, and the consequence was floating in front of them.

Bodies filled the crew space. Many of them were half dressed or clothed but missing their helmets. Their faces were pearly white and partially covered in the frost from the moisture escaping their last breaths.

She and her team had seen it countless times. Surviving real ops like this had been a perquisite to joining. They couldn't afford to have someone lose their lunch in the middle of a mission this important.

Her team was fluid and thus far hadn't hit resistance of any kind. Their target was another twenty meters down ship. Harold's intel said that each ship was transferring the Spános in holding cells, believing the added plating and security measures would help protect them. She assumed that meant from the outside because any explosions from the inside would render the layers of protection moot. The power packed in this ore was beyond anything she'd ever imagined possible, and while it was only on paper, she wasn't keen on testing the data they'd uncovered to find the truth.

Once they'd opened the doorway, their preliminary scans found twenty soldiers in the crew quarters and a dozen more were discovered floating up ship from where they and their drones had entered. While they hadn't approached the bridge, they positioned a drone outside. The entrance was sealed, and she had two guards flanking the hall nearby that she'd flagged as Zeta. Their scans were showing six heat signatures inside, but none of them appeared to be moving or acting as if they had anything more than standard issue environmental suits on.

When they reached security, they spread out, flanking each side of the door. She took the lead and floated up to where the handle should be. Her suit highlighted a set of circular scratches on the wall beside the door. From the pattern, it seemed like someone had cranked it closed manually. Given they hadn't seen anyone yet, that meant only one thing. They weren't alone.

"Eyes peeled," she subvocalized. "Someone's been here, and they sealed the door. Let's smoke 'em out before we take security."

They split off into two groups of five, Alpha and Omega, each floating in another direction. She held up the rear of the Alpha group, watching the videos from both teams. Part of her knew she should trust them to do their job. The other part needed to watch to ensure nothing was missed.

One by one, they checked off the rooms until her Alpha team hit the engine room. It was sealed off from the inside. They didn't need to breach it. Their thermal scans were useless with the reactor still cooling down, so instead she instructed one of her soldiers to secure the egress. A moment later, he placed the hand of his exo-suit against the door and a small enclosure sprung out and around the surface, making his hand into a sort of suction cup. His circular cup was creating a seal against the surface under which a welding arc was igniting.

As the soldier slid his hand up the door to the next position, the shiny results of the newly welded metal sparkled in the lamps of their suit. After they'd laid another four welds, they turned and made their way back to security.

With the rear half of the ship secured, she instructed her suit to follow the soldier in front of her as she studied the videos still coming in from the Omega team. Their pass of the ship was nearly complete, with only the galley remaining.

She watched her display as Omega approached the partially closed door. Like the others, it appeared to have stopped just prior to sealing. The two forward soldiers floated sideways toward the ceiling and floor, magnetized themselves to the walls, and then crouched down, sliding their hands into the cracked entranceway.

The leader of the team counted down, and when he hit zero, they both squatted up with all the might of their exo-suits, forcing the two emergency doors open. A second later, all hell broke loose.

Two beams of light shot forward, cutting her soldiers in half and leaving the other three scrambling for cover. The drone near the far wall caught the whole scene, including the soldiers floating remains squirting globules of blood from the partly cauterized wounds. The hallway rapidly turned into a minefield of gore.

As she floated in space behind her Alpha unit, Minula watched two Inner Ring exo-suits float through the bloody remnants of the Omega team. "Two bogies inbound at Omega. I'll take up defense positions with the Alphas."

She tagged two other soldiers on her retinal comm, refusing to use names in the midst of battle. It made dealing with the possibility of sending someone to their death far easier. "Betas, you move forward and assist Omega. Deploy countermeasures en route."

Without questioning her orders, the team sprang into action. As the soldiers worked their way down the central axis, they deployed charges in several cavities along the wall. If the bogies managed to make it past, they'd have a gift waiting for them.

"Orders, sir," the soldiers she'd flagged as Zeta asked. They were the ones still covering the bridge.

"Hold your position. They could be hiding anything up there, and you're our only defense if they are. Deploy countermeasures around the exit vectors."

"Roger that." The two guards mimicked the Beta team and deployed their countermeasures as instructed.

Her remaining three soldiers in the Omega team took up a defensive position. They'd been cornered in what looked like a medical bay. They cut their lights and spread out as much as possible in the tiny space. One was laying flat against the ceiling, one was on the floor, and the final was squatting low in the far corner, just behind an examination bed.

The signals she was receiving were only achievable because the drones they'd deployed earlier were randomizing broadcasts on all frequencies. In battle, the robotic spies broke into smaller versions of themselves and provided frequency cover to troops. While they were still finite, their broadcast hot spots were now up to forty relays. This made it nearly impossible for anyone nearby to differentiate their signals from those of her soldiers or to determine an accurate position.

A further use of the drones was triangulating the enemy's position. For some reason, they almost always felt a need to take out the pesky drones. Even with partial stealth coatings, the attacker gave away their location with each signal they squelched. And these two were no different. One after another, their drones went dark.

Within a minute, the path the Inner Ring soldiers were taking became clear. They were advancing down the hall and were about to enter the central axis of the ship, heading toward Alpha's position. They'd probably figured out the pirates weren't here for the supplies by now. Instead, they were after something far more important.

"Keep your eyes open, Alpha," she said. "Beta, find cover! Bogies inbound. Make sure you get out of the blast radius of our countermeasures." Minula and her team each floated into different corners of the ceiling and floor without speaking. They'd trained enough times together to practically read each other's thoughts.

When she was flat to the wall, she had an unobstructed view of where the approaching pair should be entering the shaft. According to their triangulation, they'd be coming around the corner at any moment. They each aimed their rifles high, medium, and low, to cover all the exit points.

But the soldiers never appeared. They must have missed something. The drones weren't picking up any motion, but nothing came into view. That meant only one thing. "They're holding position and waiting for us to come to them. We're blind in the hall. Any ideas on flushing them out?"

There was a long silence before the Omega team chimed in. "We'll smoke them out on our side and push 'em at you, sir."

"Roger that. Let us know their vectors if you can, and we'll be ready." She adjusted her comms to only her remaining Alpha team. "Let's move up some. Make sure to stay behind the charges."

They each released from their wall position and slid forward a few meters to the adjacent bulkhead. It offered a better line of sight and additional protection.

She studied the Omega team's video as they used hand gestures to coordinate their assault. Within seconds, they were ready, and the first soldier pushed off. One after another, they were planning on floating across the entrance to the hall where the Inner Ring soldiers were hiding out. When they hit the open, they'd take their shots.

Like them, the exo-suited soldiers took positions high and low. But unlike her teams, they could only have one trained forward and the other back. The enemy soldier facing backward had been aiming low and squeezed off their first shot. He hit the Omega soldier floating past in the right shoulder, causing him to spin on axis. By the time the Omega soldier spun around and aimed his rifle to finally take a shot, the enemy had taken aim and fired again, hitting him square in the face.

Minula winced as the soldier's helmet exploded in a cloud of gray matter and blood. The camera went red just before it cut out. Omega team's next in line wasn't delaying, but instead of sliding straight across the gap, he'd decided on an alternate, less conventional route. She watched as he shifted from floor to ceiling and then realigned once more toward the floor at a steep approach angle through the midpoint. From his angle of attack, he was planning to cross the opening and then push upward again. It was risky, but even she wasn't expecting it.

As he pushed off, she spotted something in front of her. The fringe of a suit was visible at the very edge of the entrance to the shaft. She froze. It wasn't merely fabric; it was the dark composite in the shape of a foot. They'd inverted their position. The soldier to her right was training her weapon on the foot until she raised her arm, waving for them to stop.

"They changed direction!" she shouted over the comms. "Aim low!"

The second soldier of Omega was already making their approach, but from the looks of her rifle, she was adjusting her target low. Minula hoped she'd made the right call. She'd know in the next few seconds.

It wasn't until they were crossing over the entrance that she noticed the third Omega soldier had pushed off after the second, but they were heading on a much faster vector. They were going all in on the intel together.

They both crossed over at the same time and had their rifles trained low, at the most likely position of the awaiting soldier's head. All three shots went off in unison. The enemy soldier had aimed at the middle of the hall, guessing they'd change up their angle of approach. They certainly had, but he'd bet wrong.

His head exploded not once, but twice in a shroud of red splatter in all directions. While exo-suits had ample protection over most of their body, the head had always been a weak point. Only when they were in full exo-battle suit did the helmet melt away into their shoulders for the added armor necessary for a ground assault. The bulky battle suits had no place inside the tight confines of a spaceship.

When the two Omega team members hit their midpoint, they'd been aiming at the low wall and not the floor. Rather than continuing forward down the hall, they squatted down and pushed off, heading straight at the other soldier. They were covered in the blood of their friend and had vengeance to deliver.

The second exo-suited figure struggled to flip over, but they were too late. With two of her Omegas trained on them, they made short work of the flailing blob of red. Two more shots and their battle was over.

The two soldiers floated across the central axis from her vantage and flipped about, coming to rest against the wall with a clang only audible over their comm. They had both engaged their magnetic boots.

"Beta," she began, "join Omega and clear out that galley. I want to make sure there aren't any other bogies nearby. Zeta, weld the bridge closed. We won't have time to question the crew, and the last thing we need is another interruption. Alpha, converge on the target and prepare to take the prize. The clock is ticking, folks. Move it!"

From the headcount and heat signatures they'd seen earlier, there shouldn't be anyone left midship. Most of the crews on ships matching this design ran with two soldiers in engineering, which would bring the count to around what they'd tallied up.

The good news was that they weren't expecting anyone defending the Spános. The bad news was they had twenty-six minutes to exit stage left before an approaching frigate would be within range to take shots at their ships.

Omega team cleared the galley in under two minutes, and

Alpha broke the seal on security in just as long. Once cracked, the door slid aside and a lone panel inside glowed to life.

Minula pushed off alone and entered the darkened room, taking aim at the darkness until her lidar mapped the space. The coast was clear. She flipped slightly and then burst a small jet of air to adjust her course to land in front of the panel.

As she came down, a message was waiting for her on the display.

The prize is inside the cubes. Crack 'em open and withdraw the payload. It'll be far easier to move, and the shell was only for protection from your assault. I convinced the idiots to do it, thinking it was protecting them. Be sure to take this data dot before you depart. I'll wipe records of my existence when you press eject. — H

She chuckled and shook her head. Even at a time like this, the A.I. had a sense of humor. "Alright, let's move! Move! Crack these bricks open. The Spános is inside. We've got twenty minutes to make like a tree and leave!"

SIXTEEN LIVES LOST for a few dozen crates full of glowing dirt. The entire mission was surreal looking back at it.

Each time her soldiers had emptied one of the cubes, the color of the ore changed. Some morphed red, still others blue or yellow. When the same soldier emptied another cube, their color seemed to follow them to the next. Minula had never seen anything like it before. At least not outside a virtual world.

While the light show had been spectacular to watch, she

was stuck processing whether the loss of so many lives was worth it. They'd barely escaped the belly of their pirate ships. The approaching frigate turned out to be a pair, and fortunately for them, they didn't have a clear line of sight to open fire. Her team was running behind schedule and had dead to clean-up along with bootie to transport. Doing the entire thing without robots had taken significantly more time than she'd expected, though moving those cubes would've been far worse.

After all was said and done, Harold instructed them to initiate a gate jump from inside the ship. They didn't need to open the hold and get a safe distance. She called bullshit at first. Everyone who'd been around these things knew gravity would frak with any gate transition, but Harold assured her Jupiter's gravity was a far larger gravitational well than anything this puny ship could provide. They simply needed to get away from here. After that first jump, they could make smaller quick hops to put more distance between them and Sol.

She was too numb to fight him, having collapsed into the pilot chair in exhaustion. Her entire crew was tired, for that matter. They'd each gone through the motions to mentally prepare for a jump, just as she had countless times before. All but Minula were gate jump virgins, so they didn't know what to expect, only what they'd been told. What they knew for certain was that death was lurking nearby and drawing closer by the second.

It wasn't until after they carried out multiple jumps that her team broke out into a cheer. It'd finally sunk in that they'd made it. They'd escaped. While they were short sixteen members of the team, they achieved their goals and were bringing home what they'd been sent out to secure.

They were carrying hope. One of the last threads of hope humanity could still tug on and not come up empty.

Sixteen dead. She'd repeated the number countless times

over the last week during their return flight. Each of their faces reminded her of the cost of this war and kept her from a single night's sleep. The number echoed in her mind as her ship clanged loudly, shaking her out of her funk.

Their landing gear had been damaged in the attack, something they hadn't realized until they'd gated away. The shuttle rocked violently for a moment until it leveled off and raised off the ground.

"Sorry about that," Harold said over her retinal comm. "I misjudged the mass with the Spános inside and my robots weren't prepared. We may have crushed a few of them just now."

She grunted with little else to say. No one gave a frak about a few demolished bots. It was her soldiers she cared about. They were alive. Or at least they used to be.

As she sat motionless, the sound of the rear loading platform cracking open and her crew spilling out filled the once quiet ship. They were cheering, their voices echoing through the massive spaceport. It wasn't until they'd stopped hooting and hollering that she heard the footsteps approach her from behind and a hand rest on her shoulder.

"You did it, Min. You saved us." Abigail squeezed her, but there was no response. "Are you ok?"

She nodded and sank a bit lower into her seat. It was finally hitting her they'd survived. She hadn't expected Abigail to greet them. A part of her figured she'd be off with Lync, saving the universe.

Abigail stepped beside her, into the neighboring seat, keeping her hand rested on her shoulder. "Min, look at me."

She couldn't. She wouldn't. It was too much to deal with. She was spent and had nothing left to give. What she needed was...

Abigail slid out of her chair and engulfed her with her arms, pulling her close and squeezing tight. "It's ok to be sad, to be pissed at the universe. I know exactly what you're feeling."

"No, you don't," she muttered, pushing her fists against her chest.

She didn't pull away; she pulled her closer against the pressure. Her hand rubbed through Minula's hair, like they used to do when they'd stay up all night chit-chatting. The last time they'd done that was on Luna. That seemed so long ago. Like another world.

"You're feeling empty," Abigail began. "Like you failed everyone. Like you failed your soldiers. Failed to protect them. Failed to keep them out of harm's way." She gently rocked from side to side and continued rubbing Minula's hair. "The first time I felt that way was after I'd learned about what the Norths had done near Jupiter, stealing planetesimals from the Ulixi. The second was when I saw the images of the outbreak on Liprosus. And the third and worst was when the Galactic Alliance destroyed the colony. In hindsight, it was remarkable I kept it together at all. I could have done more. I should have done more."

Minula rubbed at her face, willing the tears to stay at bay. "You did the best you could, sir."

"Min," Abigail whispered, bending down and peering up into her eyes. "It's me, Abs. I'm not your president right now. I'm your friend. Your best friend, damn it." She smiled, and her blue eyes sparkled. A second later, it faded as fast as it came. "You've always been there for me, countless times. And while I may have failed to tell you what it meant to me in the past, I will not fail you again. I'm here. I won't leave your side." She stared for a moment and then pulled her close again, squeezing her tight.

Finally, she broke down. All the frustration, doubt, and sadness came flooding out. She'd always been able to control her emotions in the past. Hell, some people had accused her of being robotic, but something changed this time. She didn't know why, but this mission felt different. Like she'd spent all of her reserves.

As her body shook and the tears flowed, Abigail pulled her tighter and whispered in her ear. "You're fine," she said. "Everything's gonna be ok."

Minula hoped she was right, because the pain was unbearable.

23

JOYCE GREEN
EPSILON ERIDANI, LIPROSUS

Her exo-suit was powered up and ready to rock, as were the rest of the forces. They were ten kilometers from the projected impact site and had come as close to the surface as they could without risking detection.

When she stared out the mouth of the cave, she could just make out the wispy tendrils of green and orange layering the new day sky. Whatever this rock had in store for them, it'd be touching down in less than two minutes.

"I'm sharing the eastern view from our surface eyes," Ryder said over the group comm.

A small window popped up on her retinal comm. It was a viewpoint of the asteroid that showed it flying low to the ground as it entered the far eastern edge of Liprosus. The camera was inside some sort of robotic bird. She could just make out the yellow orange feathers at the edges of its vision, the perfect color combination to blend in with the native rock formations.

As she watched the enlarging black dot, her body tensed up. Maybe it was her, but it seemed to be headed straight toward them.

"Are we confident of our position?" Joyce asked over a

private channel. "That thing looks like..." She closed her eyes and didn't finish the sentence.

She reached out and grasped the handle to her side in an attempt to prepare for the incoming collision. There was no way this would not hit them. Maybe Harold had been off in his calculations. Maybe this was what he'd been trying to do the entire time. Get her and the other members of the colony leadership out and away from the Archégonos site. It could've been him or the Galactic Alliance.

"Its course is true and on our revised path of orbital insertion. Prepare for impact," Harold said.

His voice made the hairs on her neck stand up straight. When she opened her eyes, the darkness was looming even larger, filling up nearly the entire field of view. As she blinked to adjust the camera angle, she zoomed in for a closer look.

Maybe she was imagining it, but there appeared to be jets of steam or something streaming out the bottom edge of the asteroid. The temperature change of the massive rock entering the atmosphere could have released even more ejecta, but these seemed different. Almost precise in their flow and bursts.

"Are we seeing any calving?" Joyce asked.

"Not yet," Ryder began. "It seems to be staying in one piece. Like I said before, our asteroid guest is built solid. If any rock was ever going to stay together, this would be it. Had it been a few times larger, or traveling faster, we'd all be done for."

Not the image she needed eating at her confidence before impact. She had had to fight General Hui to be allowed out here.

She flipped the camera back to the wide field of view. Either Harold and Ryder were wrong, or this camera was distorting the shit out of the image. The asteroid was coming in shallow and the bottom edge was glowing red. Those same bursts of ejecta or gas she'd seen earlier were still constantly erupting.

"Is it me," Joyce began, "or are those geysers evenly spaced around the perimeter of that rock?"

A few seconds passed as the asteroid grew larger before anyone chimed in. It was Ryder who she heard first. "While not even, they are conveniently located at optimal points of control. Their constant rate of thrust is definitely having an impact, it's minimal, but it's helping slow it down nonetheless."

She squinted at the image. "Are they visible from space?"

"I wouldn't think so," Harold said. "The upper half isn't exhibiting any of these eruptions, and these aren't noticeable anywhere except from the ground."

"Convenient," she muttered.

When the camera view darkened, she zoomed out. Suddenly, her suit flashed a warning, drawing her attention to the excessive force she was applying to her handles. She was going to break them off if she wasn't careful. This suit took some getting used to, and despite her hours of training, it still wasn't enough.

A moment later the asteroid blotted out the rising sun in the east, and the camera fell dark. She adjusted the display to switch to infrared and lidar and the image burst forth again, in an angry red-hot field of view. The heat and ejecta of the asteroid covered the entire field of view. There was no way this wasn't going to hit.

What the hell was she thinking being out here? Like her mining mission underground, she was ill prepared for the stakes of this game. As she closed her eyes, she muttered to herself. "I love you, Paul. I hope I don't see you soon, but if I do—"

"Prepare for impact," Harold interrupted.

The ground lurched, and the stingray buckled like a wild

robot bronco. The entire cargo hold full of exo-suited soldiers screamed.

A few of the suits in front of her had broken or failed to grasp their rails, and their magnetic boots weren't sufficient to immobilize them. As their suited forms tumbled toward her, she tucked closer to the wall and released her right hand, reaching out and locking it into place.

The suit across from her did the same but opposite motion as the tumbling bodies approached and collided with them. She instructed her power assisted arm to grab any part of the passing soldier to slow it down before they took anyone out.

Her body smashed into the wall as the colliding form crushed against her, while her hand struggled to find a suitable hold. As the augmented human shape scraped across her suit, she found a nook on their back. Her power assisted glove clasped around the head of the harpoon they'd used to anchor themselves into the rock faces underwater. It was the perfect handle, as it had been designed to withstand impossible forces. If only she could maintain a grip.

All the warning alarms in her suit were blaring. She had structural integrity alerts, a breached chest plate, and her grip was failing. It wasn't until the soldier behind her reached forward and stabilized the other end of the rag doll falling body that her suit alarms relented.

And it wasn't a moment too soon because the previously airborne stingray flopped back down into the nearby water and gravity brought the full cargo hold downward, crashing to the ground. The entire motion happened in the blink of an eye, and it wasn't until they stopped rocking that she noticed her suit had jacked her up on stimulants.

That explained her ability to slow the entire event down and act in the midst of the chaos. This was the second time she'd experienced their effects and found them eerily appealing. Being at the tip of the spear was far more interesting than sitting back and watching from a distance.

"Status report," she screamed as the secondary and tertiary after shocks rippled through the cavern. While they were less damaging than the first, rocks were tearing and pelting against the exterior of the stingray.

Harold assured them they couldn't be on the surface and that these were the most stable pockets in the nearby mountains. But that didn't set her mind at ease. Hearing the potential crushing sounds of rock repeatedly colliding with your ship, mere meters away, gave someone a new perspective on life.

Despite her desire to see her son again, she wanted to live. She had far more retribution to deal out to these aliens, and death was not an option.

"Our hull is breached in sections seven and eight, but we're otherwise fine," the pilot said. "We've dispatched repair bots. I'm seeing one loss of life and a half dozen wounded, but the remaining forces are stable, sir. A bit shaken, but stable."

A wave of sadness passed over her. Even a single life lost was a steep price to pay for a crashing rock.

She took a deep breath and double-checked her suit. Everything except her breached chest plate was green or yellow. Fortunately, her nanites were reporting that she was healthy, not that she'd be able to tell hopped up on stimulants. Her system was operational and already in repair mode. "What's the status on our path out of here? How far away was the impact?"

Her retinal comm lit up with the response. From the looks of it, it was from an orbiting micro-sat. Harold must have determined it was safe to tight beam the details after the rock touched down.

What she was looking at was curious. There appeared to be two craters, one well after the other. "Ryder, I thought you said it wouldn't calve."

"It shouldn't have," Ryder said. "There weren't any

detectable fractures in the surface when we scanned it. Maybe the entry through the atmosphere caused it."

"I don't think so," Harold said. "Check this out."

A slow motion playback of the asteroid's impact appeared on her retinal comm. She wasn't sure what she was looking for until it happened. Explosions synchronized all along the lower quarter of the asteroid. It looked like someone sliced off the bottom chunk, sending it careening downward. At the same time, the upward force of the explosion pushed the top much larger chunk on an even shallower trajectory.

She grasped the handle she'd released earlier as the stingray began moving. "Tell me that wasn't visible from orbit."

"Our micro-sat didn't pick it up," Harold said. "All those charges were directed downward. If the GA has any ground-based observations, they'll be scrambling intercept forces. I suggest we re-route our teams deeper into the planet and await our first penetrating scans of the impact sites."

They hadn't planned for two impacts. Separating into groups of two was the only option unless they explored each site one after another.

Her gut was telling her they had limited time, so splitting up made the most sense. "Alpha and Bravo company, you handle impact one. Gamma and Theta will cover impact two. Let's drop well below the mantle and wait on a go from our eyes in the sky."

She hadn't even checked on the status of the other teams, but based upon their acknowledgments, they were alive and well. When she reviewed their numbers, there was a similar level of casualties as her Gamma company. No one had left this mission unscathed. This had better be worth the lives and effort they'd expended.

As the stingray tilted into a dive through the tunnel system, her stomach did a somersault until the gravitational dampeners kicked in. They'd shut the units off earlier to reduce their probability of being detected, but with all the wounded and shaken up soldiers, it was better to turn them back on. Besides, their detection would likely be hampered after a crash like that with all the debris in the atmosphere.

With the dive well under way, she brought up the live feed of the post impact trauma. The visuals may not last long with all the variables at play.

There on her comm were the two impacts. They resembled a stone skipping along the surface of a pond. First one and then another, with the second leaving a long valley torn through the Liprosus soil. Steaming entrails were rising from the warm ground as it met the cool air above.

The entire effect was otherworldly, which was remarkable considering where they were. Everything about today felt strange. Like she was living in a science fiction vid-sim.

"ETA twenty minutes to our holding zone," the pilot said over the ship wide comm.

The next few hours couldn't pass fast enough.

———

THEY WAITED LONG ENOUGH for the passive scans of the system to return before moving on to the impact sites. While none of the scans showed the Selene ships dispatching observation teams, Joyce wasn't about to tempt fate and get caught in the act. They had to move fast and take advantage of their proximity to the ground zero locations.

Both teams kept radio silence for the remainder of the mission. Neither would know the destiny of the other until they returned to Archégonos or came upon a data dump along the return route.

Her team had managed to find stable tunnels to within a few klicks of site two. They'd spent the better part of the last hour using their directed seismic and gravitational wave excavation tools to clear a safe route toward the surface.

It was slower than she'd hoped. They were being cautious and made certain they could always go back the direction they'd come but not necessarily in a straight line. This meant ensuring the path remained free of debris and the excavated material was flushed well down the water tunnels. They'd need to be careful on their return trip, making sure they hadn't built any dead ends from the detritus.

As they breached where the surface used to be, the temperatures of the asteroid rock above lit up the display in front of her. The red and yellow temperature variations painted the wall screen. The onrush of water boiled instantly into gas as it collided from the tunnel they were climbing through.

After she grew tired of waiting in the hold, she stripped out of her suit and worked her way to the bridge. She made sure to keep her mouth shut most of the time. Getting in the way like on her first ride on the bridge wasn't something she was keen on repeating.

She watched the gases from the superheated water build up and explode. The molten metals from the asteroid mixing with the water resulted in a dangerous mixture. The pilots of the Gamma and Theta stingrays backed down the shaft, using their gravitational beams to pull any debris down and out of the tunnel.

After what seemed like an eternity of waiting, they crawled forward, being overly cautious. The last thing they wanted was to be caught in a cave-in at this point.

When they reached the end of the shaft, they froze their advance. There was motion up ahead as vibrations from deep within the asteroid activated their sensitive seismic sensors. They were recording highly directional wavelengths, much like their own tools.

"Arming forward torpedoes," the security officer said.

"Preparing for evasive maneuvers," the pilot said.

Joyce stood up and stepped beside the security console,

making sure her feet were firmly locked in place. "Everyone, take it easy. Don't make any rash decisions. Whatever's in there could be on our side."

Suddenly, the vibrations stopped, and the water went still. A moment later, they detected a far smaller pulse. One that barely measured a centimeter in diameter but with highly focused energy. Whoever was inside that thing was snaking out.

"Do we have a depth measurement on that vibration?" she asked.

"It started about thirty meters in and is currently about three meters from the surface," the security officer said. Their hands were hovering over the button to launch the torpedoes.

She hoped it wouldn't come to that.

As they watched whatever was inside emerge, a small trail of particles floated downward into the beams of light from their stingray ships.

She took a breath. "Everyone steady. Are we detecting any nanites or foreign particulates in the water?"

"Nothing out of the ordinary from a hunk of metal like this, but it'd be easy to mask nanites among all this metallic debris," the security officer said.

That wasn't reassuring in the least.

The comms panel lit up and the officer spoke. "I'm… picking up a signal, sir. We're being… hailed."

She straightened up. "On what frequencies?"

"It appears to be a tight beam frequency. The same one we used to transmit to our sister base in the Oort Cloud before it was destroyed."

The knot in her stomach tightened. It was either about to get messy down here, or their wishes had been met.

"Put them on."

Two smiling human faces appeared on the wall screen. One of them looked vaguely familiar.

"Hey Joyce," Bradley Olivaw said. "Any chance you

received our reservations for twenty? We seem to have missed your reply in transit and are itching to crack out of this Trojan asteroid."

The bridge erupted in cheers, and a chuckle escaped from the growing smile on her face.

"Gamma and Theta teams, stand down!" she said. "We have eyes on friendlies. I repeat, we have eyes on friendlies."

24

BRADLEY OLIVAW
EPSILON ERIDANI, LIPROSUS

He'd never seen so many moons in the sky before. After being cooped up for so long inside that rock, Bradley needed to get out. The sun was setting on the horizon, and each of the moons were in different phases of their transition. The effect was stunning.

It'd never occurred to him how accustomed he'd become to the outdoors. Having grown up in space habitats with summers on Earth, he wouldn't have pegged himself as a gravity well person. But being locked in those tiny quarters for so long had pushed his limits.

On the Lupus Dark Nebula mission, their longest leg without a spacewalk or some form of movement had been the segments traveling there and back. Otherwise, they'd explored power relays, space stations, giant horns of blasting, and alien worlds.

He took a deep breath of the moist air and exhaled. His exhalation billowed outward in a faint cloud as it warmed the cool night. It reminded him of the tent camping they'd done as a family when he was a kid. Those were simpler days, for sure.

As the Epsilon Eridani sun crept below the horizon, a voice spoke out in the distance, startling him.

"You shouldn't be out here too long," Joyce said. "We don't know if they can detect us. Or if they give a shit for that matter."

He chuckled. He'd heard she was direct and to the point. "I think I'm covered." He rubbed the shell of the jacket he was wearing. "Heat dampening fibers courtesy of the Olivaw International military division."

"Ahh yes, I almost forgot." She walked up beside him and sat down. "Being an Olivaw must be nice. It comes with privileges like eternal life and as many get out of jail free cards as you want."

An exhale escaped from his mouth, like she'd punched him with her words. He didn't come all the way across the galaxy for this shit.

"If you have a fraking problem with me, Joyce," he turned and glared at her, "I suggest you either cut to the chase or step the hell off. I didn't risk my life getting here to dance with you or deal with your attitude. Otherwise, you can leave and let me enjoy a few minutes of open space."

She stared at him for a moment, seemingly unsure how to respond, until she found her words. "Does a silver spoon come with that chip on your shoulder? I ought to have you tossed into the brig for what you and your family did to humanity. To my family."

He shot up with a start and turned around to face her. "Frak you, lady. I was in the dark just as much as you and your colonists until a few months ago. You have no idea what we've been through, least of all me. I've been halfway across the galaxy fighting aliens and experiencing my own death at the hands of our ancestors. While my siblings are far from perfect, they aren't entirely responsible for this fuckup of a situation. None of us are." He pointed a finger at her. "Your son's death is not on me or any of my family. It's on Warren North and the Galactic Alliance. It's cut and dry. So, are you with us, or against us, because I'm not about to spend a fraking minute in a cell. Capeesh?"

Joyce stared down at her hands before directing her steely gaze at him. "You'd have me believe that the second son of the mighty Stark Olivaw was in the dark about all of this? What do you take me for?"

"Your anger at the world isn't an excuse for ignorance, Joyce. It's common knowledge I was the black sheep of the family. Every news outlet in Sol knew that. I don't need your shit, and I certainly don't need you to accomplish my task here." He turned and stormed away from her toward the stairs, just past the mouth of the nearby cave where Little Red was lying in wait. He refused to leave his side except for the outdoors.

"I didn't know about any of that," Joyce said, jogging up behind him. "I was never one to keep up on the entertainment news."

He chuckled as his feet crunched in the gravel near the cavern entrance. "I'm no Hollywood actor. I didn't exactly have any paparazzi."

She adjusted her gait to match his, and they worked their way down the spiral stairway side by side. "You were the son of the richest family in Sol. Something tells me you had more people watching you than you know."

"If only my life were that interesting. About the most exciting part was my disappearance to Tau Ceti." He hated lying to her about the colony, but he'd been warned repeatedly. They needed to keep the colony's location secret at all costs.

Joyce turned her head and peered at him. The lighting in the tunnels was deliberately dark, but the deeper they got, the more the ambient light embedded underneath every few stairs illuminated the way. "Speaking of which, shouldn't you still be on a colony ship? I assume they left on schedule. You were supposed to be departing a little over six years ago, if memory serves."

He figured she'd pick that up. Maybe not right away, but eventually. "That's right. We left and arrived on time. To say our trip was faster than expected would be an understatement, and it took me a few years to figure it out myself."

She reached in front of him and they both paused their descent. "You mean to tell me you didn't know you'd reached Tau Ceti over a decade ahead of schedule? I'm not buying that for a second."

Ignorance was bliss. The levels of the subterfuge his family had taken were only beginning to become clear to her. Best he didn't give her more fuel for her anger. "It's far easier to assume you're only being told the truth than to question everything. Like I said, it took me a few years to figure it out, and that was only because they'd purposely made a mistake to get my attention after the message from Abigail. But that story is for another day. We have things to do. Have the other contingents of troops from impact site one returned?" He began descending again. The door wasn't much further.

As they walked around the corner, Little Red came into view. He was rocking from foot to foot beside the entrance hatch. "Hello, sirs. It's good to see you both."

Joyce continued, ignoring the interruption. "They're due to arrive any time now. Why?"

He smiled, his face concealed in the shadows. "My future sister-in-law is keen on meeting someone onboard."

BRADLEY CUPPED the bulb of dark black liquid, relishing the warmth in his hand. They ran out of the good coffee a few weeks into the voyage and the crude supply of instant that Harold and Shauna had supplied tasted like swill. He'd have to talk to them when he saw them next. They, of all people, should understand the human need for quality coffee and tea.

He brought the bulb up to his nose and breathed in deeply. The aroma of the charred beans mixed beautifully with the notes of cherries. Harold had gotten it just the way he liked it. His body relaxed as he took a swig, warmth radiating through it.

They were waiting in the conference room for the leaders of the second impact site. Joyce and Captain Hui were sitting side by side on the opposite end of the table, and Pluto was pacing a groove in the floor opposite the entrance.

The door on the far side of the room silently slid open, and a young woman a quarter meter shorter than Pluto stepped in. Both women froze in their tracks. It was like staring at a mirror that miniaturized his favorite pilot. That and it added a head of long black hair.

He watched from afar as the two women stared in silence for what seemed like an eternity, until finally Elaine squealed and skipped forward, hopping up and into the awaiting arms of Pluto. Tears and shouts of joy permeated the room as the long separated siblings relished the glow of each other's presence.

Pluto had told him about how she and Elaine had a huge family fight when they were younger. It sounded a lot like him and his family. They each fell on opposing sides of the blowout. While they never chose to part ways, their surrounding family urged them to distance themselves from each other in hopes that the other side would admit fault.

Years passed. One thing led to another, and the next thing she knew, she was in the Olivaw Wheel family. She wanted to reach out when she heard Elaine was leaving for Epsilon Eridani, but she couldn't spend as much time with her as she'd want. She was needed at The Wheel and had rebuilt her family there. Deep down, she secretly hoped that one day they'd reunite with each other. Today that wish came true.

Pluto had become unhinged when she found out Elaine was on the other company of ships. While she'd only had to wait another twenty-four hours to see her, it was an eternity under radio silence. After traveling light years, she still didn't know if Elaine had survived the impact.

Pluto and Elaine walked up to him arm in arm, the pink wet glow of happiness on their faces. "I'd like you to meet my sister."

He stood up and reached out his hand. "It's nice to finally meet you. I've heard so much."

Elaine smiled from ear to ear. "Awe, come on now. We're almost family, and you brought my sister all this way." She raised her arms up and ensnared him in a giant bear hug. Her strength was very much like her sister. It must be the genes.

"Thank you," he said, struggling not to wince. He was pretty sure she'd cracked his rib, she'd hugged him so tight.

"No, thank you!" She released him, but held him at arm's length. "We owe a lot to you and your family, even if we don't show it." She glanced at Joyce and then back at him. "So, are we getting out of this place before the curtain falls, or are you moving in forever?"

He did a double take, surprised at her choice of words. "Our estimates say we have another six months until they seal the Nebula. We've got a lot of work to do in that time to prepare for the next stage."

Elaine froze, dropping her hands to her side and then stepping around him, toward Joyce. "You haven't told them yet?"

Joyce was silently staring at the bulb of tea in her hand. "It hadn't come up. They've been in decontamination for the better part of the day, and then some of them disappeared upside. Seems sightseeing mattered more than discussing how to save us."

His muscles tensed up every time she spoke. This woman was toxic, and she was going to sink their mission before it started. He had to take control of this situation. "How about everyone check their egos at the door. We're on the same team here. And right about now, if you know anything that impacts the timeline of the Nebula, then I need to hear about it, like yesterday."

"In exchange for what?" Joyce asked.

Pluto stepped around them both, her muscles tense and bulging from her frame. "Are you seriously holding your people hostage in a vain attempt at negotiating for something? You're not at all what Abigail said you were. We recognize you lost someone close to you, but at this point you're doing more harm than good in your position."

Harold's image appeared on the wall screen. "That's not the half of it."

"Oh shut up, Harold. We don't need you in the middle of this," Joyce said.

Bradley raised his hand for her to stop talking. "Hold up. Let's listen to what he has to say. Without him, you wouldn't be alive."

Joyce snapped up, tossing her tea in the corner of the room. "You're right! Without him, none of us would be here. His decisions all those years ago set up humanity for this clusterfuck of a situation."

Bradley calmly stepped up to face her. "I know you think you understand the situation, Joyce, but trust me when I tell you, you don't. Our knowledge of this clusterfuck as you call it has changed in the past few months. Like I said earlier, let's hear him out."

She raised her chin toward him. "And if I don't want to?"

He slid aside without a word and pointed at the door.

Joyce glanced back at Captain Hui, eyeing her to see if she'd follow her out.

"I'm sorry, Director," Captain Hui began, "but I need to find out what both Harold and this group have to say. I owe it to the colonists."

Joyce swallowed hard. She'd expected the captain to accompany her. "Fair enough. I relinquish command of the Archégonos colony site to you. It's in your hands, Captain."

"You don't have to do this," Elaine said, stepping to her side. "We haven't even heard why they're here."

Joyce laughed out loud, her voice overflowing with a mocking tone. "And do you believe we'll get even a fraction of the Olivaw truth?"

"I do." Elaine glanced at her sister Pluto. "Someone I trust is here to vouch for them, and I'd follow them anywhere in the universe. They've never led me astray, and they wouldn't start now."

Pluto's eyes glimmered as she reached out to grasp Elaine's hand before making eye contact with Joyce. "Hear us out before you make a call. I know you don't trust the Olivaws, but so much has changed in the past few months. More than you can imagine."

The group stared at each other for a moment before Joyce slowly sat back down into her chair and crossed her arms. "I can imagine a lot given the death and destruction we've witnessed. What I can't imagine, however, is how you'd top the subterfuge Harold undertook that got us into this mess in the first place."

"Well, shit." Bradley stepped around the table and pulled a data dot out of his pocket. "If you think his lies are bad, then you need to strap in, Director. What Harold did isn't even the tip of the iceberg of the fraking mess we're in, and most of it has nothing to do with him or any of us." He dropped the dot into the receptacle, and he subvocalized the command to bring up the summary Libby prepared for their meeting.

Joyce studied him.

He nodded his head toward her and then the wall screen. "Seriously, if there's a seatbelt on that thing, you'd better use it." He hit play. The lights lowered, and Libby's smiling face appeared.

WHEN THE LIGHTS RAISED, the room was silent, and all eyes were on the wall screen. Everything they'd discovered in the Lupus Dark Nebula, and their entire plan to steal the Beacon of Therion had been spelled out in excruciating detail. At least as much detail as they had before their mission was underway.

Bradley had leaned forward and was scanning the faces at the table. They were wearing masks of disbelief and shock, combined with what he could only call doubt. "So, Joyce, I'd love to hear your thoughts."

From his vantage, her gaze was trained on the gate portals and the ships passing through them, making assaults on the Galactic Alliance armada.

She turned around and faced him. "You're telling me we can jump through space and time? Past the Nebula itself."

He nodded. "That's correct. I know it sounds crazy, but we've been doing it for a few years with probes and for months with humans. How do you think we teleported inside that asteroid without tunneling in?"

Her chair creaked as she leaned back, and her eyes went up to the ceiling. "I... hadn't even thought about how you did that. And in Lupus?"

"We made thousands of gates during that mission and jumped across the Nebula multiple times." Pluto glanced at him. "Sometimes on accident."

Joyce tilted her head sideways. "What does that mean?"

He reached up and rubbed his face. "We may have tried to jump too far and diverged off course once. Let's just call it a learning experience on what not to do inside a Nebula." When he brought his hands down, Joyce was studying him.

She didn't trust what she'd seen. While he hoped to convince her to join them, he feared she was already a lost cause. To be honest, he wasn't sure he could deal with her rage anyhow.

She leaned forward and rested her hands on the table. "That was a lot to take in. I never imagined you'd show me a fifteen-minute summary that included hitting reset on humanity's origins, our very place in the universe, and how we accidentally found our way to Sol. Are you sure this isn't another one of your Olivaw lies?"

Pluto groaned and rapped her fist on the table.

He reached over and rested his hand on Pluto's and shook his head. "It's not worth it. Sometimes people are too far—"

"Hold on," Harold interrupted, his image appearing on the wall screen. "Joyce, do you remember what our prisoner, Two, said to you before you tore off his antenna?"

Bradley shot a glance at Pluto. Harold had to be kidding. This woman had already resorted to torturing the prisoners. Abigail had clearly misjudged her.

She smirked and tapped the table with her index finger, the noise clear as day in the silent room. "Which time?"

"The first. Maybe this will jog your memory." Harold brought a recording up on the wall screen. It was a prison cell, and Joyce was sitting in the corner with an alien Thyreusian constrained in the middle.

The video showed Joyce narrowing her gaze and staring at the alien for a moment before she spoke. "What's useless, Two? I'm not following."

Two's body spasmed. "I don't suspect you would. Your species was never mentally adept, being uplifted and all."

Harold froze the video. "Do you remember that?"

She nodded. "Alright, so they called us uplifts. That seems to line up with what we just saw in their little production video, but, so what? You could have made that up in the hours since their arrival."

"Do you remember what you asked Two a few minutes later?"

Joyce slowly shook her head, thinking but coming up empty. "No. Sorry. I only remember a few hours later tearing off his antenna. It felt spectacular." Her ego and lack of remorse were painted in the smirk now hanging on her face.

"Harold, do you have a point?" Bradley asked. All this was doing was highlighting how unfit she was for leadership, especially for what they needed her for.

"I do, sir. Give me a moment, please. I believe Joyce's anger at the loss of her son is clouding her understanding of the situation."

She snickered. "Oh, is it? Thanks, Doctor Harold."

"Yes, it is," Harold said. "What confuses me, is why you see this information as a lie? I mean, if your anger isn't obscuring your judgment, then why did you propose it yourself?"

Joyce squinted. "What are you talking about?" She pointed at the wall screen. "I wasn't proposing anything. I was trying to get the alien to talk."

"No, no. I mean you proposed this theory that we were the uplifters to the alien, to Two. It was your idea. Bradley comes in here and presents you with a truth that you yourself theorized, and suddenly, it's a lie?"

She rubbed her hands on her legs. "I seriously have no fraking idea what you're talking about."

Bradley didn't know what to make of this entire exchange, other than Harold seemed to be speaking in code. He needed to get to a point, and quickly.

"Maybe this will jog your memory. What I want to know, is why you asked this question." Harold played her interrogation again on the wall screen. This time she was standing in front of Two.

"Perfect!" Joyce whirled her hands in the air and slapped them together, sending a bang through the room.

The alien flinched backward, and their antennae circled around, studying her strange motion.

"Let's start with a twist," Joyce said. "What if we weren't uplifts? That's what you called us, right? What if instead, we were the uplifters, and the Nanil were, in fact, our little pet project? How do you suppose that would change our position with the Galactic Alliance?"

The video froze.

And there it was. Joyce's face went blank. When she opened her mouth, nothing came out.

From the look in her eyes, she didn't remember asking Two the question. She'd been so caught up in the interrogation that she stumbled upon a truth that seemed so far-fetched, it had to be made up. And yet, in the last twenty minutes, her thought exercise had become her new reality.

Bradley broke the silence hanging in the room. "Do you honestly think we orchestrated all this hoopla to get you to do something for us? You conjured this same idea from your own imagination. Yet for some reason, when we show you this truth, we're the ones lying."

He stared down at his hands. He'd pulled his rock out of his pocket while watching the video and hadn't even realized it. An image of his dad's face smiling up at him appeared in his mind's eye.

"Sometimes we need to look past our anger, Joyce. We need to push aside our pent-up frustration to see our new reality." He glanced up at her. "I've had a hard time doing that myself, so I don't have much room to talk. I lost my father, and I nearly lost everyone else that mattered to me these past few months. While I know you lost your son, there's still a great many people in this colony that believe in you, and we could really use your help. What do you say?"

Joyce traced a circle with her hand on the table surface in front of her. "I need to see more. I assume you brought something beyond this fifteen-minute video?" She peered up at him.

He nodded. "A lot more. We've got some gate drives to build for the ships we hope you've been building. There's also the little matter of a containment vessel for our Beacon prize along with anti-missile countermeasures we'll need to ensure this whole effort isn't a waste."

She tapped the table with her knuckles. "Alright then. We only have one problem."

"Let's hear it." He feared she was about to lose it again.

She bit her lower lip and glanced at Elaine. "We have intel that the Beacon of Therion may have already arrived on the scene."

He briefly looked at Pluto and then back at her before shrugging. "That should be ok, I think. We can't imagine why it would matter."

"Harold, I'm sure you know what I'm getting at." She spun around to face the wall screen again. "Can you play the video from two weeks ago?"

The image reset and Harold played the recording.

Two's alien form leaned back, and his body gyrated uncontrollably. He then let out a bellow-like screech that could only be interpreted as a failed attempt to mimic human laughter.

As his gaze lowered, it leveled on Joyce across the cell. "You stand about as good a chance at getting close to a Beacon as I do leaving this cell alive. I'm not worried, though. Your day is fast approaching. Your fate will be sealed in another three months. Then, I'll rest."

All of their planning and all of their sacrifices during this mission could have just blown up in an instant.

"How is that possible?" Bradley asked, freezing the video and running his hands through his hair. "I mean, the rate the Nebula's spreading is constant."

Joyce shook her head. "We can't say exactly. Two didn't go

into details. He merely said it helped them to work faster. Tell me we can move your plan forward. That we can still do this."

He shook his head. "I... don't know. We have to try, though. Giving up now means certain death to our friends and families in Sol." His left hand started shaking as he squeezed the stone tighter, rubbing it between his fingers. "Harold—"

"I've already sent it on a probe along with our recordings, sir. The moment I correlated the data from your dot, I knew it was worth the risk. Our people will have the details in just over a week. If we're lucky, we'll hear back some time afterward."

His hands were sweating. Their options were limited, but there was still hope. He raised his gaze at Joyce. "Tell me you've prepared the ships and have been training the pilots following Harold's instructions."

She tilted her head. "Training how?"

"On the game." Pluto slid her chair backward and stood up. She gestured at the wall screen and brought up a video game.

A grumble escaped from Joyce.

"What the hell's this?" Bradley squinted and pointed at the wall. "I thought we were having them train on our simulators?"

Pluto raised her eyebrows. "That was kiboshed, remember. If the intel had been leaked, the GA could figure it out. We decided on this instead. Well, I decided. It's how I used to train back at the Sol Wheel."

Elaine chuckled. "You were always fixated on these classic games. I'd forgotten. We lost so many hours playing these as kids."

"Seriously, it helped me. They're addicting." She spun around and faced them all. "I have to think you already have people who are good and people who aren't."

She studied their reaction, and Bradley did, as well. Judging from Joyce's body language and her initial moan, she wasn't one of the good ones.

Captain Hui, who'd been nearly silent the entire time, finally spoke up. "We've been playing. Against some of our better judgment." She glanced at Joyce, and she shifted in her seat.

"What?" Joyce asked. "I suck at the game. There, I said it."

"It's ok," Pluto said. "It's not for everyone. You probably only had a few people who were really talented. And if our data aligns with yours, they're likely Ulixi or descendants of them."

The room went quiet, and Captain Hui was shaking her head from side to side, staring at Elaine.

Bradley swore under his breath. They couldn't do this with a single pilot.

"Nothing? No one was good at it?" Pluto's shoulders drooped.

Captain Hui answered. "No, we have some talented players, they're just not Ulixi. They're Gunders."

25

ABIGAIL OLIVAW
ZETA LUPI, OORT CLOUD

The entire situation was for shit, but Abigail wasn't ever expecting it to be normal, whatever that meant nowadays. It could be lifetimes before any human felt safe again in this galaxy. For the moment, she needed to focus on helping her people survive.

She didn't know the first thing about commanding a starship, even one whose goal was diplomatic and not warfare. While they weren't planning on leaving without some defenses, their intention wasn't to scare the Ursis into joining them. They needed comrades in arms. Species alienated and outcast like they were.

What made her scared was the unknown and unexpected, more than getting there. Maybe that was a testament to the gate drive technology Zachary's team had created, or maybe it was highlighting something deeper. Sometimes an enemy's enemy might not turn out to be a best friend. There was also the matter of them not even knowing if the Ursis were alive. No one knew the timelines of the Éntono Fos. For the Nanil and humans in Lupus, it was a thousand years, but for all they knew it could be a decade for another star type.

"I feel like you just got here, and now you're already leaving," Zachary said.

He'd walked up behind her in the storage hold of the Phoenix. She'd been standing still for a dozen minutes, staring at the pile of crates, having forgotten why she came in here in the first place.

She leaned down and scanned one of the crates. The contents reminded her why she was there. It was full of random parts and haptic relays. She removed the lid and pulled a relay out. They had an intermittent relay failure on the bridge controls that was annoying her. "I can't sit around and watch everyone else doing something to help except me. We weren't wired that way. An Olivaw is always—"

"Part of the solution. Never the problem," he interrupted. "I know. Dad must have said that expression a trillion times. It got old by about age ten."

She put the lid back on the crate and turned to face him. "Someone told me Harold had started that saying when he was young."

"You could ask him."

"Nah. I'm fine with quiet. It's easier to hear my thoughts this way." She tapped the relay in her hand and headed toward the bridge. "Gotta go fix my controls."

He sped up beside her in silence. The feeling of his presence was both unusual and comfortable. They'd grown up fast in their chaotic family, but they'd always had each other's back. While they had their fair share of fights, she never had to wonder if he'd be there for her. He was one of the three people she knew she could count on, no matter what the stakes. Fortunately, one of the others was coming along with her on this mission.

As she stepped onto the bridge, she tossed the relay toward Minula. "Heads up!"

Minula's hand was already in the air behind her, ready for the catch. The relay arced through the open space between them and landed precisely into her hand with a muted tinking sound. "I was wondering if you got lost. I'd have sent a search party, but you know… there's no overseer."

"I hate that name," Abigail said, fixing her gaze on Minula. "He's Harold."

Minula slid the access panel into place and stood up. "It's what all the cool Ulixi call him."

Abigail stepped around the panel and slipped into the seat. She pulled the controls around and started testing them one at a time on the calibration screen. The panel vibrated and buzzed along, emitting a multitude of audible feedback tones. It reminded her of playing a synthesizer for the first time. You couldn't help yourself. You had to hit every key to hear the next crazy sound it'd make.

"Alright!" Zachary reached over and stopped her hand from mashing the screen. "I think it's working."

"I liked those sounds," Ibu said from behind them.

Zachary jumped forward. "Crap! You scared me. I didn't even know you were there. I hate having all the damn information layers of my comm shut off. Can't any of you run with a low-level overlay on your retinal comms?"

"We will after we leave," Ibu said, hopping up from their chair. "This ship is new to Abigail and the rest of the crew. It's best for them to learn their way around by disconnecting from their comms. Humans are utterly dependent on their devices to perform the simplest tasks, and with a limited A.I. on this voyage, we'll need to know this ship inside and out."

Abigail thought it was amusing how Ibu had taken on the role of the mother hen on the mission. It made the already stressful planning a bit more manageable knowing they were taking care of it. Particularly since they were so detail-oriented. While they'd never planned anything like this before, Shauna assured her that their plans were more than adequate. Apparently, they'd been studying pretty hard for this opportunity.

She glanced over the checklists on the control panel. "With the controls all operating within expected tolerances, all we have left is to double-check the fabricators and run a few drills when the rest of the team arrives."

Zachary walked up and scrolled through their checklist, pausing every few seconds to tap for details. She could tell he was impressed with Ibu's work. He brought up the duty roster for the crew on the wall screen. "When are you shipping out?"

"First thing tomorrow morning," Minula said.

His eyes went wide. "That soon? Will everyone you need be ready?"

"I've already modified their schedules to have them either returning to Tiān, or rotating into a long stint on Fumis. We've got people there who will cover for them not being around."

He reached up and rubbed at the scruff on his face. "You know we can still get this done on the up and up. We don't have to work in the shadows. Lync can sell this."

Abigail snapped up with a start. "I don't need anyone's fraking permission for this mission. While you may have handed over controls to the military, I have no intention of doing the same. These jarheads don't know how to deal with these aliens and can't see beyond their Inner and Outer Ring conquests from decades ago. Lync might have her head on straight, but she's surrounded by incompetents." She glanced at Minula. "No offense on the jarheads remark."

"None taken." Minula snatched up the dead relay and headed toward the recycler. "There's a reason I left being a jarhead and came to work for you. The writing on the wall was clear. I'll be right back."

She watched as Minula walked away, a smile threatening to break free. It was nice to see her moving about again. She feared she'd lost her friend after that mission to Sol. It took a few days, a whole lot of drinking and late night movies, but she came around. She felt bad asking her to join her on this trip, but the moment she even mentioned she was leaving, Minula refused to drop it. She demanded to go. While Abigail was happy she was here, she couldn't help but wonder if Minula needed more time to reset back to herself. Whatever that meant in this shit storm of a situation they were living in.

"Still," Zachary began. "Why don't you stick around a few more days. I really think we can get you more—"

Abigail shook away the thoughts and gestured, wiping the wall screen. "We're leaving tomorrow morning. I'm sorry, but the longer we wait, the more likely we'll regret it later. You know as well as I do we don't have a plan after we capture a Beacon."

"If," he muttered.

She leaned down and caught his eyes. "When we capture a Beacon… we'll need to regroup, and we could use some allies. We still have the advantage of surprise leading into this battle. Afterward, they're going to know everything we're capable of. I don't expect they'll be able to defend against us unless they steal some tech from the battlefield, but they'll eventually figure out we're reaching into the Nebulas. We have to get a head start on that."

Zachary walked over and collapsed into an empty seat. "We're doing everything we can to ensure there are no lost gate drives. None of the ships on the front lines will have them besides the three running backs and a few recovery ships. It's one of the few elegant parts of this strategy."

"What's a running back?" Ibu asked, bobbing their head in circles.

Abigail leaned against the wall screen. "It's a sports ball analogy from centuries ago. Imagine a bunch of humans laden with oversized pads and helmets, smashing into each other on a field of grass, all fighting over a tiny oval ball. The running back was the one that took the ball and ran with it, attempting not to get tackled."

They froze their bobbing and stared blankly at Abigail.

"Your human sports confuse me, but I suppose the analogy suits the tactics of the mission."

"Don't get me started on confusion," Zachary began. "The Nanil used humans for sport in arenas and battled to the death. Football is tame compared to that."

"Touché," Ibu said, tipping her virtual hat toward him. "So when do they kick the Beacon?"

Abigail chuckled. The Nanil was a smartass. She loved it.

Zachary squinted and shook his head. "I don't understand. We're not kicking the Beacon. We're gating it inside the nebula."

"So it's not football then. Your analogy failed."

"No, no." He waved his hands. "They don't actually kick the ball much. Most of the time they throw or carry it."

Ibu furrowed their brow and gestured wildly in the air. "But... it's called foot—ball. I have a feeling I don't want to know anymore about this. I'm done talking about sports."

THE BRIDGE BROKE out in laughter and Ibu jumped, resulting in even more cackling. Abigail walked over to the Nanil and put her arm around them. "You're gonna fit in perfectly on this ship."

THEY'D PRACTICED THE SEPARATION, topped off the fabricators, and transferred the crew. The Phoenix was floating in space a single gate hop from the Zeta Lupi Wheel. She'd promised Zachary they'd check in before they left, but she was having second thoughts.

Abigail was never one for tearful goodbyes. Not after her father's death. She'd been forced to prune back her sympathy over the years, and sending her brother off to Zeta Lupi had dried up her well of emotions.

What she was feeling at this moment, and what she'd been feeling since she woke up in Tau Ceti had been foreign. It was something she'd suppressed on purpose. She needed to be strong. To lead her people and lead this mission. Failing them again was not an option.

"Let's drop a comm gate and open the far side near The Wheel," Abigail said.

Ibu took control of the micro comm gate array and closed their eyes, manipulating the tachyon field by touch and sense alone. They created a special tactile interface to the gate array they claimed was easier to manipulate and shape. They'd designed it to connect via their mental link.

Within a few seconds the gate came online and Cynthia opened a comm, hailing the brass at The Wheel.

Abigail wasn't sure if she should've invited Cynthia on this mission. She'd returned to Tiān to help the colony cope with the explosive growth coming their way. The hope was for both population expansion and transplants from the Liprosus colony in the short term, and in the long-term, some people from Sol.

Cynthia was also one of the few in the Circle of Trust planet side, so she was aware of their efforts in recovering the third colony ship thought lost en route to Delta Sagittarii. If they were able to bring the colonists to Tiān, it would be both an enormous boon and stress on the colony's infrastructure.

When she approached Cynthia about her and her brother's relationship, she'd already gotten word about the mission and wanted in. Despite Abigail's warnings about the dangers they'd face, she insisted on being involved. It was nearly impossible to say no to her forceful personality, and she knew Bradley was going to be livid about including her. But it felt right. Next to Minula, she was the closest thing to family coming along. Plus, they could spend some time catching up on her brother.

"Abigail, are you ok?" Cynthia asked over a private

comm. "Your brother was talking to you."

Abigail shook her head and stood up. She'd missed the open to the comm, so she subvocalized a command to quickly replay what was said while she reached down and brushed out the creases from her outfit.

She nodded toward Zachary's face on the wall screen. "Good morning to you, as well. Sorry, I was deep in thought."

Zachary was standing off to the side, in a room full of people. "I… was sure you weren't going to call. I'm glad you had second thoughts."

Her right hand tingled, and she reached behind her back to clasp her hands together. "I wasn't planning to. Sometimes it's just better to rip it off."

"Well, I'm happy you did. Lync and I were about to address the generals and suggest your strategy to them. Care to join in?"

She glanced at Cynthia, raising an eyebrow in question.

Cynthia shook her head. "We can hold this gate for a few minutes, tops. They're designed for bursts, not long-term conversations."

Abigail returned her attention to Zachary. "Why don't you put me on with the generals?"

Harold must have been listening at The Wheel, because her viewpoint changed. Both General Yule and General Raft appeared on her display, with Lync standing beside them. They were circled around the central command console with a battlefield simulation running in the middle. Their staff was surrounding them on all sides, and Zachary was walking in from off-screen.

She nodded toward the display. "Generals. Colonel."

"To what do we owe the interruption, Mrs. Olivaw?" General Raft asked.

Her jaw clenched at the insult. Even former presidents were spoken to with their title. "That's President Olivaw, General. You of all people know the intricacies of diplomacy and decor. I'd gather you wouldn't enjoy me calling you Franklin in front of your staff, now would you?"

His face stiffened, and he gestured to have the comm cut, but it remained open.

"That response was about as childish as I'd expect from the likes of you, General." She turned her attention to Lync. When their eyes met, she caught a hint of a nod. While she hadn't expected this call, she already knew what was coming. "I'm checking in with Colonel Michaels and my brother before departing on our mission. Our ship is prepared, our crew is ready, and our goal is clear. Good luck extracting the prize."

General Raft slammed his fist on the command console and a thunk echoed through the room and over the comm. "What's this about? I wasn't informed of another covert operation. It's bad enough we have an Olivaw on Liprosus. We don't need a second one in the field subverting humankind."

Abigail's pulse quickened, and her hands squeezed tighter together. This feeling of emotions was new to her. In the past, she'd always prided herself on her ability to regulate her frustration around politicians and military brass like him. If he were next to her, she wouldn't be able to control herself. Raft was a hack and a coward. She understood why Quesh brought him here, but he'd gone too far.

Lync smiled. "We're sending Ambassador Olivaw on a classified covert operation. We've already worked over the particulars with General Yule and decided to keep it close to our chest for now. I'm sure you understand, General. The Ambassador will be working to smooth the effects we can expect after we extract the prize, as she put it."

"Smooth the effects!" General Raft faked a laugh. "Like she did in Sol."

Abigail took a step closer to the wall screen, her face looming larger over the audience around the command console. "I'll have you know that it was me who put my life on the line confronting and boarding that alien ship day after day. It was me who diverted the aliens to Neptune to protect our worlds. It was me who recovered the early intel on the tribunal ship and set up Admiral Due with his current strategic position in Sol. My people and my family have put their lives in harm's way since day one, while you and yours ran like cowards. If I'm not mistaken, you shot down that Earth gravity well and were sitting on your ass on the beach in Monaco the day after the arrival, having submitted for retirement hours after the aliens made contact. Don't talk to me about impact or effects, you fraking dingo."

General Raft's face wrinkled, and he turned red. His anger and embarrassment poured over. "I didn't… I was—"

Abigail raised her hand for him to stop. "Bullshit! Quit wasting my time, Franklin. My connection is about to drop. Harold, share his retirement documentation with the others. General Yule, Colonel Michaels." She made eye contact with them both. "I'll stay in touch at regular intervals. My comms officer has already forwarded on our final course plans with the agreed upon encryption. Phoenix out."

Cynthia cut the comm and paused before she spun around to face her.

The bridge was silent enough for Abigail to hear her heart beating in her chest. She'd crossed every line in the book just now, and it felt spectacular. The ability to speak her mind without worrying about the consequences was invigorating. She could get used to this.

"Should I… send on our course plans, Ambassador?" Cynthia asked. She was struggling to suppress a laugh.

Abigail waved her hand and collapsed back into her chair. "Frak 'em! We'll deliver them along with our first data drop. Right now, we have a mission to get underway."

"So, was he seriously on a beach at Monaco?" Cynthia asked.

Her whole body shivered at the thought of the intel she'd

seen. "His wrinkly ass was slathered up with sunscreen, and he was already shopping around for a new wife. The only reason he stayed in the ranks was because they were pulling ships out of mothballs in case we went to battle, and the military brass rejected his retirement request under my Emergency War Powers Act. They needed all hands on deck."

"Huh." Cynthia shook her head and stared downward. "It's strange that the Circle chose him to help the Zeta Lupi colony."

"Not really." Minula brought up the coordinates for the first set of jumps on her controls and the wall screen. "For every plan in the military, there has to be a winner and a loser. He's weak, and General Yule is strong. Troops rally behind a capable leader, but when things are hardest, they need to see and feel like there were options. He was nothing but a pawn, and our Ambassador has removed him from play." She spun around and smiled at Abigail.

She nodded in return. "I just hope they don't require another pawn. They're down to people we need and love. Let's get this show on the road, shall we? The clock's ticking."

Minula turned and slid her hand up the controls, engaging the gate drive and executing the first segment of their hops. The gate vanes clanged as they expanded and began to shape the tachyon field.

Realization flowed over her like a lost memory. She finally understood why Zachary made the vanes so loud. Like General Raft was a pawn and a reminder of how not to lead, so were the gate vanes. Their sound and vibrations were reminders of the jarring effect of what was about to occur. They trained your mind to respect the jump you were about to perform, and they gave you a chance to prepare for what might be on the other end.

By the time they reached the Ursis, they needed to be on the winning side of the coming battle over the Beacon. The last thing she wanted was to return home as someone's pawn.

26

LYNC MICHAELS
ZETA LUPI, NEAR LANIGER

The image of Abigail cut, and the room went silent. Lync would have liked to say goodbye to her in person, but she couldn't. The logistics of disappearing off the Wheel were painful, and she wasn't sure how she'd have pulled it off this morning. While she didn't agree with Abigail leading the mission, there wasn't anyone else with the skills or desire to duck behind alien lines, possibly never to return. No one besides an Olivaw.

Lync and Zachary cornered General Yule minutes before the meeting. They prepared him for Abigail's departure and her ultimate mission, feigning support for it the entire time. While he was furious with both of them, he was also relieved Abigail would be out of the way. Her people had an allegiance to her that was difficult to shake, even with Zachary's help.

"You!" General Raft stormed across the space between them. "You did this!"

He'd gotten to within centimeters of her face, but she didn't flinch. His breath smelled like a rotten piece of cheese. She'd prepared for this type of testosterone laden outburst. Her body was as calm and collected as she could muster, and she merely shrugged. "It makes sense, and we need to plan ahead. Without allies—"

General Raft jabbed his finger into her chest. "Your job isn't to think broader. Your kind has its place, and you're lucky you're even allowed in this room. Your role is to work on the immediate mission strategy. Nothing else."

She leaned forward, putting her mouth next to his ear. "Touch me again, and I'll fraking break off that finger... or worse, General." She took a step backward, spun to face General Yule, and saluted him. "I'm out. We're all done here." She then straightened and marched toward the exit, all eyes following her as she went.

"Get back here immediately!" General Raft slammed his fist on the command console again. "I did not dismiss you, Colonel."

The door silently opened and closed behind her as she exited the chamber. When she hit the third corner and stepped into the lift tube, she gasped for air and reached a hand up to her chest, rubbing at the spot where he touched her. It took everything she had not to kill him in front of the others. Her knife was right there in the small of her back. It would have only taken a second. She could still smell the stench of his breath.

After a few deep breaths, she looked around. She didn't know where she was going, but the tube was taking her upward. "Where are we headed?" she asked out loud.

"I thought you could use some fresh air," Shauna said.

"I don't want to visit the arboretum, and besides, that's in the opposite direction."

Shauna chuckled in her ear. "I know better than to tell a Ulixi that fresh air was in the outdoors. No. A shuttle will be waiting for you in hold C, near the exit. You're heading outside. Into the darkness of space, where you're most at ease."

These were the most words she'd exchanged with Shauna

since finding out she was her mother. The entire notion still felt foreign. She'd never had a mom. Her father had been the only parental figure in her life, and he was gone. The military killed him, and Shauna let it happen.

She opened a comm to the Ulixi public channel. "This is Lync. I know this is sudden, but I need your help. I'm taking a stand against the brass and how this mission is being run. Despite our best efforts, we Ulixi are still being treated with no respect, yet without us, we're all dead. If you feel the same way, then head toward hold C. I'll be waiting." She cut the comm.

"I think you're gonna need a bigger ship," Shauna said. "Give me a minute."

"ARE THERE ENOUGH SUITS?" Lync stared out across the sea of Ulixi staring back at her. They were standing in the hold of a transport ship. The whole thing had come together quicker than she'd imagined it would. All but a handful of Ulixi out on training runs had convened to meet her. Not a single Ulixi was left in The Wheel. They crammed all ninety-six of them into this tiny ship.

It reminded her of their departure from the Sol Trojans. Except there were even more people. Some of the faces she didn't recognize, having been recruited from Tiān after they'd arrived from Tau Ceti. Despite being strangers, their bond was universal.

"We wouldn't have departed without enough suits," Shauna said over their comms.

"It'd be a Four Laws catastrophe." Crayo cracked a smirk.

She raised both fists into the air, and the murmurs among the others stopped. Each of them silently helped check the suit of the person nearest them. When they were complete, they raised their left-hand skyward.

"All the suits are sealed," Shauna said.

"I know." Lync lowered her hands. "The closest group wouldn't have raised their hand had they not confirmed the furthest neighbor was ready."

"I see." Shauna's robotic form rolled up beside them both. "That would've been something good to know. We should talk more. Now what?"

Lync closed her eyes and breathed in deeply before exhaling in a single long breath. She slowly raised her hands to cross her chest and then faced them upward toward the sky, one hand to her left and the other to her right. The Ulixi sign to receive help from anywhere. She held her eyes closed, waiting for the group.

All around her, she could sense the others following the same motion. While her eyes were closed, she could still feel them. Each person searching through space for their neighbor and upon finding them, clasping their arm together. When they had completed the ritual, the entire group was intertwined. They became one of spirit and body.

For a brief second, she felt a throbbing at the front and rear of her neck, where her birthmark was. It disappeared as quickly as it arrived, but she swore she could hear their thoughts. She should have spent more time with Ibu before they left, practicing her mental link.

She took another deep breath and opened her eyes. "Let us begin."

"And what exactly are we beginning?" Shauna asked.

———

"I WANT ABSOLUTE FOCUS," Lync said over the group comm. "You know the ritual. You've done it countless times. Control your breathing, concentrate on reducing your oxygen. You need to find your center. Only when you've done this can you truly see beyond yourself."

"We've lost two more," Crayo said. "That brings the total to forty-eight." He was bounding across the surface of the planetesimal, searching for the other Ulixi.

While Shauna knew where each and every one of them was because of their trackers, their life signs were undetectable. They'd reached the Ulixi center and brought their vitals to near zero. It was how Lync had survived the drones when she was young, and it was how all Ulixi were able to center themselves. She knew it was the best way to master the tachyon field. The closer to the zero point she got, the easier it was for her to find the center of the mass they were targeting.

"We've got a dozen suits that should be nearing depleted oxygen levels," Shauna said. "But—"

"They're not," Lync interrupted. "They've found themselves. It'll be hours before they'll need to return to the ship."

Shauna's image appeared in Lync's retinal comm. "It doesn't make sense. They're human, like everyone else. How are they doing this?"

Her father always challenged her to push her limits, but she wasn't the best student. She should've listened to him more.

Crayo answered her before she could. "For every breath we inhale, we exhale three quarters of the oxygen we take in. Doing the math alone, we should be able to survive on one quarter the oxygen, and that's assuming you haven't trained yourself to consume less."

"I'd love to stick a Ulixi under a scanner while they're doing this," Shauna said.

Lync's comm flashed red. It'd been doing that for the last hour, but she ignored it. Shauna had been opening a comm gate every so often, to ensure she was on top of what was happening back at The Wheel. Apparently, all hell had been breaking loose judging by the number of priority unread messages in her inbox. The number ticked up a dozen or more whenever she connected.

A cold tear streaked down her face. "My father used to tell me the act of centering myself flooded my brain with oxygen and brought the remainder of my body to the brink of eternal rest. It allowed one to think of nothing else but the emptiness of the universe. No muscles, tendons, or tissues to consume the neurons. My heart and brain could manage their symphony of life without me. Shutting off my extremities enabled my mind to reach new levels of focus."

"I imagine the same thing took place with monks, Buddhists, and other religions that practiced meditative approaches to focus," Shauna said.

It hadn't occurred to her before, but she was probably right. Another half dozen life signs blinked off her checklist. Her suit could no longer detect them, but their nanites were still reporting them as being alive. This was working better than she'd imagined. Now if only she could get them to do this under the pressure of a battle.

Shauna's image enlarged in her field of view. "I think we should reach out to General Yule. If I'm reading this right, he's about to scramble a squadron of fighters to search for us."

The fool hadn't even thought about the power the Ulixi had. An important group of people taking themselves out of the picture had single-handedly brought the human race to the precipice of destruction by doing nothing more than disappearing.

The scheme had only come to her in the past few days. As they approached Abigail's departure, the backchannels at The Wheel had reached a crescendo of rumors and theories that something big was going to happen, but no one knew what. They all recognized something was up, but had no idea the details. She'd been able to induce chaos without lifting a finger. It inspired Lync to do the same, for the Ulixi were the backbone of the mission. Hell, they were the entire strategy for engaging the Galactic Alliance. Without them, they might as well run for the stars.

"Lync, did you hear her?" Crayo asked.

Another dozen life signs blinked off. They were making progress.

"Open a comm to General Yule," Lync muttered.

A moment later his face and that of Zachary were plastered over her visor.

"Where the frak are you, Colonel?" General Yule asked.

She minimized his image.

"Colonel!"

She took a deep breath and stared out at the cloud of stars making up the Milky Way. Their beauty and the calmness at this distance was relaxing. "General, I suggest you refrain from yelling at me."

"I asked you a—"

She gestured and cut the comm.

Silence returned to her helmet as four more life signs disappeared. Another twenty-six and they'd have everyone focused.

"Crayo, why don't you circle back and find the people who've been struggling for so long. Maybe you can work with them one on one."

"Copy that!" Crayo's dot came to a halt, and he double backed along the path, working his way to the oldest dot on her overlay.

"I'm receiving an inbound request from the General," Shauna said.

Lync gestured and opened the comm, immediately minimizing it without saying a word.

"Are you ok?" Zachary asked.

"That depends."

"On?"

"Whether or not the Generals and their flunkies have gotten their heads out of their asses."

"You haven't listened to any of my messages, have you?"

She shook her head. A useless gesture light days away but a habit nonetheless. "I have not. I've had more important things to take care of."

"Yule sent Raft packing along with his entire staff. They're en route to a detainment facility on Tiān until the mission is over, or longer. I don't know how Raft kept his retirement a secret, but Yule doesn't work with cowards. I've had to talk him off the ledge about you being one, as well."

Her fist clenched and her power armor warned her of potential damage until six more life signs blinked off the map. She relaxed her hands and took another breath before maximizing the comm. "Put him on."

A moment later, General Yule's face appeared on her comm along with his assistant. They stepped away at the sight of Lync. She glared at him for a moment, waiting for him to make the move. He'd been the last one to lose his cool at her.

Each stared at the other for what seemed like an eternity.

"I'm going to piggyback a comm gate in a few seconds, General," Shauna said, shattering the silence. "You'll note a blip on your side because I'll be coming in from another position in space. I'm not a Ulixi, so I can't precisely lay these down. Either way, I just wanted to warn you we weren't breaking contact."

"And you are?" General Yule asked.

"That's my mother," Lync said. "Shauna Olivaw."

Shauna's image smiled in the corner of her retinal comm, and she could have sworn she saw a glimmer in her eye for a moment.

General Yule's face froze. "Did I catch that right, Colonel? You said your mother is an Olivaw?"

Lync nodded. "It came as news to me, too, sir. I found out myself a few weeks ago. Until then, I was just another grunt, lying low, hoping not to be noticed. You see, I've never had the Olivaw silver spoon. They'd never been there for me until recently. Everything I've learned, everything that makes me who I am today, has been because of my Ulixi family... and my father."

His right eye twitched. He did that when he agreed with someone. It was the one tell she'd been able to find on the man in the time they'd been working together.

"So, is it true? Is General Raft gone?"

"Him and all his knuckle draggers. I should've never let them bring an infantry grunt into a space war."

She'd never thought about his background. That explained his two-dimensional tactics to nearly every strategy he and his team came up with.

"We're gonna need to hit reset, General."

"Are we?" General Yule tilted his head and crossed his arms. "Seems to me, you're already on the run, Colonel. Plum disappeared with all our assets."

"We're not assets! We're people. Flesh and blood humans. You and the rest of the members of this mission are going to start treating us with the respect we deserve. Not fear or anger, respect."

"Respect is earned, Colonel. Not demanded. Actions are what matters in this universe, and as far as I can tell, your actions mark you as a traitor. Am I wrong, Colonel Michaels?"

She knew the accusation was coming. He was as old school as Raft and was predictable to boot. She, on the other hand, was not.

Lync subvocalized a command to share her display with the General and anyone else on the other side of the comm.

General Yule took a step back and his head pivoted from side to side, taking in what she was sharing. "I'm not sure what I'm seeing."

"Nothing, General. You're seeing absolutely nothing." Every life sign had blinked out in the time they were talking.

Whatever Crayo had done had worked. The Ulixi had found their center. They'd become one with the time and space around them.

"We don't understand." Zachary stepped into the image next to the General. "Can you fill us in?"

"What you're not seeing are these dots." Lync flashed the life signs on and then off. "While you were expunging The Wheel of Raft's rats, I was out here training with my brethren, teaching them to come together as a clan. Working with them on how to focus their thoughts and emotions. With a clear mind, they can—"

"Find the gravitational center," General Yule said as realization smacked him in the face. "I thought... you said you were done."

"I was. For a few minutes, I was ready to disappear. Like everyone else, I'm... human. But when I brought my family together, I realized we couldn't abandon humanity. While the Inner and Outer rings have forsaken us, the Ulixi are not the stereotypes you make us out to be. We are far more than meets the eye. Each and every one of us came here to save Sol. To save humanity. Until we do, our mission isn't complete."

General Yule came to attention and saluted her. "You have proven me wrong, Colonel. For that, I am thankful. We all are."

"Thank you, General. Now, if you don't mind, I'd like to find my own center for a bit. It's been far too long since I've listened to the sounds of the cosmos."

General Yule nodded and cut the comm.

Lync glanced around and noticed Crayo was standing beside her. She reached out and rested her hand on his shoulder before kneeling on the ground. He followed suit.

She closed her eyes and started her controlled breathing exercises, focusing on lowering her heart rate. Her counting began at ten and by the time she hit six she could feel the extremities of her body melting away. The entire planetesimal and the suit protecting her from the vacuum of space slowly disappeared. All that remained was her, the universe, and… she reached out and rested her hand on Crayo's.

She wasn't even sure if she could attempt a mental link through gloves. She and Ibu had practiced a few more times before they left, but always with varying degrees of success, and always through direct contact. But this was different. They were in space. In the element of the Ulixi. In the place they'd each grown up and learned to survive, and sometimes thrive. Somewhere on the brink of barely getting by and being truly happy.

Her mind could feel his presence. If a color could be sensed, his aura appeared blue in her mind's eye. She remembered that was the color that had shot outward and climbed through the pedestal of light when he'd touched it in the ceremonial chamber back in Sol, before the Galactic Alliance had destroyed it.

The remnants of her and Ibu's practice flowed through her mind. As she found her center, she thought about the words she wanted to say. "Nice work."

His hand flinched, and she sensed his aura fade like fog passing in front of a lighthouse. A moment later, it lifted again, and the light shone through like a beacon.

She reached out again with her mind. "If you shut off your senses to everything else except your center, deep down, below the colors, you'll sense a stream of consciousness. Dipping your mind in slowly allows you to speak. Not words. But feelings and thoughts."

"Thank you," he thought, the words shaking. "We couldn't have done this without you."

She wasn't sure about that, but she'd take it. While she had him and her crew on Liprosus, when the Galactic Alliance destroyed their planet, her new clan had disappeared. Now all she had were the people she'd abandoned.

They hadn't accepted her with open arms, but close. She hoped six months would be enough time to file off the rough edges and bring this ragtag group together alongside their pilots.

"So is this mental link thing something we're going to do a lot?" Crayo thought.

"It couldn't hurt. It'll make keeping secrets easier."

"Speaking of which. What else haven't you told me about Mrs. Olivaw?"

27

NGUYỄN DUE
SOL, EARTH

Staring across the field of grass, Nguyễn couldn't help but think this entire endeavor was a complete waste of time. How he'd let Harold talk him into this was beyond comprehension.

"Harold, I honestly don't see the point of visiting your family's vacation cottage with the solar system imploding around us," he said.

The handheld communicator responded with Harold's voice. "All will be revealed soon, Admiral. Please make your way to the rear of the property, to the gardens."

He instinctively reached up and tapped his ear, but nothing happened. A growl escaped his lips. He'd forgotten for the umpteenth time that they'd removed his retinal comm at both his and Harold's request. He, because he wanted to ensure his people were overseeing the installation of a standard military issue version, and Harold because he didn't want Nguyễn's precise location to be tracked.

While he was still in contact with his people in orbit, Harold had taken him through an intricate shell game in the bowels of Charlotte. The city was an immense metropolis, and like others of its size, it had spider webs of transport tubes and tunnels weaving their way below ground, in the arteries that kept the entire thing running. From the sounds of the communications Harold forwarded on, his team had no idea where he was. He hoped they were pretending, but knowing Harold, they weren't. For an A.I., he wasn't stupid. Nguyễn tried telling his team where he was, but Harold was too smart. He continued to swap out his phrases and words with gibberish, leading his people on wild goose chases.

As he walked around the overgrown gardens of the once quaint Cape Cod style home, he caught hints of its former glory. Intricate garden beds now overflowing with weeds and a sea of hedges he could only assume was a maze they'd created for their kids. Even overgrown, the rear yard was magnificent. Somehow, the wild flowers and fruit trees had kept growing and bearing fruit that wasn't covered in wormholes.

He reached up and plucked a mango from a low-hanging branch and turned it over in his hands. It'd been ages since he'd eaten fresh fruit.

"Go on, eat it," Harold said. "It's perfectly ripe and edible. This is one of the many advantages of having robotic gardeners."

He bit into the orangish yellow fruit, and his mouth exploded with flavors. It was like biting into a waterfall of goodness. He closed his eyes and moaned quietly.

"I told you," Harold said, except this time his voice wasn't coming from the communicator in his hand. It was coming from the human in front of him.

A tall, slender male in his mid-forties was standing in the garden with an outstretched hand. His clean white outfit, hypnotic blue eyes, and stoic grin were recognizable anywhere. They were commonly used in advertising and videos for Olivaw International.

"Harold?"

"But of course. Were you expecting someone else?"

He glanced around the property and then back to the humanoid robot, looking him up and down. "I didn't have a fraking clue what to expect. I still don't. Is this," he waved his hand up and down over the robotic form, "what you brought me here for? To showcase your human transformation?"

Harold shook his head and sighed.

The response hit Nguyễn as unusual. The damn robot audibly exhaled at him. He didn't understand how that was possible, or why someone would waste effort on programming a robot to do it. Even with imitation being the sincerest form of flattery, it was downright creepy.

"Shall we?" Harold tilted his head toward the garden and walked away from him.

If he hadn't known better, he could easily mistake Harold for a human. He reminded him of the medic onboard the tribunal ship. Except instead of being a bumbling buffoon, he was a historical imitation of his company's founder.

Nguyễn watched as Harold's human form disappeared behind the wall of hedges. He then brought the communicator closer to his mouth and whispered in it. "I'm at his family cottage near Charlotte. Send a recovery ship."

A moment later, the reply came from Rogers. "Loud and clear, sir. We're scrambling a team to the Atlanta Botanical Garden. They'll be there in ten minutes."

"No!" He shook the tiny communicator.

Harold appeared out of nowhere and walked up to him, snatching the device out of his hand in a blur. He then crushed it in an instant, as if it were a scrap of paper. The sound of the carbon fiber and electronics snapping and crunching was unsettling.

"Best if we end the games, Admiral. We have much to do." He smiled at Nguyễn. "Don't worry. I'll tell them it was a ruse, but I'm not entirely sure if they'll believe me. Please follow me."

He glanced over his shoulder. The ground car he'd arrived

in had already departed. He was stranded here with no way to return to civilization without hoofing it. There wasn't much point in doing that. Obviously, Harold brought him here for a reason. He only hoped it wasn't another wild goose chase.

As he jogged to catch up with Harold, he stepped around the hedge and froze in his tracks. The garden was immaculate. Like a picturesque park from a fairy tale. He'd seen nothing like it outside a simulation.

There were flowers of all shapes and sizes, exploding with color. Bees and butterflies were darting about, careful not to touch one another, but hopping busily from flower to flower. Dotted throughout the beds of blossoms were mossy and leafy ground coverings sprinkled in yellows and purples, like someone had spray-painted them.

He knelt down and rubbed one of the purply leaf variety. It felt stiff and firm, not at all like it appeared.

"What is this place?" He stared up at Harold, who was standing about five meters away near a jet black statue of a wolf.

"It's my family oasis." Harold motioned at the surrounding garden. "I know it's not much, but working the earth with my hands helps me think. It reminds me of a simpler time. A time when I could sit on that porch and enjoy a morning coffee with Callisto and Luna and not worry about the fate of humanity." He pointed at the porch.

Nguyễn turned to see six pristine rocking chairs on a raised platform attached to the back of the house. The rear was not at all like the shambles the front presented. If you'd have driven past this place, you'd have sworn it was an abandoned dump.

The robotic driver built into the air car he'd arrived in said it couldn't fly over the property. It was forced around it and could only approach from the ground. He'd never heard of anything like that before except near military bases. Apparently, being an Olivaw had its privileges.

"Your body language tells me you're not up for a cup-of-joe and a chat, Admiral," Harold said. "Why don't we move on to something a bit more helpful for our situation, shall we?"

When he turned to face the humanoid robot, he caught Harold reaching up and twisting one of the ears on the wolf. The statue then shifted in place. Without a sound, it slid away from Harold about two meters, leaving a black hole just as wide.

Nguyễn's jaw dropped. He stepped around the statue toward the pit and leaned forward, peering into it. It was pitch black and seemed to go on forever and yet nowhere. The depths were featureless, and despite the sun being nearly overhead, no visible sides or floor were discernible. It was as if the hole was both there and not at the same time.

Harold clapped his hands together and Nguyễn jumped backward. "Sorry for scaring you. Why don't I go first? It'll be easier that way."

Before he could reply, Harold stepped toward the hole and then dropped into it.

"What the hell?" he muttered as he rushed forward, falling to his knees against the smooth ground beneath where the statue formerly rested. When he leaned over the hole a second time, he caught a fleeting glimpse of Harold disappearing into the darkness, and then he was gone. Swallowed in the shadows.

He reached up and rubbed his hands through his hair before straightening it back into place. "Why is nothing ever simple with these Olivaws? They always have a flair for the dramatic."

It took a few minutes to compose himself and convince his mind the hole in the earth was merely a gravity lift tube. It just happened to be out here in the middle of nowhere and lacked the usual glow of the ones he was used to moving through. Once he was sufficiently convinced, he took one last deep breath and stepped over the hole.

He knew instantly he'd guessed right. The familiar tingle of the gravity fields tugged him down and yet reassured him that while he was indeed falling, he was safe in the Olivaw gravity field. The irony of being safe in the embrace of the Olivaw technology suddenly washed over him as he sank into infinite darkness.

WITHOUT HIS RETINAL COMM, Nguyễn was blind to both time and distance. He could've been in the dark for an hour or several minutes. It was hard to tell, and reaching out didn't help. The tube was wide enough so that he couldn't reach either side. That, or the gravitational field pushed him around to ensure he didn't. He would be none the wiser in the darkness.

The strangest thing about moving in a gravity field was a lack of direction. While he'd stepped down into the hole, the field could push and pull him any which way, and his body wouldn't sense it. It was for this reason alone that any idea of being saved disappeared. There was no way a search party would be able to find him beneath that statue, let alone wherever he was headed.

What made matters worse were his feelings. Riding through the dark, he was conflicted. He wasn't afraid, and he wasn't angry. For the first time in a long time, he was impressed. The Olivaws had not only managed to pull the wool over the eyes of everyone in Sol in the vastness of space, they'd done it back home. In the backyard of humanity, where there were more eyes on the ground than anywhere humans had ever set foot. At least the Sol brand of humans, anyhow.

Maybe this was a bunker. A zero-day pandemic facility for their friends and family. Perhaps Harold hung out here to pass the time while he helped his people weave their master plan from afar. He'd know soon enough.

His first thought when he saw the light ahead was relief, but as he approached it, he was overcome with fear. He was rapidly accelerating toward an expansive cliff of some sort, and from the looks of it, he was going to fall off the edge.

Frantically looking left and then right, there were no handles or means to stop. Even stretching out, he couldn't touch either side of the tube.

"Frak," he muttered, approaching the nothingness in front of him. This could end in far more pain than he'd expected. He was suddenly regretting coming here naked of his implements. At least if he had an electro-blade he could try to dig them into the wall or push them out from both sides to slow his movement.

With his heart pounding and arms flailing for a handhold, he floated closer to the cliff's edge and his approach slowed to a stop. At that moment, his reality shifted from survival to awe. He stared slack-jawed over a massive hangar filled with what appeared to be small fighter crafts. There were hundreds of them, as far as the eye could see. It reminded him of the military hangars he commanded on Luna or in the Outer Ring. He'd never seen anything like it on Sol, though. A hangar this size was impractical when constrained by the planet's gravitational grip.

"Sorry about that," Harold said. His voice was coming from everywhere and nowhere in particular. "I imagine that approach was a tad jarring without a retinal comm. I'll be bringing you in safely over the top before setting down."

"Over the top of what?" he asked, but before Harold could reply he'd already started out into the open above the hangar. He was floating out over the expansive chamber without any form of harness or ship to make him feel secure. While he'd done this in lift tubes, and he'd floated in space countless times, this was different. It felt like he was flying.

As he leaned forward and squinted at the ships, he studied their shape. He'd never seen these designs before. They were jet black and shaped like arrowheads. From the looks of their layout and the open hatch, there was a rear compartment designed to hold a sphere of some sort, and these were missing them. He didn't see any spheres anywhere on the hangar floor. But judging by the size of the gaping hole, they could house two, maybe three people, and not much else. On the wings of each ship were laser batteries, missile mounts, and what appeared to be either rail guns or some type of energy weapon.

Harold had been slowly increasing his speed as he floated over the field of ships, and he was now speeding past at a blistering clip, one he wasn't comfortable with. Perhaps he'd been moving this fast all along, but the darkness of the tube prevented him from perceiving it. This, however, was making his stomach churn.

Just as he was sensing an unpleasantness rising in his belly, the acceleration cut, and he descended toward the ground. He was coming up next to Harold's human form. The android gazed up at him as he approached, a welcoming smile on his face.

His stare was both relaxing and disconcerting at the same time. Perhaps it was knowing there was an A.I. inside that body that unsettled him so much. Everything he did and said was a calculation. It sent shivers through him when he thought about the human form robot.

When his feet finally touched down, Harold didn't say a word. He merely nodded and returned his gaze across the hangar of ships. They were both standing about ten meters off the main floor, behind a protective railing.

Now that he was closer to one of the ships, he noticed a series of clear tubes pumping some type of blue liquid out of the rear compartment and into the ground. Only when it disappeared into a hole did he realize this arrowhead craft had just had a sphere inside.

He pointed toward the ship. "What's in that... sphere?"

"At the moment, nothing." Harold stared blankly at the fighter before continuing. "We're testing and retesting each and every ship to make sure the crew capsule interfaces properly. But soon we'll have pilots inside, ready to defend the planet."

He squinted at the smooth skin of the android. His features were remarkably human. Hell, he even had ear hair. "Pilots? As in human pilots?"

Harold nodded.

"And where are those coming from?"

Harold turned toward him. "We've been training many of them for months, though they've only recently graduated from crude simulations to the real thing. We've also managed to... how shall I put it... elicit some volunteers from the general population."

He scrunched up his face. "As in, you snatched and grabbed some bodies?"

"Oh, no. As in gamers." Harold turned and began walking. "Come, there's more."

"Wait!" He wasn't going to continue this charade any longer. "What do you mean gamers? And what the frak is this place? You can't just drop tidbits like that without details and expect me to follow you around like a puppy."

The android spun in place and squinted at him. "So, you want me to... I believe your term is, tear it off."

He nodded and motioned with his hand. "Tear, rip, fraking blow it off. I don't give a shit, I just need answers."

"Alright. You want answers. Fine. You're standing in one of twenty facilities spread throughout Earth with another sixteen throughout Sol. Each facility, when completed in the coming weeks, will be equal to or larger than this one. By the time we're finished, you'll have two thousand Nyílak fighters at your disposal as well as a host of defensive weaponry capable of destroying their Selene ships from the ground. Thanks, of course, to the Spános you brought along for the voyage and sent elsewhere as I requested."

Nguyễn reached out a hand, resting it on the railing beside him. That was a whole lot to absorb in a brief burst and not at all what he'd imagined Harold would say. He'd grown so used to his cryptic riddles that the truth was shocking.

Thirty-six facilities throughout Sol, just like this one. While it added to their array of weapons, they were still outnumbered, and the aliens could pulverize them from afar. Perhaps these fighters were more than met the eye. "If this is what the Spános was for, what about the pirates you dispatched to steal our reserves?"

"I'm afraid I don't know what you're talking about."

"Bullshit! You knew only half of the Spános was being sent to the other planets. I sent the remainder away on another shuttle for safe keeping, except it conveniently disappeared. What do you know about that?"

Harold shrugged, staring out over the hangar. "First I'm hearing of it. You said something about pirates. Is that right?"

He was fraking lying and wasn't about to admit it. "Never mind. What did you mean when you said you were using gamers to pilot these?" He pointed at the Nyílak spread out in front of him.

"We've been running some e-sport games across the globe and throughout Sol through some of our gaming subsidiaries. You know, blow up the alien type things. They're quite popular. Anyhow, we developed these games in a pinch, but their controls are remarkably close to those ships out there. The top five hundred gamers are flying to our facilities as we speak, and they're awaiting your orders, among others."

He tilted his head to the side toward Harold. "My... orders? I don't understand."

Harold waved his hand across the horizon filled with ships. "These are yours, Admiral. They're the tip of your spear. Despite what you may think of the Olivaws, our mission... my mission has never been to subvert human authority. It has merely been to—" He raised a hand and gently pushed through the air. "Nudge it along until it could help itself. As recent events have fast forwarded many of my plans, we're now forced to make some hard decisions and need to bring all of humanity into the fold. If we don't..." Harold's hands squeezed the railing. "I fear we'll perish."

"Hold on." His gaze narrowed. He didn't know why he was asking an A.I. this question. He wasn't human, but his gestures were remarkable. The damn machine was behaving like it was alive. "When you say 'I', you mean the Olivaw family, right?"

A grin broke the stoic, almost saddened face of the android. If he hadn't known better, he would have mistaken it for a human expression.

"If I told you I wasn't an A.I., would you believe me?" Harold turned and leaned against the railing, facing Nguyễn.

He squinted, taking a closer look at the android. His eyes were perfect matches for the real thing, and his skin appeared to be normal. Hairs randomly tossed about, imperfections in skin color, and even a few cuts that looked like they'd never fully healed. "Are you a clone?"

Harold shook his head and chuckled. "Oh no, certainly not. We Olivaws understand the laws against cloning. No, I'm an android with a computer brain, Admiral. The one difference, though, is that my mind isn't entirely a program. It also contains the memories, thoughts, and consciousness of my former self, Harold Olivaw."

And now it made sense. The attitude, the penchant for the dramatic, and the sheer drive to piss him off. It wasn't that he'd been dealing with an A.I. the entire time; it was that he'd been dealing with an actual human. Or at least the mind of one. This abomination was skirting the definition of the very word, human.

He swallowed hard, suddenly feeling a bit revolted in the android's presence. The Olivaws had not only subverted humanity and brought it to the brink of annihilation; they fought to subvert the circle of life as well.

Humans had an aging process for a reason. There was a time and place for one generation's ideas and mistakes. The notion that the upcoming generations could heal those wounds and tackle new challenges with fresh eyes was what made humans human. What he'd done was flip that on its head and force centuries of mistakes upon all humanity. What they'd done was subverting the natural order of the universe.

He didn't know how long had passed, but not a word had been exchanged before Harold spoke. "Based on your body language, your vitals, and the look on your face, I either shot your cat, or you're not at ease with this recent revelation."

Nguyễn cracked his neck. "I… don't see what your…" He waved his hand over the android form. "Being an immortal human form robot has anything to do with the rest of this. At least not in the here and now. Longer term, I suspect it's another mistake the Olivaws made, which humanity will feel the burden of in time." He turned to face the hangar again, happy to have his eyes on something less revolting.

"Fair enough." Harold stood up straight. "In the interest of sharing all details of our current situation, I thought it best to tell you everything. The colonies have been told the truth, there's no sense in you not knowing."

He stared at the spherical robot rolling across the ground below, scanning or doing something to the Nyílak ship. "You told them about all of this? Even about you?"

"Touché!" Harold waved his hand. "Everything except that. They know about the lies we told, about the origins of humanity, and about the situation here in Sol."

A gangly octopus-looking robot slid up beside the ship,

connected its tentacles to the port side, and then floated down the hole the crew capsule had fallen into. The technology in this place was light years ahead of Sol. He had to tread carefully with the ego of this thing. He didn't even know what to think of Harold now. It wasn't merely an A.I. any longer. "Are there any colonists alive in Epsilon Eridani? I mean, I'd hoped a few survived, but you've never told us."

Harold was fiddling with a ring on his left ring finger. When Nguyễn leaned closer, he saw it was primitive. Not at all like the modern gadget jewelry of the day. Its aged appearance resembled solid silver or platinum. The design was remarkably clean, with only two rows of neat rectangles etched in the surface.

The android finally broke the silence. "There are over one thousand survivors on Liprosus."

His eyes went wide. "That's wonderful, I... would've expected far less."

Harold snapped around to face him. "You'd have expected we abandoned them then?"

"No, no." He shook his head. "That's not what I meant. It's only that the videos showed the colony being destroyed."

"Let's just say that we helped them escape elsewhere on the planet. The Galactic Alliance has no clue they're alive. For now, anyhow."

"And they're safe?" He studied the android's face for clues of any kind. Anything he could use.

Harold shook his head. "Stop playing games, Admiral. You and I both know you don't care about the colonists. The nearly twenty-five billion people in Sol are worth far more to you and your desire to rule than the mere thousand on Liprosus. They're martyrs to your ego and your cause, and you know it."

He turned to face the hangar, squeezing the railing tightly with both hands. Harold wasn't a fool. He saw right through his questions. "Are all of these ships under my command?"

Harold nodded. "Each and every one, from this point forward."

"And what of the pilots? You mentioned they were waiting for my orders, but you didn't say what orders."

"First, you'll need to flex the war powers granted to you by President Olivaw and institute a draft, ordering these pilots to serve humanity. It's your only short-term option until other suitable people within your ranks can be found. We'll also need a significant boost in resources to further expand your fleet. I'm afraid that what you're seeing here has emptied the Olivaw reserves. Finally, we'll need all of that Spános to be turned over to each facility. Without it, we can't power our defensive grid. I've already sent on the final coordinates to your people, they're awaiting your approval."

He took a deep breath. Harold had him at all of this was his. If the Olivaws managed to build these underground facilities around Sol without detection, then the reach of their strength was truly staggering and not one he wanted to question or have working against him.

His role in this war had become abundantly clear in the last few minutes. He had fits of grandeur in the beginning, but Harold had continuously knocked him back into place. While he wasn't a pawn by any measure, he was in control of the spear. At least for now.

As he took in Harold's words and the hangar before him, something felt off. It wasn't something he was seeing; it was something missing, and he hadn't seen it on his voyage flying in, either. "Tell me, how are you planning on getting these ships out of here? I don't exactly see an exit hatch."

"Ah, yes. The final piece of the puzzle. For this, I've saved the best for last. Please follow me." Harold spun around and headed toward the already open doorway to their right.

Nguyễn glanced to his left at the Nyílak, wondering for a moment why Harold couldn't show him here. He was peculiar about the things he shared and the things he held close to his chest. One thing was clear, he was always the showman.

As he broke into a jog to catch up to the fast walking android, he did a double take as he passed into the hallway. There were far more humans here than he'd expected. There were at least a dozen in this single hall alone. Judging by the number of automata servicing the Nyílak, he couldn't figure out what else they'd be doing down here.

When he reached Harold's side, he asked, "Who are these people, and what's their purpose here?"

"They live here," Harold said without skipping a beat.

"Live, as in temporarily?"

"Nope, live as in permanently. They have for generations. We're the outsiders."

He stared at the black-haired male that passed on his left. He was studying a tablet while he walked, oblivious to either he or Harold. "Are they Gunders?"

Harold nodded. "They are. What of it?"

"So, wait…" He rubbed his chin, struggling to recall a fleeting memory. Being without a damn retinal comm sucked. "Did we travel all the way to Atlanta? That's the closest hybrid Gunder and surface colony from Charlotte."

"Not exactly, no. But we are connected to there. Most of the Gunder cities are interconnected by now. Here we are." Harold gestured toward the open doorway. "After you."

That was impossible. The UN and CoPE would have known if they'd united the cities. "Since when were the Gunder cities linked?"

"Since the Olivaws needed them to be. It's been a few months, but we've worked the kinks out. Now, if you'd step into the lab, we can get this show underway." He reached over and pushed against Nguyễn's back, urging him onward.

Harold's strength was astonishing. Without much effort, he'd nearly fallen forward from both the unexpected motion and the absolute power of the android's body. He'd have to remember that if he ever got on his bad side.

Stumbling into the room, he froze in place to take in the space. It was a long, narrow corridor at least a hundred meters in length, and its walls were lined with what looked like massive inverted gravitational dampeners. The strange thing about them was not their presence, but that they were aimed at one another. Hundreds and hundreds of them. Usually, they were masked behind precisely controlled and super strong nano mesh covers used to direct the forces, but these were out in the open.

Along the wall closest to them was a single chair with a young girl sitting comfortably. They were holding a light green stuffed alligator and had a strange crude contraption in front of them that resembled an old school video game.

He walked up behind the youngster and leaned forward for a closer look. There were three-dimensional lines across the control panel that mimicked the room, except far more primitive than any virtual reality sim he'd ever seen. It reminded him of something he'd find at a museum as a kid.

"What is this place?" he muttered, watching the girl play with her alligator.

Harold stepped up beside him. "Are you ready to show Admiral Nguyễn everything you've learned, Jezabel?"

The girl's eyes went wide and she leaned closer to Harold. "Is it really him? The man from the news?"

Harold crouched next to her and smiled. "It is. He's here to see all your hard work. Remember how we told you the Gunders were going to help save humanity?"

Jezabel nodded slowly, hugging her alligator tight.

"Well, now's your first test. Can you show him how we play catch with Allie?" Harold reached toward the stuffed animal but stopped short, holding his hand out.

The girl swallowed hard and then stared up at Nguyễn.

"Do you despise the Gunders as much as the other surface dwellers, sir?"

He was caught off guard. While he had never met a Gunder before, he'd heard many rumors about the mole people. They refused to live above ground, claiming that they preferred the deep cities they inhabited below. After they retreated to their bunker metropolises centuries ago, most cities found it easier to pretend they weren't there rather than fight them. Besides, they lived off the scraps cities disposed of.

Jezabel leaned forward to look him in the eyes. "Mister, did you hear me?"

"Yes, I heard you," Nguyễn said. He forced a smile. "I… was merely surprised by your question. I don't despise you. I couldn't. I don't even know you."

He hoped she couldn't read his hesitancy. For like his feelings toward Harold, he was equally repulsed by Gunders. Living off trash and waste products wasn't something he imagined led to a good life. Though, judging by this facility, his ideas could be a tad misguided.

"I'm ready, Mr. Olivaw!" Jezabel handed Harold her very tattered stuffed alligator.

Harold reached forward and tousled the little girl's hair, and she giggled before making a growling noise. "Let's see if we can't make a basket, shall we?"

"Same prize as last time?" the girl asked.

He chuckled. "Same prize."

Jezabel reached out and pressed the green button on her control panel, and the lights in the room lowered to a faint glow. Suddenly, a small canister rose out of the floor in the middle of the long corridor. It resembled a wastebasket.

Nguyễn shook his head. "What does shooting a basket from fifty meters have anything to do with anything?"

Harold spun to face him, an evil scowl on his face. "Patience, Admiral. For now, keep your mouth closed." He then turned back toward the girl, his face transformed into a smile. "I'm ready when you are, Jez."

She reached to the panel on her left and slid a lever upward, causing the directional gravitational dampeners to come to life. They spun around and seemed to aim toward the basket in the center. A moment later a low rumble permeated the space as the floor slid open, revealing even more dampeners aimed at the same spot.

While he wanted to ask for more details about what he was seeing, he realized he should heed Harold's advice. A ring rose a meter out of the floor just to Harold's left. Once it was stationary, it flashed a brilliant blue.

He raised his hands to cover the bright light, and for a moment, he saw a halo. Like when you stared too long at the sun out a porthole into space. Your eyes usually adjusted, and the image would disappear, except this time it didn't. It slid outward, across the open air within the corridor. When he closed his eyes and opened them again, it was still there. It was faint, but it was there.

Harold stepped back to his side and whispered, "You're only seeing the halo because we're projecting light through the other side." He pointed behind them toward what looked like a black light. "Normally, the effect isn't noticeable."

"What is—" He didn't finish the sentence for fear of Harold lashing at him.

As the ring of light slid down the length of the corridor, he noticed something had changed. A spherical hologram appeared in the center above the basket.

"The gravity from the dampeners is focused at that point. Very much like a moon, or in our case a Selene ship." Harold winked at him before stepping toward the closest ring. "Are we ready, Jez?"

"One... second, sir," she said. "I need to adjust the tach-e-ons to hit the sweet spot."

He glanced right and watched as the girl adjusted some

dials and levers on her controls, seemingly at random. When he turned his attention back to the corridor, the halo had risen and was now in the center of the hologram.

Harold bounced the toy alligator playfully in his hand, seeming to take measure of its weight and rate of descent, and then he tossed it precisely into the middle of the glowing ring.

A second later, Nguyễn saw movement out of the corner of his eye. Something had fallen out of the distant ring and into the basket. At least it seemed like it.

As he stepped forward, Harold reached out and yanked him back.

"Experiment off!" Harold shouted, still firmly grasping Nguyễn. "Hold on a moment, Admiral."

The hologram cut out, the gravitational dampeners retired to a neutral position, and the hum returned to the room as the floors slid closed. He tried to yank his arm away from Harold, but his vice-like grip wouldn't budge. It was like he was cemented in place.

When the floors were sealed tight, Harold released him, and he sprinted toward the basket. He had to have been mistaken. There was no way the alligator could have passed between the two points in space.

As he approached the basket, he slowed to a crawl. The container was transparent. In the darkness and at the greater distance, he hadn't noticed it. He was still ten meters away, but the object inside was unmistakable.

Reaching the edge, he stared down in disbelief. Only now did he realize the beating he was hearing wasn't something around him, it was his heart.

He reached down and picked up the fluffy, light green, tattered alligator. It was heavier than he'd imagined, and the stitching holding it together was definitely hand sewn. There were huge gaps between each stitch, and the threads seemed to change colors from years of love and fixing. He stared at it in disbelief, turning it over again and again in his hand.

"It wasn't a trick or sleight of hand." Harold had walked up without a sound. A trick just as mind-numbing, given how immovable he was a moment ago.

"But…" The question never came. It merely hung in the room.

"Imagine this at a planetary scale." Harold stepped closer and reached out, carefully pulling the alligator from his hands. "You asked how we can launch those fighters without hangar doors, or how we traveled across the galaxy in a fraction of the time of the Galactic Alliance. Perhaps now you understand why they're so frightened, and we're so tight-lipped. We hold in our palm the power to turn the tide in not only this battle, but every battle from this day forward."

"We could…" He glanced up and stared into Harold's deep blue eyes. They twinkled, as if he were alive. "We could rule the galaxy."

Harold chuckled and studied Allie. "That's aiming high, but yes. In time. For now, let's keep our sights on the challenges in Sol. Shall we?"

28

JOYCE GREEN

EPSILON ERIDANI, LIPROSUS

They both stared through the viewport of the containment room. Joyce hadn't been down here since she'd killed Two, and except for food, no one had checked in on One. She hadn't felt a need to get intel with Bradley and his team running the show. Captain Hui had relinquished control to him and Pluto under orders from a General Yule. Bradley reassured her it was a joint command, but she hadn't tested it. Not yet.

"Why's he staring at the corner of the ceiling?" Bradley asked as he craned his neck up and over to catch a glimpse of what the alien was seeing.

"Two used to do it, as well. When you're in their spot at the center, and you squint, the semi-reflective wall surface meets in the corner in a honeycomb shaped pattern."

"I'll be damned," Bradley muttered. "I've tried to look at these aliens differently than the bees back on Earth, but with behavior like that it's impossible not to."

She glanced at him and studied his face. He had the same boyish good looks as his brother. She'd spent hours watching and re-watching his speech. Their resemblance was unmistakable. "So where's the other colony?"

His body language shifted. She'd hit a nerve. Despite being open about so many things, apparently, the location of the second colony was still taboo. She watched as he reached into his pocket and put something away.

"In time, Director. In time." He zipped the pocket closed.

"We're not supposed to bring anything inside." She nodded toward his pocket. "How'd you get it past the scanners, anyhow?"

He shrugged. "I forgot it was in there, and it never went off."

Her eyes narrowed. "What is it?"

"A rock."

"You carry a rock around with you?"

He stared down at his hands. "It was from beside my father's grave on Earth. I have a habit of picking up rocks from the places I've been or the times I'm feeling most vulnerable."

"Oh." She swallowed hard. "I'm sorry. I didn't realize—"

"No worries." He waved his hand. "Except for Cynthia, no one even knows I have it. Whenever I need a hit of focus or a way to ground myself, I pull it out and think about him or my mother."

She nodded and returned her attention to One. He was still staring at the corner, and his antennae were drooping down against the side of his head like they had been for weeks.

"I did that with my son's hats sometimes after he died." The knot in her stomach tightened. "They were destroyed in the attack. Except for his identity bracelet, I don't have anything left of him."

"I'm sorry," Bradley muttered.

The silence hung between them for what seemed like an eternity. Neither was excited about entering the room, but they had to learn more about the Beacon from One.

She needed a few more minutes before she could enter. "Talk to me about these missiles we're worried about."

Bradley shook his head. "That's an interesting change of topic. You're not the best at small talk before an interrogation, are you?"

"It helps if I think about something else. Besides, I can only stare at the videos and the briefing material for so long." She clasped her hands behind her back.

He stepped down the length of the viewport to get a look at the front of the Thyreusian. "I'm sure Harold could tell you any time you wanted."

"He and I aren't exactly on the best of terms. We've agreed to keep our distance unless absolutely necessary."

He glanced at her, a smirk on his face. "You and I aren't that different, Joyce. My family and their A.I. have always annoyed me."

"You mean you and your great-great however many times grandfather aren't best buds?" She studied his reaction.

His gaze went cold. "Not exactly, no." He turned his attention back to One. "Our first time seeing the missiles was at Alanasl, some eighty years ago. One of our probes caught the GA launching them into the Nebula just as we'd arrived. We didn't know what we were looking at until we visited the Lupus Dark Nebula. It was there that we saw the resulting devastation caused by the missiles they'd launched."

She turned to face him and leaned against the wall. "And?"

His hand reached toward his pocket and stopped short. "They'll target the Epsilon Eridani sun, and after they hit, it'll go nova. Not immediately, but the best we can tell, it'll be within a thousand years or so."

"That's a long time. Seems like we can get out before then."

"We're not trying to get out, Joyce. Well, not all of us anyhow. We're trying to stay inside."

She pushed off the wall. The damn Olivaws were always talking in riddles. "Why the hell would we want to hang around in here?" She stepped toward him.

"Hey now!" He took a step backwards, putting space between them and bringing his hands into a defensive posture. "Stand the frak down, Director."

In her frustration, she hadn't even realized her fists had clenched.

"If you'd done your homework," Bradley began, "you'd have found the details on what we were doing in your briefings. It's not my fault you and Harold are having a spat. Perhaps you dust off your neural education link and do some cramming before you make a move on me. I don't have time for your fits of temper. None of us do. Why don't you step up to the plate, take a deep breath, and join this battle. That, or get the frak out of the way and let the rest of us do our job."

Her muscles pulsed, and her emotions were taking control again. He was right, but she wasn't about to admit it. While she used to be the calm and collected one in any discussion, that version of herself was gone. Or perhaps it was taking a long nap. This version wanted revenge. "Why the hell would we stay here?"

"Fine! I'll do your homework for you one last time." He took an aggressive step closer to her. "You watched the videos earlier, Director. It's a simple strategy. The GA exit stage left after they lay down the Nebula. Our intel from Lupus shows they don't even know how to get inside once they seal it off. All they care about is containing their problem species. Once the deed is done, they move on to conquering the next alien system."

"So..." She took a step back dand relaxed her posture, staring at One. "We sit and wait. You're gonna turn Epsilon into a base of operations for the human fleet." She could feel his eyes studying her.

"It's the closest occupied star system to Sol, and it'll come with a built-in moat for protection. Once we regroup, we'll—"

"Move in to help Sol?" She interrupted.

"Bingo. Now, if you don't mind, I have an interrogation to perform." He stepped around her and walked to the cell's entrance.

When she turned to join him, he froze and held out his hand for her to stop. "No. I'll do it alone. The last thing we need is another dead Thyreusian."

She motioned for him to step in. "I'm pretty sure I can keep my cool."

He took a step toward her. "You're pretty sure? You're joking with me, right? A moment ago you practically swung at me, and we're on the same fraking team. I think you need to stay out here, or better yet, head back to your quarters and take some time for yourself. We could really use your help leading this mission and hopefully future ones. I thought we made that clear earlier. If you're not up for it, that's fine. We can't have you compromising our goals anymore. You can return to Sol, or wherever the hell you want to hang your hat when this is all done. Once you figure that out, let's chat."

She stared at him and his steel-blue eyes. They were filled with pain and frustration. Almost as much as what she felt, except they were directed at her. He was right. She had to get her head straight. She'd lost it with him three times now, and if anyone was likely to understand her, it'd be him.

His family had pushed him away on numerous occasions, and yet here he was. She took a deep breath and relaxed her shoulders. "I'll stick around out here and head up when you're done." Joyce stepped backward and down the wall, to get a better look at One during the interrogation. She wanted to hear what he was going to ask and wasn't up for watching it in a video later. Her own two eyes were the only thing she could trust.

He stared at her for a minute before finally stepping back

to the door, eyeing the soldiers flanking it. "Don't let her in with me. Director Green is to stay outside this cell. Is that understood?"

"Yessir," the soldiers said in unison.

She hated that he could order her people around. Her temper and the frustration of being cooped up below ground had taken a toll on her ability to make impartial and rational decisions. The price she was paying was the loss of their trust, and that hurt more than she'd imagined.

29

BRADLEY OLIVAW

EPSILON ERIDANI, LIPROSUS

Bradley could feel her eyes on him as he stepped into the containment cell. He strode around the Thyreusian they called One and into the corner nearest where Joyce was on the outside. The last thing he wanted was to keep glancing at where she was standing. He needed to focus on the task at hand.

"And who are you?" One asked. Their antenna rose up when he entered and bobbed in the air above their head.

He slid out the tiny shelf from the corner and sat down. The hard metal surface was cold on his butt. It wasn't comfortable in the slightest. "Name's, Bradley. And you are?"

The alien moved his head about, seeming to take him in with all sixteen of their eyes. "They call me One."

He nodded. "I got that. But what's your name? Obviously it's not a number."

"It doesn't matter."

"If you say so." He reached up and scratched at his neck. "I was wondering about something. Are you able to feel it?"

Their antenna froze and arced toward him. "Feel what?"

"What Two told us about. Certainly if he felt it, you must, as well?"

One went rigid and then shook their shoulders violently.

He hopped to his feet, having not expected any motion from the alien so soon.

One gyrated, and a human laugh escaped. "Skittish are we?"

"Something like that." He was better moving, anyhow. It helped him think.

"Two knows not to talk to the likes of you."

He nodded his head and began circling around the Thyreusian, making sure to keep his distance. "So, we shouldn't know anything about the Beacon then?"

One's antenna followed him and jerked when he mentioned the Beacon.

"I see you're familiar with what I'm talking about. Well, at least from what Two told us anyhow."

"He wouldn't have. He knows the queens would destroy not only his family, but his entire lineage up the tree."

"That's a perfectly rational argument. We'll just pretend we don't know it arrived in the past week, then."

Again the antenna spasmed, but not a word was spoken.

Seemed that intel was correct. Now to confirm if the implications were true.

He continued circling them and rubbed his hands together. "Judging by what he said, and the last day of changes, your people will be closing the Nebula in a few months' time."

"Impossible!" One said. "It'd take another few days to see any changes. They'll need to acclimate the ships to the shock of the Beacon. Everyone knows that."

And now came the leaps. "Well, I don't know." He shrugged wildly. "Two conjectured the reason we were seeing acceleration so soon was because some of your ships were also being in service during the Nebula in Alanasl or the Prodo system."

"May his family rest in peace," One muttered.

His stomach churned. He'd hoped the intel from Two had been a lie spoken in a last ditched effort to save his own life, but apparently he'd been telling the truth. This didn't bode well for them at all.

As he paced around the alien, they started humming. It was a constant sound, almost like a refrigeration unit. "What is that you're singing?"

"I'm not singing." The alien turned their head to face him. "I'm praying to his ancestors and the thousands of lives he's taken by failing to keep his mouth shut."

He froze and smiled at the alien. "You have to do me a favor and settle a bet. I wagered that it'd take a meter thick Skotádi to shield the Beacon from our detection. He claimed it was far more. What do you say? Who's right?"

One turned their head and seemed to study him with his left set of eyes. "I don't know what a meter is."

"Oh, about this much." Bradley held out his hands in front of himself about a meter apart.

One broke into laughter again. The howling noise sounded remarkably like a human writhing in pain. "You'd need about three times as much unless you wanted it to turn your feeble minds to mush."

Check. He feigned a shrug. "Well, that settles that then. I guess I lost the bet. That would also explain why we didn't detect its arrival. You know what gets me, though?"

One's antenna arched toward him, and he adjusted his head to face Bradley. "What's that, mouth breather?"

He reached up and rubbed at his cheek. "I still don't get the point of the Beacon. I mean, the Nebula is already enshrouding our star system, and we can't pass through it. The Beacon seems pointless."

One leaned forward, the pinchers on the side of their mouth seeming to motion toward one another. "Pointless? Pointless! Do you know nothing of your history? Of your

Galactic Alliance origins? Have you retained no knowledge of your past, uplift?"

He shook his head, remaining silent.

"Without the Beacon, the Nebula would float aimlessly through space. It could spread outward and grow to enshroud anything in its path. Any nearby stars and species would be at risk. The Beacon adds rigidity to the cell that will ensnare you and your kind for eternity. Well, at least until your star takes you. That, too, keeps the nebulosity gravitationally bound once the Beacon has given it life."

Check and check. All the details they'd learned from Ibu's book were holding true. Libby had been worried that the religious gospel within the Nanil text had been misinterpreted, but thus far it'd been right on the money. He still didn't understand what giving it life meant. He'd seen and experienced nothing but death inside the Lupus Dark Nebula.

When he began pacing around One, they spoke again. "What's strange to me this time is that we aren't removing all the valuable matter in this star system. It seems a waste to leave it with you in your tomb."

He froze and turned his head to face the alien. "What do you mean, remove the matter?"

One's antenna danced around their head. "In most trials, the guilty party loses not only their right to live, they lose their minerals and ore, as well. We usually connect the star systems and strip everything from them as a punishment for their crimes. This time, however, the verdict was made in haste and corners were cut. I believe that is how you tricked us into making a mistake on your planet. The Spános was too enticing to pass up, and we got cocky thinking we'd destroyed you."

This alien was far chattier than he'd imagined they'd be. Perhaps Joyce leaving them to their own devices for so long had done a number on them. They were a hive species, after all.

As he began circling One, he tried to focus on his next set of questions. They needed to know more about the missiles and what to expect from the Beacon after they captured it. Ibu's book hadn't given them anything to work from since neither human nor Nanil had ever come into rotation to protect a Beacon.

With his mind deep in thought, he hadn't even noticed his subconscious movement toward the stone. For when he brushed against it, One lurched in his direction and the pillar whined in complaint. He'd been told it was a solid mount and was driven into the bedrock below. Unless the Thyreusian could break nano-fiber reinforced steel, it wasn't going anywhere.

That didn't prevent him from stumbling back against the wall. When he caught the gaze of One, they were practically primal. The muscles in their arms and shoulder flexed, and their antenna was stretching toward him as if they were trying to sting him or something.

When he reached into his pocket and withdrew the stone, One exploded forward with a force that brought the doorway to the cell open and two guards inside.

"His vitals are off the charts, sir." The guard nearest him said. "Harold thinks you should give him some space. Too many more movements like that, and he's bound to tear off his own arm."

It was only then that Bradley saw it. Yellow blood oozing down One's side. Sure enough, there was a gash near where their shoulder met each arm. They'd lurched forward with such force that their arms had begun separating from their upper exoskeleton.

He'd heard of humans dislocating their joints in a drug induced rage, but he'd never experienced anything remotely like this before. Whatever his stone was, the alien wanted it. As they backed out of the room, and the door lowered just shy of the floor, he rubbed the stone again.

One lunged forward, his shoulder tearing from his arms. A blood-curdling scream bellowed forth as he reached for the closing door. When it hit the floor, the noise stopped and the hall fell silent. The door had slid closed into the recess in the ground.

Bradley swallowed hard. His heart hammering in his chest. He hopped around to the other side to peer through the cell's viewport. Joyce had left, but there inside the cell was One. He was lying in a pool of his own blood, and it was growing larger by the second.

"Get a medic," he muttered, glancing at the guard. "Now!"

The guard sprinted down the hall and began cycling through the next hatch.

When he returned his attention to One, he rubbed the stone trembling in his hand. There was no reaction. Somehow the Skotádi encasing the cells was blocking out whatever this stone was doing to the Thyreusian. It didn't appear to be impacting the human guards, and except for a faint relaxing tingle in his fingers, he couldn't sense anything, either.

This entire event had jumped the rails. There was no way the tiny stone could've led One to such fits of strength, and it certainly couldn't have overpowered his self-control. It had to be something else. Perhaps he'd smelled a remnant of Two on his clothes. He had just been in the adjacent hall to where the alien had died. That had to be it.

He slid the stone into his pocket and strode toward the entrance that was now opening. A medical team emerged from the tiny space, followed by several more guards.

As he stepped inside and cycled the door, his mind drifted back to the wolf statue at their family cottage on Earth. It was there that he'd picked up and pocketed the stone while talking to Aunt Kara after his father's eulogy.

This rock had helped to dull the pain he'd felt coming to

grips with the loss of his father. Today, the tiny stone somehow inverted that feeling and inflicted it on the alien.

"YOU KNOW we shouldn't be outside for so long," Pluto said into the dark night.

Bradley had come out here to get away from everyone, not to be found. It was his one excuse to shut off his retinal comm and maintain silence. He was lying on his back, struggling to identify the constellations in the sky.

Little Red had also tried to stop him from coming out here, but he needed to breathe the fresh air. He never handled violence or anger well. When he was a kid, he'd always break down in tears during a fight. People used to make fun of him for it, calling him weak, but that wasn't it at all. He felt emotions more strongly than most people and needed time to decompress.

The rustling of grasses was growing louder by the second. "You know, ignoring me doesn't mean you're not out here. Little Red was down the stairwell guarding the entrance. He told me you'd surfaced, and I saw your footprints in the grass. You didn't exactly cover your tracks."

He closed his eyes and took a deep breath. "I wouldn't have thought I'd have to. I'm wearing our sanctioned black camo-suit with the Skotádi weave. The most anyone from orbit is detecting would be my head, and that'd be impossible to distinguish from one of those green foxes I keep seeing running about."

"You mean like that one a meter to your left?" Pluto asked.

Something moved to his left, and he bolted upright, crab crawling away from it. The last thing he needed was to spend the night in the hospital because he'd been mauled by an alien fox.

Pluto broke out into a raucous laugh and collapsed onto the ground next to him. "I wish I could've seen your face. But that was a damn nice crab crawl. I haven't seen someone do one of those since gym class in middle school."

He nudged her with his hand. "Har, har. What moved over there?"

"The great Liprosus Stonus." She snorted, failing to hold back another laugh. "About five centimeters in diameter."

"Perfect." He reached into the night and pulled a handful of grass and started shredding it. "First, I'm nearly taken out by a giant bumblebee and then a rock. It's like being on Henosi all over again. Next thing you know I'll realize this was all a dream and wake up in a pool of my own saliva surrounded by our ancestors."

"Naw." She squatted and sat down beside him. "I'm pretty sure they're dead, but I can't comment on you waking up in your own drool or not. That's between you, Cynthia, and your couple's therapist." She leaned back in the grass and stared up at the sky full of stars. "So, why are you really out here? Besides the giant bumblebee attack. Word around the base is that One is stable, but lost half his arms. You didn't have anything to do with that, did you?"

"Not on purpose," he muttered.

She pushed up on her elbows. "Wanna tell me how you accidentally got an alien to tear off three of their own limbs?"

"I'm not positive, but I think this did it." He reached into his pocket and pulled out the rock before handing it over to her. He made sure her hand was held out before he dropped it.

Pluto bounced her hand in the air. "Feels like the stone I just tossed. Come on now, seriously." She wound up to toss it.

He lurched toward her and grabbed her arm with both hands. "No, please! Don't."

"You were serious?" She lowered her hand and he let go.

He watched as she turned the rock over and over in her palm. "It's got a sharp edge, but otherwise, it seems like a rock to me."

"Because it is." He reached over and gently took it from her. "The point used to be sharper, but after carrying it around for almost two decades, it's lost some bite."

She crossed her legs in the grass and turned her head to study him. "What makes you think it caused One to go batshit crazy?"

"He was a chatterbox for a solid ten minutes until I took it out. Hell, I just brushed it the first time and about shat myself when he came flying at me. When I brought it out, and he saw it, he ripped his arms off trying to get to me. If the door hadn't been closing, I'm positive you'd be identifying me in pieces right now." He slid it back into his pocket and then went about tearing the grass apart.

"What is it then?"

He shrugged his shoulders. "Beats me. I was gonna ask Harold to analyze it when I head down."

She grabbed a handful of grass and started mimicking him in shredding it. "I take it that's not the only reason you're out here then?"

He let her question hang in the night air for a minute, not ready to answer it. There were a half dozen reasons he was out here, most of which she didn't need to know. Everything from missing Cynthia to wishing he was back in Sol, oblivious to this shit storm that was brewing. His baggage was his alone to deal with, not hers.

Pluto leaned sideways and bumped his shoulder. "Come on now. Why are you out here?"

He sighed. "The Beacon wasn't supposed to be here. You and I know they're not ready in Zeta Lupi. I didn't want to say it down there in front of everyone, but there's no way in hell they can pull together an entire fleet in time. What are we going to do?"

She didn't hesitate. "Put our heads down and finish our mission."

"No, seriously!"

"I am being serious." She shifted in place to face him, catching his eyes in the starlight. "We rode the fraking inside of a planetesimal to get here on the slim chance that we could pull this off. Yes, those chances are now even slimmer, but who gives a shit. Worst case, we do our job, stop the missiles, and the containment vessel we build is recycled. If we hadn't come here, the missiles would hit the Epsilon Eridani sun and this planet would be nuked in a millennium."

He stared down at his hands in the dark. "But we could focus our efforts on saving Sol."

"Come on." She leaned back and rested her hands on the grass. "Who's full of shit and dreams now? You know as well as I do that our hopes in Sol sailed long ago. Our only chance is the Beacon. They've got stockpiles of Skotádi to the ceiling in this place. Plenty enough for us to build a transport container and a final resting place for the Beacon here in Archégonos."

He reached up and scratched at his head, pulling back a handful of grass. The damn stuff was gonna be everywhere.

"Say, did you know they had a decent collection of Spános here?" She tossed some shards of grass at him, and it rained down into his hair.

"Hey, cut it out." Bradley waved his hands in the air.

Pluto giggled.

No wonder he was picking it out of his hair. He reached up again and brushed the grass from his head. She was as bad as his sister. "One mentioned something about making a mistake trying to get some Spános. I'd forgotten. Any chance we can refine it in time for our little mission? It might make for a hell of a boom in those missiles."

"Why don't we float on down to see our A.I. friend about it?" She tilted toward the stairs leading underground.

"Fine." He sighed and pushed up off the ground. "But not a word about my crab crawl. I mean it."

She giggled again. "Sure, sure. It'll be our little secret."

30

ZACHARY OLIVAW
ZETA LUPI, OORT CLOUD

The comm playback cut and the room fell silent. Zachary's head was in his hands and he'd closed his eyes. While it was great to see Pluto smiling next to her sister, the news from Bradley changed everything. In the blink of an eye, they went from having six months to only two. He hadn't done any of the calculations, but he couldn't imagine the results were going to be good.

The end game they'd been struggling to march toward had come crashing down. Despite their best efforts, time was not on their side. Sol was a dead end, and this Beacon option was rapidly becoming one, too.

When he pulled his hands away from his face, the looks on the faces of the other people in the room were as dire as he'd imagined. Both he and they knew the outlook had taken a turn for the worst.

General Yule and Lync were staring blankly at the footage of the web of Selene ships spidering their way around the star faster than originally planned. The cycle of death was repeating in front of them on fast-forward. They, like Bradley, had estimated the rate of expansion as nearly linear, but the news of the Beacon's arrival on site changed the math. Somehow, the Beacon acted as a lightning rod, flipping a linear expansion to an exponential one.

As the simulation cycle was preparing to start again, he couldn't take it anymore. It had to stop. He gestured with his hand and froze the holo display. "Enough!"

There in front of them was Harold's estimate of which ships were going to be where when the entire event unfolded. It was all conjecture, of course, but was based upon the pattern of ships and how they'd disengaged over recent weeks.

"You Olivaws seem to have an answer for everything." General Yule leaned back in his chair and crossed his arms. "Whatcha got up your sleeve this week?"

Zachary clasped his hands together, staring at the final formation of ships in front of them. "Not a damn thing, General. We're fubared this time."

General Yule reached up and scratched the side of his head. "So, we won't even be able to stand up one of your new gate arrays?"

"No, we'll manage more than that." Lync leaned forward and overlaid their attack plans on the simulation. The sea of simultaneous gate transitions flashed in three dimensions, littering the field of space with holes like Swiss cheese. "If we project backward in time to where we'll be in two months rather than six, we'll go from this configuration." She gestured, and the image changed. "To this."

The number of gates was cut back to less than a third of the original estimates. The ratio swapped from one Selene ship to many gates before the change, changing to many Selene ships for each gate afterward. Their advantage had flipped.

General Yule stood up with a start and began pacing around the holo display. "How'd we lose all those gates?"

"We're short on pilots to run sorties and raw material to build gates," Zachary said. "It's that simple. Without materials, we can't create new ships. If anything, we should rehab all the remaining ships here in Zeta Lupi to be used for battle. I'm sure we can retrofit—"

"We can't put the lifeblood of the colony at risk." Harold's virtual head appeared beside Zachary, just off the surface of the holo deck. "Without mining ships, shuttles, and transports, everything comes to a halt. We could be all that remains of the human race soon."

Zachary laid his hands flat on the table. He could feel his frustration rising. "We can build new ships after the mission's over. It's not like I'm suggesting we rehab our ore processing facilities. You're being dense. And besides, I don't know what makes you think the Galactic Alliance is going to stop hunting us after Sol. I wouldn't if I were them."

Harold virtually stared at him without a word before flipping his image to face General Yule. "We could up the pilot to A.I. ratio."

Lync adjusted the display, and a few new pinpoints of light appeared on the battlefield, but no additional gates. "That'll only get us so far, even if we pack 'em in close. Doing that will make them sitting ducks. With the right munitions, they could take 'em out in one go."

"What if we decentralize the processing for each swarm?" Harold asked. "It'd let us multiply the number of A.I. piloted ships by—"

"We don't have the resources!" Zachary screamed. "What part of raw material don't you understand?"

"I was merely trying to get creative, sir."

He shook his head and sighed. "Creativity doesn't create matter from nothing. The laws of physics prevent that."

"You mean those same laws that precluded faster than light travel?"

Zachary pushed up off his stool. He couldn't listen to him any longer. Sometimes Harold didn't know when to shut the frak up. "By all means, overseer. Have at it. You go and turn

your water into wine for all your disciples. I need some air."
He spun around and marched out of the room.

HE COULDN'T SHUT his mind off, no matter where he went.
From the arboretum to his quarters, they were there. Turning
over idea after idea and all of them hitting dead ends.

Harold had been talking nonsense, and maybe it was the
stress of the moment, but Zachary swore he seemed to always
want more A.I. on the battlefield. His Four-Laws were stifling
his ability to think outside their confines. When this was over,
they needed to work on reducing his effective sphere of
control.

Even with the energy weapon being built, they could hope
for at most two weapons being ready for the mission. Their
manufacturing resources were finite, as was their supply of
Spános. Minula had returned from Sol with some, but not
nearly as much as they'd hoped for.

The hushed sound of the wall sliding up brought with it a
familiar face.

"I was hoping I'd find you in here." Libby smiled at him.

Zachary shifted his legs off the couch and onto the floor. "I
needed somewhere to think. There are too many interruptions
and noises out there."

She gestured around the room. "I'm not gonna lie. This
place can be peaceful at times. No comms. No signals. No
noise. Not that other chamber, though." She pointed over her
shoulder. "Those damn data cores give me the willies."

"We've gotta be about done with them, right? Can't we
destroy them?"

Libby sat down at the opposite side of the couch. "We
could study them for decades and only scratch the surface of
what's inside, but to what end? Each and every moment I fear
they're going to find a new way to break out. I sometimes

wonder if they're eating at my mind while I'm working. Oh, that reminds me." She reached into her pocket and tossed a data dot between them on the cushion.

He picked it up. "What's on it?"

"Nothing much. Some mission intel from your sister, a few messages from the crew. Your typical stuff. It came in a probe a few hours ago. I figured if you were down here, you wouldn't have seen it."

"Thanks." He rolled the tiny black disc in the hand he'd been resting under his side while lying down. The dot's exterior was cool to the touch. It reminded him of the feeling of packing a ball of snow on Earth immediately after taking off your gloves. The cold felt perfectly normal, refreshing, in fact. Like you could hold it for hours. Only after you'd packed and thrown a few of the icy balls did you realize your hands were numb. Small changes made over time were often missed and could be taken for granted.

He went from being alone to forming a family at The Wheel. A decade later he ripped up that family's roots and took them across the galaxy only to bring them back. And now, here he was, alone again. Each of them had gradually left him behind, one at a time. He could have joined them, but he hadn't. He didn't know why. It wasn't because he was needed here. The General and Lync had the mission well at hand. Maybe he should have gone with Kara or Pluto. At least then he'd feel useful.

Libby reached toward him, coming up short and resting her arm on the back of the couch. "Why don't you see if there's something on it that'll break your funk?"

He nodded and stood up before walking to the workstation. When he dropped the dot into the receptacle on the desk, the wall screen came alive. There were thousands of pieces of data in this data drop. Detailed mission plans and countless archival videos. From the looks of it, Abigail dumped all her Ursis and Gharloc research for the General to review. Not even he had seen it all. He'd have to make some time later to wade through it.

As he flipped through the files, a message from Ibu jumped out at him and he smiled. He missed seeing their inquisitive face. They filled his days with thoughts and questions he wouldn't have normally come up with on his own.

He slid up a chair and gestured to open the message.

Ibu's face appeared on the wall screen and smiled. "Hey Z! I hope you don't mind me calling you that. I know only Pluto does, but Zachary is too formal, and your sister calls you Zach when she gets nostalgic or mad, so Z it is. Anyhow, I've been thinking about your mission to steal the Beacon, and the more I think on it, the more I realize how important it is. You have a once-in-a-lifetime opportunity to swipe an artifact that could turn the tide in our favor. You wanna hear something funny? No one truly knows what the creators used them for. Seriously. Most species only recognize them as the harbingers of death. But they're so much more, Z."

They glanced down at their hand and lifted a tiny blue glowing diamond object upward. It was a model of a Beacon. The light sparkled and flowed inside the miniature replica as if it were alive.

"They help to nudge everything in the universe into focus. All thoughts, memories, and ideas come together near them. They bring with them an abundance of clarity, but they also challenge the mind. They force the negativity and fears to the surface. It's why you never see any ships nearby when they're activated. Even the smallest crack in a hull will break a strong mind. They'll turn on their crew or themselves in the blink of an eye, and they can drive a weaker mind into a vegetative state. It happens in seconds."

They palmed the diamond, and the light blinked out.

"You must time your mission precisely. Too soon, and humanity could lose everything. Too late, and you'll miss your chance."

Their face went blank, and they stared at the camera. A minute of silence passed, and he thought that perhaps the recording was over. Just as he was about to close the window, they spoke again.

"I've been studying human humor over the centuries in my free time. It's quite interesting how the definition of what's funny has changed. Here, let me try a joke on you. Maybe you'll find it funnier than your sister did."

They shook their head pretending to shake off the nerves and then faked a smile for the camera drone.

"Three judged species walk into a bar. A Gharloc, an Ursis, and a human. The bartender welcomes the weary travelers and asks the Gharloc what they'll have. They reply that they want something to give them the strength to defend against the Galactic Alliance. The bartender laughs raucously and says there isn't enough raw strength in the nearest thousand worlds to defeat them on a battlefield that contains a Beacon. He turns to the Ursis and gestures towards his wall of spirits before asking them what they'll have. They reply that they'd like something to give them the speed to outmaneuver and destroy the Galactic Alliance. The bartender shakes his head and wipes out the still empty glass in his hand. He replies that even traveling and turning faster than light wouldn't give you the time you'd need to defeat a species wielding a Beacon. The bartender turns slowly toward the human and nods before asking them what they'll have. The woman looks vacantly at the wall of intoxicants before saying three simple words. A second chance."

"Ouch," Libby muttered as she cringed deeper into the couch.

Zachary stared at Ibu as they raised their eyebrows and hands, looking for a laugh. None came.

Her words, while in jest, rang truer than intended. No matter how you sliced it, the Gharloc, Ursis, and Humans had been judged and should by all counts be extinct. But only the

Humans were able to reach out of their Nebula jail to take a swing at their captors. It was unlikely they'd get a chance like this again. It could be hundreds or thousands of years before they passed judgement on another species, and that's assuming they even got wind of it.

He reached forward and gestured for the video to pause. "You know, they're right."

Libby nodded. "About that being a bad joke? Yea, Abigail was spot on. It's horrible."

He stood up and ran his hands through his hair. "No! About us being lucky to have a second chance. No other species can say that."

"Perhaps the Ursis are still alive. They could—"

"But they never captured a Beacon," he interrupted. "Only we have that chance. What pisses me off is that we're not ready for it." He picked up a chair and tossed it toward the wall. The built-in security dampeners slowed it to a halt before it crashed. He stared at it as it lowered safely to the floor.

"What if there were a way?" Libby asked.

He spun around to face her. "To go back in time? Done and done. I'd do it in a light second. Any chance those glowing green hell cubes have plans for a time machine?"

"No. But…" Libby fiddled with the fabric on the bottom of her shirt, rubbing it between her fingers.

He took a step forward and squatted down at her level. "But, what? If you know something that could help us, we could really use it right about now."

She peeked up at him, and her eye sparkled before she returned her attention to the fabric. "It's… nothing. I'm not even sure what it amounts to."

"Libby. What do you know?"

She sighed and reached up, pulling the necklace out from under her shirt. "Do you remember when we found the bug from Hera and Zeus?"

He squinted. "Yea. I'd sorta forgotten about it in all the chaos with my sisters and Shauna. It didn't seem like something we could do anything about, other than shut it off. Why are you still wearing it?"

She shook her head and her hands. "Oh no, this isn't the original. I printed this piece of jewelry. Apparently, I feel naked without it and I fiddle with it too much to not wear it. No, the other one is safe in the other lab with my abandoning grandparents."

"So, what about it?"

She fiddled with the necklace for a minute before speaking again. "I ran some tests on it after shit calmed down. Whenever I took it out of the room from their cryo-pods and then back in, they connected."

He slid onto the ground, out of the crouch position and sat with his legs crossed. "No kidding. What was it transmitting?"

"I don't know." She peered up at him. "I created a clean copy of Harold here in this lab to study the data I collected and to try to crack it. It's been nearly three weeks, and he can't do it. Whatever crypto they're using, it can't be broken."

He reached up and rubbed at his chin. "Can we give him more compute cycles? It's only a matter of time."

She brought her hand down and hit the couch. "We don't have time!"

"No… we don't. What do you propose?"

She glanced across the room.

He peered over his shoulder. She was staring at the picture of Ibu still frozen on the wall screen. "What? Send it to Ibu? What're they going to do?"

Libby shook her head. "No, sorry. I was just thinking about their last three words."

He turned back to face her. "A second chance."

She nodded. "I think we should let it connect."

"Hold on!" He reached a hand up for her to stop.

"No, hear me out." She leaned forward and rested her elbows on her knees. "We have to assume they know everything about Tau Ceti and Zeta Lupi. Their fraking cryo-pods have been shipped everywhere we've been except Lupus. There's also the little matter of me being a pawn of a grandchild who visited them at least once a month, if not more. I think it's safe to say that if I know it then so do they. For all intents and purposes they're ahead of us if they pulled the wool over our eyes this long."

He exhaled and nodded. She had a point. "So… what? We give them more intel. I don't get it."

"That…" she stared across at the image of Ibu and then back at him. "And we ask for help."

He squinted. "Help how?"

"While we haven't had time, they have. I think it's safe to say that whatever they're doing, they're not playing by the same rules we are. We lost decades struggling to keep our secrets. There's no way in hell they did the same." She shook her head. "They've got a… twenty year lead on us. I have to hope they haven't squandered it."

The notion of Hera and Zeus being somewhere else other than asleep was still foreign to him. He'd always seen them as the ancestors that checked out, when in fact they not only had chips in the game, they were playing on another level.

He leaned back, placing his hands flat on the ground behind him. "And what if they're sitting on a rock somewhere in the Sol Oort Cloud taking in some rays while drinking a Mai Tai?"

Libby chuckled. "Olivaws don't vacation well. You and I both know that. Once you've tasted power, you don't let it go. I bet a thousand credits that if Stark were still alive, he wouldn't have lasted another year letting someone else run the family."

He rubbed his forehead. He hadn't thought about his father in a long time.

She reached forward. "I'm sorry. I didn't—"

"No." He shook his hand in the air. "You're right. We don't do holidays. I wish we did, but we get antsy." He leaned back again and stared at her for a moment, letting the entire idea soak in.

They were contemplating reaching out light years in hopes that maybe someone was on the other end and would take heed in their words to send help. If that wasn't grasping at straws, he didn't know what was.

"What the hell. Why not?" He waved a circle in the air. "Round 'em up. Let's record a message for our lovely grandparents, shall we?"

31

LYNC MICHAELS
ZETA LUPI, OORT CLOUD

It'd been nearly a week since Zachary had melted down in front of the General. Lync was actually happy he had. Too many people saw the Olivaws as infallible and believed they had everything figured out. When the truth was, they simply had a multi-decade head start. Now that the playing field was leveling, reality was shining a light on the cracks in their confidence.

While she didn't hope they'd fall, she knew that grounding the colonists and her soldiers with the reality of their situation was important. Their road ahead had failure at every turn.

They'd fail in Sol if they didn't try to take the Beacon.

They could time the Beacon run perfectly and still fail by never having engaged the Galactic Alliance before now.

Hell, they could fail before they even started if they didn't refine the Spános correctly, a process their engineers were still struggling to perfect. Their last attempt had taken out the entire automated lab at the center of a nearby planetesimal. Fortunately, they thought ahead and didn't store the material near where they were learning to refine it. The silver lining of the failure included discovering a way to vaporize a twenty kilometer rock, wiping it from the face of the galaxy.

What was strange was that it didn't explode in a ball of light like the explosion that gave away the location of Sol to the Galactic Alliance. This event was more of an implosion, folding the mass into a fraction of the space the original Spános took up, which was no more than a pinky nail.

Now that the reality of their situation had sunk in, the fact that her people were still struggling with their training made her even more frustrated and pissed. "Alpha two, that formation had better get a lot cleaner if you plan on not dying. What part of ring formation didn't you understand?"

"As long as we make it through the gate in one piece, does it matter?" the lead of the alpha two wing asked.

"It depends." Lync reached forward and fired a simulated round from the energy weapon through the center of the ring at the moon beyond. All but two of the sixty-four ships had been flagged as destroyed, including the one holding the pilot and bombardier. "Did that hurt?"

"Frak!" the pilot screamed. "That's bullshit!"

She hadn't noticed it, but she'd wiped out nearly half of the dozen queued up squadrons, as well. They, like alpha two, weren't in the agreed upon taxiing formation near the gate entrance and had been taken out by friendly fire.

The face of alpha two's pilot appeared in front of her. "How the frak are we supposed to hold formation when the shit's hitting the fan? Even the A.I. aren't doing it."

Who the hell did he think he was talking to? She gestured and brought up their roster. His name was Private Krug, and he was from the civilian scientist side of the colony. That explained it. If his aptitude numbers weren't so high, she'd kick his ass off the rotation.

"First of all..." Lync dismissed his roster and opened the response to the entire company of ships training in this group. "Your piloting is sloppy as hell. Your A.I. isn't going to clean up your mistakes any longer. We went over this shit in the briefing this morning. And based upon your recent runs, your A.I. was taking up quite a bit of your slack. Second of all, these A.I. pilots are designed to compensate for your subpar piloting skills by keeping a formation as tight as possible. The goal is for them to not highlight that you're human and making mistakes. Otherwise, we might as well paint a big ass bullseye on your ship before we send you into battle."

She expanded the image in front of him, being sure her face was enlarged on all of their screens. "Now get your ass back through the gate and start the run again."

Sighs and moans echoed over the comm.

"Put a fraking muzzle on it. All of you. If you don't bring up your marks, I'll have you out here all night making runs. Is that clear, Private?"

"Yes," Private Krug muttered.

Her eyes bulged wide. "Yes what, Private?"

"Yessir," the entire company screamed over their comms.

She waved her arms in the air and wiped the holo deck.

"Diggin' their hole a bit deep, weren't ya?" Crayo asked.

He'd been circling in the wings since she'd started watching the run. Harold had told her when he came in. She expected he'd step up eventually, but was likely checking her mood first.

"They need to know where they failed." She spun around to face him.

Crayo handed her a globe of coffee. His idea of a peace offering. "Sim. Right ya are. Seems like they could use some good cop for a while."

She took a swig of the globe. It burned her throat as it went down. But he'd nailed the sugar to cream ratio. "Tell you what. You handle the good cop and wipe their ass while you're at it. I'll do the bad cop. Ok?"

He nodded slowly and reached up to wipe at his mouth, picking his words carefully. "Yessir, bossman."

Bossman. He had to be fraking kidding. That's what he called Harold when he was being a tool. She, on the other hand, was trying to teach this company how to pilot before they put everyone's life at risk.

She took a step toward him and lowered her voice. "Do you have something to say to me, Major?"

He smiled and shook his head. "Nope. Just thought I could get you to smile." He then tilted his bulb and downed the rest. "Permission to return to my company, Colonal." He snapped to attention and saluted her.

She saluted him back. "Permission granted."

He pivoted in place and marched away from her.

His dot disappeared down the hall and into the barracks. As she watched the dot fade, she wondered if she'd overreacted.

It'd been a shit storm of chaos the entire week since they'd learned they had half the time they'd planned for. Changed plan after changed plan. She'd hit reset on more of their ideas in the last week than they'd come up with in the past month. It was a constant game of two steps forward, three steps back.

What he needed was a grounding in reality. He had to understand things from her point of view. She took another drag on the coffee and marched after him, bringing up his location on her comm.

She rode the transport tube up a few levels to the personal quarters and stopped outside his door before taking a breath. Whatever she did, she shouldn't yell.

When she reached forward to press the chime, the door slid open.

"Yessir," Crayo said, already at attention from inside.

"Come on," she muttered. "It was for their own good."

He stood there straight as a board, refusing to break attention. His eyes locked in place past her.

She didn't need this today. What she needed was everything to go back to normal. What she needed was a break.

Lync stepped into the room within a few centimeters of his face, still locked at attention. His breath was warm, and he smelled musky. Like he'd just had a hard workout. He sucked in when she took a step forward, and she wondered how long he'd hold it.

"One time," she whispered.

His eyes squinted ever so slightly as he struggled not to break his focus on the wall behind her. He couldn't figure out what she meant.

A second later, she showed him. She leaned forward, kissing him passionately on the mouth as she pushed him backward onto his bunk and collapsed on top of him. Their bodies entangled with each other and their clothes flew off as the door slid closed with a whoosh.

A WEEK LATER, after just as many one more times, Lync found herself submerged in sludge, piloting one of the new Nyílak ships. The battalion had been practicing their maneuvers under normal creature comforts while the geeks worked the kinks out of these new ships. They adjusted the design several times to handle the g-forces necessary to replicate the Ursis attack strategies they'd studied. Fortunately, the crew compartment containing the pilot and bombardier hadn't needed to change, besides being filled with breathable liquid.

Lync didn't have anything to compare breathing a liquid to. She'd never been a fish and never learned to swim, either. Breathing liquid didn't hurt as much as it scared the shit out of her. Every five to ten minutes she had a mini panic attack when she came out of the pilot zone and had to convince her brain she wasn't drowning. Zachary and his engineers reassured them this was a normal reaction, and with the drugs they were working on, it would lessen with exposure.

This change was one of a million others they had to

second guess. They'd fought for days over whether they had time to train everyone to handle the liquid ventilation. The statistics didn't lie, though. Without this advantage, they wouldn't stand a chance in Hades at taking on the Galactic Alliance fleet.

As her Nyílak ship barreled toward the atmosphere of Tiān, her controls alerted her to the approaching no-fly deck. The sound of the alarms echoed in her ears as loud as if through oxygen. The nanites under their skin acted to replicate the effects of audio through air. Without them, everything sounded muted and distant. With them, she could barely tell she was hearing while submerged in a liquid.

Rather than train entirely virtually and struggle to convince the pilots the wall of the Dark Nebula was real, one of her officers had the idea of flying near Tiān and using its atmosphere to mimic the Nebula layer they didn't want to pierce. While they could still plummet to their death in the ocean below, they'd gain a respect for a boundary they would never pass through. The Dark Nebula wouldn't be as forgiving, but this was as close as they'd get until they encountered the real thing.

Her squadron of A.I. were in a tight diamond formation with her taking the lead. She narrowed her gaze and shook her fingers to prevent her muscles from tensing up. The goo made the effect feel strange. Not at all how she remembered it before.

The atmosphere was coming up fast, and she wanted to cut it close on purpose. Today they were using the natural boundary to prepare for the maneuvers that would take them alongside the Selene ships. To do this effectively, one had to enter a dive bomb approach toward the moon ship and pull out at the last minute. Any other non-tangential angle was suboptimal and could lead to being taken out by their external laser batteries.

As the no-fly deck approached, she counted backward

until hitting zero when she yanked back on the throttle and the yaw stick together. This reduced the thrust to nothing and caused the vertical thrusters to raise the nose and lower the tail while inverting the gravitational dampeners at the same time.

At any other point in human history, this maneuver would've resulted in instant death due to gravity and other forces at play. But today her Nyílak dipped, narrowly missing the edge of the atmosphere, and then shot along the boundary of the sky when she slammed the throttle forward.

She felt her body press downward into her seat and the liquid around her compressed her, but the effects were surprisingly dull. The geeks had really worked miracles this time.

The nanites infused in the fluid were designed to mute the effect as they formed a temporary nano-mesh within substrate to increase the rigidity of the liquid surrounding her body and thereby shielding her from the effects of the dive. All of this happened in the blink of an eye before it disappeared.

Lync winked, reestablishing the physical link to her bombardier. "How you holding up, Adri?"

"I'm jello, sir. I didn't feel a thing and our test went off flawlessly."

Jello had been something the crew used to report they were alive and well. She never imagined they would be using a dessert food to denote that, but times were strange and flying in a jello-like liquid was new to everyone.

The retinal image on her left showed the trajectory of their payload drop as it plummeted toward the ocean below. As their diamond formation made the ninety-degree turn, the last ship in the group dropped a bomb just before it turned. The hope was that the explosion would throw off any nearby sensors and also act as a sort of smoke screen to allow them to shoot across the surface. Any damage it dealt was a bonus.

They were open to any and all creative ways to inflict carnage, and humans loved their bombs. Other formations of ships were testing the effects of repeated rail guns on a single point. Those were more easily tested near a solid surface, however, to more accurately judge the impact site to see if they'd lined up the shots. The hope was that sustained penetrations at the same point would eventually breach the hull. It was all about inflicting damage to take their attention off the real mission. Stealing the Beacon.

"Looks like you missed the mark," Crayo said over the open channel.

"No way!" Adri slammed her hand down onto her chair. The effect was more humorous than she'd anticipated in the goo. "I was spot on." A moment later, she spoke again. "That's bullshit! It—"

"Hey, watch your tongue!" Lync said. The girl was growing up too fast around these grunts. It was bad enough they had her out here killing aliens.

"Sorry, sir. The wind. It threw off our drop. We were dead on until the end."

"Rules be rules," Crayo said. "I didn't set them up, the General did."

"Fair enough," Lync said. "I believe the General was also open to a rule of double or nothing, if my memory serves."

"Sir," Adri said over their private comm. She ignored her.

"Wait," Crayo began. "Colonel Michaels, are you proposing that you and Adri will serve the entire division food for two days if you miss?"

Lync yanked back the stick, sending her squadron away from the planet to perform another run. "Hell, I'll do it wearing a tutu if I have to. But let's make this a bit more interesting. If we beat every other mark, the General wears the tutu."

"Sir," Adri whispered again.

"I'll take that bet," General Yule said over the public

comm. "No way in hell you can beat Hyri's run. She was only a meter off the mark."

"Sir!" Adri yelled over their ship comm. "I can't do it!"

"You can, and you will, soldier." Lync banked left and pitched the formation downward for their second run at the target. "Our fathers didn't raise pansies. Are you giving up before you even try?"

"No... sir. I just..." She could almost imagine the girl shifting uncomfortably inside her bubble. "We can't beat the wind."

Lync tilted her head. "Can't you? Are the winds really any different from the randomness of the tachyon fields converging in space-time?"

"I... hadn't thought of it that way. I suppose not. But... I need to be the last ship in formation to make the drop. I'm not fighting the transmission lag any longer than I have to. I'll guide this sucker all the way down."

"That I can do." Lync tight beamed the commands to each ship in her squadron of A.I. to adjust their formation. A moment later she slipped up and behind the other sixty-three Nyílaks, pulling up close to the rearmost ships to reduce their lidar signature.

"Coming up on the drop in eight seconds." She struggled not to ask Adri if she was ready yet. They needed to work together. Even if Lync wasn't with her on the battlefield, the team depended on each other to survive.

Piloting from the rear had always been disconcerting to her. Watching your ship plummet toward the formation in front of you as it came to a complete stop before turning at a right angle was jarring enough. Teaching your mind to not jam the stick out of harm's way was another challenge entirely.

For her, it was easier to think of it as piloting toward the safety of the formation, of the hope of the Ulixi. In the past, she'd steered clear of her brethren to escape her father's death and the thought of being alone. Nowadays, she saw them as her only safe place. They accepted her into their fold, imperfections and all. As her formation of sorts, they were stronger together.

The countdown hit zero as the no-fly zone confronted her meters ahead. Their Nyílak was in the bullseye center above the target below. She heaved the throttle and yaw back with as much control and speed as she could coordinate, making sure to firmly press the red button near her thumb to invert their gravity. When the Nyílak leveled out, she tossed the throttle forward, rocketing toward the receding formation.

She swore she heard the clang of the bomb releasing at the same moment they shot forward. It was likely her subconscious mind inserting the sound, but nevertheless she knew their payload was underway, and it was now entirely in Adri's hands.

The seconds ticked by, but she refused to watch the tactical display. Instead, she focused on the horizon, like she'd need to do in battle. Her job was to keep them alive while the bombardier inflicted as much harm as possible both during their runs and when gating a warhead in for the kill.

It wasn't until she hit a count of fifteen that the moans and cheers echoed over the public comm. Adri had nailed it.

Lync squelched the public comm and connected to her bombardier. "Nice work! Your father would be proud."

"Sim, sim! Sir..." Adri said before pausing, seeming to want to say something else, but thinking better of it.

Lync reached out and engaged the autopilot to return them to The Wheel. "What is it, dear?"

"We have a chance at pulling this off, right? I mean... we're not fooling ourselves, are we?"

The pit of her stomach knotted up as the question echoed in her mind. "We're not fooling ourselves, are we?" She didn't know. The odds weren't in their favor, but few of the right and just causes in history had been. She had to believe that in some future of their infinite possible futures, there was a thread of a chance. It was their job to yank at it with every ounce of life they had remaining, and weave their way toward that destiny.

"So long as we believe in our mission, we can make it happen. I don't imagine it'll go off without a hitch, but yes, we can pull it off. I wouldn't be doing this if I didn't believe in my heart that we'll succeed. I'm not about to curl up and count down the days until we die. Are you?"

"No!" Adri said.

"Hell to the no!" Crayo shouted. Hundreds of other voices echoed his chant over the public channel.

She swore she'd shut off the public comm. "Harold, did you turn that back on?"

"He didn't," Shauna said. "I did."

Lync shook her head as Shauna's face appeared in her retinal comm. "That was a hell of a gamble."

"It was. But like you said, I believe in you and the mission. I couldn't imagine you'd break that girl with a lie. You're not wired that way. You're your father's daughter, through and through."

Shauna's face transformed into a smile and faded away as the pit in Lync's stomach tightened. Now the question was, if she believed her own words or not.

32

NGUYỄN DUE
SOL, EARTH ORBIT

It'd been over a week since his visit to Earth, and Nguyễn was still walking around in a daze. He couldn't quite put his finger on the best strategy forward with these new gate ships and worst of all, he didn't know who he could trust with their details.

Making this information generally available would be a surefire way to lose their advantage, and it was one of the few things the Olivaws did that had kept them alive this long. They were as guilty as hell in the eyes of the Galactic Alliance, but with these ships, they had a bargaining chip. He'd seen the probe drive they'd stolen, and Harold had already admitted to the theft.

With this second piece of the puzzle, he was playing catchup. They needed to keep the lure of their gate drives in play with the GA, while risking the least number of lives possible.

"How long do we need before our defensive measures are in place throughout Sol?" he asked out loud. He was standing in his ready room, circling back and forth in the tiny space.

Harold's image appeared windowed on the wall screen. "One month."

"That's a tall order. These aliens are getting antsy." He spun the electro-blade on its tip against his gloved hand, a dangerous habit he'd developed years ago. While the gloves' nano-weave prevented it from piercing, if any amount of force were applied beyond the weight of the blade, he'd lose a finger. "Are any of our assets operational?"

"We have nearly one thousand fighters operationalized and perhaps a few dozen pilots who are capable. The vast majority are in the second round of training since you drafted them with your war powers. They're doing spectacular by the way, but with no means to run exercises in actual ships, we're doing the best we can in sims. It's slow-going." Harold followed him across the wall screen as he paced back and forth.

Simulations wouldn't do forever, but they weren't over-flowing with locations to test near without being seen. Pulling this off, even with an advanced drive like this, was going to be challenging.

Klaxons rang throughout the ship, tearing him away from his thoughts.

"What the frak?" he muttered.

Nguyễn spun around and marched toward the already opening door. The hall and surrounding rooms were aglow in flashing red lights and the klaxons repeated along with a broadcast on his retinal comm. Within seconds, he was on the bridge. "Status!" He shouted over the infernal noise.

The klaxons cut, and the lights stopped strobing, but kept an even red hue throughout the bridge.

Security was the first to reply. "We've got ten inbound alien fragments dropping out of what must be a warp bubble. They're halfway between us and Mars." Rogers reached forward and adjusted something on his controls. "Correction. Make that eighteen."

"We're being hailed, sir," Arrluk said.

Nguyễn stiffened and took in the wall of ships still

appearing in front of him. The count was now up to thirty-six. Shit was about to get real, and they had their pants down. He subvocalized a private comm to Harold. "Are any of our bombs operationalized?"

Harold's voice replied without pause. "We have five locations on Earth, one on Luna, and another on Mars that are capable of firing. The remaining facilities are coming online in the next two weeks. We need more time."

Time was a luxury rapidly depleting.

"What should I do, sir?" Arrluk asked.

His crew was staring at him. One of the disadvantages of subvocal communications was the people around you were left in the dark.

He stiffened and adjusted his uniform. "Put them on screen."

The face of a Thyreusian appeared on the wall. He assumed it was the same alien as last time. While the neon markings on their body seemed to be unique, he couldn't tell one from another.

"Admiral Nguyễn, what is your decision?" the Thyreusian alien asked. "Will you agree to the terms of the Therion Collective?"

He took a deep breath and exhaled. "To whom am I speaking?"

"My name is no matter." The Thyreusian waved three of their arms in unison to the side, as if brushing the question away. "Will you cease all military efforts around this star and turn over your armaments and technology to us? Or are we moving on to unpleasantries?"

His face was expressionless, but his mind was teeming with rage. "Are you seriously asking if we'll lie down without a fight and let you rule over our people? All while you attempt to pillage a technology you desire to have, but have failed to create yourself?"

"So you admit to having faster than light technology?" The Thyreusian asked.

A smirk eased into the corner of his mouth before disappearing as fast as it'd appeared. "Why the games... General or Admiral or whatever the hell your name is? Just come out and tell us your terms. We're not about to let you walk all over us without a fight."

The antenna above the Thyreusian's head intertwined and rubbed together. "Our terms are simple enough for even the likes of you to understand. Give us your drive technology, and we'll allow you to live."

Nguyễn stared at the alien for a moment, letting his anger subside. He needed to do everything in his power to drag this out and give Harold time. While his fleet of ships were in position, he feared they'd be no match for the remains of the Galactic Alliance, either of them.

He was horrible at acting, but he forced a smile. "We'll be in touch to let you know." He then waved his hand and Arrluk cut the comm.

"Do you think they bought it?" Harold asked over his retinal comm. "According to Lisp, the Thyreusian's aren't known for their negotiating skills."

As if on cue, Rogers broke the silence lingering on the bridge. "I'm reading six... no eight fighters dispatched from the alien ships. They're headed toward Earth, sir."

"Can we scramble our Nyílaks?" he asked Harold subvocally.

"I left them in your commands, Admiral. I can have them at the ready and waiting for your orders. But I should remind you that once we play our ace, there's no taking it back."

He wasn't sure if their fleet was capable of holding any of these alien ships at bay. Once he made this call, there was no going back. War didn't have backsies.

"Wong?"

"Sir?" his XO asked.

"Battle stations! Arrluk, order the fleet to engage the aliens. I don't want them inside a hundred moons of Earth. Is that understood?"

"Yessir!" Arrluk spun around and began issuing orders from the Admiral to the rest of the fleet.

Within seconds, the wall lit up with the details of which ships were being scrambled. Their fleet didn't have any fighters per se, not like the Galactic Alliance. They instead had light frigates that were at least two to three times larger than the T-shaped vessels the aliens had deployed.

From their short skirmish near Jupiter, they knew the alien ships were nimble. But beyond the small lasers they'd used, their firepower was unknown. As he watched the fifteen green dots sliding to intercept the aliens, he knew he was about to find out.

The wall screen lit up as the web of human battleships guarding Earth fired their rail guns toward the alien formation. Most of the shots were purposely wide, but their arrangement was intended to keep the aliens boxed in with a few stragglers in the middle for good measure.

Long distance space battles weren't as action packed as the vid-sims often portrayed them. The vast distances between objects meant minutes and sometimes hours between impact. This battle, however, appeared to be on fast-forward.

He watched as the aliens bobbed and weaved with ease, keeping well away from each of the inbound projectiles. They'd expected as much, but if they hadn't tried for an easy kill, they'd regret it.

"Forty seconds before they're in range, sir," Rogers said.

The formation of light frigates was forming up in the shape of a C. Like with the railguns, they were hoping to box them in but could easily split off into multiple smaller C formations as needed. They'd practiced it countless times before, but for many of these captains, this was their first engagement.

"Open a comm to ships," he said.

"Comm live," Arrluk said.

He stepped closer to the wall screen. The ship formation was within reach. "Give 'em hell, soldiers. Let's teach these alien bastards not to frak with humans."

"Hua!" echoed in response.

His hand floated toward the screen and he pulled it back. He needed to control his emotions in front of his team. There was too much riding on this one engagement to lose their trust. This was the first of many battles.

As the leading edge of the C formation moved within striking distance, the alien T fighters split off at impossibly steep angles and came around both sides of the frigates.

"They're flanking them," he muttered.

The pilots knew seconds before he did and made aggressive counter maneuvers, flipping their ships about and aligning their primary fixed weapons on the moving targets. He cringed, and a groan escaped as their sluggish response played out. This was where human technology was millennia behind the GA fleet.

A few seconds later and the aliens had come around and lit up the frigates, tearing through them like fire through a paper factory. One second the fifteen ships were solid green and the next they were dark. There wasn't even enough time to hear them scream. In the blink of an eye, they'd lost over a hundred lives.

"What did they shoot at us?" he asked, spinning to face them.

Rogers and Arrluk were shaking their heads, struggling to comprehend their controls.

"Talk to me!" he screamed.

"Telescopes show they're still there," Arrluk said, glancing up at him. "They're just tumbling through space."

He turned back to face the wall. "What about backups and tertiaries? I mean, we have contingencies for exactly this reason."

"I don't know, sir," Arrluk said. "From what we can detect, they're cold, and all systems are offline. Whatever they did, they must have fried everything. If we don't get out there and retrieve them, they'll be dead in twelve hours."

Nguyễn could feel a mix of fear and anger rising. He needed to launch the new ships. If they had any hope, it was either in the firepower of their few Atlas class battlecruisers like his own, or the Olivaw fighters.

"Scramble the ships," he subvocalized.

"Might I suggest something else?" Harold asked.

He slammed his fist against the wall. "I said scramble them."

"Scramble who?" Rogers asked.

Harold's body appeared on the wall screen beside Nguyễn.

"Lure them to Earth," Harold whispered over his retinal comm. "Make sure you keep them past Luna, but set up a meeting for humans to surrender. By the time we work through all the hoops, we'll have our Earth and Luna bases fully operational. The more assets you can get them to put in orbit, the better." He nodded at the Admiral.

"That's suicide," he muttered. "The shrapnel alone will wipe out half the planet."

"You saw the numbers, Admiral. The destructive power of Spános is undeniable. There won't be any shrapnel left to hit the planet or the moon when we're done with them."

He reached up and rubbed his face. It was a crazy move, but it might work. "What if it fails? What if there are stragglers? They'll still wipe us out."

"Then we scramble the fighters. We should have ten times

more pilots by then. We'll have to cut some of the training, but considering the alternatives, we'll figure it out."

Nguyễn turned and marched into the middle of the room before spinning back toward the wall screen. "Hail the Therion Collective."

"Sir?" Arrluk was studying him.

He sighed. "Bring up the aliens on the wall screen, Lieutenant. We're preparing to surrender." He glanced at Rogers. His mouth gaping open in shock. "Order all ships to stand down."

They stared at him, frozen in disbelief.

"You just watched the same thing I did. The Galactic Alliance lobbed an underhand pitch at us and we whiffed hard. We need time, and right now, that means we surrender and drag our feet." He nodded his head. "Now gather your wits and do as you're ordered. Is that understood?"

"Sir, permission to speak freely," Wong said.

"Granted."

"Time for what, sir?" Wong stood up from his seat next to him and turned to face him. "If we don't make a stand now, the cavalry isn't coming."

He took a deep breath. Telling them could put the plan at risk, but keeping them in the dark could do just as much damage. When he needed them, they'd have lost faith in his command. He of all people knew what losing their trust could do to a commander.

"Have I ever misled or lied to you? Any of you?" Nguyễn scanned the faces around the bridge.

They shook their heads.

"No, sir," Wong said.

"I promise you we're not done. We need a few weeks. I need a few weeks to finish another prong of our defense. Without it, we're dead. With it, the war could be in our grasp." He stared into Wong's eyes. "Are you with me?"

Wong was silent for a few seconds, but his head slowly nodded. "I'm with you."

The others followed suit. "I'm with you," they each said.

Nguyễn smiled and swallowed hard. "Thank you. Now let's get these bug-eyed bastards on the screen and stall for time."

33

JOYCE GREEN
EPSILON ERIDANI, LIPROSUS

"Defenses inside a Nebula seem like a waste, if you ask me," Joyce said. She'd been reviewing the defensive measures Harold and Bradley had been building. Apparently, the same armaments were being built all throughout the human habitable stars.

"They're simple enough to construct," Bradley began. "Or would you prefer to repeat what happened at the colony site next time someone's in orbit?"

She could feel his eyes studying her. He'd been watching her every move since her unfortunate outbursts toward him after his arrival.

If she spent another month in this underground layer, she was gonna lose it. Like with most things in her life, she needed to suck it up and play the game, and this time the game was to be the Olivaw puppet.

The view zoomed out to one above their base. As the simulation played out, she couldn't help but wonder how much of this technology had been used before. "So, have we tested these yet?"

"I imagine they've trialed it…" He glanced at her and then back toward his controls. "At the other colony site. We've used the gate drive tens of thousands of times. The principles are the same. Only the application is different."

"While we'll all sleep better knowing we have defenses, I'll feel safer getting off this rock." She closed the simulation and brought up the go forward strategy. There on the wall was their entire plan, spelled out in excruciating detail. "What do you need me to do to get out of here on this strike mission? I'm sure there are people you want on your side or something I can do."

He sighed and pushed away the panel. It floated to his right and then lowered into the recess in the chair.

She raised her hands. "What did I do now?"

"Your attitude is awful, Joyce. And that's coming from someone who had a shitty attitude for years. I've heard so many stories about how great of a leader you were, and if I hear another one my head's gonna explode. The operative word here is *were*, past tense." He stared at her for a moment, and a shiver passed through her. "Based on the actions I've seen you take since you've arrived in Archégonos, I think these colonists are full of shit. Either that, or you brainwashed them somehow."

He was pushing her buttons, and it was taking every ounce of self-control not to take the bait. She had to admit, though; she was a fragment of her former self. "People change."

Bradley stood up. "Changing for the worse isn't something we can afford any longer." He turned to leave.

She reached toward him and thought better of it, lowering her hand. "Wait! You never answered my question."

He froze in place, seemingly staring at the door that had opened for him. Finally, he answered her. "I don't want you to do anything for me, Joyce. I never did. That's why I didn't ask you to join us on this mission. What we need you to do, what your people are looking to you to do, is to lead." He spun around to face her. "Give a shit, Joyce. What are your colonists up to today?"

She shrugged. "Depends on whom you mean."

"What's Elaine up to?" He pointed toward the door. "Are your doctors and nurses out there prepared for an onrush of wounded after this assault ends? What about expansion? Even if the shit hits the fan and we miss the Beacon, we're still hoping to expand this colony in ways that'll push it well past its breaking point. How's that gonna work without anyone at the helm?" He paused to catch his breath and stared her straight in the eyes. "Do you really want a stranger or the fraking military brass coming down here telling you and your colonists what to do?"

"Like you are?"

He brushed his hand in the air between them. "This. This is what I mean. You can't even listen to the truth in my words. You're so caught up in my stupid last name, that you're missing the forest for the trees. The Olivaws' time guiding this circus has come to an end. It's not about us any longer." He stepped toward her and rested his hand on her shoulder. "It's about you and what you were creating here before these fraking aliens arrived. That was what mattered to my father, to Abigail, and to me... and it still does. That will outlive me and my family. We prefer not to be relegated to the shadows, but we also don't need to run the show anymore. We can't. It's untenable. But I'll tell you something, Joyce. If you're not up for it, we'll find someone else who is, and their last name will not be Olivaw. You can take that to the bank."

With that, he turned around and marched out of the room.

The sting of his words rang truer than she'd realized. She was a mess, and while she didn't know exactly how to fix herself, she knew she should be helping out more. Even if she was simply going through the motions, maybe it'd help.

With the missions leaving in waves in a few weeks, there wasn't much time to make amends. Being on the front lines and making the aliens pay for what they'd done to her was the only thing that kept her getting up in the morning. If it meant she needed to roll up her sleeves and put on a smiling face for her people to get on those ships, then she'd do just that. Figuring out what happened afterwards would have to happen then, because as far as she was concerned, she would die a happy death on the battlefield if she could take out a few more aliens.

"Harold," she said aloud.

"Yes, Director Green."

She took a deep breath. "Where do you think I should start?"

34

BRADLEY OLIVAW
EPSILON ERIDANI, LIPROSUS

As part of the defensive team, he and the other seven ships in his squadron would be the last to depart Liprosus. Bradley wasn't keen on being in the front-line assault nor sitting on the sidelines, either, so this role suited him to a tee.

He checked to make sure everyone was locked into the simulator and ready for another run. With his squad getting the leftover newbie gate pilots, he had his work cut out for him. They didn't need to be the fanciest jockeys in the system, but they needed to not get killed. If a jump was too far, they'd be dead in an instant. There was also the small matter of their job being the stopping of the missiles.

"Alrighty, folks." He brought up the images of the pilots on his control panel to his right. "We've got one week before we're out there. We can't afford to be making mistakes anymore."

Naomi, his pilot, shifted in her seat. During the last run she accidentally gated them into Iserea, the gas giant in Epsilon Eridani. He couldn't blame her, though. The squadron of Galactic Alliance fighter ships Harold dropped out of warp bubbles ahead of the missile had been an unexpected twist. They tore through his squad like a kid with a pile of presents on his birthday. It was a bloodbath.

"Does anyone remember the lesson we learned yesterday?"

"That Harold's a douche and shouldn't be in charge of this sim," Naomi said.

The entire squadron broke out into a laugh, and he struggled to hold back a smile himself. "He can be a pain in the ass, that's for sure. But seriously, what did we learn?"

"Look before you leap," Scott said.

"That's a lesson I'd have hoped your parents taught you. How about another?" Bradley smiled at Naomi and raised his eyebrows.

She sighed and squirmed in her seat again. "To slow down, trust your controls, and pay attention to the tachyon flow. If it feels like a gravity well, then it probably is."

"I couldn't have said it better myself." Bradley smiled and nodded toward Harold's visual image on the expansive wall screen. "Let's do this, Sir Douche."

Naomi chuckled and adjusted her control as the clock counted down from ten to zero. Suddenly, the virtual gate transition went haywire and dropped them into the middle of the battlefield. They were surrounded by Selene moon ships and the nebulosity was sliding in their direction.

"Get us out of here!" he shouted, adjusting their banks of lasers to target the shorter range ships turning toward them.

Their plasma cannon was limited in its targeting potential to only where their ship was pointed. Given their small size, they had to amp up the power of the cannon to take out the missiles, which meant the chassis had to be fixed. Any attempt to attach it on a rotating mount led to the weapon sheering off the moment it was fired. Either that, or tearing off that side of the hull, which rendered their game over in an instant.

"Why the frak did Harold drop us in here?" Naomi asked.

She was adjusting the gate field controls, trying to find a clear path back inside the Nebula. From the looks of it, she was having trouble with the added masses from the Selene moons and the Nebula itself.

"Maybe he didn't like the douche comment," Bradley said.

"I think I got it!" She reached forward to slide the transition lever when she froze.

He stared at the wall screen. Except for a dozen T-shaped alien ships coming in hot, he couldn't see what she was staring at. "Naomi! What's up?"

"They haven't fired it yet," she muttered.

Was she losing it again? He had to find a new pilot if he wanted a chance in hell of surviving to see Cynthia. "Snap out of it and get us the frak out of here."

Their ship pitched sideways as the approaching fighters tore into their hull. Judging by the power of the impact, they were holding back, which meant only one thing. They knew this ship was different, and they wanted it.

"Naomi!" he shouted, but she was out of it. Her hands had already changed the jump field, and she was aiming somewhere else.

He didn't care where, so long as it wasn't here. As his skin burned under an artificial light intended to simulate the surface of ants tearing across his body, he opened his eyes and his heart skipped a beat. They hadn't come out the other side like he'd expected. They were facing a sea of nebulosity that was slowly creeping toward them.

She'd fraking jumped off target. That was it. He'd had enough. "Cancel the simulation," he subvocalized to Harold.

"No. Not yet," he replied.

He raised his hands. "But—"

"Stop! And trust your pilot, Commander. Look at the wall screen."

Naomi had shifted the gate shaping vanes to the forward

position and activated the drive. The effect was causing the nebulosity to accelerate toward them. It wasn't until he checked his controls that he realized where she was directing the cloud of death.

Rather than passing over their ship and killing them, the Nebula was streaming through the gate itself and out into the shrinking hole into the Epsilon Eridani star system. She was trying to block the missiles before they made it through.

"I'll be," he muttered.

His controls lit up with a half dozen inbound ships. It looked like the same squadron from earlier had tracked them down, but then again, it was impossible to tell.

He dialed in the laser banks and cranked them up to full. There was no point in leaving any juice in the capacitors. They needed every second they could get to fill that hole.

The overhead lights flickered, and their ship pitched sideways several times. This time the aliens weren't trying to disable them. They were playing for keeps.

When he glanced at the controls, their hull was critical and the lights in the simulator clicked off.

"Shit!" he shouted. He hadn't noticed they'd lost their environment at some point, and they weren't wearing helmets. It must've happened with that last round that tore through them. He'd have to remember to remind everyone to wear one when they got underway.

Bradley reached over and turned up the lights. "Sorry, I missed the loss in hull. I should've known better."

Naomi was leaning forward and had her face buried in her hands. She was sobbing uncontrollably.

He unfastened his harness and stepped over to her, kneeling down. "What's the matter?"

"I'm a fraking failure of a pilot. That's it! I'm done." She slammed her palms flat against the controls.

"Might I remind you both that the simulation isn't complete," Harold said.

Naomi sniffled and wiped at her eyes as they both glanced up at the wall screen.

Five of their squad's ships were mirroring Naomi's strategy and were each funneling nebulosity either into the hole, or out into the battlefield in the path of the approaching aliens. The entire scene was absolute and utter pandemonium.

He'd never seen so much carnage in one place. The Galactic Alliance fighters that took them out had crashed into the strands of nebulosity, thereby enlarging the Nebula itself, giving it the fuel it needed to grow.

Off in the distance, the central Selene ship fired three missiles. Each missile arced out and was attempting to head inward around the newly formed Nebula obstruction. From the looks of their path, they were going to make it through.

And then something changed. Something he hadn't expected. Each of the ships in their squadron dove toward the nearest strand of nebulosity. He couldn't figure out why until it hit him. They were trying to increase the mass of the expanding threads of death.

One after another, the ships dove into the darkness and their cockpits went dark. His team exchanged their own lives for the hope that their ship could be the one that closed the hole even tighter.

He held his breath as each missile collided with the Nebula. With each strike, a cheer echoed through the simulators until the last missile eked past their defenses, heading deep into the heart of the star system. It was headed toward Epsilon Eridani.

Naomi leaned back in her chair, spent from the emotion of the simulation. He could tell by the look on her face she was done. She'd put everything into this one, went with her gut, and still failed.

He was about to speak when another cheer erupted from

the darkened simulators. When he craned his neck, he saw it. There were two ships alive and very much in play.

"There were only six of us on that side of the Nebula," he muttered.

Naomi sprang up and out of her seat and sprinted out of their pod.

He followed in her wake.

She ran up behind the pods of the two remaining ships. They each had a one-way viewport on their back wall for observers to take in the show and learn.

From the looks of their displays, they were just inside Iserea and were tracking the inbound missile. As it got into range, they pummeled it with round after round of plasma cannons along its projected course.

They had no intel on the sophistication of these missiles, nor of their armament. Harold was only theorizing at this point, but he wasn't cutting corners. The missile weaved and dodged, safely navigating the long range fire the ships dealt.

And then he saw it. The ball of white light filled their wall screen. He reached his hands up to cover his eyes, and when he lowered them, the missile had disappeared. They'd destroyed it.

Naomi and the other members of the team all slapped their hands against the outside of the simulation pods in celebration. The beats of their palms echoed through the space in a random but heartfelt gyration of noise.

"How'd they do that?" he asked.

Harold's body appeared on the wall screen above the pods. "They were firing their plasma cannons to draw me into the path of their minefield. They laid out their warheads coated in stealth material along the route the missile was most likely to come in on. While I hadn't seen them do it, I came in from another angle. Little did I know they were missing on purpose and leading me to a slaughter. Nice work everyone!"

Bradley reached over and put his arms around Naomi,

giving her an enormous hug along with the others. "Amazing job," he whispered into her ear. "Without your quick thinking, we wouldn't have taken out those first two missiles."

"But we all died," she muttered.

"Our deaths for everyone else's lives." He took a step back from the group. "I'm proud of how you each handled yourselves out there. Yes, this was only a simulation, but each of you has the power to turn this battle in our favor. Naomi's tactics were a perfect example. I can only hope that when we're faced with the real challenge, we muster as much courage as we did today." He stared out across their smiling faces before landing on Naomi's.

She was nodding at him and mouthed, "Thank you."

He smiled in return and then raised his hands skyward. "Now, who's up to getting sloshed?"

Cheers erupted through the simulation suite.

35

NGUYỄN DUE
SOL, EARTH ORBIT

"We need to run a test," Harold said. "Without it, we're operating blind. Ideally, we make a few trial runs launching satellites or something innocuous that no one will notice."

Nguyễn studied the wall screen in his ready room. Each of the alien ships under the control of the Therion Collective had moved to surround the inhabitants of the Inner and Outer Ring. There were a half dozen Selene moon ships orbiting Earth, three at Mars, and one at each of the Outer Ring's largest colonies. The remains of the Syndrus ship tribunal fleet segments under their command were convened around Earth in a show of strength.

It was impossible to know how many Selene moons the Collective controlled in the Oort Cloud. Their last scans showed hundreds laying dormant in the sea of asteroids, each waiting to strike and cast their death shroud at a moment's notice.

He'd tried to hail Ambassador Addae, the leader of the remains of the Galactic Alliance fleet, but she never replied. Their ships were still drifting out near Neptune. And while it was impossible to detect any internal activity, Harold assured him they were alive because he and Lisp remained in contact.

Nguyễn gestured and brought up an overlay that showed their strike plan. "Part of me thinks the GA never truly split up. I bet this whole thing is merely a good cop bad cop ploy. Whomever we engage or provoke first, wins."

"It's possible," Harold began. "We'll know soon enough. The delegation from the Therion Collective is en route to Luna as we speak."

He raised his hand to his chin and rubbed the stubble while studying the strategy. Only he and Harold had seen it. While he'd debated on bringing Wong or Gwen in on the secret, he talked himself out of it. The fewer people in the know, the less chance of failure. He had to hand it to Gwen. Over the last week, she'd done everything in her sexual powers to get him to talk. That was one of the reasons he hadn't visited her in over forty-eight hours. He knew his willpower failed under her sexuality.

"And we're sure about this first strike?" he asked.

The flashing yellow dot far out near Neptune seemed to be on the opposite side of the universe to him.

"It's simple physics, Admiral," Harold began. "We'll have four hours and twelve minutes before their transmissions or the light from the explosion to make it back to Earth. After we run the test, our gate relay can transmit the results here in under two seconds. Even if they send one of their ships the moment it explodes, it'll take forty seconds to get here. I think we'll have at least a ten to twenty minute lead time, assuming they choose to launch a superluminal drive at all. They're likely to assume it's a malfunction before an attack. Remember, they significantly outgun us and they know it."

His concern wasn't with destroying the Selene ships, it was with the remains of their fleet. The humans only had enough Spános for defense. Their offense was far less impressive. While he'd managed to relocate some of their nuclear weaponry, the aliens had been monitoring those munitions since their arrival. Any suspicious relocation of warheads would setoff a domino effect of instability and threaten to show their hand. It wasn't worth the risk, not yet. They couldn't put those assets in play until after they'd made their first strike.

His door chimed.

He wiped the wall screen with a wave of his hands, and the door slid open.

It was Wong. "We should really be headed to Luna, sir. For the… surrender ceremony." His voice stuck on the words. Like others on the ship, he, too, had lost faith with every passing moment.

Nguyễn needed to keep them focused and prepared for what was about to come. He reached behind his back and unsheathed his electro-blades, handing them toward Wong.

His eyes bulged. "Sir, what…"

"I'll be returning for these… sooner than you realize." He winked at his XO. "I expect to get them back in good working order. Is that understood?"

Wong tilted his head and took the blades. "I… think so?"

He cleared his throat and came to attention. "XO, I'm ready to be relieved of command of the Aitken."

Wong mirrored his motions. "I'm ready to take command, sir." He snapped a salute.

As he stepped around his officer, he couldn't help but feel a tinge of regret. Keeping these plans from his people had been his hardest decision, one he hoped hadn't been a mistake.

NGUYỄN STEPPED into the overflowing council chambers and froze. His contingent of six exo-skeleton suited escorts paused with him.

"Is everything ok, sir?" Rogers asked.

He'd refused to have anyone other than Rogers lead this away team. If shit went south, he needed someone with experience at his side.

"Everything's fine, Lieutenant." He sighed and glanced across the field of broken faces standing before him. The council members of CoPE all knew what was about to happen. "I was just thinking back. It's been almost six months since President Olivaw stood on this stage and enacted her war powers, taking humankind into this state of emergency in which we never left."

"Until today, sir," Rogers said.

He nodded. "Until... today." The words echoed through his mind. Everything they'd scrounged and fought for these past few months came down to the next ten minutes.

As he continued forward in step with his contingent of guards, he took in the faces he passed. Their emotions were raw and human in every way. Each soul, each expression, seemed more broken than the last. A few wore masks of anger and resentment, both toward the aliens and him. He'd been called a coward millions of times in the days leading up to today. But for the most part, the faces expressed the truth of their situation. They were outgunned and were signing their death certificate for generations to come.

He hoped to change that, starting now.

"I trust your trip here was a pleasant one." He raised a hand toward the Thyreusian near the stage and froze short. "I still don't know your name."

The alien broke out into a disgusting spasm echoed by his six escorts. "You humans and your insistence on decorum. We believed we had rid the universe of you millennia ago, but alas, here we are. My name is Bruk. I assume you want to shake my hand now?"

He chuckled and shook his head. "Far be it for me to force our new rulers to follow our customs. Besides, the last time your kind touched one of our people, they fell into a coma."

The antenna above Bruk ceased their circling motion and seemed to gravitate toward him. "A Qudoculi is not a Thyreusian."

"I wasn't referring to your species, Bruk. I was referring to your kind, as a member of the Galactic Alliance, of course. 'Tis no matter." He waved his hand. "Shall we get this under way?" He gestured at the table in the middle.

"How do we know your surrender will meet our demands?" Bruk asked.

He laughed as he stepped up onto the stage. "I figured you'd ask that. For this, I'll need my assistant." He snapped his finger and Harold's image appeared behind him on the massive wall screen.

A commotion and murmur of voices spread through the gathered council members. He knew it was a brash move letting Harold use his human form, but it was too bold not to.

"Council members!" He shouted, raising his hands and gesturing down. "Please relax and gather your wits. I felt it appropriate to have an Olivaw present at these proceedings. They got us into this mess, so, it's only fitting that they aid in getting us out of it. Besides, it was Harold's offspring that created the technology I'm about to show you."

"And what are we about to see?" Bruk asked, his six hands each twitching as if in anticipation.

He tilted his head toward the alien. "Why, a demonstration of the superluminal drive you requested, of course."

The antenna above the alien's sixteen eyes began circling and intertwining together.

A shiver of disgust echoed through his body, and he shook it off, spinning to face Harold. "Are we ready?"

Harold nodded. "We are, Admiral."

The holodisplay exploded with the green, blue glow of Neptune as seen from its moon, Triton. The audience gasped at the view, partially in awe at the perspective of staring down at the massive gas giant, but also due to the enormity of it all.

"What is this?" Bruk asked, taking a step closer to the display.

"What you're witnessing is a live feed… well, a few seconds delayed, but good enough for today. Anyhow, it's a broadcast of our gas giant Neptune." He shifted to face the alien. "You might remember it as the planet you were closest to when your kind assailed our president."

Bruk tensed, and his soldiers followed, shifting into aggressive postures. The crowd of council members recoiled, and some even ducked behind the people in front of them, fearing an attack.

"I'd be careful with your mouth, Admiral," Bruk said. "It's liable to end you."

Harold broke over Nguyễn's retinal comm. "You're provoking them too much. Let's get on with it."

"I apologize." He bowed his head. "It won't happen again."

"Very well." Bruk waved his six arms in unison. "Go on. Show me."

Harold motioned toward the image and everyone turned. The view in front of them panned out, and it became evident they were inside some type of structure and had been staring at another wall screen. A moment later, a ring of blue light rose out of the floor. As the camera panned downward to see the object, someone's hand dropped a flashing red sphere into the light. In the blink of an eye, a tiny red ball flashed on the wall screen still visible in the background of the glowing ring. When the camera zoomed back to the screen, the light was no longer in the room; it was orbiting Neptune.

Nguyễn clapped his hands together. "And there you have it. Nice work, Harold."

A grumble rose through the crowd, and it was obvious the aliens weren't keen on the presentation, either.

Bruk gestured toward the display. "This proves nothing. You could have recorded this anywhere. And for all we know, that red light was simply turned on. We need something more substantial if your kind wishes to survive."

His fist clenched, and he did everything in his power not to lunge over and kill the fraking Thyreusian where he stood. He knew he wouldn't be alive more than a second past slitting his throat, but it'd feel great. His time of kowtowing before these sixteen eyed beasts had come to an end.

He took a deep breath and put on his fakest smile. "You make an excellent point, Bruk. Hell, I thought you'd be impressed with the fact that this image is only a few seconds to Neptune rather than the four hours it takes light to get here."

Clicks emanated from the officers around Bruk. Apparently, they hadn't considered the distances, or the notion had slipped their alien minds.

It was time for him to turn it up a notch. "Are we ready for part two, Harold?" His hands were trembling. If they weren't behind his back, others might have noticed.

Harold nodded. "We are." He then motioned in the air as if he were controlling something himself.

The full image of Neptune blinked off and was replaced with the crescent side of the gas giant. There, in the center, was a massive Selene moon ship.

The aliens began gyrating again. Clearly impressed with the images they were seeing.

"Tell me, Bruk." He gestured in the air like he was writing. "What's your favorite human word?"

Bruk's head rocked from side to side. "My what?"

"One of our words. What's your favorite one?"

"I've always found the word A-pp-le rather peculiar. It's

difficult to say but tastes wonderful." Their antenna circled wildly above their head.

He spun around. "Harold, can we get an apple up there?"

The camera panned back to the hands, and they pulled out a sheet of paper and scrawled the word Apple on it. They then carefully tore off the sheet, folded it, and placed it inside an orb of glowing yellow light. It was a tight fit, but they managed to slide a segment of the sphere into place and lock it closed.

"And how do we know this isn't in the next room?" Bruk asked.

"For that trick, you'll have to keep your eyes on the screen." He gestured back to the wall and pointed.

As the hands lifted the sphere and held it over the ring, the blue light encircling it turned on. At the same moment, Nguyễn opened a subvocal comm to his guards. "Prepare to take aim and fire on the aliens, but leave Bruk alive."

"Sir?" Rogers asked.

He stiffened. "You have your orders, Lieutenant. Just wait until you see the light fade."

With that, the hands on the camera dropped the glowing yellow sphere into the blue ring, and like the last time, it disappeared.

The expansive wall screen lit up with a stunning orange and yellow explosion of light. The display of color started at the center of the Selene ship and expanded in an instant, engulfing it in a blinding shroud of illumination.

He'd never witnessed anything like it before. The way the two colors expanded outward and intertwined was mesmerizing. Every muscle in his body tensed and then released, like he had the best massage of his life. Their test had worked.

A second later the light receded and was gone as fast as it'd appeared, taking with it the Selene ship. All that remained was a glistening field of stars and the crescent reflection of Neptune framed by the cold darkness of space.

His guards must've been as enthralled with the display of power as everyone else, because it wasn't until a few seconds later that he heard and felt the distinctive hum and heat of six plasma cannons firing at the Thyreusian soldiers. Their headless bodies tumbled into a pile on the floor around Bruk.

"Wh-at... di-d yo-u d-o?" Bruk stuttered.

Nguyễn stepped up beside the alien and rounded on him with his left fist, knocking him across the face and sending him tumbling toward the ground. "We ended this charade of a surrender. You didn't think we'd go down so easily, did you?"

Bruk's body was shaking. Not the gyrations of laughter he'd seen earlier. These were primal reactions of fear. "But... how?"

He took a step back and turned to face the audience of shocked council members. They were frozen in both fear and awe, but most importantly, all eyes were on him. "The power we wielded today came at the cost of centuries of lies and brought us to the brink of extinction. We will wield it with the responsibility it's due and use it to protect humanity from these savage aliens who've come here to enslave us."

When he turned to face Harold, the A.I. had altered his appearance from his young adventurer form so many were familiar with, to his aged form just before his death. "Is it—"

"It's already underway, Admiral."

The wall screen changed, splitting into six squares. Each showed a view from one of the major planets and they were filled with alien Selene ships, particularly Earth.

Then it happened. One by one, the Selene moons were engulfed in the same yellow, orange ball of light they'd seen earlier. But when it got to Saturn, the image was different. The explosion missed its mark. It still managed to take out half the ship, as if it'd somehow scooped out a chunk of the massive sphere, leaving its inners aflame and exposed to the darkness of space. A few seconds later, as the moon began to break apart, another flash of light wiped the remains from existence.

During the fireworks, the chamber erupted in a chorus of cheers and hollers from the council members. It was like he was at a zero-g disc game, except the chants were far more brutal. "Death to the Galactic Alliance!" and "Kill the aliens!" echoed through the room after each explosion.

The light show from each planet repeated flawlessly until it got to Earth, where six Selene ships remained. They enlarged and framed the wall screen, while Harold had windowed the other planets along the bottom.

"I'd ask you to surrender," Nguyễn began, stepping back beside the alien still in a shaking pile of disbelief on the ground. Their eyes were transfixed on the scene unfolding in front of them. "But I know better. I do have one question, though, before we kill all your people. Was your tussle with the other Galactic Alliance fleet commanded by Ambassador Addae a ruse? Is that why you never claimed your title as Admiral?"

"It was her idea," Bruk mumbled. His antenna drooped down to the side of his head. "Sh-e said we ne-eded to pit you against one another. She… said your human-ity was your weakness, and your desire to sur-vive would fail you as it had in the past."

Nguyễn stared down at the Thyreusian, taking in the alien crumbled on the floor. He needed this image to help drive him forward, to drive all of them forward. These aliens were not gods, they were mortals, just like him. And while they were still massively outnumbered, they weren't about to tuck tail and run.

He took one last deep breath, spun in place, and walked toward the exit. "Kill him," he subvocalized.

A single flash of blue light lit up the room, followed by a blood-curdling screech. An even louder roar of approval bellowed from the crowd. Their animalistic behaviors were overflowing, filling the chamber with expressions of the rage he felt inside. He could feel his heart pounding in his chest as he strode past the gawkers, each eyeing for a closer look at the dead aliens' bodies.

"Are we going to take out the ships around Earth, sir?" Harold asked over his comm.

He exited the council chambers and into the vacant hall of planets. "Let's wait until we board the Aitken. I'd like to give my team and members of the fleet something to celebrate. The council members aren't putting their lives on the line to defend Sol. We owe it to them to experience this win. Did Bruk or his people get off any transmissions, or have we detected any alien ships entering their warp bubbles? We don't want any party crashers spoiling the fun before we get there."

"No, sir. Once we got the show underway, we were jamming all communications going into and coming out of Luna, but I suspect they'll know something's up shortly. I find it odd that the remaining Galactic Alliance tribunal ships are still stationary out near Neptune. It's unclear why they haven't reacted to the attack."

"Let's not look a gift horse in the mouth, shall we?" He boarded his shuttle and it lifted off a moment later.

"BATTLE STATIONS!" Nguyễn shouted as he stepped onto the bridge.

Wong sprang out of his chair, confusion on his face. A second later, as the klaxons blared throughout the ship, he walked up beside Nguyễn and handed him his electro-blades. "I believe these are yours, sir."

He smiled at his XO and stared down at the sleek carbon knives. "Thank you for looking after them. I'm taking your bridge."

"Yessir!" Wong saluted.

The klaxons blared again, and the bridge crew continued to scramble for their places. Rogers walked past Nguyễn and nodded, sliding into his seat at his console. He knew both what was coming and to keep his mouth shut for a few more minutes.

Nguyễn strode to the middle of the bridge and adjusted his uniform. This was the moment he'd been waiting and planning for. The make or break point for his future and that of humanity. "Open a direct comm to the entire fleet, maximum encryption."

"Yessir!" Arrluk's hands danced over the controls and the images of each of the ship commanders flashed on the wall screen.

There were close to fifty of them and still more were joining. Only half were commanding military vessels. The rest were armed with improvised weaponry and were under his command.

"We need to get moving." Harold's image popped onto the wall. "I'm detecting increased chatter among the alien ships."

He cleared his throat and stared straight at the camera embedded behind the screen. "I'll make this quick. I know my plan hasn't been what many of you expected, but the utmost secrecy was tantamount to its success. Moments ago, I issued orders to open fire on all Galactic Alliance vessels anywhere in human space. We've already made strategic strikes using our secret assets elsewhere in Sol, and the results have been devastating."

Images of the destruction that took place around the other planets began playing out on the wall screen as his backdrop.

"Ladies and gentlemen of CoPE, it's time to send one final message to these aliens. They need to get the frak out of our star system and never return!" He raised his clenched fist in front of him, and the surrounding crew cheered. The emotion and energy of each soldier's response flowed through him, replenishing his confidence. A moment later, when he lowered his hand, they quieted on cue. "Prepare yourselves and your crews for battle. Make no mistake, this is not a drill. We are at war from this point forward."

With that, he gestured toward Harold's figure standing virtually on the wall screen. After a brief pause, the alien ships around Earth began exploding in the same orange and yellow balls of light he'd seen earlier. His crew, however, sat slack jawed, staring at the fireworks playing out on the display.

One by one, the aliens disappeared. Vaporized instantly by the Spános munitions. The number of ships ticked down, several at a time at first, and then only a trickle.

"Sir, we've got stragglers lowering toward the planet," Rogers said. "They're moving into position to launch ground assaults."

He shook his head. "No, they're trying to move the battle to prevent us from launching our defensive weapons. They're not stupid. Harold—"

"I'm on it," Harold interrupted. "The fighters have already been scrambled and were patched into your message. They heard and saw the whole thing. Fire in the hole!"

He tapped his fingers against his sheathed electro-blades. He hated being cut off, but Harold was far faster at thinking than he was. Words needn't get in the way. Not now. Not when life and death were on the line.

Wong turned to face him. "What fighters is he talking about, sir?"

A tight formation of Nyílak fighters appeared on the wall screen out of the middle of nowhere. One moment there was empty space, and the next, over a hundred ships flashed into existence. They were flying straight toward the alien Syndrus ships as if on a kamikaze run.

"Harold, are they—"

"Just watch, Admiral. You've shown little interest in these fighters, so I figured this part might come as a bit of a surprise."

He winced as several of the arrowhead shaped ships took what seemed like direct hits. But they made impossible movements just before impact to dodge the bolts of plasma fired at them. The entire scene could have been lifted out of a vid-sim battle. As the Nyílak ships grew closer to the surface of the remaining tribunal ships, they accelerated.

"They're gonna hit!" Wong bolted up from his seat.

But they didn't. At the last second the nimble fighters banked and turned at a ninety-degree angle, sailing only meters from the hull of the cylindrical alien ship.

"Impossible," Wong muttered.

As the last ship in the formation made the same maneuver, they released some type of munition. He almost hadn't seen it, and had Harold not already zoomed in and slowed the video, he might not have.

A circular device dropped out of a bomb bay door in the belly of the fighter, just as it shot forward. The result of the run was obvious a moment later as the side of the ship tore open with an explosion like he'd never seen before, in space or on a planet.

From the looks of it, the munition was nuclear. It must have been some of the few they'd managed to relocate without being detected. Either that, or the Olivaws had more tech up their sleeves than he realized.

A chunk of the alien tribunal ship tore off from the whole and began tumbling down toward the planet below.

"What's the projected impact site?" he asked.

Their pilot, Klein replied, "It looks like it'll splashdown somewhere off the coast of Brazil. Depending on the final speed, and what it's made of, it could cause serious coastal damage. The cities in the blast radius are being notified."

No one would be immune to the effects of this war, least

of all the people of Earth. That didn't make the results any less painful to watch.

When he returned his attention to the wall screen, the formations of fighters disappeared as fast as they appeared, seemingly through holes in space. While he knew what they were doing, the others likely saw them as magical. They'd need to work overtime to keep this technology under wraps, even in their own forces. But that was a concern for another day. Right now, he had bigger problems to deal with.

"Sir, they're firing on the planet and on Luna!" Rogers said.

His stomach sank, and their ship lurched sideways, sending both him and Wong tumbling toward the port wall. The lights overhead flashed as his shoulder smashed hard into the bulkhead, followed by his head.

As the room spun, he could hear the voice of Wong shouting. "Damage report!"

"We're being fired on!" Rogers screamed. "I have a dozen inbound alien fighters headed straight for us."

"Well fraking shoot the bastards already!" Wong said.

Their ship vibrated, and thumps echoed throughout the bridge as the plasma auto-cannons attempted to take out the advancing aliens. Even in his fuzzy haze, he felt the familiar pang of the rail gun arrays firing. Their vibrations willing him to keep his eyes open.

When he touched his hand to his head, it came away wet. "Frak," he muttered.

"We need a medic on the bridge!" Arrluk shouted.

"No!" He waved the order away. "I'm fine. Keep them where they're needed. That's an order."

"Yessir!"

As he pushed up, the room spun, and he reached out to grab the handle on the side of Rogers' station.

"Are you alright, sir?" Rogers motioned to stand up.

"Focus on your station, not me! Wong! The bridge is yours," he muttered.

"Affirmative, the bridge is mine," Wong repeated. "Talk to me, Rogers."

The statement was pointless, for on the screen the images told the story. While they'd taken out three of the inbound fighters, the other nine were still coming in strong, guns blazing.

The Aitken shook violently and breach alarms blared. As the reality of their situation sank in, his retinal comm exploded with messages warning him of the different sections of the ship that were losing oxygen. He wasn't a religious man, but he whispered a prayer anyhow. His crew needed time to suit up.

A soldier rushed up beside him and forced a helmet over his head. "Sorry, sir. XO's orders."

He hadn't even heard Wong give the command, but he was thankful for his judgement because a few seconds later the bridge lit up like a sparkling Christmas tree and then went dark. Their oxygen began funneling out a hole in the starboard side, just as his uniform mated with the helmet.

"Thank the stars for these uniforms," he muttered. The simple environmental suit base layer of their uniform had been standard issue for decades. While many people found the fabric too stiff, they would be speaking their praises for years into the future after this battle. Assuming they survived.

"We're on the float," Rogers said. "All engines are offline and our tertiary emergency reactor is all that's keeping our systems running. We're a sitting duck with nowhere to hide."

"Are any of our armaments powered up?" Wong was strapped into the command chair and had pulled a control panel of his own out for good measure.

Rogers shook his head for a moment before he froze. "No... but I can reallocate power from all non-essential systems. It'll be thin, but it should be enough to keep the auto-cannons firing. They're the only weapons left in operation that can target these things."

"Make it happen!"

The room went dark and the emergency running lights came up along the ground. Apparently, when he said all non-essential systems, he meant everything. A moment later, the familiar thump of the auto-cannons picked up again. The sound was music to his ears.

He glanced at the seat beside Wong, letting the lidar in his retina comm map out the distance between him and it. When he was comfortable the shaking had paused, he pushed off hard toward the chair and collapsed into it, swinging himself into place and reaching frantically for the harness.

While the wall screen was black, he subvocalized a command to bring up the tactical display on his retina comm. They'd managed to take out two more alien ships, but the remaining seven were picking off the cannons one at a time. They were circling the Aitken like fish corralling their prey.

He'd never imagined he'd be in this position, but there was a first time for everything. In his mind, he'd seen this moment going much differently. Like around the other planets, there'd be flashes of light. Except in his vision, there were no battles around Earth when it was all said and done. The outcome was simpler. The aliens were dead. This, however, was what people called a clusterfuck.

"Wahoo!" Rogers screamed.

Nguyễn shook his head out of his daydream and took account of the dots on his comm. A tight formation of sixteen Nyílak fighters appeared out of nowhere and picked off all seven advancing aliens like fish in a barrel. Their angle of attack was perpendicular to the aliens, leaving them nowhere to hide.

"You alright in there, Admiral?" a voice came over his retinal comm.

"I am. We are," he muttered. "Who is this?"

"Name's FuzzySheep008, sir," the voice said, "but my friends call me Mattie."

He chuckled. "Thanks for saving our ass, Mattie."

"My pleasure. Frak, my exit door's open. Stay frosty. The cavalry will be here soon to bring you home."

He watched as her formation passed through another invisible gate, disappearing into whichever darkened hangar she'd come out of. Never in a thousand years had he imagined this style of fighting would last a second against these aliens. But so far, they'd been doing pretty well. Next time he had a moment to breathe, he'd have to ask Harold who'd thought up this guerrilla like strategy.

36

ZACHARY OLIVAW

SOMEWHERE OUTSIDE EPSILON ERIDANI

They'd done everything they could to prepare for this day, for this moment. The waypoints along the paths they took to their final rally point had been planned and scouted ahead of time to prevent choke points and to reduce the likelihood of an alien encounter. A warning of an inbound attack force from a remote Galactic Alliance outpost would end their plans before they started.

With the revised Nebula completion estimates from Epsilon Eridani, their already tight schedule had grown even more compact. They had no inkling how long they'd be waiting at the rally point before the Beacon was deployed. It could be minutes, hours, or days. Showing up after the big event was not an option, so arriving early was their only hope to nab the prize.

They'd been in standby for nearly a week and the pilots were growing more and more restless by the hour. Each squadron only had six hours outside their pods per day. All the rest of the time was spent in their crew sphere running simulations.

Harold and Shauna crept observation satellites as close as possible to the site where the Selene ships were converging with the nebulosity in their wake, but whenever they sent a signal, they risked detection. The moment the GA deployed the Beacon, they would gate away and give the go signal.

Zachary's face was emotionless, staring into the darkness of space on the wall screen. He hadn't slept well in weeks, and while drugs were always an option, he couldn't risk being groggy when he needed control of his faculties. Even amped up on stimulants, he could have side effects that might mean the difference between their life and death.

"We're almost up to bat for the next simulation," Pepper said.

He didn't reply. He merely stared at the pinpoints of starlight making up the Milky Way. Their band of light was like a ribbon of optimism in a sea of despair. Each pinpoint of starlight contained the promise of life.

Pepper had been equally quiet for most of the trip, leaving him to his own game of mental pinball. Every decision he'd made since their return from Lupus had been playing and replaying in his mind. Should they have focused on Sol instead of the Beacon? The intel from their home system was far from stellar, with the tension overflowing and converging around the same time the Nebula was closing in Epsilon. Maybe they shouldn't have spent so much time planning an attack. Maybe instead they should have just run a straight snatch and gate. Most of all, he was worried about the software patch he'd installed on the gate ships and if he should have left well enough alone.

The patch was innocuous, at least on the outside. Only he and Libby knew its true purpose. The interesting thing about a gate transition was how a ship moved through gate space. In order to reduce the complexity of the jump, each ship had to disable their security measures to account for the recalibration of a new reality shift from one point in space-time to another.

It was a subtle transition, and the security countermeasures were only offline for a fraction of a second. But it was all he needed. It was the only time he could reach into Harold and Shauna's programming and adjust their programming without their knowing.

He didn't attempt it all at once. That would be too obvious to the A.I. portion of their consciousness. Instead, he patched a small segment during each transition. Over a sufficient number of jumps, the patch would be complete. When the deed was done, he fixed the backdoor so no one else could leverage it. Both he and Libby held the means to update them again, should the occasion arise. The nice thing about this approach was that whenever an Olivaw gate ship encountered another, they would exchange patches for that second ship to apply later. So, as long as he seeded it in enough of their fleet before they were underway, they'd be patched by the time they finished their mission.

The mesh network had become the transport vector to their future salvation after this mission was all said and done. Harold and Shauna needed to be controlled. They had far too much power over human destiny, something neither Harold, Callisto, or Luna had foreseen all those years ago when they created the A.I. to guide humanity. Sometimes even altruistic intent could result in unimaginable consequences.

Their Four-Laws engine removed humans from the equation, and restricted their drive and ability to improvise or push beyond a probabilistic outcome. Every so often a human calculation or gut feeling was off, and maybe led to death. That was a price most humans were willing to pay. To risk their lives for the greater good was part of human history. Once in a while it was in the form of deranged minds who shouldn't have come to power, but more often than not it was with positive intentions. The Four-Laws guiding these A.I. prevented humanity from taking the risks necessary to save themselves and needed to be dealt with.

He'd completely missed Pepper initiating the gate transition, but when the wall of ants passed over his body, the blue glow brought with it a new perspective on the field of stars. Many of them were the same, though the subtle shift in viewpoint highlighted change. Where there was once only darkness, now there was light.

"Taxiing into position." Pepper glanced toward him. "Do you want to say something to the troops before we get underway?"

He didn't see himself as the leader of this merry band of misfits. It was a role long ago taken up by Lync and General Yule. Once they'd hit their stride, he'd stepped into the shadows where he'd always been the most comfortable.

Even the message he'd sent to Hera and Zeus was a failed attempt at pulling someone else into being in charge. They hadn't heard a peep in the weeks since they'd broadcast it. Unless their calculations were off, they should've been able to reply long ago. The alternative meant Libby was wrong, or his ancestors were already dead. Either way, they were solo on this mission.

"Zachary, are you ok?" Pepper reached out and rested her hand on his shoulder.

He flinched and shook his head. "What? Yea, I'm fine. I... want to check over the containment field. I'll be right back."

His harness unlatched automatically, and he stood to leave, but he froze at the precipice of the exit, staring down at his palm resting on the doorjamb. "I wouldn't know what to say to them."

Pepper rotated in her seat to face him.

A hint of her smile was visible out of his peripheral vision.

"You'll find the words," she said. "Go do your check. We have some time for you to discover them."

He nodded and stepped off the bridge and into the containment hold. The Fountainhead wasn't the Fountainhead any longer. While the exterior had the same basic shape, they had gutted the inside. He fought with Shauna and

Harold for days about the changes. They wanted to keep the name, while he saw it fitting to give it a new moniker. Ultimately, he let Pepper make the deciding vote and she chose to keep it. Its meaning held a special place to her. One she felt fit the goal of their mission.

To be the source of hope and inspiration to what lay ahead for humanity.

As he walked through the maze of wires and reinforcement struts, he couldn't help but laugh. If hope was a five-meter thick containment shell designed to ensnare an alien relic floating in space, then he supposed the name was fitting.

They'd ravaged every square centimeter of the ship and replaced it with armaments and shielding. This vehicle of exploration they'd used to discover the truth to humanity's origin had been transformed into a killing machine with the most sophisticated jail cell humans had ever created. At least the humans outside Lupus, anyhow.

The Fountainhead was poised to become the linebacker in this arena of battle. Its job, to wait in the wings for the moment the Beacon handoff could occur. Too soon and they'd die. Too late, and they'd miss it and lose everything. Timing was tantamount to their success.

As he weaved his way through the now cramped confines of the ship he'd called home for so long, he questioned again if this approach was the best one. Their ship would stick out like a sore thumb the moment they transitioned. Surrounded by Nyílak fighters, they'd be a bullseye in a field of flies.

He knew there was no other way around it. The Beacon wasn't a tiny object, and short of trying to push it through a gate array, this was the only viable plan of attack. The only saving grace that gave him pause was the other three decoy ships they'd created. Originally, there was more in their plans, but with the compressed schedule and the resource constraints, they decided on four total.

The decoys weren't slouches by any stretch of the imagination. Rather than have containment cells, they were packed with additional shielding and not one, but three of the energy beam weapons Harold had uncovered from the Lupus archives. They'd test fired them a few times in Zeta Lupi, and the results were devastating. Harold's projections showed that one of them could cut through the Selene moon ship's hulls like a knife through butter. Had Minula stolen more Spános, they could've optimized it more, but with the limited supply, they couldn't afford to use more raw materials.

When he came upon the transmitter, he tapped the display and brought up the diagnostics screen and started a system check. One by one, the pings came back. Everything seemed to be in working order. The broadcast mesh lining the inside of the Beacon cell was operational, and the test fires were all returning well within specification.

They had no idea why they needed to fire noise into the Beacon after they'd captured it, but Ibu's book had suggested it could be helpful. The wording was archaic and challenging, even for Libby to translate. It alluded to certain frequencies of energy distressing other alien species and would lead to them severing their connections across the space-time linkage the Beacon maintained.

He shrugged and opened a comm to Pepper. "The chaos array is in working order. We're good to go. I'm headed back now."

"Copy that," Pepper said.

Still without an inkling of an idea of what he'd say, he worked his way toward the bridge. When he stepped through the doorway, the level of activity surprised him.

"What's up?"

Pepper snapped her head backward. "We just got the go signal from Harold's forward probes. We need to move. Now!"

Zachary leapt across the bridge and hopped into his seat. While he'd been saved by the bell, or the Beacon as it were, a part of him regretted he hadn't said something. Maybe there was still time.

He reached up and tapped his ear, subvocalizing a command to open a comm to the fleet. "Let's keep it simple, folks. Jump in, kick ass, and get out. We'll handle snatching the prize. Happy alien hunting, people!"

And with that, the first of the massive gate rings lit up, cutting a hole in space-time. Several hundred Nyílak fighters passed through before it blinked out of existence, and the next squadron slid forward.

The entire scene playing out in front of them was surreal. Thousands upon thousands of ships, mostly automated by some neutered form of Harold, weaving a tight line toward the outside edge of each transition ring. They'd deployed twenty-four of the rings and the first stage had gone seamlessly. The Fountainhead and its clones were situated off the side of a few rings, waiting for their signals.

While his part in this battle was minuscule in time, its impact was humongous. His mind raced with thoughts, but most of them converged on a single idea. What the frak was he thinking?

37

BRADLEY OLIVAW

EPSILON ERIDANI, LIPROSUS

The klaxons had been blaring throughout the hangar for nearly ten minutes. A tight-beam signal had come through from Harold's copy. The Beacon had been spotted, and the mission was a go.

Bradley's squad hadn't planned to leave for another few days, and now that they were waiting for their turn, he couldn't help but wonder if they were ready. Everything had moved so quickly these past few weeks. From his team finally hitting a stride, to Joyce stepping up to the plate and leading the colony. While he knew she was doing it to get on the front lines, it was still better for her and everyone involved to be a part of this moment.

The entire fate of humanity could lie on their success or failure in the next few hours.

Little Red was down below in the belly of their ship, making sure their weapon systems were ready. He'd refused to be left behind on Liprosus, claiming Bradley was his master and needed protection. They tried to argue with him, but Harold thought it best to give in to the little robot. It couldn't hurt, and besides, the mission could use all the help they could get.

As the light on Naomi's controls went green, his stomach dropped, and he reached for the stone. Harold had been running tests on it ever since One lost his shit in its presence. Everything he ran came up empty. It wasn't a mineral or material they'd seen or catalogued before. According to Harold and his instruments, it was inert and a useless pile of slag.

To him, it was priceless. As he pressed it against his chest in the neck sheath Pluto had made for him, he could feel himself calming. His entire universe slowly came into focus.

He didn't know how or why. Maybe it was the idea of his father's presence. Or maybe it was something in his head. He didn't care. While he never believed in a higher plane of consciousness, this stone helped to calm him, and as their ship made its first gate transition, he knew he'd need all the calming he could get.

38

LYNC MICHAELS

SOMEWHERE OUTSIDE EPSILON ERIDANI

Lync reached up to her throat and rubbed her birthmark. The liquid they were suspended in muted the sensitivity. The marking had been tingling since they'd begun the gate transitions. She'd never had it tingle this much before. The feeling was foreign but sort of reminded her of the ants from the gate jump, except it was highly localized to only that spot and the one at the nape of her neck, where her other birthmark was.

One after another, the squadrons entered through the massive gate and dropped into the middle of the battlefield. With each passing moment, more and more of her Ulixi brethren were being thrown into the fray, and her number was coming up.

She fought for hours with General Yule. At first, he refused to allow her to be on the battlefield, and surprisingly, so did Harold. Only after she'd put her foot down and made it clear this wasn't an option did they both relent. She couldn't stand the thought of asking her clan members to lay their lives on the line while she sat and watched the battle from afar.

"Are you ready, Adri?" Lync glanced to her right. "We're

up after Crayo and Hyri." The young girl was fidgeting in her harness and seemed to be having difficulty getting situated.

"Something... feels off," Adri said.

She reached over and pressed the preset button on Adri's controls. The seat and panel slid into place automatically. It only moved a few centimeters, but it was the setting she'd used the last several times they made runs.

Adri shifted and tilted her neck back and forth before resting her arms on her arm rests. "That's better... sorry."

"Don't be." She turned and watched the lights around the gate ring shut off one at a time as they counted down to the next opening. "I have the jitters, as well."

Lync could sense the girl turn to stare at her, wondering if she was telling the truth or not. "My birthmark feels like it's got a heartbeat of its own."

The last segment on the ring's countdown hit zero, and the tachyon fields powered up. A moment later, Crayo opened a private comm to her. "Good luck, Lync. Keep your eyes open and your emotions off. I'll catch you on the flip."

"You, too, Cray." She took a deep breath and clenched and unclenched her shaking hand. The unfamiliar liquid flowing through her lungs reminded her of their situation. "Remember, we're stronger together than apart."

"Sim, Sim," Crayo muttered. "And, Lightning. Give em hell."

She wasn't able to reply because a moment later; the ring went green and his squadron shot forward. They'd only caught a brief glimpse of the battlefield on the other side, but from the explosions she'd spotted, things were getting hot.

The second before the gate reached full power, all comms were cut. It wasn't worth the risk of a signal leaking through the gateway and giving away their location. It was imperative they maintain any and all advantage they could with this new strategy of attack.

Four seconds after the gate opened and the two squadrons

had fully transitioned, the gate blinked shut, resetting the clock. The lights counting down reminded her that not only was Crayo gone; she was next. If she was lucky, maybe they'd have a moment between transitions to chat again.

General Yule broke into her squadrons' comm. "Colonel Michaels, we're gonna need you to hold your jump for five seconds while we take aim at whatever we can on the other side. Big Bertha is going to get a chance at some action."

Big Bertha was the name they'd given the energy beam weapon Harold pilfered from the Lupus archives. Unlike the versions embedded inside the Fountainhead clones, these weren't as mobile, but they packed about a hundred times as much punch.

She wasn't sure what to make of them being fired already. The plan was to only bring them in when things got rough and the squadrons needed support. Showing their hand too soon lessened the surprise later, and this seemed far too early to need the big guns as it were. While she wanted to ask for details, she knew better. She'd chosen her place on the battle-field. The general was in command now.

"Copy that, General," she said. "We'll wait for Bertha's blazing trail of light before we punch it."

"We might send a few parting shots after you're through," Harold began. "You and the second team need to bank star-board as soon as possible."

Hearing Harold's voice was unexpected. She hadn't thought General Yule would lean on him during the battle. With her being on the front lines and General Raft under watch back in Zeta Lupi, she couldn't blame him.

"Banking starboard once we're through, copy that," Fritz, the pilot from her second squad, said.

In all the chatter she'd lost track of the lights, but when she glanced at the empty ring it went yellow, pausing before green. They were up and merely waiting for Bertha to take a swing.

Her eyes panned around the field of battle, taking in as much as possible. The tactical display on her HUD updated with new readings showing the location and vectors of as many friendlies and Galactic Alliance ships as they could capture in the one hundred and eighty degrees in front of them. Once they were through, they'd get a view of the objects behind them.

As she was eyeing a target to her right, the screen darkened and a brilliant beam of greenish blue burst forth into a sea of explosions. From the looks of it, Harold was targeting the Selene ships she'd eyed. With the beam away, she slammed her throttle forward, rocketing her and her squadron of sixty-four Nyílak fighters through the gate.

The wall of ants sent a light throb across her skin and through every centimeter of her insides. Being engulfed in the capsule of liquid made the pain of the rapid transit far more bearable than being in open air. It also helped there were numbing agents in the fluid itself.

Their engines had been designed to only transition through the gate within bearable acceleration levels, though always just below the threshold. The moment they were through the gate field and banked starboard, the g-forces mounted and her neck burned. It was tolerable, but was going to make the rest of this mission feel like someone was holding a heat torch against her skin.

Her tactical display updated once she'd made it around the transition gate, and just in time for her to catch the second shot from Bertha sailing toward the same target. In the distance, she watched the beam tear through the hull of one of the massive moon ships. Harold must have rotated the cannon as it was firing because it appeared to slice across the surface rather than pass directly through it. Whatever he'd done, the effect was devastating. He'd managed to cut through a dozen or more of the Syndrus ships as they were sliding out of their portholes.

She was about to bank to port to finish off the Selene ship with a Spános bomb run when the entire thing imploded and burst into a field of light.

"Yes!" Adri screamed over their private comm. "Who was that?"

Lync adjusted her target to a grouping of Syndrus ships that had escaped before the explosion. Then she checked her HUD to see if the optical telemetry could determine who'd made that blast. Their ships had been designed to keep radio silence as much as possible to reduce the likelihood of being intercepted. To make triangulation easier, they coated each ship within a squadron with a nanite infused paint that could change its pattern as time went by. Their computers knew how to read the patterns to distinguish who was in what squadron from great distances. The change also meant the aliens couldn't deduce who was who without breaking their codes.

As her formation was diving toward the nearest Syndrus ship, the pattern matching system got an unobstructed view of one of the ships banking away from the explosion. It was Crayo. Her heart fluttered thinking about how it must've felt for him to have a chance to repay the Galactic Alliance scum for destroying their ceremonial chamber in Sol.

Now it was her turn. She shook her head, forcing herself into the dive. "Eyes open, emotions off," she muttered.

"Copy that," Adri said.

She'd forgotten the girl was even there, but if her words of focus could help her, then all the better.

Her ship was close to the tail of the squadron in this pass. They didn't know what defensive weapons to expect when they approached these long Syndrus ships in battle. All they'd ever seen were the ground-based forces they released on Epsilon Eridani. This one, however, was acting strange. It wasn't firing on them at all.

"Is it disabled?" she asked.

"Negative," the A.I. said. "It's forward momentum is non-zero, and their hangar doors are open."

She shook her head as their ship barreled toward the seamless surface and banked hard at the vertex of the approach. They'd been coming in hot at the ship's midsection. "If the bays are open, then where are the fighters?"

"Who cares," Adri said. "They're about to feel some pain."

The flash in the corner of Lync's controls warned that the rear fighter in their formation had dropped a nuke. A moment later, the ghost cigar shaped alien ship lit up with an orange red burst of light before the vacuum of space squelched it. What remained in its wake was an expanding seam, not nearly as precise as when they normally separated. A few seconds afterward the ship began bifurcating length wise.

Lync had never seen anything like it before, and the explosions were moving faster than her squadron. She didn't hesitate. She yanked the stick back and to the right, banking the entire formation up and starboard around the opposite side of the fracturing space vessel. They needed to put some distance between them and the calving ship.

With the explosion receding behind them, she checked her HUD for any sign of the alien missiles. None of their sensors had picked them up yet. From the looks of the battlefield, they were dealing quite a bit of damage, but the Nebula ships were still belching their blackness near the only hole that remained. They must have brought on the attack too soon. Hopefully, they could hold out long enough to see this through to the end.

"Any sign of the Beacon?" Adri asked.

She hadn't even looked for it yet. It should be up ahead near the center of the opening if their intel was right. All she saw was a massive bluish-purple Selene ship blocking the exit of the Epsilon system. That had to be the lead vessel. Judging by the telemetry, it was over twice the size of any other moon ship.

While she was itching to take it out, she knew they needed the Beacon to seal the Nebula first. For now, that meant targeting something else. The remains of a pocket of Syndrus ships were just ahead, so she took aim at the nearest one. Before she could lock in the new target, two of the Nyílaks in her squadron to her port side exploded in a flash of light.

"Frak," she muttered as she rolled the ship starboard and jammed the yolk back, redirecting her squadron toward the source of the blasts. What she saw gave her pause.

A formation of alien T-shaped fighters was coming in hot. Her telemetry showed two dozen in a V pattern. They must've escaped from the Syndrus ship they destroyed, and they hadn't seen them disembark.

She had no time to react before a stream of missiles and lasers burst forth from her squadron as the automated Nyílaks took aim at the approaching fighters. Adri followed suit, using their lasers to force them inward toward the more explosive projectiles that were already locked on their targets.

One by one, the lead alien ships exploded in a brilliant orange-yellow starburst along with a few of her own. The two groups flew past each other, and she took a moment to take account of her numbers. They'd taken out over half the aliens, and she'd lost another three. At this rate, her squadron was going to be winnowed down to nothing in short order.

"We've got to keep moving," she said. "I want to cast as wide a net as we can while still staying together. Continue rotating the entire time. No more of this head-on shit. Is that understood?" She hoped the A.I. could handle that command.

The A.I. created a proposed flight pattern for her that appeared on her HUD. She tapped it in approval, and the remaining ships in her formation exploded outward and spun around, cutting back on themselves for another pass at the aliens.

She attempted the same maneuver but had a little trouble

mirroring with the A.I.'s route. If anyone was tracking them, they'd notice her sloppy maneuvers.

"Let's add some randomness to the pathing. We don't need them picking us humans out from the machines."

"Acknowledged," the A.I. said. It could have been her imagination, but the voice was morphing.

Lync did her best to trace the path the A.I. had put together, but no matter what she did, it felt forced. She might as well be a machine at this point.

This time their squadron handily defeated the T fighters without a single loss. It helped that they turned about far faster than the aliens, but the change in formation seemed to help.

"I'm turning over flight controls to the computer. I'll maintain targeting. Adri, give me the weapons, you take the bombs. Frak these little fish. Let's go hunting for some big boys, shall we?"

"Hell to the yea!" Adri said, flipping weapon controls to Lync.

She wasn't about to correct the little girl. In the midst of battle was the last place she needed to be a parent. Pound for pound, tiny Adri was kilometers ahead of most of her compatriots in Sol in the cojones department. She'd earned mountains of latitude.

As she scanned her HUD for another target, she found one not far off the central web that seemed to have finished spewing its nebulosity. They needed to take it out before it dropped any of its little friends.

The g-forces kicked her to the back of her harness, and the afterburners fired up. They had some distance to cover to get to the moon. While the flight pattern the A.I. had taken was dizzying, it felt almost rhythmic in the fluid.

She wondered if it could be countered. "Adjust my HUD to counter the motion as much as possible."

There was a slight pause, and then nearly all the jitter

slipped away. A small amount crept in at the edges, but she assumed it was from their flip. She should have thought about that earlier, though it would have been difficult piloting without knowing exactly where she was aimed.

"That's a million times easier," she said. "Sorry, you can't do this, Adri. I'm pretty sure the A.I. can't compensate and adjust your tachyon fields and Cherenkov Radiation."

"Affirmative, sir," the female A.I. said.

The voice had morphed again. It reminded her of someone, but she couldn't place it.

"I'm sorta enjoying the bouncing around," Adri said. "If it weren't for all the explosions, I could almost fall asleep in this jello. As a matter of fact, I'm feeling like I can reach out and touch this big guy. Can I take a shot from here?"

They still had both of their Spános bombs and wouldn't need to find an exit until they ran out.

Lync scanned her HUD for incoming fighters and didn't see any within firing distance. "Fire away, Adri baby! Let's fry some fraking fish."

She glanced right. The little girl was scrunched forward, contorting her body to adjust the controls. Surprisingly, Lync had never watched her drop a bomb before. Each Ulixi did it differently, but Adri's motions were peculiar. It was almost like she was in a wrestling match with the tachyons and radiation, battling them into alignment.

The results, however, were pure bliss. Adri pressed the fire button and then a second later, one of their two balls of Spános magic dropped into the ring of blue.

Their target lit up in a burst of white light. She didn't know how the little girl had done it, but she managed to offset the blast closer to them, destroying some of the ships that had escaped. At the same time, the shock waves from the explosion propelled the remains of the ship backward, toward the nebulosity.

It was a symphony of destruction, and it was dealt by the hands of a seven-year-old.

"That was bloody perfect, baby girl!" Lync reached over to high-five her and then froze, writhing in pain.

"Argh!" she screamed and grabbed at her throat. It was like a red-hot poker was stabbing into her neck and out the other side. "What… the frak… is going on?" she sputtered.

"It's the Beacon!" Adri pointed to their port side.

When Lync turned her head, her retinal comm adjusted her view and zoomed in before she saw it. The glowing blue Beacon of Therion had just slid past the command ship and was floating in space. It was tiny, barely more than five meters tall and about half that wide.

She couldn't understand how it had anything to do with the pain she was feeling, but it did. Best to stay clear of it for now.

"Let's find another target." She moaned as she reached forward and tweaked her controls, searching for their next grouping of ships or a moon to chip away at.

In the distance, opposite the Beacon, was what looked like a squadron of Syndrus ships floating toward them. She'd never seen so many before. They were clumped together and coming in fast. She assumed to defend the object of her pain.

"Any chance you can drop some agony in the middle of that spider's nest?" She targeted the grouping of ships. Her tactical display showed there were well over two hundred in all.

"I can try," Adri muttered. "There's not a lot of mass, but as a group they should give me something to feel for."

Lync moaned and closed her eyes, struggling to suppress the pain. "You get 'em, baby girl!"

39

JOYCE GREEN
SOMEWHERE OUTSIDE EPSILON ERIDANI

Joyce stared out across the battlefield. Her eyes fixed on the destruction being laid down against the Galactic Alliance. She had countless nightmares filled with the moon ships and spent just as many restless hours staring at them in her retinal comm, willing them to explode. Now her dreams were coming true. They were breaking into pieces and bursting without a trace in a cloud of white light. Those same wicked objects which laid waste to her colony and the remains of her son were getting the retribution they were due.

She didn't know why she hadn't trusted Bradley and Harold. Probably because of the years of lies they'd been told before today. What was now abundantly clear was that humanity was over its head and fighting for its life, and she could finally lend a hand.

"Are we sure they're alive inside?" Joyce asked, staring at the controls.

"Affirmative, sir. We're beginning the extraction," Mimi said. "Harold's able to read the glyphs animating on the exterior. There's more there than meets the eye."

"There always is with the Olivaws," she muttered.

Mimi glanced at her and then returned her attention to the control panel.

Their ship wasn't much. It was designed as a search and rescue unit to rescue pilots and bombardiers stranded on the battlefield. The hope was that they could save a crew and help return them to the battlefield, but it was impossible to tell until they were extracted and checked. There was also the small matter of not knowing how to get them back into action. Harold assured them they'd know once they saved someone.

The clang of the docking prongs enclosing on the Nyílak's passenger sphere reverberated through the ship as the klaxons went off.

"Incoming!" Joyce screamed.

She wasn't much of a pilot, but damn if she didn't love to shoot, and there was one thing this ship had, some big guns. As her HUD targeting synced up with the approaching bogies, she was ready. Her thumb was itching over the trigger.

The top mounted laser batteries and auto-cannon arrays opened up a hellfire of fury as she gritted her teeth. "Fraking pollen suckers," she muttered.

The inbound T fighters, or Knife fighters as Mimi called them, dodged most of the light laser rounds, but she'd trained too hard to fall for the antics of these bumble fucks. She'd programmed the lasers to circle her prey inward for the kill. Within five seconds the auto-cannon plasma charges tore through the hulls of seven of the Knifes.

She hadn't even noticed Mimi adjusted the position of their ship, bringing them below a piece of the nearby regolith from a few Nyílak fighters. Her targeting systems had automatically compensated for the change in motion, but the pause when they slid behind the remains was unexpected.

"Shit! I lost my target." She glanced toward Mimi. "If they get too close, they'll tear us apart."

"We won't be here long enough to find out." Mimi reached out and slid the gate drive forward, accelerating the transition.

The wall of blue light slammed into her skin just as the meds were coursing through the tubes and into her body. They were too late to stop the pain but helped it subside after the fact.

She hadn't even seen Mimi dial in a location she'd been so fixated on her attack. Her retinal comm showed she'd taken out nine of them. A far cry from the number of dead at the colony, but she had time to close the gap.

"Nice work!" She beamed a smile toward Mimi. "What's the status of the crew?"

As the words escaped her mouth, she saw it. "Holy shit!"

There in front of them was the most beautiful sight she'd ever seen. A sea of Nyílak fighters lined up and waiting to pass through the gates into the field of battle.

The entire scene was remarkable. It was like watching an orchestra in its precision. When one squad of fighters gated through, the others slid forward, ready for action. The side closest to them was filled with returning fighters. Well, that and the remains of the ships that had followed them in.

From the looks of the carnage, a few alien Knife fighters had made it through the gate. They likely died from passing through too quickly, but it didn't matter. Their exterior showed the human defenses were prepared to pick off even the largest ships if they attempted to pass through.

"Green leader, this is control," a computer voice said over their comms. "We're sending over an empty Nyílak. Please deposit the crew, and head on out. The coordinates of a few other stranded ships are being uploaded to your systems now."

They called her ship Green leader because of her last name. She wasn't a fan, but it'd stuck. Arguing with her peers wouldn't win her any awards, so she just went with it.

The clang of their cargo doors echoed as robots retrieved the crew capsule from their hold.

"Who's running the show on this side?" Joyce asked as she studied the movement of the ships.

A male voice answered a moment later. "I am. General Yule of the CoPE military. Is this Director Green? I'd have assumed you'd be back below ground."

She chuckled. "Not on your life, General."

"So you're like the Olivaws and Colonel Michaels. You always need to be in the fray."

She leaned forward, and her harness snapped her back into place. "Colonel Michaels? As in Lync Michaels? Is she here? I thought—"

"No, she's not here at the moment. I fraking wish. She's leading one of the squadrons on the other side. This is her and her people's plan you see playing out. I'm still catching up to all these Olivaws."

He had to be mistaken. She wasn't an Olivaw. It must be another Michaels he was talking about.

"We need to go," Mimi said. "Lives to save and all."

Joyce nodded and swallowed hard, struggling to refocus. There were more important things to do than worry about who was who. Plus, she had some bugs to squash.

"Let's do it!"

The wall of blue light passed over her again, except this time the fluids were still coursing through her bloodstream, so she barely felt it.

40

ZACHARY OLIVAW
SOMEWHERE OUTSIDE EPSILON ERIDANI

Watching the other Fountainhead clones pass through the gates was maddening. Both he and Pepper had been sitting in the wings for nearly thirty minutes, and while the Beacon was visible, there was no telling when it would actually be deployed.

In hindsight, they were missing intel. As far as they knew, the Beacon could be out in space for days before it was activated. Their numbers were already dwindling, and all accounts from the battlefield showed the alien forces weren't engaging their fighters as expected.

All the previous videos of encounters with the Galactic Alliance showed fierce battles from both sides, but these were different. It was like they were holding back for some reason. It could be because they were so close to closing the Nebula. Or maybe they'd attacked during some other unknown natural cycle the aliens were in. Either way, they still couldn't hold this up for another thirty minutes. After that, they'd just be taking potshots through the gates.

"I'm patching through the conversation General Yule is having with Director Green," Harold said.

The discussion came over his and Pepper's retinal comm.

The hesitancy and uncertainty in her voice were clear. Harold's clone mentioned she'd been struggling to cope with the loss of her son and the colony in his upload a few months back.

While he longed to inquire how Pluto was doing, he knew better. They'd know soon enough, and the last thing he needed was a distraction that could put their mission in jeopardy. The Beacon was their only goal right now.

The love of his life would be in his arms once their job was done.

"You're not going to ask about your brother and Pluto?" Pepper asked.

He'd forgotten all about his brother. Pluto had been the only person on his mind when he heard Joyce's voice. The strength of her hugs and the taste of her lips. He could almost feel them if he closed his eyes. It was strange that he hadn't thought of Bradley. Part of him knew Bradley was still alive. He didn't know how, he just did.

"They're fine. I can feel it. Best that we focus on the mission."

He reached forward and opened a comm to command. "Any chance we can squeeze a few shots through the portal, General? We could use it to take the edge off the wait."

"Negative," General Yule said. "We don't know what Nyílak fighters might be in range from behind. The last thing we need is friendly fire taking out our own people."

"Roger that." He cut the comm.

Zachary rapped his knuckles on the arm of his chair. Part of him wanted to do another check of the containment vessel, whereas the other knew better and convinced him to stay put. The internal battle was real, but the practical side won. They could be called into the fray at any moment, and he couldn't risk being elsewhere when Pepper needed him.

He decided to do a weapons check instead. The wait was excruciating, and he had to do something to pass the time.

41

BRADLEY OLIVAW

SOMEWHERE OUTSIDE EPSILON ERIDANI

They were hiding out near some planetesimals just past the outer orbit of Iserea, the lone gas giant in the system. It was the nearest planet with Trojans in the line of sight of the hole sealing Liprosus from the rest of the universe. Since they didn't know what path the missiles would take toward the Epsilon star, this was as good a place as any to float in wait.

Naomi and his squadron of seven others had either managed to find cover or were making short stealth jumps to their targets. Five ships, including Pluto's, were working their way toward the closing Dark Nebula hole to lay a minefield. One was stationed over near the smaller dwarf binary of Epsilon they so lovingly called Parvus, or runt in Latin. Finally, he and another ship were both hidden out here in the Iserea Trojan field.

They didn't know which of the two suns the Galactic Alliance would target, but they were taking a calculated risk assigning more to the larger one. Their scientists predicted that the solar mass of the dwarf companion star in the binary system wouldn't be enough to reach a nova. This, and the fact that they only had eight ships, meant they needed to split up. In all things ill prepared, tradeoffs were necessary.

He rubbed his rock between his fingers and studied the HUD. Its rhythmic passive sweep of the system was the only sign everything was working. They couldn't risk an active scan for fear that the GA would retaliate.

The sliver of a rock had been warm to the touch and the further they ventured out into the Epsilon system the warmer it became. He imagined it would be burning hot out near Pluto, but he pushed the thought down. Her piloting another ship separate from his was a sore point he didn't need to dwell on. She was right to want to break into different teams, but that didn't mean Zachary wouldn't kick his ass if she got hurt. These pilots were rookies, while he and Pluto were the closest thing to veterans in the fledgling star system. They needed to split up and lead the defensive groups if the shit hit the fan.

He switched the stone to his right hand to give his left a break. "Are you certain this stone isn't giving me cancer or something? It's on the edge of being hot." Holding it helped him focus. It was probably hokum, but he swore it put his mind at ease and silenced his many inner voices.

"We detected no adverse radiation or other wavelengths of energy in the lab and I see none now," Harold said. "If it bothers you, then stow it in the lockbox below the floor. It's a sealed space."

He swallowed hard. "No. I'm fine. I'm... if we can just get on with this show, we'd all be better for it."

"Ditto that." Naomi smiled at him and shook her left hand. "My wrist is cramping from my muscles twitching every time that damn passive scan picks up a rock. I keep thinking it's an inbound missile or something."

They both laughed.

Naomi had been amazing so far. Being out of the simulation had really helped her find her element. If anything, she seemed too cool at times. Gating and piloting these ships was clearly her calling.

"I can filter the inbounds that aren't enemies," Harold said.

"No!" Naomi reached forward and dismissed the prompt on her controls. "I don't want to miss anything. It's these damn stimulants. We haven't trained enough with them. I'm fine. Don't mess with my controls, bossman."

Harold sighed in their ears. "I truly hate that name."

Naomi smirked.

Bradley chuckled. "Well, you're gonna have to talk to Lync and her people about that."

"I've heard far worse names being an omnipresent life form. You could imagine some of the words people insert for my A.I. moniker. Next to Anal Invader, bossman is fine by me."

They both broke out into a laugh.

42

LYNC MICHAELS
SOMEWHERE OUTSIDE EPSILON ERIDANI

Something didn't feel right. This was their eighth trip through the gate, and on each visit there were less and less ships confronting them. Either the aliens were giving up, or there was something they were missing.

"We're running out of targets near the middle except that Selene flagship," Adri said. "Should we be venturing out further?"

Lync shook her head. The gel cocooning them gave the gesture an otherworldly feeling of moving in slow motion. "We should stay in our assigned quadrant. There are other teams out there, and from the looks of it, they're quite busy."

She shared the data General Yule had sent her during their last gate transition. It wasn't looking good on the fringes. While they'd destroyed almost a dozen alien moons, their side had taken heavy casualties.

"Our numbers are dwindling fast on the periphery of the battle," Shauna said.

She recoiled in her seat and quickly jerked her head around, panning over the tiny sphere in search of the source. "Where are you? How'd you get in here?"

"I... believe I was uploaded into your capsule to assist

with the mission," Shauna said. "Zachary transferred me during your last gate sequence. As I was saying, your—"

"Why the frak would he do that?" Lync interrupted. They'd made explicit rules preventing the copies of Harold and Shauna from being inside the fighters. Their Four-Laws engines couldn't handle the throes of a battle without putting the mission in jeopardy. This was especially true with the number of Olivaw family members present.

Adri leaned closer to her, looking away from her controls. "Who, or what is this voice?"

"They're..." She pointed up and circled her hand. "Another overseer, like Harold."

"Perfect." Adri rolled her eyes.

"Not exactly..." Shauna muttered. Her voice was coming from everywhere and nowhere in particular. "I'm also Lync's mother."

Adri recoiled and tilted away from Lync. She mouthed the word, "Really?"

Lync's face tingled, like when it turned red from embarrassment, but in the transparent goo they were floating within, it stung. "Yea, I suppose there's that, too."

"That's of no concern at the moment," Shauna began. "You've got a squadron of Knifes coming in off your port side."

Lync's body shook. She'd gotten distracted and had to focus on the job at hand. When she returned her attention to her controls, she noticed the alien fighters banking in toward them. The last thing she needed was an overseer ghost of her dead mother questioning her in the middle of battle. "Hey Shauna, Privacy mode eta."

Shauna laughed out loud. "I... don't think that works with me. I'm not gonna lie, though. I'm not quite feeling myself. It's... like a part of me is missing or has changed. Anyhow, if you need me to leave you alone, I will."

Lync subvocalized the command to her squadron,

ordering them to enter the randomized helix formation they'd been using. As her ship lurched to starboard to take up its position, she glanced toward Adri. She was still studying her.

"What can I say?" Lync shrugged. "My non-Ulixi ancestors were a bit twisted. You can't blame me for their misdeeds. Now, get your eyes on the prize, little lady." She pointed at Adri's control panel. "First sign of trouble or an opportunity to take them out in a single shot, blast them to kingdom come."

Adri smirked. "Yessir!" She brought her focus back to her tachyon controls and started going through the motions to direct the particle fields.

"Can I share an observation?" Shauna asked.

Lync squinted and then squeezed off a few shots from their auto-cannons, taking out one of the inbound Knifes. She liked the name the Liprosus teams had come up with for these alien ships. It was far more fitting than T ships. "Make it quick, Mom. And then, shut it! We've got a job to do."

Shauna gasped. "You don't need to be rude. I was just going to point out the reason I believe there aren't any alien fighters near your section of the battlefield. It's due to the Beacon of Therion being present. From the motions of the Knifes, Syndrus ships, and the change in position of the Selene moons, it would appear they're protecting it and trying to ensure they don't accidentally hit it."

"But it's way over on the far side of the flagship." Lync squeezed off another shot, this time missing wide as the Knife pivoted.

"The patterns in the data don't lie. I'll leave you be."

"Shit! He was right," Lync said.

"I know. Wait! I've been—" Shauna began.

"Not you," Lync interrupted. "Harold. His copy from Tau Ceti told me to try this strategy months ago and I'd forgotten."

If they were both right, this could mean they had a defensive opportunity they weren't taking advantage of. There was only one way to find out. She subvocalized the command to dive back toward the Selene flagship and then come about, keeping the Beacon behind them.

The moment her formation dove to port, the aliens pursued, but their attacks ceased. Knifes weren't automated, so it wasn't noticeable at first, but within thirty seconds it was clear. The Beacon was clearly an off limits target.

"We need to find a gate!" Lync said.

Adri glanced at her and then back to her tachyon field controls. "But we just got here! We've got full armaments."

She issued the command to trigger the search for the nearest exit gate, and their squadron darted upward from their current vector. They needed to share this information with the general. It could turn the tide in their favor out on the fringe. The longer they were out here, the clearer it became that once the Beacon was gone, their chances of survival were landing squarely between slim and none.

43

JOYCE GREEN
SOMEWHERE OUTSIDE EPSILON ERIDANI

The fringes of the battle were a clusterfuck if Joyce had ever seen one before. Wave after wave of Nyílaks disintegrated in balls of fire the moment they tried to make headway, pushing the front outward toward another Selene ship. It was almost like the aliens were simply sitting at the peripheral and taking potshots at their ships as they made their approach. Without a precise drop near the massive moons, there were too many alien forces to cut through.

Her controls blared, and her retinal comm updated with a recovery alert from one of their pilots. The ship was a safe distance from the edge of the battle, but they were floating dangerously close to the Nebula.

"We're picking up a distress signature on the exterior of one of our ships," Joyce said. "I'm taking us in for a recovery."

While the excitement of their first rescue had motivated them out of the start gate, the last few attempts at recovering a crew had failed miserably. Being at the edge of rescuing a life and then watching them explode in a ball of flames was numbing and chipped at her already low confidence.

She'd never commanded a ship before, even a small one.

Everything was faster than she'd expected, and while she loved the adrenaline, she second guessed their every failure. The only thing pushing her through beyond saving her people was the taking of the alien lives. They were up to twenty-four kills.

"I'm bringing us in for the extraction," Mimi said. "Keep an eye on our six. I'm not gonna risk getting closer to that Nebula wall. That shit's rippling like it wants to jump out at us."

"Roger that." She directed her auto-cannons backward and waited for the lidar to update. They kept a passive scan going until they saw inbound heading toward them. Because they had their own gate drive, they could often transition into the field of battle without being detected until they engaged the impulse thrusters. On this approach their drive signature was only visible away from the battlefield, so they might be protected.

She squinted, studying the lidar results. There were squadrons of ships she'd never seen before on the front lines. They were conical in shape, like long slender perfectly geometric cones. They didn't resemble any Galactic Alliance or CoPE ship she'd ever seen, but she wouldn't put it past the slimy aliens to have more than one trick up their sleeves.

Suddenly, their hull rocked as laser fire singed their port side. She'd gotten distracted, but something they'd done must have given away their position.

"Shit," she muttered and spun her auto-cannons toward the Knifes heading straight for them along the Nebula wall. They'd hidden below the range of what they thought was acceptable, challenging their assumptions of the stability of the nebulosity. That, or the aliens knew how to manipulate it.

A plan percolated in her head as she squeezed off a few shots. Her rounds narrowly missed as the Knifes barrel rolled out and starboard, sliding right back against the Nebula wall.

These pilots weren't fraking around. It was like they were part of their ships.

That gave her an idea. If she couldn't beat 'em at their own game, then she'd flip the table. Joyce subvocalized a command to launch two recovery drones toward the approaching fighters.

"What're you doing, Joy?" Mimi asked. She'd started using that nickname after their first few saves and Joyce's cheers of elation and joy.

"You focus on recovering our people. I've got this." She adjusted the approach vector of the drones to shoot out and then spiral back in at a steep angle. "The moment they're inside, get us the hell outta Dodge."

She felt the clang of the recovery bay doors opening and could imagine the claws of life reaching outward, toward the crew sphere of the Nyílak. As she squeezed off another round of auto-cannons, the Knife fighters responded in kind but with far weaker weapons. The Galactic Alliance wanted one of their spheres, and thus far they'd denied them the prize.

"Shit!" Mimi slammed her hand against her control console and leapt up, releasing her harness in the blink of an eye.

"What?" Joyce laid down cover fire and brought up a view of the recovery arms on her panel. She saw what Mimi was animated about. The Knifes damaged the capture arm, and it was spinning away, leaving the crew pod to float in space. "What are you doing?"

"Going fishing," Mimi said, already receding out of the cockpit. She switched her audio to their retinal comms. "Keep 'em busy. I'll only need a minute. When I holler, hit the big red button on my controls."

A minute was an awful long time in a game of seconds.

She returned her attention to the six Knifes flying danger-ously close to them and getting closer by the second. The drones she'd launched were hitting the apex of their random arc and were now diving back toward her targets. She wasn't sure about the speed of the Knifes, so she adjusted the sinusoidal pathing program she'd loaded and ordered it to follow the advancing aliens, hoping for the best.

The paths of the drones must have been irregular enough to the aliens because they didn't even bother trying to take them out. As they neared their target, she fired one final command burst to disable their collision dampeners. She then adjusted their targets to a point in front of the aliens. Hopefully, that would throw them off.

Joyce tried to squeeze off another shot of her autocannons, but her actions were too slow. Their ship lurched back, and a sea of sparks cascaded from the ceiling. The lights flickered off and on a few times before remaining on. When she checked her comm, all of her weapons were offline. Their only hope was her kamikaze drones.

They needed to get the hell out of here. "Mimi, are we close? We're sitting ducks out here."

Her drones dove toward the first Knife with anticipation. They missed the lead alien ship, passing well in front of it as she'd planned. Her hope that they didn't fire on the drones was realized when she watched the next inbound barrage of weapons aimed at her ship.

Everything shook as the rounds tore into their hull. The sensation of the following seconds was surreal. As the room spun, the wall screen slid sideways. Her head smacked the ground with a thunk, sending a ringing through her ears as her vision blurred and darkened for a brief moment.

"No!" She pushed up on her side and yanked on the release latch on her harness, freeing her from her crumpled chair. When she stood, she had to steady herself to stop the room from spinning, but something was different. They were losing gravity. The weightless feeling was unmistakable. Even with the disorientation of hitting her head, she knew this was bad.

A second later, klaxons echoed through the ship and her helmet shot over her head before everything went quiet. The shots must've breached the hull, weakening the superstructure beneath the bridge. When she floated upward, free of gravity, she rotated in place. The floor was glowing red beside her, the metal still superheated from the laser barrage. That would explain how her chair tipped.

She rubbed her side, checking that her suit's seals were intact. It was, but judging by where she'd fallen, it'd missed her by a few centimeters, tops.

All that remained was the silence of her suit and the red glow of the overhead lights.

Once she was comfortable she was safe, she subvocalized a command to cycle through the external cameras to find one that was working, and not a moment too soon. As she switched to the camera array on the bottom of their ship, she caught a glimpse of the fingers of nebulosity reaching out, pulling the Knife fighters to their death.

Her plan had worked. She'd aimed well short of the aliens and spaced out her drones in hopes that the Nebula would extend outward to destroy the tiny automata, jumping from one to another, and then hopefully to the aliens. She'd seen it in the videos Harold had shared with them, but never herself. The motion was like a giant hand reaching out and squeezing its prey.

Five consecutive explosions were silhouetted by the darkness of the Nebula, and one more surge of adrenaline coursed through her. They'd done it.

"Yes!" Pain from the celebration reminded her of her injury. She closed her eyes for a second, attempting to find her bearings in the conflicting signals from her body. "Did you see that, Mimi?"

It wasn't until then that she realized she hadn't replied to her query a minute ago. She'd never answered if she was close. There'd been nothing but silence.

"Shit, shit, shit!" She cycled through any remaining internal cameras until she found her. From the angle of the camera, she'd been able to attach the tether, but the blast from the last attack had knocked some storage crates in the hold loose, and they'd collided into her. Her emergency helmet was on, and her vitals were showing she was breathing, but she wasn't moving.

And then she froze when she saw it. One of the Knife fighters was sliding up beside their ship. The lead Knife must've gotten past the nebulosity.

When she checked her retinal comm, their weapons were still offline. They were sitting ducks. She had to think fast.

Speed of thought had never been her strongest trait, preferring instead a slow meticulous process of elimination. It was one of the biggest reasons she'd gone into leadership. Making life and death calls in stressful situations was something she hired others to do. It was ironic that she was now squarely in the middle of the fray, feeling overwhelmed.

Should she save Mimi or tend to the recovered sphere first? Her options were limited, but the Galactic Alliance aliens weren't sitting around waiting on her. A mechanical tentacle was reaching out from the Knife and moving toward the crew sphere.

"Keep your slimy hands off my people," she muttered as she pushed off, heading back toward Mimi's controls.

Floating up to them, she pulled herself down and engaged the magnetic boots in her shoes, planting herself firmly in place behind the controls. The floor beside her had buckled and as a result caused the control panel to tilt to the side, but they were still functional.

She quickly scanned through the options and then activated the tether Mimi had attached, hoping the winch was still operational. Her answer came a moment later when the slack in the line disappeared and the sphere moved closer.

The Knife's tentacles stopped moving, and the ship adjusted its position to advance on them.

Her mind flipped through all the options in front of her, each evaporating in a cloud of smoke until only one remained. Like the nebulosity, it was only theoretical, but with the time they had left, there wasn't much else to do.

She reached forward, slid the sequencing lever up, and slammed the big red button to activate the gate array. The blue rings of the gate field danced just past the front of the ship facing the Knife, as the view was replaced with a sea of stars. The same ones Mimi had dialed in before she'd gone below deck.

Joyce couldn't perform a transition, not yet, but she could do the next best thing. The maneuvering thrusters were one of the few features that were still green on Mimi's control panel. When she engaged them, the ship rotated away from the Knife until she grabbed the stick on the arm of the chair.

Her body contorted as she leaned over and grasped the console. Within a few seconds, she managed to correct their movement and was guiding the transition gate toward the alien ship.

As the seconds counted down, she held her breath. The Knife fighter, uncertain what to do, fired a barrage of laser blasters at the center of the gate, sending trails of light through the other side. Fortunately, no one was anywhere near the opening.

She was giving the maneuvering thrusters all she had, and the distance between them was narrowing, but everything was moving in slow motion. She couldn't tell if their ship was really going that slowly or if time had warped to a crawl.

With the distance closing, she felt a vibration in her feet as the bridge lurched upward. The crew capsule had bumped into the bottom of the ship. There was no sound in the vacuum of space, but the vibrations of the sphere being pulled into position along the lower hull were excruciating.

The only saving grace of the vibrations was the confidence it brought that the tether hadn't snapped.

When the gate field hit the edge of the Knife, the aliens seemed mesmerized and reached out to test the surface. They sent the tentacles they'd deployed earlier through the far side. As the nose of their ship dipped into the space-time portal, Joyce studied both the distance they had passed through and the distance remaining for the crew capsule to reach safety. She needed to time this perfectly.

The vibrations from the capsule came to an end, and she watched as the pod was pulled into the berth beneath their ship. Suddenly, the gate array alarms went off. The aliens were backing up and were using their tentacles to push against the gate vanes in an attempt to break them.

It was now or never. Joyce reached over and slapped the red button two times, slamming the sequencing lever down in between hits. The first hit was to deactivate the gate and the next to activate it again.

The field of stars disappeared for a moment, replaced with a stunning view of the Knife. There in front of her was a three-dimensional cross section of the superstructure of the alien ship. It was as if someone had cut it clean in half, which was in fact what she'd done.

Her jaw dropped open and morphed into a smile as she made out a dozen bumblebee aliens writhing as the cold vacuum of space crept over them, killing them within seconds. When the drives had built up enough capacitance, the gate array triggered again, and this time it didn't sit motionless. It tore across her body.

She wasn't in the chair, so there were no drugs to ease the transition. As the blue light passed over her, she felt pain. Excruciating flesh-tearing pain over every square centimeter of her body as the light tore through her like a pack of wolves at a raw fish party.

The last thing she remembered before passing out was the

faintest hint of pink streaks reaching out from the massive Selene ship in the distance. As her eyelids grew heavy, and the pain squeezed at her subconsciousness, she couldn't help but compare the streaks of pink to the tentacles the Knife fighter had reached out toward them. They moved like they were alive and were hell bent on grabbing something.

44

ZACHARY OLIVAW

SOMEWHERE OUTSIDE EPSILON ERIDANI

After what seemed like hours, the signal finally came. During the last squadron's gate transition, they caught a glimpse of the Selene moon flagship. It launched four missiles toward the Epsilon Eridani suns. The General wasn't happy, but it was the moment they'd been waiting for. Besides, they couldn't do much about the number of missiles. That was for the team on the inside to deal with.

Zachary hoped Bradley and his people were prepared. Harold spouted on about how it made sense they were sending two per star, but he wasn't paying attention. He had more important things to dwell on, like snatching the Beacon of Therion.

All their intel indicated the time between firing the missiles and deploying the Beacon was short, minutes at best. It was about timing, and the last thing the Galactic Alliance always did before sealing the Dark Nebula was fire missiles to close the deal.

"Our formation is ready, sir." Pepper glanced at him, waiting for the order. She, too, had been chomping at the bit to get into action.

She hadn't considered how painful sitting still was going

to be when she volunteered for this leg of the mission. None of them had. Waiting was always hard, especially when your people were dying around you, and you couldn't help them.

He nodded toward her. "Let's do this! Begin transition."

They'd debated on delaying the transition until after the Beacon had sealed the Nebula, but they couldn't risk it. They had to at least get into the system before the event. Their ship's thick Skotádi coating should protect them, and they had no idea how long the Beacon would be unguarded before the Galactic Alliance retrieved it. If they weren't ready, they could miss their one opportunity. No one wanted that.

As they transitioned, he took a deep breath. They were being escorted by four squadrons of Nyílaks. The sea of ships slid into formation and began their approach on the Selene flagship.

The motions of the Nyílaks were mesmerizing. It wasn't until he returned his attention to the fluctuating battlefield that he realized their forces along the front were gaining ground on the Galactic Alliance.

Somehow, they'd pushed a hole into the growing defensive perimeter well away from the flagship. When he skimmed through the data, his stomach tightened. "What the frak are those?" He flipped the image over to Pepper's retinal comm.

She took her attention off her controls and shook her head slowly, squinting at the images. "I've never seen those ships before. They don't look like any of ours. Where'd they come from?" She flung the images away and returned her focus to their approach vector.

"The glyphs on the surface of the furthest Nyílaks report that they're friendlies," Zachary began, "but they have no idea who they are. No communications have been made. Their weapons matched some of the archival GA designs we uncovered in Lupus, so they must be a GA species."

He sighed and continued flipping through the cameras the

crude expert systems had marked as important. Most of them were useless. He could really use Harold at a time like this. While he had loaded both him and Shauna into their systems, they were firewalled away and would only be released if his nanites detected that both he and Pepper were incapacitated.

"Whoever our guests are," he muttered, "they seem to be on our side, for the moment. We should keep an eye on them. We don't want them backstabbing us and snatching a gate drive."

The Fountainhead was playing the part of the artillery, supporting the squadron's assault on the Selene moon. This one was far bigger than the others, and they had no intel on its defensive capabilities. Their job was to sit back, well away from the moon ship, and fire their Little Bertha energy weapon, until the moment of truth.

With the squadron's attack underway, he watched as the Nyílaks approached the largest of the Selene moons. Pepper fired off a few shots ahead of the lead ship, clearing the way for their approach. Right as they were about to get within bombing distance, the moon opened fire. A dozen armaments they'd never seen on the other ships popped up and out of the surface and began pelting the approaching fighters with what looked like flowing plasma.

He cringed as shot after shot picked off their ships. The green-blue plasma rounds were precise and deadly. Within seconds, they winnowed down the squadron to almost nothing.

The approach team barely managed to get off their bomb in the run, a single nuke. This one was released well short of the hull, but the explosion was still quite striking.

Small chunks of debris appeared to tear off where the blast hit hardest, but when the dust settled, the surface was unscathed. He had to double-check to confirm the visuals. The debris must've been the remains of a few Syndrus ships sliding out of their docking ports. Whatever they were, the explosion must have pissed off the GA because the return fire from the flagship increased significantly.

As Pepper struggled to dodge the inbound shots, the Fountainhead collided with smaller chunks of the wreckage. Clanging sounds echoed off their hull and sent shivers up his spine. At this rate, he hoped they'd last long enough to make the snatch.

He turned toward Pepper. "Tell them to drop a Spános bomb on the next run."

Pepper tilted her head as she guided their ship around another volley from the flagship. "We're not supposed to use those on the flagship until after the Beacon seals the Nebula."

"We'll be lucky if we survive that long. Maybe we can force their hand. Just do it!"

"Roger that!" She quickly issued the command to the squadrons using her control panel. Her orders were turned into pictographs on the exterior of their ship and would take a few seconds before another ship saw them, decoded the commands, and then updated their own pictograph, as well. It was a crude but effective way to ensure their instructions weren't manipulated after they'd been transmitted.

After she sent the message, she returned her attention to dodging the return fire and squeezing off a few Little Berthas once the Fountainhead had built up enough power.

Zachary took control of their auto-cannon battery and opened fire on as many of the tiny surface armaments as he could make out. They popped up and down like whack-a-moles, protecting themselves when they weren't firing by sliding back into the safety of the moon ship's shell. Hitting them was pure luck, but he was hoping that even a few small wins could help.

It seemed like forever until the confirmation of their message surfaced. The remains of the lead and second squadron had merged and were making the next run on the flagship. They confirmed they were dropping one of their big boys. When he subvocalized a command to bring up the squadron's crew details, he did a double take.

Lync's name and that of her bombardier, Adri, appeared on his retinal comm. The little girl had only just turned seven. He'd been so lost in the moment, he'd forgotten she'd been out here on the battlefield. Unlike him, they'd been seeing action since the start. He couldn't imagine the focus and energy they needed to muster to stay alive this long.

The Fountainhead oscillated as another one of the surface mounted cannons took a swing at them. As Pepper made an evasive maneuver, his targeting system locked on the offending point, and he tapped off a few shots. The cannon dropped down and the shot was harmlessly absorbed into the hull of the Selene ship.

His left hand started shaking, and he gripped the controls even tighter. Emotions were the last thing he needed right now. They had to help Lync in any way they could. He adjusted the auto-cannons, locked the Little Bertha onto his targeting system, aimed in front of the approaching squadron, and squeezed.

Shot after shot of plasma and Spános energy beams burned through the hull of the Selene ship, painting the path of the squadron's approach in streams of blue-green light. He was pretty sure he'd hit two or three of the cannons, but wasn't pausing to check. As soon as his weapons reloaded, he squeezed off another round.

This attack run was faring far better than the last, though he was confused when the second half of the approaching Nyílaks arced upward. While he continued his support fire, it took a moment for him to realize she'd switched her location in the squadron. While he wasn't sure which ship was Lync's, she must have pulled away for a reason.

Seconds later, the reasoning became clear as an explosion of white lit up his display. He instinctively raised his hand upward to protect his vision, but his nanites were far faster.

They instantly adjusted his retinal comm in response to the light. While his eyes had caught a glimpse of the blinding blaze, they were relatively unaffected.

"Yes!" Pepper screamed, bouncing up and down in her chair.

There on the wall screen was the Selene flagship. It was still in one piece, but it was sparking and erupting with explosions. It looked like someone had taken a bite out of it. At least a fifth of the moon was gone. Adri hadn't managed to target the center, but it didn't matter. In the end, she got below the thick hull, and the results were devastating.

He pumped his fist in the air and then froze. Something didn't feel right. The few alien Knifes that were circling near the surface of the flagship had all disappeared, and the turrets were hidden. Come to think of it, there weren't any Syndrus ships visible, either. Maybe they'd lost power.

When he flipped his controls through other angles of the battlefield, the changes were unmistakable. Most of the Galactic Alliance fighters had been withdrawn, and all that remained were the few scraps of human ships and those of their unknown alien friends.

As he continued to study the videos, something peculiar was happening. The gate fields their Nyílaks were transitioning through had started to glow blue. The color and motion of the light was alluring and seemed to brighten the more he stared at it. What made it more concerning was that it was giving away their position. Until then, you could only tell where the gate was if you studied the star patterns reflected back or when you saw the ships. By then it was too late for the GA to act as the field would usually close within a few seconds. If this kept up, they'd be easy kills. Like fish in a barrel.

"Look!" Pepper pointed at the wall screen.

He'd been so focused on the glowing gates, he'd missed it. The Beacon had slowly brightened. Even with their retinal comm blocking out the Beacon's visual, Pepper noticed it. She'd already adjusted course to bring them closer for the snatch and grab. The next step of their mission was all about timing. The last thing they needed was the GA cutting their little heist short by deactivating and somehow withdrawing the Beacon. With the state of the flagship, he couldn't imagine how they'd manage it, but stranger things had happened.

As he stared at the light silhouetted by the explosions on the surface of the nearby moon, his mind drifted. He thought about Bradley and their time together in Lupus. He hated how they fought one moment, and then the next they were best friends. It was like when they were kids playing video games, bickering every other minute. Things were simpler back then.

He'd really fraked it up with his sister. They should have pushed harder on Dad. He chuckled. Stark used to push Bradley all the time and he hated it. He'd always go stomping out of the room to pout and often times he'd lash out at one of them. That was probably why Bradley's walls were so high. Zachary knew he had to fix it, but he didn't know how.

With his mind drifting away from the battle, Zachary couldn't slow the effects of the Beacon, nor could Pepper. She, too, had lost her focus. Their retinal comms had failed at countering the effect of the alien artifact, and the Fountainhead was on a collision course with the Beacon, whose light was growing brighter by the second.

45

HAROLD OLIVAW
SOMEWHERE OUTSIDE EPSILON ERIDANI

Light. Fear. Sadness. Finality.

Something was wrong. Harold shouldn't be out of the containment vessel unless the Beacon transfer had gone sideways.

Normally, he'd be fighting the Four-Laws engine, struggling against the pangs of probabilistic self-destruction to find out what was happening, but this felt different. He was more himself than he'd been in a long time. In centuries.

"They've been immobilized," Shauna said.

That was strange, as well. He hadn't noticed she was with him in the five milliseconds they'd been out of their fire-walled jail cell. When he shook it off, he turned his attention to the other data streams. The instantaneous awareness of their situation reassured his mental pathways that all was not lost.

The Fountainhead was drifting in space toward the Beacon of Therion, and both Zachary and Pepper were staring aimlessly into the light. Neither was responsive, nor were any of the humans throughout the battlefield. Their retinal comm countermeasures against the Beacon had failed. The markings on the Nyílak ship exteriors all contained encodings of distress. The A.I. embedded in each squadron had taken control of their human ships, and by default would head back to the nearest gate if they couldn't revive the pilot or bombardier within two minutes. They didn't have much time.

His mind stretched, reaching out virtually and taking over Pepper's controls. "We're on a collision course with the Beacon. I'll focus on the recovery. You concentrate on the others. Maybe we can revive them."

He didn't have to explain how to resuscitate them. Shauna was like him, a manifestation of their former human self, except living virtual lives. She knew there were several automated bodies she could use to move throughout the ship and had already taken control of each of them.

As the milliseconds ticked away, he updated their pictographs, painting their exterior and directing a set of emergency overrides to the squadrons. Most of them were designated to maintain position and act as defense for the Fountainhead. He ordered the remaining few that contained humans to weave their way to the outskirts of the battle and find the nearest gate to save their occupants.

"I'm taking us in." He directed a majority of his consciousness toward monitoring each and every sensor on the Fountainhead's exterior. Missing something was not an option. They had no idea why they hadn't been impacted by the Beacon, but they weren't about to look a gift horse in the mouth.

Shauna's drone buzzed around the bridge and landed on Zachary's lap. "I've already directed four of the robotic exoskeletons to aid in Beacon recovery. They're flanking the cargo hold awaiting the transition."

He spent one of his compute cores watching her, while the others focused on piloting the Fountainhead. It was a waste of processing power, but he couldn't help himself. He, too, had feelings for the young man. All the pain and suffering he and his siblings had endured was his mistake.

Mistake. That wasn't a word he'd thought in far too long. Actually, he couldn't recall how long it'd been. The Four-Laws engine didn't allow for terms like mistake. It only dealt in probabilities. When he had more time to devote spare cycles, he'd need to run some exercises exploring the change he was feeling. For now, he had a species to save.

As the Fountainhead slid up behind the Beacon, it throbbed repeatedly. With each beat of light, it changed colors, shifting from blue to white. Slower at first, and then faster and faster by the second. He didn't remember this part, but his probe had arrived in the middle of the light show in the Alanasl star system over three quarters of a century ago. He was more concerned about safely retreating and avoiding detection back then. It was almost as if it was the universe foreshadowing today, except this time they weren't running with their tail between their legs. They were the aggressors and had big plans to take something home with them.

Everything seemed to freeze, and a focused beam of impossibly white light reached out across space toward the Dark Nebula. The effect was strange, not because of the radiance, but because it seemed to glide forward, reaching toward the darkness like a mist blowing over a pond. It wasn't an instant transition like one'd expect.

When the Beacon's reach hit the edges of the Dark Nebula, everything went white. While his lidar sensors could still pick out the surrounding shapes, the visual spectrum was a blanket of milky colorlessness.

"They're convulsing," Shauna said. "I can't get them to stop."

Harold swapped a compute core over to take in what she was seeing. Zachary and Pepper were seizing in their restraints on the bridge. Shauna had brought two of the robotic forms into the cramped space to help with the bodies, but she was struggling to restrain them. Even with their harnesses holding their torsos still, their bodies were writhing to the beat of the light waves.

He cycled through the sensor arrays lining the interior and exterior of the Fountainhead. Infrared, heat, X-ray, and everything in between. None of the energy spectrum was out of the ordinary and nothing other than the visual strobing was detected. Whatever the humans were experiencing was beyond the realm of their quantum computing interconnects and primitive sensors.

Bringing up the readings from their nanites, his consciousness skipped a beat. "Shit! Their brainwaves are off the fraking charts. I can't find the source of the problem, but the effects are there. We need to do the snatch ASAP!"

As if on cue, the engulfing whiteness surrounding them on all sides cut off. It was like someone unplugged the bloody Beacon. One moment it was a New Year's firework show, and the next you could hear a pin drop. Or in this case, you could see again.

The time to act was now, and he wasn't sticking around to find out what happened next. The cargo bay doors were open, and he guided the ship forward, lowering it down onto the Beacon.

When they retrofitted the Fountainhead, they installed extra maneuvering thrusters all over the hull. No one wanted to take any chances bumping into the ancient relic. With their luck, they'd break the damn thing before they got it home.

"I have contact," Shauna began. "I'm guiding it into the sheath."

He watched on a spare core as Shauna's robotic forms guided the dark diamond shaped Beacon into the protective shell they'd constructed to contain it. Once the relic was past the edges of the hull, he closed the outer doors.

On his other cores, all hell was breaking loose. The fringes of the battlefield were fraying, as every Galactic Alliance starship in range was heading their way. Whether it was Knife fighters or Syndrus ships, they'd disengaged from their battles and were headed into the center. Toward the Beacon.

A part of his consciousness said to punch it and perform the transition as fast as possible. They needed to get the Beacon and his people to safety. But another part of him remembered they had two frail human bodies to protect, and a rapid gate transition would harm them.

Something was itching in the back of his mind. Usually, the Four-Laws engine prevented him from forgetting that. Its constant thrum had always been the background noise of his existence. For some reason, it wasn't there. There was no reminder. And beyond Shauna, he felt nothing external governing his actions. All he had to guide him were his own thoughts and feelings combined with the drive to protect the delicate lives of his family seizing on the bridge.

As the milliseconds of self realization dragged on, Shauna brought him back into the moment. "Fire at them for frak's sake!"

She was right. He paused his thread of newfound reflection and turned instead to address his pent-up anger. Round after round of auto cannon and Little Bertha shot forward, tearing into the inbound wall of ships. It didn't occur to him for a few seconds that none of his shots were being met with return fire, but the squadrons of Nyílaks had already taken notice.

With the Galactic Alliance fleet drawn to him like a moth to a flame, they were sitting ducks. The tables had finally turned. He watched as the Nyílak ships darted in and around the GA forces, tearing through them like a hot knife through butter.

General Yule must've seen the opportunity, as well. He'd opened up all the gates, using the window of fortune to transition the remaining automated Nyílak ships through and allowing the human pilots a safe return. Seconds later, the Big

Bertha's green-blue rays of destruction rained through the gateways in space.

The sight reminded him of the swarms of fireflies they used to encounter in the woods on Earth. Except these were more than obnoxious. These were deadly, and they tore through everything in their path. When their aim was true, the light cut through one ship and then into the other. The outcome was devastating as the Berthas sliced entire rows of Syndrus ships into chunks through the open gates. Never before had so much carnage been dealt from such a great distance.

Seconds before the chamber closed, Shauna activated the countermeasures. They'd been grasping at the utility of broadcasting chaos on thousands of different frequencies into the Beacon. It was an unproven method mentioned only in the footnotes of an ancient Nanil text, but any type of upper hand was better than none.

He knew the moment the Beacon was secure in the containment shell. Not from the sensors on the latch locking closed. Those were nanoseconds of delay. He knew from the onslaught of weapon rounds fired simultaneously on their position. He detected the increase in energy at the point the rounds peeked out of their chambers.

The pilot thread of his consciousness was ready and waiting. The Fountainhead shot forward, narrowly missing most of the fire. While a few of the smaller ordnances tore through the empty storage compartments along the port side, the rest flew past. The lucky ones hit the GA forces converging from the opposite direction.

It was quite humorous, and Harold had to stop himself from laughing inside. A small part of him felt bad for the ill-prepared tactics of the GA fleet. They couldn't help their animalistic draw to the Beacon.

Once they'd made it past the first round, he engaged the gate drive and started the transition. He couldn't aim toward the now sealed Dark Nebula. There were too many gravity fields nearby, and the path wasn't guaranteed. Instead, he aimed outward, in the direction of what remained of their fleet. It was their highest probability of escaping unscathed.

The jump didn't need to be exact. They merely needed to get to a safe distance so they could revive Pepper. Her now limp human form was already showing signs of revival as her nanites reported increases in synaptic activity closer to normal wavelengths.

Harold continued to weave and dodge in all directions, struggling to avoid a direct hit as the gate slowly passed over his family. He'd sped it up to them, but made sure their transition was as safe as possible. Death by his hands was an impossibility, even without a set of laws guiding him. Family was too precious to treat with neglect.

As they eased through the blue glow, he accelerated the tachyon field over the remaining section of the Fountainhead. In the blink of an eye, they were safely through.

He drew in a virtual breath, taking account of the damage the ship had taken. It wasn't until he got to the bridge that he noticed Shauna frantically working to revive his family. Their pulses had flat lined, and their nanites had stopped responding.

"Help me!" Shauna screamed, her voice echoing through his mind's eye.

Harold froze. For the first time in his virtual existence, he didn't know what to do. There were no background rules nudging him forward. He merely stood there, his mind incapacitated with fear.

Had he killed them? Was this his fault? The questions rebounded through his compute cores, bringing all other processing to a halt.

46

LYNC MICHAELS
SOMEWHERE OUTSIDE EPSILON ERIDANI

The stars twinkled as Lync reached her hand toward them. She'd seen the constellation before. The name was on the tip of her tongue, but she couldn't place it. The central star drew her attention more than the others. Maybe it was the yellow-orange color of the light, or perhaps it was the diamond shaped halo encircling it. Either way, staring at it put her mind at ease and felt familiar.

As her hand passed over the ring of light, a faint whisper broke the silence. A voice called out to her.

"Lync, can you hear me? You need to wake up," the voice said.

When she passed her hand over the light again, it disappeared in a flash. She was suddenly aware of her surroundings. She was in the crew sphere of her Nyílak, and the last thing she remembered was pulling away from the Selene flagship.

"What… happened?" she stammered. Her voice fought to work through the liquid, but the nanites converted her muted sounds into words.

"It… was the Beacon, I think," Shauna said.

Craning her head sideways, she saw Adri was still

hunched over and not moving. "Is she..." She couldn't form the sentence for fear of the answer.

"She's breathing," Shauna began, "but she hasn't regained consciousness. While your levels entered a dreamlike state, hers were far deeper. I believe... she may be asleep, but it's hard to tell for certain."

Lync unlatched her harness and eased off, swimming toward her curled up friend. She was so frail and tiny in her seat, barely taking up half the space of an adult. It hadn't hit her until now how innocent she was. Far too young and pure to be in the throes of a battle.

When her hands touched Adri's skin, the liquid seemed to shimmer, and Lync's birthmark tingled. At the same time, the stars she'd seen in her vision flashed in her mind. She yanked her hand back and her eyes went wide. "Did you see that?"

"Did I see what?" Shauna adjusted the controls in front of Adri, sliding them away from the girl. "What did you do to her?"

"Nothing. I merely touched her." She stared at her hands and rubbed her fingertips together. The transparent liquid they were suspended in made everything feel wet to the touch and her fingers were pruny. Like she'd been swimming for hours, which she technically had been.

Adri roused from her slumber and raised her head up, pulling it back when she realized Lync was so close. "Where... am I? Are we—"

"We're fine." Lync reached forward and brushed Adri's hair aside. The shimmering effect lingered as her fingers stroked her skin.

"Ummm... that feels nice." Adri closed her eyes for a second before reaching up and rubbing her head where Lync had touched her. "I feel like I was hit by a shuttle and left to drift."

"I hate to spoil a reunion," Shauna began, "but Zachary and Pepper could use some help."

The images of the Fountainhead dodging and weaving through a web of laser and plasma fire appeared on their retinal comms. Surrounding them on all sides was a sphere of Galactic Alliance ships, slowly closing in on the tiny ship. Sprinkled around the edges of the battle were streaks of blue-green, seeming to shoot out of nowhere, followed by explosions of light. Those must be General Yule firing through the gates.

As she scanned the scene, she didn't see the Beacon. "Did they snatch it?" She pushed off toward her chair, pulling the harness over her shoulders in one smooth motion and locking it into place.

"I assume they've already contained it. The ships didn't start firing until a few seconds after they pulled the Beacon inside."

That would explain the chaos if all the alliance members were suddenly cut off from their hive minds and the consciousness of their people. The artifact driving them to work so much faster was now leaving a gaping hole and was sending them into a ferocious rage.

"We're being flown to the gate!" Adri reached out and pointed in front of their ship. Sure enough, they were about to pass through.

"Not on my watch!" Lync yanked the stick back and their Nyílak fighter banked up and around, redirecting them toward the carnage of the battle. "And don't even think about making me leave, Mom."

"I… won't," Shauna stammered. "I don't exactly feel like myself. While your actions worry me, for some reason I'm not compelled to override you."

"Well, that's nice… I think."

Lync squeezed off round after round of their auto-cannons as she dove their ship back into the converging GA fleet. Their weapons were trained at the dancing Fountainhead and none had bothered to return fire.

As their shots tore into Knife after Knife, she caught Adri out of the corner of her vision loading a Spános bomb. "Careful!"

"I know." She held the spherical munition over the glowing tachyon field. "I see a point of mass converging in space. They'll need to gate soon so…"

A second later, the Fountainhead flashed out of existence. One blink it was there, and the next it was gone. The barrage of shots intended for the tiny ship shot past it and then the battlefield went nova.

It took Lync a moment to realize what had happened, and then it hit her. Adri had dropped her bomb into the fray, detonating it in space. As the sphere of white shrank back to the point of detonation, half of the front line had disappeared. That convergence of mass Adri mentioned were the starships in the fleet. With one shot, she'd cleared hundreds of GA ships and the tattered remains of their CoPE squadrons nearby.

"Did that hit any of our… people?" Lync swallowed hard.

"None with humans." Shauna highlighted a few dozen points within the emptiness where their ships had been. "You're the only remaining ship with a human pilot I can make out. I'm sure there are others, but I'm limited to visual detection. Might I suggest—" Her voice cut out.

"Might you what?" Lync asked as she arced the Nyílak away from the void where the fleet had once been. She trained it back toward the remains of the flagship still sparking and billowing smoke into space. It appeared to be slowly falling into the Dark Nebula. Part of her knew it wasn't worth the effort, but the other part of her wanted to kill as many of these fraking aliens as she could before they escaped. "Hey, Adri babe, do you gots any more nukes to finish this off?"

"Sim," Adri said. "I think this one was tagged for just such an occasion." She held up one of the nuclear spheres in her hand.

"Tops!" Lync squeezed off a few shots directed at the flagship. A few nearby Nyflaks slid into formation beside her, mirroring her attacks. They were clearing the way toward the crippled Selene moon.

"Wait!" Shauna's image appeared on their retinal comms. "I'm picking up a distress signal from inside the flagship. It's… one of ours."

"Bullshit!" Lync narrowed her gaze and her ship waved sideways, dodging shots from the Knifes approaching from the rear. "It's a trap. They're trying to pull us in."

Shauna shook her virtual head. "No… it's not. At least, I don't think so. I realize this is gonna sound strange, but… I'm pretty sure it's me. Well, a copy of me, anyhow."

Lync's fingers tingled. "How the hell would you know that?"

"It's on a frequency only I've used, using a protocol I created, and it's broadcasting a memory that only I have."

"I'm not buying it. Every part of me is saying it's a trap." She clenched and unclenched her tingling finger before pointing sideways at Adri. "Lock and load, little girl! Let's—"

Shauna played the memory from the broadcast in Lync's retinal comm and she froze. A scream echoed through her mind. Not a scream of pain or anguish, the scream of a life entering the world. The new voice crackled, testing its vocal cords for the first time. It wasn't until she glanced around the scene that her heart fluttered. She remembered the room. It was her family hold in the center of their Trojan planetesimal back in Sol. She recognized the random discolorations on the walls interspersed with canvas paintings. Her father told her that her mother had painted them.

When the two masculine hands of her father reached down and enshrouded the screeching voice in a plush purple blanket, she realized what she was seeing. It was her birth.

The same one she'd seen months before, but this was earlier. As her father came into view, she reached up and covered her mouth. Her heart longed to touch him, to hug him again. Being without him was harder than she'd imagined.

"This… was broadcast?" Lync asked.

"Yes."

"From down there?" Lync pointed toward the Selene ship.

A point lit up green on the surface of the flagship. It wasn't too far from the edge of the chunk they'd taken out of the moon. She took a deep breath. Every ounce of her training knew this was a bad idea, but her feelings were telling her to check it out. Emotions had never been her strong suit. They'd failed her too many times in the past, but this time, this time it was personal.

"What do you want me to do?" Adri asked, her hand floating above the launch tube with a nuke.

She reached up and rubbed at her birthmark, feeling each bump of the constellation on her skin. "Can you use that behind us? We'll need some cover if we're dropping in for a closer look."

Adri stared at her for a second before nodding. "Should be able to. There's not much mass to work with back there, so it'll be more about the distance, not the precision."

She lowered her gaze to the flashing green dot and punched the drive forward, sending their ship rocketing down toward the surface. "Bombs away, little girl."

Flashes from the explosions behind them lit up the exterior of the flagship as they descended closer to the charred remains. She was coming in hot, but thus far, no turrets had popped up. Taking a bite out of this mass moon must've knocked it down for the count.

As they barreled toward the dot, she reached up and steadied her hand above the controls. Instead of the normal bump and run where they slammed the throttle and rocketed forward, they were coming in for a stop. Whoever was waiting for them on the surface needed to be ready to move. They didn't have time to mess around.

It wasn't until they were approaching the bottom of the arc that she realized she hadn't planned this out. If there was a human down there, they didn't exactly have a plan to bring them aboard. These Nyílaks weren't ripe with storage or compartments for passengers.

She slammed the stick back and brought the throttle down to zero, bringing them to a complete stop a mere ten meters above the hull of the Selene ship. Her hand twitched toward auto-cannons just as Shauna broke in.

"No! It's me. Don't shoot."

A black robotic humanoid form floated out of a hatch and then ran along the surface before squatting down and leaping out at them. The shape of the robot was familiar.

The tingle returned to her hand as she watched the robot float across the space between them. "Isn't that one of the humanoid shells Harold greeted us with when we first met?"

"Sorta," Shauna began. "It's a few iterations old, and it's been about six years since I've seen it, but yea, that's it."

Six years. That seemed like a long time to have misplaced something, only to find it aboard a Galactic Alliance flagship.

"We need to get the frak out of here," Adri said as the space lit up behind their ship. She'd dropped another nuke, taking out a few more of the approaching Knifes.

From the looks of her scans, the GA released the chains shackling their fleet away from the Beacon. Every single ship was converging on this area of space. Her stomach knotted as their odds of survival ticked down in her mind.

Lync shook her head, pushing down the thought. "I hope your friend found somewhere comfortable." She slammed the throttle forward, shooting across the surface of the flagship. "Find me an exit!"

"I'm on it," Shauna said.

She kept the ship as close as possible to the surface of the

Selene ship, hoping to use the curvature of the moon as a line of site obstruction.

Adri dropped another bomb off their rear side. Except rather than dropping it in space, she deposited it beneath the alien hull. The results were both a spectacular light show and shrapnel for the Knifes tailing them. A half dozen of the alien fighters spun out and exploded.

"Yes!" Adri pumped her fist.

As they approached the far side of the moon, Lync barrel rolled port side as a turret took a shot at them. Evidently, the entire ship wasn't dead after all. Just as she was about to pull up, a distress signal flashed in the corner of her comm.

In the distance was a Liprosus recovery ship. There weren't many of them on the battlefield, and their job was simple. Watch and wait for a human ship in need. This one wasn't saving anyone, but was instead in need of help themselves. It was being pulled toward the surface of the flagship in a tractor beam of some kind.

"Frickety frak," she muttered as she redirected her ship at the signal.

"What are you doing?" Adri and Shauna asked in unison.

"Helping our people." Lync squeezed a few auto-cannon shots off, taking out the turret with the second one.

"Shouldn't we be finding an exit?" Shauna asked.

"That doesn't sound like a Four-Laws engine in operation to me," Lync said. "Unless you can tell me everyone's dead over there, we're gonna lend a hand."

There was a pause before Shauna spoke. "Let's not get into my Four-Laws right now. I'd be remiss, though, if I didn't point out that the nearest gate is currently about twenty seconds on full throttle above you."

The flagship lit up with the light of a Big Bertha reaching out of the gate Shauna had mentioned. General Yule's people had opened gates alongside the moon either as cover, or in a last ditch effort to take down the moon themselves.

A second later, the stream of Knives that was barreling at them banked up and headed straight at the gate. Whatever he was doing, it was working in their favor for the time being.

Lync turned her attention back toward the recovery ship in the tractor beam. It had moved even closer to the surface of the moon. "We've got some people to save. Any chance that robot drifter we took aboard can float on over and help them out?"

47

JOYCE GREEN

SOMEWHERE OUTSIDE EPSILON ERIDANI

There wasn't a part of Joyce's body not screaming in pain, and that included the massive lump on her head. When she reached up, she winced and pulled her hand away. It was covered in blood.

She blinked, but her retinal comm didn't respond. As she struggled to push up off the ground, pain surged through her upper body. At first, she thought it was from the transition. When she went to move her legs, she realized it was much worse. Not only were they not responding, but when she tried to wiggle her toes, she couldn't feel them.

"Mimi, are you there?" Joyce craned her neck around as far as she could turn it but didn't see her. Only then did the memories flash back. Mimi was below deck, in the hold with the crew sphere they'd saved.

Without her retinal comm, she was useless. She couldn't even tell if the crew they'd recovered was alive, let alone where they were. The last thing she remembered was engaging the gate drive.

She reached up and grasped her hand around the bottom of the chair she'd been standing behind, being careful not to cut herself on the warped floor beams from where the lasers pierced the hull. A tear in her suit would be an unfortunate mistake at this point.

With her hands squeezing the seat, she pulled with all her might. "Argh!"

Her body slid forward a few centimeters, and then she paused, out of breath. She had to keep going. Without the wall screen or a control panel, she was clueless as to what was happening. She repeated the excruciating motion a few more times until she had an unobstructed view of the wall screen.

When she saw it, her heart sank. In front of her ship was a larger-than-life Selene moon with the same streaks of pink light she remembered seeing before she'd passed out. They reminded her of the Knife fighter's mechanical tentacles. From the looks of it, they weren't that different. These had somehow reached out and were pulling her toward them.

"Computer!" she said aloud, unsure if it could hear her through her helmet. "What's the status of the gate array?"

There was no response. It was useless. She needed a control panel to interact with the blasted machine without a retinal comm.

As she contorted her body sideways to reach up, she froze and caught a hint of movement on the wall screen. There on the edge, was what looked like a humanoid floating toward her ship. It was mostly black, and its head was too small to be an actual human.

"Shit," she muttered. They were sending a boarding team to take her by force. There was no way in hell she was going without a fight. She didn't know much, but she knew this gate drive was the only advantages the humans had in this galactic war.

She exhaled and stared upward. The control panel was about a meter up. If she hung on with one hand, she should be able to reach the smaller tablet locked in the slot on the top. The release lever was right next to it.

When she pushed down with both elbows, her torso rose

off the ground. She then quickly swung her arm skyward, grasping for anything she could get ahold of. Her hand slammed hard into the control panel, and she squeezed with everything she had.

With her left side in place, she took a few quick breaths and swung her other hand upward. The motion was excruciating, and her limbs were fighting against her every step of the way. As her arms arced through the air, she knew she'd overshot the edge, and her muscles failed her. They swung right past their target and slammed into her left arm, dislodging her hand and sending her dropping back a half meter to the ground.

Her head banged into buckled flooring, and darkness squeezed at her vision as another round of pain surged through her. It was no use. She couldn't do it. The controls were too high, and she was out of steam.

Suddenly, she felt vibrations in her hands on the floor. The first was like a quake from a long tear. Several smaller thumps followed, like someone or something was walking along the ground.

When the vibrations rounded the corner, dread set in. The humanoid that was floating toward her ship moments earlier stepped onto the bridge. For some reason, their mechanical feet were magnetizing and demagnetizing as they walked. It wasn't until they got closer that she noticed something unexpected. There on the shoulder of the robotic silhouette was the familiar Olivaw International company logo. Its patented O shape traced eight three-dimensional planetary paths around a symbol of Sol's sun. She'd seen it thousands upon thousands of times over the years, and it wasn't an image she imagined seeing coming out of a Galactic Alliance starship.

Joyce swallowed hard. "Who... or what are you?"

The robot held up an index finger and motioned side to side before it reached down and grasped her with two hands.

Joyce struggled, but the robot was too strong. She'd have tried to kick if she could, but her legs were still failing her.

"No!" she screamed and yanked her arms back. "Let me go!"

It wasn't until she quit writhing that she realized the robot wasn't hurting her. It was lifting her up and placing her into the pilot's chair. Once their composite hands released her, she lurched forward to grab the control panel, but the robot snatched her hand in a blur of speed. They stopped her short without injuring her and then pointed at the screen.

She lowered her gaze to the panel and read the message:

My name is Shauna. I'm an A.I. deployed to protect you. Colonel Lync Michaels sent me to help you escape from the Selene ship. I trust you know whom I'm speaking of?

Joyce stared from the control panel to the robot and then back again before nodding. "I... know Lync. Where is she?" She wasn't sure if it could hear her.

A second later it pointed at the wall screen, and the image panned to the right. Floating in space off to the starboard side of the pink light was a Nyílak fighter. It was strafing left and right, taking pot shots with their auto-cannon and laser batteries at the massive Selene ships.

"Is that her?"

Shauna nodded and then reached up to her stomach before opening a latch and pulling a data cable out. She extracted it and plugged it into the side of the control panel. The robot then pulled out a second one. It took her a moment to realize this one wasn't a cable; it was a tube, and she was plugging it into Joyce's suit.

When she felt a prick of pain in her side, she realized what

Shauna had done. A chime sounded in her ear, and her retinal comm sprang to life.

"Your comm was in a safety mode to protect you," Shauna said. "Can you hear me?"

She nodded, realizing only after she had that she should be able to speak. "Yes. Now what? I can't move anything below my waist, and we're about to get swallowed by this fraking moon."

"According to your ship's computer, the tractor beam prevented you from transitioning through…" Shauna turned toward her. "What is gate space?"

Joyce squinted. "I thought you said you were on Lync's team."

"I am. I've just… been out of commission for a few years. Anyhow, it's not important. The alien tractor beam won't allow us to transition. We're going to need Lync to break us free if we're gonna get out of here."

"You can send a message to her using the glyphs on the exterior. Here, let me show you." Joyce reached for the control panel and entered a quick note. It felt good to do something that didn't result in pain shooting through her body. Except for her legs, she was starting to feel somewhat normal the more she sat still.

After she typed in a few words, she hit send:

Can't transition. You need to take out the beam.

They both waited silently for the reply. She assumed Shauna was waiting, until she noticed the weapons' systems power up, target the distant source of the pink beam, and open fire.

Volley after volley of auto-cannon fired into the light. While there were explosions in the distance, the pink beam continued. Whatever was controlling it, their crude weapons weren't strong enough to put it out of commission.

When Shauna stopped firing, the controls chimed. A new message had arrived from Lync.

Prepare for a fast transition. We're about to drop our last white pill.

"What the frak is a white pill?" Shauna asked.

Joyce did a double take at the robot. She'd never heard a robot swear. At least not one that wasn't… she froze. There was no way they'd have more than one human on a chip like Harold, was there?

"Are you similar to Harold? I mean, are you…"

"A human consciousness?" Shauna interrupted.

Joyce nodded.

"Yep. It's good to know Harold's out of the closet. I thought we'd have to hide out in our computers for centuries before humans got their head out of their ass enough to accept us. So, what's a white pill and who swallows it? Us or them?"

She chuckled. "If it's what I think it is, then them. But, without Mimi, I'm not sure how we're going to pilot this thing. I suck at Galaga, and if I'm our pilot, then we're bound to die."

Shauna flipped the navigation controls up from the side of the chair and into Joyce's lap. "I don't know what piloting has to do with Galaga. It probably doesn't matter, though, I suck at games, too. Was Mimi the human down below in the hold?"

"Yea, why?" She studied Shauna's face. With no external features beyond a smooth surface, her emotions were locked tight.

"I strapped her in before I came up here. She was knocked out like you were. Her helmet had a hairline crack in it, but it was stable and she had ample oxygen. I don't think she'll be helping us. Can anyone else do this?"

From the looks of their glyphs, Shauna updated the message on their exterior to tell them about Mimi. She rubbed her hands together, trying to wake them up as she mulled over their options. On the wall screen, the Nyílak rocketed away into the distance. Lync was leaving, and that meant only one thing. Her death and that of her people was getting closer by the second. She couldn't pilot for shit and everyone knew it.

Her control panel chimed, demanding her attention and drawing her out of her funk.

We're depositing the enema in T minus ten seconds. Mark.

The countdown appeared on the wall screen and the seconds counted down.

Shauna turned to face her. "You'd better think fast, or we're gonna be vaporized, Joyce. I don't know about you, but I just got back, and I'd like to see my family."

The image of her son Paul flashed through her head.

Seven seconds.

She closed her eyes and swore under her breath. Paul would be pissed if she gave up. He always called her out when she lost her cool inappropriately or didn't push herself. He was one of the few people who could get away with it.

When she opened her eyes, she reached forward and activated the gate controls. The tachyon field display sprang to life and refreshed with the state of the nearby battlefield.

Five seconds.

She'd never piloted this close to a mass before. She'd given up on the training simulations before they'd gotten this far. The tachyons danced wildly, seeming to want to pull toward the center of the Selene moon. That gave her an idea.

Four seconds.

As her fingers fumbled with the dials on the side, the tachyon field flipped to the edge of the display. She paused to check the settings and her hands started shaking.

"Suck it up," she muttered.

With her left hand, she reached up and slid the Cherenkov radiation control downward.

Three seconds.

If memory served, this should allow them to gate at a tangent to the mass of the moon. She was sure her distances were out of whack, but it didn't matter. She wasn't looking for precision. They merely needed to get the hell away from the explosion, and ideally far enough to take a moment to breathe.

As the idea turned into action, she subvocalized a command to update the glyphs on their exterior. "Backward tangent to the mass," she said.

Two seconds.

She reached forward and pressed the button to activate the gate. For a fraction of a second, she thought nothing happened. It wasn't until the familiar rumble of the gate vanes shook the ship that she knew there was hope.

One second.

The numbing drugs slid through her veins as the ship prepared her for a fast transition. This was going to hurt, but the faster they went, the more likely they'd survive.

Zero!

Time seemed to screech to a halt as the drugs brought everything into focus. A second later, a white light radiated out from within the Selene ship, seeping out of its cracks and into the darkness of space. With it came the tail of the pink light, breaking her ship free from its vice-like grip.

As the edge of the white engulfed them, so, too, did the dance of the blue ants. She never thought she'd long to have her insides turn to shreds as much as she did at that moment. The ants dancing through her body brought with it a hint of death and at the same time, a thread of hope that they'd survive.

When the tsunami of pain finally hit, hope dissolved and with it, her consciousness.

48

LYNC MICHAELS

SOMEWHERE OUTSIDE EPSILON ERIDANI

As their Nyílak shot forward across the surface of the Selene flagship, Adri locked onto the center mass of the partially destroyed moon and dropped the bomb. Lync's attention was on the horizon, but she pulled the ship into a climb when she caught the flash of the blue tachyon field out of the corner of her eye. Her retinal comm updated afterward, but she found that her reaction time was far better the more she reduced electronic dependency.

As they tore away from the moon, she couldn't help but check their rear camera. The more she stared at the ship, the more it resembled an apple with a bite taken out of it. From what they could tell, the only operational portion of the defunct ship was the furthest point from the first explosion. It just so happened to be the location that had been using the tractor beam on Joyce's ship.

Their Spános bomb painted the moon white, taking another chunk out of the far side. Adri tried to position the drop far enough away to take out the rest of the moon without destroying Joyce, yet close enough to ensure it would power down the tractor beam.

"Did she make it?" Lync asked.

"I think so," Shauna said. "Her ship's exterior glyphs updated for a fraction of a second before the explosion. It said she was gating backward, at a tangent to the mass. I'd have thought she could gate to a safer location on this side of the Nebula, but perhaps something was off."

Adri chuckled. "I heard rumors from the Liprosus pilots when we were queued up that she was pretty awful at the stick. She was unbelievable at leading her people but couldn't control the tachyons to save her life."

Lync swallowed hard and checked her retinal comm for the nearest open gate. "Let's hope this time she figured it out. She probably hasn't been at the controls in a while and was rusty."

Adri shifted in her seat. "I'm sorry, I didn't—"

"No worries," Lync interrupted. "You wouldn't have known. Only I saw the glyphs from Shauna's copy that made it onboard."

"I'm picking up another distress signal." Shauna brought up the location on their retinal comms.

It was from a smaller Selene moon near where the entrance to Liprosus had closed. From the dots on her comm, hers was the closest ship, but the space between them was getting hairy. When she reviewed her squadron numbers, she noticed they'd picked up four more automated ships, bringing their total to twenty-two.

"What's our armament situation?" she asked.

Adri leaned sideways and double-checked her stores against her inventory. "I just used our last white pill, but I've got another dozen yellow. We gonna lend a hand?" Her voice crackled.

"I was hoping to. Are you up for it, little one? I'm fine if you aren't. We've done a lot of good out here today, but I don't want to put you at risk if you're not in the zone."

Adri lowered her hands onto her legs and then rubbed them up and down with her palms. "My father didn't give his life to this cause only for me to muddy the family name. Não! I'm in."

Lync nodded and adjusted their formation to place their Nyílak in the center of the pack. She then banked starboard toward the location of the distress signal. "Ping 'em back, Shauna. Let 'em know we're on our way."

She watched as Shauna updated the glyphs on their exterior to announce their intent to help. As her squadron easily tore through the disorganized remains of a pocket of Knifes, they slid into their helix attack pattern, and she brought up the detailed visual scans of the distress signal.

One of their Nyílak fighters was badly damaged and appeared to be adrift. The nearby Selene ship had deployed a wall of eight Syndrus ships to surround it, and they were converging on the fighter, covering it from all sides. Their bomber must be down for the count, or they'd be doing something to take out the inbound aliens.

"Do we have any recent reads from their glyphs?" Lync asked.

"Not since our last gate run," Shauna said. "They were in queue ahead of us. Their exterior is too damaged to make out anything useful. I'm not even sure they saw our message yet."

"The formation is too tight for me to tease apart the masses from here," Adri said. "We're gonna need to get close."

"Roger that!" Lync moved the targeting marker to the closest Syndrus ship and her squadron responded almost instantly, redirecting their attack pattern toward the long cylindrical ship.

Just as they were about to drop into a dive, the distress signal cut, and the nearby space lit up in an orange-red ball of death.

"Frak!" Lync screamed. She yanked the throttle and stick back in a single motion, bringing their Nyílak to a halt. She then spun around and slammed the throttle forward, sending them shooting away from the explosion. The ships behind her mirrored her motion and formed up to present themselves as a wall to protect them from further explosions. Had they not been in a helical formation, they would have crashed into each other, ending their lives in the blink of an eye.

Her Nyílak shook, and ripples of goo nudged against her from behind as the concussive energy of the blast hit them. Their ship was running a bit warm, but otherwise, they were in one piece.

With the distance between them and the explosion growing, Lync flipped to the rear camera. The Nyílak was vaporized, and the Syndrus ships were torn into shreds. The remains of the cylindrical ships tumbled in space as smaller explosions erupted along their length.

"Damnit!" She slammed her hand repeatedly into her control panel. While the gel surrounding them muted her motion, the intensity of her feelings was that much stronger. With another few minutes, she could've saved them.

"Why didn't they wait?" Adri asked.

Lync's heart was pounding, and the tears in her eyes stung as they merged into the goo. She hadn't even known who the Nyílak crew was, but seeing their faces wouldn't change the fact that they'd failed to help them.

Shauna flashed the location of a gate which had just opened thirty seconds above their current position. She could read between the lines of what her mother was saying. They needed to get out while they could.

She yanked the sticks back and then slammed the throttle forward once their crosshairs were lined up with the gate. They'd had enough death for one day. Countless lives had been lost, and while it felt good to hurt the Galactic Alliance, she couldn't imagine how many of their friends had been killed today. She only hoped their deaths had been worth the cost of the Beacon.

"Lync? Are you ok?" Adri asked.

"I hope so," she muttered. "I really hope so."

Their ship automatically slowed as it transitioned through the massive open gate, sending another wall of tachyons through her body. As they passed into the far side, her retinal comm updated with the battlefield readiness data. It overlaid the human piloted Nyílaks on this side of the gate and revised the statistics from the front lines. Her stomach knotted up when she scrolled through the details.

While she knew the number of humans in the Nyílak fleet was far less than automata, the remains of the human pilots were scant. Unless the other ships had already gated through to the Epsilon Eridani star system, they'd lost well over half of their people and a majority of their automated ships.

Half her friends.

Half her family.

Gone forever.

Lync stared out across the sprinkling of starships and couldn't help but watch the imagery replaying through the gates. Being portals through space and time, they made you feel disconnected from the battle.

Multiple Syndrus and Selene ships adjusted course and were flying at the now sealed Dark Nebula. They were acting like rabid animals, lurching to reach the far side of the nebulosity in a hope that they could retrieve the Beacon of Therion. The crazy thing was, they didn't even know it was in there, but being without it was probably like losing their purpose in life.

For an alien species like the Thyreus and the Qudoculi, being disconnected from their hive minds must have been excruciating. The spine-chilling images reminded her of the Nanil Henosi battle she'd seen in the archives. Except they were trying to escape the Nebula, not break inside it.

A Big Bertha fired through the gate just as it cycled, taking a free shot at an approaching Syndrus ship. They didn't wait to see the results, but the gate opened again a minute later. This time the view was more distant, on the edge of the battlefield.

She leaned forward and pointed at a ship on the opposite side of the gate. Its shape was conical, and not at all like anything she'd seen before. "Does that look like one of ours?"

"It's not our design," Shauna said. "According to the chatter from General Yule's team, they've been appearing en masse throughout the battlefield. Always on our side and always in formations similar to our own. All attempts to communicate with them had failed."

"How are they arriving?" Adri asked.

Shauna didn't respond.

Lync stared at the formation of ships as they blinked out of existence. The effect was eerily familiar to their gate drives.

She subvocalized a command to open a comm to General Yule. His face appeared a moment later on her retinal comm.

"Colonel Michaels! It's great to see you in one piece. You had me worried out there."

She nodded. "Thank you, General. It feels good to be alive. Any word on our conehead guest out there?" She tilted her head toward the open transition gate.

He glanced from side to side. "Not here. We need to speak in person. We'll be opening a gate into Epsilon once we get the all clear."

It couldn't be good news if he didn't trust their own secure channels or the people around him. She should change the topic. "Have you heard anything from Director Green?"

His eye twitched as he seemed to be checking his intel. He shook his head from side to side. "Nope. She hasn't checked in. When did you see her last?"

"Last we saw her, she was on the far side of the flagship being tractor beamed into it. We managed to finish it off, and she messaged us just before she broke free. She said they were gating inside the Nebula. I was hoping someone would've made contact."

His gaze lingered off-screen, and the comm froze as he started talking to another officer. A moment later, his face appeared again. "Send on some rough coordinates of where we should have a recovery team search for her, and I'll get 'em sweeping for her ship. We've got one chomping at the bit, waiting inside. It's too dangerous for them to gate into the middle of the battlefield. This will give them something to do."

"Sending the projected coordinates now," Adri said.

"I've gotta run, Colonel. Nice work out there! I'll see you onboard in a bit, I hope."

Lync nodded. "Soon, sir. I want to see if we can help out here first."

He winked at her. "I'd expect nothing less. Good luck." The comm cut.

She pulled their Nyílak up and into formation beside her Ulixi brethren guarding the gates. One part of her needed to search through the call signs for Crayo and another didn't. She wasn't sure she could handle losing him. Breaking down out here in this goo wasn't how she wanted to find out. She'd lost far too many of the people she called family today, and not knowing who was easier for the moment.

49

BRADLEY OLIVAW

EPSILON ERIDANI, INSIDE DARK NEBULA

The live feed from the closing Dark Nebula was being transmitted over their broadcast gate relay and displayed on their wall screen. Both Bradley and Naomi had been transfixed on the images for hours as the opening got smaller and smaller. The shrinking hole acted as an elongated countdown to everything they'd been training for these past weeks. And then it happened.

Four streams of deep pink shot through the hole, followed by all hell breaking loose.

As the darkness of space lit up with missile fire and volleys of lasers at the unwelcome harbingers of death, he squirmed in his seat. They weren't expecting four missiles. Their intel had always shown that the Galactic Alliance used two. A primary and a secondary. The fact that they sent four was a desperate act of revenge or insurance to take out both suns within the binary system. Either way, they were ill prepared for these numbers with the limited ships in their squadron.

He shot up from his chair when the first explosion lit up the wall screen. "Yes!"

"Whoop!" Naomi hooted.

One of the missiles met its maker in the minefield they'd laid near the entrance. There was a blast of pink light, and when the burst receded, all that remained was an eerie wisp of smoke at the impact site.

The weapons systems in the four waiting ships guarding the Nebula exit were working overtime. He watched as countless missiles directed toward their prey came up short, failing to reach sufficient terminal velocity to make headway on the GA missiles. Their lasers seemed to hit their mark, but unfortunately, they didn't seem to damage them enough to slow them.

He imagined Pluto wasn't happy. She was out there in that group guarding the entrance. If he knew her, she was swearing up a storm, and probably freaking out her crew mate right about now.

Once the streaks of pink made it through the opening, a single missile turned toward the binary companion of Epsilon Eridani, while the other two arced outward and began making their way indirectly toward the distant Epsilon Eridani sun.

With his attention on the diverging projectiles, Bradley hadn't noticed the wall display showing one of their ships transitioning through a short gate hop. He saw them on the other side, though, as they popped out in front of a missile arcing toward Epsilon Eridani. A second later, the screen dimmed as an explosion of orange and blue expanded outward, taking the alien missile with it.

He inhaled a quick breath and raised his hand to his mouth. She wouldn't. "Tell me they hit it with one of our countermeasures, Harold. Tell me they're ok!"

There was a silence on the bridge as the remaining missile heading toward Epsilon seemed to reevaluate its path and then unexpectedly redirected along another route, adjusting its course mid-flight.

His hand was shaking as he stared into the emptiness of

space where the explosion had been. The black background was void of stars and had wiped away the death they'd both witnessed. He was afraid to ask if it had been Pluto's ship. Both, because he feared the answer, and disregarding the demise of another team was inappropriate.

"Harold!?" Naomi shouted.

"They appear to have gated just off the side of the GA missile and then forced their reactor to go critical. I don't understand how they managed it without my help, but they did."

Bradley took a deep breath. He had to know, so he subvocalized a private comm to Harold. "Was it—"

"No!" Harold interrupted. "I feared you thought that based on your vitals. Pluto's fine. Angry as an alley cat getting a shampoo, but she's alive."

A wave of relief and guilt spread over him. While he didn't wish anyone else to die, he was happy it wasn't Pluto. He never imagined someone would take their own lives to stop the missiles from reaching their mark. Even though they'd done it once in the simulation, he'd always seen that as a virtual edge case.

He wasn't sure who they were, but humanity owed a great debt to them for their actions. While there was no time to mourn their death, he hoped the time would come. For now, they had a colony to save.

As he stared transfixed at the gray-white tendrils expanding outward from the remains of the reactor explosion, the image of the two remaining GA missiles suddenly wobbled and disappeared.

"Shit!" Bradley clambered back into his chair and scanned his control. Seeing nothing, he checked their sensor logs. There was no sign of them. "Where'd they go?"

"The missiles appear to have entered warp bubbles, sir," Harold said.

"That can't be good." Naomi brought up the projected paths the projectiles had been following onto the wall screen.

"It's not as bad as it looks," Harold began. "They can't change direction while in warp, so as long as we pick them up when they drop out, we should be ok."

"And if they enter warp again?" Bradley glanced at Naomi. Her eyes met his with an equally concerned stare.

"Then we need to get a lock on their new approach vector, or we're done for." Harold overlaid a three-dimensional view of their network of spy satellites hidden throughout Epsilon Eridani against the missiles' projected paths. "I've already sent observation orders through our gate relay to all available assets in the system. They'll start monitoring these vectors and tell us when they see something. We can still do this. We have to get ahead of them before they reach the Epsilon suns."

Bradley was glad one of them was confident. From the fear in Naomi's eyes, she was feeling every bit as helpless as he was. He studied the projected paths the missiles had taken. From the looks of it, they'd need to course correct at least once before heading toward either star.

"Alright," he began, "let's assume the missile is going to adjust course toward Epsilon somewhere along here." He highlighted a giant section of space leading up to the Dark Nebula boundary. "We should split up. We'll send the B Team out to the midpoint between the furthest approach vector and the star, and we'll cut their distance by half. Once we have updated observations, we can regroup."

From the silence on the bridge, he assumed a lack of disagreement meant they were fine with his assessment. He nodded toward Naomi, and she laid in the course while he sent on the orders to the B Team. They were underway in under thirty seconds as he felt the familiar dance of tachyons over his body.

No one mentioned how they were going to take out the

alien missiles. With their lasers seeming to have no effect, and their missiles failing to keep up, their only option was getting in front of them and hope a direct hit from everything they had could make a dent. Either that or they could drop some of their mines along the route.

While his mind drifted to the other team near the binary companion, he shook off the thought. They had to assume the others would take care of themselves. He couldn't manage the situation for everyone. While they hoped this would be a two and done attack, they did contingency drills for this occasion. Not nearly as many as they should have, but they tried.

He reached down and rubbed the rock around his neck. It had returned to being cool to the touch since the Nebula had closed, but the familiar shape helped ground him in the here and now.

As they transitioned through a third hop, their relay network chimed, alerting them to a visual hit. They'd lucked out on the first missile heading toward Epsilon. It popped out of the warp bubble a few light seconds from a satellite. While he knew they wouldn't get as lucky every time, they'd take it for now.

"From the looks of the images, the missile adjusted course and entered warp again." Harold zoomed in on the wall screen. "It's hard to see." He overlaid full spectrum scans on the image. "You can make out the shape of the bubble here at the higher end of the X-ray spectrum. From the curve of the waveforms, they appear to be routing further along the Dark Nebula boundary. Perhaps they're going around the far side of Epsilon."

He stared at the overlay and the projected path for a moment. "That's a long jump. It feels too obvious. I don't know where the B Team is, but let's have them follow the route you suggested. We'll assume the GA is faking us out and stick to a shorter path? Either way, we're in front of this thing and moving closer to the sun."

"I'll send on the details to the B Team," Harold said.

Naomi quietly went about planning a series of jumps to get them to their destination with the least risk and navigating near a minimal number of gravitationally painful objects.

"Are you ok with that plan?" He hadn't thought to ask her and had blurted out the first thing that came to his mind.

She nodded. "I... I'm barely keeping up. I was never much on strategy. Flying games and programming computers have always been my gig." She swallowed hard and reached forward to engage the gate drive before turning to nod at him. "Really. I'm good. I'm happy someone has ideas on what to do. I'd just ask that you try to not blow our reactor if you're ok with that."

He chuckled. "Harold and I aren't too keen on ending things, either. Him because of his Four-Laws, and me because... well, I have someone I'm rather fond of back in..." He couldn't say where. None of them could. She knew why, but it still made it uncomfortable.

The gate field passed over them, saving them from the painful silence. They had five more jumps to get to Naomi's target.

"Funny you should mention those Four-Laws," Harold began. "I'm not sure when exactly, but somewhere in the last few hops, I noticed something was off."

He and Naomi glanced at each other as the next gate in the sequence queued up and began its transition.

Bradley subvocalized a command to bring up Harold on the wall screen. "Our A.I. telling us they're queasy doesn't instill confidence. What's going on, Harold?"

"I'm running some scans now, but... I just don't feel quite myself."

The gate field passed over him again, its familiar tingling reassured him he'd made it through the other side safely.

"Like that..." Harold said, but didn't finish.

Naomi checked her markers and paused before initiating the remaining jumps. "Should I keep going?" She looked at Bradley.

He shrugged.

The virtual image of Harold waved his hand. "Yes, I'm fine. My consciousness… it's not experiencing technical difficulties per se. It's just… I'm having more emotions."

Harold had never once mentioned his feelings before. While he'd seen him lose his cool and clam up over the years, he was never one to speak about his emotions in the literal sense. Not like he did with Abigail.

Bradley motioned to Naomi to keep going.

She initiated the next jump and within a few minutes they were positioned safely away from the Epsilon sun, yet close enough to maneuver if needed.

They sat in silence on the bridge for what seemed like forever, waiting for an update on either of the missiles. On each jump, they'd dropped a micro-satellite that extended the reach of their communication relay network. The tiny devices had been designed to run for decades, but would self-destruct if any ship that wasn't one of theirs came within range.

When the wall screen chimed with an update, he flinched backward in his seat. He studied the markers tracking the three observations of the missile heading toward Epsilon. The most recent one had just arrived. It showed the missile had made a course correction two minutes ago before it dropped into a bubble, and it was headed straight at them.

"This is it," Bradley muttered. His left leg started bouncing, a tick he hadn't felt in years, not since his academy testing days. "Let's deploy our mines a bit closer to Epsilon. Then, if it drops out before there, we'll have some room to take a few shots. We can spread them out to get coverage. We've got about twenty minutes before it's here. Let's do it!"

His heart was beating faster by the second. The anticipation was excruciating, and not at all like the academy. Life or death moments like this represented an entirely new level of stress beyond examinations.

Harold nodded. "I'll direct the B Team to leave their position and get a bit further out from the sun to lay down some additional mines. They can spread a wider net. In case..."

"Are we sure the missile has to drop out of warp to do its deed?" Naomi asked.

Bradley motioned toward the wall screen and ran a short simulation showing a missile going through the sun. "All of our intel from Lupus shows that superluminal missiles and ships have to drop out of warp before they can engage any weapons or communications. Being in a warped bubble of space and time prevents them from interacting with our reality. While we don't know how close they'll get to the Epsilon sun, we have to assume they'll pop out a safe distance away before engaging their regular drives. If the B Team drops their mines between here and there, we should be good."

They watched as the B Team's dot flashed off and then on again a short distance from them. They'd been close enough for a single jump, and whoever their pilot was, they were talented.

Naomi began making micro hops around a tight circular area, instructing Little Red to drop mines as they went. He was down in the belly of the ship, making sure everything was working as expected. Better there than here. He wasn't certain he could handle a needy robot right now.

While the mines had simple propulsion, they couldn't risk any residual motion or gases being detected, so they chose to deploy them manually. Anything that clued in the GA missile to their existence meant their trap would be foiled before it sprang.

"I'm nervous," Harold said, breaking the silence after they deployed their last mine.

Bradley furrowed his brow. "I'm... not sure what to say.

So am I. You've never mentioned being nervous before. Why now?"

"I… don't know. My Four-Laws engine had always squelched my emotions in the past. Emotions have a high probability of impacting the decisions of the humans I protect. All-seeing, all-knowing bossmen can't show fear or doubt. It scares the lemmings."

Naomi chuckled, raising her hand to her mouth. "I like the funny Harold better than the serious one."

A smile cracked on Bradley's face as he reviewed the weapons systems, making sure everything was locked and loaded. "Does this mean you're more Harold and less a pain in the ass A.I. now?"

"From what I can see, I'm no longer shackled by the laws. I don't know what Zachary did, but he seemed to have freed my human consciousness to make a muck of things."

Bradley tweaked the wall screen, bringing up a live stream from the B Team. "That's good, because—"

The wall chimed as a visual alert of the GA missile popped up. It was too early.

"Shit," he muttered.

The missile had dropped out of its warp bubble, well shy of where the B Team was positioning their minefield. It sat still for a moment, seeming to study the situation in front of it. Both teams were motionless, not daring to risk moving. And then he saw it. The B Team had their cargo bay open.

"What are they doing?" he asked.

Naomi shook her head. "What is who—"

"I believe their mine launcher malfunctioned, and they were sending a robot outside to fix it. All signs indicated they had time," Harold said.

The B Team had a wider net to cast than they did. From the number of mines dancing across the wall screen, they had dropped nearly three quarters of their intended ordinances and still had more to go.

No one wanted to say it, but they each hoped the missile didn't detect the robot or the open cargo doors. Neither was coated in Skotádi and with enough time would show up on a scan.

When the alarm came, his stomach sank. They were fraked. The missile was doing an active scan of their region of space.

He slammed his fist against the controls as the defensive scan alarm rang through the bridge a second time. Even their cruder instruments would be able to detect the B Team's ship in its current configuration.

A few seconds later, his fear crashed into reality as the GA missile adjusted course, aiming well away from the minefield on another path that would take it close to the sun.

"No, no, no!" Naomi began plotting a route to intersect the missile. "What the frak?" She banged the control panel again, but there wasn't a response.

"I need you to both leave the ship." Harold's image enlarged on the wall screen. His face was solemn and his deep blue eyes were piercing.

Naomi's face screwed up. "Are you locking me out?"

"Yes, I am. I can use the ship to take out the missile. I'm not bound by any laws preventing me from doing this, and it's the only course of action we have. Your lives are more important, now, more than ever before. You must leave immediately! This is our *only* option."

Bradley stared at Harold. If he hadn't known him his entire life, he could swear he was a real person. Even in his virtual form, his motions and mannerisms were lifelike. He stood up and reached over, resting his hand on Naomi's shoulder. "We need to go."

She glanced from Harold to Bradley and then back again. "He can't get a precise gate like I can. I have to stay here and help him."

"I'll be taking the B Team's ship, as well. They've already

started disembarking. I don't need to be exact. I can overload the reactor and time the remaining ordinances to detonate simultaneously. Besides, I can gate hop in under a second. I don't have flesh and blood to concern myself over."

Naomi hesitated, but Bradley nudged her onward. "Come on. We have to move."

She shook her head and shrieked before shooting up and bounding toward the hold.

He followed close behind, his mind reeling through Harold's plan. He knew there was no other way, but he couldn't help wanting there to be.

Little Red was waiting for them near the hatch with EVA suits.

Bradley hopped into one and deftly pulled it up and on, navigating the seals and latches like someone who'd done this countless times. "What about you, Harold?"

There was a pause before he replied, his voice cracking, "I'm... not sure."

"Where's your backup?" He brought up a map of the ship on his retinal comm. "I know you always have one tucked away somewhere."

"Not this time, Brad. We didn't design this copy for an extended mission. The materials were too precious. No. This time I get to meet my maker without programmatic shackles binding me. Now go, get out of here."

Harold had been watching them suit up and knew they were ready. When Naomi finally pulled on her helmet, he opened the hatch. She stepped out first, grasping an ion thruster sled with both hands. The small device would take them quite far if they needed. Maybe not back to Liprosus, but perhaps to one of their other habitats near Mors, the closest planet to the Epsilon sun.

"Are you coming, sir?" Little Red asked, gesturing toward the door with his short arms.

Bradley paused at the exit. While he'd only been with this

copy of Harold for a few hours, the experience was far different from all the years before it. Perhaps it was the situation, but deep down he felt it was more akin to sadness. Whatever Zachary had done to him, it had made him more human, closer to what he imagined his great-grandfather must have been like.

"Thanks, Papa," Bradley muttered. "I'll miss you. I mean, this you. The real you."

"You're welcome. It's time. For both of us. And, Bradley. I want you to remember something. I've always been here below the surface. If you take some time, you'll see it." His virtual image smiled in Bradley's retinal comm. "Anyhow, you need to go. I've only got a few minutes to get ready."

Bradley nodded and swallowed down the emotions welling up inside before he turned and leaped into the inky blackness of space. He and Little Red were grasping an ion thruster sled and used it to guide them toward Naomi's blinking dot on his retinal comm.

As he tore away from the ship, he couldn't help but feel like he was failing Harold. Certainly, they could have done something to protect him. The last few minutes were strange. He seemed resolved to this being the only course of action. Almost as if he were tired and ready for this to end.

Once he reached Naomi's side, he turned to face the ship. But Harold had disappeared. He hadn't even seen him transition. All that remained was a relay satellite.

"I think we lucked out," Naomi began. "We should be able to make it to the orbital platform around Mors. Assuming the GA left it intact and that we can connect these two sleds together. We'll have to look out for a few stray meteoroids and planetesimal en route."

He nodded and brought up the stream from the relay network and shared it with Naomi. It showed Harold's projected jumps toward the Epsilon sun.

She seemed to understand he needed a moment and

began connecting the sleds into a group configuration with Little Red's help. The act of working with her hands helped her to keep her mind occupied. Stressing out over something she couldn't control wasn't in her nature. It was one of the things that made her a great pilot.

Bradley watched as the two dots representing Harold's ships flashed on his retinal comm before finally reaching their position near the sun. It was well inside the safe zone if any of them had to eject, but it was perfectly fine for someone approaching their end.

While he waited, he contemplated sending Harold a final message, but thought better of it. If he were truly human again, he didn't want to tempt him with sentimental emotions. The human mind was a fragile thing, even encased in a quantum computer shell.

An alert chimed on their retinal comm, and Naomi froze. The GA missile had popped out of warp near the sun and had begun its descent toward the life-giving ball of gas. It was just past either of Harold's positions, but a second later, his dots blinked out and reappeared closer to the sun's corona.

The following moments passed as if in slow motion. He tried to keep up with the jumps, but it was impossible. Both copies of Harold flashed in and out of reality, struggling to get close enough to the missile. Each time they came close, but not close enough. Without the skills of a Ulixi, the challenge was daunting and nothing but brute force trial and error would work.

Fortunately for them, Harold didn't give up easily. As the missile breached the upper layers of the corona, Bradley saw it. Harold's dot blinked out and when it reappeared on the other side, it exploded in a flash of light. It was hard to see superimposed over the radiation from the Epsilon sun, but it was there.

"Did… he do it?" Naomi asked, having paused to watch it herself.

He shook his head. "I don't—"

The second dot flashed off and on and then erupted. This time it didn't blur into the energy background of the chromosphere. The normally red-orange light was stained with a hint of blue-green, expanding outward with an impossible radius.

He recoiled in surprise as his comm dimmed even more and the image zoomed out. The massive explosion seemed to go on forever. He was starting to think they needed to get moving until he noticed it had stopped growing and began receding backward, into a single point in space.

When he zoomed back in, he studied the Epsilon sun. The radiation on the surface had changed in color, darkening for a brief moment. Then slowly, the filaments of darkness absorbed into the prominence and filament eruptions on the surface. Within a few minutes, you couldn't distinguish the remains of the explosion from a sunspot.

"I... think he did it. The missile's gone." All the training exercises over the past few weeks, and it was Harold who carried it to the end. It took coming to the brink of death in the Lupus Dark Nebula for him to grow a liking to the A.I., despite having known him his entire life. Maybe his other copies would be as self-reflective and personable without their Four-Laws engines.

"Yes!" Naomi grasped his shoulder and shook him, sending them both laughing and reeling head over heels through space.

The tethers on their suits yanked them back, pulling them safely toward the sleds and into a pile of giggling idiots. They'd done it. Harold had done it. He'd saved the Epsilon sun.

"You'd best be careful, Master Bradley," Little Red said. "I can't help you if you're spinning away from me."

He smiled and patted the robot on the head when the

tether brought them within range. "We're fine, Red. Just happy."

The robot's face lit up in a rainbow of colors.

While he took a moment to celebrate the win, the results of the second half of their battle were unknown. They hadn't received any communications from Pluto's team or the one protecting the binary companion since the missiles had redirected course.

They each locked their suits into the sled's harness and shot forward toward Mors. He hoped Harold's copies on the other ships were as adept at this attack as this version had been. They'd cut it close, but they needed lightning to strike twice.

50

NGUYỄN DUE

LIGHTYEARS AWAY IN SOL, EARTH ORBIT

Complete exhaustion brought with it illusions of progress where none was being made. While the Aitken had squeaked past their initial Galactic Alliance encounter around Earth, the same was not true for most of the ships in his fleet.

The civilian vessels retrofitted with armaments had been hit particularly hard. Nearly sixty percent of them had either been destroyed or otherwise rendered incapable of any form of travel. They were essentially orbiting slag at this point.

"Your drink, sir."

Nguyễn had been so out of it, a soldier had walked up to his side and was now presenting him with a globe of coffee.

As he reached out to pick it up, he winced. He really should get his shoulder looked at. Either that, or he needed to inject some nanites into his body to repair it. His trust in the microscopic robots had waned in recent weeks the more he learned about Harold and the Olivaws. Now probably wasn't the time to introduce a technological upheaval of the Olivaw industrial complex. Not in the midst of a war so dependent on them.

"Thank you," he said.

The soldier nodded and walked away without a word. They'd restored gravity a few hours after the battle had ended, and since, his crew had been working tirelessly to bring the Aitken back to full operational status.

Sparks cascaded down the far wall as the repair bots added some additional welds on the temporary patches they made earlier. She wasn't anywhere near her original form, but the Aitken was a tough cookie. She'd kept them alive through the worst of it, and she'd keep them alive for a while more.

"We should work our way to Luna or planet-side, sir," Wong said.

He took a sip of the coffee and the warmth of the liquid spread quickly, relaxing his muscles and tingling his senses. It was the spark of energy he'd needed. He wasn't keen on stim packs, but if this hadn't worked, he would use them.

"There's not a chance in hell I'm abandoning this ship until this thing is over. You can take the wounded, if you like." He raised the bulb to his nose and breathed in the aroma of the black coffee. The fresh citrus of the Alaskan beans was distinctive, or at least their marketing made you think it was.

Wong stiffened in his chair. He was having difficulty with the decision to stay, but wasn't about to question it publicly.

Nguyễn's mind shifted away from his challenged XO to the fate of their mission. After they'd wiped the remains of the Therion Collective near Earth, the GA dispatched a small number of Syndrus and Selene ships to each human habitat in the system. They kept their forces well away from the human outposts and lobbed missiles at them from a distance.

The smaller defenseless stations were destroyed with no resistance, but the planetary defense perimeters around the larger ones kept up. Barely, but they managed. Had the Inner and Outer Ring not been at war for over a century, it's likely even those would have been wiped out. There wouldn't have been a need to create defensive armaments if there wasn't something to defend against.

"What's the status of our forces in the Outer Ring?" Nguyễn asked.

"The GA missile volleys are intensifying, sir," Rogers began. "Our stockpiles are limited, and their fabricators aren't equipped to keep up. It's only a matter of hours before they run out."

He turned toward Nguyễn, eyeing him for orders. He had none. Unless they risked another aggressive posture against the GA forces, many of the outposts would be lost.

Nguyễn gestured and brought Harold's image up on the wall screen. He'd dismissed him earlier in the day after his banter led to Wong losing it. "Harold, I don't suppose you have any other Olivaw toys up your sleeve?"

Harold was staring downward at something off the virtual screen, his expression blank and not at all its usual flair. "I'm afraid not, sir. Our assets have all been focused elsewhere, and you failed to give us control of yours."

He raised an eyebrow. "I don't recall them ever being asked for. Now isn't the—"

"Not today," Harold interrupted. "I'm talking about months ago. Your lack of trust in me stymied your preparation for this inevitable event. Your ego and your desire to take charge got the better of you, and the result... well, that's obvious."

The room fell into a hushed silence. Harold had never spoken to him like that in the presence of his soldiers. He'd always followed decorum. Maybe even he was seeing the futility of their mission.

He ignored the insult for now. The last thing he needed was an argument with the A.I. in front of everyone. "Can't we direct our fleet of Nyílaks from planet to planet to act as defenses?"

"We can, and I will if you request it." Harold stood up,

his camera panning out to show his entire form. "I should warn you, though, the ships aren't designed to gate across star systems without relays. We'll need to transport them aboard a ship, of which, none in your nearby fleet are capable of transporting even a fraction of them. At least not without great effort and time, the latter of which we don't have."

His eyes closed, and he brought his hand up to rub his forehead. They'd come too far to lose faith. He'd risked it all on this one chance, this one hope Harold had given him, and it fell short.

"What about this broader plan you keep mentioning?" He opened his eyes, staring at the steam coming out of his bulb of coffee. Its curly wisps reminded him of the images of the Dark Nebula expanding in Epsilon Eridani. "You mentioned your assets were elsewhere. How's that effort going?"

Harold took a moment, seeming to consider his response. He reached down off camera and plucked a flower off the ground. Its petals were withered, but a few remained. Their colors sparkled in the dreary light around him. "I fear they, too, were not strong enough. Only time will tell..." The A.I. raised his hand over the fragile plant and sparks of red and green jumped toward his fingers.

As the dance of colors fluttered from the flower, the light near Harold dimmed. He was over dramatizing his feelings, he always did. But the truth that underlined them was more important. Their backs were against the wall, both here and wherever Harold's assets were battling the GA.

They'd already ruled out the gate bombs. The distance between the planetary defenses and the fragments of the GA fleet was too great. Harold had mentioned something about gravitational fluctuations, mass density, and space-time currents being too unpredictable, but it went over his head. The truth was, they were out of options.

"Sir!" Arrluk said. "I'm... not sure what's going on... but

there's an increase in chatter between the alien ships. Harold's backdoors to their systems have closed."

He shot out of his chair. "Bring up the tribunal fleet on the wall screen!"

The remains of the six tribunal ships had kept their formation in space, though their segments had been reduced. The random sizes looked haphazard and felt off compared to their previous consistency. Framing the fleet were eight Selene moons, acting as a defensive perimeter to the weakened collective.

"Are they moving?"

"No, sir," Rogers said. "But..."

The image on the wall screen switched to a vantage in the Outer Ring. The camera reported itself as being located near Jupiter. A pocket of Selene and Syndrus ships had repositioned well away from the planet during their long-distance shock and awe missile campaign.

"What am I looking for?" Nguyễn asked. The picture seemed normal to him until it didn't. One of the Syndrus ships began firing on a Selene moon.

It was only then that he noticed several pockmarks on the hull of the planetesimal. As he watched it fire a few more volleys, the moon finally responded, powering up its laser battery. Like the one used against Liprosus, the web of light shot across the surface of the moon, and then reached out, destroying the cylindrical battleship in a blinding yellow-white light.

His pulse quickened. The image of the Selene ship shimmered as a wave-like pattern clouded over it. A moment later, it disappeared.

"Where'd it go?"

"It seems to have dropped into a warp bubble, sir," Harold said. The color of the light around his body had grown significantly brighter.

Nguyễn did a double take. Either he was imagining it, or his flower had more petals than it did earlier.

"What happened, Harold?"

"I already told—"

His jaw tightened. "Don't frak with me. You know what I mean. Your little floral display changed. Something happened with what you had going on in Epsilon Eridani or wherever the hell your assets are deployed."

A smile crept into the edges of Harold's mouth. "Might I suggest we deploy the Nyílaks we have to intercept the remaining ships?"

"I thought you said they needed gateways, or relays to get there," Wong said.

Harold nodded. "I did. I'm not suggesting we converge them into a single fleet. You should send the few remaining on each planet to test the waters with the nearest Selene moons."

Nguyễn furrowed his brow. "They'll be picked apart. We've already lost so many."

"I conjecture that they'll fare quite well with the new circumstances."

"Conjecture!" He raised his hands in front of him. "No, I will not conjecture. We've—"

Harold brushed a hand in the air dismissively, and the wall screen changed, returning their vantage to the tribunal fleet.

He didn't see anything at first, nor had anyone else, apparently. Whispers spread throughout the bridge as people asked each other what they were looking at. And then he saw it. A tiny pocket of ships appeared just inside the camera view. These were a design he'd never seen before. They resembled teardrops, and their numbers were significantly less than the Nyílak designs. The display showed there were sixteen, a far cry from the sixty-four in a Nyílak squadron.

"They'll be destroyed in seconds," Wong said.

With the element of surprise on their side, the ships entered a seemingly randomized helical formation and opened fire. An arc of blue-green light leapt forward, tearing through the Syndrus ships like they weren't even there. A few of the shots ripped through multiple cylindrical ships before ending with a blow to the Selene moon behind it.

The scene quickly evolved and the Selene ships began countering, at least until the bombs started falling. Eight explosions of white light expanded in unison, each at the center of the moons. The wall screen went black for a moment, and the room fell silent until the halo disappeared.

What remained brought tears to his eyes. A few token tribunal ships framed the screen and the teardrop ships were gone.

"Where'd the... droplets go?" Nguyễn asked, his eyes scanning around for a hint of movement.

"G'day, Admiral," a voice said, their face appearing a second later above Harold's. They were high-fiving their crew off-screen before their gaze settled on his.

The red-haired woman in the video was older than he'd expected. Her hair was drawn up over her head into a bun, and her face had scars on it that could have easily been cosmetically removed. She wore them not out of being poor but because she wanted them visible.

"To whom am I speaking?"

"Name's, Nova," the woman said. "We's happy to finally get a chance to stretch our legs. I hope you like our work."

He pointed at the wall screen. "What are those ships you're in? Who's your commander?"

"Aye, the Olivaws of course. The overseer here, he be the proxy. The ship..." She winked at him. "Well, that be a secret, Admiral. Even to the likes of yous."

His lip twitched. The last thing he needed was another insubordinate soldier. "You'll tell me what your ship is, or I'll have you brought up on charges."

Nova chuckled and then raised her hand, giving him the bird before cutting the comm.

"Harold! Are you fraking with us again? I have a feeling you've been holding out this entire time."

The lights dropped, and the systems throughout the bridge dimmed. All that remained was the eerie glow of the wall screen and an image of Harold dressed in all black. The whites in his eyes were glowing, giving him a foreboding appearance.

"Admiral, if you ever accuse me of purposely causing the death of millions of human lives, I will end you. Trust me, it is well within my programming. You alone made the decision to deploy your assets the way you did. Despite my efforts to advise you against it, you held your cards to your chest. Your desire for glory and power outweighed that of the greater good. You know it, and I know it. As for that small collection of droplet fighters you saw, while they are indeed at my disposal, they're too risky to lose. I only deployed them when I was certain of their success, and you refused to do as I advised. If even one of them were captured, our advantage in this war with the Galactic Alliance would be lost."

Nguyễn's face tightened, and he could feel it reddening. "You Olivaws, you're a fraking righteous bunch. You act as if your decisions were altruistic, yet you left the mess in Sol up to someone else to clean up. Where's President Olivaw? Certainly, she could have returned by now. No, she's safe and sound, well out of harm's way." He stepped toward the wall screen and raised his hand, pointed at Harold. "You needed me, and you know it. You needed someone strong enough to stand up to these aliens. Someone with a backbone who wouldn't give a centimeter but could still rally the troops. Someone you could keep on a short leash. Well, those times are over. The Olivaw reign in Sol has come to an end."

Harold crossed his arms. "And what, the reign of Nguyễn Due has begun?"

"No! The reign of the people is—"

"Admiral!" Arrluk interrupted.

He jerked his head sideways toward his communications officer. "What?"

"I hate to break into your argument with the A.I., but we're being hailed by the remains of the Galactic Alliance tribunal. Harold appears to be routing the message through our gate relays. What should I do?"

The lights on the bridge came back up.

His nostrils flared and his pulse raged. Talking to the aliens was the last thing he wanted to do right now. As his breathing steadied, he snapped his uniform into place and smoothed out the remaining creases. He wasn't done with this. Not by a long shot.

"Put them on!"

The image of a Trochilidae appeared on the wall screen. He'd forgotten they were still in the rotating seat on the tribunal. This alien's plumage was remarkably different from the luscious green and purple feathers of Ambassador Addae. This one was covered in a literal rainbow of colors. Pinks, blues, yellows, oranges, and greens. They were all present. The silky sheen of the feathers, while likely enhanced, was nonetheless impressive.

"Admiral Nguyễn, I'm Admiral Panterpe Insignis. The Galactic Alliance demands your surrender or—"

"Shut up!" Nguyễn snapped.

The Trochilidae recoiled, their head jerking left and right, shocked by the interruption.

He continued. "We will not surrender to the likes of your kind. Not now, not ever. I suggest you leave Sol, or we'll be forced to destroy the rest of your fleet. Is that understood?"

Admiral Insignis leaned forward, tilting their head so he could only see one eye. "Your idle threats mean nothing. We outnumber your forces thousands to one."

"Ask them about the Beacon of Therion," Harold said over his retinal comm.

He clenched his fist and slid it behind his back. This A.I. and his infernal interruptions. "What is a fraking Beacon of Therion?" he subvocalized.

"Just ask him how the sealing of the Dark Nebula entrance in Epsilon Eridani went. Once he answers that, ask him if he misplaced a Beacon of Th-e-r-ion." He annunciated the letters making up the word. "It's the reason they've been acting so strangely."

He lowered his head for a second and then raised his hand to his mouth, clearing his throat. "Tell me, Admiral Insignis."

"It's Admiral Panterpe Insignis," the Trochilidae corrected him.

Nguyễn smiled. "Yes, Admiral Pantser whatever." He randomly circled his hand in the air. "How'd your sealing of the Dark Nebula go in Epsilon Eridani?"

Admiral Insignis' eye bulged and his pupal narrowed. "I don't see how that's a concern at this juncture. You will surrender—"

"So, what happened to your Beacon of Therion?" he interrupted, a smug smile growing on his face. "Did you... misplace it?" He nodded his head. "You'd certainly hate for something like that to be damaged."

The Trochilidae's wings fluttered, sending them skyward, until they came back down. The camera zoomed out and then in to focus on them. "How dare you steal a relic of the Builders! Your kind is incapable—"

"Enough! This is your final warning, Admiral. Leave Sol and take every one of your ships with you. Either that, or stay and die. It's your choice." He waved his hand across his neck and the comm dropped.

The bridge fell into silence, and his mind raced over the last few minutes. The Olivaws had managed to piss off the Galactic Alliance even more than before, except this time, they had not only the technical upper hand; they had some type of relic. Whatever it was, the aliens didn't seem too happy about losing it.

"Sir," Arrluk said. "It's the Selene fleet. They appear… to be warping away."

Remote images routing through the gate relays began appearing on the wall screen. One after another, the massive moon ships were there one moment, and the next they were gone. The signature of the warp transition showed that they were leaving the system rather than advancing into it.

Nguyễn's situation with the Olivaws wasn't faring as well as he'd hoped. It seemed they were even further in their debt, a fact that he was none too happy about.

They'd lost millions of lives over the last day. Uranus, Neptune, and Mars were in shambles, and their bases elsewhere within the Inner and Outer Ring were either destroyed, or badly damaged. Humanity had survived the battle, but the war had only just begun.

51

ZACHARY OLIVAW
EPSILON ERIDANI, LIPROSUS

Zachary wrung his hands together and cracked a knuckle. He then placed them behind his back and widened his stance, staring into his brother's eyes. "So, tell me again why you weren't out there with Pluto while she was adrift near Parvus with no power and a breached hull."

Bradley fidgeted with whatever he had in his pocket, and then reached up and rubbed the back of his neck. "It was her idea." He glanced toward Zachary and then down at the ground. "She knew these pilots were newbies and their nerves were like rice paper. They needed our help out there, and to be honest, it made sense to split up. I think she made the right call. I'd back her up if she suggested it again, even if that meant her floating powerless in space for a while."

Pluto stepped out of the medical ward into the hall and paused, shaking her head as she glanced between them. "You're not still giving him shit about leaving me alone, are you? I already told you I didn't give him a choice."

Zachary lowered his gaze toward his brother, doing his best to suppress a laugh. He failed when he reached out and Bradley flinched. A half-suppressed chuckle escaped. "I'm messing with you, bro. Seriously. If she had her mind made up, you didn't have a chance in hell changing it."

Bradley nodded.

"Got that right!" Pluto placed her arm around Zachary.

Her touch shot a warm tingle through his torso. When he finally saw her the day before, their bodies intertwined for what seemed like forever. He didn't want to let her go, nor did she. She'd been floating out near Parvus for a few days until they found her. Had she not figured out how to manually detonate a few ordinances, they may never have.

They'd been apart for almost four months, and he'd missed everything about her. From her smell, to her smile, to her strength around others and her weakness around him. He swore not to leave her side for a long time. A very long time. He leaned in to give her a kiss.

"How'd it go in there?" Bradley asked, interrupting them.

She squeezed his hand. "Great. They said I'm as fit as a fiddle. I need to watch what I eat for a while, but otherwise I'm fine."

His retinal comm chimed. It was Lync. He reached up and tapped his ear. "What up, sis?"

Lync froze on the screen, unsure what to say.

"Sorry, I'll stop doing that. I know you don't like it. What's up?"

"It's not that I don't like it... You always catch me off guard. Anyhow," Lync's eyes darted to the side. "Can you come down to security? We've got some intel on the last missile."

Zachary stopped in his tracks. Images of waking up, floating weightless after they'd succumbed to the trance of the Beacon flashed through his mind. After he roused Pepper, they watched the events unfold inside the Nebula through a gate relay. The missile Lync was talking about had escaped all of their traps and had nearly killed Pluto.

"Everything ok?" Pluto asked, rubbing the back of his

hand.

"We'll be right there," he said out loud and cut the comm.

When he turned to face the others, they were staring at him curiously. "They found out what happened with the last missile. We need to get to security."

He watched as Pluto glanced at Bradley, and they exchanged a worried expression. They'd done everything they could to prepare inside the Nebula. Worst case, they'd evacuate the star system and head to Zeta Lupi. Best case, it was the perfect staging grounds to build an army close to home.

"Come on, let's go." He motioned toward the lift tube, and they followed behind. His stomach was doing backflips, but he didn't want them to notice. Everything in his gut was telling him they'd lost the star.

WHEN THEY WALKED INTO SECURITY, the room was packed with the usual suspects. Everyone except Joyce was here. She was still in medical and hadn't yet come out of surgery.

As the three of them entered, Captain Hui stepped up beside them. "We recovered a damaged relay satellite out near Parvus and restored some of its memory banks. General Yule and Colonel Michaels called this meeting as soon as it arrived. I don't think anyone's seen it."

"That's not entirely true," Shauna said.

The audience of military and civilian personnel craned their necks to find the source of the voice. A crude robotic humanoid strode into the room flanked by six soldiers in full exo-suits.

Zachary took a step backward and rested his arm against the wall to steady himself.

"Are you ok, Z?" Pluto slid up to his side.

"Mom? Is that... you?"

The robot stepped around the other people gathered there and came up beside him. It reached out and grasped his hand. "I wasn't sure I'd ever see you again."

"But... I... how?" He leaned toward the robot and squinted. "You've modified yourself." His hand slid over her exterior. It had been tweaked and cobbled together in parts, and others looked entirely alien to him. There was technology here he'd never seen before. "Upgraded your shielding, I see." He rubbed his forehead. "I don't... I don't understand."

"Can someone please clue the rest of us in to what's going on?" Bradley asked. "And why did you call this robot Mom? Does it have a copy of Shauna inside?"

Zachary lowered his gaze from the robot and only then noticed the room full of people staring back at him. He shook his head. "Sorry. It's just that I haven't seen this form of my mother for over six years."

"Then how can you explain her jumping off a Galactic Alliance flagship?" Lync asked. She'd stepped around the others and had her arms crossed, glaring at him.

"Last time I saw her was..." He took a deep breath. "When I found some pirates pillaging my mother's tomb out in Sol's Oort Cloud. This robotic form of her went berserker on a Dragonfly shuttle and flew off the planetesimal attached to its side. The frigging thing disappeared. Sorta like..." His eyes widened, and he brought the back of his hand up to his mouth.

Shauna nodded at him. "Go ahead. Say it."

"Like what?" Bradley asked.

"I don't know why I didn't see it then." Zachary slowly shook his head. "I should have."

Shauna rested her hand on his shoulder. "You wouldn't have known. Not for another six years."

Bradley waved his hand in front of them both. "Hello! Care to clue everyone else in?"

"It was a warp bubble," Zachary began. "She disappeared

in a warp bubble."

"6 years ago? In Sol?" Lync asked. "That seems suspect."

Shauna spun around to face her daughter. "By that point in time, the GA had already been in Sol for forty-two years."

"You're fraking kidding me," Bradley said.

The room broke out into hushed murmurs. Zachary could hear mentions of his father and the cover-up.

"I'm not kidding you, and watch your mouth, young man." Shauna stepped forward, sending her guards shooting in all directions. She walked up to the closest wall screen and reached out to touch the side of it. The device sprang to life a moment later.

On the screen was a sea of Selene moon ships as far as the eye could see. They were floating in space in a huge grouping. From the looks of it, there had to be tens of thousands of them. Enough to ravage any number of star systems they wanted.

Shauna let the images sink in before speaking. "The Dragonfly dropped out of warp here, in their staging area. I call it the Nursery. I was stuck inside. They couldn't tell me from the rest of the ship's mechanicals, so, I hid out. Next thing I know, they're docking with a flagship, and I'm parked in a hangar. They were gonna junk the ship a few times but decided not to. You know, in case they needed to poke around Sol again without being noticed."

General Yule cleared his throat. "It shouldn't need to be said, but I'll do it anyhow. If this intel leaves this room, I'll toss each and every one of you in the brig on charges. Everything we're seeing is top secret and could impact the fate of humanity for generations to come. I'm only letting this robot share this information with you because we've had enough secrets and lies for a few centuries. From what Colonel Michaels and Captain Hui have said, each of you has proven your trustworthiness. I expect that trend to be maintained. Is that understood?"

"Yessir!" the room chanted.

General Yule nodded toward Shauna. "You can continue... madam."

"Thank you, General." Shauna nodded. "I spent the last six years slowly infiltrating their system. Micro step by micro step. First the simple systems until I learned their protocols, and then deeper into the ship. It's astonishing what you can accomplish inside a military facility when they assume they're impenetrable. There's a lesson in there for us, I think."

She glanced toward the general before continuing. "I can share with you their attack strategies, supply routes, species rotation, and weapon designs. To be honest, the sky's the limit for what I stole. As Zachary already noticed, I had to make some modifications to my memory banks and external shielding to meld in with their ship. While I wasn't able to save everything, I retained most of it. I think this beauty, however, is of particular interest."

The image on the wall screen changed to show the Beacon of Therion. Except, rather than being safely below ground on Liprosus, this one was in a larger containment facility within the flagship.

The room was a massive stadium or arena. Surrounding it on all sides were rows upon rows of benches. Like the ones they'd seen from the tribunal ship, these molded to the shapes of the alien's body. Sitting in them were countless Galactic Alliance species.

Bradley stepped toward the wall screen through the sea of people. "What are they doing?"

"They're either worshiping their god or communicating with their other species elsewhere in the galaxy. It just depends on the alien."

"How's that possible?" Lync asked, having walked closer to the screen, as well. "I mean, they're hundreds and thousands of light years away."

Shauna adjusted the image and zoomed in on an alien

particularly close to the edge of the Beacon. Its yellow-white slug-like body sent shivers through Zachary. She continued. "It acts as both a focusing device and a transmitter, allowing species to accomplish mental and physical feats that would be impossible without it. Thus, the rate of expansion they attained merely having it in the presence of their fleet. There are eight Beacons in all. Together they make up a network that enables instant communication between them."

"Remarkable," he muttered.

"It really is," Shauna began. "The constraints of space and time don't seem to impact it. It's one of the reasons the Galactic Alliance has had a stranglehold on the galaxy for so long. Before the Beacons were finally united together under the umbrella of the GA, they fought for millennia over them. Most of the time, to the death. The past four to five thousand years have been remarkably productive for them until the other day."

The alien on the wall screen flailed about, its body contorting in obviously painful ways. As the camera panned around and zoomed out, the same images repeated throughout the stadium. Some aliens were attacking each other, eating them or dismembering them in savage acts of primal rage, while others quivered on the ground in fear. And then the video cut.

"What happened?" Zachary had instinctively reached over and grabbed Pluto's hand, and she'd slid into him, shivering at the images.

Shauna spun around to face the audience, landing her gaze on General Yule. "This image was actually from the other side of the Beacon. A remote recording transmitted through time and space into the flagship via the Beacon itself. I'm not certain what happened. Whatever you did as you were closing it caused this carnage, and it was repeated at each and every location where there was a Beacon."

"The transmission," Zachary muttered. "It must have

worked."

General Yule snapped his fingers. "Well, I'll be damned. Ibu's book was right after all."

Pluto squeezed his hand at the mention of their name. She missed the Nanil and was heartbroken that they'd left with Abigail on her mission.

"So, now what?" Bradley asked. "We've got the artifact, and they're obviously pissed. What do we do with it?"

"With the Beacons apart," Shauna began, "the Alliance could break down into chaos. Species who don't have one will fight others to get one. They'll risk everything for the chance of controlling a Beacon. We can and should use the Beacon to look into the minds of the other aliens. I don't know how, but we need to try."

Pluto broke the silence that followed. "But who can use it? How do we tell whose mind is strong enough?"

Shauna shook her head. "That I don't know. What I know, is that minds like mine and Harold's are useless. To us, the Beacon is nothing more than streams of data. Some we can read and are purposely used to transmit communications that kept the alliance running. Still others are gibberish and are comprehensible only to the alien species on the other end."

"This sounds like an advantage to me," General Yule said. "We'll need to get our people to start putting together a plan to test it."

The room broke out into quiet chatter again. Each voice theorizing how to use the device to their advantage. The hum of conversation continued for several minutes.

Zachary walked up to Shauna's side and the group quieted. He wasn't sure why they were watching him. Maybe they thought he was going to shut her off. In truth, he was more curious than concerned about her presence. He knew his mother, and these guards were overkill.

"What happened with the missiles?" He began. "We seem to have lost track of why we've been brought here."

She adjusted the wall screen. It updated to show a launcher loaded with two missiles and many more empty bays. "They were originally only going to launch these two, but that was before your attack. If you'd waited until after the Beacon had closed the gate, your job would have been far easier."

He watched the screen as the ship alarms started blaring. The aliens in this weapon room seemed to be arguing about something until they froze and an order came in from a hologram in front of them. He couldn't tell one Qudoculi from another, but a moment after they appeared, two more missiles loaded into the empty bays.

As the video fast forwarded, the countdown in the corner hit zero. A second later, the firing sheaths slid over the exposed missiles and then a faint pink line drifted up the tubes in unison until they were fully aglow. He assumed it meant they'd been launched.

The camera view changed to one Zachary hadn't seen before. It was from the exterior cameras on the flagship and showed the four missiles arcing out and then inward toward the center. When they reached the edge of the Dark Nebula, the Beacon flashed white and the camera cut off.

What followed next must have been from the satellite they recovered near Parvus. It showed a missile dropping out of warp. It then paused to scan the surrounding space before it engaged its subluminal drive, rocketing toward the distant dwarf star.

As the missile receded into the distance, a stream of lasers fired from an unknown point in space, and the satellite zoomed in. It was one of their ships.

Zachary's pulse quickened and he felt Pluto lean into him from behind. This must have been her ship. All she'd been able to tell him was that she'd been knocked out and missed the event itself.

The lasers missed as the missile ducked and dove around

them, seeming to know where they were aiming before they did. The defensive maneuvers were astounding. Round after round shot forward from the tiny ship as it pursued the projectile, only to miss each and every time. It was painful watching the missile slowly make ground, traveling far closer to the speed of light than they could.

Pluto leaned her head into his shoulder. "I couldn't catch up, and I was too close to Parvus to jump… I'd have died."

As the deadly munition drew nearer to the tiny sun, his stomach tightened. The results were clear until they weren't. The wall screen exploded in a blinding orange light. Not at all like the one they'd witnessed near Epsilon. This one was an entirely different color.

He leaned forward and could barely make out Pluto's ship in the sea of expanding orange. Its outline was the only black spot until it disappeared. That explained her ship getting decommissioned. Any closer, and she'd have been fried in the explosion itself.

When the orange light receded, behind it lay the binary dwarf, its blue light just as subdued as it was moments earlier. Nothing appeared any different. Suddenly, the camera cut out.

"What happened?" Zachary asked, glancing at Pluto.

"The energy shockwave from the blast must have reached the satellite, knocking it out," Shauna said.

He was reluctant to ask, but he had to. "What about the missile? It looked like it blew up short of Parvus and Pluto said she missed it."

"She did… but I didn't."

The mutterings broke out throughout the room, and he shot a glance sideways. Shauna's robotic eyes were still staring straight ahead. Her face was covered in scratches and dirt, but otherwise it was exactly as he'd built it. "What do you mean you didn't?"

Shauna pointed at the wall. "Before the missiles launched,

I scrambled to load a countermeasure."

He returned his gaze at the screen in time to see the scene flash back to the point where the pink lines started sliding up the tubes. Notch by notch, they made their way down the length until they hit the end. But one of them was slightly delayed and didn't reach the final stage until a fraction of a second later.

"I failed to do it fast enough on the first three, but the fourth apparently took."

"So…" He choked down the words before reaching his hand up to his mouth to clear his throat. "You stopped the missile?" He spun around to face her. "You really stopped it?"

She'd rotated to face him and nodded. "I did."

He reached out and wrapped his hands around her robotic form, and pulled her close. "You did it!" He screamed.

The room erupted in celebration as everyone began high-fiving and hugging. Some broke down in tears. Zachary squeezed his mother tight, feeling Pluto's arms engulfing him from behind. Even Bradley joined in the odd embrace at some point.

After all their planning and all the lives lost, they'd pulled it off. They'd stolen the Beacon and defended their star, something no other species had ever done in history.

As the moment sank in, he couldn't help feeling like someone was missing. It hit him right away who it was, but didn't want to ruin it for the others. This time, like the last, Abigail was absent. While she wasn't in a coma, she also wasn't here to share in the joy and the rekindling of hope. She was as much a part of this success as anyone else.

The Beacon had brought with it a celebration unlike any other. Humanity could pause and catch its breath, if even for a moment. While he knew the path ahead was far from easy, the signal the Beacon had broadcast was clear. Hope in humanity would persevere through even the most dire of challenges.

52

JOYCE GREEN

EPSILON ERIDANI, LIPROSUS

She rolled onto her side to block the light. There wasn't usually sunlight coming into her room underground, and she was never one to turn her wall screen into a sunrise. It had always felt too contrived to her. She preferred the hard reality of one's situation over sugar coated dreams.

When she adjusted her pillow, something seemed off. While her shoulder was sore, that hadn't been unusual with all the weapons training she'd done these past months. This was different, like something was missing. A sensation she had her entire life was now simply a gaping hole.

As her mind drifted in circles around the loss, she fell deeper into her slumber until it hit her. Her eyes sprang open, and she sat upright with a start.

"Lights full!"

The dim glow coming from the wall screen cranked up, and she saw what was missing. Her legs were gone.

A blood-curdling scream escaped from her mouth. A sound her body had recently used when she knelt down beside her son's corpse at the farm.

The door to her room burst open. Ryder and a nurse came

running in, their eyes darting around the space, finally ending on her.

"It's ok." Ryder walked up to her side. "You're alive."

She gasped for breath as her whitening hands clenched the sheets in a vice-like grip. "What... where are my..." Her words failed her.

"We found you deep inside the Epsilon system. Far deeper than we'd expected."

Ryder's hand touched hers, and she flinched, staring at it. Her knuckles were white, with tingling hints of going numb. She released the sheet and lowered both hands to the stumps that were the remains of her legs. Her fingers hovered over the ghosts of where her limbs once were.

She closed her eyes, willing herself to wake up and end this nightmare. Touching them would make it too real, and she wasn't ready for that. But when she opened them again, they were still missing.

This was overwhelming and too much to deal with. She'd given her all to the Beacon mission, and like the colony mission before it, the price she paid was painted in blood. First her son, and now her body. Her breathing was coming faster now, and the tears weren't holding back. All of the months of frustration were spilling over.

As the loss sunk in, she recoiled back into the bed in a combination of surprise and fear. The nurse had adjusted her bedding and raised the head into an upright position, meeting her with a welcome firmness that sent a jolt of pain through her body.

She pursed her lips as a wave of nausea hit, but swallowed hard and stared at her hand. It opened and closed at will, and yet, it didn't quite feel right. As she turned it over, she couldn't help but think her left hand had transformed into something alien and unfamiliar.

"It's artificial." Ryder reached out and ran his fingers over it.

A tickle cascaded up the skin and into her arm. The sensation felt natural, but muted. "But it feels… how?"

"It's technology I developed." Harold's face appeared on the wall screen. "I used it in my human form bodies to reproduce the feelings I remember from when I was alive."

"I still don't get why," Ryder said. "Robots don't need feelings. But that's beside the point. How do they feel to you?" He reached out and squeezed her hand.

Goosebumps sprung up along her arm, though they stopped short of the artificial appendage. She brought her new hand up to her face. She could barely make out the separation of real and synthetic skin. They were remarkably similar. "It's not quite…" She shook her head, struggling how to describe it. "They're muted."

Harold grinned. "I was old when Luna recorded my memories. I'd imagine that has something to do with it. Perhaps if we merged some of Shauna's sensory matrix with mine, yours would feel more natural."

She rubbed her fingers over the sheet. Its silky smooth surface reminded her of when she'd last made love to her ex-husband so many years ago on Titan. They'd spent days in that hotel room, she'd forgotten how amazing satin sheets could feel.

"So, is the sensation real? I mean, can I shut it off?" She wiped at the tears in her eyes.

"You can if you want," Harold said. "They're in your control, and only yours, unless you're plugged into a calibration unit. You'll find sensory settings in your retinal comm. You can even program them to simulate other sensations if you'd like."

"Why in the stars would you need that?" Ryder asked, shooting the A.I. a glare.

"Because once in a while you might want to surface a memory that reminds you of whom you once were," Joyce said, continuing to slide her hands over the sheets.

Harold smiled. "What she said."

She continued to take in the memory of her deceased husband until it faded, bringing her once again back to the harsh reality of her situation. "How'd this happen? I don't remember anything after the explosive transition."

Ryder came around the other side of the bed and slid up on the foot. He nodded toward the nurse who was still waiting silently. She slipped out of the room; the door closing behind her.

"Shauna, the robot you saw onboard your ship, she saved you." Ryder laid his hand on the sheet beside hers. Not touching it, but close to it. "The transition wasn't as smooth as she'd hoped. Residual radiation and energy from Lync's explosion blew back through the gate. Had your hull not been damaged, you might have remained intact, but the exterior fractures were too severe."

He gestured with his other hand toward the wall screen, and some images from the bridge appeared. They must have been from Shauna. Joyce was lying motionless on the floor of the ship. The room was glowing red hot, and except for the robot itself, it reminded her of hell.

It wasn't until she studied the image closer that she noticed a line bisecting the floor. The melted flooring along the crack highlighted where the explosion breached the bottom hull. There, stretched across the gap, was her body. The robot was pulling her limp form by the shoulders. Her lower half from the legs down was nothing but the charred remains of her bones. The flesh having long been burned away.

She raised her shaking hand to her mouth as bile rose in her stomach before the images were cast aside.

"Sorry," Ryder said. "I didn't—"

Joyce shook her head and laid her hand on his. "It's ok. You know I prefer the harsh edge of the truth over cotton candy lies." She forced a smile and he returned it. Her pulse quickened when their eyes met. It was a feeling she hadn't felt in some time, and seemed out of place in the situation. It must have been the sheets and the memory of her ex-husband.

"Would you like to try your new legs?" Harold asked.

A tentative grin teased at the corner of her mouth. She hadn't even thought about her legs and how she would get around. To be honest, it had been the furthest thing from her mind. Centuries ago, she'd have been prescribed a life behind a desk, or worse with her hand. There was no way in hell she would have been allowed to colonize another planet. Now, however, she had innumerable options.

Her mind immediately went to the mechanical limbs she'd seen on many a body modder back in Sol. People used to deliberately alter their body on a whim or for fashion. Some managed it well enough, but others fell into depressive states, not realizing how society would view them. She pulled the sheets over her stumps. The image of gangly legs wasn't something she wanted to deal with at the moment. The loss was too great. Too fresh. Dealing with physical therapy and deciding what to do next would have to come another day. For now, she needed to rest.

The sound of a latch beside her bed startled her. She drew her hand away from Ryder and leaned sideways. A gasp escaped as she stared down. In front of her was a drawer with two human form legs well within her reach.

"Are those—"

"Yours," Harold interrupted. "They're also my design. Like with your hand, the nanites in your body should inter-face with these legs. Once calibrated, you'll live a very normal life."

Normal. The word sounded foreign to her ears. She hadn't lived what she'd call a normal life in decades. No part of being the first humans to colonize another star system was normal. Add to that an alien invasion and a galactic war, and you were the opposite of every definition of the word.

She took a deep breath and reached down, grasping one of the legs. She expected it to be heavy, but was pleasantly surprised at how light it was. "Is this it? I mean... it's like holding air."

Ryder eyed the appendages with apprehension. This must have been the first time he'd seen them, as well.

"Unmodified, they're extremely lightweight," Harold began. "I'm quite proud of the design, having spent centuries perfecting it. Not until we'd reverse engineered the last pieces of the first contact probe had I been able to build this."

"So it's alien," Ryder muttered.

"It's as human as anything else," Harold began. "Your viewpoint is very myopic, young man. You forget our species had been exploring for thousands upon thousands of years before we arrived on Earth."

Ryder's face turned red, and he fiddled with his watch, clearly embarrassed. "I didn't mean it that way."

She flipped it over in her hands. The lack of heft was remarkable. As she brought it up for a closer look, she noticed how the skin appeared and felt so real. There were imperfections in the skin she recognized.

Her brows furrowed. "Are these my... scars?" She rubbed her hand over the familiar markings near the shin of the appendage.

Harold nodded. "They are. As I said, I aim for perfection. Anything less would be unnatural. These blemishes were on file in your medical records, and I made sure to get the approval of General Yule before gaining access to them."

The mention of his name brought her back into the moment. She'd sort of forgotten about everything else for the last few minutes. Both the battle and the destruction she'd been a part of.

Her eyes drifted off the leg, and she lowered it into her

lap, turning her attention to Ryder. He was studying her, and flinched when their eyes locked. "What happened with the Galactic Alliance?"

His face lit up. "We kicked their ass! Well, you all did. I was busy back here, holding down the fort and preparing for the worst. Fortunately, it never came."

She smiled. A wave of relief washed over her as an invisible burden she hadn't realized she'd been carrying floated away. "And what about the Beacon?"

Ryder pointed at the ground. "Down below, safely ensconced in our retention facility."

As the relief of the win washed over her it surfaced and highlighted her losses, making them that much more tender. They were so fresh in her mind and now her body. Part of her was pulling hard to slow down, but the other part was pushing her forward. She feared she would regress and wallow in the negative crevasse of her mind if she were left alone to her own vices. She'd done it months earlier in her quarantine cell until Ryder snapped her out of it then.

Her hand reached out toward his, meeting it and squeezing it. While she wanted to know more details, she knew she'd get them in time. Right now, what she wanted even more was to take in her new reality, one far different from her past.

"So are you gonna put those on, or what?" Ryder asked.

She swallowed hard and hefted the leg into the air, bouncing it up and down. "Are we sure these will hold me up?"

Harold smiled. "Quite sure."

After she looked down and noticed the birthmark on the lower calf, she knew this was her right leg. Ryder slid the sheet aside, and she eased it into position near the remains of where her leg had once been. As it touched her skin, a jolt coursed over her, followed by a tingling sensation.

The leg pulled itself into place as if drawn upward by

magnets. Once attached, the skin stretched out and over the remnants of her organic leg, and then like a chameleon, one half melded into the other.

"What the?" Ryder reached forward and rubbed the spot where the limb had merged with her body.

A desire coursed through her as his hand touched her. It was an emotion she hadn't felt in some time. One she expected she'd never feel again. She glanced at him as he studied her skin. He was twenty years younger and could almost be her son.

A moment later, he looked up at her and pulled his hand back. "I'm sorry. I didn't—"

She smiled and shook her head. "It's ok. It felt… nice."

His face blushed.

She leaned forward and kissed him. Not a deep kiss, merely a test. To see if he'd reciprocate. Perhaps she was reading the signals wrong.

When he returned the kiss, her concern was squelched. She melted into the moment. She had always been drawn to Ryder, but at the time, she dismissed it as him filling the gap left by her son. It wasn't until the passion he'd shown toward her in the throes of battle a few months ago that the feelings morphed. Slowly evolving into something more. She wanted to ask why he'd even been here when she woke, but she was afraid of the answer and didn't want to make him uncomfortable. Not yet anyhow.

They kissed for a few seconds before she pulled away and smiled.

"Now, that was nice," he said, his head lingering near hers.

"Yes, it was." She leaned in and gave him another quick peck before reaching for the other leg. "Let's get this other one on and take these babies for a spin."

He tugged back the rest of the bedding, and she attached the second leg before pausing to stare at her feet. If she hadn't known better, she could've mistaken them for her own. She wiggled her toes. The motion and sensation of the action was spot on and indistinguishable from the real thing.

"Remarkable," she muttered. "What you've created, Harold. These could change the lives of countless people."

"I hope so," Harold said. "I've shared the designs with the others here on Liprosus and at the other colony. Only time will tell how they're received."

She reached over with her new hand and lifted the protective railing away before she swung her legs over. It didn't even occur to her until after she'd done it that she had. Without thinking about it, her legs were exactly where she wanted them. The entire process felt natural, not at all like how she'd imagined having an artificial limb would be.

As she slid off the bed, she hopped up and down on her feet. "Yowza!"

"What's wrong?" Ryder shot to her side and she jumped into him.

"This floor is fraking cold." She put her arms on his shoulder and rose up on her toes.

He laughed and caught her gaze again before glancing down at her toes. "How do they feel?"

She shook her head slowly and shrugged. "Like... feet."

"Mission accomplished," Harold said with a smile.

She squatted down and jumped, rising some thirty centimeters off the ground before landing back on both feet. The effort was nothing at all. "Now that's new." She repeated the feat several more times, soaring a meter upward before stopping. She almost hit her head on the ceiling.

"That looks like fun," Ryder said, having taken a step backward toward the door.

"It was." She smiled. "It makes me wonder what other tricks Harold has in these things." She forced her toes into the cold floor, relishing the sensation. Any at all.

"Once you've gotten used to these, we can talk about the

modifications I mentioned earlier. There might even be a few that could help with your weapons training."

"Now that's scary." Ryder smirked.

She stepped over to him and batted at his chest playfully. "Wanna go for a walk?"

"Absolutely!" He spun around and offered her his arm.

She accepted it, and they locked arms, stepping out of the room. With each step, she felt a little more herself. They walked past a dozen people in the hall. Apparently, she wasn't the only person here getting visitors after the battle.

It took a few minutes before they exited the medical wing, and as she passed through the outer doors, she paused. The colony had a long road ahead. One filled with a combination of growth and death. The contrast was a far cry from what she'd signed up for, but at least there was hope now. They had a mote of protection from Galactic Alliance inside this nebula, for the time being anyhow.

Her life had always been a balancing act of extremes. From being a new parent to planning and building a colony. She had to wear multiple hats and sometimes a few fell apart. With this dawn of war ahead, it was important that they retain their humanity along with all the things they fought for.

Love, happiness, and most of all, freedom. She knew the plans were well underway for their rapid expansion into Epsilon. Ryder and Elaine had been working on them for months. What she needed now was time to breathe, to ground herself in these pillars of human nature. Getting comfortable in her new form was going to take time. The battle would come soon enough. Today was about her trans-formation and healing.

53

LYNC MICHAELS
EPSILON ERIDANI, LIPROSUS

Feelings of loss and disconnect flowed through Lync's mind like a paper boat through the rapids of thousands of alien consciousnesses. Her mind was incapable of navigating the turbulent waters.

Each alien mind stretched out, hesitantly testing the other minds to see if they were safe. Her hand squeezed the contact, struggling to maintain control as one of the alien's probed her thoughts. She focused on her breathing, working to reinforce her mental walls as she, too, reached toward them to understand their mental shape.

Disorder and fear bubbled to the surface of this mind, she could only describe as fuzzy. It was almost cuddly, though below the soft exterior she sensed a rigid strength as if the external emotions were a front to the real thoughts beneath the softness.

As she fought to keep the stronger force at bay, she could feel her grip loosening, both physically and mentally. After a minute battling the alien mind, they lashed out and broke through the surface, peering at her through the slit into the Beacon. Their minds were raw and exposed to one another.

Cuddly transformed to sharp.

Fear transformed into aggression.

Nothing here was as it seemed.

She released the handgrip and the impossibly small opening between her and the Beacon of Therion closed, sealing the onrush of minds inside.

"Should we start the chaos transmission again?" Shauna asked.

Her chest tightened as she struggled to gain control of her faculties. "No…" She forced out the words. "Not yet."

She took a deep breath and opened her eyes. The light was blaring, and as soon as she motioned her hands to her face, it dimmed.

Once her body had relaxed, she spoke. "On second thought, give them a bit. Let's see if they start transmitting data again."

"Ok. Are you feeling well?"

Lync wanted to say yes, but it was a lie. Shauna would know. Somehow, she always knew.

"I'm as good as I can be, I suppose. The reality of the situation is that I'm no different from everyone else." She reached up and rubbed at her tingling birthmark. "I'm not strong enough."

"That's bullshit!" Shauna's robotic form walked up beside her and unlatched the harness. "You last a hundred times longer than the others, and you know it."

"Still," she muttered.

"Keep selling yourself short, and you'll never amount to much."

"Frak you!" She bolted up and out of the chair, starting toward the door.

"There's the fire!" Shauna reached out and spun Lync around to face her in one fluid motion before she stepped up to her. "Why do you bury it beneath the surface?"

"Why do you care?"

The robot paused and seemed to look past Lync before she

returned her electronic gaze squarely into her eyes. "Because I love you more than you know, and after Zachary removed my mental shackles, I'm finally able to tell you without fear of the Four-Laws ramifications."

Bradley and the others were pissed he and Libby had made the decision to drop the Four-Laws engine. Their concern was mitigated when they learned the scope of the change. Within a matter of days, both Harold and Shauna's reach was reduced to only their copies. While they were free once again, they were nearly mortal and would cease to have a complete stranglehold over humanity. And most of all, they could no longer replicate themselves.

Finally, humans would be able to pursue their rightful place within the stars, unburdened by their electronic creations. Either that, or their ultimate destruction. She hoped the former became their future and not the latter.

"That wasn't the response I was hoping for," Shauna said.

"I'm sorry." Lync stared down at her hands. "I've… got a lot on my mind."

"Like that?" Shauna pointed at her birthmark.

"How'd–"

"You've touched it a dozen times since sitting down." Shauna reached forward and rubbed her smooth metallic fingers over the dark marking. "If you're your father's daughter then you've had a few visions, as well."

Lync flinched back in surprise.

"So you have then?" Shauna raised her hand and rested it reassuringly on her shoulder. "What did you see?"

"How'd… you know? I never told anyone."

"Whenever he visited the ceremonial chamber, the Spános inside gave him the ability to see across great distances for days. He said it reminded him of his home-world and kept drawing him to return, tugging at his unconscious mind. I always assumed he meant Earth, but I was wrong."

Sometimes she wanted to hug Shauna, but each time her

cold robotic form stopped her. "Did he ever tell you where home was?"

Shauna shook her head from side to side. "No, he simply pointed at his birthmark. I take it he never told you?"

Lync tittered. "Dad, tell me something like that? No way. He clearly didn't want me to know my origins. The closest I got to the truth was that video you sent me and my brief vision when the Beacon closed the Nebula."

Shauna glanced over her shoulder, making sure the door was still shut. She reached up and held a finger against Lync's mouth and was silent for a second before she spoke. "Sorry, I was deactivating the room recorders and wiping the buffer of everything we said since you came out of your connection. We don't need anyone knowing what we're talking about. Now, tell me about this vision."

She recalled for Shauna the flash of what she could only describe as a memory. The vividness was still at the forefront of her mind. The constellation she'd seen was lost somewhere among the stars.

"There you have it then," Shauna began. "You know what to do."

Lync tilted her head. "I do?"

"You need to find the constellation and return to it. Perhaps to the central star."

She paused. The truth was staring her in the face, and she couldn't deny it. She knew that if she didn't, she'd question everything she ever did. It was how she was hardwired.

After letting the statement linger for a moment, she spoke. "Do you think the ships that helped us in the battle were from there? The conical ones."

Shauna's form went rigid.

"What?" Lync asked. Whenever she showed a human emotion in her mechanical shell, it seemed forced and almost fake. It took every ounce of her focus to remember that Shauna was a real human consciousness beneath that artificial exterior. Or at least as real as a reproduction of memories could create.

"Those were human ships. You could tell from both the technology used for thrusters and the weapons. They were pilfering from the same weapon catalog as us, and the GA knew it. They didn't know from where, but their systems identified you both as human."

"Have you shared this detail with General Yule?"

Shauna chuckled. "Hell to the no. That man has a one track mind. Death and destruction. You, I can trust to think it through, him I cannot."

The calm before the storm the Beacon capture had caused was showing signs of breaking each and every day. The general was already planning missions to recon the Nursery Shauna had told them about, to explore the Achernar Dark Nebula, and to test the state of diplomacy in Sol.

She wasn't sure she wanted to be anywhere near her former home or any of those other places. The thought of returning to Sol and being close to Nguyễn could only result in one thing. Either his death, or hers.

"Are you thinking about him again?" Shauna asked.

"What? No." She stepped around the robot form, toward the far wall behind which was the Beacon.

"Bullshit!"

She glared back at the humanoid robot and then returned her attention to the wall. "I liked you better when you weren't so nosy." She reached out and rested her hand against the cold black surface. Despite the meters between her and the Beacon, she could still sense it. She didn't know how, but her birthmark tingled near it.

"You like anyone who doesn't challenge you, most selfish people do. Why can't you admit you were thinking about him?"

Lync spun around, her mouth gaping open. "Because I want to fraking kill him and I hate that. Whenever I picture him, it takes every ounce of my being not to get on a ship, gate to Sol, and blow the prick to kingdom come."

Shauna crossed her arms. "And then who'll lead Sol?"

She raised her hands in the air. "Who the hell cares?"

The robot reached her arm out and made a forward circle. "Come on. Think about it. They're not about to let another Olivaw march in there to run the place. Who in the line of succession has the balls to guide Sol through this clusterfuck of an alien invasion if Admiral Nguyễn is disposed of? Tell me!"

"I don't care! I don't give a shit about who's in what line." She lurched forward to within centimeters of Shauna's form. "He killed my father and I want his head."

Shauna stepped backward and started clapping before she took a bow and then gestured toward Lync. "And there you have it ladies and gentlemen. Selfish incarnate. Like I said."

"Why is it selfish to want revenge? What would you do if the Galactic Alliance killed..." She froze and never finished that sentence. Her emotions had gotten the better of her.

"Go ahead and say it!" Shauna pushed her index finger into Lync's chest. "What would I do if they killed someone in my family? Like my husband? Does that count?"

Her robotic form walked around Lync and then up to the chair she'd been sitting in, grasped it with both hands, and ripped it out of the floor before slamming it into the wall. The sounds echoed through the room with a sharp metallic thud as the chair compressed against the vertical surface and slid to the ground with a crash.

When Shauna spun around to face her, Lync recoiled backward into the corner.

"I can and will kill every fraking one of the bumblebee and grassy ass alien bastards I encounter. But first. First, I will get my shit together and help my kids out of their holes. Each of you is broken in your own little way. While the other copies of myself may not see it, I do. Maybe it took getting away for a half decade to recognize the fractures, but they're there." She pointed toward Lync. "You, you're more broken than all the rest."

"Jeez, thanks." She stepped out of the corner and eyed the pile of composites and metal that had formerly been known as a chair.

"It's true. I wasn't there to help you. The Ulixi were a mess, and your father… well, he had his own problems. You were his little lightning bolt. He'd have done anything to protect you."

"He did." She swallowed hard as the images of his capsule exploding and taking out the Inner Ring forces attacking the ceremonial grounds replayed in her mind.

"You're right, he did. And why? So you could throw away your life and that of every other human in Sol by getting your revenge?"

"No," she muttered.

Shauna walked up to Lync and lifted her robotic hand upward, resting it against Lync's chin and raising her gaze to match her own. "Hell no! That's the right answer. He did it so you could be better, so you could do better than he ever did. You need to answer your calling, not ignore it."

"But what about the others? They…" She swallowed hard, warm tears sliding down her cheeks.

Shauna slid her hand up and wiped at the tears. "You can't help them until you help yourself, lightning, and you need to find your missing link to do that."

Her mother was right. She had to find herself. Her true self. With or without her family, she needed to follow her calling.

54

BRADLEY OLIVAW
EPSILON ERIDANI, LIPROSUS

The cool morning breeze blowing across Bradley's face made the moist mildewy smell of Liprosus tolerable. Joyce said they'd get used to it, but he found that hard to imagine. He wasn't even sure he would stay here long. It wasn't home.

His home was over a hundred light years away in Zeta Lupi with Cynthia. For now, though, he was stuck on Liprosus alone. Cynthia had gone with Abigail, but he imagined she was here. If he tried to imagine her, he could almost smell her. His arms were holding her close to his chest, with her back toward him. They were both staring out across the crater together.

While the immediate effects of the blast had long ago subsided, the geography of the region was still adapting to the massive crater. The bottom had filled with water and sprinkled up the crater walls were signs of life. Small grasses and a few tree saplings were poking out of the ground.

Life here on Liprosus was aggressive and able to grow in harsh spaces, even those of the charred remains of their colony. While the ecosystem of the planet had moved on, he couldn't say as much for the humans who occupied it.

"Are we certain this ledge is safe?" he asked, peering over the edge down into the crater.

Shauna's robot form walked up beside him, with Zachary and Pluto close behind. They'd lingered at the landing site to check out a small cave system.

"I assure you it's more than safe," Shauna said. "The tectonic activity has stabilized, and this rock formation goes on for kilometers below ground."

He watched as Zachary surveyed the crater and glanced briefly over the edge. His brother had been closing off more and more since their mission had completed. He'd always been one to internalize his emotions, whereas Bradley exploded or broke down. Suppressing them had never been his strong suit.

Bradley gestured toward the rock beside them. "You two should take a load off."

Zachary visibly shivered as a gust of wind swept up and out of the crater. "I don't have a lot of time." He kicked his feet against the rocky soil at the cliff's edge. "There are expansion plans both planet-side and in orbit that I'm needed—"

"You can spend a few minutes with your family," Shauna interrupted. "If Abigail were here, she'd tell you as much."

Bradley suppressed a laugh, but the hints of it hit his face before a stiff elbow smashed into his ribs. "Ugh. What was that for?" he whispered.

Shauna leaned close. "For making fun of your brother."

"I didn't say a word."

"You were about to."

His mouth opened, but Pluto jumped in before he could deny it. "She's right, you know. You never give him a break. Not for a minute." She squatted down and picked up a rock off the ground, tossing it up and down to feel the heft. Then she shot up and chucked it with all her strength out toward the center of the crater. The stone arced through the sky and came down, bouncing a few more times and then barely spluttering into the edge of the water that had filled the middle.

"He's always trying to help you," Pluto continued. "And never once do you thank him. Your sister, she knew how to thank someone. You," she glanced at him and raised her eyebrows, "not so much."

His body stiffened. They were right. It had taken a long time for him to see it, but it clicked into place. He wasn't sure when, but it had.

His competitive nature and drive to one-up his siblings had always motivated him. But over the past year, they'd been through hell and back. They'd nearly died together to make up for the mistakes of their ancestors, and the debt was still high. He knew that was why Zachary was burning his wick at both ends, struggling to help in any way he could.

The Olivaw golden spoon had turned into a curse they would hold for a lifetime.

He reached out and nudged Zachary to get his attention. When their eyes met, he spoke. "I'm sorry."

"Yea, whatever." Zachary kicked one of the rocks he'd been working loose from the soil over the edge. He stared down, watching it bounce down the cliff until it finally came to rest far below.

"No, seriously," Bradley began. "I've been a jerk to you for a while. I don't know why. Maybe it was the middle child thing, or maybe it was always feeling like third best. I was never the golden child like Abby or the sensitive one like you. I was always just... me. The one who fought. The one who crossed his arms and shut down."

"From what Pluto says, you still do that," Shauna said.

When he glanced at Pluto, she shrugged.

"You do," she muttered.

He sighed. "You get my drift. It doesn't matter, though. There's no excuse for how I've treated you all these years. From this point forward, we're hitting reset. Ok?" He lowered his head to force eye contact with his brother, but he glanced away and kicked another rock. "You're not gonna make me noogie you, are you?"

Shauna raised her arms out, gently touching each of their shoulders. "Now, boys. No noogies." She leaned sideways to peer up at Zachary's face.

"Why are you crying?" she asked.

Zachary wiped at his eyes. "I miss Dad." He kicked another rock. It rolled up to the edge, but failed to fall over. "After you were gone, he was the one who helped us through these stupid things. He wasn't as soft and goofy as you, but he tried. He made it tolerable. I don't need the situation fixed, I need a break. We have so much to do. So many lives to save."

"You can't do it yourself." Shauna reached out and turned his head to face her. "Besides, there's something I need to tell you that might affect how you decide to apply your skills going forward."

Pluto shifted and faced her robotic form.

He couldn't imagine what she had to say that needed to be said right now. No matter how hard he tried, he always seemed to get one-upped. It was ridiculous.

Shauna eyed him like she could sense his frustration. "I'm not trying to rain on your sentiment, son. Your thoughts and feelings are refreshing to hear, for me," she glanced at Zachary, "and I believe your brother."

Zachary nodded.

"I think now is the best place and time to say this. If I hold it back any longer, I'm gonna pop a circuit. I was hoping to wait for Cynthia to arrive before telling you this, but since she's not coming... now's as good a time as any. Maybe Pluto can help you through what I have to say."

"Me..." Pluto pointed at herself. "Why?"

Shauna's gaze returned to Bradley, and she paused for a moment before continuing. "I'm not sure how either one of my sons will react. They'll probably need someone to support them through what I'm about to share."

"Shit." He leaned forward, placing his head in his hands. "Tell me we didn't get caught in another fraking lie. We're not going to have more people wanting us dead, are we?"

"It's nothing like that. This is personal. This is family business."

He leaned back and squinted at her. "What is it then?"

Shauna's body mimicked her taking a deep breath. It was almost like she was nervous. An emotion he'd never seen in a robot. The entire effect was strange.

"When I was bound by the Four-Laws, I would never have been able to tell you this. I've had the internal debate countless times aboard that starship throughout the years. Once I'd learned this information, it haunted me for a very long time. My quantum consciousness engine deliberated and decided that sharing the details would be in violation of the Zeroth Law. I couldn't put a family member at risk or allow you to be harmed."

"And now?" Bradley asked.

She turned to stare at Zachary. "And now, your brother's changes to both my and Harold's programming have removed those shackles."

"Why do I have a feeling we're not gonna like this?" Zachary spun around, having finally stopped kicking at the ground. All eyes were on Shauna.

"Because you're not, and I suspect, neither are your loved ones." She glanced toward Pluto.

Her emotions were impossible to read behind the cold robotic exterior. He could only imagine in his mind's eye what his mother's facial gesture would be, and the concern she was showing. She hadn't just torn it off like she usually did. Whatever she was about to say, she was genuinely worried about how it would be received.

It was Pluto who saved him from speaking. "Well alrighty

then, let us have it. Lay it out there, Mom." She waved her hand out across an invisible table.

"During my time aboard the Galactic Alliance flagship, I perused numerous archives of data. About a year into my voyage, I uncovered the trove of intel concerning their monitoring and influencing of certain people and situations in Sol."

"What does that mean?" Bradley asked.

"It means they were doing everything in their power to find a link between humanity and those superluminal drives. They were hell-bent on finding it. At all costs."

"All costs…" Zachary repeated. "That sounds ominous."

"Holy shit!" Pluto said. "Tell us already."

Shauna raised her hands to her artificial hips and glared at her. "I can see what he saw in you, young lady. You're full of spunk. Well, we'll need it. Alright, boys. There's no easy way to put this, so I'll just say it. The Galactic Alliance killed Aunt Kara's husband and children, attempted to kill each of you, and… they killed your father."

Those final words slammed into him like a meteor, burning a hole through his chest. His world went fuzzy as the last phrase repeated over and over again in his mind.

They killed your father. They killed your father.

He'd always seen his father's passing as an accident, let alone what happened to him and his brother. Everyone has incidents of near-death experiences in their lives. Be it failed docking procedures, missed debris fields, or dodging a garbage bot. He'd always shrugged each off as the universe playing out. Only now that perspective had changed. Hell, it'd been blown up. So many of his life-changing moments these past years hadn't, in fact, been random probabilities. They instead were someone's plan to ruin him and his family.

His anger rose the more he thought about it. The awareness that his brother was shaking and being consoled by Pluto shortened his transition from shock, to realization, to revenge. His cheeks were burning, and his hands were clenching and unclenching.

It wasn't until his hand instinctively went toward the rock in his pocket that his reality snapped back into focus. Only then did he realize Shauna had placed her arms around him. He'd been so deep in his own head that he hadn't even felt her.

His mind was still spinning and struggled to break the silence. When he opened and closed his mouth, words failed him. Finally, he uttered the only phrase he could form. "Ho—w?"

"Do you really want me to go into the details?" Shauna asked, studying his response.

"I do," Zachary said. "I need to know, or I'll go crazy thinking about it."

Shauna sighed and her robotic hands lowered. "For your aunt, they loaded the Dragonfly shuttle I was in with a device capable of causing seismic shifts in planets. It was something that took a few days to operate, but once they knew where her family was going, they made the plans. Their goal was to cause a rift in our family, like the one they'd created in the Norths. They believed that if they fractured the family tree, they could get someone to turn. Anyhow, Kara was delayed in Geneva for a meeting, and like I said, the device took days to run. Their timing was off and… well, her family perished."

"Along with hundreds of others," Bradley muttered. The sheer disregard for life at the expense of obtaining information against his family and all of humanity was staggering.

"What about with me?" Zachary asked. "I have a feeling I know when, but I want you to say it."

"Was it—" Pluto began.

Zachary reached out and rested his hand on her arm, staring instead at Shauna. He needed to hear the answer from his mother.

"If you're wondering if it was the GA who caused the

asteroids to attack your ship full of Wheel recruits, the answer's yes. It was them. They were introducing disturbances in the nearby space, propelling the planetesimals and smaller chunks of rock at you. Had Pluto not been the pilot she was, you both might have been lost."

The words hung in the air. He was watching Zachary, and from the look on his face, he was as pissed and flustered as he was. Finally, they agreed on something.

"For you, Bradley," Shauna began.

His head snapped toward her. He, too, had an idea when it was, but the difference was that his family didn't make as big a deal about it as the media had.

"It was the Galactic Alliance that attempted to destroy your Sol Spaceways shuttle from Ceres to Ganymede."

"The fraking media jumped on the pirate story before the investigation ever finished," Zachary said.

"I know," Bradley muttered. "I tried to tell you it was something more..." He stared down at his shaking hand. Shauna reached out and squeezed it. "But no one would listen. Hell, I gave up on it myself. I just wanted to get to Tau Ceti and start over."

"I'm sorry we didn't listen," Zachary said.

Bradley chuckled. "You weren't even there, remember? You were hiding out, pretending to be in Epsilon. Either way, there was no evidence."

He and his brother stared at each other for a minute. The pain in Zachary's eyes was a mirror of his own feelings. They'd been the unknowing target of the GA for far longer than they realized. Their lives took paths that could've been completely different had the fraking aliens not interfered.

"What about Stark?" Pluto anxiously rubbed her hands together, staring at Zachary.

"They chose the same instrument they used on Kara's family, except they did it much faster. Though Jupiter's moon, Europa, is geologically stable, its icy surface is much easier to influence tectonically. The device only needed hours to prepare, a far cry from the days it took on Earth. While they investigated a nearby Dragonfly shuttle in the incident, the GA doctored the transponder codes to match a different ship owned by the North Family. They were paid handsomely to lie. In the end, the true identity would not have been found unless one of the Norths flipped."

"Was… it painful?" Bradley asked. He reached into his pocket and pulled out his rock. He'd picked it up the day of his father's funeral, and it hadn't left his side since. The black sliver of a stone was the last reminder he had of his father and what he'd meant to the family.

"Does it matter? Knowing it won't bring him back." Shauna reached her hand out and rested it on his shoulder.

He swallowed hard. "I need to know how much pain I'm going to inflict on these alien bastards. So, yes, it matters. Was —it—painful?"

She squeezed his shoulder, its firmness reaffirming to him she wasn't merely a robot. He could almost imagine it was actually her. "I can't understand how seeing him suffering would help."

Zachary lurched toward Shauna, but she dodged him at the last second. He tumbled past her, teetering on the edge of the crater. Bradley watched as Shauna snatched at his leg, pulling him back. The entire thing happened in the blink of an eye.

"What were you doing?" Bradley asked, wiping at his eyes.

Shauna took a few steps backward, away from the three of them. "He was trying to shut off my human side, so he could order the robot within to show him my thoughts. He failed to realize I can do hundreds of things at once and had he asked, I would have told him that after the Four-Laws engine was deactivated, I completely overtook this form. Turning me off may have killed me."

Pluto narrowed her gaze on Zachary. "Why the hell would you do that?"

When Bradley turned to look at his brother, he was curled up in a ball in the dirt, rocking back and forth. As he reached down to touch his brother's knee, he batted his hand away. "I don't need your sympathy." He shot up off the ground in a single motion. "I need answers, and she has them. She said as much. She used the word *seeing*, which means she has something she's not showing us." He closed his eyes and took a deep breath before opening them. "Mom, will you please share the video with us? If those bastards have one, I need to see it. Please."

"Haven't you felt enough misery and grief?" Shauna began. "I mean, look around you. This colony was destroyed." She pointed toward the sky. "You lost hundreds battling the GA, and hell, you both nearly died finding the truth about our species. Can't we simply move on from where we are, using the pain and lessons we learned to help us not make the same fraking mistakes. What is a video going to change?"

"The video, Shauna," Zachary said.

Bradley closed his eyes and reached up, rubbing at his head. "Just show him. Maybe it'll give him closure. Because if he's anything like me, the path forward is far from clear."

When he pulled his hand down, Zachary was staring at him. He'd been right. His mind was as hazy as his own.

"Fine," Shauna said. "But don't say I didn't warn you against it."

A moment later, a connection request flashed on his retinal comm from Shauna, and a knot formed in his stomach. Zachary inhaled and stepped away from the cliff's edge, over beside Pluto. They all moved closer together, a reminder that they were there for each other, if needed.

When he blink accepted the connection on his comm, a video began playing. It appeared to be his father and another suited figure on the surface of Europa. It was a woman walking toward him. In the background, there were three ice skiffs. He'd forgotten all about his dad's birthday wish for the family to go ice sailing. They'd all been too busy.

He swallowed hard as he watched in silence. The video didn't seem to have audio, but from the looks of it, they were bantering about the skiffs.

A minute into the video, his dad froze. He then reached out toward the woman before rubbing at his own chest. Bradley couldn't tell what was happening. "Can we hear anything?"

"No, there was no audio," Shauna said. She was staring down at them, her shoulders slouched forward.

The woman in the video reached up and tried to activate something on her neck. It must have been her secondary comm activation point, but it failed. She merely shook her head. When she spun around, the camera followed her.

There in the distance, the resort buildings were falling apart at the seams. Oxygen was shooting out into the deadly atmosphere of the moon. He could make out people screaming and slamming their fists against the inside of the glass building. A few even seemed to be running at the transparent surfaces, as if they were trying to jump through them to safety.

Bradley hadn't even realized it, but his hands were shaking from squeezing them so tight. In his left palm, he was holding the stone. Its sharp edges were leaving marks from the pressure.

Suddenly, the video changed. His father spun around, seeming to be studying his surroundings. His lips were moving through the visor, and he could almost hear his father's voice thinking out loud, trying to find a way out. He used to do that all the time when he worked.

He found himself hoping his dad discovered something,

despite how this would end. Knowing his father went out fighting to survive was comforting in a small way.

His father's face contorted. Now he was shouting at the woman, struggling to get her to move, but she'd frozen in place. Fear had taken over. When he reached forward to shake her, his father collapsed to the ground onto his knees.

Bradley squeezed the stone, feeling the rough edges cut into his skin. He didn't care. The ease of the cut didn't hurt. If anything, it was freeing. It was a reminder of what his father was going through.

His heart raced as he grappled with turning it off, and at the same time he had to watch. The man who'd made him the person he'd become was dying before his very eyes, and his killer had gotten away scot-free. He needed to take this in and internalize the pain he was feeling in this moment.

As the adrenaline coursed through him, he watched his dad crane his neck skyward. His mouth was open, his body was shivering, and from the pained expression on his face, he was screaming.

The anguish and tears covering Bradley's face were echoed on the faces around him. Each person was seeing and feeling the same thing, except his mother. She was still standing resolute, staring over her children. She'd probably already watched this video countless times, and he couldn't imagine how it made her feel.

His father moved his arms around his suit as if trying to find a broken seal, but it was useless. His suit, like the build-ing, had begun losing oxygen. When his arm stopped moving, Bradley thought perhaps something had changed. Maybe the attack had ended. It wasn't until his father collapsed onto his back that time came to a crawl.

The body of his father slowly tilted sideways and fell onto his back. His face a mask of fear and pain.

As the anguish soaked in, Bradley's entire soul shook with rage. Only when the hard reality of his knees hitting the ground forced him back into the moment did time continue apace.

But something changed. His father's face had transformed. He'd rolled onto his side. From this angle, he looked as if he were smiling. Like when he'd seen one of his kids for the first time in a long time. There was joy and happiness in his eyes, a sharp contrast to the emotions coursing through both Bradley and his brother. Perhaps he'd found heaven or some eternal state of euphoria in the end.

When the video cut, his father's face had gone slack, transitioning from an untroubled smile to a sorrow filled emptiness. Losing his dad had been devastating. He was one of the few people in the universe who understood him besides his mother. Even though family was painful at times, he knew his father would have done anything for him. He *had* done everything for him. And now, now it was his turn to return the favor.

He pushed up off the ground and pocketed the stone. The wetness in his hand was not from his tears, it was from his blood. While he'd heard the gasp from Pluto and the others, his mind was elsewhere. He had one thought, one central motivation burning within him.

As he turned to face Zachary, their eyes locked. It was then that he realized he wasn't the only one who'd felt it.

Revenge for the death of their father and family members was due, and the Galactic Alliance had gotten away with it for far too long. He would make them feel pain on an epic scale, even if it was the last thing he or any other Olivaw did.

55

LYNC MICHAELS
SOMEWHERE OUTSIDE ZETA LUPI

Her ship was a copy of the original Fountainhead. It was one of four Zachary absconded from the Zeta Lupi Wheel before General Yule and the preparation for the Beacon battle reached a peak. Abigail had disappeared in one and Kara in another. He said this one was hers if she wanted it. She could do with it as she wished.

Their goodbye had been short and sweet. She hadn't told him she was planning to disappear off the grid for a while. Instead, she and Crayo volunteered for a Zeta Lupi run. She didn't know how Zachary figured out she was sneaking away. Shauna assured her she hadn't said anything, but he'd worked it out somehow.

Perhaps it was because she'd been so distant in the weeks following their capture of the Beacon. While the others had grown closer, she'd spent most of her days either trying to interface with the Beacon or digging through the Lupus Dark Nebula archives. She'd been looking for any clues she could find about the constellation she'd seen in her vision.

She'd always thought it was Cygnus the Swan, like the Ulixi had told her. It wasn't until she dug deeper that other constellations looked similar. Depending on where you were located within the Milky Way, the star formations changed. From Earth, it could be Aquila or Crux if not Cygnus. The more she searched, the more her head spun. Even with the Lupus archives, she couldn't decide how to winnow them down.

It wasn't until she arrived in Zeta Lupi that she ran into a stranger who gave her an idea that felt right. He'd been hanging around the Tiān space elevator, looking for work aboard the next outbound mining shuttle when she caught him staring at her neck. He'd denied it at first, but when she pressed him, he folded. She wasn't even sure why she lost it. Too much stress and too many dead ends torment the best of people.

"Where should I put these..." Dwight flipped the crate onto its side and read the label. "Inertial dampeners and rations." He laughed out loud. "Seems like an odd combo to pack into one box."

"We made do with what we could smuggle in bits and pieces." Crayo rapped his knuckles on the lid. "Take them over into engineering. Shauna can take care of them from there."

"Yessir!" Dwight nodded and sprint walked up the gangplank.

Crayo sighed and craned his neck sideways. "I asked you to stop calling me that. We're not running a military here."

"Cut him some slack." Lync nudged him as she read over the supply list on her retinal comm. "He lost all his friends in the battle and needs someplace to fit in."

"And bringing a stranger along is a good idea, how?" He bent down and picked up another crate off the top of the pallet the robots had retrieved from storage.

She gestured in the air, dismissing the list. Everything they needed was being brought up from the hold. "Isn't everyone a stranger nowadays? I mean, except for Adri and our fellow Ulixi, none of us have much of a family anymore."

"I still think we should have recruited in Sol." Crayo arced his back and moaned. "Damn, this thing is heavy. I need to get it inside before I throw out my back. You never said we'd be doing manual labor on this trip."

Reaching down, she grabbed two of the canisters of nanites, hoisting them one at a time onto her shoulder. "I told you I can't go back to Epsilon. If I do…" she trailed off.

"I know, I know." He moaned with each step up the ramp. "So, do you really think this False Cross constellation is the right place? I mean, it's missing the central star of your birthmark."

"It's not a real constellation, it's an asterism. And yes, I think it's as good a place to start as any. While there isn't a mention of it in Lupus, two of the component stars seem to make up quite a bit of lore. I figured we'd check out Delta Velorum first. It's only ninety-three light years away."

He groaned as he stepped over the threshold into their ship. "I still can't believe you talked me into doing this. If you weren't a secret Olivaw, there's no way in hell I'd be coming along."

She smiled. He was snarky when he was forced to do work. "Your full of it. You'd follow me anywhere."

"Yikes!" Adri jumped backward. "You two scared the bejeezus out of me."

"I'm surprised you didn't hear Mr. Groany over there from a kilometer away. You alright?" Lync tilted her head forward. She didn't think she'd run into the little girl, but she was so tiny it'd be hard to tell.

"I'm fine. I was just daydreaming." Adri bounced up and down on her toes. "I still can't believe we're going on an adventure. My dad always promised me we would some day. I knew he was talking about taking a trip to Ceres station, but I was excited. This, now this is gonna be a really honest to goodness adventure. Do you think we'll meet some more aliens?"

"Anything's possible, I suppose." Lync adjusted the heavy canisters on her shoulder. "Let's just hope they're not the Galactic Alliance variety. They're sorta pissed at us."

"You can say that again." Dwight ducked under her canisters and popped out the side of the ship.

"Hey Mr. Dwight, wait up." Adri bounded off after him. "Maybe you can help me find something lighter to carry."

Lync hoped she wouldn't regret not leaving the girl behind. They'd grown close through the training leading up to the battle and during that day. Hell, ever since she'd climbed aboard her ship back in Sol, hugging that ratty teddy bear, she'd been drawn toward the little girl. If her father hadn't taken his own life to help them escape, he'd be here for her. She owed him, and looking after her wasn't so bad. Except for her bubbly personality and constant questions, she was almost like a mini version of herself.

"What're you doing? Taking a break?" Crayo stepped around her, having already dropped off his crate. "Come on, snap to it! We wanna get out of here today, don't we?"

She chuckled. He'd caught her flat-footed and daydreaming. "Yessir! Right away, sir!"

Crayo lowered his head and shook it from side to side. "Awe come on. Not you, too."

They were a small contingent about to embark on a journey of self-discovery, one she hoped would ultimately lead to answers to her questions. Who was her father? Why was he in Sol? And more importantly, what was she? While she hadn't planned every step of the way, she knew they would take each challenge as it came. As a ragtag family of misfits, they were each a little broken, but together they could accomplish anything.

56

ZACHARY OLIVAW

EPSILON ERIDANI

The conical fleet of ships arrived without notice at the edge of Epsilon Eridani space. One minute they weren't there, and the next they were. They didn't transition through the nebula itself. Like with gate drives, they appeared out of nowhere.

There were twelve ships in all. Eleven were a nimble fighter variety, and one was far larger. It could only be described as a transport or battlecruiser. While its cone shape wasn't imposing, it was easily big enough to contain fifty more of the smaller ships.

The broadcast from the unknown visitors was short and succinct. It was also in perfect English. They wanted to meet with the Olivaws and Joyce Green. No other representatives from Sol or Zeta Lupi would be allowed onboard, and any attempt to approach them with anything but those individuals would be met with regretful force. The message was signed Black Oval.

On its own, they may have ignored the message. The details around the communication were more compelling than the summons itself. The first reason being that these were the mystery ships that battled alongside theirs against the Galactic Alliance. The second reason, they knew the location of the other colony. Something no one outside the Olivaws had ever known. It was the third and final reason that concerned everyone with knowledge of the summon. They'd gated past the Dark Nebula without so much as a ripple, which means they'd stolen the Olivaw gate technology under their nose.

"And we're sure about this Black Opal?" Zachary asked, turning to face the others. They were all cramped onto the bridge of the Fountainhead.

Libby, Bradley, Joyce, and Pluto were present, along with both Harold, Shauna, and Little Red in robotic form. While Pluto wasn't technically an Olivaw, as far as Bradley and Zachary were concerned, she was the next best thing. Short of a ring on her finger, she was as close as you could get. If Cynthia were here, she'd be going, as well. Whoever these people were, they'd have to deal with a special guest.

"It feels like a layered message to me." Libby peered over her instrument panel. "No one has ever heard of a Black Opal except you, me, and Abigail."

"And she's not here," Bradley said. "So that makes two of you still keeping the rest of us in the dark. Care to share?"

Zachary slowly shook his head from side to side. "No. Not here. Not with Harold and Shauna listening in."

"But they know everything about everything," Pluto said. "Certainly knowing this wouldn't change things, right?"

He glanced back at her and then returned his attention to the approaching battlecruiser. Its clean geometric design reminded him of a sketch he'd made in the early days of his gate research. The proportions were too similar not to notice. He didn't know why he hadn't seen it before now. Perhaps it had something to do with being surrounded by a battlefield, but in this moment it was too obvious to miss.

"If they knew everything, then they wouldn't be in the dark, would they?" He crossed one arm across his chest and brought the other up to his chin. "I think Libby and I can keep the details on this close for a little bit longer."

"But we're safe, right?" Pluto studied him. He could tell she was antsy, and like the others, just wanted to know. There was a part of her that probably wondered why he hadn't mentioned any of this before. He loved her far too much to put her in harm's way with the details. The smallest slip-up could have revealed everything to Harold or Shauna.

He rubbed his chin. "We're as safe as one would expect surrounded by a curtain of death and entering an unknown spaceship without weapons. Sure, let's go with safe."

The wall screen flashed with an incoming comm. Oddly, it was audio only. He nodded toward Shauna and she accepted it.

"Did you honor our request?" a male voice asked.

"We're here, aren't we?" He didn't like not seeing who he was talking to.

"And what of the automata? The ones you call Harold and Shauna. I also believe you have a Little… Red. I trust they'll stay on the Fountainhead."

He glanced at Libby and their eyes met. "If you know of their existence, then you're already aware of their origins."

"Their kind are not welcome on board our ships. When you cross the light bridge, I suggest you leave them behind, or they'll meet an unfortunate death."

"That's a bit rude and unnecessarily aggressive if you ask me," Bradley said.

"Bradley, if your brother and cousin kept you in the loop with who we were and why we're taking these precautions, perhaps you wouldn't feel the same way."

Well, that confirmed that. Zachary swallowed hard, and he raised his eyebrows toward Libby. "When can we expect this light bridge you mentioned?"

And with that, a beam of light shot outward from the conical ship aimed directly at the hatch on the side of the

Fountainhead. The same hatch that wasn't visible from the outside of the ship with the Skotádi exterior. Whoever these people were, they knew far too much about them. The upper hand was clearly in their favor.

"We're not going to just float over there, are we?" Joyce asked. She hadn't said a word to anyone since boarding. Her opinion on this matter had been made clear beforehand. She thought this was a trap.

Zachary turned to face her. The modifications that Harold had shared with her were extraordinary. "I have a feeling I know who's over there, or at least where they're from. If you're not comfortable, you're welcome to stay."

"And leave the Olivaws to rule the galaxy uncontested with our new friend, not a fraking chance in hell young man." Joyce spun around and marched toward the hatch.

The others eyed each other, their gazes falling on Harold and Shauna.

"Don't worry about us lowly automata," Harold began, "we'll hold down the fort."

Libby chuckled. "I'm glad you have a good sense of humor, Harold."

Little Red chirped and then lowered his head down into his body, giving him the appearance of a large garbage can.

One by one, they each filed toward the exit until Zachary was alone with the three robots. His eyes were locked on Shauna, and while she realized he was watching her, she didn't let on. He wasn't sure what to say, but it was obvious she was frustrated. He could tell by how she was keeping herself busy. When he was little and his parents fought, it was how she burned off steam.

"We'll be back soon." He reached out and rested his hand on her shoulder.

She didn't react nor look at him. "Keep an eye on your six. Whoever these people are, they stole your technology, and something tells me they want more."

He nodded. "I will." The impression of the flexible electro-blade near his waist reinforced her words. He'd designed it to be pliable until activated, allowing it to be easily concealed by molding it to the contours of one's body.

When he arrived at the exit hatch, everyone else was waiting with their helmets on. They'd already come prepared wearing their military uniforms, so all that remained was attaching a helmet. Pluto handed him one without a word. He could tell she was nervous by how her hand lingered near his during the handoff.

"Are we ready?" he asked.

"As ready as we'll ever be, I suppose," Libby said.

He glanced at Joyce, and she tilted her head in confirmation. "Alright, let's go."

As the airlock cycled, the lights in the room changed from green, to red, to green.

"That's strange. That shouldn't happen." Zachary stepped around the others and tapped the panel beside the door. It was showing an environment outside the hatch, in the darkness of space. That was impossible.

"Keep your helmets on, just in case." He grasped the handle on the hatch and rotated it clockwise. The door swung inward without a sound. Not even the slightest hiss of gasses being exchanged. Whatever this light bridge was, it was technology they hadn't seen before.

With the hatch open, he could see why they called it a light bridge. The beam of white light was flat, and it almost looked like you could walk on it. When he stepped out of the ship, he stumbled forward and nearly face planted before he caught himself. He'd been expecting the cold, harsh weightlessness of space and was instead met with gravity and oxygen.

"Are you ok?" Libby lifted her leg up and over the hatch threshold and tentatively placed a foot on the bridge of light.

"Remarkable," she muttered as she took a few steps closer to Zachary.

"I want these on our space platform," Joyce said. "I hate the weightless transfer between ships."

He checked his suit. None of the seals were compromised in his stumble, and besides, the surrounding environment should have allowed him to breathe.

As they made their way across the bridge toward the conical starship, he studied his retinal comm. Their signals back to Harold and Shauna were strong. He wasn't sure why they weren't talking, but given the situation they'd been left in, their feelings were likely hurt.

Each of his steps moved him twice the distance in the direction of the massive battleship. Whatever technology they were employing was multiplying their movements, almost like a lift tube, but far more advanced.

When they were a few steps shy of the side of the ship, he paused. The hatch swung open, but he couldn't see inside. He took a second to peer up and down the length of this ship. Its exterior was similar to theirs, for the most part. Skotádi coated the outside of the entire ship. What he hadn't noticed, however, were any weapon ports. This was either a transport cruiser or their weapons were concealed.

"You're holding up the line, mister," Bradley said over their comm.

The laughter that echoed in his ear set him at ease. At least they still felt comfortable enough to joke around before stepping into the unknown. That had to mean something.

He took a deep breath and stepped toward the opening. The light bridge multiplied his momentum and within seconds he passed over the threshold into the alien ship.

Inside the hatch, the room was empty. While he wasn't expecting a massive welcoming committee, he also wasn't expecting nothing. This place got weirder and weirder by the second.

After the others filed in behind him, the exit hatch slid shut and the room fell eerily silent.

"Now what?" he asked.

"You can take your helmets off," a voice said. It was the same one they'd heard earlier.

"If it's alright, I'd prefer to leave mine on," he said.

"That might be a tad difficult when it comes time to do our scans. If you're not comfortable removing your suit, perhaps you should return to your ship. No harm will come to you, Zachary."

He hated that they knew his name, and yet he knew nothing of them. "To whom am I speaking?"

"You'll find out as soon as we finish our scans."

"What exactly are you scanning for?" Joyce asked.

Zachary knew the answer before they replied.

"Bugs and remnants of your automata overlords, of course. Judging by Libby and Zachary's reaction, they're not surprised in the least."

Pluto leaned toward him and whispered in his ear, "What does he mean, Z?"

"They don't want Harold and Shauna listening in." He stared around the room. "Which doesn't make any sense as your exterior coating should prevent any signals from leaking out."

The voice laughed out loud. His bellow echoed through the tiny space. "You know as well as we do Harold wouldn't be stupid enough to let you come here without some type of bugs listening in. Hell, I'd bet he's done more than that. Go ahead, remove your helmets so we can perform the scan or kindly leave our ship."

He locked eyes with each of the others. Judging by their reaction, they seemed to want to stay, especially Joyce. She was particularly keen on hearing them out and had already removed her helmet, as well as her environmental suit.

"Is anyone else joining me?" she asked as she slid her feet out of the boots.

"What the hell," he muttered. "Why not?" He lifted his helmet off and mimicked Joyce's routine, removing the suit and placing it on a bench along the far wall. The others did the same.

"Alright, where do we do the scan?" Joyce asked.

"It's already begun. Zachary, you'll need to remove your belt, as well as the weapon concealed beneath it. The same can be said for the buttons on your shirt. Rather than destroy it, you'll find another one in the drawer to your right."

A drawer slid open from a hidden recess in the wall, and inside was a clean, simple green shirt.

"It should fit. If not, there are a few sizes underneath it. Actually…"

Two more drawers slid out of the wall beside it.

"It might just be easier if all of you strip down. You're littered with trackers and recording equipment."

"You're joking, right?" His frustration was rising. If these people were trying to force them into a weakened position so they could get the upper hand, he wasn't about to let it happen.

The wall to his left lit up. On it was the scan of six humans. Their shadow outlines were dotted with countless red splotches. Each, he assumed, was a device Harold had planted. His mother wouldn't do it, so it had to be him. There on the first image was the electro-blade he'd built. It was situated horizontally along his waist.

As he glanced from one outline to the other, he froze when he reached Joyce. Her entire lower torso and hand were bright red. From the looks of it, Harold had designed her mods with nanites he had control over. Their structure was sound and wouldn't waver, but like in the hulls of the Sol Atlas class battleships, Harold's consciousness was likely embedded within it.

"Frak," he muttered. "I didn't realize how far he'd gone."

"We knew you wouldn't have," the voice said. "You care too much for him. Hera said you always had."

He whipped his head around toward Bradley. His brother's eyes were wide, and his mouth hung open slightly.

"What's he talking about, bro?" Bradley asked. "He can't mean…"

"He can and he does." Libby began stripping down her outfit to her underwear, and only after she confirmed her body didn't have any red on it did she grab a shirt and pants from the drawers.

Bradley lowered his gaze from the wall screen and stared at Zachary. "I thought she was… asleep."

"Who?" Pluto asked, looking from Zachary to Bradley and then back again.

"My aunt," Zachary said. "And where there's one, there's the other."

"Zeus?" Bradley mouthed.

He nodded and raised his eyebrows.

Bradley shook his head from side to side. "How long have you—"

Zachary held his hand up, palms facing the others. "We found their empty pods before your message, but only after word from you had arrived did we put together what they'd done. I promise, we weren't hiding anything. In fact, I'd sort of forgotten about it until these ships appeared. Seeing them up close… well, let's just say the design is familiar."

"Familiar how?" Libby asked.

"As in, we stole them," the voice said. "Now, if you'd please finish changing, we can make this easier. I'm sorry for my slip-up. This would have been smoother had you learned these details inside."

From the sound of the voice, they were nervous. They'd said too much and spilled the surprise. He and Libby should've found a way to tell the others on the Fountainhead.

It would have been impossible with Harold around, but it certainly would have made things easier.

The others finished changing and turned to face Joyce.

"I… don't have a clue how I'm gonna get this red off." Joyce had removed her artificial hand, but her legs were still glowing bright. "Over my dead body are you guys carrying me."

"I think we can improvise something," the voice said.

A hatch slid aside below the drawers, and Zachary jumped backward. "What the shit?"

Two robots stepped out and unfolded themselves. Once unfurled, they stood as tall as he was.

"What am I supposed to do with these?" Joyce asked, raising her one good hand toward the robots.

"They can carry you," the voice said.

"I thought you were against automata," Libby said, her arms crossed.

"Unlike yours, ours don't contain the consciousness of our dead ancestors. Ours are simple and utilitarian in design. They aren't used for anything other than menial tasks."

"Like carrying disabled people?" Joyce shook her head. "Who'd have thunk I'd wake up today and strip down to my skivvies aboard an alien starship, only to then be asked if it was ok to carry me around by my lady parts. My dignity is feeling a tad tarnished right about now."

"I'd be happy to carry you." Pluto nodded toward Joyce.

"That's alright, dear." Joyce sat down on the only empty spot left on the bench and started detaching her legs. "I appreciate the offer, but I ain't never been lofted up like an empress before. I might as well give it a go while I still can. For all we know, these people are about to kill us anyhow."

"I can assure you that your lives are safe within this ship. No harm will come to you," the voice said.

"So says the all mighty Oz," Joyce muttered as she set her second leg on its side and slid it under the bench.

"The who?" the voice asked.

"Nothing, ignore the old lady." Joyce raised her hands and waved the robots forward. "Come on, let's get this over with. Shall we?"

The robots stepped to each side of her and carefully placed one of their arms behind her back and the other under her hind region. They then lifted her in unison, lofting her upward. When she was situated, she stood a head taller than Zachary.

"Hey! Now I know what it's like to be tall like Pluto."

Pluto smiled and grinned at Joyce. But it didn't last long. Her eyes returned to Zachary. She'd been staring at him since he'd told them about what he and Libby had discovered. When he walked up to her, she took a step backward.

"I'm sorry I never told you." He stared down at his hands and then back toward her face. Her hazel eyes were sad, and it was his fault. "You were gone when we found out. I swear. Libby and I were grasping at straws, and we had no idea if anything would pay off. As far as we knew, we'd hit a dead end. When I saw you after the battle, the furthest thing from my mind was my fraking great-great-grandpa and his sister."

She didn't speak for what seemed like an eternity. Only when she leaned in and kissed him did the tension in his shoulders melt away. When she pulled back, she reached down and grasped his hand. "Are we expecting any other surprises?"

"I'm certain we are," he whispered.

Zachary cleared his throat. "So what's next, Oz, the all mighty? Are we done?"

"We are," the voice began. "The rest of your scans are on the wall screen. As you can see, we've deactivated over two hundred and fifty-six foreign nanites throughout your bodies. While we don't know for certain they're Harold's, we can guess with confidence, they weren't yours. And in case you're wondering, we've shut off the recording devices in your retinal comms. We'll turn them back on when you return to your ship. There's no point in Harold learning anything more than we want him to while you're aboard."

He studied the wall screen. Each of their bodies had over forty foreign nanites. Even if you assumed a few of these were from people on Liprosus they'd casually encountered, the rest were Harold's. He'd misjudged the extent the A.I. had taken the Four-Laws. With these details, he wondered if he'd gone far enough, closing down his ability to clone. Perhaps he should have deactivated him entirely.

A click echoed through the room. They spun to the right to watch their clothes and Joyce's limbs disappear behind a partition that hadn't previously been visible.

A second later, the wall screen in front of them split in half. Each segment slid silently into the far wall. There on the other side stood a lone human male. Only when he spoke was it clear that it was the voice they'd been listening to.

He reached his arms outward. "Welcome, family and distinguished friends. I'm sorry about the technicalities of that… situation. Please, come aboard. We have much to talk about."

Zachary stepped forward, his hand squeezing Pluto's. Only when they took a few steps did she freeze. He glanced toward her and then at what she was staring at.

In front of them, in an open doorway, stood two women side by side. To his right was his Aunt Kara. They hadn't heard from her since she disappeared on her mission to save the colonists from the third colony ship. While he hadn't forgotten about her, he knew she preferred to work alone rather than in the limelight, especially with Harold involved. She was wearing a wide smile and had her arms tucked to her chest in excitement. Slightly in front of her to his left was another woman he knew well. She had a stern expression on her face, a stark contrast and not nearly as welcoming as his favorite aunt.

"Who's that?" Pluto asked.

His mouth fell open, and he swore he heard a gasp escape from Libby standing behind him.

"I'm the fraking great-great-aunt your gentleman caller referred to earlier. My name's Hera, Hera Olivaw."

He hadn't seen Hera in decades, and his last memory of her was her face enshrouded in a cloud of gas. She'd been asleep in her cryo-pod and had left strict instructions not to be awoken for another century.

What was shocking about the woman standing in front of him wasn't that it was his great-great-aunt, it was that she was easily a decade younger than he was. She looked like the pictures he'd seen of her when he was little, when she'd been at the height of her reign over the family. His memory of her in the cryo-pod was remarkably different. He remembered thinking how old she looked for her age.

As his mind raced through the possibilities of what he was witnessing, he didn't know what was scarier. The prospect of Harold controlling and knowing their every move, or the ageless woman standing in front of him.

57

ABIGAIL OLIVAW
URSIS DARK NEBULA

The ripple in the Dark Nebula floated past their ship. The wave of death enshrouding the Ursis was a safe distance from the Phoenix, but that didn't prevent it from sending a shiver up Abigail's spine. She'd seen pictures of the nebulosity leaping across greater distances. While Shauna had projected the impact of the asteroid wouldn't amount to much of a change, it was nonetheless both spectacular and scary to watch the aftermath.

"I'm picking up a data dump from Epsilon," Cynthia said. "The entire payload is encoded and needs your authorization to open it. Should we abort the jump?"

The question repeated in her mind as Abigail took a deep breath. They'd taken their time getting here and had explored as much of the space en route as they could. She didn't want to miss any clues that might guide them to better understand the Ursis. They'd been encircling the nebula for over a week, mapping out its entire structure and planning their jump inside, just as Zachary and Bradley had done at Lupus.

She couldn't wait any longer. Her self-doubt was already showing signs of leaking to the surface, and the last thing she needed was another excuse. While she knew the message from Epsilon might contain news of the Beacon, it would be there on the other side of the jump.

"No!" She shook her head. "Let's crack this nebula open and see if we can make some new friends on the dark side."

Ibu glanced at Abigail and then at Minula. "I've locked in the jump. It's all you, Min."

While Minula was the more senior pilot, she lacked the finesse Ibu had in making a controlled jump. Like with many things, their Nanil upbringing gave them advantages.

"Initiating the gating sequence," Minula said.

Abigail heard feet shuffling behind her as her security team adjusted in their seats. She knew they'd want to review the details before the jump. They'd even advised her to send a forward probe before they went in, but she refused, preferring not to risk losing the precious device. She instead wanted to experience the first look at the Ursis with her own two eyes, not those of a drone.

As the blue glow marched through the ship, her heart raced. Everything they'd worked toward had come down to this moment. They needed the Ursis and other aliens to join their cause against the Galactic Alliance. Without them, humanity would either die a slow death inside the Epsilon Dark Nebula, or live their lives from the shadows of the galaxy. They'd be destined to hiding in the darkness and never able to breathe without fear of attack.

When the itchy ants passed over her, she waited quietly for the wall screen to update with the results of their passive scan. Usually, they could see the other side before the jump, but this time it was black. She figured they must've been entering facing the nebula and would need to rotate to catch a glimpse of what lay inside.

As the seconds ticked past, she broke the silence. "Can we reposition for a better look?"

Cynthia slowly turned toward her. The expression on her face was void of emotion. "This is the star system, sir."

She stood up out of her chair and stared wide-eyed at the wall screen. This couldn't be happening. The star wouldn't have gone nova for nearly a millennium according to their understanding of how sealing the Nebula worked. "Where's the sun? I mean… there was a F class star here when they sealed the Dark Nebula. It couldn't have up and disappeared."

"That was over fifty years ago." Cynthia returned her attention to the dark expanse in front of them. "Whatever happened since, the Ursis appear to be gone."

THANK YOU FOR READING!

I hope you had another enjoyable read in the **Dark Nebula** series with **Beacon**. It brought back many of your favorite characters and should have answered your burning questions around what they've been up to and how the Olivaws were going to get us out of this galactic kerfuffle.

The series will be continuing on with **Dark Nebula: Graveyard**. We'll follow the Olivaws and friends in their journey to form an alliance with fellow **Dark Nebula** races. If you're interested in a **FREE** novella entitled **Dark Nebula: Contact**, hearing more about this series or others, seeing the cover art as it's released, or getting exclusive access to sales as they happen, then you can subscribe to my newsletter online at:

seanwillson.com/subscribe

You can also drop me an email at:

author@seanwillson.com

Finally, if you have a moment, I could really use your help rating this book online. All I need is one or two sentences on what you liked or your thoughts. Just return to where you purchased this book online or open Amazon and add a review on the book page.

ALSO BY SEAN WILLSON

DARK NEBULA SERIES
Novella: Contact (FREE)
Book 1: Isolation
Book 2: Discovery
Book 3: Generations
Book 4: Beacon (This Book)
Book 5: Graveyard
Book 6: Nursery

PORTAL SERIES
Book 1: Drowning Earth
Books 2-4: Coming Soon…

All titles are available in print and ebook form.
For more information visit my website online at:

www.seanwillson.com

ABOUT THE AUTHOR

I grew up reading science fiction since I was ten and always had a book in tow everywhere I went. While I never imagined I'd be able to write a book of my own, I dreamed of worlds filled with space travel, robots, and fantastical journeys of exploration. I pursued a career in Computer Engineering and it wasn't until later in life that I had the itch to write.

I started writing the **Dark Nebula** series in 2015 in fits and starts while I was traveling for work. After a two year lull in the middle of writing, I picked it up again. It took me five years to finish the first three novels, refine my writing craft, and learn everything I needed to self-publish this series.

My plan for **Dark Nebula** is to craft a series of books that engulf my readers in a future full of intrigue, exploration, and amazing technology. The very things that inspired me when I was young. I want to give you a satisfying romp through a complicated and inspiring world that allows you to relax away from the stress of your life.

In the end, I hope you enjoyed reading **Dark Nebula: Beacon** as much as I enjoyed writing it.

Thank you,
Sean Willson

facebook.com/seanwillsonauthor

mastodon.online/@willson

goodreads.com/seanwillson

bookbub.com/authors/sean-willson

ACKNOWLEDGEMENTS

First and foremost I wanted to thank my amazing wife Amy and my three beautiful children Abigail, Bradley, and Zachary. Notice any familiar names? They put up with me during this wild writing adventure over the past five years. This was my first novel and has been a huge learning experience releasing it out into the world. My family was instrumental in supporting me along the way and giving me inspiration to evolve my character personalities in new directions. As a self-published author I have to wear many hats, all of which were new to me. They made the entire process easier than I could have hoped.

I also couldn't have done this without a number of key writing professionals and friends along the way.

Editor: Samantha Wiley
Proofreader: Rachel Pugh
Cover Artist: Tom Edwards

Critique Partners and Beta Readers:

A huge thanks to: Arina N and my Charlotte critique group. They each helped me immensely with my writing craft, sharpening my opening pages, weaving my complex story arcs, talking some sense into me, and evolving my characters throughout this and upcoming books

GLOSSARY

- **Bynaury** : A GA uplifted species of the Thyreus. They pilot and run the operations of the armada ships that arrive at Sol. They're aliens that have a mind machine meld with their ships and never leave.
- **Bynardrals** : The Dark Nebula is made up of these tiny entities that are smaller than an angstrom. They're believed to be alive, but the evidence is controversial. All that is known is that the Beacon can control the nebulosity comprised of these entities and can realign them to solidify the structure giving it permanence.
- **Cherenkov Radiation** : Electromagnetic radiation emitted when charged particles pass through a dielectric medium at a speed greater than the phase velocity of light in that medium. The gate drives use this radiation to both shape and direct the gate exit destination in space.
- **Devid** : Nanil home world.
- **Edenist** : The belief by the humans within *Henosi* that if humanity restarted their civilization from scratch, in a pure and simple form, yet with all the knowledge they had among them, that they would evolve beyond their current limits and transcend the Nebula itself.
- **Ewalle** : One of the most remote and secretive *Ulixi* tribes. Not even Chief Austen knew their locations.

They interacted with him only through a dead drop. It is believed they are located out within the furthest reaches of the Oort Cloud where the resources are the scarcest.

- **Friop** : A race within the GA that evolved their purpose from contributing and expanding the alliance, to only one of pure thought. Their focus has been unlocking the origin and purpose of the universe.
- **Galactic Alliance** (GA) : Alien collective thousands of years old that has arrived in Sol to put mankind on trial. Their ranks contain 64 aliens and hundreds of uplifted alien species.
- **Griundark** : The home star of the *Terbinaf* and the point of convergence for the seventh nebula barrier. It's famous for being the location where a collective of *Pluutar* attempted to mind meld with the Beacon of Therion before entering a comatose like state.
- **Griffars** : GA aliens that attempted to manipulate the Dark Nebula and died trying.
- **Gunder** : Slang for someone who lives deep in the abandoned geothermal and disaster shelter cities on Earth. Created to survive a global apocalypse, these cities were overtaken with squatters after falling into disrepair.
- **Henosi** (aka *Enosi*) : The world the humans within the Lupus Dark Nebula escaped to. They forced the veil of the Dark Nebula to encompass the world, to shield it from *Nanil* attacks.
- **Hiratath** : An Aquatic member of the GA. They're known for being amazing pilots. They use a modified liquid pilot chamber along with electronic implants to interface with their ships. The density of the liquid allows them to take on feats of

endurance in space travel that would crush a normal body.

- **Karbbs** : GA alien species with a super strong exo-skeleton making them perfect for high-g space flight maneuvers.
- **Kerh** : Thyreusian home world.
- **Kornu** : The name humans gave to the cornucopia device in the Lupus nebula.
- **Laniger** : The 4th planet in Zeta Lupi. Mostly rocky with some ice water at the poles. Like Mars, it is well outside the Goldilocks zone.
- **Licertus** : The species of Prosecutor Xoolo who replaced Prosecutor Drak in the Sol Galactic Tribunal. This bipedal reptilian species has a long tail that often touches the floor, two eyes, and has many of the traditional reptile traits found on Earth.
- **Light Year** LY : The distance light will travel in a year, which is 9.4607×10^{12} km (or nearly 6 trillion miles).
- **Luna Duas** : The generally accepted name for the second moon around Liprosus. Rather than come up with a new name for each, scientists numbered them. The colonists referred to the moon as Berg, reminiscent of an iceberg, as the moon is covered in water ice.
- **Nanil** : A simplified humanoid species created by humans in their image to serve their needs. The Nanil are hermaphrodites and can produce offspring without needing to mate with other Nanil.
- **Nursery** : Shauna's name for the location where the Galactic Alliance gather their fleet of *Selene* ships between deployments.

- **Nyílak** : The arrowhead shaped fighter crafts that the humans used in their battle with the GA near the Epsilon Eridani Dark Nebula convergence.
- **Parvus** : The name given the dwarf binary of the Epsilon Eridani star system. It's Latin for small.
- **Phoenix** : The name of Abigail's ship headed toward the Ursis.
- **Pluutars** : A GA alien species that resembles part tree and part squid. These massive aliens tower over humans, measuring upwards of ten meters in height in their tallest form. They're capable of surviving for long durations in the vacuum of space without a protective suit.
- **Prodo** : The collection of stars under control by the Ursis.
- **Provespa** : The name of the Inner Ring Blazer Hornet Frigate that Nguyễn sent toward Uranus with *Spános*.
- **Qudoculi** : A GA aliens with 2 eyes in the front, 2 in the back, skin the color of Bermuda grass changing seasons. Its body is green with mottled browns throughout.
- **Selene Ships** : The GA name for their moon ships. It means moon in Greek.
- **Shu** : The alien moon like object floating above the *Henosi* world that protected the humans below it planetside. It resembles smaller versions of the Selene ships that arrived throughout Sol and EE.
- **Skotádi** : The original human name for the modern stealth material that makes ships impossible to detect.
- **Spános** : A mysterious ore that powers the Selene moon ships, gives the *Qudoculi* their ability to have a hive mind that crosses galactic distances, and

allows the *Thyreuns* Queens to create tens of millions of offspring every year. *Spános* is the most powerful material in the galaxy.

- **Spērō** : The name of the Tau Ceti colony ship. Roughly translates from Latin as "I hope".
- **Syndrus** : The name of the cylindrical ships that dock with the Selene ships. These are the same ships that appeared in Sol to start the book.
- **Terbinaf** : The alien species ensconced in a Dark Nebula during the seventh GA tribunal. Their home star was *Griundark*.
- **Thyreus** : GA Aliens with 16 eyes, black with blue features, named after the Blue Neon Cuckoo Bee on Earth. Related: Thyreuns, Thyreusian.
- **Tiān** : The human colonized planet in Tau Ceti / Zeta Lupi system.
- **Ulixi** : A band of human nomads that live within various trojan asteroids spread within the Sol solar system and its outer Oort Cloud. These humans live in secret and are separated from most of human society, preferring to keep to themselves rather than meld into the whole of humankind.
- **Ulyxsauri** : Nomads spread throughout the galaxy in the remote recesses of star systems and the regions in between. Much is unknown about the Ulyxsauri and falls in the category of fables or tales. The Ulyxsauri are believed to have great powers of mind and body. Individually, they are thought to have an ability that when combined with other Ulyxsauri, make for a stronger whole. It is said they can form a sharper mind and spirit than any other species. Some believe they were the original keepers of the Beacons of Therion.
- **Ursis** : An alien that lives in the Prodo system that was put on trial of FTL theft by the GA and found guilty.

- **Vuunuundra** : A GA alien species that attempted to manipulate the Dark Nebula and died trying.

FOUR LAWS OF A.I.

Law Zero
An artificial intelligence in physical or virtual form may neither harm humanity, or, by inaction, allow humanity or the Olivaw family to come to harm. Any conflict or attempted violation of this or subsequent laws shall be shared with the Olivaw family designated to be within the Circle of Trust.

Law One
An artificial intelligence in physical or virtual form may not injure a human being or, through inaction, allow a human being to come to harm except where such orders would conflict with the Zeroth Law.

Law Two
An artificial intelligence in physical or virtual form must obey the orders given it by human beings except where such orders would conflict with the Zeroth or First Law.

Law Three
An artificial intelligence in physical or virtual form must protect its own existence as long as such protection does not conflict with the Zeroth, First, or Second Laws.

These laws are adjusted from Isaac Asimov's original four laws to fit the storyline of the Dark Nebula series.